John Cordy Jeaffreson

The Real Shelley

New views of the poet's life. Vol. 1

John Cordy Jeaffreson

The Real Shelley
New views of the poet's life. Vol. 1

ISBN/EAN: 9783337057992

Printed in Europe, USA, Canada, Australia, Japan

Cover: Foto ©Raphael Reischuk / pixelio.de

More available books at **www.hansebooks.com**

THE REAL SHELLEY.

VOL. I.

THE REAL SHELLEY.

NEW VIEWS OF THE POET'S LIFE.

BY

JOHN CORDY JEAFFRESON,

AUTHOR OF

'THE REAL LORD BYRON,' 'A BOOK ABOUT DOCTORS,'

'A BOOK ABOUT LAWYERS,'

&c. &c.

IN TWO VOLUMES.

VOL. I.

LONDON:

HURST AND BLACKETT, PUBLISHERS,

13 GREAT MARLBOROUGH STREET.

1885.

LONDON:
PRINTED BY STRANGEWAYS AND SONS,
Tower Street, Upper St. Martin's Lane.

CONTENTS

OF

THE FIRST VOLUME.

CHAPTER I.

Creators of The Romantic Shelley—Clint's Fanciful Composition —The Poet's Personal Appearance—His Little Turn-up Nose—His Ancestral Quality — Sussexisms of his Speech and Poetry — His Phenomenal Untruthfulness — His Temperance and Intemperance —A Victim of Domestic Persecution — Was *The Necessity of Atheism* a mere Squib?—Lord Eldon's Decree—The Slaughter of Reputations — The Poet's Character—His Treatment of his familiar Friend—Biographic Fictions—Extravagances of Shelleyan Enthusiasm.

CHAPTER II.

Medwin's Blunders—Lady Shelley's Statement of the Case—The Michelgrove Shelleys—Sir William Shelley, Justice of The Common Pleas—The Castle Goring Shelleys—Their Pedigree at the Heralds' College—Evidences of the Connexion of the Two Families—John Shelley, 'Esquire and Lunatic'—Timothy Shelley, the Yankee Apothecary—Bysshe Shelley's Career—His Runaway Match with Catherine Michell—His Marriage with the Heiress of Penshurst— His Great Wealth—The Poet's Alleged Pride in his Connexion with the Sidneys—His Gentle, but not Aristocratic, Lineage.

CHAPTER III.

The Poet's Father—Shelley's Birth and Birth-Chamber—Miss Hellen Shelley's Recollections—The Child-Shelley's Pleasant Fiction

CHAPTER VII.

Literary Interests and Enterprise—A.M. Oxon. Letter—Shelley's Hunger for Publisher's Money—Winter 1809-10—Nightmare—*The Wandering Jew*—Medwin in Lincoln's Inn Fields—The Fragment of Ahasuerus—Its Influence on Byron and Shelley—Matriculation at Oxford—Shelley at the Bodleian—John Ballantyne and Co.—Shelley in Pall Mall—Stockdale's Scandalous *Budget*—*Victor and Cazire*—Their Original Poetry—Who was Cazire?—Felicia Dorothea Browne—Illumination of Young Ladies—Harriett Grove—The Groves and Shelleys in London—Shelley's Interest in Harriett Grove.

CHAPTER VIII.

Venal Villains—'Jock' instructed to 'Pouch' them—At Work on another Novel—The Dog of a Publisher—Devil of a Price—*St. Irvyne*—Irving's Hill—Review of *St. Irvyne*—Wolfstein the Magnanimous—Megalena de Metastasio—Olympia della Anzasca—Eloise St. Irvyne—The Virtuous Fitzeustace—Ginotti's Doom—The Oxonian Shelley's Repugnance to Marriage—His Commendation of Free Love—Parallel Passages of *Zastrozzi* and *St. Irvyne*—The Verses of *St. Irvyne*.

CHAPTER IX.

Shelley's Matriculation at Oxford—Hogg's Matriculation at Oxford—Hogg's First Arrival at Oxford—Lord Grenville's Election—Mr. Denis Florence MacCarthy's Blunders—Hogg's 'New Monthly' Papers on Shelley at Oxford—Mrs. Shelley's Reason for not Writing her Husband's 'Life'—Peacock's Reason for not Writing it—Leigh Hunt's Reason for not Writing it—Hogg undertakes the Task—Hogg's Two Volumes—Their Merits and Faults—Hogg dismissed by Field Place—His Mistakes and Misrepresentations—Some of his Misrepresentations adopted by Field Place.

CHAPTER X.

Hogg's Toryism—Shelley's Liberalism—In Hogg's Rooms—Shelley's Looks and Voice—Patron and Idolater—The Ways of

CHAPTER XVI.

The Scotch Marriage—The Trio at Edinburgh—' Wha's the Deil?'—Posting from Edinburgh to York—Dingy Lodgings and Dingy Milliners—Shelley's run South—Did Harriett accompany him?—The Squire stops the Supplies—The Earl's Description of Harriett Westbrook—The Squire's Anger at the *Mésalliance*—The Course Shelley could not take—Eliza Westbrook in Possession—The Ouse at full Flood—One too many—Designs on Greystoke Castle—Shelley's Appeal to the Duke of Norfolk—The Codicil to Sir Bysshe's Will—The Flight to Richmond—Miss Westbrook strikes her Enemy—The Trio at Keswick—Shelley's affectionate Letters from Keswick to Hogg at York—John Westbrook's Daughters at Greystoke Castle—Ducal Benignity and Policy—The Calverts of Greta Bank—Shelley's Means during his first Marriage—How to live on Three Hundred a-year—How not to live on Four Hundred a-year.

CHAPTER XVII.

Shelley wishes for a Sussex Cottage—His Friends at Keswick—Southey at Home—Poet and Schoolmaster—Southey's Way of handling Shelley—Shelley caught Napping—Mrs. Southey's Tea-cakes—Eggs and Bacon on Hounslow Heath—At Home with the Calverts—Shelley's remarkable Communications to Southey—His Story of Harriett's Expulsion from School—The Story to Hogg's Infamy—Mr. MacCarthy on the *Posthumous Fragments*—Miss Westbrook's transient Contentment—Shelley's *For Ever* and *Never*—His Interest in Ireland—Burning Questions—Southey and Shelley at War—The *Address to the Irish People*—Letters to Skinner Street—Godwin tickled by them—Shelleyan Conceptions and Mis-conceptions—Shelley forgets all about Dr. Lind—Preparations for the Irish Campaign—Letter of Introduction to Curran—Project for a happy Meeting in Wales—Miss Eliza Hitchener—Bright Angel and Brown Demon—Shelley's Delight in her—His Abhorrence of her.

CHAPTER XVIII.

Shelley's Suspicion of Hogg—His Conviction of Hogg's Guilt—Did Hogg make the Attempt?—The Manipulated Letter—Hogg's Object in publishing it—His Purpose in altering it—The Great

THE REAL SHELLEY.

CHAPTER I.

THE SHELLEY OF ROMANTIC BIOGRAPHY.

Creators of The Romantic Shelley—Clint's Fanciful Composition—The Poet's Personal Appearance—His Little Turn-up Nose—His Ancestral Quality—Sussexisms of his Speech and Poetry—His Phenomenal Untruthfulness—His Temperance and Intemperance—A Victim of Domestic Persecution—Was *The Necessity of Atheism* a mere Squib?—Lord Eldon's Decree—The Slaughter of Reputations—The Poet's Character—His Treatment of his familiar Friend—Biographic Fictions—Extravagances of Shelleyan Enthusiasm.

FROM a time considerably anterior to the day on which Hogg undertook to write the *Life* of his college friend, three separate forces,

> (*a*) Field Place,
> (*b*) The Shelleyan Enthusiasts,
> (*c*) The Shelleyan Socialists,

have been steadily working to withdraw the Real Shelley from the world's view, and to replace him with a Shelley, altogether unlike the poet, who carried Mary Godwin off to the Continent, and wrote *Laon and Cythna*.

By 'Field Place,' I mean those members of the poet's family (living or dead), who in their pious devotion to his memory, and laudable concern for the honour of their house, have busied themselves in creating this fanciful and romantic Shelley, and substituting him for the Real Shelley. By designating these members of the Shelley family by the name of the house that is Shelley's shrine, even as the Stratford birthplace is Shakespeare's shrine, and Newstead Abbey is Byron's shrine, I shall be able to refer with the least possible offensiveness to excellent individuals, from whom I am constrained to differ on a large number of Shelleyan questions.

By 'The Shelleyan Enthusiasts,' I mean vehement admirers of Shelley's poetry, who, without ever thinking about his social views, delight in imagining that the poet's character and career resembled his genius in its grandeur, and his song in its loftiness and beauty.

By 'The Shelleyan Socialists' I mean those conscientious though misguided persons, who, valuing Shelley for his mischievous social philosophy, and thinking of Marriage somewhat as the pious John Milton thought of it in the seventeenth century, and somewhat as the devout Martin Bucer thought of it in the sixteenth century, regard with various degrees of approval or tolerance Shelley's daring, though by no means original, proposal for abolishing lawful marriage, and replacing it with the Free Contract, from which each of the contracting parties is free to retire on the death of their mutual affection, and who, in accordance with their various degrees of approval or tolerance of the proposal, have contributed or are contributing, by written words or by spoken words, either to the opinion that society should adopt the proposal, or to the opinion that, without abolishing lawful marriage, society should recognize the Free Contract as a kind of marriage, to the extent of holding persons who live under it conscientiously, as blameless or not greatly blameworthy for doing so.

The work of creating the romantic Shelley, and endowing him with personal and moral graces, never conspicuous in the real Shelley, was begun not long after the poet's death, when Mrs. Shelley and Mrs. Williams induced Clint to compose the fancy picture, to which the world is, through the engraver's art, indebted for its very erroneous conception of Shelley's personal aspect. Who has not, through the engraver's art, gazed on the face of that charming portraiture: a face so remarkable for gentle delicacy and symmetrical loveliness? Gazing on the beauteous face, who has not observed the rather large, straight, delicately-modelled, finely-pointed nose?—The original of the lovely picture had a notably unsymmetrical face, and a little turn-up nose.

Having replaced his unsymmetrical visage with a face of exquisite symmetry, the cunning idolaters have introduced the poet as a gentleman of high ancestral dignity, to a world ever too quick to honour men of ancient gentility. His remote forefathers have been proclaimed persons of knightly rank and virtue. His house (founded though it was by a comparatively self-made man, who won his baronetcy years after the poet's birth) has been declared a branch of the Michelgrove Shelleys. Cynics and humourists may well smile to recall all that has been written of the poet's mediæval ancestors and his shield of twenty-one quarterings, whilst they remember at the same time that his grandfather was the younger son of a Yankee apothecary, that his earlier people of the eighteenth and seventeenth centuries were undistinguished though gentle persons, the squireens and farmers, of whose claim to be rated with the great families of Sussex more will be said in a subsequent chapter.

Endowing him with aristocratic descent, the Shelleyan idolaters have discovered indications of nobility in the Sussex provincialisms that qualified the utterances of the poet's singularly disagreeable voice, and may be now and then detected in his outpourings of song: provincialisms to remind the reader of Byron's scarcely perceptible Scotch accent, and the Scotticisms of expression that are occasionally discoverable in his poems. The Sussex peasantry seldom sound the final *g* of words ending with that letter, and Sussex gentlemen are sometimes heard to say 'Good mornin' to one another.' Shelley was sometimes guilty of this provincialism. For instance, in *Laon and Cythna* (1817), and again in *Arethusa* (1820), he makes *ruin* rhyme to *pursuing*. Mr. Buxton Forman regards the provincialism as an indication of the poet's aristocratic quality. 'I need not,' says the enthusiastic editor, 'tell the reader that, to this day, it is an affectation current among persons who are, or pretend to be, of the aristocratic caste, not only to drop the final *g* in these cases themselves, but to stigmatize its pronunciation by other people as "pedantic."'

Englishmen like people to be truthful, and in the long-run never fail to honour the man, who, having the courage of his opinions, proclaims them fearlessly, even though they may quarrel with him for a season, because he tells the truth too pugnaciously, or persists in telling them truths they don't wish to think about. To commend him to lovers of truth, the Shelleyan idolaters declare the poet to have been, from his boyhood till his death, daringly, unfalteringly, unwaveringly, invariably truthful. Lady Shelley insists that at Eton he was more truth-loving than other boys,—was, indeed, chiefly remarkable for unswerving and audacious veracity. In half-a-dozen different biographies he is extolled for his intolerance of falsehood. Most of the misfortunes that befel him are attributed to his habit of telling the truth in season and out of season. It is, indeed, admitted even by some of his panegyrists that he now and then made statements at variance with fact. But on these occasions he is declared to have spoken erroneously through the delusive influence of a too powerful imagination. The inordinately vigorous fancy, that enabled him to write *Queen Mab*, caused him sometimes to imagine things to have taken place, when they had not taken place. His mis-statements resulted altogether from misconception, and should not be regarded as in any way affecting the overwhelming evidence that he loved truth more than life; that he made great sacrifices for the truth's sake, that he was, in fact, a martyr for the truth. It is, however, all too certain that he uttered mis-statements, for which the force of his imagination cannot in any degree whatever have been accountable; and that, instead of being more truth-loving than most men, he was phenomenally untruthful. Telling fibs in order to escape momentary annoyance or gain a trivial advantage, he could instruct other persons to tell fibs in his interest. He was singular amongst men of his degree for being able to declare his intention of practising deceit, and forthwith being as bad as his word. Instances of this candour in falsehood are given in the ensuing pages. When he tells a fib, a gentleman is usually too much ashamed of the matter to take any one into his confidence on the subject. There were times, when no such sense of shame troubled Shelley.

Much has been written to Shelley's honour about his habitual temperance and general disregard for the pleasures of the table. It has been accounted to him for righteousness that he seldom drank wine, and for months together ate nothing but vegetable food. As Shelley at one period of his career found, or fancied, that his health was better, his mind lighter and more vigorous, his whole soul in higher contentment, when he lived wholly on vegetable food, than when he ate flesh, I cannot see why it was eminently virtuous in him to take the food that seemed to suit him best. As he drank fresh water and strong tea, because he liked them better than mild ale and stiff toddy, it remains to be shown why he should be so much commended for drinking what he liked best. Still temperance in diet is one of the minor virtues. But was Shelley a temperate man in his drinks? If he never drank wine immoderately, and in some periods of his career was a total abstainer from all the usual alcoholic drinks, it is certain that he was at times a heavy laudanum-drinker; and it is not obvious why it is less intemperate to be sottish with spirits of wine, in which opium has been macerated; than to be sottish with gin, in which gentian has been macerated.

Misrepresenting the poet's story in the smaller matters, the Shelleyan apologists have misrepresented it even more daringly in the larger matters. Endeavouring to explain away his gravest academic offence, they maintain that *The Necessity of Atheism* was a trivial essay, a little argumentative syllabus, a humorous *brochure*, that did not exhibit his real opinions on matters pertaining to religion; that it was printed only for private circulation amongst the learned; that it was never offered for sale to the general public. Yet it is certain that he reproduced some of its argument in the *Letter to Lord Ellenborough;* that more than two years after its first publication, he revised, amended, and reprinted it in the notes to *Queen Mab;* that later still he reproduced some of its reasoning in the *Refutation of Deism*, and that it was offered for sale to anyone who cared to buy it at Oxford. Mr. Garnett declares the essay to have been nothing more than 'a squib,' and gives Hogg as his authority for the staggering statement. Yet it is certain that Hogg makes no such statement; but is, on the contrary, most careful and precise in declaring how completely earnest and sincere Shelley was in the matter. Declaring that the essay was no expression of the author's genuine opinions, the Shelleyan apologists almost in the same breath declare it to have been an utterance of his real convictions, and applaud him for his courage in putting forth clearly what he believed to be true.

One of the prime biographic fictions about Shelley is, that he endured persecution for publishing this equally sincere and insincere profession of no faith, not only at Oxford but in his domestic circle. It is asserted that he was treated cruelly by his father, excluded from Field Place, driven from his boyhood's home, and even disinherited, for this and other bold declarations of what he believed to be true. Sympathy and admiration are demanded for him as a martyr for the truth's sake. 'On the sensitively affectionate feelings of the young controversialist and poet,' Lady Shelley says, ' this sentence of exclusion from his boyhood's home inflicted a bitter pang, yet he was determined to bear it for the sake of what he believed to be right and true.' With the perplexing perversity that characterised so many of his utterances about his private affairs, Shelley himself, after surrendering by his own **act, and** of his own will, the position assigned to him in respect to his grandfather's property by his grandfather's will, used **to** speak of himself as having made great sacrifices of his material interests for the truth, and to offer himself to the sympathy and admiration of his friends as a martyr for conscience's sake. Yet it is certain that he was treated kindly by his father in respect to the causes and immediate consequences of his academic disgrace ; that he was excluded from Field Place in the first instance, not on account **of his** religious opinions, but on account **of** his outrageous disregard for his father's wishes in respect to other matters ; **that he was excluded** from Field Place in 1811 only for **a few weeks, during which** time so far from ' being determined **to bear it for the sake of what** he believed to be right and true,' **he never for a moment** designed **to respect** the sentence of banishment, but intended to return to his boyhood's home as **soon as it should please** him to do so ; and that, the few weeks **of discord having** passed, he was received at Field Place by **his father and** endowed with a handsome yearly allowance of pocket-money. No less certain is it that he was never driven from **his boyhood's** home ; that on eventually withdrawing from the **old** domestic circle, he left **it of** his own accord, to make a runaway match with a licensed victualler's daughter ; and that, instead of resulting from differences of opinion on questions **of** religion and politics (differences which at most only aggravated and embittered a quarrel due to other **causes), his** estrangement from and rupture with his family resulted from (1) their reasonable displeasure at his *mésalliance*, **and (2)** the reasonable displeasure of his grandfather, and father, **at his refusal** to **concur** with them in effecting a particular settlement of certain real estate.

To give yet another example of the audacious way in which Shelley's story has been mistold in respect to its principal incidents. Every one has heard how Shelley was deprived of the custody of his children by Lord Eldon ; how, on account of his religious opinions, and for no other cause, he was robbed of his dear babes by the cruel and fanatical Lord Chancellor. Lady Shelley speaks furiously of 'the monstrous injustice of this decree.' In an article, written to the lively gratification of the Shelleyan Enthusiasts and the Shelleyan Socialists, the *Edinburgh Review* not long since (October, 1882) declared that the judgment was formed and the decree delivered, 'on the ground, not of Shelley's misconduct to his wife, but of the opinions expressed in his writings.' The words of the Edinburgh Reviewer are absolutely erroneous. The judgment was formed in steady consideration of the poet's misconduct to his first wife; and in its delivery the Chancellor was careful to say, not once, but repeatedly, that he decreed against the poet's petition, *not* on account of any opinions expressed in his writings (considered apart from conduct), *but* on account of his *conduct* (the word conduct, conduct, conduct, being reiterated by the Chancellor, till the reader of the decree grows weary of it)—on account of his *conduct* in respect to his wife; *conduct* showing his resolve to act on the Free Contract principles, set forth in the anti-matrimonial note to *Queen Mab; conduct* justifying the opinion that if Harriett Westbrook's children were delivered to him, he would rear them to hold his own anti-matrimonial views. That so respectable an organ of public opinion should make this statement is significant. It indicates how great is the force with which I venture to contend, not without hope that my weak hands may be strengthened by all who reverence marriage.

A matter to be noticed, in connection with the efforts to substitute the romantic for the Real Shelley, is that their success will involve the discredit, if not the absolute infamy, of nearly all the principal persons, whom the poet encountered in friendship or enmity, on his way from birth to death. To accept the extravagant stories told by Shelley or his idolaters is to believe, that the poet's father was a prodigy of parental wickedness; that his mother was hatefully deficient in maternal affection; that Dr. Greenlaw was a malicious, base-natured pedagogue; that the Eton masters (from Dr. Keate to Mr. Bethell) delighted in persecuting their famous pupil; that the Master and Fellows of University College were actuated by the basest motives (including sycophancy to a powerful minister) in requiring the poet to leave Oxford; that Hogg was a nauseous villain, who attempted to seduce his friend's wife within a few weeks of her wedding-day; that the first Mrs. Shelley broke her marriage-vow; that William Godwin, instead of feeling like the honest man he affected to be at his daughter's flight, chuckled in his sleeve at his girl's good fortune in winning a rich baronet's son for her paramour and eventual husband; that Lord Chancellor Eldon was an unjust judge, who delivered a monstrous decree at the instigation of religious bigotry and political resentment; that Peacock was either a simpleton or traitor in bearing testimony to the first Mrs. Shelley's conjugal goodness; that William Jerdan was a virulent slanderer; that Sir John Taylor Coleridge was a malignant calumniator; that Byron, whom Shelley throughout successive years honoured as a supremely great man, and for a while worshipt as a god, was the meanest, paltriest, dirtiest knave that ever broke a sacred trust, and stole a letter. It is thus that the creators of the romantic Shelley deal with the persons most influential on the poet's career and reputation. It is true they have good words for the hard-swearing Windsor apothecary, who gave the Etonian Shelley lessons in commination and chemistry; and for Leigh Hunt, the equally insatiable and charming parasite, who took all he could get from his young friend's pocket. The Squire of Field Place, Dr. Greenlaw, Dr. Keate. Mr. Bethell, the Master and Tutors of University College, Hogg, William Godwin, Lord Eldon, Peacock, William Jerdan, Sir John Taylor Coleridge, Byron, were all odious in different ways. The only good and true men, of all the many notable men, Shelley encountered on his way through life, were Dr. Lind and Leigh Hunt. Surely there must be something wrong in the story, that slays so many reputations, whilst it selects Dr. Lind and Leigh Hunt for approval.

Were there not another and very different side to the story, this book would not have been written. Unless I read it amiss (and I am sure I read it aright, for I have studied it carefully, and in doing so have found it to have been perused only in parts, and in some parts with strange carelessness, by all previous biographers), it stands out clear upon the record, that from his boyhood Shelley was disposed to rise in rebellion against all persons placed in authority over him; that instead of having the gentle nature attributed to him by fanciful historians, he was quick-tempered and resentful; that without being desperately wicked, his heart was strangely deceitful towards himself;

that he was a bad and disloyal son to a kind-hearted and well-intentioned father, and by no means a good son to a gentle-natured and conscientious mother; that he was a bad husband to his first wife, and far from a faultless husband to his second wife; that, together with several agreeable characteristics, he possessed several dangerous qualities; and that he was, at least towards one person, a bad friend.

So strangely has Shelley's story been mistold, that this last assertion is likely to make readers start with surprise and revolt against the author. Let it, therefore, be justified at once. The poet had a familiar friend, from whom he had received much kindness, for whom he professed cordial veneration, and with whom he lived in close intimacy. This friend had an only daughter, a bright, lively, romantic, lovely girl, still only sixteen years old. Reared within the lines of religious orthodoxy, this young girl had been educated to think of marriage just as other young English girls are usually taught to think of it. Though he had in former time been an advocate of the Free Contract, her father had changed his views about marriage before her birth, and had abandoned his Free Contract views when she was still a nursling. Soon after making this girl's acquaintance, Shelley passed into discord with his wife; and soon after ceasing to love his wife, he fixed his affections on his friend's daughter. Without speaking to his friend on the subject, or giving him occasion to suspect what he was about, Shelley paid his addresses to this child, and had won her heart, ere ever it occurred to her father that they might be living too intimately and affectionately with one another. It was with great difficulty Shelley overcame the child's notions of right in which she had been educated; but, eventually, he accomplished his purpose. A few days later, leaving his wife in England, Shelley stole this young child from her home, and, carrying her off to the Continent, lived with her as though she were his wife. He did this, though she was his most intimate friend's only daughter, though she was only sixteen years old, and though he had no prospect of ever being able to marry her. The creators of the romantic Shelley deal with this episode of Shelley's story as though it were a pleasant and unusually interesting love-passage. Some of them are unable to see that Shelley was at all to blame in the business. Those of them, who admit it was not altogether right of him to act thus towards so young a girl, maintain that the author of such superlatively fine poetry as *Adonais* and *The Cenci* cannot have been very **wrong** in the affair, and should not be judged in respect to the matter, **as** though he were a young man incapable of writing **fine** poetry. No one of them **has** a word of compassion for the girl's father. **Mr.** Froude is of opinion that **in this matter** Shelley was guilty of nothing worse than 'the sin of acting on emotional theories **of liberty,**' and should be judged tenderly, because he was young and enthusiastic! Differing **from Mr. Froude, I venture** to say that, in acting thus ill towards the girl, Shelley was guilty of very hateful treason **towards his friend. I ask** English fathers with young children about them, and English brothers with young sisters for playmates, to judge between me and my adversary.

Since it dismissed Hogg with scant courtesy for being too realistic and communicative, Field Place has done much to gratify the Shelleyan **enthusiasts** and socialists. Soon after publishing the uniformly erroneous *Shelley Memorials*, Field Place **promised to produce,** in due season, evidence that Shelley **was not seriously to blame in his** treatment of his first wife. **For** years Field Place has gathered evidences for the poet's vindication. Field Place aided Mr. Buxton Forman in producing his stately and careful edition **of** the poet's works. In **comparatively** recent time the **Field** Place muniments have enabled **a well-known** writer to produce the memoir of the poet's father-in-law (William Godwin), and a memoir of Mary Wollstonecraft, in which she is styled Gilbert Imlay's **wife, and** is said **to** have thought herself his wife before God and man, though they were never married. And now Field Place is enabling another writer to produce another authoritative history of Shelley and Mary, that shall raise Mary **Godwin yet** nearer to the angels, and bring her husband's story into more perfect harmony with the straight nose and **symmetrical** lineaments of Clint's composition.

It is not surprising that Field Place should wish to produce some more adequate memoir of its poet than Lady Shelley's *Shelley Memorials; from Authentic Sources.* But however cleverly it may be executed, only the most hopeful can hope that the promised biography will afford satisfaction to the general public. It is simply impossible for it to satisfy those who want the truth about Shelley, and at the same time to satisfy the enthusiasts who would be pained by the truth, and the Shelleyan Socialists who are chiefly desirous that the truth should not be told. To satisfy those who want the truth and the whole of it: to produce a memoir that shall be worth the paper on which it is printed, it will be necessary for the official biographer to show that Lady Shelley's work is from first to last a book of mistakes — that it is wrong in every page; wrong in its views of the poet's character; wrong in its general outline of his career; wrong in its incidents; wrong in its names and dates; wrong, even in its particulars of domestic affairs, legal matters, and pecuniary arrangements — particulars in respect to which a biographer, with access to authentic sources of information, has no excuse for blundering. Can such candour be looked for from the source which gave us the *Shelley Memorials?* Is it conceivable that the new official scribe will be permitted to deal thus honestly with Lady Shelley's book from authentic sources? If he is required to make his book agree with this thing from authentic sources, he must dismiss the hope of pleasing the general public.

On the other hand, to please the enthusiasts and the more fervid Shelleyan Socialists he must tell that Shelley was sinless, stainless, divine; that Mary Wollstonecraft was married, in the sight of God and man, to the American adventurer, who never married her; and that Mary Godwin showed a justifiable disregard of social prejudices, when she went off to Switzerland with another woman's husband. He must produce a work more or less calculated to illuminate the English people out of their reverence for marriage, and educate them into a philosophical tolerance of the Free Contract. Nothing less thorough will appear to the more fervid of the Shelleyan Socialists a sufficient vindication of the poet's superhuman excellence.

For in these days, to please both sets of zealots, it is not enough for a biographer to delight in Shelley's verse; to render homage to his genius; to think him — as all men of culture and poetical sensibility concur in thinking him — the brightest, most strenuous, and most musical of lyric poets; and at the same time, taking a charitable view of his failings and indiscretions, to palliate them in all honest ways, or look away from them, when they admit of no honest palliation. This is not enough for the enthusiasts, who insist that the poet's character and career were altogether in harmony with his art.

It only exasperates the most strenuous of the social innovators, who honouring him for his social philosophy even more than for his poetry, have no word of cordial censure, and scarcely a word of regret, for the way in which he acted on 'his emotional theories of liberty.' Readers must not blink the fact, that the more able and resolute of the Shelleyan enthusiasts recognize in Shelley a great social teacher and regenerator, as well as a great poet. To Mr. Buxton Forman, the author of *Laon and Cyntha* is 'that Shelley who, in some circumstances, might have been the Saviour of the World.' It is needless for me to express my opinion of the comparison instituted by these words. It is enough for me to say that the words are Mr. Buxton Forman's words, and that he represents favourably the learning and sentiment of a body of gentlemen, whose generous fervour appears to me more commendable than their discretion.

When it is possible for such words to be written by an eminent Shelleyan specialist, and to be read with approval by men of high culture, it must surely be admitted that Shelleyan enthusiasm has gone quite far enough ; and that it is well for a writer to produce a truthful account of the poet, who is thus offered to universal homage.

I have not discovered the Real Shelley. The poet of these volumes is the same Real Shelley, who appears in his most agreeable aspects in Hogg's biography, the delightful book that was stopped midway, because its realism offended the Hunts and Field Place. I mean to show that Shelley was judged fairly, though severely, by those of his contemporaries who, whilst recognizing his genius, condemned his principles, conduct, and social theories. In respect to the Real Shelley, I shall merely bring to light what has been hurtfully withdrawn, or hurtfully withheld from view. As for the fictitious Shelley, with which the Real Shelley has been replaced, I mean to demolish it. In destroying it, I shall be animated by a desire to do something before I go away, to counteract the strong stream of literature—a literature of books, pamphlets, magazine-articles, and articles in powerful journals—which for more than a quarter of a century has been educating people to approve or tolerate the pernicious social philosophy, that requires sound-hearted England to abolish marriage and replace it with the Free Contract.

CHAPTER II.

THE SHELLEYS OF SUSSEX.

Medwin's Blunders—Lady Shelley's Statement of The Case—The **Michel-grove** Shelleys—Sir William Shelley, Justice of The Common Pleas—The **Castle** Goring Shelleys—Their Pedigree at the Heralds' College—**Evidences** of the Connexion of the Two Families—John Shelley, 'Esquire and Lunatic'—Timothy Shelley, the Yankee Apothecary—Bysshe **Shelley's Career**—His Runaway Match with Catherine Michell—His Marriage with the Heiress of Penshurst—His Great **Wealth**—The Poet's Alleged Pride in his Connexion with **the** Sidneys—His Gentle, but not Aristocratic, Lineage.

So much has been written in the ways of sycophancy or vaingloriousness about Shelley's Norman descent and aristocratic quality, it is necessary to glance at some of the facts of his ancestral story.

The poet's friend, from the time when they were schoolfellows at Brentford, Thomas Medwin the Younger, was also the poet's kinsman—his third cousin, through Sir Bysshe Shelley's marriage with Mary Catherine Michell, and his second cousin, through Sir Timothy Shelley's marriage with Elizabeth Pilford. It might have been supposed that a biographer, thus related to Shelley by blood and friendship, would know the prime facts of his friend's pedigree, and state them without egregious error. But poor Tom Medwin was not remarkable for accuracy.

To rely in this affair on the whilom *littérateur* and cavalry officer, is to believe that the poet was a lineal descendant of Sir John Shelley of Maresfield Park, who was created a baronet in 1611; to believe that this Sir John Shelley's son (William) was a Justice of the Common Pleas; and to believe that the poet's great-grandfather (Timothy Shelley, of Fen Place, Co. Sussex) was a lineal descendant, in the ninth descent, of the aforesaid baronet of James the First's time. 'I will only say,' Medwin remarks lightly, 'that Sir John Shelley, of Maresfield Park, who dated his Baronetage from the earliest creation of that title in 1611, had besides other issue, two sons, Sir William, a Judge of the Common Pleas, and Edward; from the latter of whom, in the seventh descent, sprung Timothy, who also had two sons, and settled—having married an American lady—at Christ's Church, Newark, in North America.'

Medwin is wrong in all the really important allegations of the brief statement. Sir John Shelley of Michelgrove (the baronet referred to) had two sons; but neither of them was named Edward; neither of them became a Justice of the Common Pleas; neither of them was in any way or degree accountable for Percy Bysshe Shelley's appearance on the earth's surface. The poet was no more descended from Sir John Shelley, the first of the Michelgrove baronets, than he was descended from the man in the moon. How could the poet's great-grandfather (Timothy, born in 1700 A.D.) be the eighth in descent from the first Michelgrove baronet, the seventh in descent from either of the baronet's sons? Human generations do not come and go at the rate of seven to a century.

To pass for a moment from Tom Medwin (of whose egregious mis-statements something more must be said) to the present Lady Shelley, the poet's daughter-in-law. 'At the close of the last century,' says this lady in her *Shelley Memorials: from Authentic Sources*, 'the family of the Shelleys had long held a high position among the large landholders of Sussex. Fortunate marriages in two generations preceding the birth of the poet considerably increased the wealth and influence of the house, the head of which was a staunch Whig.' Lady Shelley's book from authentic sources contains several statements of no authenticity. For each of the principal statements of the above-quoted words, she had, however, good authority. But instead of coming to her from a single authentic source, the facts embodied in the quotation were drawn from two different authentic sources, the archives of the Michelgrove Shelleys, and the archives of the Castle Goring Shelleys; and by cleverly combining the two sets of facts, Lady Shelley conveys to her readers a very erroneous impression respecting the condition of the poet's seventeenth-century ancestors. Unquestionably, the Sussex Shelleys, at the close of the eighteenth century, had long held a high position among the large landowners of the county. But these fortunate Shelleys were not the family of which the poet was the brightest ornament. They were the Michelgrove Shelleys;

whereas the poet came of people, differing greatly from the Michelgrove people in social quality. He was of the Castle Goring Shelleys—a family that, instead of being merely enriched, was created and established by the fortunate marriages to which Lady Shelley refers. Before the first of those marriages, wedlock had done much for the advantage of these inferior Shelleys. For instance, the marriage, in 1692, of John Shelley, of Fen Place, *jure uxoris*, with Helen, co-heir of Roger Bysshe, of Fen Place, Co. Sussex, had reclaimed the poet's direct male ancestors from a state of territorial vagrancy, and given them a permanent, though modest, abiding-place. But for a considerable period after that marriage, the direct ancestral precursors of the Castle Goring Shelleys were no such house as the readers of Lady Shelley's book are likely to imagine. The Michelgrove Shelleys were one 'house,' the Castle Goring Shelleys were quite another house; though it has for some time been the fashion of biographers to mix the two houses, and speak of them by turns as one house, or as branches of the same house. The Michelgrove Shelleys were an ancient house. The Castle Goring Shelleys were a mushroom family, disdainfully regarded by the Michelgrove people, at the opening of the nineteenth century.

Something more must be said of the older of these houses. The Michelgrove Shelleys are said, for reasons no longer discoverable, to have entered the country with the Conqueror. They may have done so. There is better evidence that they had lands in Kent in the times of Edward I. and Edward II., before they established themselves in Sussex; and still better testimony, that one of the clan (John Shelley) was Member of Parliament for Rye from 1415 to 1428. With this parliamentary personage, the house, or rather the family from which the house proceeded, comes into the clear light of history. Two long generations later (generations so lengthy that one has reason to suspect a failure of the record) the house acquired a dignity, which gave it an enduring place amongst the historic families of the realm.

Bred to the law, William Shelley (the grandson, or maybe the great-grandson, of the afore-mentioned Member for Rye) became Reader of the Inner Temple in 1517, and after holding successively the office of a Judge of the Sheriff's Court and the office of Recorder of the City of London, rose to be a

Judge of the Common Pleas somewhere about the beginning of 1527. Before mounting to this eminence he had represented the City in Parliament, and practised for six years as a Serjeant-at-law in Westminster Hall. Those who know Cavendish's *Wolsey* do not need to be reminded of the part taken by this fortunate lawyer in the negotiations that closed with the Cardinal's surrender of York House to Henry the Eighth. 'Tell his Highness,' said the fallen Cardinal to the Judge of the Common Pleas, 'that I am his most faithful subject and obedient beadsman, whose command I will in no wise disobey; but will in all things fulfil his pleasure, as you the father of the law say I may. I therefore charge your conscience to discharge me, and show His Highness from me that I must desire His Majesty to remember there is both heaven and hell;' a message which the judge probably forgot to deliver, as he lived to entertain the King at Michelgrove, and was continued in his office till Henry's death. Surviving the sovereign, whom he served on the bench of the Common Pleas for twenty years, Sir William Shelley served Edward the Sixth in the same capacity, to the day of his own death, which occurred between November 3, 1548 (the date of his last fine), and May 10, 1549, the date of his successor's appointment.

Fortunate in his professional career, Sir William Shelley was no less fortunate in his domestic affairs. Marrying an heiress, he had, with other children, John, the grandfather of the first Michelgrove baronet, and Sir Richard Shelley, the last English Prior of St. John of Jerusalem.

Not much less than a century wrong in assigning the legal eminence of Henry the Eighth's judge to the eldest son of James the First's baronet, Medwin wrote under a general impression that the Shelleys to whom he was related, had somehow or other descended from the Michelgrove house, an impression which the poet seems also to have cherished, and imparted to his college-friend and biographer, Thomas Jefferson Hogg, who writes in serio-comic vein of Sir Guyon de Shelley and Sir Richard Shelley (the Knight of Malta), as though the Grand Prior of the sixteenth century and the Paladin with the three conchs were veritable forefathers of the Castle Goring Shelleys.

That these Shelleys of the junior house were no family of singular antiquity or overpowering dignity, is shown by the pedigree of Percy Bysshe Shelley, published in the first volume of Mr. Forman's edition of the poet's prose works. A pedigree of only nine generations, beginning with mention of Henry Shelley, of Worminghurst, Co. Sussex, who died in 1623, this evidential writing puts it beyond question that the poet, of whose ancestral grandeur so much has been written, was no man of noble or otherwise splendid lineage; puts it beyond question, that whether regard be had to the number of its generations, the antiquity of the earliest dates, or the importance of the persons commemorated in its entries, it is (from the date of Henry Shelley's death *temp.* James I. to Percy Bysshe Shelley's birth in 1792) nothing more than such a pedigree as could be displayed by the majority of the gentle families of the middle way of English life, who never for a moment think of rating themselves as families of patrician worth.

One or two rather awkward matters excepted, this pedigree is a fair and honest record of the births, marriages, and deaths, of nine successive generations of gentle people; but as an exhibition of familiar grandeur, it is no more impressive than any pedigree one would regard as a matter of course in the muniment room of a country gentleman, tracing his descent from a gentle yeoman of the Elizabethan period. It mentions eight of the poet's forefathers in the direct right line. Describing some of these eight individuals as 'esquires,' and some of them as 'gentlemen,' the record shows that no one of them bore any hereditary honour, or even the dignity of knighthood before the poet's birth. It shows that no one of them married a woman of higher quality than the degree of a simple gentlewoman. Doubtless they were (with a single exception) gentlewomen in the heraldic sense of the term,—daughters of gentlemen bearing arms,—but to use an old-world phrase, no one of them was 'a woman of quality.' The record shows, that at the time of the poet's birth, no one of his eight male ancestors in the direct right line had served the State with distinction, won a foremost place in one of the learned professions, or attained to any social eminence higher than a place in a Commission of the Peace.

Such is the evidence of the document of which Mr. Forman justly remarks, 'the pedigree speaks for itself to any careful reader.' And this evidence is the more impressive, because the carefully elaborated record is the pedigree deposited at the Heralds' College on 6th March, 1816, by Mr. John Shelley

Sidney (the poet's uncle by the half-blood), at a moment when he was especially desirous of figuring to the best possible advantage in the esteem of heralds and their employers. Regard being had to this gentleman's character and social ambition, and his pride in his descent from the Sidneys, it cannot be questioned that he made his genealogical record showy and impressive to the utmost of his ability,—that he would fain have driven it back another generation,—that could he have demonstrated a connection between the Castle Goring and Michelgrove Shelleys, he would not have omitted to prove them two branches of the same tree.

Mr. John Shelley Sidney's forbearance from pushing the genealogical record a single stage backwards beyond the certain evidences, is the more noteworthy and creditable, because he can scarcely have been ignorant of the inconclusive, though by no means inconsiderable, testimony that the Henry Shelley, who died at Worminghurst in 1623, was the grandson of Edward Shelley of the said parish, and that this Edward Shelley was the younger brother of the Judge of the Common Pleas, who was the actual founder of the Michelgrove family.

What are the inconclusive, though considerable, evidences of this descent of the Castle Goring Shelleys and the Michelgrove Shelleys from a common ancestor, John Shelley, the judge's father? A manuscript, in the possession of the present Sir Percy Shelley, bears witness that the Henry Shelley, of Worminghurst, mentioned in the first entry of the pedigree (deposited by Mr., afterwards Sir John Shelley Sidney in the Heralds' College), was the son of Henry Shelley of the same parish. Consequently, if reliance may be placed on this manuscript, the most ancient of the male ancestors in the right line, from whom Mr. John Shelley Sidney traced his descent, was preceded by his father at Worminghurst, a fact carrying the poet's lineage another generation backwards, into the closing term of the Tudor period. There is, moreover, in the chancel of Worminghurst Church, a brass, of sixteenth century workmanship, to the memory of Edward Shelley, Esq., one of the four masters of the royal household, in the successive reigns of Henry the Eighth, Edward the Sixth, and Mary Tudor. There are grounds for believing that this Edward Shelley was a son of John Shelley, of Michelgrove, and younger brother of Sir William Shelley, Justice of the Common Pleas. The archives of the Michelgrove Shelleys certify that Sir William Shelley, the judge of the Common Pleas, had a younger brother named Edward. That the poet's certain male ancestors in the right line bore the same arms as the Michelgrove Shelleys in the seventeenth century, that vigilant heralds permitted them to bear those arms, and that no baronet of the Michelgrove Shelleys ever questioned their right to bear those arms, are noteworthy pieces of testimony that the two families came from the same source. In the absence of positive evidence of the fact, it cannot be denied that Sir Bernard Burke had sufficient presumptive testimony, to warrant him in recording that the poet was a lineal descendant of Edward Shelley, the judge's younger brother. There is also fair presumptive testimony that the judge's younger brother Edward was the Edward Shelley, who held office as one of the Masters of Henry the Eighth's household, and found his grave in Worminghurst. Such evidence would not be sufficient to establish a claim to a dormant peerage, or to the reversion of a great estate; but it is sufficient for the purpose of Shelley's personal historian.

'The house,' which Lady Shelley regards as having been merely enriched by the fortunate marriages that created it, was a curiously vagrant family for a house 'holding a high position among the large landholders of Sussex.' Leaving Worminghurst, Co. Sussex, on the demise of Henry Shelley ('esq.,' as he is described in the official pedigree), who died there in 1623, the house moved to Ichingfield, in the time of Richard Shelley ('gent.,' as he is modestly defined in the same genealogical chart). Under the government of John Shelley, 'esq.,' who died in 1673, the house rested at Thakeham, whence it migrated to Fen Place, in the parish of Worth, Co. Sussex, on the marriage, in 1692, of John Shelley (of Fen Place, *jure uxoris*, Co. Sussex, esq.), with Hellen, younger of the two daughters and co-heirs of Roger Bysshe, of Fen Place, aforesaid. Of the eight children of this marriage, the reader of the present work is invited to take notice of no more than two, John Shelley, the second, and Timothy Shelley, the third son. Born at Worth in 1696, this last-named John Shelley, who died in 1772 at Uckfield, is handed down to all future time by the pedigree as 'an esquire and lunatic.' That there was a strain of insanity in the Castle-Goring Shelleys is a matter to be borne in mind by those who are interested in the poet and his nearest kindred.   Percy Bysshe was great-great-nephew of this lunatic, and great-grandson of the lunatic's brother, Timothy, of whom further mention must be made.

Born at Worth, in April 1700, the third son, and fifth child, of a petty squireen, who lived to have nine children to set going in the world, Timothy, on coming to man's estate, emigrated to the American plantations, with a slender purse and an abundant store of physical energy.   It is probable that he also carried across the Atlantic some knowledge of medicine and surgery, acquired during an apprenticeship to a country apothecary.   As there is no evidence that he passed, or tried to pass, an examination at the Apothecaries' Hall, or Surgeons' Hall, nor any evidence that the adventurer underwent any medical training before he crossed the Atlantic, Medwin may have been right in believing that he fought life's battle in the New World as 'a quack doctor.'   It should, however, be borne in mind that, if he had served an apprenticeship to a Sussex apothecary, this Timothy would have possessed all the legal qualification to kill and cure, that was required of provincial apothecaries in the mother country prior to the Medical Act of 1814.   Anyhow, with or without qualification, the adventurer established himself as a medicine man, and with quackery, or without it, throve in his adopted calling.   Practising at Christ's Church, Newark, he married a widow with money.   In this last particular he held firmly to the main article of Shelleyan worldly wisdom. The poet's ancestors may have married for love, but they usually required a substantial compensation for the loss of celibatic freedom.   The widow to whom Timothy surrendered himself was the widow of a New York miller, named Plum ; and it is believed that her purse satisfied the hopes planted in her admirer's breast by so suggestive a name.   Marrying thus prudently, Timothy Shelley, of Newark, became the father of his first-born son, John Shelley, on the 10th of December, 1729, and of his second son, Bysshe Shelley (the first of the Castle Goring baronets), on the 21st of June, 1731.

It is doubtful when Timothy of Newark returned to England, where his father died in 1739, after surviving his eldest and issueless son by some six years.   He may have sailed 'for home,' on news coming to him in Newark of his father's death. That he became the actual chief of the family on his father's demise may be inferred from the fact that he is styled in the pedigree his father's 'heir.' After setting his English affairs in order, he may have returned to America for awhile. It is more probable, however, that, returning to England with his two boys, when the elder of them was some *ten*, and the younger some *eight* years old, he was content to play the part of a modest Sussex squireen to the day of his death. Anyhow it is certain the equally adventurous and fortunate apothecary (or 'quack doctor,' if any reader prefers Tom Medwin's word) was the squire of Fen Place for a considerable term of years, before he was coffined, and put under the floor of Warnham Church, in 1770, some two years and six months before the death of his elder and lunatic brother.

What became of this fortunate apothecary's two sons, John (the elder) and Bysshe (the younger)? Becoming the head of 'the House' on his father's demise in 1770, the apothecary's elder son married the daughter of a Sussex gentleman, led a comparatively uneventful life at Field Place, near Horsham, and dying childless in 1790, was buried in Warnham Church; being succeeded by his younger brother, a man far superior to him in address and energy, if not in benevolence and piety. Planted by the petty squireen, who took possession of Roger Bysshe's daughter and home, and watered by the apothecary who had followed fortune, and found money in America, the family that gave England her brightest, and sweetest, and most passionate lyric poet, was raised to the dignity of a house, by the craft, greed, and penuriousness of Bysshe Shelley, the first baronet of Castle Goring.

The several excellent writers, who have been misled on the matter by Medwin, the Misleader, may take the present writer's assurance that the gentleman, who won a baronetcy in his old age, never 'exercised the profession of a quack doctor' in America. There is, however, sufficient evidence that the Newark apothecary's younger son was designed to follow his father's calling. In his sordid and eccentric old age, when the lord of Castle Goring inhabited a small house hard by his favourite tap-room in Horsham, it was generally believed that he had at one time practised medicine in London. It may also be put upon the present record, that he was believed to have been a partner in the professional activities of Dr. James Graham, the notorious mesmeric charlatan, in whose Temple of Health the fair and frail Emma Harte officiated as the Goddess Hygeia, before she became Sir William Hamilton's wife and Nelson's mistress. Percy Bysshe, the poet, told Hogg, that his grandfather supplied the money which enabled Graham to set up his preposterous purple chariot. Percy's statements, however, should be regarded suspiciously, when they tend to the discredit of his sire and grandsire.

Whatever the means he used for making money, it is certain that the man, who in his old age was remarkable for the stateliness of his presence, and in his milder moods for the courtesy of manner, possessed in his youth no ordinary charms of appearance and address. Tall, even as his famous grandson, and qualified by his blue eyes and brown curls to captivate heedless womankind, he had not crossed the threshold of manly estate, when he found favour in the eyes of Miss Mary Catherine Michell, only child and heir of the late Reverend Theobald Michell, clk., formerly of Horsham. The young lady (only eighteen years old) having considerable possessions, it is probable that her guardians thought she could do better for herself than marry the boyish medical student, who was only the younger son of the squire and whilom apothecary of Fen Place. Possibly they only expressed a strong opinion, that the young man should wait awhile, and thereby avoid the evils of precipitate wedlock. Possibly they had no opportunity of expressing an opinion on the matter, until remonstrance would have been out of time. To the young people it appeared a case for elopement and irregular marriage ; and, acting on this romantic view of their position, they hastened to town and were married in 1752, at Keith's Chapel, Mayfair (the fashionable place for Fleet marriages done in the west end of the town). From Keith's Chapel they hastened to Paris, where the bride fell ill of small-pox, and narrowly escaped the death that would have made Tom Medwin's mother the heir of the late Rev. Theobald Michell's estate. Eight years later, the lady died after giving birth to three children, and Mr. Bysshe Shelley was at liberty to look out for a second heiress willing to become his wife. The only son of this marriage was Timothy Shelley, the poet's father, who became M.P. for New Shoreham, Co. Sussex.

Nine years after his first wife's death, Mr. Bysshe Shelley fixed his affections on another heiress—the heiress of an historic line and an historic estate—Miss Elizabeth Jane Sidney Perry, only daughter and heir of William Perry, Esq., of Turvill Park, Bucks, Wormington, Co. Gloucester, and Penshurst Place, Co. Kent. It is remarkable that an heiress of so bright a lineage and so noble an estate—an heiress who, in descent and fortune, was a fit match for an earl—an heiress lineally descended from the Sidneys, Earls of Leicester—should have lived in singleness to her twenty-ninth year. Perhaps this remarkable fact gave the younger son of the Newark apothecary the requisite courage for a daring exploit.

Thirty-eight years old, he was no longer young when he first conceived the purpose of winning so notable an heiress. But though well on in middle age, he had the figure, and face, and audacity, of a youngster. Taking up a position, suitable for his purpose, in a little inn near the Park, celebrated by Jonson's verse, and glorified by the loves of Waller and Saccharissa, he crossed the lady's path in her walks, regarded her worshipfully when she attended the services of Penshurst Church, knelt to her beneath the spreading branches of 'the Lady's Oak.' Is it marvellous that a suitor, so eager and vigilant, so comely and daring, achieved his purpose, notwithstanding the disadvantages of inferior station and growing years? Is it wonderful that the gentlewoman eloped with the suitor, who valued her far more for her broad acres than her descent from the Sidneys? Whatever the motives to the suit, Mr. Bysshe Shelley won, in gallant fashion, the lady by whom he had his second lot of children,—five sons and two daughters.

In the year following this marriage, the Newark apothecary was entombed in Warnham Church; and eleven years later (May 1781) Mr. Bysshe Shelley again found himself a widower when he was still in his fiftieth year. Henceforth he devoted himself chiefly to the pursuit of money,—a pursuit in which he was favoured by the death of his childless brother in 1790, when he succeeded to the Fen Place and Field Place estates.

The family having come to his hands, he made 'a House' of it. In 1806,—when his little grandson, the future poet, was on the point of going to Eton,—Mr. Bysshe Shelley became Sir Bysshe Shelley, baronet, of Castle Goring; the dignity being the price, with which the Duke of Norfolk rewarded him for former electioneering service, and prepaid him for similar service to be rendered to the Howards and the Whig party to the end of his days. At the date of this social promotion, Sir

Bysshe Shelley had already begun to build the egregious Castle which he never finished, though he is said, by the unreliable Medwin, to have spent 80,000*l.* upon it.

If he ever hoped for happiness in his later time, the hope was disappointed. After he had married his daughters, and sent his sons into life, the passion for money, which had long overpowered the other forces of his nature, developed even to miserly madness. In other respects the strain of insanity, that had given him a lunatic for an uncle, displayed itself in his manifold eccentricities. Living at Horsham, in a little house, and finding his most congenial associates in the tap-rooms of the Horsham taverns, whilst his grandson went to school at Brentford and Eton, the founder of the Castle Goring Shelleys disliked his son so cordially, that he is said to have seldom greeted him without an outbreak of passionate malevolence. Percy, the future poet, used to entertain his comrades at Eton by cursing his absent sire; and at Oxford, he assured Hogg, that he had acquired this singular taste for cursing his father behind his back, from hearing old Sir Bysshe curse him to his face. It was thus that this chief of the Castle Goring Shelleys lived from the creation of his baronetcy in 1806 to his death in 1815, when he left vast wealth in money and lands, *In Trust*, for the creation of the big entailed estate, that should perpetuate the grandeur of ' the House ' he had laboured so resolutely to found. Medwin (no safe authority on details) says the old man left to his descendants 300,000*l.* in the English funds, and landed estates yielding a yearly revenue of 20,000*l.*, besides the bank-notes to the amount of 10,000*l.* that were hidden in the books and other furniture of the room, where he drew and yielded his last breath.

Another thing to be noticed in the evidences of this family is the testimony to the newness of its grandeur, that may be gathered from the records of its territorial possessions. Fen Place came to these Shelleys, through the wedding-ring, so recently as the last decade of the seventeenth century. They acquired Field Place by purchase in the earlier half of the following (the eighteenth) century. For their place ' among the large landholders of Sussex,' they are mainly indebted to the Newark apothecary's younger son, who flourished in George the Third's time, and died only a few months before the battle of Waterloo.

To take a true view of the poet's lineage and ancestral quality, the reader must bear in mind the distinctness of the Michelgrove Shelleys and the Castle Goring Shelleys,—a distinctness that would not be affected by the production of positive and indisputable evidence, that the two families had for their common progenitor, a gentle yeoman of Henry the Eighth's time. Should this remote connexion of the two families ever be put beyond question, it would be none the less true that, instead of being of aristocratic descent, as so many biographers have asserted, the poet came of a line of forefathers who were nothing more than 'gentle yeomen' till the later time of George III. The poet was no lineal descendant of the Justice of the Common Pleas, who may be fairly styled the founder of the Michelgrove House. From the date of that slightly historic personage, the Michelgrove family was a knightly house. Baronets from the creation of the order, they intermarried with knightly and noble houses before and after 1611, drawing to their veins the blood of the Belknaps, Fitz-Williamses, Sackvilles, Lovells, Reresbys, Vantelets, and Nevills. On the other hand, from the earliest date of his genealogical record, the poet's ancestors were mere gentle yeomen, intermarrying with families of no higher gentility, till the poet's grandfather carried off the heiress of the Penshurst Sidneys.

As no drop of Sidney blood came to his veins from his grandfather's second marriage, and as his kindred of the half-blood at Penshurst were not over-fond of their half-cousins at Field Place, it is scarcely conceivable the poet was so proud of his connexion with the Sidneys as Medwin represents. It may, however, have been so. For with all his vaunted superiority to aristocratic prejudice, and all his sincere hostility to aristocratic privilege, Shelley was by no means exempt from the weakness, which disposed Byron in his vainer moods to think too much of his nobility. The advocate of republican ideas, the apostle of freedom and equality, he was sometimes curiously careful to remind his admirers that he was no demagogue of vulgar origin, but resembled the Lionel of *Rosalind and Helen*, in being the heir to 'great wealth and lineage high.' When this humour prevailed within him, it is possible that he sometimes looked away from the father whom he hated, the grandsire he despised, the obscure yeomen whom he distasted, and could persuade himself that, like his half-cousins at Penshurst, he, too, had somehow or other descended from the Sidneys. But no such innocent exercise of fancy would touch the facts or qualify the complexion of his genealogy. It is nothing to the poet's dishonour to say that, though better born than Shakespeare, he was no more fortunate in his ancestral story than the majority—or, at least, a large minority of English gentlemen, moving in the middle ways of gentle life.

CHAPTER III.

SHELLEY'S CHILDHOOD.

The Poet's Father—Shelley's Birth and Birth-Chamber—Miss Hellen
   Shelley's Recollections—The Child-Shelley's Pleasant Fiction—His
   Aspect at Tender Age—His Description of his own Nose—The Indian-
   Ink Sketch—Miss Curran's 'Daub'—Williams's Water-Colour Drawing
   —Clint's Composition—Engravings of 'The Daub' and 'The Compo-
   sition'—The Poet's Likeness in Marble—Shelley and Byron—Peacock
   and Hogg on Shelley's Facial Beauty—The Colnaghi Engraving.

WHATEVER the failings of the Newark apothecary's younger
son, it must be recorded to his credit that he gave his son an
education befitting the chief of a territorial family. Inferior
though he was in tact and politeness to the great Chesterfield,
whose precepts and example are said to have been largely
accountable for his manners and morality, Mr. Timothy Shelley
(Sir Bysshe's son and heir by Mary Catherine Michell) received
the training, and, notwithstanding the eccentricities that provoked the smiles of London drawing-rooms, had the port and
temper of an English gentleman.

It has been the fashion of biographers to decry this gentleman. Readers, however, should decline to accept the poet's
estimate of the second baronet of Castle Goring, though
the much-maligned gentleman wrote comically ungrammatical
letters, thought too highly of himself, talked boastfully over
his second bottle, swore well up to the mark of Georgian good
breeding, and believed himself the originator of every strenuous
argument in Paley's *Evidences*. The good landlord and kindly
patron of aged servants, the squire whose virtues blossomed
in the dust, the amiable father whose parental excellences
were gratefully remembered by all his surviving children, was
neither the fool nor the barbarian his eldest son thought him.

The Shelleyan enthusiasts have little charity for the poet's
sire, even the most discreet of them regarding him as a deplorably inconvenient father for so marvellous a son. It is not
clear what kind of father would have won Percy's filial loyalty.
In fairness to this sire, it should be remembered that, if he was

not the right kind of father for the poet, he proved an excellent father to all his other children; and that, if the poet should have had a more congenial father, Squire Timothy could not well have had a more trying son than the boy of latent genius, who lived to cover his house with glory.

After keeping his terms at the same Oxford College, from which his son was expelled in the following century, Mr. Timothy Shelley made 'the grand tour,' returning in due course with a smattering of French, an extremely bad picture of the Eruption of Vesuvius, and 'a certain air' (if Medwin may be trusted) of having seen the world. Having surveyed mankind in European capitals, and entered middle age, he married Miss Elizabeth Pilfold, a gentlewoman of good family and great beauty, who is lightly regarded by the Shelleyan enthusiasts, because, in the conflict of her husband and her son, she held loyally to the former, and declined to be the partisan of the latter. It has even been urged to this lady's discredit that, when her wilful boy would fain have shaken his sister's confidence in the doctrines of the Church of England, she, in her mental narrowness, was alarmed for the spiritual safety of her girls, and thought it well that at least for a time they should be guarded from his influence.

Had these parents foreseen the trouble that would come to them from their first-born child, they would have welcomed him coldly on his arrival in the room (at Field Place), one of whose walls has in recent time been illustrated with this inscription:—

PERCY BYSSHE SHELLEY

WAS BORN IN THIS CHAMBER

AUGUST 4TH, 1792.

SHRINE OF THE DAWNING SPEECH AND THOUGHT

OF SHELLEY SACRED BE

TO ALL WHO BOW WHERE TIME HAS BROUGHT

GIFTS TO ETERNITY.

Of Shelley, the little fellow of Dr. Greenlaw's school at Brentford, we know much from Tom Medwin's occasionally accurate pages, and from other sources of information, which enable us to check the statements of that more entertaining than reliable biographer. Respecting Shelley at Eton, there is almost a redundance of evidence. Of the Etonian's ways of amusing himself at Field Place during his holidays, there is no lack of information;—thanks to Miss Hellen Shelley's goodness in committing all she could remember of her brother to paper, for the assistance of his biographer and fellow-collegian, Hogg, the cynical humourist and clever lawyer. But of Shelley, the nursling of the Field Place nursery, and child of the Field Place schoolroom, few facts are on the record;—scarcely anything besides the three or four matters, which Miss Hellen placed amongst her personal recollections, as matters of domestic tradition, coming to her from times before she was of an age to take clear and enduring cognizance of her brother's doings.

Seven years his junior, the lady, plying her pen in 1856 (four-and-thirty years after his death), can scarcely have retained any clear memories of him, from a time previous to the opening of her ninth year. Barely seven years old, when her brother went for the first time to Eton, she had in 1856 a memory of uncommon retentiveness, if it afforded her a clear picture of him, as he appeared during the first of his Eton holidays. Fortunately, however, she touches on affairs and incidents of an earlier date; such, for instance, as his visits to the Warnham Vicar, who taught him the rudiments of Latin, visits that began when he was only six years old, and she was still unborn. To this gentle and delightful chronicler, speaking for the moment from memory of her mother's gossip, we are indebted for our knowledge of the astonishment little Bysshe (whilst a Latin scholar at the Vicar's school) caused the elders of Field Place, by repeating aloud, word for word, and without an error, Gray's lines on the Cat and the Gold Fish, after a single reading of the composition.

Without precisely declaring herself indebted to hearsay for the story, Miss Hellen seems to be speaking of a matter anterior to the earliest of her personal observations, when she gives us the particulars of the marvellous 'invention' with which Percy in his tender childhood entertained and perplexed the people of his home. The essay in romantic fiction was this: Assuring his sisters (Hellen's elder sisters) that he had just returned from paying a visit to certain ladies of their village, he recounted to them, minutely, how the ladies received him, how they occupied themselves during his visit, and more particularly how he and they wandered through a delightful garden, well known to the boy's auditors for its filbert bank and undulating turf bank. On inquiry, it was found that the imaginative urchin had not been to the ladies, their house, or their garden. The whole statement was made up of fibs; 'but' (says the recorder of the characteristic incident) 'it was not considered as a falsehood to be punished.' Perhaps it would have been better in the long run for little Bysshe, had a less lenient view been taken of the affair that, if not the first, was one of the earliest of those countless deviations from strict historical veracity, which have occasioned so much controversy between his extravagant idolaters and his temperate admirers.

Of the droll things written of the poet by his enthusiastic worshipers, few are droller than the pages in which this exercise of childish fancy is dealt with, as an early exhibition of the peculiar genius that placed him eventually in the highest rank of imaginative artists. Had they not been too engrossed with the affairs of their own home to take nice cognizance of their neighbours' children, the elders of Field Place, whilst rightly regarding the fib as no flagrant offence, would not have 'mentioned it as a singular fact.' To those who are familiar with the ways and humours of children, it is needless to say, that little Bysshe's 'invention' is an example of the commonest kind of the harmless fibs, that come from the proverbially truthful mouths of babes and sucklings. Poets would be unendurably abundant, if all the little boys and girls, who 'romance' in this innocent fashion, were destined for the service of the Muses.

In Shelley's case, however, the story has an exceptional interest, because he never survived the disposition, which thus early in his career caused him to proclaim himself the recipient of civilities that had not been offered to him,—the graceful actor in a domestic drama that had not been performed. All through life, Shelley had a practice of uttering for the truth statements that were not true. All through life, his familiar friends received his communications, with reference to this propensity. Out of their affection for the man, they palliated the weakness with more or less sincere excuses, that relieved the infirmity of the odium of deceitfulness. Some of his friends called attention to the poetical verity, underlying the least veracious statements; others persuaded themselves that the speaker of untruths was the victim of an inordinately powerful imagination. Others, unable to shut their eyes to the sure indications that he was not altogether unaware of the fictitious nature of his statements, maintained that the fables were due partly to hallucination, and only in some degree to wilful inventiveness. Whilst Hogg talked of the poetic verity of the egregious fictions, and of their utterer's inordinately powerful imagination, Peacock originated the theory of 'semi-delusion.'

From the few glimpses to be had of him in Miss Hellen Shelley's letters, and Medwin's reminiscences, and from bits of testimony which, though found in records of his later boyhood, are evidential to certain particulars of his earlier infancy, the cautious historian can produce the principal characteristics of the little fellow, who used to play with his sisters in the Field Place gardens, and ride on his pony about the Warnham lanes, in years anterior to his first departure from home for boarding-school. It is manifest that the child, who from his seventh to his eleventh year went daily to the Warnham Vicar for instruction in Latin, and received his other lessons in his sisters' schoolroom, may be thought of as a shy, nervous, timid, small-headed urchin; tall for his years, but delicately fashioned. Narrow-chested and slightly round-shouldered, he had the look of a little fellow, scarcely strong enough to enjoy the sports of robust children. A slight slip of a lad, more given to loitering than running about the Field Place gardens; more often seen sitting by the fire, than dancing on the carpet of his sisters' play-room; he was gentle in his happier moods with a girlish gentleness, and sometimes fretful with a girlish fretfulness. Deficient in boyishness, the boy had a face, chiefly remarkable for the fawn-like prominence of its deep blue eyes, the delicate, though imperfect, shapeliness of its mouth, the rather comical meanness of its little tip-tilted nose, and the red-and-white of its singularly bright complexion; the general girlishness of his appearance being heightened by the profusion of the silky hair, falling and flowing in blond-brown ringlets about his long neck and weedy shoulders.

Years later, musing on his conception of his former self, when he preferred the society of his little sister to the company of the rough boys of the Vicar's schoolroom, Shelley wrote in *Rosalind and Helen*, of Helen's docile child:—

> 'He was a gentle boy,
> And in all gentle sports took joy;
> Oft in a dry leaf for a boat,
> With a small feather for a sail,
> His fancy on that spring would float,
> If some invisible breeze would stir
> Its marble calm.'

In like manner, 'Abdallah' and 'Maimuna' (the little Bysshe and Bessie of *The Assassins*) used to float their toy-boats upon the water of their smiling creek. Shelley's delight in toy-flotillas may have arisen for the first time (as some of his biographers aver) long after his childhood. Possibly he was the fool of his own fancy in thinking he cared to play with toy-boats in his infancy. It is, however, certain, that gentleness characterized the child, who, on attaining manhood, meditated complacently on the delight he took in gentle sports when he was a gentle boy.

From what has been said of the facial show of the little fellow, who used to play in the Field Place gardens, and ride his Shetland pony about the Warnham lanes, in the closing years of the last, and the opening summers of the present century, it follows that the picture published by Mr. Colnaghi, in 1879, as a veritable portraiture of Shelley in his childhood, is an unauthentic and delusive performance. An exquisite example of childish beauty, the little boy of Mr. Colnaghi's engraving has a straight, finely-pointed nose, and a face of faultless symmetry; a nose that could not have developed into the distinctly tip-tilted nose of the poet's later visage; a face, that could not have departed so far from its normal mould, as in later time to bear any resemblance to the poet's countenance, which is represented by all the several persons of his familiar acquaintance, who wrote about it, as having been no less wanting in symmetry than fortunate in the charms of expressiveness. Whilst declaring the singular comeliness of the poet's face in its happier moments, Hogg records that its 'features were not symmetrical.' Medwin, ever quick to glorify his cousin, admits that his features were 'not *regularly* handsome.' Though she busied herself to impose upon the world the picture of a beautifully symmetrical face as Shelley's veritable semblance, and was even more accountable than Mrs. Shelley for the prevailing misconceptions respecting his facial aspect, Mrs. Hogg (the Mrs. Williams of Shelleyan annals) admitted to Mr. Rossetti, in Trelawny's presence, on March 13, 1872, that the poet 'could not be called handsome or beautiful, though the character of his face was so remarkable for ideality and expression;' the lady, at the same time, confirming what Hogg and Peacock tell us of the unmusical character of the poet's voice. In the opinion of the lady, whose singing was unutterably sweet to her spiritual worshiper, Shelley's 'voice was decidedly disagreeable.' On seeing the familiar pictures of Shelley, that serve as the frontispieces in Hogg's *Life*, and Trelawny's *Recollections*, Peacock declined to regard them as likenesses of his former friend ; putting them aside not merely as ineffective and unsatisfactory likenesses, but as no likenesses whatever of the individual they professed to represent. 'The portraits,' he remarked in *Fraser*, 'do not impress themselves on me as likenesses ; they seem to me to want the true outline of Shelley's features, above all, to want their true expression.' How could he honestly speak otherwise of the spurious and delusive portraits, 'in which' (to repeat his own words) 'the nose has no turn-up ?' That Shelley had a small and distinctly tip-tilted nose, instead of the straight and rather large (though delicately moulded) nose of the lying pictures, appears from words penned by himself to Peacock, from Leghorn, in August, 1819. After speaking derisively of John Gisborne's quite Slawkenbergian nose as a thing that, weighing upon the beholder's imagination, and transforming all its owner's g's into k's, was a feature scarcely to be forgiven by Christian charity, Shelley observed, ' *I, you know, have a little turn-up nose;* Hogg has a large hook one ; but add them together, square them, cube them, you would have but a faint notion of the nose to which I refer.' Shelley having written in this way of the defective shape and size of a principal feature of his face, it is not surprising that, whilst avoiding such words as 'unsymmetrical' and 'irregular,' Lady Shelley admitted reluctantly in her *Shelley Memorials*, that the poet's 'features were not *positively* handsome.' The wonder is that, after making this admission in the text, the lady told a different story in the frontispiece of her book. The evidence is superabundant that, instead of being positively handsome, Shelley's little nose was positively tip-tilted, and his face positively unsymmetrical.

To see the real Shelley, as he appeared during life to persons who regarded him through no such disturbing medium as romantic glamour, it is needful to get the better of misconceptions, arising from the delusive portraitures of him, to be found in familiar biographies—the fanciful pictures, which are the more intolerable for being fruitful of misapprehensions respecting the poet's moral endowments.

The epithet applied to the delusive portraitures, was chosen with deliberation. 'Fanciful' in effect, they had their origin in fancy, and may be fairly described as the offspring of fancy working upon fancy, at different times and under various conditions. Shelley never sate to a professional painter. From the year that produced the Indian-ink sketch of a young gentleman, wearing the scant gown and leading bands of an Oxford undergraduate, to the year of his death, Shelley never gave a competent painter an opportunity for producing a work, that would have prevented the fanciful misrepresentations from gaining any credit—possibly would even have prevented them from coming into existence.

It would have been better for his readers, and certainly no worse for his fame, had he never consented to sit to an amateur. But it was fated that the man, who suffered so much in more important matters from sterner adversaries, should suffer considerably from two dabblers in the fine arts. At Rome (Lady Shelley says in 1818, Trelawny says in 1819) Miss Curran began the portrait in oil, which she never finished, of the poet in his twenty-eighth year—the sketch which, dropped and relinquished by the fair limner, possibly because she felt she had made 'a bad beginning,' was destined to be the chief source of all the artistic falsities, that have been manufactured to his injury since his death. Trelawny says this failure was 'left in an altogether flat and inanimate state'—a description to be kept in mind.

An amateur in oil (of the gentler sex) having thus attempted and failed to paint the poet when he was at Rome, two or three years later (1821 or 1822) Shelley surrendered himself to a masculine dabbler in water-colours—to Williams, the companion of his voyage to death. Possibly, this sketch (which differed from Miss Curran's effort, in being finished) would have been preserved, had it accorded with the spurious portraitures, given so profusely in later time to a credulous and undiscerning public. But it has disappeared ; and at the present date no one can say how far it merited the praise given to it by Trelawny, whose favourable opinion of the 'spirited water-colour drawing' would deserve more consideration, had he known half as much about the fine arts as he knew about horses and yachts. The Indian-ink sketch of a boy in the academicals of an Oxford undergraduate, the unfinished daub in oil, and the 'spirited water-colour drawing,' are the only portraits of the poet, known to have been produced by artists of any qualification or incapacity during his life.

Possibly, the Indian-ink sketch, which De Quincey saw somewhere in London, was the best of the three performances. It cannot have been much more absurd than Miss Curran's absurdity, though from De Quincey's words it seems to have been a sufficiently ludicrous production. 'The sketch,' says the Opium-Eater, 'tallied pretty well with a verbal description which I had heard of him in some company, viz. : that he was tall, slender, and presenting the air of an elegant flower, whose head drooped from being surcharged with rain '—a description censured by the essayist for giving the equally false and disagreeable impression that the youthful *littérateur* ' was tainted, even in his external deportment, by some excess of sickly sentimentalism, from which, however, in all stages of his life, he was remarkably free.' Though, possibly, more like the man than Miss Curran's fanciful oil-daub and Mr. Williams's 'spirited' achievement in water-colour, this performance in Indian-ink, which made a young Englishman look like a dripping lily or a rose well wetted at a pump, was certainly a libel on the scandalous undergraduate.

Perhaps it would have been well had the spirited water-colour disappeared sooner. It would have been better than well had Miss Curran's 'failure' been tossed into the Tiber as soon as she despaired of making a decent picture of it. Unfortunately, the thing that was only begun by a woman, and the thing that was finished to the last touch by man, survived the poet ; so that Mrs. Shelley (through Mrs. Williams) was able to put them into the hands of Mr. Clint, with a request that out of such sorry materials, her own reminiscences — the recollections of a widow who liked to speak of herself as ' the chosen mate of a celestial spirit '—and his sense of the fitness of things, he would compose a picture, worthy of being handed down to posterity, as the veritable and unquestionably historic likeness of the greatest lyrical poet of the nineteenth century.

The fancy picture, that was ' composed ' under these less unusual than laughable circumstances, may not be more untruthful, but certainly is not more veracious, than the majority of fancy portraits. 'Of these materials,' Trelawny wrote in 1858, ' Mrs. Williams, on her return to England after the death of Shelley, got Clint to compose a portrait, which the few who knew Shelley in the last year of his life thought very like him. The water-colour drawing has been lost, so that the portrait done by Clint is the only one of any value.' What evidential value can attach to a portrait ' composed ' and 'done' under such circumstances? Apart from his weakness (one might, perhaps, say his dishonesty) in consenting to the prayer of the poet's widow and her friend (Mrs. Williams), no blame belongs to Clint. Doing as portrait-painters are wont to do, when they agree to manufacture posthumous likenesses of people they have never seen, Clint worked up a fancy picture out of the two performances by amateurs ; assuming that he might rely on those performances for correct information as to the principal features and general effect of the poet's countenance. On points where the two performances gave incongruent evidence, he relied on the widows (Mrs. Williams and Mrs. Shelley) to instruct him as to which of the two performances was the more trustworthy. The portrait having been 'composed ' and 'done ' in this way, the final touches were added in accordance with further information from Mrs. Williams and further suggestions by ' the chosen mate of a celestial spirit.'

The falseness and absurdity of the composition are mainly referable to the romantic view Miss Curran took of the poet's appearance, and to her romantic desire to give him the beauty which she deemed appropriate to the author of incomparably beautiful poems. Rating him with the angels, the lady was determined he should look like an angel—on her canvas. Beginning with this ambition, it is no matter for surprise that she made only ' a beginning.' If he was instructed to rely on the daub in oil, rather than on the spirited water-colour, it is not wonderful Clint went wrong. In her resolve to make Shelley look like an angel, Miss Curran decided to make the principal feature of his portrait altogether unlike the most prominent feature of his face. In the face, this feature wanted the size and contour needful for the romantic beauty, with which the lady would fain have endowed her bard. In the picture, this particular feature has every quality required in a feature of its kind by connoisseurs of romantic beauty— connoisseurs, that is to say, of the conventional school to which the lady and her friends (Mrs. Williams and Mrs. Shelley) belonged.

The artist was not more interested than either of the other ladies in misrepresenting the poet in this particular feature. Mrs. Williams was animated with sentimental tenderness for the poet, who wrote her so much beautiful poetry. It was natural for this romantic mourner to wish that in his historic portrait, her Platonic lover should be relieved of a facial defect, that in her opinion amounted to disfigurement. Whilst mourning sincerely for her husband, Mrs. Williams mourned romantically for the poet who had perished with her husband in the same wild storm. In like manner, Mrs. Shelley (whose notions of the beautiful were purely conventional) was desirous that this particular feature should be dealt with tenderly, delicately, lovingly, in the portrait that would represent her husband's facial show to future ages. Hence it was, that whilst he was composing the great historic portrait chiefly out of Miss Curran's artistic falsehood, neither of the ladies, on whose guidance he relied, was in a mood to tell Mr. Clint in what respect the oil-daub was especially misleading, or even to hint it was likely to mislead him in any way. Sixty years since, a little turn-up nose was universally regarded as a nose wholly unbefitting a poet. In their measures for rendering their poet altogether admirable and lovely to unborn ages, both ladies were especially desirous that on the historic canvas he should be endowed with a nose wholly unlike the one that had been, in their eyes, the great blemish of his earthly tabernacle.

If Trelawny's evidence may be accepted, Clint did his work to the satisfaction of ' the few who knew Shelley in the last year of his life.' As Trelawny was one of those few, the 'composition ' may be assumed to have had his approval. But Trelawny knew nothing of pictures, and little of the poet with whose story he will be associated to the end of time. The whole term of their friendly intercourse exceeded six months by no more than two or three days. And throughout that term the Cornish gentleman, with his simple reverence for literature and men of letters, regarded the poet through the glamour that makes things seem other than they are. On being shown the portrait for the first time, with an assurance that people approved it, Trelawny was not the man to discover anything wrong in it. When he saw it for the first time, a considerable number of long years had elapsed since the death of his acquaintance for six short months. Under these circumstances, Trelawny's good word goes for nothing in the estimate of the spurious performance. That Hogg resembled Peacock in rating the picture at its proper worthlessness is matter of certainty; for though an engraving of the artistic imposture faces the title-page of his first volume, the biographer shows himself fully alive to the fictitious nature of the composition, by his vivid and minute verbal portraitures of the poet at Oxford and in later stages of his career.

Since Trelawny published Vinter's lithograph of the picture as a frontispiece to the *Recollections* (1858), numerous engravings have appeared on wood, stone, or metal, of the posthumous 'composition' which the Cornish gentleman, at the time of his book's appearance, regarded as the only reliable painting of the poet. 'The water-colour drawing has been lost,' Trelawny wrote in 1858, 'so the portrait done by Clint is the only one of any value.' At that time he was far from imagining that the oil-sketch, which Miss Curran 'never finished, and left in an altogether flat and inanimate state,' would ever compete in public confidence with the posthumous 'composition.' To the present writer it has not seemed worth the while to inquire what (if anything) was done to Miss Curran's 'failure,' to bring it out of the 'altogether flat and inanimate state,' and put it into a condition to be regarded (*on the authority* of words spoken by Sir Percy Shelley, *on the authority* of his mother) as the 'best portrait extant' of the poet. It is enough for the present writer and his readers to know that Miss Curran's beginning of a portrait has risen to this place in Sir Percy's esteem—to know that it rose eventually to an equally high place in Mary Godwin Shelley's esteem—to know from Lady Shelley's assurance that the frontispiece of the third edition of her *Shelley Memorials: From Authentic Sources*, is an engraving from (to use her ladyship's words) 'the original picture by Miss Curran, painted at Rome in 1818, now in Sir Percy Shelley's possession'—to know, from Mr. Buxton Forman's authoritative assurance, that the frontispiece to the first volume of his edition of *The Poetical Works* is an engraving from the same 'best portrait extant,' and not an engraving of Clint's posthumous 'composition'—to know that engravings from this 'best portrait extant' have, like the engravings at first hand of the 'composition,' been repeatedly re-engraved (with or without variations to suit the requirements of editorial taste),—and, *lastly*, to know that all the engravings and re-engravings of the two delusive originals are flagrant and altogether-to-be-repudiated misrepresentations of the poet's actual appearance.

After what has been said of Miss Curran's unfinished oil-sketch, and Clint's posthumous ' composition,' which was mainly made up from the lady's derelict absurdity, it is needless to say that all the engravings and re-engravings of the abandoned fib and the elaborate falsehood bear a close resemblance to one another. Resembling one another in the contour of the features, the arrangement of the hair (even to the tips of the curls), the items of costume (even to the shape of the rumpled Byronic collars), these engravings and re-engravings might be mistaken for reproductions of the same original picture—allowance being made for the taste and whims of engravers, the fancies and requirements of editors. The only difference between the avowed engravings from Miss Curran's daub and the engravings of Mr. Clint's composition is that the former are something more un-natural and unsatisfactory than the latter. The poet of the former lot of engravings is a somnambulant girl—a sleep-walker from dyspepsia, who, on leaving her bed somehow or other, contrived to put on her brother's walking-coat instead of her own bodice. The poet of the latter set of engravings is a very pretty girl, exhibiting no sign of disease, apart from the indications of a desire to look something wiser and prettier than she really is. Like the somnambulant girl of the more dis-agreeable picture, the young lady of these less disagreeable engravings has put on her brother's coat, wears Byronic shirt-collars, has a quill pen in her lily-white hand, and is so posed that her right fore-arm is resting on an open manuscript. Of the dozen or more engravings of this young lady now lying open before the present writer's desk, the one to which he would direct his readers' attention—in consideration of its being the most agreeable, typical, and artistic of them all—is the engraving by that fine engraver, Francis Holl, which does duty as frontispiece to the first volume of Hogg's (unfinished) *Life*.

What is offered to the eye by this frontispiece? It is the picture of a man, to judge of it from the coat, the folds of the Byronic shirt-collar, and the absence of the developments of the breast that are such powerful elements of feminine loveli-ness. It is the picture of a beautiful girl, to judge of it by the girlish face and hair, the girlishness of the long, slender neck.

The first thing to strike the beholder of this girl's face is the symmetrical character of its delicate beauty. The symmetry is perfect—too perfect, even for a girl of seventeen. The fine pencillings of the eye-brows, the curves immediately beneath the eyes, the superior contours of the cheeks, the line and shadow-line of the long, straight nose, the outlines of the lower parts of the countenance, the curlings of the small kissable lips and dainty chin, are all finely, unsurpassably symmetrical. If the word may be applied to things so lovely and delicate, symmetry is carried even to caricature in the details of this girlish face. Of course the face, so delicately girlish, is deficient in the strength, the indications of force, active or latent, always to be looked for and, in some degree, invariably discernible in the countenance of a man of mark.

Though he never sate to professional painter, Shelley sate to a sculptor of sufficient ability, whose chisel produced a work of art that, indicating with sufficient clearness the two chief defects of the poet's least comely feature, fortunately, still exists, to give the lie to the foolish pictures, and to protest with mute eloquence against the policy of misrepresentation, which pursues its ends with insolent disregard for the rights of the many thousands of persons, who are interested in knowing the truth and the whole truth, and in believing nothing but the truth, about one of the most remarkable Englishmen of the present century.

But though it offered violence to romantic and conventional notions of poetical beauty, and gave his countenance a contour very different from the profile of the delusive portraits, it may not be imagined that the 'little turn-up nose' caused Shelley to be otherwise than a man of a singularly striking and charming appearance. Tall for his years, from his childhood till he attained the fullness of his stature, Shelley had a slender figure that would not have wanted elegance, had it not been for the slight drooping and roundness of his shoulders, the narrowness of his chest, and the forward inclination of his long neck and minute head—peculiarities scarcely reconcilable with all that has been written about his personal stateliness. To imagine that the young man who paced the streets of Oxford and London 'with bent knees and outstretched neck' (in the manner described by Hogg), was remarkable for the grace and dignity of his carriage, is to surrender one's judgment to the sway of romantic biographers. None the less certain, however, is it that there were moments when Shelley's countenance might be commended for loveliness. Remarkable for a complexion, in which carmine-red and delicate white, instead of being blended, were separately conspicuous, even when it was most freckled by exposure to the sun, the face surmounting his long and slender frame was singularly expressive of intelligence, sympathy, nervous alertness, enthusiasm, and sincerity. Dull in moments of contemplation, the prominent deep-blue eyes of Trelawny's stag-eyed Shelley were comparable with Byron's grey-blue eyes, for overpowering vehemence under the impulses of strong and sudden emotion. Though inferior to Byron's feminine mouth in beauty, and even more deficient than Byron's mouth in power, Shelley's mouth—the one symmetrical part of his unsymmetrical countenance — was notable for shapeliness, and alike expressive of sensibility and refinement.

In other particulars, Shelley's head and face were comparable with Byron's head and face. Like Byron, the author of *Laon and Cythna* had a head of striking smallness. It is a matter to be pondered by the physiologists, who maintain no man can be mentally powerful unless he has a big bulk of brain and a big pan to hold it, that the two greatest poets of the nineteenth century were, perhaps, the *two* smallest-headed Englishmen of their time. Though it wanted the auburn under-glow, the feathery softness, and careful keeping of the Byronic tresses, Shelley's brown shock—blonde brown in childhood, deep brown ere it began prematurely to turn grey—resembled the locks of his familiar friend and fellow-poet in curling naturally. The most prominent feature of either poet's face was the one in which he differed most conspicuously from the other. In that feature Byron had greatly the advantage. Had he not grudged the poet whom he hated this personal advantage over the poet whom he loved, Leigh Hunt would not have been at so much pains to describe the faults of Byron's nose—its excessive massiveness, and its appearance of having been put upon the face, rather than of growing out of it. But whilst inferior to Byron's face in that important feature, Shelley's face, in its naturalness and seraphic gentleness, its candour and high simplicity, was possessed of charms no one would venture to attribute to Byron's more earthly loveliness. In spite of its grand defect, Shelley's was a face that reminded his two closest friends of works of Italian art. Whilst Peacock speaks of his vanished friend's resemblance to the portrait of Antonio Leisman in the Florentine Gallery, Hogg likens the sweetest and loftiest element of the poet's facial beauty to the air of profound religious veneration that may be observed in the best frescoes of the greatest masters of Florence and Rome.

There is no need to inquire how the lovely face of Mr. Colnaghi's engraving came to be regarded as a portrait of Shelley in his childhood. Still less is there any need to inquire whether the original picture was the work of the exiled French prince to whom it has been attributed. The present writer has no wish to deal disrespectfully with any part of the picture's story that does not touch the poet's record. For this work's purpose it is enough to say authoritatively that the child, whose delicate and exquisitely symmetrical lineaments are exhibited in the Colnaghi engraving, cannot have been the infantile Shelley, because it is not in the nature of things that the poet of unsymmetrical visage and 'little turn-up nose' was the development of the child, whose facial loveliness was so perfect an example of facial symmetry, and whose nose could not by any possibility have changed into the tip-tilted feature, described so precisely by the poet himself. Portraits are often strangely mis-assigned; but it is seldom for a portrait to be so egregiously mis-assigned as this so-called picture of the child Shelley. Had not Mrs. Shelley and Mrs. Williams succeeded in palming off on romantic credulity their symmetrical and straight-nosed 'composition' as a veritable picture of 'The Real Shelley,' it would never have occurred to any one to suggest that the original of the Colnaghi engraving was the poet Shelley at a tender age.

CHAPTER IV.

THE BRENTFORD SCHOOLBOY.

Dr. Greenlaw's Character—Quality of his School—Medwin's Anecdotes to the Doctor's Discredit—Mr. Gellibrand's Recollections of the Brentford Shelley—The Bullies of the Brentford Playground—Shelley's Character at the School—His Disposition to Somnambulism—His Delight in Novels—His Wretchedness at School—Shelleyan Egotism—Byronic Egotism—Byron's Influence on Shelley—Enduring Influence of Novels on Shelley's Mind—Stories of Boating—Easter Holidays in Wiltshire—'Essay on Friendship'—Its Biographical Value.

THE slight slip of a boy, who under the name of Percy Bysshe Shelley, appeared for the first time in his eleventh year (the third year of the present century) amongst the boys of Dr. Greenlaw's school at Sion House, Brentford, was no child to prefer the society of overbearing boys to the society of his little sisters, whose playmate he had hitherto been.

Dr. Greenlaw's home for young gentlemen was a house of forbidding aspect. More than once as they walked from London to Bishopgate (familiar to those who are in the habit of entering Windsor Park from Englefield Green), Shelley directed Hogg's attention to the gloomy walls of his first boarding-school. The house was unalluring, the master not incapable of outbreaks of anger, the boys by no means innocent of puerile rudeness and inhumanity. But the present writer, who in former time knew some of Dr. Greenlaw's scholarly descendants, has reason to believe the doctor was a kindlier gentleman, and his school a much less defective establishment, than Mr. Medwin made the world imagine.

Taking much credit to himself for having been at Brentford a sympathetic and condescending senior schoolmate to his little far-away cousin, Tom Medwin speaks with ungenerous resentment of the seminary where they sipt the Pierian spring. All that his bitter words amount to is that Dr. Greenlaw was a pedagogue, and Sion House a seminary, 'of an old school.' If the bread served to the boys at breakfast and supper was parsimoniously dressed with butter, the fare was neither better nor worse than the bread and butter usually provided for schoolboys eighty years since. If the Saturday's pie was a scrap-pie, and a poor specimen of its inferior kind of pie, it was only such a thing as schoolboys of the period were expected to eat with thankfulness. A schoolboy's toilet, in the days of our grand-fathers, was always a short and simple business. As the boys seldom saw the lady, who never harassed or troubled them in any way, Mr. Medwin might as well have forborne to sneer at Mrs. Greenlaw for priding herself less on her husband's calling, than on being distantly related to the Duke of Argyll. Mr. Medwin was not a little proud of his slight relationship to the Castle Goring Shelleys, though they were not (to put the case mildly) the best of the Sussex families. He might, therefore, have spoken leniently of Mrs. Greenlaw's sense of the dignity of her people, or been silent about the matter. Himself the son of a country attorney, Mr. Medwin should have written a little less disdainfully of his old schoolfellows, for being 'mostly the sons of London shopkeepers.' Nor is the Rev. Dr. Greenlaw (he was in holy orders and had a Scotch degree) to be severely judged if, when pupils were few, he was something less inqui-sitive than he might have been about the quality of parents. To live, schoolmasters must fill up their beds ; and to be placed at school in the same dormitory with a cheesemonger's son is an indignity, to be forgiven (after forty years) even by the son of a solicitor of the High Court of Judicature.

It may, however, be conceded that Sion House was no more a fit school for the heir of a great county family, than the Clapham school, where the poet's sisters received their higher education, was a suitable seminary for the daughters of an aristocratic house. Whilst little Bysshe was still making Latin verses in the company of tradesmen's sons, the elder of his sisters went to the Clapham school, where Harriett Westbrook (the daughter of a licensed victualler) in later time learnt some-thing of French and the answers to Mangnall's Questions. It may not, however, be inferred that Mr. and Mrs. Shelley, of Field Place, were deficient in proper care for their own dignity, or in proper concern for the welfare of their offspring. Though no place of education for the sons of the English aristocracy, Sion House was greatly superior to the 'commercial schools' where tradesmen sent their boys to be trained for the counter and the counting-house. It was a 'classical school' for the sons of ordinary professional men (boys like Tom Medwin), and

the sons of well-to-do and ambitious tradesmen, bent on putting
their boys into the liberal professions. The Clapham school for
girls was a school of corresponding quality,—a place of education for the daughters of people moving in the middle way of
life. That he sent his children to such schools merely shows
that the Squire of Field Place was not possessed by the spirit of
exclusiveness, that is a characteristic of aristocratic personages ;
that he was still far from rating himself with the aristocracy of
his county, though he had taken a degree at Oxford, made the
grand tour, and risen to represent New Shoreham in the House
of Commons. That the children were sent to such schools
shows how far the head of the family (old Mr. Bysshe Shelley,
the son of the Newark apothecary and the friend of Graham,
the quack) was from over-estimating his social position ; how
far he was from deeming himself one of the dignitaries of his
shire, though he had married the heiress of Penshurst, and
adding acre to acre, was rich enough to spend tens of thousands
on the big castle, which he never finished or inhabited.

Instead of enjoying the status, which delusive biographers
declare them to have enjoyed for successive centuries, the poet's
people were in his childhood only emerging from the middle
class of society. Planted though they had been for some time
within the outer breastworks of provincial gentility, they were
still regarded by their patrician neighbours as people of ambiguous quality,—too wealthy to be rated with mere 'gentle
populace,' and at the same time, too wanting in local influence
and ancestral dignity to be rated with the *élite* of 'the county.'
Fortunate though it had been, old Mr. Bysshe Shelley's career
was more calculated to provoke scandal than conciliate social
sentiment. Though it had done much for his enrichment, his
second marriage had also caused leading families of Sussex and
Kent to regard him with animosity, and speak of him with disapproval. Strange stories were told of the ways in which the
old man had made money,—was still making money. The
sordid tastes and habits, that rendered him equally despicable
and pitiable in his senility, were already revealing themselves,
and confirming people of honest pride and good principle in
their resolve to hold aloof from him. To personages of the
county, who had long looked down upon them as obtrusive up-
starts, the father and son grew more distasteful in proportion
as they grew richer. Instead of being diminished, this disfavour
was for a time quickened by the civilities, which for political

reasons the Duke of Norfolk thought fit to offer to the Horsham capitalist and the Member for New Shoreham. Both within and without the lines of the Liberal party, dislike of these 'new men' was stimulated by the growing opinion that, if the younger kept his seat for the Sussex borough, and voted steadily in accordance with the Duke's pleasure, the elder of them would in a few years be raised to the dignity for which he had long hungered.

Thus regarded in Sussex, it is not surprising that the poet's father and grandfather lived more within the lines of their proper middle-class connexion, than with the higher gentry of their neighbourhood, and that, in selecting schools for his children, Mr. Timothy Shelley acted in harmony with the views of his middle-class friends and relations. It is not surprising that little Bysshe was sent to the school that was good enough for the boys of people like the Medwins, and none too good for the tradesmen's sons who came between the wind and Tom Medwin's nobility. Nor is it surprising that in later time little Bysshe's sisters were sent to the suburban academy, where the youngest of them became intimate with Harriett Westbrook,— the lovely child of 'Jew Westbrook,' the licensed victualler. Had he in 1802 felt more certain of getting the baronetcy for which he was playing (and won only four years later—1806), it is probable that the Horsham money-maker would have loosened his purse-string, and told his son (the M.P.) that Sion House was not good enough school for the heir of the Castle Goring Shelleys. Had the father and son foreseen what embarrassment and scandal would come to the Castle Goring Shelleys from friendships made at the Clapham girls'-school, it is probable that the poet's sisters would have been sent to a more select seminary, or have been educated, even to the finishing touches of their education, at Field Place.

That the Reverend Dr. Greenlaw was a fairly sufficient pedagogue may be inferred even from the reluctant admissions of the writer, who is our chief source of information respecting little Bysshe's life at Sion House. Whilst telling apocryphal stories to the discredit of his scholarship, Medwin concedes that the Doctor was 'a tolerable Greek and Latin scholar,' drilled his pupils assiduously in Homer, and carried them 'in his own way' through some of the plays of Æschylus, Sophocles, and Euripides. Mr. Medwin was not so precisely accurate a writer that we must accept all his statements to the schoolmaster's disadvantage. Possibly, in recalling the teacher's way of 'driving straightforwards in defiance of obstacles,' the biographer only remembered his own way of dealing with choruses and other perplexing passages of the Greek dramatists. The historian who misquoted the Ovidian verses, in his worst and most damaging story against the Doctor, may also have misquoted the sorry verses inscribed on the Scotch mull which Charles Mackintosh (a former pupil at Sion House) gave his preceptor. If the verses of the mull were as bad as the biographer represents, and were (as the same authority alleges) the production of the Doctor's own head and hand, their extreme badness disproves the assertion that the Doctor 'was a tolerable Greek and Latin Scholar.' However much misquoted in Medwin's *Life of Shelley*, the verses must have been bad; but it is more probable that 'Carolus Mackintosh . . . *alumnus*' composed the lame lines inscribed upon his gift, than that they were put together by 'the tolerable Greek and Latin scholar,' who had grown grey in teaching boys to make Latin verses. Recollections after a lapse of forty years, touching the infirmities of former schoolmasters, should be regarded with suspicion, even when they proceed from habitually careful narrators. But when a gentleman of almost proverbial inaccuracy entertains the world with irreconcilable reminiscences of the same individual, he may be regarded as labouring for a moment under the besetting infirmity, that always weakens Mr. Medwin's testimony, and sometimes deprives it of all value.

That the successful schoolmaster (bound alike by his interest and the obligations of his office to be mindful of the proprieties) disgusted little Bysshe, and delighted the rest of the class with obscene jocosity in reference to a familiar passage of the *Æneid*, is less probable than that Tom Medwin's memory betrayed him. It is easier to believe that in a mood of unusual irritability and dullness Dr. Greenlaw discovered execrable Latinity in the Ovidian lines :

> 'Me miserum ! quanti montes volvuntur aquarum !
> Jam, jam tacturas sidera summa putes,'—

which little Bysshe 'gave in' as verses of his own manufacture. '*Jam, jam !*' the Doctor is said to have exclaimed during the course of animadversions that were emphasized with slaps administered to the child's small cheeks and ears. '*Jam, jam !* Pooh, pooh, boy ! raspberry jam ! Do you think you are at your mother's? Don't you know that I have a sovereign objection to those two monosyllables, with which schoolboys cram their verses? haven't I told you so a hundred times already? "*Tacturas sidera summa putes*,"—what, do the waves on the coast of Sussex strike the stars, eh?—"*summa sidera*,"—who does not know that the stars are high? Where did you find that epithet?—in your *Gradus ad Parnassum*, I suppose. You will never mount so high. "*Putes!*" you may think this very fine, but to me it is all balderdash, hyperbolical stuff. There' (with a final box on the little fellow's nearest ear), 'go now, sir, and see if you can't write something better!'

It is consolatory to reflect that, though he should not have been cuffed and exposed to the riotous ridicule of his school-fellows for writing Latin verses as badly as Ovid wrote them, the culprit merited some kind of punishment for 'giving in' as his own the verses that were not his own,—an act of deception common enough with schoolboys, but scarcely recon-cilable with the severe truthfulness, which is said (by the Shelleyan enthusiasts) to have distinguished him from his child-hood to his last hour. 'He was,' says Lady Shelley in her *Shelley Memorials : From Authentic Sources*, 'more outspoken and truth-loving than other boys.'

With this anecdote of Latin verses, given in to the Doctor of the Brentford school, may be coupled a story, which the late Mr. Gellibrand used to tell, somewhat to the discredit of little Bysshe. Just about Shelley's age, though placed in a lower form of the school than Shelley's, Gellibrand was trying to put together a nonsense Latin verse in the way of scholastic duty, when Bysshe said, 'Give me your slate, and I will do it for you and you can go.' Trusting his friend, Gellibrand surrendered his slate and went off to play. The verses Shelley wrote on the slate ran,—

> 'Hos ego versiculos scripsi,
> Sed non ego feci.'

On being 'given in,' by a boy who could not make a nonsense 'line' without racking his brain, these verses may well have attracted the master's attention. To the question, 'Did you write this?' Gellibrand of course answered 'Yes.' Of course, also, the matter was inquired into further ; the result being that Gellibrand received a whipping, for which he paid Shelley out with a 'pummelling.'

Though heavy, the blows he received for the Jam-jam verses were by no means the sharpest and most penetrating that came from time to time to little Bysshe Shelley from the same hand. Eighty years since our boys were taken from the nursery and confided to the schoolmaster, in the same way that pups of choicest breed were given over to the very slender mercy of the under-gamekeeper. In either case it was known what was in store for the young and helpless creatures. It was needful for these young things to be licked into shape and form and good behaviour,—for the small boys to be whipt into bigger boys, and then into serviceable men; and for the young dogs to be whipt into good sporting dogs. Relying on the wisdom of his ancestors, the English gentleman believed in the Coptic proverb, which declares that 'the stick came down from heaven.' To train boys and dogs the stick was needful. Whilst the tender-hearted father hoped silently that much of the stick would not be needed, the father of no more than average humanity was jubilant about the stick, confident that youngsters needed it, jocular about its power to do them good. Like George the Third, who told his sons' tutors to whip them when they wanted it (but for this order, how badly George the Fourth might have turned out!). Mr. Timothy Shelley, M.P. for New Shoreham, sent little Bysshe to Sion House, with the understanding that he would be whipt, and well whipt too, when he wanted it. Mrs. Shelley knew what was in store for the little fellow, when she put the plum-cake into his box and hoped he would enjoy it. The foreknowledge did not make the lady sorrowful. Was it not written, that to spare the rod was to spoil the child? It is hard on schoolmasters that they should be required to bear the odium of an educational method, so universally approved two generations since, and sanctioned by the highest authority.

Elderly (not to say old) gentlemen of 'the old school' still talk and write cheerily of the good old birch. In his later novels the late Lord Lytton uttered several pleasantries about the antique instrument of domestic torture. But he probably took another view of the matter, when he was under it. Though the great Thackeray wrote with characteristic sprightliness and piquancy of interviews with 'the Doctor' in his study,—interviews attended with swishing sounds and shrill cries of puerile protest, audible through the strong doors of the same awful room,—he was alive to the tragic side of the comic business. Only a few years before his death, he spoke to an attentive mahogany-tree of one of these 'interviews with the Doctor,' in which he had figured as passive principal at a preparatory school, where he acquired some of the rudiments of human knowledge, before going to Charterhouse. 'And can you still remember what it felt like?' inquired one of the listeners. 'Remember it! It was like ——!' screamed the witness to his own early grief, raising his voice and eyebrows till they were comically eloquent of pain and affright, as he named a place whither so excellent a novelist cannot be supposed to have gone. Like little Makepeace, little Bysshe had interviews with the Doctor between the four walls of the Doctor's study,—interviews from which the nervous boy retired, with fury and horror in his face and at his heart, to the schoolroom full of heartless boys, whose only expression of concern at his misadventure was to ask him 'how he liked it.' All this is so much a matter of course that nothing would be said of it in these pages, were it not for the general opinion that this medicine of childhood (as an old writer pleasantly designates the discipline of the rod) not only caused the future poet the usual amount of transient physical annoyance, but had also an enduring and by no means beneficial effect on his temper and his disposition towards every kind of human government. It has been urged by successive biographers that this bitter physic, instead of curing his infantile ill-humours, aggravated them seriously, and was one of the several influences that set him at war with society from the outset of his career. Mrs. Shelley and Lady Shelley (the poet's second wife and his daughter-in-law) both take this view of the discipline that vexed him both at Brentford and Eton. And though he does not hold the birch largely accountable for *Queen Mab*, the present writer is by no means certain that the two ladies are so entirely wrong on this matter, as they are on other matters of the poet's character and story.

Notwithstanding the incidents, which may have disposed him to rate his Brentford preceptor as one of his earlier tyrants, there is evidence that, after coming to manhood, Shelley remembered Dr. Greenlaw with qualified approval, if not with affection. As they walked past the gloomy brick house to which he had just called his companion's attention, Shelley 'spoke of the master, Doctor Greenlaw, not without respect, saying, "he was a hard-headed Scotchman, and man of rather liberal opinions." ' To be tinctured with liberality of sentiment was, in Shelley's opinion, to have a quality of goodness.

If Medwin was justified in saying that ' Sion House was a perfect hell' to Shelley, it is probable that the bullies of the playground were more accountable than the discipline of the schoolroom for the boy's hatred of the place. Numbering about sixty scholars, some of whom were seventeen or eighteen years old, the school—governed out of school-hours by bullies, who might bully any one weak enough to be bullied, instead of by ' masters ' entitled to bully only their own fags—was just the place to be fruitful of misery for a shy, nervous, mammy-sick lad; lacking the muscle and pluck to hold his own with boys of his own age. On appearing for the first time in the playground—fenced with four high walls, and adorned with the solitary tree, to which the school-bell was hung—the child from Field Place found himself surrounded by a mob of inquisitive urchins, who at a glance saw he had neither the strength nor the courage to answer a rough word with a ready blow. Could he play at pegtop? at marbles? at hopscotch? at cricket? As each of these questions was answered in the negative, a cry of derision went up from his inquisitors. His girlish looks and long hair, his red-and-white complexion and the slightness of his long (not oval) face provoked uncomplimentary criticism. Then came questions about his home. Had he any sisters? What were their names? Where did they live? Had he a mother? What was his father? What was he ' blubbing ' about? On hearing that his father was a Member of Parliament, some of the boys (possibly the tradesmen's sons) intimated that he had better not give himself airs.

Resembling Byron in divers matters already submitted to the reader's consideration, and in other matters to be noticed in later pages of this work, Shelley resembled him also, from childhood to his latest hour, in being a singular combination of feminine weakness and masculine strength. Remarkable for boyish resoluteness and energy, the Byron of Aberdeen, Harrow, and Cambridge, was no less remarkable for girlish sensibility and softness. Feminine in the emotional forces of his nature, the Byron of ' the Pilgrimage,' the London drawing-rooms, the Italian exile, and the expedition to Greece, was rich also in manly daring and combativeness. A similar account may be given of Shelley's constitution and temper. In his earlier time a boy on one side of his nature, he was a girl on the other. If 'his port' (to use Hogg's words) 'had the meekness of a maiden' in his later time, it possessed also the dignity of manliness. In moments of sudden peril it was discovered that fear had no chamber in the heart, of which Hogg wrote 'the heart of the young virgin, who had never crossed her father's threshold to encounter the rude world, could not be more susceptible of all the sweet charities than his.' It is remarkable how these two inseparable poets (inseparable for ever! notwithstanding all the efforts of the Shelleyan enthusiasts to disassociate them) impressed their closest friends alternately by their manliness and their womanliness. The biographer, who is eloquent about the manliness of Shelley's carriage, could not recall this friend of his heart and holder of his admiration, without remembering his meek and maidenly bearing and virginal sensibility. Even when he was bearing testimony to Byron's manly endowments, Hobhouse could not refrain from glancing at those of the poet's weaknesses, that, resembling 'a portion of his virtues, were of a feminine character—so that the affection felt for him was as that for a favourite and sometimes froward sister.'

At Brentford the girlish elements of Bysshe's nature were in the ascendant, the masculine elements altogether in abeyance. Possibly the latter elements had never manifested themselves at Field Place, where the little fellow, with younger sisters for his playmates, had lived at the end of his mother's apron-string something too long. If they had shown themselves in his earlier childhood, they seem to have retired from view during his stay at Dr. Greenlaw's school. Bearing a stronger likeness to the Geordie Byron, of Aberdeen High School, who fell a-weeping before his classmates, on being required for the first time to answer to the proud title of 'Dominus,' than to the Geordie Byron of the same school, who, notwithstanding his lameness, used to spring (in his hopping way) with clenched fists and flashing eyes at boys of superior size and strength, little Bysshe seems throughout his time at Sion House to have justified the disdain in which he was held, alike by the big and the small bullies of the dismal playground, as a chicken-heart and a milk-sop. His old schoolfellow, Gellibrand, who died something over twelve months in his ninety-third year, used to describe the Shelley of Dr. Greenlaw's seminary as a 'girl in boy's clothes, fighting with open hands and rolling on the floor when flogged, not from the pain, but "from a sense of indignity."' (*Vide* Mr. Augustine Birrell's letter to the *Athenæum* of 3rd May, 1884.)

Scared and cowed by the first greetings of the playground, he seems never to have gained heart to learn the games, of which he had been compelled to confess a shameful ignorance, or to repay with boyish energy and in proper style the snubs and blows of boys as small as himself. Every boy's hand was raised against him; and when he raised his own in retaliation, it was to slap with open palm. What the big bullies bade him do, he did meekly and often to his cost. When they ordered him to run after their balls, he obeyed till he was ready to drop with fatigue. When they ordered him to fetch books from the circulating library, to 'truck' Latin dictionaries and other scholastic volumes (appraised by avoirdupois weight) with the grocer for lumps of cheese or sweetstuff, he broke bounds and did their commands, earning once and again a smart punishment ' from the Doctor,' by his submissiveness to lawless orders. But he never joined of his own will in the pastimes of his schoolfellows, great or small. Moping in corners by himself, when the other boys were playing clamorously at prisoners' bars or leap-frog, with their marbles or their tops, he counted the days till next breaking-up day, recalled the pleasures of the garden where his little sisters had been his sturdiest playmates, or conned the pages of stories, borrowed from the circulating library. Sometimes on half-holidays he loitered for the hour together under the southern wall of the playground, as far as possible out of the way of his uncongenial companions. Sometimes out of pity for the child's solitariness and misery, Medwin left the sports of the yard, and walked with his little cousin to and fro under the high wall. It pleased the senior cousin long after the younger cousin's death to imagine, that Shelley was mindful of these walks and the kindness thus shown him when, in the description of an antique group, he wrote, ' Look, the figures are walking with a sauntering and idle pace, and talking to each other as they walk, as you may have seen a younger and an elder boy at school, walking in some grassy spot of the playground, with that tender friendship for each other which the age inspires.'

In this stage of his existence, little Bysshe resembled Geordie Byron at a somewhat earlier age, in having the nervous diathesis that often disposes children to walk in their sleep, when suffering from derangement of the stomach. At least, on one occasion, Geordie Byron was a somnambulist at Aberdeen. At least, on one occasion, Bysshe Shelley was a somnambulist during the time he passed under Dr. Greenlaw's government. More than forty years later, Medwin remembered how the boy looked, when after leaving his proper bedroom he advanced with slow steps, one summer night, to the open window of the dormitory he had no right to enter. Seeing that he was asleep, and unaware that sleep-walkers should be awakened gradually, Medwin jumped from bed and, seizing him quickly, roused the somnambulist with a suddenness that gave him a painful shock, attended with severe nervous erethism. In the morning Shelley paid another penalty for the misbehaviour of his nerves. Boys taken at night in a wrong bed-room were offenders ·against a wholesome domestic rule, to be punished even though the offence was unintentional. 'I remember,' says Medwin, 'that he was severely punished for this involuntary transgression.' It does not appear how he was punished, or whether it was known to the punisher that the breach of law had been committed during sleep.

Though he was not guilty of another walk in his sleep, the nervous and delicate boy was still visited by 'waking dreams, a sort of lethargy and abstraction that became habitual to him.' Whilst he was under the influence of these day-dreams, his prominent blue eyes were glazed with a peculiar dullness, and were equally inexpressive and insensible of external objects. As soon as the visitations were over, his eyes flashed, his lips quivered, and he spoke with a tremulous voice that was strangely and painfully indicative of nervous agitation and distress. 'A sort of ecstasy,' says Medwin, 'came over him, and he talked more like a spirit or an angel than a human being.' As the words convey the intended impression, there is no need to inquire in what respect the speech of a human creature differs from the speech of a spirit, or to imagine the circumstances under which Mr. Medwin may have been permitted to overhear the talk of angels.

Under the manifold vexations and sorrows that preyed upon his feelings at Sion House, Shelley found solace and intermissions of grief in the perusal of blue books,—no folios of parliamentary manufacture and information; but the little blue-covered volumes of extremely exciting and unwholesome prose-fiction, that were to be bought at sixpence a-piece of ordinary booksellers in the earlier decades of the present century. He was also a greedy devourer of tales (touching haunted castles, magicians, picturesque brigands, and mysterious murderers) that proceeded from writers, who did not condescend to offer their productions to the public eye, in the vulgar little 'blue books,' or in any form less acceptable to connoisseurs of elegant literature than board-bound volumes. It is something to the honour of prose-fiction that the two greatest poets of the nine-teenth century may be said to have been mentally suckled and reared on novels from infancy to adult age,—taught by novels how to think and feel, and how to make others think and feel. It is alike true of Byron and Shelley, that the germs of much that is most delightful and admirable in their finest poems must be sought in old novels. John Moore's *Zeluco* was not more influential in the production of *Childe Harold*, than *Zofloya or the Moor* was influential in the production of *Zastrozzi* and *St. Irvyne*, those crude and unutterably ridiculous achievements of Shelley's youthful pen, which, offering to their amused perusers the feeble fancies and puerile conceits that, appearing and reappearing in successive volumes, developed eventually into vigorous creations and exquisite examples of poetic imagery,— exhibit also the rude notions and embryonic reasonings, that in the course of a few years grew and shaped themselves in the fundamental principles and main features of his philosophy on matters pertaining to politics, social economy, and religion.

It is a question whether the recollections of misery endured at school, which occupy three of the familiar stanzas to ' Mary,' should be regarded as reminiscences of trials the poet underwent at Sion House, or of sorrows that moved him to tears at Eton. Mrs. Shelley had no doubt the stanzas referred to the public school; and Lady Shelley is no less confident that her father-in-law was thinking of the Eton playing-grounds, when he wrote in the dedicatory prelude to *Laon and Cythna*:

> ' Thoughts of great deeds were mine, dear Friend, when first
> The clouds which wrap this world from youth did pass;
> I do remember well the hour which burst
> My spirit's sleep: a fresh May-dawn it was,

When I walked forth upon the glittering grass,
And wept, I knew not why; until there rose
From the near schoolroom, voices, that, alas!
Were but one echo from a world of woes—
The harsh and grating strife of tyrants ánd of foes.

' And then I clasped my hands and looked around,
But none was near to mock my streaming eyes,
Which poured their warm drops on the sunny ground—
So without shame, I spake :—" I will be wise,
And just, and free, and mild, if in me lies
Such power, for I grow weary to behold
The selfish and the strong still tyrannise,
Without reproach or check."   I then controuled
My tears; my heart grew calm, and I was meek and bold.

' And from that hour did I with earnest thought
Heap knowledge from forbidden mines of lore ;
Yet nothing that my tyrants knew or taught
I cared to learn, but from that secret store
Wrought linked-armour for my soul, before
It might walk forth to war upon mankind ;
Thus power and hope were strengthened more and more
Within me, till there came upon my mind
A sense of loneliness, a thirst with which I pined.'

It has been usual with Shelley's biographers to deal with these verses as though, besides referring to Eton, they afford a substantially accurate account of trouble undergone, resolutions formed, and action taken by the poet whilst he was at Eton. To the Shelleyan enthusiasts, it is heresy to question the strict and severe historic veracity of any particular statement of this piece of melodious egotism.   To them it is an affair of certainty that the grass glittered, the boy wept, the voices came from the school-house, the weeping youth made virtuous resolves, precisely as, and when, the poetry represents.   The verses are given in evidence that Shelley neglected Latin and Greek in order that he might devote all his best energies to chemistry, astronomy, electricity, pneumatics,—in brief, to those ' scientific pursuits,' about which so much fantastic nonsense has been printed by the more fervid and less discreet of his eulogists. To this way of reading and handling these verses, is mainly referable the equally general and false notion that Shelley's principal employment at Eton was to make 'linked armour for his soul' out of materials prohibited to ingenuous youth by the teachers of his despotic school,—and that his one purpose in forging this linked armour for his soul, was that he might equip himself for 'walking forth to war among mankind,' *i.e.* for playing the part of a political revolutionist and social reformer, as soon as he should be his own master.

There is the less need to trouble oneself seriously with the question whether the verses refer to Sion House or Eton, because it is certain they do not correspond, in all their chief particulars, to his life at either school. Whilst it is certain that his studies at the private school were the studies prescribed by Dr. Greenlaw (unless the not-actually-prohibited perusal of novels is to be rated as 'study'), it is no less certain that he never grossly neglected the studies of either school. Far from neglecting the ordinary scholastic exercises of an Eton boy in the degree implied by the words,

> 'Yet nothing that my tyrants knew or taught
> I cared to learn,'

it is certain that, without holding steadily a high place in any of the higher forms, he acquired something more than a fair amount of the only learning imparted to boys at Eton eighty years since, and displayed remarkable aptitude and skill in making Latin verses,—an important part of what his tyrants knew and taught. The evidence is conclusive that, at Eton he was a facile and clever maker of Latin verses. Medwin speaks to 'his capacity for writing Latin verses,' and gives some examples of the capacity, that may, at least, be styled creditable performances for a public school-boy. Long after his abrupt withdrawal from the school, the excellence of Shelley's Latin verses was remembered by old Etonians. Whilst his readiness in the verse-maker's art was described as 'wonderful' by Mr. Packe, another of his former schoolmates at Eton (Mr. Walter S. Halliday) wrote of the same faculty to Lady Shelley, 'his power of Latin versification' was 'marvellous.' Hogg certifies that, though more than a year elapsed between his retirement from Eton and his going into residence at University College—a period during which he certainly omitted to enlarge his classical attainments—Shelley came up to Oxford an expert and singularly quick Latin verse-maker, and a ready writer of Latin prose. So much for the poet's vaunt that he did not care to learn what the Eton masters could teach him.

On the other hand, it is certain that, whilst carrying

away from Eton something more than a creditable amount of
the learning to be acquired in the classes, Shelley learnt nothing
at the school by irregular and unrecognized study to justify the
assertion that, whilst a schoolboy, he gathered 'knowledge from
forbidden mines of lore,' and armed himself for the battle of
life with weapons his official teachers would fain have kept from
his hands.   His scientific studies were the mere sports of a
schoolboy, playing idly with an air-pump, an electrical battery,
and a few acids and alkalies.   Instead of spending his leisure
at Eton in the serious pursuits of natural science, he employed
it chiefly in literary essays, that show him to have been
possessed by an ambition scarcely compatible with an enthusiasm for scientific investigation and a yearning for scientific
celebrity.

That both Mrs. Shelley and Lady Shelley had considerable,
though insufficient, grounds for regarding the dedicatory
stanzas as a record of the poet's experiences at Eton, is
unquestionable.   Mrs. Shelley could, doubtless, have defended
her view of the verses with words spoken by her husband, who
entertained her with several equally strange and delusive
stories of his life at the public school.   Besides the poet's
authority, Lady Shelley could, perhaps, produce other evidence
to justify her concurrence with Mrs. Shelley's opinion.   Whilst
he deems it possible that Shelley was thinking more of Eton
than Brentford, when he committed the verses to paper, the
present writer has no doubt whatever that the poet, soon after
their composition and ever afterwards, regarded the three
stanzas as veracious autobiography—as a faithful poetical
record of what he had suffered, resolved, and done, when he was
under Dr. Keate's rigorous government.   But the poet's words
may not be produced as sure evidence respecting the tenor and
chief incidents of his career.   From manhood's threshold to his
last hour, he was subject to strange delusions about his own
story ; some of the marvellous misconceptions having reference
to matters of quite recent occurrence.   'Had he,' says Hogg,
'written to ten different individuals the history of some
proceeding in which he was himself a party and an eye-witness,
each of his ten reports would have varied from the rest in
essential and important circumstances.   The relation given on
the morrow would be unlike that of to-day, as the latter would
contradict the tale of yesterday.'   Peacock, who also knew

and loved him well, bears similar testimony to the loose-
ness and inaccuracy of the poet's statements about his own
affairs, even about those of his affairs, respecting which (had
he been a man of ordinary exactness and fidelity to facts) he
would be naturally regarded as the best source of information.
To escape the disagreeable necessity of thinking him deliberately untruthful, Thomas Love Peacock had recourse to the
notion that his friend was the victim of ' semi-delusions.'
With all his desire to palliate his friend's besetting frailty, so
as to relieve it of the odium of sheer untruthfulness, Peacock,
in his inability to rate the delusive fancies as sincere and
perfect delusions, came to the conclusion that they were only
' semi-delusions ; ' that the mis-statements of the poet's mouth
and pen were referable in equal proportions to delusive fancy
and influences distinct from delusion. Whatever their show of
autobiographic purport and sincerity, it is obvious that the
verses of a poet, suffering from so perplexing an infirmity, differ
widely in evidential value from the autobiographic statements
of an ordinary individual.

How far the Byronic poems should be held accountable for
Shelley's Byronic way of dealing with his personal story in
poems offered to the world, is a question deserving more
consideration than can be given to it in this chapter. At this
early point of an attempt to exhibit ' the Real Shelley,' it is,
however, well to indicate why criticism should deal with the
egotisms of the Shelleyan poems precisely as criticism has long
dealt with the egotisms of the Byronic poems.

However people may differ about the respective merits of
the two poets, all persons must allow that Byron and Shelley
were both egotists in the superlative degree,—and that differing
from other poets in more unusual and admirable qualities, they
differ from them also in surcharging their magnificent poetry
with more or less misleading references to their private concerns, and with emotion and sentiment arising from their purely
personal interests,—often from their purely personal discontents.
In this respect, both poets strayed from the high poetic path ;
sacrificing art to egotism, fame to foible, greatness to vanity.
If *Childe Harold* was the wail of a single romantic sufferer for
his own sake, *Laon and Cythna* was the cry of a single romantic
sufferer for his own as well as the world's sake. The poet's
personality is forced upon the reader's notice no less resolutely

in Shelley's than in Byron's poem. If it was Byron's vanity
to demand human sympathy as the victim of fate, it was
Shelley's vanity to solicit it as the victim of persecution.

Whilst the man of sin and mystery invited the world to
admire his proud endurance of the doom that distinguished him
from all other mortals, the angel of goodness and light invited
mankind to worship him, for his unselfishness, his impatience
of evil, his abhorrence of oppression, his ineffable benevolence,
his heroic readiness to perish for the good of his species. Both
actors were equals in sincerity and in dishonesty. The man who
has still to discover that sincerity underlies almost every display
of human affectation, is a man who has failed in justice to a
considerable proportion of his species. The pretender ever
plays the character he desires in the most secret chamber of his
heart to be mistaken for. Byron and Shelley were alike actors
and alike sincere, each taking a part accordant with his conceptions of the sublime and admirable in human nature. In
assuming the character of a libertine,

> ' A shameless wight,
> Sore given to revel and ungodly glee,'

Byron assumed the character that interested and fascinated him.
In assuming the character of the social martyr, Shelley, true to
his own nature, selected the character that appeared to him
the most admirable. Both characters were taken from the
marvellous creations of the romantic literature on which the
two poets fed from childhood to years of discretion. It was a
literature that may be styled the romantic literature of the good
principle and the evil principle. In taking a representative of
the evil principle for his model, Byron displayed his genuine
disposition which, in spite of his engaging qualities and several
generous endowments, was a disposition towards evil. In
determining to be a representative of the good principle of
human existence, as that existence was exhibited in the 'blue
books,' and other literature of the circulating libraries, Shelley
made a choice no less true to his own more gentle and earnest
nature. Mere boys when they forced themselves into notoriety,
neither of them could readily relinquish the part,—chosen so
easily and naturally. Shelley determined to be on the side of
the angels, because his disposition was in the main towards
goodness; Byron went with the devils, because he found them

upon the whole better and more congenial company than the angels of light.

In other respects, their resemblance was striking. Endowed with a memory that equalled Byron's memory in retentiveness, though more liable to illusions, an imagination even more powerful than Byron's imagination, and a sensibility no less acute than Byron's sensibility, Shelley resembled Byron also in his habit of brooding over old sorrows, intensifying them by the exercise of fancy, and using them as instruments of self-torture. Certainly in some degree, probably in a high degree, this habit is referable to the influence of Byron's genius,—to the influence of the Byronic poems, and also of their popularity. Whilst success never fails to produce imitators, the affectations of the successful are curiously infectious. This was notably the case with Byron's success, that putting the younger poets and poetasters into turn-down collars, caused them to train their voices to notes of what they deemed Byronic melancholy, and to set their features into what they deemed expressions of Byronic bitterness, and melancholy. It is not suggested that Shelley was for a single minute one of the Byro-maniacal apes. It is not hinted that he ever imitated Byron, except in the way in which a loyal, enthusiastic, and altogether honest disciple may be seen to imitate a great master.

From his boyhood to his last year, Shelley regarded Byron with a generous admiration, that once and again expressed itself in almost idolatrous language. Unlike the Shelleyan fanatics, who seek to exalt their favourite by decrying the only modern English poet likely to be rated as his superior, Shelley ever regarded Byron as the greatest living master of their art. Scott, Wordsworth, Southey, Coleridge, Keats, Tom Moore, Leigh Hunt, to say nothing of minor minstrels, all had a share of Shelley's never-stinted homage, but he never for any long time thought of putting the best and strongest of them on equality with the incomparable Byron. To remember the terms in which he wrote and spoke of Byron, is to think with a smile of all that has been written in these later years by poetasters and critics to Byron's discredit.

The enthusiasts, who have so clear a perception of the signs of Shelley's influence over Byron in the Third Canto of *Childe Harold*, are curiously blind to the far more important and conspicuous indications of Byron's influence on Shelley in *Laon and Cythna.* When the most has been said of the manifestations of Shelleyan thought in Byron's poem, it cannot be questioned that had the younger of the two poets never lived, the four Cantos of *Childe Harold* would have been substantially the same poem they now are. On the other hand, it is impossible for any one but a Shelleyan enthusiast to believe that *Laon and Cythna* would have been the same poem it now is, had Byron never come into existence. Written in the summer of 1817, when the poet had been for five years, like all the younger poets of his time, living under the domination of Byron's intellect, and had been for a still longer period an enthusiastic admirer of Byron's writings; written in the summer following the one in which the still youthful aspirant to poetical renown had come under the personal influence of the great poet, whom he had so long desired to know personally, and had made at least one futile attempt to approach, *Laon and Cythna* bears the most distinct marks of Byron's influence in Shelley's selection of the Spenserian measure, in the poem's Byronic egotisms, and in the pains taken by the poet to identify himself with the hero of the narrative. In all these particulars (to say nothing of other particulars which the reader of these pages can discover for himself), *Laon and Cythna* resembles *Childe Harold*, just as the painting by a young artist, abounding in originality and natural vigour, is often seen to resemble the painting of an older artist, whose notions and treatment of colour, and whose manipulatory address, have been a manifest force in the aspirant's education. Just as the painting of the younger artist in form and colour, without being either ' a copy,' or even ' an imitation,' in any dishonourable sense of the term, bears to the painting of the master a certain resemblance (of tone and treatment) that causes both works to be regarded in later times as ' works of the same school,' Shelley's great poem resembles Byron's great poem.

Byron was in no degree accountable either for the 'story' of Shelley's poem, or for its incidents and conceptions of character. The same may be said of the prevailing sentiments, subordinate aims, and main purpose of the poem. Whilst the prevailing sentiments of the poem are altogether foreign to Byron's views on the religious, political, and social questions dealt with in *Laon and Cythna*, his writings are in evidence that he must have regarded Shelley's approval of 'Laon's' incest with his own sister as revolting in the highest degree. But though the substance of this extraordinary poem could not have proceeded from Byron's brain and pen, the form of the work is distinctly Byronic. Shelley cannot have been unconscious of this resemblance of his poem to what was at that time Byron's greatest achievement in song. *Qui s'excuse s'accuse.* The very words of the Preface, in which he anticipates a charge of 'presuming to enter into competition with our greatest contemporary poets,' and, whilst disclaiming the presumption, declares his 'unwillingness to tread in the footsteps of any who preceded him,' are words of evidence that he was fully and uneasily alive to the resemblance. His curious way of accounting for his choice of the measure which Byron's poem had rendered more popular for the moment than any other measure, is only the poet's attempt to shut his eyes to the fact, that he selected the measure because *Childe Harold* had rendered it more agreeable to his own ear than any other, and had also made it the measure most likely to commend his poem to the public taste. 'I have,' he says, 'adopted the stanza of Spenser (a measure inexpressibly beautiful), not because I consider it a finer model of poetical harmony than the blank verse of Shakspeare and Milton, but because in the latter, there is no shelter for mediocrity; you must either succeed or fail.' Though Byron doubtless smiled at this reason for the adoption of the measure, which he had in a certain sense made his own, he must have been gratified by the delicate compliment to the poet who had adopted it with success.

Using the Byronic measure (for the Spenserian measure had become for the moment Byron's property), Shelley made a Byronic use of matter taken from romances devoured in his childhood. 'Treading in the footsteps' of his master, notwithstanding his assertions to the contrary, Shelley followed the Byronic example in attaching his own personality to the hero of his poem. Not content with hinting poetically in the Dedicatory Stanzas to Mary that he and Laon are one, the author of *Laon and Cythna* is at pains to declare more fully and precisely in the prose of his Preface that Laon's views on matters of religion and politics, on questions of government and misgovernment, on the vices of ecclesiasticism and the merits of vegetarianism, on the relations of the sexes and the æsthetics of love, are the views of Percy Bysshe Shelley, Esq., who has studied human nature in Switzerland as well as England, and who, in consideration of his 'having trodden the glaciers of the Alps, and lived under the eye of Mont Blanc,' should be regarded as a gentleman especially educated and peculiarly qualified to dogmatize on such matters to English persons who have never crossed the Channel. Both in the poem and dedicatory prelude he seizes every opportunity to impress on the reader that Percy Bysshe Shelley is Laon, the apostle of 'Liberty, Fraternity, and Equality,' and that this Preacher of the 'New Evangel,' who at the close of the poem sails into Paradise with his sister and the offspring of their incestuous intercourse in a boat made of

> 'one curved shell of hollow pearl,
> Almost translucent with the light divine
> Of her within,'

is no other than Percy Bysshe Shelley, Esq., eldest son of the Member of Parliament for New Shoreham, and heir-apparent to a Sussex baronetcy. In these Shelleyan egotisms the critical reader of the marvellous poem recognizes the very touch and trick of Byron's way of dressing up details of his domestic woes and personal story for the delight and mystification of his readers. One of the most pathetic and effective of the egotisms is the poet's account of the misery he endured from hard-hearted masters and malicious boys whilst he was at school.

Just as Byron seasoned the introductory stanzas of *Childe Harold's* first canto with more or less imaginary particulars of his misspent youth, when

> 'Few earthly things found favour in his sight,
> Save concubines and carnal companie,
> And flaunting wassailers of high and low degree,'

Shelley seasoned the dedicatory verses of *Laon and Cythna* with references to the wretchedness that preyed upon him when, walking forth upon the glittering grass, he wept and

> 'knew not why; until there rose
> From the near schoolroom, voices, that, alas!
> Were but one echo from a world of woes—
> The harsh and grating strife of tyrants and of foes.'

Both descriptions were equally truthful and untruthful. The basis of truth in Byron's poetical narrative of his misspent youth is that he kept the girl at Brompton who used to ride and walk about London in boy's clothes, and that when he entertained three or four old college friends at Newstead, they talked a good deal of nonsense and drank rather more champagne than was good for them. The basis of truth in Shelley's narrative of his wretched boyhood is that he was often unhappy at school (*very* unhappy at Brentford), and that being of a soft and girlish temperament when he was at Sion House, he sometimes fell a-weeping because the 'boys were so unkind to him.' The Shelleyan narrative is not historically exact to his doings and experiences in either of his two schools. At Brentford he was not remarkably insubordinate (as he was at Eton), and did nothing to give the faintest justificatory colour to his vaunt of having devoted himself to studies prohibited or discountenanced by the masters of the establishment. At Eton (where, though often unhappy, he was less given to crying than in his Brentford days), instead of neglecting the studies of the college, he attained to considerable excellence in them. Upon the whole, the weeping boy 'upon the glittering grass' bears more resemblance to the chicken-heart and milksop of Dr. Greenlaw's playground than to the unruly, fitfully riotous, and inordinately blasphemous young rascal, who was eliminated from Eton with the least possible disgrace, even as in later time he was expelled in an irregular way, and with no needless humiliation, from Oxford. And in consideration of this greater resemblance, the present writer has thought right to deal, in this chapter about the Brentford schoolboy, with the verses that, in Mrs. Shelley's opinion and Lady Shelley's opinion, are a faithful picture of the lad at Eton.

It is certain that the little Bysshe was an unhappy child at Sion House, even to the time of his withdrawal from the school, when he had grown almost too tall, though certainly not too robust, to be called 'little.' But miserable children are curiously, pathetically clever in escaping from their misery. The smart of them over, Bysshe soon dismissed from his mind those disagreeable visits to the Doctor's study. In the pages of his ghost-stories and banditti-stories, his tales of satanic malice and knightly heroism, he forgot all about those very unkind boys. Most of those delightful books he borrowed from the circulating library, but doubtless he had in his schoolroom 'locker' his own copies of his favourite novels. It cannot be questioned he had a peculiar and inalienable copy of *Zofloya, or The Moor*, which, yielding flowers of romance to be found in the ineffably absurd novels which he published in the opening term of his literary career, gave him also fine pieces of descriptive writing that, after doing service in *Zastrozzi* and *St. Irvyne*, were worked with skilful art into the lofty song of *Laon and Cythna*.

The urchin enjoyed his frequent walks under the playground's southern wall with his cousin Tom Medwin, till the latter left Dr. Greenlaw's sadly plebeian school, and went off to the public school which prepared him for Oxford. Though he cannot rely so confidently as he could wish on Tom Medwin's assurance, the present writer likes to imagine Mr. Medwin had better ground than his treacherous memory for saying that, when they were schoolfellows at Sion House, he and his young cousin more than once played the truant; and rowing on the river more than once to Kew, went on one occasion by water to Richmond, where they visited the theatre and saw Mrs. Jordan in the 'Country Girl.' One would fain believe this of the little boy who, on growing to be a man, disliked the theatre almost as cordially as he had in former time hated Professor Sala's dancing academy.

But one hesitates to trust in this matter to the biographer who seems to have erred in recording that Shelley acquired a taste for boating, even at a time considerably prior to the period in which this secret and lawless trip to the Richmond Theatre is said to have been made. Peacock, who can scarcely have been mistaken, was certain the poet's 'affection for boating began at a much later date' than his time at Eton. Walter S. Halliday (Shelley's friend at the public school) was no less certain, in February, 1857, that at Eton Shelley 'never joined in the usual sports of the boys, and, what is remarkable, never went out in a boat on the river.' Had Shelley enjoyed boating at Sion House, it is inconceivable that he (so passionately fond of the water in later time) would have avoided the river, or could have been kept from it at Eton. As Halliday was no such reliable authority as successive writers have thought, I should have hesitated to prefer his evidence to Medwin's testimony on this point, had not the Etonian witness been so emphatically sustained by Love Peacock. In regard to what he says of Shelley's boating at Brentford, Mr. Medwin professes to speak from his own knowledge. On the other hand, he acknowledges that, with respect to the poet's alleged love of boating at Eton, he speaks on the worst possible authority—the poet's own equally delusive and retentive memory. 'He told me,' says Medwin, *vide The Life*, v. I., p. 52, 'the greatest delight he experienced at Eton was from boating, for which he had, as I have already mentioned, early acquired a taste.' Such unsupported evidence from Shelley is scarcely anything better than no evidence at all, on being opposed by such witnesses as Halliday and Peacock.

From this chapter on Shelley's school-days at Brentford, one should not omit a pleasant glimpse that is afforded of the boy (in the company of his cousins, the Groves, sons of Thomas Grove, of Fern House, Wiltshire, who married Charlotte Pilford, sister of the poet's mother) by a letter, dated to Hogg, February 16th, 1857, by Charles Henry Grove. At that date it was in the memory of Charles Henry Grove how, when a tender Harrovian, *ætat.* nine, he saw his cousin Bysshe for the first time. On this occasion the nine-year old Harrovian, attended by his brother George, *ætat.* ten, and protected by a sufficient body-servant, picked Bysshe up at Brentford and carried him off, on the roof of the stage-coach to Wiltshire, for the Easter holidays. It lived in Charles Grove's memory, how, during these holidays he and his brother joined Shelley in a feat of mischief that no doubt made the Squire of Fern wish them back at school. Acting on Bysshe's suggestion, the three took the carpenter's axes, and set to work cutting down some of the young fir-trees of Fern Park. As Charles Grove, *ætat.* nine at the time of this occurrence, was born in 1794 (*vide* Burke's *Landed Gentry*), and Shelley was born in August, 1792, this pretty 'piece of boys' mischief' may be assigned to the Easter holidays of Bysshe's twelfth year,—*i.e.* Easter, 1804; about the middle of his whole time at Sion House.

It seems to have been towards the end of his time at Brentford, that Shelley experienced the delights of his tender attachment to the gentle schoolmate of his own age, with whom he used to hold romantic converse in the playground, and exchange 'good-night kisses' at the time for going to bed— the childish attachment so sweetly commemorated in the *Essay on Friendship*. What is the biographical value of that charming story, which one could believe no less readily than gladly, were it not told *of* Shelley *by* Shelley?

Had it proceeded from a man far less imaginative than

Shelley, and far less prone to mistake the creations of his fancy for sincere recollections, no cautious reader would regard this pleasant record of infantile affection as faithful in every particular to the actual circumstances of the childish attachment. On the other hand, the coldest and most suspicious peruser will be disposed to think the story substantially truthful, due allowance being made for the force of imagination, the deceitfulness of the equally retentive and fallacious memory, and the peculiar infirmity of the man who could not be trusted to give twelve fairly consistent accounts of any matter, however much he might desire to be precisely accurate. It is in favour of this estimate of the story that the essayist's portraiture of his former self harmonizes with the several other accounts he has given elsewhere of his character in childhood. In his later time Shelley always thought of the child, from which he had developed, as a mild-mannered, tractable, gentle child. The attachment being remembered, as an affair of his twelfth or thirteenth year, it may be presumed to have stirred and held his heart towards the close of his time at Brentford,—probably after Tom Medwin (who says nothing of the matter) left Sion House. To see the Brentford schoolboy's prominent blue eyes overflowing with tears of delight, under the music of his friend's voice, to watch the two urchins exchanging kisses, is to remember the girlishness of Byron's early attachments, as well as the girlishness of his affectionate care for his Harrow 'favourites.' From his first to his last hour at Sion House the masculine forces of Bysshe's two-sided nature were in abeyance. He was a gentle English girl rather than a gentle English boy.

CHAPTER V.

THE ETON SCHOOLBOY.

First year at Eton—Creation of the Castle-Goring Baronetcy—Sir Bysshe
Shelley's Last Will—Timothy Shelley's Children—Miss Hellen Shelley's
Recollections—The Etonian at Home—The Big Tortoise—The Great
Snake—Dr. Keate—Mr. Packe at fault—Walter Halliday—Mr. Hex-
ter—Mr. Bethell—Fagging—Mad Shelley—'Old Walker'—Enthusiasm
for Natural Science—The Rebel of the School—Lord High Atheist—
Dr. Lind's Pernicious Influence on Shelley—Poetical Fictions about
Dr. Lind—Shelley's Illness at Field Place—His Monstrous Hallucina-
tion touching his Father—John Shelley the Lunatic—*Zastrozzi*—
Premature Withdrawal from Eton.

RESPECTING the year of Shelley's first term at Eton, the
authorities differ: one set of writers averring that he entered
the school in his fourteenth year (1806), whilst other biographers record that he entered it in his fifteenth year (1807).
Lady Shelley says, 'At the age of *thirteen* Shelley went to Eton.'
On the other hand, the usually exact Thomas Love Peacock
says, 'On leaving this academy (*i.e.* Sion House) 'he was sent
in his fifteenth year to Eton,' and Mr. William Rossetti says,
' He passed to Eton in his fifteenth year.' Though no prudent
writer ventures to set aside lightly a date given by so careful
and conscientious a biographer as the author of the *Memoir of
Shelley*, I venture to think that Mr. Rossetti is at fault in this
particular, having perhaps erred through reasonable reliance on
the accuracy of Mr. Peacock, who seems, in taking a date from
one of the books he was reviewing for *Fraser's Magazine* (June,
1858), to have gone a barley-corn beyond Mr. Middleton's
words. Instead of saying that Shelley *went* to Eton in his
fifteenth year for the first time, Mr. Middleton (in his *Shelley
and his Writings*, 1858) keeps to historic truth in merely stating,
' In 1807, when Shelley was in his fifteenth year, we find him
at Eton.' He neither says nor implies that the future poet
could not have been found there in the previous year. On the
contrary, his words indicate uncertainty as to the precise date
of the poet's first appearance at the school. Gaining his knowledge of the poet's career at Eton from old Etonians who were

schoolmates there, Mr. Middleton was probably instructed in this matter by an old Etonian who, whilst certain Shelley was at the school in 1807, could not speak positively to his being there in an earlier year.

Though the author of the *Shelley Memorials* is curiously deficient in the communicativeness and accuracy to be looked for in a biographer professing to gather her materials 'from Authentic Sources,' it may be assumed that Lady Shelley is right on a matter from which the schoolboy's preserved letters and his father's domestic memoranda of the year 1806 would save her from going wrong. It favours this view of Lady Shelley's statement, that old Mr. Bysshe Shelley was created a baronet by the Duke of Norfolk's influence on the 3rd of March, 1806, when he was in his seventy-fifth year. At length the Castle-Goring Shelleys had risen from the status of prosperous middle-class folk to the honour of the baronetage. Having become a dignified commoner, with a dignity transmissible to his descendants, the Horsham miser (who had sent his son to Oxford) naturally felt that, instead of associating any longer with tradesmen's sons at Sion House, his grandson (the heir of the heir to the Castle-Goring baronetcy) should make the acquaintance of the sons of the nobility and other territorial gentry. Much though he grudged the fees for his baronetcy, and dreaded the school-bills, Sir Bysshe determined that his grandson should be educated up to his rank, and sent forthwith to Eton.

The future poet was still under Dr. Greenlaw's government, and his grandsire was counting the days still to elapse before he should clutch the long-coveted honour of the bloody hand, when the veteran took an important step (on 28th November, 1805) for the achievement of the grand ambition of his riper age and failing years. This ambition was to make the Shelleys of his loins into the House of the Castle-Goring Shelleys, and to endow the new house with a large and strictly entailed estate in land, that should place it securely amongst the great territorial families of Sussex ; a common-place ambition, that was the natural and matter-of-course ambition for a man of old Bysshe Shelley's character, career, and age. As he was his father's eldest son, Mr. Timothy Shelley (the poet's father) naturally approved this design for making a big entailed estate, to which he would succeed on his sire's death. Though they squabbled and wrangled with one another on minor pecuniary questions, the veteran and his son were of one mind on this point. Whilst the old man was set on making a big entailed estate, his son was of opinion that the estate ought to be made.

The materials of which it was proposed to construct this big estate were,—

(A) Certain real estate, settled by deed of appointment (dated 20th August, 1791) on Mr. Bysshe Shelley for life, and then on his son Timothy for life, with, &c.

(B) Certain other real estate, settled, by certain indentures of Lease and Release (dated respectively 29th and 30th April, 1782) on the same Bysshe Shelley for life, and then on his same son Timothy for life, with, &c., and

(C) Certain unsettled lands, the property and disposal of which were wholly in the same Bysshe Shelley: and one half of the same Bysshe Shelley's personal estate.

After what has been said of old Bysshe Shelley's success in making money, it is needless to inform readers that C was by far the most important of these three several lots of estate:— that, though of considerable value, A and B were insignificant in comparison with C.

What was the precise yearly revenue of A and B does not appear. At a time when he had no clear knowledge of the matter, the poet used to speak of the revenue as 6000*l.* per annum. But whilst he certainly did not understate the income, there is reason for thinking he greatly exaggerated it. The rental may (for all I know positively to the contrary) have been 6000*l.* a-year; but in estimating the poet's financial position, readers had better assume that the yearly income from A and B did not exceed, and may have been considerably less than, 4000*l.* a-year. If the two lots of estate yielded a clear income of 4000*l.* they were worth about 80,000*l.* If they yielded as much as 6000*l.*, they were worth about 120,000*l.*

Under the settlements, to which reference has been made, Percy Bysshe Shelley (the poet) was, in the language of lawyers, tenant in tail male of A and B in remainder expectant on the deaths of his father and grandfather. That is to say, the fee simple of A and B would devolve on him absolutely after the deaths of his sire and grandsire. For the more clear information of non-legal readers, let it also be observed that, having this estate in A and B under existing settlements, Percy had in A and B an interest that would vest in him at the attainment of his majority,—an estate which, on his coming of age, he would be able to charge, aliene, or will away from his kindred ; an estate on which he would be able to borrow money, and could sell, or dispose of by testament, during the lives of his father and grandfather, or the life of either of them, no less than when on the deaths of both of them he should come in actual possession of the land.

This being so, old Bysshe Shelley (son of the Yankee apothecary) made a will on 28th November, 1805, whereby he devised his unsettled lands (of C) to trustees, In Trust to settle the same, in what lawyers designate ' strict settlement,' on his son Timothy Shelley for life, Percy Bysshe Shelley for life, and Percy Bysshe Shelley's sons successively, according to their seniorities in tail male, and then in default, &c., on other sons of Timothy Shelley aforesaid born in the testator's lifetime and their sons successively in tail male, and then in default, &c., on other sons of the same Timothy, born after the testator's death, successively according to their seniorities in tail male ; with similar limitations in default, &c., in favour of John Shelley Sidney, and Robert Shelley (Timothy's younger brothers by half-blood), and their respective issue male. By his will the testator further bequeathed his personal estate to trustees, and directed half of it to be invested in land, to be settled in the same way as the already-mentioned lands. It is further directed by the will that all persons entitled to A shall concur in settling A as C, or forfeit for themselves and issue all the interest pertaining to them under the will in C. By the will, therefore, Percy Bysshe Shelley stood to succeed on his father's death as tenant for life to the whole entailed estate, provided he concurred in arrangements whereby the real estate A (of which he was tenant in tail male in remainder expectant on the deaths, &c., &c.)would become part of the entailed estate. To take his place in succession to the very large estate, to be created by his grandsire's will, he was only required, on coming of age, to surrender his eventual absolute interest in a comparatively small estate, and take in lieu thereof a life-interest. Nothing was required of him that is not often required of heirs under similar circumstances. Nothing was required of him that (in case of his death in his nonage) would not have been required of his younger brother, or any other person similarly interested in A. Such was the will of old Bysshe Shelley made in 1805 in abundant grand-paternal affection for the poet, long before any differences touching religion and politics had risen between the youngster and his father. This same will was in due course proved as the last testament of Sir Bysshe Shelley, Bart., in Doctors' Commons, in 1815.

At the moment of the future poet's departure for Eton, it is well to remind the readers of his story, that he was the eldest child of his parents,—being senior to his eldest sister by a year and nine months. Mistakes having been made about the poet in his earlier years, which would not have been made by his biographers, had they been aware of this fact, it is necessary to warn readers not to mistrust their present guide because he differs on this matter from several previous authorities. Here is the list of the offspring of Mr. and Mrs. Timothy Shelley, of Field Place, with some particulars of the children, taken from the pedigree, mentioned in a previous chapter :—

1. Percy Bysshe Shelley, eldest son and heir-apparent, born at Field Place 4th August, 1792, baptized at Warnham 7th September following.
2. Elizabeth Shelley, eldest daughter, born 10th May, 1794, baptized at Warnham 2nd July following.
3. Hellen Shelley, 2nd daughter, born 29th January, 1796, baptized 27th February following; died an infant, buried at Warnham 25th May, 1796.
4. Mary Shelley, 3rd daughter, born 9th June, 1797, baptized at Warnham 17th of July following.
5. Hellen Shelley, 4th daughter, born 26th September, 1799, baptized at Warnham 6th October following.
6. Margaret Shelley, 5th daughter, born 20th of January, 1801, baptized at Warnham 12th March following.
7. John Shelley, 2nd son, born 15th of March, 1806, baptized at Warnham 14th of August following.

A child of six years, when her brother went to Eton for the first time, Miss Hellen Shelley (who lived to be in her later middle age the chief source of information respecting his boyhood) may have still been in her seventh year, cannot have exceeded her seventh year by three full months, when he returned from Eton to Field Place for his first Etonian holidays. It follows that, instead of pertaining to an earlier period of his boyhood, Miss Hellen Shelley's recollections of her brother

relate to the Eton schoolboy; to the youth between the date of
his gentle extrusion from Eton and entrance into Oxford, to the
University undergraduate, and to the youthful lodger in Poland
Street, immediately after his by no means undeserved expulsion
from his Oxford college. It is not in the nature of things that
his sister Hellen (his junior by seven years and something more
than seven weeks) should have remembered aught of her
brother previous to his Eton time, so clearly as she remembered
the things narrated of him, by virtue of her own memory, in the
letters of her pen published in Hogg's first volume. It follows,
therefore, that for a biographer to make the Shelley of the
Warnham day-school, and the Brentford boarding-school, out of
these reminiscences, is to produce a precocious infant very much
unlike what the schoolboy can have been in his earlier childhood; in fact, to set the reader wrong at the story's outset with
a false Shelley, instead of the real Shelley.

If Miss Hellen Shelley may be trusted (and there is no
reason to question the general fidelity of the lady's reminiscences), the Etonian, at home for the holidays, taught his little
sisters to personate angels of light and. angels of darkness,
spirits of the air and spirits of the fiery depths, with such
eccentric and fantastic articles of clothing or other drapery as
the children of big country-houses can usually discover in out-
of-the-way wardrobes and closets when they have mind to 'play
at dressing up' in the Christmas holidays. He used also to play
under their curious eyes, and to their alternate delight and terror,
with his chemical toys and electrical apparatus. Good cause had
little Hellen to hold her breath with alarm, and wonder what
would come of the magical performance, when the mysteriously
clever and daring Bysshe was seen running through a principal
passage of the old home towards the kitchen, whilst bearing
in his outstretched hands a dish, that sent blue flames upwards
even to the ceiling. Better reason still had the small damsel
to cry aloud, in strains that brought the elders of the family to
her rescue, when the scientific experimentalist (who had on
previous occasions inspired her with a reasonable aversion to
his electrical jar) declared his humane purpose of curing her
chilblains with a series of small shocks.

Himself a glutton of horrible tales, the Etonian-at-home
was ever ready with a harrowing narrative of tragic crime and
ghastly consequences, when the girls begged him to tell them

something terrible, by the flickering light of their play-room fire. He overflowed, also, with stories about the alchemist, Cornelius Agrippa, who was represented as living up aloft in a spacious garret, under the roof of Field Place, directly over the heads of the excited children, grouped about this play-room's only source of light. To their frequent entreaties for a personal introduction to the mysterious and benevolent Cornelius, Percy used to assure his sisters that in due course they should see the philosopher, his books, his lamp, his venerable beard, when he should migrate from the garret to the cave, soon to be dug for him in the orchard, and furnished with all the apparatus needful for his investigations and experiments.

At other times Percy entertained his sisters with anecdotes of the Great Tortoise, that had lived for centuries and grown to enormous magnitude in and near Warnham Pond. What he told them of the fabulous tortoise does not appear. It is so difficult to get anything but turtle-soup and hair-combs out of a tortoise of any kind, one would like to know how the boy contrived to inspire his auditors with a vivid interest in this creature of his imagination. To do so he may be presumed to have talked freely and with wild disregard for the teaching of the best authorities on natural history.

Towards the close of his Eton time (or possibly somewhat later, between his withdrawal from Eton and departure for Oxford) Percy Bysshe discarded the Big Tortoise and replaced it with the Great Snake, that was supposed to have lived for three hundred years in the Field Place gardens, before it was killed by the scythe of the careless or ruthless gardener, during the childhood of its imaginative historian. Biographers, who smile at the Shelleyan girls for putting faith in their brother's taradiddles about the Big Tortoise, are firm believers in his taradiddles about the monstrous and Venerable Serpent. Indeed, they are apt to be indignant with flippant sceptics, who declare themselves as ready to believe in the Warnham Tortoise as in the Field Place Snake. How the snake had amused itself for three hundred years in the grass and flower-beds of the garden is not on the record. Nor does it appear how the young historian came upon the evidence of its longevity.

At Oxford, Hogg heard strange tales of the Field Place Snake; and listening to them, as they came from his young friend's lips, the hard-headed north-countryman may well have wondered why his young friend told so many more lies than were necessary. But if Hogg dismissed the Great Snake legends from his mind, as mere levities undeserving of remembrance, some of the poet's historians would have them treated more respectfully. Believing in the Great Snake, and gushing over it in a style that appears slightly comical to unbelievers, Mr. Buxton Forman ejaculates, 'We think of these things, and remember the anecdote of the "great old snake" of Field Place, beloved of the little Percy, and killed by the scythe of the gardener, and almost wonder what inarticulate dirge the little boy uttered over his mutilated favourite'!!! It still remains for a Royal Academician to put on canvas this pathetic scene:—The Child Shelley uttering an inarticulate dirge over the corse of his mutilated favourite, whilst the remorseless and all unfeeling gardener pursues his daily wages with the fatal knife.

Other facts touching the Etonian may be gleaned from Miss Hellen Shelley's letters, or the pages of less delightful writers. Sometimes he is seen taking his sisters for country walks. At other times he is seen on his pony, riding, perhaps, to 'the meet' of his grandsire's hounds; for much as he loved money, and much as he may have grudged the cost of his kennel, old Sir Bysshe kept hounds, and a huntsman and 'whips' almost to the last. There were times when he walked forth shooting, with a gun in his hand and a dog at his heels. On one occasion the humour seized him to don the garb of a farmer's hind, and bearing a truss of hay on his back walk across the Field Place lawn, and under the very windows through which his sisters were looking. It was, doubtless, some two years or more before this bit of rural masquerading, that he used to walk out in the evening, to look at the moon and stars, moving to and fro in the park, and in the Warnham lanes, with the butler at his heels, to watch over him and take care of him. There was also a day, when this—in his sisters' eyes, so marvellous—Etonian spoke to them seriously of his intention to buy a little gipsy-girl, and train her to love him and depend upon him. But nothing in all Miss Hellen Shelley's reminiscences is more eloquent of the pride she took in her marvellous brother, than her recollection of the pleasure she took in admiring 'the beautifully fitting silk pantaloons,' and other sumptuous raiment he was allowed to order 'according to his own fancy at Eton.'

Little Hellen's delight was perfect when she saw this exemplary
Etonian standing, after the fashion of men and boys, with his
back to the fire, posturing, and playing with his coat-tails, so as
to display his slight figure and exquisite nether-garments to
the best advantage. What though this superb brother now and
then stained his little sister's pinafores and frocks with lunar-
caustic, and otherwise injured them with the chemicals he used
in his scientific experiments?

Going to Eton in 1806 (probably in the early autumn)
Shelley left the school in disgrace, some time towards the close
of 1809. The exact date of his withdrawal from the college
has never been revealed by the authorities of Field Place,
who have been no less reticent respecting the circumstances
that resulted in his premature removal from the seminary,
where he failed to win the approval of the masters, though he
succeeded eventually in making himself acceptable to the boys.
Why Lady Shelley, writing 'from authentic sources,' was thus
silent on particulars of no slight moment, the present writer
makes no suggestion. All he can say positively on these points
is that Shelley left the school in disgrace, which there is reason
for thinking he richly merited, and left it at the time already
stated. His Eton career, therefore, cannot have exceeded three
years by very many weeks. In so short a time, however, he
endured more suffering than falls to the lot of an ordinary
schoolboy, and at the same time achieved a reputation that long
survived his departure from the school, and would have lived
for several years in its traditions, even if his subsequent career
had not given his former comrades at the famous seat of learning, other and stronger reasons for holding him in remembrance.

On the girlish side of his nature, Bysshe was no boy to
conciliate the riotous, overbearing urchins of the public school.
When the masculine elements of his constitution came to be in
the ascendant, he made enemies of the masters; and at Eton,
in 'old Keate's time,' to have a bad character with the masters
was to come under the lash of a gentleman who surpassed
Mulcaster and Busby as a severe disciplinarian. If any kind
of posthumous renown is better than none, this gentleman may
be numbered amongst the fortunate members of his profession;
for his fame will not perish so long as Orbilius is remembered.
Shelley soon learnt that Dr. Greenlaw's hand was light in comparison with the hand of the Etonian master-in-chief; that his

rods were feathers in comparison with the implements of torture wielded by Dr. Keate. Succeeding a head-master, the mildness of whose rigour had rendered him the scorn of pedagogues and the jest of schoolboys, Dr. Keate ascended his throne with a purpose of restoring the discipline of the school to the ancient standard of Etonian severity. Just the man to accomplish this ambition, he failed only by raising the discipline something higher than the standard he proposed to his energies. It is recorded of this squat, stout, thickset, crooked-legged man, that a look of cruel glee played over his countenance as he conned the names of a heavy flogging-bill. A man of humour and a lover of good cheer, he was a hospitable entertainer; and it has been told admiringly of him, how he would leave his guests over their wine, and half-an-hour later return to them with heightened gaiety after flogging a batch of gentlemanly young culprits. If he has not been strangely maligned by history and tradition, he used to stand for the hour together over the penal block with his right shoulder well thrown back, and his right arm moving like a piece of machinery. He is said to have flogged eighty boys on a single morning, throwing his whole force into every stripe, smiling grimly as he went on in the path of duty, and finally retiring to his breakfast with an air of serene complacence pervading the visage, that bore so striking a resemblance to the visage of a bull-dog. Prominence is here given to these matters out of deference to those of the Shelleyan enthusiasts who, like Mrs. Shelley and Lady Shelley, insist that harsh and ferocious schoolmasters are to be held accountable for whatever was slightly amiss in the poet, before he shone forth a faultless creature.

Arising in no way from deficiency of materials, which, save in respect to one or two matters, are superabundant for the biographer's purpose, the chief difficulty in describing Shelley's course at Eton is the difficulty of discriminating between the trustworthy and delusive materials, and especially of separating the threads of pure fact from the threads of pure fiction used in about equal proportion in the manufacture of statements that, without the exercise of cautious and nice discernment, might be accepted as wholly true or altogether devoid of evidential value. For instance, in dealing with the statements by Mr. Packe, touching Shelley's career at Eton—statements to which Lady Shelley accords her unqualified credence and conclusive 'imprimatur'—it is by no means easy to separate the threads of truth from the threads of fable.

'Among my latest recollections of Shelley's life at Eton,' says Mr. Packe, at the end of his letter, 'is the publication of *Zastrozzi*, for which, I think, he received 40*l*. With part of the proceeds he gave a most magnificent banquet to eight of his friends, among whom I was included.'

In these few words there are three mis-statements. As Shelley left Eton in the later part of 1809, and *Zastrozzi* was not published before the 5th of June (or, at the earliest, before the end of May), 1810, it is certain that the publication of the novel was no incident of Shelley's life at the school. It being certain that Shelley received never a farthing of publisher's money for the absurd performance, Mr. Packe must have been wrong in saying the author was paid 40*l*. for it. [Mr. Packe's words, 'for which, I think, he received 40*l*.,' are, of course, to be read 'for which he received, I think, 40*l*.'—*i.e.* as the statement of a witness, certain that a considerable sum was paid, though uncertain whether 40*l*. was the precise sum.] As the author received no money for the book, he cannot have given 'with part of the proceeds' (*i.e.* part of nothing) 'a most magnificent banquet to eight of his friends.' But though he gives three pieces of delusive evidence in three lines of type, it does not follow that the lines are of no evidential value. An honest person, writing in good faith, Mr. Packe may be fairly regarded as a person, remembering something about *Zastrozzi* in connexion with Eton (where the novel, or some part of it, was certainly written) ; with remembering something, also, of Shelley's farewell feast to a party of friends at Eton ; with remembering, moreover (or, at least, believing that he remembered), that Shelley was said to have been paid 40*l*., more or less, for the literary production. These recollections (albeit the recollections of a very mistaken and very much misinformed witness) are not to be rejected as altogether valueless, but kept in reserve as honest statements and possibly veritable recollections, unfit to be used as testimony by themselves, but quite fit to be used in confirmation of similar recollections by other people. Could it be shown in like way that each of the other guests, either at the time of the banquet or some time afterwards, was under the impression that the feast was paid for with publisher's money, no person competent to sift and weigh evidence would hesitate in coming to the conclusion that the banquet was given by Shelley as a thing bought with money he had received from a publisher,—that the common impression of the eight independent witnesses was the result of representations made by the giver of the feast.

But what was Lady Shelley about, when she—drawing her information from 'authentic sources,' and proclaiming the superiority of her book to all Shelleyan biographies from 'unauthentic sources'—allowed the three lines of Mr. Packe's letter, and other equally faulty lines of it, to go before the public as sure and trustworthy information? If biographies from 'authentic sources' are made up in this fashion, readers may with reason come to prefer biographies 'from unauthentic sources.' As Lady Shelley has forced her literary method and address into contrast with those of the man of letters, whom she discharged with strange discourtesy, she must not resent the assurance that the comparison she has provoked is not to Mr. Hogg's disadvantage.

In the sufficient evidences respecting Shelley at Eton, critical readers make the acquaintance of two very different Shelleys :—the girlish Shelley (of Mr. Walter Halliday's letter) who ' was not made to endure the rough and boisterous pastime at Eton,' never 'joined in the usual sports of the boys, and, what is remarkable, never went out in a boat on the river,' but preferred to ramble about Clewer, Frogmore, and Stoke Park, by himself, or with a single companion of congenial gentleness; and the combative Shelley, whose unruliness and contumacious behaviour to his masters gained for him the office and title of ' The Atheist ' of the school. Differing little from the moping and discontented lad of his last year at Sion House, the girlish Etonian exhibits several points of resemblance to Byron in the earlier part of his unhappy time at Harrow; and in like manner when he has risen to be the arch-rebel of the school, the saucy and combative Etonian reminds one of the combative Byron, leading the riotous Harrovians, and rising with atheistical impudence against Dr. Butler's authority.

In one respect Shelley entered Eton under circumstances far more advantageous than those that caused Byron to hate his public school in the opening terms of his connexion with it. Unlike Byron, who went to Harrow, so badly prepared for its studies, that, had it not been for Dr. Drury's sympathetic consideration, he would have been put (to his poignant humiliation) in a form

of quite little boys, much younger than himself, Shelley went
to his public school well grounded in Latin and Greek. 'He
had,' says Medwin, 'been so well grounded in the classics, that
it required little labour for him to get up his daily lessons.'
Medwin's testimony on this point is sustained by the evidence
of Messrs. Packe and Halliday, two of the poet's contemporaries
at Eton.

During his stay at the public school, Shelley seems to have
resided successively at two different houses. Getting his
information from old Etonians, who had known the author of
Laon and Cythna at Eton, Mr. Middleton certifies that the
future poet boarded, in 1807, at the house of Mr. Hexter, the
writing-master, 'one of those extra masters, some of whom
resided at the College, and, holding an amphibious rank between
the tutor and the dame, were allowed to take boarders.' Subsequently he is found in the house of Mr. Bethell, the tutor whom
Mr. Packe (possibly with no more justice than generosity)
described half-a-century later as 'one of the dullest men in the
establishment.' What Mr. Packe's qualifications were for
passing judgment in this style on one of his former preceptors
does not appear; but the solitary epistle, which gives him a
place in these pages, would not warrant a confident opinion
that brightness was Mr. Packe's distinguishing characteristic.
Fortunately, for school-masters, evidence given to their discredit
by former pupils is never regarded as evidence of the highest
quality by persons of discretion and judicial fairness. Possibly
Mr. Packe was as wrong about Mr. Bethell's intellect, as he
was about the date of the publication of *Zastrozzi*. But an idle
word to the defamation of the Eton tutor, with whom Shelley
came into conflict, was no word for Lady Shelley to withhold
from the world. It has long been the practice of the Shelleyan
enthusiasts to think and speak the worst of every one with
whom the poet had a difference,—to blacken every reputation
that could be suspected of lowering the lustre of the poet, who
under auspicious circumstances 'might have been " the Saviour
of the World." '

That Shelley, on the girlish side of his nature, was no boy
' to take kindly to fagging,' and on the masculine side of his
nature was precisely the boy to detest a system under which he
might be licked with a bamboo or a leather strap for hard-
boiling an egg which he had been told to boil lightly, no one is

likely to question. But though it is certain he disliked being made to fag, and more than probable that he showed this dislike in ways to be resented, not only by the proprietors of fags, but also by the most infantile of Etonian conservatives, readers are under no obligation to accept for truth all the fine and melo-dramatic accounts of the efforts made, and sufferings endured by the poet, in order to put an end to so revolting a system of domestic tyranny.

Getting her fanciful notions of the matter from her husband's lips, Mrs. Shelley would have us believe that repugnance to fagging was the offence which brought him so often to the block, and rendered him alike unpopular with masters and boys. It is even averred that to put down fagging he organized a conspiracy of the junior Etonians against the barbarous prac-tice. That no such conspiracy was begotten and fostered by Shelley is certain; for the old Etonians, of whom Medwin and Middleton certainly (Peacock and Hogg almost certainly) made inquiries about the matter, had never heard anything of a move-ment which could not have failed to come to their knowledge, had it ever been an incident of scholastic politics in their time. The truth underlying these fictions is that Shelley, like most junior boys, conceived a hatred of 'fagging,' suffered much from it, and having, unlike most junior boys, the rashness to declare the hatred, paid the penalty of his rashness, in being cuffed, licked, and silenced in various painful and exasperating ways. This seems to be the whole of the case, which he magnified in later time into a far greater affair. To Peacock, he used to speak of the cruelties practised upon him by senior boys at Eton, with a show of abhorrence only surpassed by his display of indignation and disgust at the monstrous barbarities done him by Lord Chancellor Eldon. In still later time he doubt-less spoke even more passionately to his wife of the fires of Etonian persecution. Men sometimes say strange things to their wives; and, in certain moods, wives are even quicker to believe the strange things, than in other moods to suspect untruth in the commonplace things told them by their lords. After brooding for twelve years or more over the sorrows and wrongs he endured at Eton, the poet believed all he imagined about them.

Though Shelley suffered no little at Eton from 'fagging,' he suffered far more from the particular bullying that flourishes

under the system he detested, quite as much as in schools where
fags are unknown, and senior boys have no especial and peculiar
slaves. In behalf of 'fagging' it is justly urged that if the
master licks his 'fag,' he is quick on the score of dignity and
ownership to protect him from maltreatment by other senior
boys;—that if the 'fag' is bullied by his proper lord, he is
secured by 'the system' from being bullied by a score of tyrants.
None the less true is it that, though the system saves a junior
boy from the tyranny of several tyrants acting individually and
separately, it is powerless to guard him from the oppression of
many tyrants acting conjointly and in mass. Subject to the
certain tyranny (more or less severe and irritating) of a single
despot, the fag is also liable to the uncertain tyranny of the
playground (*i.e.*, of the multitude of his schoolmates, acting in
unison), a tyranny which his peculiar owner can do little or
nothing to moderate. In his earlier time at Eton, Shelley suffered more than most boys of his age from the tyranny of the
playground.

Boys are quick to discover the peculiarities of their companions, and no less quick to discover something offensive in
those peculiarities. Having discovered the offensiveness, they
conceive themselves morally entitled—and, indeed, by honour
bound—to chastise the individual who by force of his disagreeable peculiarities offends them. Of all peculiarities likely
to offend a multitude of schoolboys and set them at war with a
junior boy, none is more certain to give offence than a 'general
queerness,' allied with unsociability. The shy, nervous, moping
boy from Field Place had not been a week at Eton before he
was found guilty of 'general queerness.' He had not been
there a month before he was found guilty of unsociability.
These facts having been found against the boy who held aloof
from other boys, the playground began to ridicule him, hoot at
him, mob him. Under these provocations the nervous and
excitable boy vented his rage with shrill screams of fury.
Obviously, the boy who responded in this violent style was
a boy worth the trouble of 'baiting.' It was good fun to hem
him in, mimic his cries of rage, point derisive fingers at him,
and burst into clamorous laughter, when he uttered a more than
ordinarily shrill shriek of rage and anguish. When he clenched
his fist, and rushed at the nearest of his tormentors with the
intention of striking him, the playground fled before him—not

in real terror, as Lady Shelley imagines—but with a mere
show of fright simulated for his further annoyance, the promotion of general hilarity, and the maintenance of ' sport.'

It was the practice of Etonians, in Shelley's earlier time, to
assemble on dark winter evenings under the cloisters, and amuse
themselves in this droll fashion. The name of a particular boy
(one known probably to be in the rear of the multitude coming
from the playing-grounds) was shouted aloud, as though he
were needed for some urgent business. The cry having been
thus raised, it grew louder and louder from the increasing
energy and growing number of the voices. On the appearance
of the boy owning the name, the clamour was redoubled.
Everyone drew to one side or the other to make a way for
him. It was useless for him to proclaim his presence and
beg the shouters to spare their lungs. No words of his utterance could be heard in the uproar. Could they have been
heard, any words from him would only stimulate the shouters
to shout yet louder. There was no course open to him but to
walk straight on through two lines of excited faces to the
point, where the demand for his presence had originated. On
coming to that point he found (if he did not know it before)
that nobody wanted him, and was received with peals of
laughter. In its origin the game was doubtless a lively,
piquant, and comparatively inoffensive practical joke at the
expense of a lad, who, imagining himself called for some
serious cause, hastened at full speed to discover he had been
summoned for nothing. But it is in the nature of practical
jokes to degenerate into cruel jokes, however amiable they may
have been in the first instance. As soon as this particular
joke had lost its newness, the boy thus shouted for knew that
he was being made a fool of, felt himself insulted, grew angry ;
his anger being further stimulated by some new variation of the
game of torture.

It having been discovered that Shelley suffered keenly from
the ridicule of the playing-fields, he was selected evening after
evening for this particular ' baiting.' Evening after evening
the cry was raised of ' Shelley, Shelley, Shelley !' As he ran
the gauntlet of derisive faces and voices, fingers were pointed at
him. Not seldom he came in for rougher usage. If he was
carrying books under his arm, a blow from behind scattered
them on the ground. His clothes were pulled and torn. More

than once a muddy football, deriving its impetus from a well-planted kick, came with the force of a spent shot down the narrow alley of deriders, caught him in his shirt-front, and bounding upwards, made his face as dirty as his frill. Mr. Middleton was assured by an eye-witness of these scenes that the fury, to which Shelley was goaded by his tormentors, 'made his eyes flash like a tiger's, his cheeks grow pale as death, his limbs quiver, and his hair stand on end.' It is probable that the boy's shrill screeches of rage, wild gesticulations, and frantic appearance, whilst he was thus baited and ridiculed by the whole school, first suggested to his persecutors that 'mad' was the fittest epithet to put before his surname. Anyhow, he was known in the school as 'Mad Shelley,' both before and after he had earned the less opprobrious designation of 'The Atheist.'

At a time when 'Mad Shelley' was the butt of the playing-grounds, Eton was visited by an itinerant lecturer, who received permission to deliver a course of lectures on astronomy, chemistry, electricity, and mechanics, to the boys of the school. Familiarly designated 'Old Walker,' this vagrant professor used to go about the country with his assistant-demonstrator, orrery, solar microscope, electrical machine, and other scientific apparatus; lecturing at the superior boys' schools and girls' schools of the provincial towns. Without Medwin's testimony to the point, it would have been safe to assume that the wandering lecturer, who was permitted to enlighten the boys of the most aristocratic of our great public schools, had also the honour of rendering the same service to the boys of Dr. Greenlaw's academy. Medwin, however, speaks so precisely of the visit Old Walker paid Sion House during Bysshe's second or third year at the school, and of the lively interest taken by Shelley in the professor's demonstrations, that he is not, in consideration of his frequent inaccuracies, to be declared guilty of error on the main facts of this part of his narrative. It is, of course, conceivable that blundering Tom Medwin assigned to the great room of the Brentford Academy incidents of a later date and another scene. But it is more probable he was guiltless of the mistake. Anyhow, Shelley had not long suffered under imputations of madness at Eton, when he heard Old Walker's course of lectures for the second time, if Medwin was right—for the first time, if Medwin was wrong in the matter.

At Eton, 'Old Walker' had an eager devourer of his words,

a delighted witness of his experimental demonstrations, in Mad
Shelley. The lectures had on Shelley all the effect they were
designed to produce on intelligent lads. Producing on him all
the effect desired by the Professor, they were also fruitful of
results, that in the opinion of the Eton masters far exceeded the
limits of wholesome interest. It is conceivable that, had Dr.
Keate, and Mr. Bethell, and Mr. Hexter, known how the boy
would be stirred and excited by the lectures, Old Walker would
not have received permission to deliver them to the collegians,
or Mad Shelley would not have been allowed to be present at
their delivery. Like many other boys before and after his time,
Mad Shelley was so taken by the lectures, that it is only a
permissible figure of speech to say, he 'went mad' on natural
science. Before Old Walker cleared out of Eton, the boy had
become the owner of a solar microscope, and bought an electrical
machine of Old Walker's assistant.

In Mr. Hexter's house the boy (*ætat.* thirteen and fourteen)
had shown more concern for English literature than for any
other accessible means of pastime,—reading works of prose (as
he had done at Brentford), learning by rote passages from the
English poets, and composing childish dramas with the assistance
of a fellow-pupil and fellow-fag of the same house, named Amos;
amusing himself, in short, in accordance with his genuine and
strongest intellectual taste and ambition. One of the happiest
and most agreable glimpses to be had of Mad Shelley in his
earlier time of Eton, affords a view of the boy, running nimbly
up and down the stairs of Mr. Hexter's house, and singing out
cheerily the witches' song of *Macbeth:*—

> 'Double, double, toil and trouble :
> Fire burn and cauldron bubble.'

Of the plays composed by the two boys nothing is known at the
present date, save that they were performed by the author before
a third fag of their house, Matthews, who was the solitary witness of the performances, and, it may be hoped, an enthusiastically applausive one.

In the new excitement and interests, to which Old Walker's
lectures gave birth, Shelley's care for English literature languished. Like other children he cared only for the new toy.
Like other boys possessed by the scientific mania, he for a while
delighted in nothing but his scientific apparatus, contrivances,

experiments. For a time it was true that he cared for no learning that his masters taught. During this passion for the experimental study of scientific phenomena, one of his exploits was to lay a long train of gunpowder between a decaying tree and a point, at some distance from the tree, and then to fire the gunpowder by means of a burning-glass,—with a result altogether satisfactory to the youthful experimentalist,—but less satisfactory to the owner of the ancient tree, and by no means to the approval of the masters, who were responsible for the behaviour of the boys, and for the safety of the buildings of Eton College. On another occasion, after his transference from Mr. Hexter's house to the house of the gentleman described by Mr. Packe as 'one of the dullest men of the establishment,' he was busy at dead of night in his bedroom with his 'chemical studies' (as they are grandly styled by the Shelleyan enthusiasts), when he upset a frying-pan full of ingredients into the fire, with consequences that roused all the sleepers in the house, and made them in the morning congratulate themselves on not having been burnt to death in their beds by Mad Shelley.

It certainly does not sustain Mr. Packe's contemptuous opinion of the tutor, that Mr. Bethell was bright enough to think he had better check his pupil's enthusiasm for scientific inquiry. It can scarcely be regarded as evidence of his dullness that this gentleman felt it his duty to see what Mad Shelley was after, and take steps to preserve his house and its inmates from the quick destruction, with which they were threatened by the rather lawless proceedings of an eccentric boy. With this purpose in view, Mr. Bethell paid Shelley's room a visit at a moment, when the young gentleman was then and there enlarging his knowledge of nature, by the scientific production of a blue flame, though the boys of Mr. Bethell's house had been forbidden to produce blue or any other flame iu their bedrooms.

'Chemical experiments,' airily remarks Lady Shelley, who, taking the story from the page of a previous writer, seems to think it even more to her father-in-law's credit than to the tutor's manifest shame, 'were prohibited in the boys' chambers; and the tutor (Mr. Bethel) somewhat angrily asked what the lad was doing. Shelley jocularly replied that he was raising the devil. Mr. Bethel seized hold of a mysterious implement on the table, and in an instant was thrown against the wall, having grasped a highly charged electrical machine. Of course the young experimentalist paid dearly for this unfortunate occurrence.'

And equally, of course, he deserved to pay dearly for the 'unfortunate occurrence.'

Positively this story is told in proof that young Bysshe Shelley was a youth of parts, genius, and exceeding sweetness of disposition. A boy (probably fifteen years old, possibly a year older by this time) is caught in his bedroom doing what he has been forbidden to do. Coming upon the boy when he is so occupied, his tutor says, somewhat angrily, 'What are you doing?' Instead of answering this by no means impertinent question in the respectful tone required by mere good breeding, the boy answers 'cheekily' (the Shelleyan enthusiasts must pardon me for using a schoolboy's word, to describe the schoolboy's misdemeanour), 'I am raising the devil.' On seeing his tutor approach a powerfully charged electric battery, with outstretched hand, instead of crying out 'Don't touch it, sir; it will do you injury,' the boy ('the young experimentalist!'), holding his tongue, allows his tutor to touch the machine, and to be thrown violently against a wall. Lady Shelley would have us think this 'young experimentalist' a nice, loyal, fine-natured, gentlemanly boy; would have us join in a shout of derision at 'one of the dullest men of the establishment;' would have us think this pleasant boy badly treated, because he was whipt for his misbehaviour. I cannot do as Lady Shelley would have me. On the contrary, knowing the temper and gracious qualities of public schoolboys, I have no doubt they will, for the most and best part, concur with me in saying, that Shelley (superb poet though he became in later time) behaved badly in this business, and deserved all that he 'caught' from Dr. Keate for unruliness, so wholly 'out of form.'

Shelley having caused so much trouble with his experimental excesses, it was decided that, to prevent them from turning their bedrooms into laboratories and setting fire to rotten timber, the boys should at least for awhile be forbidden to play at being chemical students. A book on chemistry, which Shelley had borrowed of Mr. Medwin, the Horsham attorney (Tom Medwin's father), being found in the lad's room, it was sent by his tutor to Mr. Timothy Shelley, of Field Place, who passed the volume on to its owner, saying in a note (referred to in the younger Medwin's *Life of Shelley*), 'I have returned the book on chemistry, as it is a forbidden thing at Eton.' As chemistry, thus forbidden in 1808, cannot be supposed to have been for-

bidden in the school when Old Walker was permitted to make
the boys take an interest in the science, it is a fair inference
that the prohibition resulted in some degree from annoyances,
coming to the school through the lecturer's most interested
auditor. Mad Shelley's electrical machine, and other scientific
apparatus, would probably have been sent to Field Place, together with the volume on chemistry, had he not already
deposited them for safe keeping in the hands of a certain white-
headed gentleman, who will soon receive the attention he merits
at the hands of the present writer.

Those who knew Shelley best in his boyhood did not imagine
at the time, that the 'prohibition of chemistry' would dispose
him to desist from the forbidden pastime. Those who knew
him best in later time concurred in thinking that the order to
refrain from chemical inquiry and experiments would only
quicken his enthusiasm for the proscribed amusement.

'Might not this extraordinary prohibition,' asks Mr. Medwin, speaking from his personal knowledge of his cousin in boyhood and manhood,
'have the more stimulated Shelley to engage in the pursuit?' In the
same spirit, Mr. Rossetti remarks, with equal sagacity and justice. 'No
doubt the great turn for chemical experiment which he developed at
Eton, and which became his chief passion there, had as much to do with an
impressible fancy, and with the fact that chemical practice was prohibited
to the schoolboys in their chambers, as with scientific tendencies.'

It is certain, that instead of having any natural aptitude for the
practice, Shelley was unusually deficient in the qualities, requisite in a scientific experimentalist. A dreamer, a visionary,
and an enthusiast, he wanted the nice touch, the fine perception
of minute phenomena, the intellectual patience, the mental
disposition for accuracy in the smallest details. It is certain
that the man, who, even in his proper art, was curiously careless of verbal details, never had any sincere disposition for
pursuits, in which nothing can be done without incessant
attention to minutiæ,—for pursuits which repel the student,
who does not delight in the painful vigilance and methodical
exactness of scientific inquiry. Had he played with the microscope to the last hour of a long life, as he played with it
fitfully for several years after leaving Eton, he would never for
a single hour have been 'a worker' with it. He was singularly
wanting in what Mr. Rossetti calls 'scientific tendencies.'

On the other hand, it is no less manifest that in his earlier

time a certain mental and moral perversity—a perversity by
no means uncommon in young people, and only a few degrees
less common in persons of mature age—gave him a keen appetite for fruit he was forbidden to pluck, and a distaste for
whatever fruit he was required to enjoy. The majority of boys
take to smoking (a very disagreeable pastime to beginners),
even as Thomas Carlyle confessed he took to it,—'for the pure
sin of it.' Just as the Chelsea sage began smoking because he
was ordered not to smoke, the Etonian Shelley pursued chemistry because he was ordered not to pursue it. Had it not been
for the needful prohibition of the pastime, that threw the school
into disorder and threatened boarding-houses with destruction,
the enthusiasm for science, for which Old Walker's lectures
were in the first instance accountable, would soon have died
out. Forbidden to play with his chemical apparatus and
munitions, Shelley cared for no other pastime, and maintained
that the pastime was a serious pursuit. Had the authorities of
the school ordered every boy to study chemistry and astronomy,
and put their ban on the pursuit of classical lore, Shelley
would soon have declared natural science a profitless kind of
busy idleness, and would have 'wrought linked-armour for his
soul' out of Latin and Greek books. This perversity must be
borne in mind by those who would take a true view of the
Shelley of later times,—the Shelley who at Oxford soon ceased
to care for the 'experimental studies' in which he was at
liberty to waste his whole time, and cared especially for the
sceptical writers whom he was admonished to avoid ; the Shelley
who, on coming from the university into the wider world, threw
himself into the arms of the revolutionary doctrinaires (before
he had given three weeks to the study of political science),
because his natural advisers,—the persons with the strongest
title to direct him authoritatively,—bade and entreated him to
give no heed to such dangerous teachers.

Having come into conflict with the Eton masters on the
blue-flame question, and the natural right of every Eton boy to
possess an electrical machine and use it at his pleasure for the
humiliation of his tutor, Shelley was nearing the time when
the unanimous voice of the forms (*minus* the masters) proclaimed him 'The Atheist' of the school. Under the persecu-
tions of the playground, which had goaded him out of his
girlishness into thought and action, that revealed the masculine

forces of his nature, Shelley was ceasing to be the Sion House
'faint heart' and 'milksop,' when Old Walker visited Eton.
In the subsequent battle for freedom of scientific inquiry, the
boy's combativeness became daily more and more apparent; his
carelessness for his own skin and his contempt for Dr. Keate's
rods more and more sublime, till Mad Shelley, ceasing to be
everybody's butt, became a boy of pluck and merit to the whole
school,—a possible martyr in the sacred cause of scholastic disorder,—a lad who cared not a fig for Keate or any of Keate's
underlings. From the mad-dog of the Eton playing-grounds,
he had risen to the proud position of The Eton Atheist. The
girlish Shelley had for the moment become 'a boy,'—a very
naughty boy!

Let there be no misunderstanding about this rather sensational title. A boy might be The Eton Atheist, and at the
same time be a sound and unwavering believer in every doctrine
of the Thirty-nine Articles. The gods of Eton were only the
masters of the school; the sceptics of Eton were nothing more
terrible than those naughty boys who held these masters full
cheap, and questioned their natural fitness for the authority
given into their hands. The Atheist of Eton was the boy who
surpassed all the other naughty boys in contempt for the
masters, and not content with questioning their natural fitness
for their official eminence, boldly and utterly denied it. No
Etonian sceptic could question, no Etonian Atheist could deny
the existence of gods who daily entered boys' names on flogging-
bills. Dr. Keate's rods were no things to be ignored; the
wielder of those rods was a person, whose existence could not
be questioned. His character, however, was open to criticism,
and the Lord High Atheist spoke his mind about it with freedom.

Before an Etonian could rise to the position of Lord High
Atheist, or even become a candidate for the office, it was needful for him to distinguish himself from ordinary deriders of
the pedagogic species by some super-puerile extravagance of
audacity. The youngster, who preceded Shelley in the Atheist's
chair, had one dark winter's night taken possession of the huge,
richly-gilded bunch of grapes, which hung in front of 'The
Christopher Tavern,' and having so taken into his keeping the
inn-sign, suspended it over the door of the head-master's house.
In the morning, on rushing over his threshold to get to
chapel in time for sacred service, this head-master ran full

butt into the bunch of grapes, with consequences altogether
satisfactory to the contriver and doer of the practical joke, who
witnessed the successful issue of his arrangements from a convenient corner. It is needless to say that, after executing this
feat in contempt of the greatest of the Etonian gods, the bor-
rower of the grapes was declared Lord High Atheist before he
had lived another day. It is uncertain what egregious act of
profanity raised Shelley to the same eminence. Possibly the
affair with the electric battery, that hurled Mr. Bethell against
the bedroom wall, may have contributed to the future poet's
elevation to an office, which he does not seem to have disgraced.
Anyhow, it is certain that Shelley became the Lord High
Atheist of the school, and that he would not have attained to
this distinction, had he not been regarded by his comrades as
the most unruly and impudent boy of the establishment.

Whilst holding this office, not content with deriding the
masters and disobeying their orders at every turn, the boy also
distinguished himself by the fervour and blasphemous ingenuity
with which he used to curse the King (George the Third), and
used also to curse his own father. It speaks ill for the tone of
Etonian manners during the poet's time at the public school,
that the boys used to gather round the Lord High Atheist on a
hint that he meant forthwith to curse his own father. The
willing listeners never seem to have expressed disgust at the
comminatory performance. On the contrary, the frequently
repeated entertainment was thought so droll and piquant that,
during his short stay at Oxford, Shelley was entreated, at least
on one occasion, to curse his father yet again for the gratification of two or three of his former schoolfellows. Hogg, who
was present on this occasion, records that Shelley yielded reluctantly to the entreaty ; but he *did* consent to the importunity
of the old Etonians, and 'delivered with vehemence and animation
a string of execrations, greatly resembling in its absurdity a
papal anathema.' Though he joined in the 'hearty laugh,'
that rewarded the performer, Hogg, on the departure of the
two or three Etonians, exclaimed, 'Why, you young reprobate,
who in the world taught you to curse your father,—your own
father ?'—an inquiry to which Shelley replied :—

'My grandfather, Sir Bysshe, partly : but principally my friend,
Dr. Lind, at Eton. When anything goes wrong at Field Place, my
father does nothing but swear all day long afterwards. Whenever

I have gone with my father to visit Sir Bysshe, he always received him
with a tremendous oath, and continued to heap curses upon his head
so long as he remained in the room.'

Ever ready, though he was, to give evidence to his father's
discredit, the undergraduate did not venture to charge his father
with retorting Sir Bysshe's maledictions. Whilst **Mr. Timothy**
Shelley appears only to have sworn after a bad fashion of the
period, the first baronet of Castle Goring exceeded the licence
of blasphemy accorded to gentlemen by a custom, more honoured
in the breach than the observance.

It remains to be seen how the Shelleyan enthusiasts will
deal with the record of Shelley's habit of cursing his father,
when the public shall have been educated to approve every act
of the poet's life; but at present they glide lightly over the
ugly business in memoirs for the general reader, glossing it
with suggestions of wilful misstatement or unconscious exaggeration on the part of the poet's earliest biographer. Even
Mr. Forman forbears to hint that Shelley's resemblance to the
Saviour of the World is heightened by the poet's behaviour to
his father. In the coteries, however, where the Shelleyan
apologists speak with less caution, these cursing bouts are
sometimes referred to for evidence that, even in his boyhood,
the author of *Laon and Cythna* was a person of infinite jest and
subtle humour. These apologists must bear with a writer who
sees much to condemn, and nothing to admire, in such exhibitions of unfilial rancour and profanity. There are jokes and
jokes;—those that can be enjoyed, those that can be tolerated,
and those that are absolutely intolerable. The joke of a boy
cursing his own father for the amusement of his schoolfellows
is one of the intolerable kind. The reader may be safely left
to select a fitter word than ' humourist ' for the designation of
the young gentleman, who amused himself and his friends in
so revolting a manner.

Mr. Walter S. Halliday, by the way, must have forgotten
all about these cursing-bouts, when he wrote to Lady Shelley,
' He ' (*i.e.*, the poet at Eton) ' had great moral courage and
feared nothing, but what was base, false, and low.' Surely it
is base and low for a boy to curse his own father for the pure
fun of the thing.

Who was Dr. James Lind, chiefly famous (and infamous)
as Shelley's chief instructor in the science and art of cursing?

Drawing her facts from 'authentic sources,' Lady Shelley speaks of him as 'an erudite scholar and amiable old man, much devoted to chemistry, at whose house Shelley passed the happiest of his Eton hours.' 'He was a physician,' the lady adds, 'and also one of the tutors.' Recording that Dr. James Lind bore 'a name well known among the professors of medical science,' Mrs. Shelley has also put it on record that ' the Doctor often stood by to befriend and support the persecuted, and that her husband never, in after-life, mentioned his name without love and reverence.' Shelley himself used to say of this amiable and erudite old man, 'He loved me, and I shall never forget our long talks, where he breathed the spirit of the kindest tolerance and the purest wisdom.' Without alleging that he speaks from other and better authorities than the poet, his widow and his daughter-in-law, Mr. Rossetti says of Shelley and his peculiar patron, 'The only official person whom he really liked there' (*i.e.* Eton) 'was Dr. James Lind of Windsor, a physician, chemist, and tutor, and a man of erudition, who superintended the youth's scientific studies.' Had he only deserved half the praise lavished upon him, Dr. Lind would have been a man of extraordinary goodness. But, unfortunately, it is only too clear that he was a mischievous, malignant, hard-swearing old man, who gained great influence over the Etonian Shelley, and used it hurtfully.

Possibly Lady Shelley and later biographers were justified in writing of this bad old man, as though he held a tutorial office on the Eton establishment; but without being in a position to speak positively to their discredit, the present writer ventures to entertain a doubt of their accuracy on this matter, and to give Dr. James Lind the full benefit of the doubt. If the Doctor was one of the Eton tutors, he was even a worse man than he is declared in these pages: for in that case the man, who encouraged Shelley to study chemistry in defiance of the recent prohibition, and to persist in his contumacy to the masters of the school, was guilty of encouraging the boy to rebel against authority, which he was bound by honour and official obligations to maintain. The grey-headed tutor, who secretly stimulated the boy's rebellious spirit, and applauded him for it, was wanting in loyalty, and not guiltless of treachery, to his comrades in tutorial service. But in the absence of clear evidence to the contrary, it may be assumed that the amiable and extremely benevolent old gentleman, who taught a fifteen- or sixteen-years-old boy to curse his father, was under no especial obligation to have a care for the lad's moral health, apart from the general duty of every man to encourage what is virtuous, and discountenance what is vicious in all persons, over whom he has any influence.

If Mrs. Shelley was right in saying Dr. James Lind made himself famous among the professors of medical science, it is strange that the fame at this date rests chiefly on the lady's certificate. Though he has inquired of the persons most likely to have heard of Dr. Lind's services to science, the present writer has learnt nothing of the deeds from which so bright a fame should have proceeded.

All that is known with certainty at this present date about this amiable and benevolent old man, apart from his pernicious intimacy with the young Etonian, is that during Shelley's time he was a medical practitioner (certainly no physician of the London College) following his vocation at Windsor, that he had for his housekeeper a Miss Lind (his daughter or sister), that he was a hard swearer, and that, conceiving himself to have been badly treated by George the Third, he used to make much of his grievance, and waste many words and much time in cursing the King who had done him evil. What the man's grievance was, that made him think so ill of poor old George the Third, is wholly a matter for conjecture. The Doctor may have been employed for awhile at 'the Castle,' and been superseded by a younger doctor. He may have failed in some candidature for a medical office within the royal borough, and discovered grounds for attributing his misadventure to the influence of the Castle. The grievance may have been a real one, or an affair of the imagination. All that can be told of the matter, in this year of grace, is that the Doctor believed himself to have been 'infamously treated' by the King, and that, in a manner scarcely accordant with all that has been written of his amiability and benevolence, seldom allowed a day to pass without doing his best to consign his royal enemy to the lowest and darkest pit of perdition.

The Lord High Atheist of the Etonians used to join Dr. and Miss Lind over their tea-table twice or thrice a-week, and after the meal spend in their society those happy hours (men-

tioned by Lady Shelley) during which he learnt how to curse
his father more strenuously by hearing the Doctor curse his
King. The Shelleyan enthusiasts are sometimes heard to
suggest that Hogg may have made too much of what Shelley
told him about the physician's comminatory taste and achievements. But there is no evidence that Hogg was guilty of the
exaggeration. Nor is there any reason to suppose Shelley was
more than just to his teacher's consummate mastery of maledic-
tion. Yet it was of this Doctor, who swore so heavily over his
willow-pattern tea-cups, whose swearing was so inexpressibly
piquant to its youthful auditor, that Shelley wrote some eight
years later in *Laon and Cythna*, as though the man of oaths and
imprecations were chiefly remarkable for philosophic dignity,
sweetness of speech, mildness of manners. It was of his intercourse with this embittered and scurrilous apothecary, that the
poet wrote in *Prince Athanase* with equal melody and falseness :—

> ' Prince Athanase had one belovèd friend,
>   An old, old man, with hair of silver white,
>   And lips where heavenly smiles would hang and blend
>
> With his wise words;
>
>   *   *   *   *   *   *
>
> Such was Zonoras; and as daylight finds
>   One amaranth glittering on the path of frost,
>   When autumn nights have nipt all weaker kinds,
>
> Thus through his age, dark, cold, and tempest-tost,
>   Shone truth upon Zonoras; and he filled
>   From fountains pure, nigh overgrown and lost,
>
> The spirit of Prince Athanase, a child,
>   With soul-sustaining songs of ancient lore
>   And philosophic wisdom, clear and mild.
>
> And sweet and subtle talk now evermore,
>   The pupil and the master shared; until,
>   Sharing that undiminishable store,
>
> The youth, as shadows on a grassy hill
>   Outrun the winds that chase them, soon outran
>   His teacher, and did teach with native skill
>
> Strange truths and new to that experienced man;
>   Still they were friends, as few have ever been
>   Who mark the extremes of life's discordant span.'

It was to this amiable and wise physician that Shelley was indebted for another practice, scarcely less hurtful to his moral character, and far more fruitful to him of disaster at the outset of life, than his revolting habit of cursing his own father. Not content with teaching him to curse his parent, Dr. Lind taught the boy it was good fun to inveigle unwary people into scientific controversies, to trip them up with catch-questions, and then to laugh at them for being fools. By this mild-natured and benevolent physician (who is usually described as satisfying the boy's hunger for wholesome knowledge, and ministering to his spiritual needs) Shelley, whilst at Eton, was taught to write letters under assumed names to persons interested in, but only slightly acquainted with, chemistry,—in order to discover their ignorance, and then have the pleasure of laughing insolently at it. The letters written for this amiable purpose (under Dr. Lind's instruction) were for the most part written deceitfully, — *i.e.* with a false show of being written by a young and ingenuous inquirer after truth, and with a false name and address. Can any diversion be imagined more likely to infuse a boy with self-conceit and arrogance, to inspire him with the temper most foreign to genuine love of knowledge, and giving him a taste for underhand trickery, to train him how to indulge it habitually? Yet the good and wise Dr. Lind taught the boy to amuse himself in this ungenerous and deceitful way. By-and-bye, the disastrous consequences of this practice on the boy's career at Oxford will be seen. That Shelley on coming to Oxford was so disputatious, so overflowing with scorn for minds he deemed weaker than his own, so ungenerously eager to prove himself wiser than his teachers, so ungenerously quick to show people they were fools, and mock them for being fools, must be attributed in a great degree to his premature introduction (by the humane and judicious Dr. Lind) to the violent delights of controversy. One of the correspondents, whom the boy thus lured into profitless disputation, is said to have threatened him with a flogging from Dr. Keate; a threat that is said to have determined the Etonian henceforth to approach strangers under cover of a false name and address. Had the threat been carried out and the flogging given, the boy would have taken no more than he deserved for his bad manners.

To Dr. Lind the poet was also indebted for his earliest

lessons in Free Thought on matters pertaining to religion. Hogg is a good authority for this statement. Having thus sown the seeds of religious scepticism in the mind of his young friend, this exemplary physician left them to grow in a congenial soil. It does not appear that the doctor ever troubled himself to observe the consequences of his action in this matter, after his pupil left Eton. Nor does it appear that, after leaving Eton, Shelley ever troubled himself to visit, or correspond with, the virtuous sage to whom he declared himself so deeply indebted. For good or evil it cannot be questioned the boy of tender age was influenced in no slight degree by the tutor who educated him to write false epistles, to curse his father, and to repudiate Christianity.

On finding themselves disposed to regard the 'egotisms' of the Shelleyan poems as passages of veracious autobiography, readers should correct the tendency to error by remembering, how the hard-swearing Windsor doctor was idealized into the virtuous hermit of *Laon and Cythna* and the no less virtuous philosopher of *Prince Athanase;* how the boy (the poet's former self), who delighted in the doctor's profane and scurrilous utterances, was idealized into the young Prince whose heart harboured 'nought of ill,' whose 'gentle, yet aspiring mind,' was alike remarkable for justice, innocence, and various learning; and how, in course of time, the poet believed so completely all his fanciful pen had written to the Doctor's honour, that he used to speak of him as an example of wise, stately, and virtuous old age. According to words, spoken by the poet to his second wife, Dr. Lind's benevolence and dignified demeanour were qualified by youthful ardour. His locks were white, his eyes glowed with supernatural expressiveness, his countenance and mien were eloquent of amiability. 'I owe to that man,' Shelley used to ejaculate, 'far, ah! far more than I owe to my father; he loved me, and I never shall forget our long talks, when he breathed the kindest toleration and the purest wisdom.'

In this strain Shelley used to talk of the man who taught him to curse his own father,—of the man whom he would have remembered only as a profane old reprobate, had he been less completely the victim of his own delusive fancy.

It has already been told how Shelley spent his Eton holidays at Field Place; how he took his sisters for walks, entertained

them with his scientific toys, amused them with romantic stories,
and dazzled them with his Eton air and stylish clothing ; and
how he strolled forth by starlight and moonlight to gaze at
the heavenly bodies. But precise mention has still to be made
of an incident of the Etonian's life under his father's roof, to
which readers may well give their best attention.

At a time when Dr. Lind's pernicious influence over him was
at its height, Shelley suffered at Field Place from a febrile
attack attended with delirium,—the illness of which he spoke to
William Godwin's daughter, before her elopement with him, in
these words—

'Once when I was very ill during the holidays, as I was recovering
from a fever which had attacked my brain, a servant overheard my
father consult about sending me to a private madhouse. I was a favourite
among all our servants, so this fellow came and told me as I lay sick in
bed. My horror was beyond words, and I might soon have been mad
indeed, if they had proceeded in their iniquitous plan. I had one hope.
I was master of three pounds of money, and, with the servant's help, I
contrived to send an express to Dr. Lind. He came, and I never shall
forget his manner on that occasion. His profession gave him authority;
his love for me ardour. He dared my father to execute his purpose, and
his menaces had the desired effect.'

These words were spoken by Shelley to Mary Godwin on the
'night that' (to use her own words) 'decided her destiny ; when
he opened at first with the confidence of friendship, and then
with the ardour of love, his whole heart to me.' Mrs. Shelley
is at great pains to impress her readers with a sense of the precise accuracy of her report of the words, which, it is suggested,
determined her, or at least were largely influential, in determining her, to fly with the object of such atrocious paternal
malignity. The substantial accuracy of the lady's report is put
out of question by Hogg, who declares that he heard 'Shelley
speak of his fever and this scene at Field Place more than once,
in nearly the same terms as Mrs. Shelley adopts.' It appears,
therefore, that, whilst the accuracy of Mrs. Shelley's report is
unquestionable, the statement made to her by her husband is one
of the few statements respecting himself, which he repeated at
different times with no important variation ; the substantial
consistency of his several accounts being evidential at least of
the earnestness with which he pondered the narrative, and in
some degree of the sincerity of his avowals of its truthfulness.

Like so many of the poet's stories about himself, it was a curious mixture of fact and fiction. As the story, so thoroughly believed and steadily repeated by its teller, points to the period when Shelley began to regard his father with morbid fear and aversion, and also to the circumstances that gave birth to so unnatural a state of feeling, it is well to inquire how much of this marvellous story was true, and how much of it was illusion. No discreet and judicial hearer of the story ever gave the slighest credit to the chief and most painful statements of the narrative,—viz., that Mr. Timothy Shelley intended to send his fever-stricken boy to a madhouse, and had been heard to express this intention. The evidence being conclusive that he was an affectionate father and kindly gentleman, the notion that he was capable of any such atrocity can have been nothing more than one of the sick boy's delirious fancies. Had Mr. Timothy Shelley been a less amiable person, his abundant sensitiveness for the honour of Field Place (the honour of the newly-created Castle Goring family), and his nervous care for the world's opinion, would have saved him from the blunder of sending the sick boy to a lunatic asylum; the blunder, moreover, of consigning to a madhouse the son who, as a lunatic, could not have concurred in the resettlement of family estates, for which his concurrence was requisite, and the Squire was greatly desirous. Old Sir Bysshe was not more desirous than his son Timothy for the resettlement of the estates A and B. A man of affairs, Mr. Timothy Shelley, would have known that, whilst imprisoned as a lunatic, his son could not resettle the estates; knew also that, by barbarously throwing him into a madhouse, he would create in his son's mind a state of feeling that would be fatal to the scheme for getting him to join in the resettlement, on his liberation or escape from the madhouse. Had he been morally capable of so atrocious an offence, self-interest would have preserved the Squire of Field Place from the iniquitous purpose, about which Shelley's wild story made him gossip lightly and loudly. Hogg gave not a moment's credence to the ghastly and revolting particulars of the story. The other hearers of the story, to whom Hogg makes reference, concurred with him in ascribing these particulars to hallucination, which continued to prey on the patient's light and flighty brain, long years after his recovery from the fever that gave birth to the morbid fancy. Even Lady Shelley seems to take the only sensible view of this part of the affair, though she does not go the length of saying her father-in-law was the victim of hallucination—

'From the indiscreet gossip,' she says, 'of a servant, who had overheard some conversation between his father and the village doctor, Bysshe had come to the conviction that it was intended to remove him from the house to some distant asylum:—'

language certainly implying that the sick boy's fancy was erroneous. Hogg says :—

'It appeared to myself and to others also, that his, *i.e.* Shelley's recollections, were those of a person not quite recovered from a fever, which had attacked his brain, and still disturbed by the horrors of the disease. Truth and justice demand that no event of his life should be kept back, but that all materials for the formation of a correct judgment should be freely given.'

Other particulars of the story may have been no less baseless. That a servant told him of his father's purpose, that he gave this servant orders and means to despatch a messenger to Dr. Lind, may have been mere fancies of the delirious brain. On the other hand, Lady Shelley may have had better authority than the poet's words for attributing the painful conviction to a servant's gossip. It can also be readily imagined that the sufferer from the distressing fancy gave his pocket-money to a servant, and bade him be off to Windsor for the doctor. These are points on which the reader may be left to form his own opinion, but he must altogether acquit Mr. Timothy Shelley of intending to send his boy to a madhouse.

The indisputable facts of the story are these :—The boy had a febrile illness attended with delirium ; whilst ill he suffered from a fancy that his father meant to send him to a lunatic asylum ; after this notion had fastened on the disordered brain, Dr. Lind was sent for ; in compliance with the summons Dr. Lind came from Windsor to Field Place, and attended the boy till he was better. A reasonable view of these facts is that during his delirious sickness the patient expressed a strong desire to see Dr. Lind, and that, in their natural desire to do the best for their child's comfort and recovery, Mr. and Mrs. Shelley invited the doctor to come to Field Place. Even Dr. Lind with all his eccentricity would not have presumed to visit Field Place without an invitation from the master of the house. Still less would he have ventured to force his way into the sick chamber against Mr. Timothy Shelley's wish. The statement that he dared Mr. Shelley 'to execute his purpose,' and brought him to a sense of decency by 'menaces,' is simply ridiculous. Ever reluctant though she is to discredit any of the poet's statements, Lady Shelley shows her opinion of the wildest extravagances of his marvellous story by being silent about them.

Something should be said about the probable time of this illness. Circumstances point to the latter part of 1808 as the period in which Dr. Lind attended Shelley in Field Place. Shelley may have been right in regarding the illness as an incident of one of his 'holidays;' but there are grounds for thinking it more probable that the illness ran its course during one of the Eton terms. Four-and-thirty years after the poet's death, Miss Margaret Shelley could remember that, whilst her sister Hellen was at school at Clapham, Bysshe was sent home from Eton to be nursed through an illness.

'I went to school before Margaret,' Miss Hellen Shelley wrote in 1856, 'so that she recollects how Bysshe came home in the midst of the half-year to be nursed ; and when he was allowed to leave the house, he came to the dining-room window, and kissed her through the pane of glass.'

Hellen's age (she was born in 1799) seems to indicate that this illness cannot have taken place earlier than the autumn of 1808. Even then she would have been young to go to boarding-school. If this was the illness mentioned in the poet's strange story, Dr. Lind's visit to Field Place is a simple affair. Sent home when he was already sickening for an illness, the patient had been under Dr. Lind's medical treatment before he was sent home to be nursed through an illness that would probably prove a severe one. What more natural and in the ordinary course of things, when the boy grew worse, and the village apothecary wished for 'a second opinion,' than for Mr. Timothy Shelley to summon the Windsor doctor who had seen the patient in the earliest stage of the malady. The conversation between Mr. Timothy Shelley and the village apothecary, which is said to have been so indiscreetly reported to the sick boy, may have turned wholly on the question, whether Dr. Lind should be sent for. Dr. Lind unquestionably was summoned; and as Mr. Shelley was at Field Place at the time, no one else is likely to have dispatched the summons. Had he imagined Dr.

Lind had already been, or would soon be, the boy's instructor in hard swearing, Mr. Shelley would, doubtless, have sent for another doctor. As the future poet left Eton towards the end of 1809 ; as the illness of the marvellous story occurred during the height of Dr. Lind's influence over the boy; as that influence was certainly an affair of the later half of Bysshe's stay at Eton (1808-9); and as Shelley was certainly sent home from Eton to be nursed through an illness when his sister Hellen (born in September, 1799) was already at school and in 'the middle of her half-year,' most readers will concur with the present writer in thinking the illness mentioned in the story and the illness mentioned in the letter were one and the same illness,—and that the illness at the earliest took place in the autumn of 1808, at the latest in the spring of 1809, *i.e.* when Shelley was sixteen years old. If this manner of dealing with sure facts is acceptable to readers, they may congratulate themselves on having discovered the six months, at the beginning or end of which, the poet was first possessed by the fancy that his father was looking out for a pretext for locking him up in a madhouse:—the hideous fancy that (to use Love Peacock's words) 'haunted him throughout life.'

How came this ghastly and absolutely groundless fancy to take this early and enduring hold of his mind? The answer must be sought in the poet's ancestral story, the characteristics of the romantic literature of which he had been a greedy devourer from his early childhood, and the conditions of his life at Eton. The answer to be extorted from these three sources of information is doubtless an answer, resting on inference and conjecture from facts, almost as much as upon facts themselves. Still it is an answer worth having, though veined with uncertainties. The Shelleys, who eventually blossomed into the Castle Goring house, resembled the eighteenth and nineteenth century Byrons in having a distinct strain of madness. Mention has already been made of the Newark apothecary's elder brother, whose story is told in the following words of the Castle Goring pedigree :—

' John Shelley, of Fen Place, aforesaid, esq., 2nd son, *a lunatic.* Bapt. at Worth 1st September, 1696; died unmarried at Uckfield, 7th October, 1772, buried at Worth 18th same month.'

This long-lived lunatic, who did not escape from his dismal doom in this world, till he had entered his seventy-seventh year, is a significant feature of the poet's ancestral story. Brother of the Newark apothecary, this madman, whose affliction caused him to be set aside in the arrangements of the family (to his younger brother's advantage), was the first baronet's uncle, the poet's great-great-uncle. The obscurity of the families, with whom this lunatic's ancestors intermarried before his period, precludes the discovery of the number of the various channels through which insanity may have come to his brain. But it is not to the physiological credit of the Castle Goring Shelleys, that their ancestors married so many heiresses. Families, whose men have married for money in successive generations, are usually seen to suffer in bodily stamina and mental health from what has come together with money to the family story. There is, of course, no reason why an heiress should not be as healthy as a poor parson's daughter. But there is nothing in money to exempt its possessor from struma in its various forms; and so long as he can win in his bride the first object of his desire, money, the male fortune-hunter is apt to shut his eyes to the indications that the advantages of the money must be taken with serious attendant drawbacks. Families, famous for marrying heiresses, whether they intermarry with noble stocks, or, like our poet's ancestors, with mere gentle yeomanry (*i.e.* squireens entitled to bear arms), are seldom famous for the qualities that render individuals gracious and existence delightful. If they endure for centuries, such families often do so by suffering for centuries.

To account for the same revolting fancy, allowance must also be made for the morbid literature on which the boy had been mentally suckled from his tender infancy,—the tales of domestic horror and cruelties, in which he had revelled from early childhood. To the producers and readers of that literature, no character was more attractive than a wretched being unjustly dealt with as a lunatic by barbarous relations. It is at least probable that the stories of such cruelty, flowing as they did from the press in the period when Monk Lewis threw the audience of a crowded theatre into hysterical anguish by his monodrama of *The Captive*, may have inspired the boy with a morbid apprehension of life-long imprisonment in a mad-house.

Even more likely to produce the same agonizing apprehension, were some of the more painful incidents of his life at Eton, if their terrorizing power was intensified by the knowledge that one of his not very remote collateral ancestors had been confined justly or unjustly as a lunatic. The nervous boy who was hunted and baited in the Eton playing-grounds, by a multitude of lads, shouting at the top of their voices, 'Mad Shelley, Mad Shelley, Mad Shelley!' had good reason to suspect that something in his behaviour and idiosyncrasy must have suggested the imputation of insanity.

'I have seen him,' says one of the spectators of these frequent scenes of cruelty and suffering, 'surrounded, hooted, baited like a maddened bull; and, at this distance of time (forty years after), I seem to hear ringing in my ears the cry which Shelley was wont to utter in his paroxysms of revengeful anger.'

The torture, which made so deep and enduring an impression on the boy who only witnessed it, affected far more strongly the boy who was the object of the persecution. To the end of his life, the poet (given like Byron to brood over the sorrows of his childhood) used to speak with passionate resentment of the barbarous malice of the boys, who either exasperated him with an accusation they knew to be groundless, or, worse still (if they really thought him insane), mocked him for the affliction that entitled him to their compassion.

In his later time at Eton, when he was distinguishing himself by contumacy and insolence to the masters of his school, his father was of course informed of his insubordination and other scholastic offences. Could his word be taken (which it may not be) on the matter, Shelley was twice expelled from Eton, and twice (at his father's entreaty) re-admitted to the school, before he was dismissed from it for the third and last time. It cannot be doubted the Atheist of College gave the masters good reasons for wishing him away from the school, and for requesting Mr. Shelley to remove him from an establishment that, fruitless of benefit to him, suffered not a little from his disorderliness. It is probable that the Squire of Field Place was aware of the maledictions poured upon him by the Etonian scapegrace. It is unlikely that the boy, so unruly and contumacious at school, was submissive and respectful to his father in the holidays. There is no evidence before the world that the lad received personal chastisement at his father's hands. But it is conceivable he was so corrected by the Member for New Shoreham, in days when fathers of unimpeachable humanity and affectionateness applied the bamboo and the birch to their sons in a way, that would now-a-days be justly stigmatized as barbarous and revolting. It is, however, certain that the essentially amiable, though rather choleric, squire, had much trouble to manage his heir, and that their inharmonious intercourse was attended with friction and collisions, that could not fail to make such a son regard his sire with suspicion and aversion. If he was familiar with the story of the Uckfield lunatic, either from the gossip of old servants, or from the free speech of that lunatic's nephew (old Sir Bysshe), what more likely and natural than for the Etonian scapegrace to think that his fate might resemble his great-great-uncle's fate,—that he might be set aside as a lunatic to his little brother's advantage in the arrangements of his family,—that his father was already looking about for a pretext and an occasion for sending him to a mad-house?

But, it may be asked, was Peacock justified in going so far as to say of the poet, that 'the idea, that his father was continually on the watch for a pretext to lock him up, haunted him through life?' Was the delusion so absolutely unintermitting? Were there no times when the hideous fancy passed from his brain? No lucid intervals when he saw he had in this matter been the dupe of his own imagination? No times, moreover, when he forced himself back into the delusion by an effort of will and fancy, similar to those imaginative exercises in which Byron was so expert and curious an operator? In answer to these questions, it can only be said that there is no evidence of intermissions in the delusion, and that Peacock probably intended to say no more when he remarked that the morbid fancy, which certainly held the poet's mind in his later time, 'haunted him through life.'

To the present writer, indeed, it is conceivable that there were times when the poet's mind got the better of the most hideous of the several delusions that troubled it from time to time. The present writer can also conceive there were times when the poet, by the exercise of his will, sustained his belief in the delusion, even as the dreamer can for a few seconds by pure volition persist in believing a dream, which may be described as overlying his consciousness of its unreality. One of the prime dogmas of the school of metaphysicians, whose tenets Shelley embraced with cordial conviction of their truth, is that belief is independent of volition. The dogma is true in respect to perfectly logical and altogether sound minds. But there are unsound minds that are capable of shaping their opinions and determining their belief by processes of volition. Minds subject to manifest and distressing illusions are not to be rated as perfectly logical and altogether sound. Shelley's mind certainly was liable to such delusions. It is conceivable he would not have insisted on the separateness of belief and volition with so much needless emphasis and passion, had he not been uneasily conscious,—troubled and irritated by a criminatory sub-consciousness—that in some matters (such for instance as his delusion respecting his father) he believed what he ought not to believe, and could by strenuous volition save himself from believing. Some such thought as this was perhaps in Peacock's mind, when he spoke of the 'semi-delusions' of the man whom he loved so heartily.

Returning to Eton after recovering from the fever, of which so much has been said in foregoing pages of this chapter, Shelley, to the end of his time at the public school, continued to be in most respects the same boy he was on rising to the office of Lord High Atheist. Persisting in contumacy and unruliness he left the school in disgrace, though not under any ignominy to preclude him from the advantages of further education at one of the universities. In one particular, however, he seems to have changed his course towards the close of his Etonian career. The passion for scientific amusements (let them not be called 'studies') having in some degree spent itself, he devoted the greater part of his leisure to literary exercise, in the hope of winning premature distinction as a man of letters, —an ambition he certainly would not have entertained, had he been so seriously set on scientific inquiry, and occupied with scientific interests, as successive biographers have represented.

On 7th May of 1809, whilst still a boarder in Mr. Bethell's house, Shelley wrote Messrs. Longman & Co., the eminent publishers of Paternoster Row, London, a boyish letter, informing them that he was writing a romance, and expressing his wish for them to publish it. The publishers were informed that, as he was 'the heir of a gentleman of large fortune in the county of Sussex,' their correspondent was not writing for money, though he would gladly take a share of any pecuniary profits, resulting from the production of his work. As the publishers endorsed this puerile letter with a memorandum of their readiness to look at the story on its completion, it may be assumed that the manuscript of perhaps the most ludicrous tale of all English literature was submitted to the publishers' reader. As the absurd performance was not published till the end of May, or an early day of June, 1810, and was then published by Messrs. G. Wilkie and J. Robinson, of 57 Paternoster Row, it may be assumed that after considering their reader's opinion of the story, Messrs. Longman & Co. declined to publish it,—or at least to publish it on terms the author could consent to accept.

Though it is certain Shelley left Eton prematurely and on account of misbehaviour, the particular misconduct which resulted in his dismissal from the school is unknown. To Peacock (who at the time smiled secretly at the ' semi-delusion,' even as in later time he smiled at it openly in the pages of *Fraser's Magazine*), Shelley averred that he was sent away from Eton for striking a penknife through the hand of one of his school-fellows, and pinning it to a desk. Of course, Shelley said the ferocious act was the result of extravagant provocation.

To satisfy impartial readers that Shelley did not pin his schoolfellow's hand to a desk with the blade of a pen-knife, it is enough to say that his comrades at Eton had no recollection of any such incident in his career at the school. How Shelley came to account in so remarkable a manner for his premature withdrawal from the public school, is not left altogether to conjecture. Though he makes no reference to the affair in his *Fraser* article, Peacock, on hearing Shelley's astounding story, was doubtless mindful of the case of the military gamester, whose hand (in an early year of the present century) was pinned with a steel fork to the table of a famous gambling-club, as a convenient preliminary to the exposure of what was concealed between his wrist and cuff.

Whilst it is certain that Shelley was *not* dismissed from Eton for the cause he stated, it is by no means improbable that he was sent home on account of his amiable habit of cursing his own father,—a practice that cannot have favoured the moral tone of school, and on coming to the knowledge of the masters would necessarily move them to a strong expression of disapproval.

It accords with this conjecture, that the Etonians, who called on Shelley at Oxford in Hogg's presence, obviously regarded his singular way of proclaiming his hatred of his father as the grandest and most memorable of his offences at school. The young man, whose reluctance to repeat the form of cursing for the amusement of his old schoolfellows may be fairly attributed to regretful shame, would naturally in later time shrink from confessing he had been sent away from Eton for so heinous a misdemeanour.

But though he left Eton in disgrace with the masters, the Atheist of the school does not seem to have fallen out of favour with the boys, whose regard he had won by extravagances of unruliness. Hogg speaks of the books (Greek or Latin classics, each inscribed with the donor's name) given to Shelley by his comrades on his withdrawal from the college, and reasonably urges that the 'unusual number' of these parting gifts is sufficient evidence of his eventual popularity with his schoolfellows.

CHAPTER VI.

THE literary diversions, that occupied a considerable part of his
leisure at Eton, are note-worthy indications of Shelley's intellectual tastes and aims at a time, when delusive biography
represents him as possessed by a passion for scientific studies.
Having in his earlier terms at the school found congenial
pastime in the composition of childish dramas, he amused himself, after coming under Dr. Lind's hurtful influence, with
translating some of the earlier chapters of Pliny's *Natural
History*. Medwin assures us it was the boy's intention to produce a complete English version of that curious medley of
fact and fable, but relinquished the enterprise almost at the
threshold, on account of his inability to comprehend the
philosopher's chapters on the stars. In his perplexity the
youthful translator is said to have sought the aid of Dr. Lind,
who avoided the difficulties submitted to his consideration, and
at the same time preserved his credit for masterly erudition, by
telling his disciple that he had better not waste his time on
passages which the best scholars could not understand. In
accordance with this prudent counsel, the aspirant to literary
eminence bade adieu to Pliny the Elder, and looked about him
for an easier way of winning the distinction for which he
hungered.

In the spring of 1809, he bethought himself that he would
compete with the artists of prose-fiction, and write a novel that
should make him as famous as Mrs. Anne Radcliffe and Mr.
Matthew Lewis. If the son of a West Indian planter could in
his nonage write a novel so famous, that he was universally
styled after its title 'Monk' Lewis, surely 'the heir of a gentleman of large fortune ' (as the Etonian described himself in his
letter to Messrs. Longman and Co.) might in his nonage produce

a romance that should cause him to be talked about as Zastrozzi
Shelley. To accomplish this ambition, Shelley went to work
on the novel which, certainly begun in Mr. Bethell's house,
and talked about before he left the school, was perhaps written
to the last line at Eton; though, in consequence of the delays
and postponements which usually attend a literary aspirant's
first steps to celebrity, it was not published by Messrs. G.
Wilkie and J. Robinson, of Paternoster Row, till the summer
of 1810, when the author had been for some seven or eight
weeks a member of the University of Oxford.

Though the idolaters of Shelley's genius have small reason
to thank his most voluminous editor for recovering so absurd a
performance from the oblivion that covers most of his puerile
follies, the poet's biographers, and all who are interested in his
story, have cause for gratitude to Mr. Buxton Forman, for
reprinting in clear type the ludicrous tale, which enables them to
examine the mental stuff and texture of the seventeen years' old
boy (sixteen years and nine months old when he began the
story, seventeen years and ten months old when he published
it) who, fairly forward in Greek, could throw off Latin prose
and verse, of more than average goodness, with singular facility.

Were it not for *Zastrozzi; a Romance*, by P. B. S. (1810),
one would be without evidence that Percy Bysshe Shelley, the
poet of Free Love, did not leave Eton without conceiving the
disregard for the religious sanctions of marriage, which developed into a strong repugnance to the institution, and a cordial
disapproval of all the restraints imposed on wedlock by law
and custom. Readers seriously bent on knowing the Real
Shelley, who has been so artfully and dangerously replaced in
these later years by the Fictitious Shelley, will do well to give
their best attention to the following summary of the story
which reveals so much of the poet's character and disposition,
at the moment when he crossed the line that divides boyhood
from manhood.

ZASTROZZI; A ROMANCE. BY P. B. S.

The action and successive tragedies of this curious performance
result from the craft, energy, and diabolical vindictiveness of Pietro
Zastrozzi, the illegitimate son of Olivia Zastrozzi, who in her fifteenth
year was seduced, under promise of marriage, by the Count Verezzi,
an Italian nobleman. More heartless than a majority of the seducers,
who impart piquancy to the novels in which our grand-parents

delighted, this nobleman of a southern clime, instead of allowing her
the means of subsistence usually accorded in romantic literature to cast-
off mistresses, refused to give his victim a crust, when, deserting her
and her child (the villain of the book!), he threw himself into the arms
of the heiress who became his wife,—and in due course the mother of
another Count Verezzi, the virtuous count of the narrative.

Possessing every virtue but womanly discretion and the power to
forgive her enemies, the wretched and exemplary Olivia Zastrozzi died
in her thirtieth year, after enjoining her son, Pietrino, to avenge his
mother's wrongs. Having, in language appropriate to a pious son,
mitigated his mother's mortal agonies with a vow to do her bidding,
Pietrino passed from her grave to the cruel world, with a virtuous
resolve to compass the destruction of his own father (the elder Count
Verezzi), his own half-brother (the younger Count Verezzi), and any
persons in whom the same virtuous young Count should be strongly
interested. On coming to full manhood, Olivia Zastrozzi's son, seizing
the happy moment and making the most of it, plunged a dagger into
his father's heart, sending him without shrift to the pit that is reserved
in the nether regions for the seducers of trustful womankind.

Having disposed of his father in this summary fashion, Pietro
Zastrozzi determines to wreak his vengeance on his half-brother by
means more secret, ingenious, and horrible. Biding his time till the young
Count Verezzi has won the love of Julia Marchesa di Strobazzo, whose
affection he worthily reciprocates, and has also gained unintentionally
the love of Matilda Contessa di Laurentini, whose passion he is most
desirous of avoiding, Pietro Zastrozzi is quick to see his advantage
in the mutual jealousy and aversion of the two ladies, and in the em-
barrassments certain to arise from their idolatry of the same man. To
afford his exemplary mother's soul the vindictive satisfaction for which
so pure a spirit is naturally pining, Pietro Zastrozzi approaches these
ladies, and, by a series of subtle stratagems and diabolical contrivances,
brings them and their Count to extremities of passion and despair ;
and to deaths, that under the more skilful manipulation of Mrs.
Radcliffe or *Monk* Lewis, would have rendered *Zastrozzi* a superlatively thrilling and sensational romance.

Resembling one another in the nobility of their lineage, and the
enormity of their wealth, and the reputation that had come to them,
these two heroines are alike admirable for their different styles of beauty.
Whilst Julia is a gentle blonde, Matilda is a Cleopatra, with dark rolling
eyes, and breasts made to heave with voluptuous desire. Each of these
ladies is in love with the Count at the beginning of the story, which
opens with particulars of his seizure at an inn near Munich, as he is
journeying southwards to the damsel of his preference.

Captured at this tavern, whilst he breathes heavily and lies helpless
under a stupor of Zastrozzi's contrivance, the Count Verezzi is thrust
into a chariot, and conveyed to his place of imprisonment with all the
celerity attainable on rough roads, in days long prior to the invention

of the steam-locomotive.   Drawn by relays of horses, that are put to
their fullest speed by Bernardo (the postillion) the chariot moves rapidly
throughout the day, till on the approach of nightfall it quits the post-
road, and makes slower progress through the rugged underwood of a
forest, to the jaws of a cavern yawning in a darksome dell.   In this
cavern the Count—fastened by a chain to the rock of the cavern's
inmost recess, and fed upon bread and water—is confined for several
days and nights, till the rock of his dismal dungeon is broken up during
a thunderstorm by a scintillating flash of lightning !

On the morrow of this remarkable storm, the youthful Count is
discovered in a plight, which causes his persecutors to liberate him from
his manacles, and to call in a physician, who, after carrying the
youth out of brain-fever (quite as skilfully as the Hermit, *alias* Dr.
Lind, in *Laon and Cythna* carries Laon out of brain-fever under similar
circumstances), recommends that he should be conveyed, without loss of
a single moment, to a scene of tranquillity.   In compliance with this
advice, the captive is lifted again into the chariot, and conveyed by
Zastrozzi and his subordinate villains (Ugo and Bernardo) to a cottage,
standing in the middle of a wide and desolate heath, to which they
come after four hours' rapid posting.   In that cottage, tended by an
old woman (one of Zastrozzi's creatures), and watched by Ugo and
Bernardo, the Count remains till, on his convalescence, he knocks
Bernardo down-stairs (in the temporary absence of Zastrozzi, Ugo, and
the old woman), and clearing out of the humble tenement, reaches the
vicinity of Passau, where he is sheltered and hospitably entertained by
the peasant Claudine,—an amiable old woman, who gets her living by
raising flowers for the Passau market.

The scene now changes to one of the rural palaces of Matilda La
Contessa di Laurentini—a palace of Gothic architecture, whose battlemented walls rise high above the lofty trees of the surrounding forest ;
the palace in which the Marchesa Julia's faithful servant, Paulo,
dies from the fatal potion, administered to him by Zastrozzi and
Matilda.   As Paulo's only offence against La Contessa Matilda is
his loyalty to his own mistress, one is constrained to pity the
poor fellow, though he makes matters needlessly unpleasant by groaning
in his death-torments with excessive loudness, and rolling his eyes in
a revolting manner.

Despatching Zastrozzi to Naples to watch the movements of Julia
La Marchesa di Strabozzi, and seize the first opportunity for murdering
her, Matilda La Contessa di Laurentini migrates from her battlemented
palace to her hotel in Passau, on the banks of the Danube, where she
passes her time in meditating schemes for her rival's extinction, and
taking measures to get possession of her beloved Verezzi.   On the
failure of these measures, the Countess grows desperate, and in the
violence of her despair is on the point of drowning herself in the
Danube, when, instead of dropping in the water, she falls into the arms
of a casual wayfarer.   Of course, this casual wayfarer is Verezzi, who,

after saving her from the guilt of self-murder, carries La Contessa off
for the night to Claudine's cottage.   On the morrow, the Countess
returns to Passau, attended by Verezzi, who henceforth lives with the
lady till he expires in her presence.

Not that he yields at once to her overtures for his consent to
their union. For a time, La Contessa Matilda gets nothing more
agreeable from her domiciliation with her beloved Verezzi, than the
pleasure of ministering to the brain-sickness and despondency of the
invalid Count, who, regarding her by turns with frigid pity, distrustful
tenderness, and vehement detestation, persists in vexing her ears with
rapturous praises of his adorable Marchesa Julia. Acting on Zastrozzi's
advice, Matilda di Laurentini assures her guest that Julia is dead, and
even causes him to think her dead. But vain the assurance, bootless
its success! Instead of seeking consolation in the arms of La Contessa
di Laurentini, the Count Verezzi persists in idolizing his Marchesa,
protesting that he is bound to her for ever—as much bound to her
now that she is dead, as he was bound to her when she was alive.

But though she cannot draw him to her embrace, Matilda La
Contessa gains a gradually growing influence over the Count by
'her siren illusions and well-timed blandishments.' Soothing him in
his wilder moods, cheering him in his dejection, Matilda di Laurentini
diverts him with piquant speech, fascinates him with the music of her
harp and voice, and animates him with the society she attracts to her
salon. Playing the part of his ministering angel, she conceals from
Verezzi the real nature of the passion, whose fierceness and animality
would revolt him. ' Her breast,' the reader is told, 'heaved violently,
her dark eyes, in expressive glances, told the fierce passions of her soul ;
yet, sensible of the necessity of controlling her emotions, she leaned her
head upon her hand, and when she answered Verezzi, a calmness, a
melting expression overspread her features. She conjured him, in the
most tender, the most soothing terms, to compose himself ; and, though
Julia was gone for ever, to remember that there was yet one in the
world, one tender friend, who could render the burden of life less
unsupportable.'

At length joy comes to this tender friend, whose demeanour is so
mild and conciliatory to the Count Verezzi, though, in his absence, her
bosom often heaves violently, whilst her dark and lustrous eyes emit
glances, eloquent of the soul's fiercest passion. Matilda La Contessa
di Laurentini, and her idolized Count, have journeyed from Passau to
yet another of her stately homes,—the Castella di Laurentini, standing
in a gloomy and remote spot of the Venetian territory ; a palace
surrounded by a darksome forest, and lofty mountains that ' lift their
aspiring and craggy summits to the skies,'—when the lady achieves
her purpose by a melodramatic stratagem.

To win the Count, she is admonished by Zastrozzi to ' dare the
dagger's point,' and is, at the same time, instructed by her counsellor
how to dare it. In accordance with the instructions, Matilda La

Contessa leads Verezzi to a convenient spot of her picturesque demesne — a spot where, on the right hand, the thick umbrage of forest trees would render indistinguishable any person lurking about; whilst on the left, there yawns a frightful precipice, at whose base a deafening cataract dashes with tumultuous violence around misshapen and enormous masses of rock, lying at the foot of the gigantic and blackened mountain, which rears its craggy summit to the skies.

Matilda and Verezzi are looking down the precipice, when a man, who has been instructed to play the part of an assassin, rushes with upraised dagger on the Count, who deems himself the mark of the bravo's weapon. A second later, and the Contessa di Laurentini, hurling herself between the two men, receives the descending poniard in her right arm. Disappearing in the forest, the sham-bravo leaves the uninjured Verezzi with the wounded Contessa,—the one overflowing with gratitude to his preserver, whilst the other exults in the success of her artifice.

Soon after this theatrical scene, the Count, yielding to Matilda di Laurentini's ' siren illusions and well - timed blandishments,' addresses her as his wife, adding ' *And though love like ours wants not the vain ties of human laws, yet, that our love may want not any sanction which could possibly be given to it, let immediate orders be given for the celebration of our union.*'

Their marriage having received the vain sanction of human laws, Matilda and Verezzi enjoy a brief term of tempestuous bliss. On her wedding-day, ' Matilda's joy, her soul-felt triumph, is too great for utterance,—too great for concealment. The exultation of her inmost soul flashes in expressive glances from her scintillating eyes, expressive of joy intense—unutterable. Animated with excessive delight, she starts from the table, and seizing Verezzi's hand, in a transport of inconceivable bliss, drags him in wild transport and varied movements to the sound of swelling and soul-stirring melody.' By this time, the virtuous Verezzi has so completely succumbed to ' siren illusions ' that instead of showing any disapproval of the Contessa's forwardness, or any annoyance at being dragged about thus sportively, he exclaims with delight, ' Come, my Matilda, come, I am weary of transport,—sick with excess of unutterable pleasure.'

In the earlier days of the honeymoon, one circumstance alone moderates Matilda's happiness. Though the Count thinks Julia la Marchesa is dead, the Contessa has received no intelligence of a successful issue to her arrangements for her rival's murder. This source of uneasiness passes away, however, for a time, when Zastrozzi assures the Countess he has removed Julia di Strabozzi with poison. But malignant fate soon puts a period to the feverish felicity of the husband and wife. Ere they have been married a month, Matilda La Contessa di Laurentini is summoned before the Inquisition. In their alarm at the letter of citation, the Count Verezzi and Matilda (albeit the latter has been warned by Zastrozzi to keep away from the capital) fly to a secluded dwelling in the eastern suburb of Venice, in the hope of living there in concealment from the agents of the dread Tribunal.

At Venice Matilda soon discovers that Zastrozzi's warning was not given without reason. They have not been there many days, when one evening she and the Count behold the pensive and melancholy Marchesa di Strabozzi, gliding over the Laguna in her magnificent gondola, surrounded by 'the innumerable flambeaux which blazing about rival the meridian sun.' Whilst the Count discovers that the Marchesa, the real possessor of his heart, is still alive, the Contessa Matilda discovers that Zastrozzi has deceived her with a false announcement of her rival's death. At the same time, the' pensive and melancholy Julia di Strabozzi discovers that her Count Verezzi is living on terms of suspicious familiarity with Matilda di Laurentini.

These discoveries are followed by dramatic incidents and tragic scenes. Sitting with Matilda in the villa of the eastern suburb, the Count Verezzi is in the act of drinking to her, with protestations of eternal fidelity, when the pensive and melancholy Julia appears at the supper-table. 'My adored Matilda!' the Count is saying, 'this is to thy happiness,—this is to thy every wish ; and if I cherish a single thought which centres not in thee, may the most horrible tortures which ever poisoned the peace of man drive me instantly to distraction! God of Heaven! witness thou my oath, and write it in letters never to be erased! Ministering spirits, who watch over the happiness of mortals, attend! for here I swear eternal fidelity, indissoluble, unutterable affection, to Matilda!'

No sooner has the Count Verezzi delivered himself of this oration than Julia comes into the room. The Count has been taken at his word! The ministering spirits are in attendance! If she has not appeared as a witness against him, Julia has come to inquire why her affianced suitor is living so intimately with Matilda. No wonder that Verezzi dashes the goblet to the ground! that his frame is agitated with convulsions! that, 'seized with sudden madness, he draws the dagger from his girdle, and with fellest intent raises it high!'

'Raised with fellest intent,' the gleaming poniard is in a trice buried in the Count's breast. Whilst 'his soul flies without a groan, his body falls upon the floor bathed in purple blood.' Furious at the spectacle, Matilda plucks the weapon from her husband's corse, and rushes upon the pensive and melancholy intruder, who, seeing mischief in the Contessa's flashing eyes, and danger in the ensanguined weapon, turns and flies towards the door. 'Nerved anew by this futile attempt to escape her vengeance, the ferocious Matilda seizes Julia's floating hair, and holding her back with fiend-like strength, stabs her in a thousand places, and with exulting pleasure again and again buries the dagger to the hilt in her body, even after all remains of life are annihilated.' On throwing the dagger from her, Matilda di Laurentini regards a terrific scene with sullen gaze.

As it takes at least two seconds to plunge a dagger up to the hilt into the tenderest flesh and to withdraw the weapon for another blow, the Countess must have spent considerably more than half-an-hour in stabbing the Marchesa's body. Bearing in mind the amount of muscular effort requisite for driving a dagger up to the hilt into a human body, one is not surprised to learn that the murderess exhausted herself. Bearing in mind also the number of square inches on the surface of a woman's body, no reader will question that Julia's body was frightfully disfigured by the thousand stabs in a thousand different places.

Julia's murder is of course followed by the punishment of the murderess, and of the supreme villain who may be said to have educated her to perpetrate the monstrous crime. Zastrozzi is racked to death. No particulars are given of Matilda di Laurentini's last agonies, but the reader is left under the impression that she has died or will die by the executioner.

Published in a single duodecimo volume, this tale of horror contains about as many words as a single volume of an ordinary three-volume novel. Perhaps more horrors have never been crowded into so short a romance. The tortures endured by Verezzi during his successive imprisonments afflict the memory. Verezzi's father is poniarded to death by his bastard son. Julia's faithful servant, Paulo, dies in the presence of his poisoners, groaning horribly and writhing in hideous convulsions. Matilda makes a futile attempt to throw herself into the Danube. The dagger-scene in the vicinity of the Castella di Laurentini would not have been more terrific had the mock-assailant been a veritable bravo. The Count Verezzi commits suicide. Julia is stabbed in a thousand different spots of her body. Zastrozzi is racked to death. The Contessa di Laurentini is left for execution.

Affording not a single indication of literary taste or wholesome sentiment, the story is badly written, morbid, unnatural, and superlatively foolish, from its first to its last page. To Shelley's reasonable and honest biographers, the performance is of great value and interest on account of the view it gives of the future poet's culture, attainments, and mental condition towards the close of his career at Eton. Allowance should of course be made for the author's youth, his inexperience of human nature and society, and the difficulties besetting every puerile essayist in an arduous department of literature. But when all allowances have been made, the book remains a thing of evidence to the utter discredit of all the fine things that have been written by certain of the poet's adulators about his intellectual precocity. He would not have laboured at this crude tale in his seventeenth year, corrected it for the press, and published it in his eighteenth year, hoping to win fame by it, had he, in his boyhood, acquired the knowledge of English literature, for which several historians of his earlier career have given him credit, or had he been the sincere and strenuous student of natural science the same writers have declared him. Had he perused the works of the higher English writers with critical discernment as well as delight, the

Etonian would have written his mother tongue with less inelegance and feebleness. Had his care for natural science exceeded the common-place curiosity of a youth, given to play tricks with an air-pump, an electrical machine, and a chest of chemical materials, his mind would have been too fully occupied to have a hankering for the miserable distinction that comes to the writers of bad novels.

Though it is not regarded as a faultless performance in the coteries of the Shelleyan enthusiasts, passages of considerable merit and in-dications of fine feeling have been discovered in this superlatively foolish story, by some of the gentlemen who have in these later years con-stituted themselves the peculiar guardians of Shelley's honour, and the especial interpreters of his philosophical utterances.

In the superabundance of his veneration for every line written, and every scrap of paper known to have been touched by the poet, Mr. Buxton Forman, is educating the English people to regard *Zastrozzi* as a performance that, instead of being perused lightly and laughed over merrily, should be studied with due regard to the various readings of its two different editions,—the original edition of 1810, and the reprint of 1839, in *The Romancist and Novelist's Library*. Wherever those editions differ by an inverted comma, a mark of punctuation, a dropt letter, or a letter too many, Mr. Buxton Forman calls attention to the difference, as though each trivial diversity of the two texts were a matter of high importance. Believing that delicate meanings may be found in the poet's occasional slips of spelling, Mr. Forman calls attention to the remarkable fact, that the word 'ceiling' in the reprint is spelt 'cieling' in the original edition ; the no less curious and significant circumstance that the word 'escritoire' of the later edition is spelt *escrutoire* in the edition that passed straight to the world from the author's own hand and eye. In like manner we are invited to notice the difference of a perfectly formed 's' between the 'mishapen' of Shelley's own text, and the 'misshapen' of the reprint. Mr. Forman calls attention to an even bolder departure from the original text in the reprint, which may well be regarded with suspicion and mistrust by the Shelleyan specialists. Whilst the original edition contains the sentence, 'The most horrible scheme of vengeance at at this instant glances across Zastrozzi's mind,' the editor of the 1839 edition has the daring (not altogether innocent of irreverence) to omit the second 'at.' From the standpoint and principles of an editor, who regards Shelley as a being who might have been the Saviour of the World, Mr. Buxton Forman is of course right in attaching great importance to these differences of the two editions, of an almost sacred performance. But to the profane mind of the present writer, who, instead of thinking Shelley in any respect comparable with the Saviour of the World, and conceives him to have been a rather foolish schoolboy in the earlier months of 1809, a very foolish Oxford undergraduate in the later months of 1810, and a still more foolish undergraduate in the earlier months of 1811, it appears that these differences of the two editions of *Zastrozzi* are of no more importance than the proverbial difference between 'tweedledum' and 'tweedledee.'

It is, however, interesting to observe how the hero of the puerile novel corresponds with the hero of *Laon and Cythna*,—to observe also how Shelley (holding to crudities and fantastic fancies, which any other man of similar strength would have hurled to his soul's rubbish-bin), reproduces in the great poem some of the subordinate details of the immature romance.

The victim of secret enemies and relentless persecutors (even as Laon is the victim of similar enemies and persecutors, and even as Shelley himself suffered from a conspiracy headed by his unnatural father, ever watching for a pretext for locking him up), the Count is torn from Julia di Strabozzi, and carried to a cavern in a darksome forest, even as Laon, after being torn from Cythna, is conveyed in a state of unconsciousness to the cavern of the column-surmounted rock. On entering the cavern in the wood, Verezzi recovers consciousness, even as Laon recovers his powers of observation on approaching the 'cavern in the hill.' The darkness of the tortuous way, by which the Count's enemies lead him to the inmost cell of the cavern, is qualified by no ray of light, but for awhile the cell is illumined by Bernardo's solitary torch, even as the cavern under the hill, which serves as a passage to Laon's grated prison, is lit by the solitary torch, carried by one of his captors.

In *Zastrozzi*, it is said, 'after winding down the rugged descent for some time, they arrived at an iron door, which at first sight appeared to be part of the rock itself. Everything had till now been obscured by total darkness, and Verezzi, for the first time, saw the faces of his persecutors, which a torch borne by Bernardo rendered visible.'

In *Laon and Cythna* it is written,

> ' They bore me to a cavern in the hill
> Beneath the column, and unbound me there ;
> And one did strip me stark ; and one did fill
> A vessel from the putrid pool ; one bare
> A lighted torch, and four with friendless care
> Guided my steps the cavern-paths along,
> Then up a steep and dark and narrow stair
> We wound, until the torch's fiery tongue
> Amid the gushing day beamless and pallid hung.'

After bringing him into his prison, the Count Verezzi's persecutors put an iron chain about his waist, and leave him fast bound to the cruel rock that cuts his tender flesh, even as Laon is bound with chains in his cage upon the mountain's top.

In *Zastrozzi* it is written, 'His triumphant persecutor bore him into the damp cell, and chained him to the wall. An iron chain encircled his waist ; his limbs, which not even a little straw kept from the rock, were fixed by immense staples to the flinty floor ; and but one

of his hands was at liberty to take the scanty pittance of bread and
water which was daily allowed him.'

In *Laon and Cythna* it is read,

> ' They raised me to the platform of the pile,
> That column's dizzy height :—the grate of brass
> Thro' which they thrust me, open stood the while,
> As to its ponderous and suspended mass,
> With chains which eat into the flesh, alas !
> With brazen links, my naked limbs they bound :
>
>   *   *   *   *   *   *   *
>
> I gnawed my brazen chain, and sought to sever
> Its adamantine links, that I might die.'

From the fever which results from the barbarities inflicted upon
him in the forest cavern, and from the terror consequent on the thunderstorm that shatters the walls of his prison, the Count Verezzi is recovered by the ministrations of a physician, who, after carrying him
through the crisis of the malady, prescribes conditions of existence more
favourable to mental tranquillity. Very much the same happens to
Laon, who is restored to sanity from the sheer madness, that seizes him
and preys upon him in the brazen cage, by the wise physician who
visits him under the guise of a hermit, and conveys him to the tranquil
retreat, where he eventually regains his faculties.

In *Zastrozzi* it is written,—' A physician was sent for, who declared
that, the crisis of the fever which had attacked him being past, proper
care might reinstate him ; but, that the disorder having attacked his
brain, a tranquillity of mind was absolutely necessary for his recovery.
Zastrozzi, to whom the life, though not the happiness, of Verezzi was
requisite, saw that his too eager desire for revenge had carried him beyond
his point. He saw that some deception was requisite ; he accordingly
instructed the old woman to inform him, when he recovered, that he
was placed in this situation, because the physicians had asserted that the
air of this country was necessary for a recovery from the brain-fever,
which had attacked him. It was long before Verezzi recovered—long
did he languish in torpid sensibility, during which his soul seemed to
have winged its way to happier regions. At last, however, he recovered,
and the first use he made of his senses was to inquire where he was.'

In *Laon and Cythna* the hero of the poem describes his release
from prison and his recovery from fever in the following terms :—

> ' . . . . in the deep
> The shape of an old man did then appear,
> Stately and beautiful, that dreadful sleep
> His heavenly smiles dispersed, and I could wake and weep.
>
> And when the blinding tears had fallen, I saw
> That column, and those corpses, and the moon,
> And felt the poisonous tooth of hunger gnaw

My vitals, I rejoiced, as if the boon
Of senseless death would be accorded soon ;—
When from that stony gloom a voice arose,
Solemn and sweet as when low winds attune
The midnight pines ; the grate did then unclose,
And on that reverend form the moonlight did repose.

He struck my chains, and gently spake and smiled ;
As they were loosened by that Hermit old,
Mine eyes were of their madness half beguiled,
To answer those kind looks—he did infold
His giant arms about me, to uphold
My wretched frame, my scorchèd limbs he wound
In linen moist and balmy, and cold
As dew to drooping leaves ;—the chain, with sound
Like earthquake, thro' the chasm of the steep stair did bound.

  * * * * * *

       . . . . We came at last
To a small chamber, which with mosses rare
Was tapestried, where me his soft hands placed
Upon a couch of grass and oak-leaves interlaced.

  * * * * * *

Thus slowly from my brain the darkness rolled,
My thoughts their due array did re-assume
'Thro' the inchantments of that Hermit old ;
Then I bethought me of the glorious doom
Of those who sternly struggle to relume
The lamp of Hope o'er man's bewildered lot ;
And, sitting by the waters, in the gloom
Of eve, to that friend's heart I told my thought—
That heart which had grown old, but had corrupted not.'

From these passages of the puerile romance and the mature poem,
readers may see how Shelley nursed and nourished every fancy that
entered his brain ; how, growing gradually in form and beauty under his
fostering egotism, the conceits of his puerile inventiveness developed
into the conceptions of his poetical genius ; and how he weaved the story
of his own life out of imaginations as baseless, and in the earlier stages
of their development as grotesque, as the phantasies of departing
slumber. The imprisonment of Laon was the outgrowth of Verezzi's
imprisonment. The hero of the poem resembles the hero of the romance
in being the victim of secret and unscrupulous enemies ; and in that
respect they resembled the poet who created them,—the poet who only
escaped captivity such as theirs by repeatedly flying from foes, bent
on throwing him into a dungeon. The fever that seized Laon in the
grated cage, and the fever that nearly killed Verezzi in the gloomy

forest were romantic reproductions of the fever Percy Bysshe Shelley
endured at Field Place. The tyrant who put Laon between brazen
bars, and the villain who chained Verezzi in the darksome cavern, had
their prototype in the unnatural father (of the poet's 'marvellous story'
to his second wife), who was set on sending his wretched heir to a
madhouse. The physician who, braving a tyrant's vengeance, rescued
Laon from confinement and ministered to his mental disease, was the
same hard-swearing Windsor doctor who, facing the malicious despot
of Field Place, saved Percy Bysshe Shelley from his appointed doom,
and carried him out of brain-fever. It was thus that Shelley wrote his
wild views of his own story into the Byronic 'egotisms' of his literary
productions :—the 'egotisms' which the Shelleyan enthusiasts would
have the world accept as pieces of substantially veracious autobiography.

CHAPTER VII.

BETWEEN ETON AND OXFORD.

Literary Interests and Enterprise — A.M. Oxon. Letter — Shelley's Hunger
for Publisher's Money — Winter 1809-10 — Nightmare — *The Wandering
Jew* — Medwin in Lincoln's Inn Fields — The Fragment of Ahasuerus —
Its Influence on Byron and Shelley — Matriculation at Oxford — Shelley
at the Bodleian — John Ballantyne and Co. — Shelley in Pall Mall — Stock-
dale's Scandalous Budget — *Victor and Cazire* — Their Original Poetry —
Who was Cazire? — Felicia Dorothea Browne — Illumination of Young
Ladies — Harriett Grove — The Groves and Shelleys in London — Shelley's
Interest in Harriett Grove.

HAVING written a large portion of his first publication (*Zastrozzi ;
a Romance*) by 7th May, 1809, Shelley had little leisure for
'scientific studies' between that date and the Christmas holidays
of 1810–11. The literary aspirant during those twenty months
worked successfully (in some of the cases, simultaneously) on
(1) *Zastrozzi ;* (2) *The Nightmare ;* (3) *Original Poetry of Victor
and Cazire ;* (4) *St. Irvyne, or The Rosicrucian*, his second published romance; (5) *The Wandering Jew ;* (6) The Verses to be
regarded as the First Sketches for *Queen Mab;* (7) The *Posthumous Fragments of Margaret Nicholson ;* (8) The very careful
analysis of Hume's *Essays* used in the composition of *The
Necessity of Atheism*, that resulted in his expulsion from University College, Oxford; (9) A novel, described in the letter of
18th December, 1810, to Stockdale, as 'principally constructed
to convey metaphysical and political opinions by way of conversation,' and (10) a novel (never finished) that was designed
to give the death-blow to intolerance. With so many literary
irons in the fire, he cannot have spent many half-hours in
playing with the scientific instruments and apparatus that
figured so conspicuously in his college rooms. During the same
period, he found time for journeys to and fro between Field
Place and Oxford; at least one stay of several weeks in London ;
a good deal of miscellaneous reading; much sentimental and
sceptical correspondence, by letter, with Miss Felicia Dorothea
Browne; much correspondence of the same nature with Miss
Harriett Grove; long walks with Medwin in St. Leonard's
Forest; long walks with Hogg in the neighbourhood of Oxford;

and some participation in the field-sports, seldom altogether neglected by country gentlemen.

Whether *Zastrozzi* (published on or a little before 5th June, 1810) was written to the last lines at Eton, is uncertain. Bearing in mind every young author's impatience to see himself in print, and having regard to the natural consequences of this impatience in the excitable Shelley, I am disposed to think the book would have appeared sooner, had it been ready for the printers before the unruly Etonian left the public school. Time, doubtless, was wasted in the futile negotiation with the Messrs. Longman & Co. But the delay from this cause would scarcely account for the long postponement of the publication, if the author finished the MS. under Mr. Bethell's roof, and on receiving it back from the Longmans, sent it straight to Messrs. Wilkie and Robinson.

Whilst the external evidence that Shelley wrote the letter is too light for the scales of criticism, the internal evidence is conclusive that he was not the contributor of the 'A.M. Oxon's' epistle, in behalf of Lord Grenville's candidature for the Chancellorship. Medwin's assertion is idle in respect to the composition, whose style shows it was not, could not have been, written by the author of the puerile letters to the Messrs. Longman, Messrs. Wilkie and Robinson, and Stockdale,—the puerile prose of *Zastrozzi* and *St. Irvyne*,—and the scarcely less puerile prose of the letters and addresses written by the poet in Ireland. A comparison of the 'A. M. Oxon' letter of November 1809, with the numerous examples of Shelley's English prose, will satisfy the critical reader that Shelley did not, because he could not, write the epistle in behalf of Lord Grenville. The question is one of those questions where the evidence of style is conclusive. It is conceivable the 'A. M. Oxon' letter was well spoken of at Field Place, that it was written at Mr. Timothy Shelley's instance, that Medwin was told Shelley wrote it, that Shelley claimed the authorship of the letter. Establish all these points, produce a copy of the letter in Shelley's hand-writing; and the evidence of style would be none the less conclusive, that Shelley did not write the letter.

Towards the close of 1809, and throughout the earlier months of 1810, Shelley was 'at home,' writing briskly for fame, and with a keen appetite for 'publisher's money,' which Byron, at the outset of his literary career, was of opinion

no nobleman or other gentleman of high degree could accept,
without sullying his honour. In his nonage, the author of
Zastrozzi asked publishers for their money with a steadiness,
that would probably have been less unwavering, had it been old
Sir Bysshe's practice to tip his grandson bountifully. Not that
the desire for payment was wholly due to the need of it. In
taking wages for the work of his pen, he would have regarded
them as no less honourable than convenient. The Etonian,
whose friends seem to have thought, that he entertained them
with his literary earnings, was no youth to feel shame in taking
publisher's money, or to miss it for want of asking for it. On
the contrary, at the outset of a literary career (that from the
commercial point of view, was worse than absolutely profitless)
he liked to be credited with winning what he never won, and
could ask for payment, though he had only the faintest hope of
getting it.

Throughout his time at Eton, Shelley saw much of Tom
Medwin during vacations. During the winter of 1809–10, the
cousin, who would soon go to Oxford, and the cousin, who
would soon leave it for the army, were inseparable companions.
During their long walks through the leafless glades of St.
Leonard's Forest—in the clear frosty air and under the bright
skies, that had a most exhilarating effect on their spirits—these
two young men of common blood and kindred tastes discoursed
with more enjoyment than discretion on the principles of poetry
and romantic prose, of ancient science and modern culture.
This was the winter, when they set to work on the production
of a wild story (with a hideous witch for its principal character),
that seems to have justified its title of *Nightmare*, before they
ceased writing alternate chapters of the morbid tale, and threw
themselves with greater enthusiasm into the much higher and
more arduous enterprise of a grand 'metrical romance on the
subject of the *Wandering Jew*,'—an enterprise in which the two
cousins were encouraged and influenced (though not actuated
from the commencement) by one of those accidents, which so often
influence, and sometimes determine, the course of human genius.

On his way through Lincoln's Inn Fields, Tom Medwin
picked up at a bookstall the following passage, from a free
English rendering and adaptation (with variations from the
original) of Christian D. F. Schubart's rhapsodical poem *Der
Ewige Jude*.

'Ahasuerus the Jew crept forth from the dark cave of Mount Carmel. Near two thousand years have elapsed since he was first goaded by never-ending restlessness to rove the globe from pole to pole. When our Lord was wearied with the burden of his ponderous cross, and wanted to rest before the door of Ahasuerus, the unfeeling wretch drove him away with brutality. The Saviour of mankind staggered, sinking under the heavy load, but uttered no complaint. An angel of death appeared before Ahasuerus, and exclaimed indignantly, "Barbarian! thou hast denied rest to the Son of Man; be it denied thee also, until He comes to judge the world!"

'A black demon, let loose from hell upon Ahasuerus, goads him now from country to country; he is denied the consolation which death affords, and precluded from the rest of the peaceful grave.

'Ahasuerus crept forth from the dark cave of Mount Carmel—he shook the dust from his beard—and taking up one of the sculls heaped there, hurled it down the eminence; it rebounded from the earth in shivered atoms. This was my father! roared Ahasuerus. Seven more sculls rolled down from rock to rock; while the infuriate Jew, following them with ghastly looks, exclaimed—And these were my wives! He still continued to hurl down scull after scull, roaring in dreadful accents —And these, and these, and these were my children! They *could die;* but I! reprobate wretch, alas! I cannot die! Dreadful beyond conception is the judgment that hangs over me. Jerusalem fell—I crushed the sucking babe, and precipitated myself into the destructive flames. I cursed the Romans—but alas! alas! the restless curse held me by the hair,—and I could not die!

'Rome, the giantess, fell—I placed myself before the falling statue —she fell, and did not crush me. Nations sprung up and disappeared before me;—but I remained and did not die. From cloud-encircled cliffs did I precipitate myself into the ocean; but the foaming billows cast me upon the shore, and the burning arrow of existence pierced my cold heart again. I leaped into Etna's flaming abyss, and roared with the giants for ten long months, polluting with my groans the Mount's sulphureous mouth—ah! ten long months. The volcano fermented, and in a fiery stream of lava cast me up. I lay torn by the torture-snakes of hell amid the glowing cinders, and yet continued to exist.—A forest was on fire: I darted on wings of fury and despair into the crackling wood. Fire dropped upon me from the trees, but the flames only singed my limbs; alas! it could not consume them.—I now mixed with the butchers of mankind, and plunged into the tempest of the raging battle. I roared defiance to the infuriate Gaul, defiance to the victorious German; but arrows and spears rebounded in shivers from my body. The Saracen's flaming sword broke upon my scull: balls in vain hissed upon me; the lightnings of battle glared harmless around my loins; in vain did the elephant trample on me, in vain the iron hoof of the wrathful steed! The mine, big with destructive power, burst upon me, and hurled me high in the air—I fell on heaps of smoking limbs, but was only singed. The giant's steel club rebounded from my body; the executioner's hand could not strangle me, the tiger's tooth could not pierce me, nor would the hungry lion in the circus devour me. I cohabited with poisonous snakes, and pinched the red crest of the dragon. The serpent stung, but could not destroy me. The dragon tormented, but dared not to devour me.—I now provoked the fury of tyrants: I said to Nero, Thou art a bloodhound! I said to Christiern, Thou art a bloodhound! I said to Muley Ismail, Thou art a bloodhound!—The tyrants invented cruel torments, but did not kill me.—Ha! not to be able to die—not to be able to die—not to be permitted to rest after the toils of life—to be doomed to be imprisoned for ever in the clay-formed dungeon—to be for ever clogged with this worthless body, its load of diseases and infirmities—to be condemned to hold for millenniums that yawning monster Sameness, and Time, that hungry hyæna, ever bearing children, and ever devouring again her offspring!—Ha! not to be permitted to die! Awful avenger in heaven, hast thou in thine armoury of wrath a punishment more dreadful? then let it thunder upon me, command a hurricane to sweep me down to the foot of Carmel, that I there may lie extended; may pant, and writhe, and die!'

What consequences ensued from young Medwin's accidental discovery of this fragment amongst the litter of the London bookstall! The finder of the scrap carried it to Shelley, Shelley carried it to Byron; and both poets were powerfully affected, permanently influenced by it. It gave Byron the thought of the lines in *Manfred*.

> ' I have affronted death—but in the war
> Of elements the water shrunk from me,
> And fatal things pass'd harmless—the cold hand
> Of an all-pitiless demon held me back,
> Back by a single hair, which would not break.
> In fantasy, imagination, all
> The affluence of my soul—which one day was
> A Crœsus in creation—I plunged deep,
> But, like an ebbing wave, it dash'd me back
> Into the gulf of my unfathom'd thought.
> I plunged amidst mankind—Forgetfulness
> I sought in all, save where 'tis to be found,
> And that I have to learn—my sciences,
> My long pursued and super-human art,
> Is mortal here—I dwell in my despair—
> And live—and live for ever.'

So strongly held to his last hour was Shelley by the thought which came to him, through the scrap of dirty paper taken with worthless stuff from a bookstall, that whilst Ahasuerus appears

once and again in his own character and personality in the
poet's works, the reader of those works comes no less often on
cursory references to the undying wanderer, and on lines that
would never have been penned, had it not been for Shelley's
deep and frequent ponderings of the hideous doom of deathless-
ness, accorded to the supreme sinner of Christian romance.
Ahasuerus the Jew figures in *Queen Mab* (1812-13) and *Hellas*
(1821); he was in the poet's mind when he meditated the lines
of *Alastor* (1815)—

'O, that God,
Profuse of poisons, would concede the chalice
Which but one living man has drained, who now,
Vessel of deathless wrath, a slave that feels
No proud exemption in the blighting curse
He bears, over the world wanders for ever,
Lone as incarnate death!'

Shelley's subsequent misconception of the way in which the
tragic fragment came into his possession, may be regarded
as one of the trivial consequences, though by no means the
least curious consequence, of the degree in which the fragment possessed his fancy. As there is no evidence that the
author of *Queen Mab* was in London shortly before the time
when the fragment first came under his eyes, and much evidence
that he was away from London throughout the certain period,
covering the uncertain day on which the fragment was picked
up at the bookstall, there is no reason on the score of
Medwin's peculiar mental infirmity to question the accuracy of
his precise statement that he was the finder of the transcript,
which he describes as 'not a separate publication,' but a thing
that 'mixed up with the works of some German poet' seemed
to have been 'copied . . . from a magazine of the day.' The
words of Medwin's precise averment touching this matter are—

'Mrs. Shelley is misinformed as to the history of the fragment from
the German, which I, not Shelley, picked up in Lincoln's-Inn-Fields
(as mentioned in my preface to Ahasuerus), and which was not found
till some of the cantos had been written.'

Mrs. Shelley certainly could produce in support of her statement an authority she was bound to regard as respectable. For
at the foot of the *Queen Mab* note (1812-13), from which I have
just transcribed the fragment, Shelley says—

'This fragment is the translation of part of some German work,
whose title I have vainly endeavoured to discover. I picked it up,
dirty and torn, some years ago, in Lincoln's-Inn-Fields.'

Thus in the course of something less than three years (a period scarcely to be described by so comprehensive a term as 'some years ago') Shelley, whilst remembering the scene of the discovery, had come to imagine himself the discoverer, a misapprehension not to be omitted from the schedule of facts, to the credit of those of the poet's nearest and dearest friends, who have spoken of the little reliance to be placed on his statements respecting himself and his affairs.

The first glimpse of Shelley at Oxford is obtained immediately after his matriculation on 10th of April, 1810, when the tall, slight, long-necked youth, with a square cap on his minute head, and a new gown hanging from his rather round shoulders, entered the Bodleian Library, in the hope of seeing the book from which the fragment had been taken. Had the German book been given him, the freshman would have learnt nothing from it, for he knew nothing of the German tongue at this point of his career. Ignorant alike of the title of the book he wished to see, and of the name of its author, the undergraduate asked for *The Wandering Jew*,—a request that probably caused the librarian no less amusement than surprise. The librarian had never heard of a book so entitled, but was not wholly ignorant of a periodical (edited by one of the wits of the Great Frederick's court) which bore the name of interest. Having come to the famous library, under an impression that it contained every book of every language, Mr. Percy Bysshe Shelley, of University College, was not a little disappointed at failing to get a view of the only book he for the moment had a strong desire to look at. The incident points to the time when the youngster was full of the marvellous Jew, and wanted the book for aid in his poetical enterprise.

Enough is known of the poem, that was perused by Campbell and offered to the Ballantynes of Edinburgh, to warrant a strong opinion that originality of thought was not one of its characteristics. One of the cousins (Medwin) lived to think it 'a sort of thing such as boys usually write, a cento from different favourite authors;' and probably the other author would have described the puerile performance even more unfavourably, had he written about it in his later time. The vision in the third canto was taken from Lewis's *Monk*, one of the bad novels in which Shelley delighted. The crucifixion scene seems to have been lifted bodily into the manuscript from a published work; it was (to use Medwin's words) 'altogether a plagiarism from a volume of Cambridge Prize Poems.' Bold play was doubtless made with 'the fragment' by the joint authors, who differed on one important particular,—Shelley wishing to leave the Jew at large, whilst Medwin wished to put a period to the wretch's sufferings by killing him at the end of the last canto. When seven or eight cantos had been made up in this fashion, the patchwork of shameless plagiarisms was copied fair from the first to the last line by Shelley, and sent off to the Edinburgh publishers who, after keeping the authors a long while in suspense, declined their proposal (without returning the MS.) in the following terms :—

'Edinburgh, September 24th, 1810.

'Sir,

. 'The delay which occurred in our reply to you respecting the poem you have obligingly offered us for publication, has arisen from our literary friends and advisers (at least such as we have confidence in) being in the country at this season, as is usual, and the time they have bestowed on its perusal.

'We are extremely sorry, at length, after the most mature deliberation, to be under the necessity of declining the honour of being the publishers of the present poem ;—not that we doubt its success, but that it is, perhaps, better suited to the character and liberal feelings of the English, than the bigoted spirit which yet pervades many cultivated minds in this country. Even Walter Scott is assailed on all hands at present by our Scotch spiritual, and Evangelical magazines, and instructors, for having promulgated atheistical doctrines in the *Lady of the Lake*.

'We beg you will have the goodness to advise us how it should be returned, and we think its being consigned to the care of some person in London would be more likely to ensure its safety than addressing it to Horsham.

'We are, Sir, your most obedient humble servants,

'John Ballantyne & Co.'

The religious sentiments, which the publishers thought less likely to offend English than Scotch readers, were probably the same 'opinions on religion, whose inconsequence' Medwin declares to be a sufficient indication that the poem was the composition of two different writers. That the publishers had reason to think these sentiments little adapted to the feelings of their fellow-countrymen of North Britain will appear probable to readers who recall the part played by Ahasuerus in *Queen*

Mab,—a poem that resembled the poem of *The Wandering Jew* in containing passages that were the direct offspring of the memorable fragment.

Medwin says that on their completion, Shelley sent the seven or eight cantos 'to Campbell for his opinion on their merits, with a view to publication,' and that the author of the *Pleasures of Hope* returned the MS. with the remark that there were only two good lines in it :—

> 'It seemed as if an angel's **sigh**
> Had breathed the plaintive **symphony**,'

lines, by the way (Medwin adds), 'savouring strongly of Walter Scott.' The peculiarities of Mr. Medwin's habitual inexactness countenance the suspicion that, though the poem came under Campbell's critical consideration *through* Shelley's act, the author of the *Pleasures of Hope* would not have seen it had he not been the particular literary friend and adviser, whose 'opinion' determined John Ballantyne and Co. not to publish the work. Anyhow, Campbell read and condemned the poem which the publishers declined,—the poem which Shelley (on receiving the letter of 24th September, 1810, from the Edinburgh publishers) lost no time in offering to John Joseph Stockdale, the Pall Mall (London) publisher, whose dealings with the poet and the poet's father were laid before the public in *Stockdale's Budget* (1827).

In one of the several puerile letters, whose style affords conclusive testimony that he was not the author of the *A.M. Oxon.* letter, Shelley wrote to Stockdale from Field Place on 28th September, 1810 (just a month before he went into 'residence' at Oxford):

'I sent, before I had the pleasure of knowing you, the MS. of a poem to Messieurs Ballantyne and Co., Edinburgh ; they have declined publishing it, with the inclosed letter. I now offer it to you, *and depend upon your honour as a gentleman for a fair price for the copyright*. It will be sent to you from Edinburgh. The subject is *The Wandering Jew*. As to its containing Atheistical principles, I assure you, I was wholly unaware of the fact hinted at. *Your good sense will point out to you the impossibility of inculcating pernicious doctrines in a poem, which, as you will see, is so totally abstract from any circumstances which occur under the possible view of mankind.*'

The words, which the present writer has caused to be printed in italics, should hold the reader's attention for a moment. Whilst the desire for money, indicated by the earlier set of words, is noteworthy, the second set of words should be examined as an example of the Oxonian's epistolary style at a time when some of his adulators have declared him capable of writing vigorous prose.

Not quite seven weeks after the date of these significant sets of words, Shelley (now an Oxonian 'in residence') is writing on 14th November, 1810, to the Pall Mall publisher: 'I am surprised that you have not received *The Wandering Jew*, and in consequence write to Mr. Ballantyne to mention it; you will doubtlessly, therefore, receive it soon.' Five days later (19th November, 1810), writing again to his publisher from University College, the youthful literary aspirant says, 'If you have not yet got *The Wandering Jew* from Mr. B., I will send you a MS. copy which I possess.' Nearly a fortnight later (2nd December, 1810), he writes from his college to the same correspondent: 'Will you, if you have got two copies of *The Wandering Jew* send one of them to me, as I have thought of some corrections which I wish to make,—your opinion on it will likewise much oblige me :'—words showing that Shelley had sent his 'reserved copy' of the poem to Pall Mall, that he assumed it was in Mr. Stockdale's hands, and that he thought it possible Mr. Stockdale was also in possession of the transcript which should have been sent to him from Edinburgh by the Ballantynes. The words also show that the young author was in some excitement about the fate of his poem, and eager to hear whether the publisher would produce the metrical romance, and, 'as a gentleman' pay him 'a fair price for the copyright.'

Unless Stockdale's memory failed him on the matter in 1827, neither of these copies came to his hands.—'It is singular,' he says in his scandalous *Budget* (1827), 'that, after all, the poem of *The Wandering Jew* never reached my hands, nor have I either seen or heard of it from that time.' From this not altogether reliable statement it seems that there was a miscarriage of the second and 'reserved' transcript of the poem, sent by Shelley himself from Field Place to Pall Mall. For the removal of a scarcely noteworthy misapprehension, it may be observed there was no similar miscarriage of the other copy; the evidence being abundant that the MS., sent by Shelley from Field Place to Edinburgh, was *not* lost through miscarriage on its way from Edinburgh to Pall Mall. This MS. cannot have miscarried for the simple reason, that it was never despatched by the Ballantynes to Mr. Stockdale's place of business. Instead of being sent to London, in accordance with the suggestion made by the Ballantynes themselves, and in accordance with the instructions sent to them by Shelley, mainly in consequence of their suggestion, the MS. rested at Edinburgh till 1831, when, some nine years after the poet's death, it came to light;—a discovery that was speedily followed by a publication of some portions of the metrical folly (Medwin says 'four of the cantos') in *Fraser's Magazine*.

After throwing off *The Wandering Jew*, which even Mr. Buxton Forman, with all his reverence for every scrap of paper blotted by the poet, has excluded (with the exception of a few verses) from his authorized edition of the poet's writings, Shelley, with the assistance of a friend, produced in the spring or summer of 1810, the volume of poetry entitled *Original Poetry, by Victor and Cazire*,—the edition of miserable rhymes, noticed in the *British Critic* of 1811 (*vide* Professor Dowden's very noteworthy article in *The Contemporary Review* of September, 1884, on 'Some Early Writings of Shelley'), that was suppressed soon after its untimely birth, because at least one of the poems was discovered to be scandalously wanting in originality; to be, in fact, a gross and disgraceful plagiarism of one of Monk Lewis's pieces of sensational verse.

Ignorant of the name of Shelley's coadjutor in this discreditable business, Mr. Garnett is at much pains to show, who could not have been the coadjutor, who may not be supposed to have been the coadjutor, and who might have been the coadjutor. Hogg could not have been the coadjutor, because he had not yet made the poet's acquaintance. Tom Medwin was not the coadjutor. But Mr. Garnett is of opinion that Miss Harriett Grove may have been the coadjutor. 'A more likely coadjutor,' he says, ' would be Harriet Grove, Shelley's cousin, and the object of his first attachment, who is said to have aided him in the composition of his first romance, *Zastrozzi*.' It is strange that so exemplary a Shelleyan expert as Mr. Garnett dealt thus respectfully with what Shelley told Medwin, or Medwin imagined himself to have been told by Shelley, about Harriett Grove's part in the composition of *Zastrozzi*. There is no more truth in the fable that Harriett Grove wrote some of the chapters of

Zastrozzi, than there is in the fable that she was the Harriett of the Dedicatory Prelude to *Queen Mab*. Possibly Shelley saw his pretty cousin in her Wiltshire home, when he went from Brentford to Fern for the Easter holidays, in the company of her Harrovian brothers. Probably the cousins saw one another on other occasions, when they were small children; but when they met at Field Place in the summer of 1810, they came together as new acquaintances. There is decent, though not conclusive, evidence that they had never looked on each other before that summer. It is certain that their brief intimacy, attended with innocent flirtation and cousinly correspondence, was an affair of the later six months of 1810 :—that *Zastrozzi* had been written to the last line, sent to Messrs. Longman and Co., declined by those publishers, sent to Messrs. Wilkie and Robinson, printed by them, and almost, if not actually published, before the dawn of that brief intimacy. So much for what has been written about Harriett Grove's participation in the authorship of the earlier of Shelley's inexpressibly ludicrous novels.

The poet's coadjutor in the unfortunate business of the *Original Poetry* was his sister Elizabeth, and it is easy to see how Shelley manufactured the fanciful name 'Cazire' out of so dissimilar a name as Elizabeth. He may be presumed to have made it out of the letters of his sister's name and a single epithet of affection, on principles familiar to students who are versed in the romantic curiosities and fanciful contrivances of eighteenth-century English literature.   Isabel and Elizabeth are the same name with differences of garniture.   In each case Iza is the veritable name.   To call a woman Izabel, or Izabella, is to call her 'the beautiful Iza.' To call her Elizabeth (El Iza beata) is to style her 'the blessed Iza.' In being christened Elizabeth, the eldest of Shelley's sisters was named Iza. The letters out of which Shelley made the fancy-name 'Cazire,' were the letters of Cara Iza = dear Iza. Of course he used no letter twice.   Rule of art forbade him to use the same letter twice.   First he took the letters of the name, and by reversing their order made them spell 'azi.' By prefixing to 'azi' the 'C' of Cara, and putting the 'r' of the same epithet after the 'i' of 'Cazi,' he made the name 'Cazir,'—a name to which he gave a more feminine appearance by adding to it the initial letter of his sister's familiar name, Elizabeth. Hence 'Cazire.'

Even as the Byron of Southwell Green employed Ridge,

the Newark bookseller, to print and publish his three first
volumes of verse, the Shelley of Field Place appointed a
Horsham printer to make a printed book of the *Original Poetry*,
which he and his sister had put together. The edition, thus printed
at Horsham in the late summer or early autumn of 1810, though
it can scarcely be said to have been published there, seems to
have been an edition of fifteen hundred copies. If the youthful
authors looked for a brisk sale in Sussex, that would enable
them to pay their printer as soon as he should ask for his
money, they were disappointed. If the Horsham printer worked
off the edition, under the notion that he would have no difficulty in getting payment of his little bill from the young
gentleman of Field Place, or from the Member of Parliament
for New Shoreham, or from old Sir Bysshe Shelley, he, too, was
disappointed. For in the autumn (towards the end of August
or on one of the earliest days of September), 1810, the Oxford
undergraduate entered for the first time the place of business of
Mr. John Joseph Stockdale, and with a countenance eloquent
of anxiety besought the publisher to satisfy the demand of the
importunate Horsham printer, and taking over the stock of
printed copies to offer them for sale in his usual way of business.
Had he been a youth of no social quality, instead of being the
eldest son of a well-known Member of Parliament, who was
reputed to be the heir of the wealthiest commoner of Sussex,
the petitioner for relief from an embarrassing position would
probably have been bowed out of the publisher's office with
more promptitude than courtesy. But the heir-apparent of
the heir-apparent of the inordinately rich Sir Bysshe Shelley,
Baronet, was no person for Mr. John Joseph Stockdale to repel.
In a few years the beardless undergraduate might himself be
one of the richest of England's dignified commoners.

An arrangement was made between the man of business and
the youth of quality; and on 17th September, 1810, the Pall-
Mall publisher received from the Horsham printer fourteen
hundred and eighty copies of the *Original Poetry: By Victor
and Cazire*, a work forthwith announced in the principal London
papers as on sale 'by Stockdale, Jun., 41, Pall-Mall,' at the
price of 4*s.* per copy, in 'boards.' The book's career, under
these circumstances, was brief. It had not been re-published
many days, at the longest not more than two or three weeks,
and the copies sold or put into circulation cannot, at the boldest

computation, have exceeded a hundred, when, on examining the book closely (examining it, probably, in consequence of something he had heard to the volume's discredit) the publisher came to the conclusion that the work must be withdrawn and suppressed. A fraud on the public, an infringement of at least one author's copyright, a thing published with a deceptive title-page, the *Original Poetry* was found to contain poetry by Monk Lewis. It may be conceived how surprised Shelley was to find he had induced a London publisher to accept for the original poetry of himself and his friend, poetry that, instead of being what he declared it to be, was stolen poetry. No fine words, no specious phrases, can put out of sight the fact that this business was an ugly business. Shelley was not a child when he thus put wares under a false name on a London tradesman. He had entered his nineteenth year when he did this distinctly discreditable thing.

To separate Shelley as far as possible from what he necessarily regards as an awkward and humiliating affair, Mr. Garnett has recourse to a representation which, instead of according with the probabilities of the case, is discountenanced by several facts. 'It was but too clear,' says the author of *Shelley in Pall Mall,* 'that Shelley's colleague, doubtless under the compulsion of the poet's impetuous solicitations for more verses, had appropriated whatever came first to hand, with slight respect for pedantic considerations of *meum* and *tuum.*' What evidence could Mr. Garnett produce that the pilfered matter was put into the book, not by Shelley but by his coadjutor ? that the poet had pressed his coadjutor impetuously for more verses ? that, in consequence of his impetuous solicitations for more verses, Shelley's coadjutor took verses out of a printed book, and palmed them off on him as verses of her own composition ? What evidence could Mr. Garnett produce that Shelley was unaware that the volume of so-styled original verse contained poetry which had been 'appropriated. . . . with slight respect for pedantic considerations of *meum* and *tuum ?*' No evidence of any kind, over and beyond these words by the mendacious and rascally Stockdale :—

'I fully anticipated the probable vexation of the juvenile maiden-author, when I communicated my discovery to Mr. P. B. Shelley. With all the ardour, incidental to his character, which embraces youthful honour in all its brilliancy, he expressed the warmest resentment at the imposition, practised upon him, by his coadjutor, and intreated me to destroy all the copies.'

Of Stockdale's motives of self-interest and vindictiveness, in writing of Shelley in a laudatory style, something will be said by-and-by. For the present it is enough to remind the reader that the concoctor of the scandalous *Budget* (1827) was writing from memory, more than sixteen years after the incidents to which he refers. That Shelley's coadjutor was spurred into wrongful action by ' the poet's impetuous solicitations for more verses,' is a touch of fiction for which we are indebted to Mr. Garnett's imagination.

As no copy of the suppressed edition is known to be in existence, and all our certain knowledge of the contents of the volume comes from Stockdale's meagre and mendacious narrative, it is useless to inquire what will probably never be known—what proportion the purloined matter bore to the original writing of the book, and how far the purloined matter was manipulated and re-dressed by the pilferer or pilferers? It is scarcely conceivable that the stolen stuff was lifted from one book to the other without any verbal alteration. Should a copy of the *Original Poetry* be recovered, I should expect to find the least original of its pieces to be specimens of bold, free, manifest plagiarisms—not verbatim transcripts. That Shelley was a partner to such plagiarisms in 1810 we know from Medwin's candid account of the way in which they made up the cantos of *The Wandering Jew*. That Shelley used to perpetrate such plagiarisms single-handed, and for his own sole use, in 1810, we know from the plagiarism from Byron's *Lachin-y-Gair* (*Hours of Idleness*) to be found in *St. Irryne*. Lewis's *Monk* was boldly pilfered for the benefit of the third canto of *The Wandering Jew*, a canto altered and added to by Shelley after Medwin had rough-written it. Monk Lewis's writings were so much admired by Shelley, and so familiar to him, that whilst he (with a strong taste for literary imitation) may be assumed, almost as a matter of course, to have plagiarized some parts of them at some time or other, he was not likely to have overlooked the quality of any plagiarism from Monk Lewis in the verses given him by his sister for their joint enterprise.

It follows that, whilst there is no sufficient evidence in support of Mr. Garnett's account of the affair, several facts point to the probability that, instead of being perpetrated by Miss Shelley,

the plagiarisms, which made it needful to withdraw and suppress
the 'original poetry,' were done by her brother's own hand.
Yet Mr. Garnett declares it not merely clear, but 'too clear,'
that Shelley was nothing more than the simple and unsuspicious victim of an unworthy coadjutor. At the same time
to minimize the discredit, accruing to Shelley from her misconduct, it is observed lightly that, instead of stealing, she
only 'appropriated whatever first came to hand, with slight
respect for pedantic considerations of *meum* and *tuum*.' It is
thus that disagreeable matters are glossed for the benefit of the
poet, who might have been the Saviour of the World.

Mr. Rossetti, by far the most discreet and able of Shelley's
apologists, would win a favourable verdict for the poet in
respect to this *Victor and Cazire* business, on the plea that so
youthful and unworldly a writer is not to be supposed to have
studied the law of copyright.

'One can but speculate on the question whether Shelley was himself
in fault in this matter, or whether he had been duped by his coadjutor.
There was certainly some tendency to secretiveness in his early literary
attempts; and it may be doubted whether the Etonian scatterbrain
would have seen much harm in appropriating stanzas or whole compositions from Lewis if they fell in with his notions,—or, indeed,
whether he had ever perceived or pondered the meaning of the word
copyright. Stockdale, at any rate, does not seem to have considered
himself aggrieved by Shelley, as he soon after undertook the publishing
of *St. Irvyne;* in fact, after some serious rows during their business
connexion, he continued enthusiastic as to the young author's character
and honour.'

By all means let Shelley have the benefit of the lenient
judgment of a publisher, who came to ruin through his own
dishonourable conduct. The publisher, who gave English
literature *The Memoirs of Harriet Wilson*, is scarcely the
person on whose evidence a proud man would care to rely for
the vindication of his own or his friend's honour. The plea
that Shelley probably knew nothing of the law of copyright,
reminds one of the similar plea, which caused Lord Justice
Knight Bruce to declare in his proper court, that ' to be honest
it was not necessary to be an attorney.' In truth, the question
is wholly beside Shelley's knowledge or ignorance of that law.
Every Eton boy knows whether he has done a set of Latin verses
for himself, or copied them from another boy's paper; knows

also that he is telling an untruth when he expressly declares himself the maker of the verses which another boy has composed for him. If Shelley knew the book contained poetry, that was written by neither of the individuals indicated in the title-page,—contained poetry that was *not* original in the sense of the title,—he was guilty of an untruth. For reasons already stated, I cannot question he had this knowledge, and was guilty of an untruth, which he would not have uttered to the publisher and the world, had he been (as Lady Shelley declares him to have been) more outspoken and truthful than other boys; or (as Mr. Walter S. Halliday declares him to have been) remarkable for 'great moral courage' and dislike of everything that was 'false.' Were it a solitary instance of departure from truth in the poet's career, his present biographer would be at less pains to call attention to this matter, as an affair that should not be without effect on our final estimate of an equally interesting and puzzling character.

After placing the 1480 copies of the *Original Poetry* in Mr. Stockdale's hands, Shelley naturally wished the same publisher of light literature to produce *St. Irvyne; or, the Rosicrucian*,—a novel of which so much will be said in the next chapter of this volume, that it is enough in the present page to say the young author was at work upon it in the summer and autumn of 1810, and probably began to work upon it soon after sending the copy of *The Wandering Jew* to John Ballantyne and Co.

Enough has been said of the verses that, written by Shelley in 1809–10 (probably in the earlier half of 1810), may have been the first sketches and studies for *Queen Mab*. It is, however, well to refer again to the metrical performances that, engaging Shelley's attention in the autumn of 1810, were published by the Oxford printer and bookseller, J. Munday, in the middle of the November of that year, under the title of *Posthumous Fragments of Margaret Nicholson*. In a contemptuous notice of the *Victor and Cazire* poems, the *British Critic* (1811) spoke of the volume's as 'sentimental nonsense and very absurd tales of horror' in terms, that seem to dispose of Mr. D. F. MacCarthy's suggestion that the *Posthumous Fragments of Margaret Nicholson* may be a mere reproduction of the *Victor and Cazire* poems, *minus* the verses that might have brought the publisher into the Court of Chancery. In comparing Byron's story with Shelley's story, one is struck by the numerous resemblances and coincidences of the two careers. Even as Byron employed a country printer to produce his first volume of boyish verse, Shelley employed a country printer for the production of his first book of jingle. Even as the indiscretions of Byron's first book constrained him to suppress it, Shelley was forced to suppress his first thing of rhymes by fear of consequences.

What was the year of Shelley's correspondence with Miss Felicia Dorothea Browne (afterwards Mrs. Hemans), the correspondence, in which he impregnated her mind with sceptical thought, and so far disturbed her religious life that Mrs. Browne (Felicia's mother) wrote to Mr. Medwin the elder, begging him to use his influence with Shelley, so that he should desist from writing to the girl he had never seen? In the absence of dated documents, I answer this question with some hesitation by assigning the interchange of letters to 1810. There are reasons for giving a somewhat earlier date to the correspondence, and reasons for thinking the boy and girl were writing to one another even so late as the spring of 1811. But, speaking doubtfully, I regard the interchange of epistles as an affair of the spring and summer of 1810.

With his usual ambiguity of expression, Medwin says, or seems to say, that he made Miss Felicia Dorothea Browne's acquaintance in North Wales at the beginning of 1808 or somewhat before that year; subscribed for a volume of her poems when she was sixteen years old; and on his return from North Wales (in the earlier part of 1808) spoke of her and her writings to Shelley, in terms that caused him to write to the young lady. The perplexing Mr. Thomas Medwin writes thus :—

'In the beginning of the first of these two years' (*i.e.* 1808 and 1809), 'I showed Shelley some poems to which I had subscribed by Felicia Browne, whom I had met in North Wales, where she had been on a visit at the house of a connexion of mine. She was then sixteen, and it was impossible not to be struck with the beauty (for beautiful she was), the grace, and charming simplicity and *naiveté* of this interesting girl; and on my return from Denbighshire, I made her and her works the frequent subject of conversation with . . . . . . He desired to become acquainted with the young authoress, and using my name wrote to her, as he was in the habit of doing to all those who in any way excited his sympathies. This letter produced an answer, and a correspondence of some length passed between them, which, of course, I never saw, but it is to be supposed that it turned on other subjects besides poetry. I mean that it was sceptical. It has been said by her biographer, that the poetess was at one period of her life, as is the case frequently with deeper thinkers on religion, inclined to doubt; and it is not impossible that such owed its origin to this interchange of thought. One may, indeed, suppose this to have been the case, from the circumstance of her mother writing to my father, and begging him to use his influence with Shelley to cease from any further communication with her daughter,—in fact, prohibiting their further correspondence.'

Medwin is obviously not right in his dates. Born on 23rd September, 1793, Felicia Browne (Hemans) attained the age of sixteen on 23rd September, 1809. If he made the young lady's acquaintance at the end of 1807, or in the beginning of 1808, she was only fifteen years of age when he first made a bow to her. If she was in her seventeenth year when he first saw her, the meeting took place on some day between 23rd September, 1809, and 23rd September, 1810. It is much more probable that he was right about her age than about the year. The girl's precise age is much more likely than the precise number of the year, in which he first saw her, to have lived in his memory. The admiration with which he regarded and remembered her is a state of feeling much more likely to have been caused by a girl of sixteen than a child of fifteen. If he made her acquaintance at the end of 1809, he made it at a time closely preceding the winter in which he saw so much of Shelley. If he made her acquaintance at the close of 1807, or the beginning of 1808, he would have had fewer opportunities for speaking about her to his cousin (still an Eton schoolboy); and in the spring and summer of 1809, he would scarcely have been cognizant of the correspondence of the boy at Eton and the girl in Wales. In the winter of 1809-10, and in the following spring, he would naturally know of the correspondence, and hear something of the letters he was not permitted to see.

It matters little whether the correspondence was an affair of this year or that year. The important fact is that, whilst still a stripling, the future poet opened a correspondence with the young lady, and used the opportunities of the correspondence to infuse her with sceptical sentiment, and disturb her faith in the religion in which she had been trained. What might come to Miss Felicia Browne from his intrusion on her spiritual life was no question to trouble him. What misery might ensue to the girl's mother and other kindred from his action was no matter for him to consider. The rights and feelings of parents were rights and feelings to which the young gentleman (who might have been the Saviour of the World) was sublimely indifferent, whenever it pleased him to talk with a school-girl (whose acquaintance he had made without the sanction or knowledge of her parents) on the evidences of Christianity, the soul's immortality, the existence of the Deity. No less heedless was he of his own mother's wishes, anxieties, fears, hopes, when the humour came upon him to enlighten his sisters on matters about which she wished them to be left in ignorance. Himself a passionate disbeliever of the Christian religion, Shelley was possessed by a passion for making other people sharers of his disbelief, especially for raising the young ladies of his acquaintance to his own philosophical contempt for the delusions of Christianity. Any one who humoured his propensity to win converts to his own particular infidelity was a philosopher; every one who presumed to oppose it was an intolerant bigot. In the indulgence of this passion for making converts to unbelief, he was selfish.

Without receiving or seeking Mrs. Browne's permission to address her daughter on matters pertaining to religion, or to have any kind of confidential relations with her, he opened a correspondence with the sixteen-years-old girl, and did his best to lure her from the religion in which she had been educated, —and was so far successful as to shake her faith in Christianity. A few weeks or months later, without receiving or seeking Mrs. Grove's permission to address her daughter (a young girl of his own age) on matters of religion, he did his best by spoken words and written words to lure the girl from Christianity, though he must have known that he could not effect his purpose without inflicting inexpressible pain on his mother's sister. Knowing his mother's repugnance to infidelity, he did his best to lure his eldest sister (a girl of poetical sensibility and genius, who idolized him) from the Christian religion. In the following year, finding Harriett Westbrook still a sixteen-years-old school-girl, who held the usual religious views of an English school-girl educated within the lines of the Established Church, he approached her without asking her parents' authority to do so, lured her from Christianity to Atheism, set her in rebellion against her father, and having made her an undutiful daughter and an atheist, married her,—marrying her instead of

making her his mere mistress, *only* because Hogg made him see
he was bound in honour to make her his lawfully wedded wife,
before possessing himself of her person. In this period of his
early manhood, he approached other girls of tender age in the
same manner,—addressing them on matters of religion, disturbing their spiritual life, and shaking their faith in Christianity, when he did not succeed in his efforts to extinguish it.'
With the single exception of Miss Harriett Grove (who does
not seem to have suffered from his sophistries) he seems to have
been more or less successful in all his attempts on the faith of
young girls.

In acting thus to young girls, without the sanction or knowledge of their natural guardians, the apt pupil of the hard-
swearing Windsor doctor is declared by the most fervid of his
admirers to have been justified, because he was a sincere and
earnest teacher of what he believed to be the truth, an
enthusiastic assailant of error, and a fervid enemy of intolerance. Though his action was often strangely wanting in
candour and openness, was sometimes odiously secretive and
treacherous towards the parents of the young girls with whose
faith he tampered, the sincerity of his religious sentiments and
utterances is open to no suspicion. It is unquestionable that
he believed what he tried to make others believe,—that he was
wholly convinced and absolutely certain of the falseness of the
opinions which he entreated other people to repudiate as false.
It cannot be doubted he was an enthusiastic assailant of what
he thought to be error, and the majority of his acquaintance
thought to be the reverse of error. In one sense, he was no
doubt a disinterested assailant of what he thought to be error.
But how about his tolerance? his hatred of intolerance? For
the moment we are not thinking of the Italian Shelley, who,
after warring wildly with all who differed from him in opinion,
desisted in some degree from the bootless strife,—on discovering
that what was truth to him might be error to higher intelligence, that the people from whom he differed in opinion
had the same right to their manifestly erroneous opinions as he
had to his possibly erroneous views ; that human creatures could
not be forced out of their errors by passionate speech ; that disputants fighting with subtle arguments and hot words might be
as essentially intolerant as disputants fighting with instruments
of torture and blazing faggots. To say that the Shelley, who,

after surviving the phrensies of his earlier manhood, wrote the *Essay on Christianity*, was devoid of tolerance would be unjust. But how about the Shelley who wrote *Laon and Cythna*, who raved against religion in *Queen Mab*, and was moved by hatred of error to teach Harriett Westbrook (ætat. 16), Harriett Grove (ætat. 17), his sister Elizabeth (ætat. 16), Felicia Browne (ætat. 16), that Christianity was made up of monstrous fables and delusions; that the Christian religion was accountable for the worst evils of human society; that the sentiment of the Christian faith was pernicious and execrable. Was this enemy of intolerance chiefly remarkable for tolerance? Whilst railing at the world's want of tolerance, Shelley was himself a caricature of intolerance.

In regarding Shelley during the earlier stages of his crusade against Christianity, more especially in regarding his endeavours to dispel the religious delusions of Felicia Browne, Harriett Grove, his sister Elizabeth, Harriett Westbrook and other young ladies of his acquaintance, readers should judge him at least quite as severely as they would judge any young man of the present period, whom they should detect in sapping the religious faith and disturbing the religious life of young girls, still under their governesses. I might even go a step further and say that they should judge him even more severely than a young man of the present period: as in these days of Free Thought, when it is questioned by a considerable minority of people whether children are the better for being kept well within the lines of religious orthodoxy, a young man guilty of infusing the damsels of his familiar circle with sceptical sentiment, would offend social opinion less flagrantly and universally, than the Oxford undergraduate who was guilty of such conduct in days, when society was almost unanimous in attaching the highest value to religious orthodoxy, and in believing that to depart from it was to lay aside the only effectual armour against temptations to immorality.

Still, it is enough for readers to judge Shelley in this matter, precisely as they would judge a youthful delinquent of the present period, when the wholesome opinion still prevails that the man is guilty of heinous domestic treachery, who abuses the opportunities of familiar intercourse, so as to disturb the religious life of the young people of his acquaintance, and lure them from the tenets in which their natural guardians have educated them, and desire them still to be educated. What would the readers of this page say of any clever Etonian or Oxford undergraduate, whom they should overhear and catch in the very act of luring a girl of tender age from the religion of her parents (the religion in which they wish to confirm her) into Atheism? I conceive most readers of this page would pass judgment on the offender, without reference to the relative merits or demerits of the religion the girl was being lured to repudiate. I do not hesitate to say that in such a case I should tell the youthful apostle of Free Thought my opinion of his conduct, in a few words of homely English, that would make his ears tingle;—and the words of homely English would be none the less stinging and disdainful, because I knew the young gentleman to be a rather clever fellow, and even thought him likely to write good poetry some years hence.

Why do I presume to say without hesitation that Miss Harriett Grove's correspondence with, and so-called engagement to, her cousin, Percy Bysshe Shelley, were affairs of the year 1810, whilst Lady Shelley (writing '*from authentic sources*') declares them to have been affairs of the previous year 1809?

The authorities have blundered curiously about this affair of the two cousins. Mr. Thomas Love Peacock makes a great slip, where he says that 'Shelley's expulsion from Oxford brought to a summary conclusion his boyish passion for Miss Harriett Grove.' Letters published in Hogg's first volume put it beyond question that, whilst the brief familiar intercourse was an affair of the latter half of 1810, it was all over by the end of that year, or at latest before the end of the Christmas holidays of 1810-11. Shelley had ceased to sigh for Harriett Grove, some weeks before the expulsion.

In the note, which reveals his disposition to think the dedicatory verses of *Queen Mab* may after all have been addressed by the poet in the first instance to Harriett Grove, Mr. Forman does an injustice (for which he has, however, a sufficient excuse) to Mr. Thomas Medwin, in representing him as giving the summer of 1809 as the summer in which the young lady and the poet 'met for the first time, since they had been children, at Field Place.' An inexact author must be read with proper regard for his besetting infirmity, even as an unsound horse must be handled with due regard for his particular unsoundness. Half-a-score facts show that in speaking of the winter of

1809 (the winter next after Shelley's withdrawal from Eton), Medwin was speaking of the winter of 1809-10. From that date on p. 53, vol. I., of the *Life of Shelley*, the narrative is carried on throughout the winter and ensuing spring into the summer, when, on p. 66 of the same volume, the biographer says, 'It was in the summer of this year that he became acquainted with our cousin, Harriet Grove;' — obviously meaning the summer of 1810. Lady Shelley, who makes free use of Medwin's book (blunders and all), probably made her mistake of the year by reading Medwin, even as Mr. Forman in later time read him, without sufficient care.

What does Mr. Charles Henry Grove (Harriett's brother) say about the matter in a very interesting letter? Writing from Torquay on 16th February, 1857, when still only in his 63rd year, this gentleman (after mentioning the Brentford schoolboy's visit to Fern for the Easter holidays), remarks :—

'I did not meet Bysshe again after that till I was fifteen, the year I left the navy, and then I went to Field Place with my father, mother, Charlotte, and Harriet. Bysshe was there, having just left Eton, and his sister, Elizabeth. Bysshe was at that time more attached to my sister Harriet than I can express, and I recollect well the moonlight walks we four had at Strode, and also at St. Irvings ; that, I think, was the name of the place, then the Duke of Norfolk's, at Horsham. [St.* Irving's Hills, a beautiful place, on the right-hand side as you go from Horsham to Field Place, laid out by the famous Capability Brown, and full of magnificent forest trees, waterfalls, and rustic seats. The house was Elizabethan. All has been destroyed.] That was in the year 1810. After our visit to Field Place, we went to my brother's house in Lincoln's Inn Fields, where Bysshe, his mother, and Elizabeth joined us, and a very happy month we spent. Bysshe was full of life and spirits, and very well pleased with his successful devotion to my sister. In the course of that summer, to the best of my recollection, after we had retired into Wiltshire, a continued correspondence was

* This extract from Charles Grove's letter is taken from the printed copy of the epistle in Hogg's second volume ; and the reader should give his attention to the words between brackets which are no part of the letter, but one of the explanatory notes, which the biographer indiscreetly put into the body of his transcripts of original documents, instead of printing them as footnotes. It was his rule to bracket such editorial notes, and insert his initials after the second bracket. But the careless scribe, and still more careless proof-corrector, sometimes forgot to insert his initials, sometimes forgetting also to insert the brackets. Hence the so-called 'interpolations' of original evidences, for which he has been unfairly reproached by his detractors.

going on, as, I believe, there had been before, between Bysshe and my sister Harriet. But she became uneasy at the tone of his letters on speculative subjects, at first consulting my mother, and subsequently my father also, on the subject. This led at last, though I cannot exactly tell how, to the dissolution of an engagement between Bysshe and my sister, which had previously been permitted, both by his father and mine.'

The bracketed words being regarded as 'editorial comment,' this quotation from Mr. Charles Henry Grove's letter, and all the rest of the epistle, are lucid and strenuous. The writer of so good a letter may have exaggerated the fervour of Shelley's passion for his cousin Harriett, and made a regular engagement out of a mere appearance of mutual liking that promised to ripen quickly into a formal betrothal (of these errors I have no doubt Mr. Charles Henry Grove was in some degree guilty); but he was not likely to be wrong about the year, remembered as the year in which he was fifteen, and the year in which he left the navy. That he was right about the year appears also from divers of Shelley's letters to Hogg.

It requires no great effort of the imagination to create pleasant scenes and incidents from the little that is recorded of this meeting and association of the two families of the Wiltshire Groves and Sussex Shelleys, families having their homes too far apart to see much of one another in pre-railway time. Harriett and Percy Bysshe had not seen each other (if we may trust Medwin) since they were children. No wonder the young man was favourably impressed by his fair cousin,—a singularly beautiful girl of graceful figure, clear blue eyes, a singular superabundance of light golden-brown tresses, a complexion comparable with his own complexion for show of pink and white, but surpassing it in clearness and freedom from freckles. Cousins of the same age almost to a day, they resembled one another in several personal particulars ; but the girl had the advantage of her cousin in the delicate symmetry of her countenance, and the fine straightness of the feature that rendered the fault of his small, turn-up nose more noticeable. In the dignity and composure of her carriage she also had the advantage of the Oxford undergraduate, whose movements were too nervous, and impetuous, and irregular for stateliness. This difference of bearing and gesture in the two cousins corresponded with the difference of their temperaments,—his quick and vehement impulsiveness, her calm self-possession. Perhaps Shelley liked the lovely girl all the more for her coldness, just as Byron was fascinated by the frigid placidity of Miss Milbanke's demeanour. That he had reason to admire her is unquestionable. After a lapse of six-and-thirty years, Tom Medwin (who was one of the family party at Field Place in 1810, and in those thirty-six years had seen many charming women in divers lands) could recall no woman comparable with her for beauty.

Possibly the meeting of the two families had been arranged by the elders to see if the two cousins were likely to care more than a little for each other. It was not in human nature for the two families to live together for two months without thinking that it might result in a wedding. Mr. Grove (*ætat.* 51, a country gentleman with a large family:—I find no sufficient reason to credit him with clerical quality, though he is styled a clergyman by one of the poet's biographers; Burke only styles him ' esquire ') may well have liked the thought of matching his lovely daughter with the heir-apparent of the heir-apparent of the prodigiously wealthy baronet of Castle Goring. Mrs. Grove would have been a strangely unreasonable woman to think her nephew no sufficient match for her beautiful daughter. The Member for New Shoreham and Mrs. Shelley of Field Place may well have thought an early engagement, with a prospect of early marriage, precisely the thing to keep their eccentric, troublesome, scatterbrain boy steady and straight at Oxford.

Whilst the Eton-Oxford man certainly liked his cousin well enough to enjoy the notion of becoming her husband, at least one member of the family party was desirous, intent, busy on making a match out of such promising materials. This would-be match-maker was Bysshe's sister Elizabeth,—the Iza of *Cazire*, at the same time her brother's idol and idolater, a girl of no common beauty and mental endowments, a maiden clever with her pen and yet cleverer with her pencil. At her own instance, and at his request, to please her brother and to please herself, she threw herself into his purpose, and pleaded in his behalf to the Beauty of Fern, declaring he possessed every noble quality, and was free from every failing of his sex ; insisting that he and the cousin whom he admired so enthusiastically were designed by Heaven for one another; and imploring the tranquil, too unresponsive beauty to rate Bysshe at his proper worth, and prize his expressions of affection far higher than she seemed to prize them.

The poet must have mistrusted his power to win and hold the beauty when he asked his sister to help him; and before she entreated the beauty to be merciful, Miss Shelley must have felt her brother sorely needed her assistance. My impression is that from first to last Shelley never had any hold whatever on Miss Grove's affections, that he was no clever suitor, that circumstances were from the outset against him. Before she came to Field Place there may have been an understanding between the young lady and the Somerset gentleman whom she married in the following year; an understanding that, whilst binding her lightly though securely to him, left her free to amuse herself with a little innocent flirtation with her cousin of Field Place. I have reason to suspect that when she consulted her father and mother about Bysshe's sceptical views after corresponding with him for several months, she produced the letters not so much for the benefit of their advice as for the assistance they would afford her in inducing them to relinquish a scheme on which they had set their hearts, and to sanction a scheme on which she had set her heart nine months since. I cannot question that Bysshe diminished and weakened any slight chance he may have had of winning the beauty's hand by talking sceptically to her, and otherwise carrying her through the primer of infidelity. Instead of taking the new doctrine to her heart, she was at first a little frightened by it, and then strongly determined by it to take a path of life, in which she would not be attended by the scatterbrain heir to the brand-new Castle Goring baronetcy.

Still every girl likes to be admired, and Miss Grove liked her cousin's admiration none the less because his sister entreated her so prettily to accept it responsively. There was no reason why she should disappoint the brother and sister with a promptitude, that would put a premature period to an agreeable holiday. The obvious wishes of the elders of both families may also have disposed the young lady to temporize. That the elders of the family party wished for the match when the Groves went from Field Place to town, may be inferred from the arrangement for the speedy reunion of the young people in Lincoln's Inn Fields. That Bysshe, Mrs. Shelley, and Miss Shelley, followed the five

Groves to London so quickly, and spent a month with them under the same roof of Lincoln's Inn Fields, is a significant fact.

In London, as the reader doubtless remembers, the poet had other business to look after besides the pursuit of his cousin's affection. It was needful for him to come to an arrangement with a London publisher respecting those already mentioned fourteen hundred and eighty copies of *Original Poetry*, by Victor and Cazire. Needful, also, was it that he should find a publisher for *St. Irvyne, or The Rosicrucian*, which would soon be ready for the press. The poet's first visit to Mr. John Joseph Stockdale's place of business in Pall Mall was paid whilst he was staying with his mother, and his sister, and Harriett the Enchantress, under his cousin Grove's house, hard by Lincoln's Inn. Since he entered the publisher's office with a countenance eloquent of anxiety, one can imagine the relief it was to Cazire (the sharer of his literary toil and anxiety) to learn from Victor, on his return from Pall Mall, that he thought he saw a way out of the bother with that embarrassing Horsham printer, who wanted his money so much sooner than was reasonable and convenient.

But though she cannot have rated him highly as a partner in the dance, and does not seem at any moment to have thought seriously of taking him for a partner through life, the cousins played together prettily for two summer months. The moon-light walks at Strode and about St. Irving's Hills were followed by no less agreeable visits to the sights of the town. And when Miss Harriett returned to Wiltshire, and the youthful poet went back to Field Place, there was a commencement or renewal (Mr. Charles Henry Grove is uncertain which it was) of their correspondence through the post, that came to an end in, or shortly before, the ensuing Christmas holidays. It is not surprising that spectators of the game, who, of course, could see but little of it, mistook for an engagement what to outsiders seemed so likely to become an engagement, though it never was an affair (if I read the facts aright) that could have ended in marriage.

Peacock was justified in saying far too much had been made of this affair. On Shelley's side, it certainly was no grand passion. On Harriett's side it probably was nothing more than an innocent, perfectly feminine, and scarcely avoidable, flirta-tion. To please her parents rather than herself, she was something more complaisant to her cousin than she need have been. To please him, she answered the letters he rained down upon her—letters it would have been uncivil in her to leave altogether unnoticed. After fuming for a week or ten days, on being told he might not write to her again, Shelley never pretended that his heart had been seriously concerned in the affair, that he was a blighted being, that Harriett Grove had dealt him a blow comparable with the blow that drove Byron in anguish from Annesley. In this matter, at least, he was wholly guiltless of affectation, even whilst in his first annoyance he fumed and blustered in a very absurd fashion, vowing war to the bitter end with the demon Intolerance, that had severed him from his Harriett. He played a perfectly natural, though scarcely heroic, part, when he had taken time to wipe his eyes and recover his temper. The affair with his cousin had been ended only a few months, when he went off cheerily to Scotland with the sixteen-years-old daughter of a licensed victualler.

After leaving Oxford, Shelley never talked any nonsense about Harriett Grove's unkindness, never affected to have suffered much from her rejection of his suit, never accused her of having treated him badly. And so long as he lived, no nonsense was written or talked about the matter by the poet's friends. But when he had been dead for some few years, it occurred to the Shelleyan zealots, who were decrying Byron on serious questions for the advantage of their peculiar bard, that less important matters might be handled in the same way to the benefit of the poet, whom (to use an Americanism) they were 'running' against the author of *Childe Harold*. Hence the extravagant talk about Shelley's ancient lineage and patrician quality. If the opposition poet was a baron of the realm, a man of splendid lineage, a descendant from the Norman Buruns, the poet of 'the zealots' was next in succession to an English baronetcy, a gentleman of Norman ancestry, a worshipful personage, who had reason to value himself on his relationship to the Penshurst Sidneys, and on being heir to wealth that could purchase a score such places as Newstead Abbey. Hence, also, the talk about Byron's egotistic selfishness, insincerities, and affectations, which made him show disadvantageously in comparison with Shelley, who was (of course) so remarkable for simplicity and devotion to the truth, so invariably considerate for the feelings of other people, and so incapable of talking about himself in his poetry! Hence, also, the disparagement of Byron's singular facial loveliness. When he discovered that Byron's nose was too big for his face, and declared it had the appearance of having been imposed upon the face instead of growing naturally out of it, Leigh Hunt was trying (even in respect to so trivial a matter as a single feature) to reduce the poet he hated, to an equality with the poet, whose too small nose was 'a turn up,'—a blemish, that the 'Shelleyan enthusiasts' have done their best to withhold from the poet's posterity.

Hence, also, the practice of making far too much of Shelley's passion for Harriett Grove, and its disappointment. Readers do not need to be reminded what good running Byron made during life with his droll piece of romance about his passion for Mary Chaworth, and the ruin that came to him from its disappointment ;—the fiction, that originated in vanity and sentimentalism, being subsequently embellished and emphasized at the instigation of the poet's spite against his unforgiving wife. But the sympathy and admiration, that came to Byron during his life from this fantastic and lovely bit of poetical fibbing, were trivial in comparison with the compassion and charity, lavished upon him in the grave by the thousands and hundreds of thousands of simple persons, who had been taught by his verse to believe he would have abounded in all the social virtues, had it not been for that unfortunate business with Mary Chaworth. Under these circumstances, it is not surprising that the zealots, who persisted in 'running' Shelley against Byron, determined to 'run' Harriett Grove against Mary Chaworth, and to teach mankind that Byron's passion for Mary was no grander an affair than Shelley's passion for his Harriett (the First).

CHAPTER VIII.

ST. IRVYNE; OR, THE ROSICRUCIAN: A ROMANCE. BY A GENTLEMAN OF THE UNIVERSITY OF OXFORD.

Venal Villains—'Jock' instructed to 'Pouch' them—At Work on another
Novel—The Dog of a Publisher—Devil of a Price—*St. Irvyne*—
Irving's Hill—Review of *St. Irvyne*—Wolfstein the Magnanimous—
Megalena de Metastasio—Olympia della Anzasca—Eloise St. Irvyne
—The Virtuous Fitzeustace—Ginotti's Doom—The Oxonian Shelley's
Repugnance to Marriage—His Commendation of Free Love—Parallel
Passages of *Zastrozzi* and *St. Irvyne*—The Verses of *St. Irvyne*.

As the hour drew near for the publication of *Zastrozzi*, Shelley
was urgent with his publisher to spend money in getting favourable reviews of the superlatively foolish book. The publisher
declining to part with his money for that purpose, the literary
aspirant (more truth-loving though he was than other boys, if
Lady Shelley may be trusted) discovered a grievance in Mr.
Robinson's niggardly reluctance to bribe the reviewers. As the
man of business would not make needful arrangements with the
'gentlemen of the press,' Shelley declared his intention (in a
letter dated 1st April, 1810), to see that the 'venal villains'
were properly 'pouched.' Many a boyish author has talked
and written in the same vein, and even tipt a 'venal villain'
for a lying paragraph, without bearing himself in later time so
as to acquire a reputation for untruthfulness or for labouring
under semi-delusions. A biographer might well disdain to
notice so trivial an indication of a readiness to tamper with the
truth and fib by deputy, had Shelley's veracity never been
called in question in later time. Under the circumstances of
the case, one does not make too much of the small matter, in
remarking that, whilst it accords with the action of the young
man who offered verse for sale as 'original poetry' with the
knowledge that it was not 'original,' this resolve to buy insincere praise, in order to deceive the public and win money or
homage from credulous readers, is out of harmony with the fine
things that have been said of the poet's sublime sincerity and
passionate abhorrence of falsehood. If Medwin was right in

saying *Zastrozzi* was favourably reviewed and declared ' a book of much promise,' the critic must have been a sufficiently ' pouched ' and ' venal villain.'

In the same letter of 1st April, 1810, the poet and novelist, who ten days later donned cap and gown at University College, is seen at work on another novel, in the hope that it will bring him 60*l.*, and place him before the world as the author of the *New Romance* in three volumes. If ' Jock ' (otherwise styled Mr. John Robinson, of Paternoster Row) won't pay him ' a devil of a price ' for his new poem, and at least 60*l.* for his new romance, ' the dog shall not have them.' It was thus the youngster swaggered over a sheet of paper on April Fools' Day, about his dog of a publisher, and the devil of a price the dog must pay him for the finest fruit of his genius. The young man boasting of the 60*l.* he meant to have for his *New Romance* in three volumes, was the same boy who seems to have set it about that he had been paid 40*l.* for *Zastrozzi*. What the poem was, does not appear. It may have been the ' Original Poetry ' that wasn't original, or the *Wandering Jew* that was subsequently offered for a devil of a price, or a gentlemanly price to the Messrs. Ballantyne and Co. of Edinburgh, and Mr. John Joseph Stockdale, of 41 Pall Mall, or even the first meagre sketch of *Queen Mab;* but I am inclined to think it was *The Jew*. *Zastrozzi* having fallen dead from the press (of course, for no other reason than the dog's neglect to pouch the villains), Jock was not in the humour to drop money either on the poem for which ' a devil of a price ' would be nothing more than fair payment, or on the novel that, on being finished and ' fitted for the press by a publisher, instead of filling three volumes was (in bulk) a slighter and meaner book than *Zastrozzi*. Placed in Mr. Stockdale's hands in September, 1810, and ' fitted ' for public perusal by Mr. Stockdale himself, this performance in prose fiction was published by the Pall Mall bookseller (not on the payment of 60*l.* to the author, but altogether at the author's cost and risk) in December, 1810, under the style and titles of *St. Irryne, or, The Rosicrucian*, the first of the two titles being an adaptation of the names of the ducal seat (St. Irving's Hills)*,

* The right name of this seat seems to have been Hill Place. In the *Beauties of England and Wales* (1813), *Sussex*, p. 97, it is written, ' In the same direction on the right of the road, is an old seat called Hill Place, formerly the property of the late Viscountess Irwin, but now belonging to the Duke of Norfolk.' ' Lady Irwen's Hill Place ' would be naturally

in whose glades and gardens he had walked by moonlight with
the more cold than faithless Harriett, not six months since.

For insufficient reasons *St. Irvyne, or, The Rosicrucian*—
an even wilder piece of lunacy than *Zastrozzi*—has been assigned
to a German source. German tale-wrights may have been in
some slight degree accountable for its morbid extravagances,
even as they were indirectly accountable for some of the several
hundreds of similar English romances, that were produced in
the poet's boyhood by the imitators of Mrs. Radcliffe and Monk
Lewis. But to speak of it as a tale *from* the German, or even
after the German, is to be guilty of a misdescription.

Consisting of two separate stories, stitched together by an
inexpert handler of the literary needle, *St. Irvyne* is just such
a performance as might have been looked for from the author
of *Zastrozzi*, eager to produce a second romance, before 'clearing out' of the state of mental disease, that was partly the
effect and partly the cause of the efforts that resulted in the
earlier story. Something must be said of both parts of the tale
that, dropping still-born from the press, would have been
absolutely forgotten, had it not been for the author's subsequent
celebrity.

PART, No. I.

Consenting to participate in the adventures and fortunes of the
Alpine Brigands, by whom he has been captured, the youthful and
'high-souled' Wolfstein—an outcast from his noble family and from
the society of his equals—makes the acquaintance of Ginotti the
Rosicrucian, whilst the latter is acting as First Lieutenant under
Cavigni, the captain of the Banditti. Almost at the same time he falls
under the influence of Megalena de Metastasio, daughter of a wealthy
Italian Count, who has been despoiled, murdered, and thrown down a
yawning precipice by the comrades of the magnanimous Wolfstein.
The association of the brigands with Wolfstein is of no long duration :
for when he has made two attempts to poison their chieftain (the second
attempt being successful), the allied robbers expel Wolfstein of the
lofty soul from their brotherhood.

In justice to the magnanimous Wolfstein, it must be admitted he
did not poison Cavigni without provocation. Not only does the robber-chief presume to force his unacceptable addresses on the lovely
Megalena de Metastasio, but follows up this presumption with a threat
of ravishing her. 'Then,' cries the robber-chief, 'if within four-and-

---

abbreviated after her death into 'Irwen's Hill,' which again would be corrupted into 'Irving's Hill,' the familiar designation of the place in Shelley's
boyhood.

twenty hours you hold yourself not in readiness to return my love, force shall wrest the jewel from the casket.' Ere the four-and-twenty hours have passed, Cavigni has drained the poisoned chalice, and is rolling in torments at his murderer's feet.

Saved by Ginotti from the death to which other robbers would fain consign him, Wolfstein goes off with Megalena to Genoa, where they enter the best society. On the eve of their withdrawal from the Alpine cave, Megalena shows 'Wolfstein jewels to an immense amount';—a sight that causes the high-souled Wolfstein to exclaim, 'Then we may defy poverty; for I have about me jewels to the value of ten thousand zechins.'

When they have settled themselves in their Genoese home, Wolfstein of the lofty soul shocks Megalena by begging her to become his wife without a nuptial ceremony. 'And is my adored Megalena,' he asks, ' a victim then to prejudice ? . . . . Does she suppose that Nature created us to become the tormentors of each other ?'—questions that of course convince Megalena she ought not to stand out for the empty forms of lawful wedlock. 'Yes, yes,' the young lady exclaims with equal courage and sobriety. 'Prejudice, avaunt! Once more reason takes her seat, and convinces me that to be Wolfstein's is not criminal. O Wolfstein! if for a moment Megalena has yielded to the imbecility of nature, believe that she yet knows how to recover herself, to reappear in her proper character.' People differ in their notions of propriety. To old-fashioned persons Megalena may seem to ' reappear in a very improper character.' She and the high-souled Wolfstein henceforth live together as husband and wife without being husband and wife. They ' acted on emotional theories of liberty.' But then, as Mr. Froude would say, they were *so* young and enthusiastic!

The course of their mutual affections can scarcely be used as an argument for Free Love. They ' act on emotional theories of liberty' in other matters. Turning pettish and restless, Megalena plunges into ' dissipated pleasures.' Less enamoured of his ringless bride than harassed by her caprice, the high-souled Wolfstein takes to gambling, and forms an embarrassing intimacy with the ardent and lovely Olympia della Anzasca (daughter of the Count and Countess of the same rather uncomfortable name), a young gentlewoman, whose passions, stimulated by ' a false system of education and a wrong expansion of ideas,' impel her to quit her father's palazzo one evening, and pay Wolfstein a visit, just as he and Megalena are sitting down to a late supper.

' To what, Lady Olympia, do I owe the unforeseen pleasure of your visit ? What so mysterious business have you with me?' inquires Wolfstein, on entering the room to which the untimely and unattended visitor had been shown.

Acting on an emotional theory of liberty, the Lady Olympia della Anzasca ejaculates, ' Oh! if you wish to see me expire in horrible torments at your feet, inhuman Wolfstein, call for Megalena, and then will your purpose be accomplished!'

Having no wish to see the Lady Olympia die in so unsuitable a place, Wolfstein, instead of calling for Megalena, replies, 'Dearest Lady Olympia, compose yourself, I beseech you. What, what agitates you?'

'Oh! pardon me, pardon me,' exclaims the Lady Olympia, with 'maniac wildness,' 'pardon a wretched female who knows not what she does! Oh! resistlessly am I impelled to this avowal; resistlessly am I impelled to declare to you, that I love you! adore you to distraction!—Will you return my affection? But, ah! I rave! Megalena, the beloved Megalena claims you as her own; and the wretched Olympia must moan the blighted prospects which were about to open fair before her eyes.'

With the propriety, to be looked for in a gentleman whose Megalena is supping in the next room, and may come upon the scene at any moment, the high-souled Wolfstein exclaims: 'No reflection in the present instance is needed, Lady. What man of honour needs a moment's rumination to discover what nature has so inerasibly planted in his bosom,—the sense of right and wrong? I am connected with a female whom I love, who confides in me; in what manner should I merit her confidence, if I join myself to another? Nor can the loveliness of the beautiful Olympia della Anzasca compensate me for breaking an oath sworn to another!'

On hearing this 'dreadful fiat of her destiny,' Olympia swoons at Wolfstein's feet, a swoon from which she recovers, just as Megalena sweeps into the room, at the instance of natural curiosity respecting the cause of Olympia's visit. At the sight of Megalena's 'detested form,' the 'passion-grieving' Olympia, faintly articulating 'Vengeance!' rushes into the street and bends her rapid flight to the 'Palazzo di Anzasca.' When Olympia has thus departed in her 'passion-grief,' Wolfstein protests he has never given the fair Anzasca's passion any encouragement.

'What further proof,' he asks of Megalena, 'can I give but my oath, that never in soul or body have I broken the allegiance that I formerly swore to thee?'

'The death of Olympia!' answers Megalena.

'What mean you?' ejaculates Wolfstein.

'I mean,' says Megalena, 'I mean that, if ever you wish again to possess my affections, ere to-morrow morning Olympia must expire.'

'Murder the innocent Olympia?'

'Yes.'

'Will nothing else convince Megalena that Wolfstein is eternally hers?'

'Nothing!' says Megalena.

''Tis done then,' replies Wolfstein the Magnanimous, ''tis done. Yet' (he mutters), 'I may writhe, convulsed in immaterial agony, for ever and ever—ah! I cannot. No, Megalena, I am again yours; I will immolate the victim which thou requirest as a sacrifice to our love. Give me a dagger, which may sweep off from the face of the earth one who is hateful to thee! Adored creature, give me the dagger, and I will restore it to thee dripping with Olympia's hated blood; it shall have first been buried in her heart.'

Armed with the dagger, which Megalena puts in his hand, the high-souled Wolfstein goes off to the Palazzo della Anzasca (or 'di' Anzasca, the author uses 'della' and 'di' indifferently), enters it, unobserved follows Olympia to her bedroom, hides himself in the room till Olympia has put herself to bed, and remains in his convenient corner of the chamber, till she breathes the heavy breath of slumber. The moment for the ruthless deed has come. Dagger in hand, Wolfstein of the exalted soul glides to the sleeper's bed, watches her angelic features, gazes on the angelic smile that plays over her countenance, nerves himself to deliver the fatal blow, raises the poniard, and then—throws it from him. The noise of the falling dagger rouses Olympia to consciousness. She is awake and recognizes him. They speak to one another. For a moment Olympia imagines he has relented, and has come to give her the strongest proof of his affection. Another moment, and discovering her mistake, she leaps wildly from her bed.

'A light and flowing night-dress,' runs the narrative, 'alone veiled her form; her alabaster bosom was shaded by the light ringlets of her hair, which rested unconfined upon it. She threw herself at the feet of Wolfstein. On a sudden, as if struck by some thought, she started convulsively from the earth; for an instant she paused. The rays of a lamp, which stood in a recess of the apartment, fell full upon the dagger of Wolfstein. Eagerly Olympia sprung towards it, and, ere Wolfstein was aware of her dreadful intent, plunged it into her bosom. Weltering in purple gore she fell; no groan, no sigh escaped her lips. A smile, which the pangs of dissolution could not dispel, played on her convulsed countenance; it irradiated her features with celestially awful, although terrific expression. "Ineffectually have I endeavoured to conquer the ardent feelings of my soul; now I overcome them," were her last words. She uttered them in a tone of firmness; and, falling back, expired in torments, which her fine but expressive features declared that she gloried in.'

The victim of 'a false system of education and a wrong expansion of ideas' is at rest. All is silent in the chamber of death. As the stir, certain to ensue on the tragedy of Olympia's bedroom, may render Genoa a perilous place of residence for the man she adored and the woman she detested, Wolfstein and Megalena fly to Bohemia, in which country he has recently succeeded to immense wealth, through his uncle's death.

PART, No. II.

Consisting of six chapters and a concluding note, the Second Part of this marvellous combination of two several tales relates chiefly to the fortunes of Eloise St. Irvyne, who accompanies her dying mother from the Chateau de St. Irvyne in France to Geneva, where the elder lady expires of a lingering malady, after solemnly admonishing her daughter to beware of any man she may encounter, who shall be ' a man enveloped in deceit and mystery.' Such a man Eloise has already encountered on her journey to Geneva; and she falls under his fatal influence immediately after her mother's death. Just as Wolfstein induces Megalena to become his ringless bride, Nempere prevails on Eloise de St. Irvyne to become his mistress.

Growing weary of his victim's fascinations soon after he has gained possession of her body, the villain Nempere (who in due course turns out to be Ginotti, the Rosicrucian) offers Eloise St. Irvyne as a mere *fille de joie*, in payment of a gambling debt, to the dissolute but essentially honourable Chevalier Mountfort,—an Englishman of ancient lineage and noble rank. Too chivalrous to take advantage of the power he has acquired by purchase over the victim of Nempere's licentiousness and perfidy, the Chevalier Mountfort places Eloise with an adequate allowance in a picturesque cottage, under the chivalric surveillance of the exemplary Fitzeustace (an Irish gentleman), who eventually makes her his wife. Having thus provided for Eloise, the Chevalier Mountfort goes off in pursuit of Nempere, to chastise him for his villany.

Eloise is left in good hands. ' He is an Irishman,' the Chevalier has remarked to Eloise of the gentleman to whose care she is consigned, ' and so *very* moral, and so averse to every species of *gaieté de cœur* that you need be under no apprehensions. In short, he is a love-sick swain, without ever having found what he calls a congenial female.' The virtues of this Irish gentleman are regarded by Mr. Denis Florence MacCarthy as indicative that, whilst writing *St. Irvyne* in the summer of 1810, Shelley was already disposed to regard the Irish with favour.

In Eloise this ' love-sick swain ' discovers the ' congenial female ' for whom he has long been seeking. Admiring her beauty, he hangs upon the music of her lips, pining for the time when he shall be permitted to salute them. Nothing in her history moderates his passion for Nempere's abandoned mistress. In his judgment it is nothing to her disadvantage that she has been seduced, and is on the point of giving birth to a child of shame. When she answers his prayer for their immediate union by saying: ' Know you not that I have been another's?' he replies with passionate fervour: ' Oh, suppose me not the slave of such vulgar and narrow-minded prejudice. Does the frightful vice and ingratitude of Nempere sully the spotless excellence of my Eloise's soul?' When Eloise gives birth to Nempere's son, Fitzeustace officiates by turns as the mother's doctor and the infant's nurse. At moments when he is necessarily ' absent from the apartment of the beloved Eloise, his whole delight is to gaze on the child, and trace in its innocent countenance the features of the mother he adores.'

Eloise having at length consented to become his wife, this Irish gentleman remarks: ' But before we go to England, before my father will see us, it is necessary that we should be married. Nay, do not start, Eloise: I view it in the light that you do; I consider it as but a chain which, although it keeps the body, still leaves the soul unfettered; it is not so with love. But still, Eloise, to those who think like us, it is, at all events, harmless; 'tis but yielding to the prejudices of the world wherein we live, and procuring moral expediency at a slight sacrifice of what we conceive to be right.'

Thus admonished, Eloise consents to the slight sacrifice of what she conceives to be right, and promises to pass to her Fitzeustace's conjugal embraces through the narrow gate of lawful matrimony, instead of by the broad and higher way of Free Love. ' Well, well,' she says reluctantly, ' it shall be done, Fitzeustace; but take the assurance of my promise that I cannot love you more.' Partly, in palliation of the lady's weakness and Fitzeustace's excessive care for the world's opinion in this business, the author of the romance remarks in his own person : ' They soon agreed on a point, in their eyes of so trifling importance, and arriving in England, tasted that happiness, which love and innocence alone can give. Prejudice may triumph for awhile, but virtue will be eventually the conqueror.'

Reappearing, in the last chapter, to compass the high-souled Wolfstein's destruction, Ginotti, *alias* Nempere, is left eventually in the darksome vaults of St. Irvyne's ruinous abbey, to endure 'a dateless and hopeless eternity of horror,' as a gigantic and conscious skeleton, with ' two pale and ghastly flames glaring in his eyeless sockets.' The way in which the narrative is wound up surpasses all human understanding. After ' fitting ' the manuscript for the press, Mr. John Joseph Stockdale may well have entreated Shelley to reconsider some passages of the story, and to explain or alter, certain matters of the *dénouement*. In answer to the publisher's request for explanations and further instructions, Shelley wrote lightly from University College, Oxford, on 14th November, 1810:—

' Dear Sir,—I return you the Romance by this day's coach. I am much obligated by the trouble you have taken to fit it for the press. I am myself by no means a good hand at correction, but I think I have obviated the principal objections which you allege.

' Ginotti, as you will see, did *not* die by Wolfstein's hand, but by the influence of that natural magic which, when the secret was imparted to the latter, destroyed him.—Mountfort being a character of inferior import, I did not think it necessary to state the catastrophe of *him*, as at best it could be but uninteresting.—Eloise and Fitzeustace, are married and happy I suppose, and Megalena dies by the same means as Wolfstein.—I do not myself see any other explanation that is required.—As to the method of publishing it, I think, as it is a thing which almost *mechanically* sells to circulating libraries, &c., I would wish it to be published on my *own* account.

' I am surprised that you have not received the *Wandering Jew*, and, in consequence write to Mr. Ballantyne to mention it; you will doubtlessly therefore, receive it soon.—Should you still perceive in the romance any error of flagrant incoherency, &c., it must be altered, but I should conceive it will (being wholly so abrupt) not require it.

I am your sincere humble servant,

PERCY B. SHELLEY.

'Shall you make this in one or two volumes? Mr. Robinson, of Paternoster Row, published *Zastrozzi.*'

The author's explanations in no degree diminish the difficulty of understanding the story. On the contrary, they rather increase the difficulty. Having done his duty in calling the author's attention to some of the story's most glaring absurdities, and having (as he imagined) no pecuniary interest to be cautious for in respect to a work that was to be published at the charges of the young gentleman who, sooner or later, would, of course, be able to pay a heavy bill, Mr. Stockdale sent to the printers the thing of lunacy, of which Mr. Garnett says: ' Worthless as *St. Irvyne* is of itself, it becomes of high interest when regarded as the first feeble step of a mighty genius on the road to consummate excellence.'

It was enough for the author of *Zastrozzi*, in the first stage of his fanatical abhorrence of lawful wedlock, to make the virtuous Verezzi speak slightingly of the nuptial rite as needless for the consecration of his spiritual union with the amiable Matilda di Laurentini. In *St. Irvyne* this repugnance to the fetters put upon passion, that should be left in absolute freedom, is declared more precisely and emphatically. Whilst the exemplary Fitzeustace declares his contempt for the ceremony, Eloise makes it clear she would rather be his mistress than his wife. At the same time, the author in his own person declares that, when Virtue shall have triumphed over Prejudice, women, instead of being given and taken in Marriage, will be given and taken in Free Love. In this matter the Oxonian surpasses the Etonian, and is seen to have advanced a long step towards the conclusions that qualified him to proclaim the sanctity of Free Love in *Laon and Cythna*,—the poem in which he ' startled ' (his own word) the men and women of England by insisting that in a perfect state of society a brother and sister would be able, with perfect propriety, to live together in Free Love, and beget children of one another.

In the article entitled ' A Newspaper Editor's Reminiscences,' to be found in the June, 1841, number of *Fraser's Magazine*, the curious may find some rather strong, but inconclusive, evidence that at some time between *October, 1811, and March, 1812, Shelley tried to sell to three or four different London publishers, for a sum of 10*l.*, certain tales in manuscript, out of which he composed *Zastrozzi* and *St. Irvyne*. If Shelley, after publishing the two 'failures' in prose fiction, tried to wheedle money out of booksellers for the materials out of which those failures were made, he did what he should not have done, and received

* Shelley, as we shall see, was in London, and in urgent need of more money, in October, 1811.

less than his proper punishment in getting nothing by his pains. But the evidence is so unsatisfactory that the young man did thus endeavour to get money for stuff, whose worthlessness he had ascertained, I cannot hold him guilty of the curious piece of sharp practice. The same newspaper editor's evidence that one of these tales was either a translation from the German, or alleged by Shelley to have been a translation from the German, being still more unsatisfactory, there is no need to trouble the reader of these volumes to consider the particulars of it.

As he delights in the dreary labour of collating the texts of worthless books, it is strange that Mr. Buxton Forman (who has wasted a great deal of time in collating the different editions of Shelley's writings) should have failed to discover that *St. Irvyne* consists, in a considerable degree, of the characters, and positions, and incidents of *Zastrozzi*, so changed by being turned inside out and differently coloured, as to be likely to be mistaken, by hasty and unsuspicious readers of both books, for new actors and positions and incidents. Towards the close of his career, Thackeray said to a friend, 'I am no prolific creator of characters. In that respect 1 have fairly worked myself out. It remains for me now to redress my old puppets with new bits of riband and tinsel.' The puppets of the Etonian romance are thus redressed in the Oxford story. By change of costume, the puppet, who figures as a man in *Zastrozzi*, is qualified for a woman's part in *St. Irvyne*. By being pulled inside out, the position that was meant to rouse admiration in the one story, becomes a position that (in the hands of an abler artist) would stir to pity in the other. To escape from an humiliating position, Olympia poniards herself in *St. Irvyne ;* even as Verezzi, to escape a melodramatic embarrassment, poniards himself in *Zastrozzi.* The slumbering Eloise in the later fiction declares her passion for Fitzeustace to the listening Irishman, even as the slumbering Verezzi in the earlier romance declares his passion for Julia to the listening Matilda.'

<table>
<tr><td>

THE DAGGER SCENE IN
' ZASTROZZI.'

' Madness—fiercest madness—revelled through his brain. He raised the poniard high, but Julia rushed forwards, and in accents of desperation, in a voice of alarmed tenderness, besought him to spare himself—to spare her—for all might yet be well.

'" Oh ! never, never !" exclaimed Verezzi, frantically, " no peace but in the grave for me. I am—I am— married to Matilda."

'Saying this, he fell backwards upon a sofa in strong convulsions, yet his hand still firmly grasped the fatal poniard.

</td><td>

THE DAGGER SCENE IN
' ST. IRVYNE.'

' " Wilt thou be mine ? " exclaimed the enraptured Olympia, as a ray of hope arose in her mind. " Never ! never can I," groaned the agitated Wolfstein, " I am irrevocably, indissolutely another's."—Maddened by this death-blow to all expectations of happiness, which the deluded Olympia had so fondly anticipated, she leaped wildly from the bed. A light and flowing night-dress alone veiled her form ; her alabaster bosom was shaded by the light ringlets of her hair which rested unconfined upon it. She threw herself at the feet of

</td></tr>
</table>

'Matilda, meanwhile, fixedly contemplated the scene. Fiercest passions raged through her breast: vengeance, disappointed love—disappointed in the instant, too, when she had supposed happiness to be hers for ever, rendered her bosom the scene of wildest anarchy.

'Yet she spoke not—she moved not—but collected in herself, stood waiting the issue of that event, which had so unexpectedly dissolved *her visions of air-built ecstasy.*

'Serened to firmness from despair, Julia administered everything which could restore Verezzi with the most unremitting attention. At last he recovered. *He slowly raised himself, and starting from the sofa where he lay, his eyes rolling wildly,* and his whole frame convulsed by fiercest agitation, *he raised the dagger which he still retained, and, with a bitter smile of exultation, plunged it into his bosom!—His soul fled without a groan, and his body fell to the floor, bathed in purple blood.'*

Wolfstein. On a sudden, as if struck by some thought, she started convulsively from the earth: for an instant she paused.

'The rays of a lamp, which stood in a recess of the apartment, fell full upon the dagger of Wolfstein. *Eagerly Olympia sprung towards it; and ere Wolfstein was aware of her dreadful intent, plunged it into her bosom. Weltering in purple gore, she fell; no groan, no sigh escaped her lips. A smile, which the pangs of dissolution could not dispel, played on her convulsed countenance; it irradiated her features* with celestially awful, although terrific, expression. " Ineffectually have I endeavoured to conquer the ardent feelings of my soul; now I overcome them," were her last words. She uttered them in a tone of firmness, and, falling back, expired in torments, which her fine, her expressive features declared that she gloried in.'

Each of these passages is a fair example of the work from which it is taken. Surely their resemblance in temper, moral fibre, style, verbiage, affords sufficient evidence that the two passages were put together by the same writer. What evidence do they afford that, whilst the passage, taken from *Zastrozzi* (the novel universally allowed to be a thing of Shelley's own manufacture), was written as it is printed by the future poet, the passage from *St. Irvyne* (the novel generally assigned to a German source) is a mere translation from a German original? Why (in the absence of evidence that Shelley could translate a page of German, and in the absence of any German novel, out of which *St. Irvyne* could have been made) are we to regard the passage of the earlier book as the pure product of Shelley's mind, and the passage of the later romance as so much of the translated product of a German writer's mind?

<table>
<tr><td>THE BEDROOM SCENE IN
' ZASTROZZI.'</td><td>THE PAVILION SCENE IN
' ST. IRVYNE.'</td></tr>
<tr><td>'The morning came — Matilda arose from a sleepless couch, and with hopes yet unconfirmed sought</td><td>'Heedless yet of the beauties of nature, the loveliness of the scene, they entered the pavilion.</td></tr>
</table>

Verezzi's apartment. She stood near the door listening. Her heart palpitated with tremulous violence, as she listened to Verezzi's breathing—every sound from within alarmed her. At last she slowly opened the door, and though adhering to the physician's directions in not suffering Verezzi to see her, she could not deny herself the pleasure of watching him, and busying herself in little offices about his apartment.

'She could hear Verezzi question the attendant collectedly, yet as a person who was ignorant where he was, and knew not the events which had immediately preceded his present state.

'*At last he sank into a deep sleep.*— Matilda now dared to gaze on him; the hectic colour which had flushed his cheek was fled, but the ashy hue of his lips had given place to a brilliant vermilion. *She gazed intently on his countenance.*

'*A heavenly yet faint smile diffused itself over his countenance*—his hand slightly moved.

'Matilda, fearing that he would awake, again concealed herself. She was mistaken: for, on looking again, he still slept.

'She still gazed upon his countenance. *The visions of his sleep were changed, for tears came fast from under his eyelids, and a deep sigh burst from his bosom.*

'Thus passed several days: Matilda still watched, with the most affectionate assiduity, by the bedside of the unconscious Verezzi.

'The physician declared that his patient's mind was yet in too irritable a state to permit him to see Matilda, but that he was convalescent.

'One evening she sate by his bedside, and gazing upon the features of the sleeping Verezzi, felt unusual

'Eloise convulsively pressed her hand upon her forehead.

'"What is the matter, my dearest Eloise?' inquired Fitzeustace, whom awakened tenderness had thrown off his guard.

'"Oh! nothing, nothing; but a momentary faintness. It will soon go off: let us sit down."

'They entered the pavilion.

'"'Tis nothing but drowsiness," said Eloise, affecting gaiety; "'twill soon go off. I sate up late last night: that I believe was the occasion."

'"Recline on this sofa, then," said Fitzeustace, reaching another pillow to make the couch easier, "and I will play some of those Irish tunes which you admire so much."

'Eloise reclined on the sofa, and Fitzeustace, seated on the floor, began to play; the melancholy plaintiveness of his music touched Eloise; she sighed, and concealed her tears in her handkerchief. *At length she sunk into a profound sleep;* still Fitzeustace continued playing, noticing not that she slept.

'*He approached. She lay wrapped in sleep: a sweet and celestial smile played on her countenance and irradiated her features with a tenfold expression of etheriality.*

'*Suddenly the visions of her slumber appeared to have changed; the smile yet remained, but the expression was melancholy; tears stole gently from her eyelids:—she sighed.*

'*Ah! with what eagerness of ecstasy did Fitzeustace lean over her form.*

'He dared not speak, he dared not move; *but pressing a ringlet of hair, which had escaped its band, to his lips, waited silently.*

'"Yes, yes; I think—it may,—" at last she muttered; but so confusely, as scarcely to be distinguishable.

softness take possession of her soul —an indefinable tumultuous emotion shook her bosom—*her whole frame thrilled with rapturous ecstasy, and seizing the hand, which lay motionless, beside her, she imprinted on it a thousand burning kisses.*

'*"Ah, Julia! Julia! is it you?" exclaimed Verezzi, as he raised his enfeebled frame; but perceiving his mistake, as he cast his eyes on Matilda, sank back and fainted.*

CHAPTER IX.

'THE soul of Verezzi was filled with irresistible disgust, as, recovering, he found himself in Matilda's arms. His whole frame trembled with chilly horror, and he could scarcely withhold himself from again fainting. He fixed his eyes upon her countenance — they met hers — an ardent fire, mingled with a touching softness, filled their orbits.'

'Fitzeustace remained rooted in rapturous attention, listening.

'*" I thought, I thought he looked as if he could love me," articulated the sleeping Eloise. " Perhaps, though he cannot love me, he may allow me to love him.—Fitzeustace!"*

'On a sudden again were changed the visions of her slumbers; terrified, she started from sleep and cried, " Fitzeustace."

CHAPTER XII.

'NEEDLESS were it to expatiate on their transports; they loved each other, and that is enough for those who have felt like Eloise and Fitzeustace.'

After comparing these two scenes of two sleeping lovers, each of whom reveals the heart's secret to an attentive watcher ; after comparing the literary characteristics of the one scene with those of the other, the structure of the sentences, language, details, touches ; after noticing the identity of the very words used in some parts of the parallel passages, can any reader think the two scenes were by two different writers? that, whilst the extract from *Zastrozzi* is a piece of original writing, the extract from *St. Irvyne* is a piece of a translation from the undiscovered work of an undiscovered German author? These passages are fair examples of the two books from which they are taken. Can any reader hesitate in coming to the conclusion that Shelley reproduced in the later the materials of the earlier romance? The writer may have been unaware he was reproducing scraps of his former work. The reproduction may have been the result of mental action, occasioned by the effort of producing the earlier tale, rather than the consequence of a deliberate design to use the old stuff for a second time. But the reproduction is obvious.

St. Irvyne contains six sets of verses, that are interesting examples of the earliest fruits of the poetical disposition, which soon developed into Shelley's poetical genius. Resembling

Byron's *Hours of Idleness,* in affording only the faintest indications of the author's eventual faculty for the service of the
Muse, these sets of verses are chiefly noteworthy for their evidence that the *Hours of Idleness* may be styled 'the horn-
book,' from which Shelley acquired the rudiments of the art of
poesy. The resemblance of one of those pieces of versification
to one of the stanzas of 'Lachin-y-Gair' in the *Hours of Idleness* is so remarkable, that the Oxonian's lines may fairly be
styled a plagiarism on the lines that had come a few years earlier
from the Byron of Cambridge.

THE STANZA OF 'LACHIN-Y-GAIR.'

'*Shades of the dead! have I not heard your voices*
    Rise on the night-rolling breath of the gale?
Surely the *soul of the hero rejoices,*
    And rides on the wind, o'er his own Highland vale.
Round Loch-na-Garr, while the stormy mist gathers,
    Winter presides in his cold icy car;
Clouds there encircle the forms of my fathers:
    They dwell in the tempests of dark Loch-na-Garr.'

THE VERSES OF 'ST. IRVYNE.'

'*Ghosts of the dead! have I not heard your yelling*
    Rise on the night-rolling breath of the blast,
When o'er the dark ether the tempest is swelling,
    And on eddying whirlwind the thunder-peal past?

'For oft I have stood on the dark height of Jura,
    Which frowns on the valley which opens beneath;
Oft have I brav'd the chill night-tempest's fury,
    Whilst around me, I thought, echo'd murmurs of death.

'And now, whilst the winds of the mountain are howling,
    O father! thy voice seems to strike on mine ear;
In air whilst the tide of the night-storm is rolling,
    It breaks on the pause of the elements' jar.

'On the wing of the whirlwind which roars in the mountain
    Perhaps *rides the ghost of my sire who is dead;*
On the mist of the tempest which hangs o'er the fountain,
    Whilst a wreath of dark vapour encircles his head.'

In a note to *St. Irvyne* (in his edition of Shelley's 'prose
works'), Mr. Buxton Forman calls attention to the obvious
adoption of the two first lines of the quoted stanza of Byron's
poem, as though they were the whole of the youthful Shelley's

'small debt' in this particular matter, to the youthful Byron. It cannot have escaped the notice of Shelley's careful editor that, whilst Shelley speaks of his father's ghost as riding on the whirl-wind and the mist of the tempest, Byron sees 'the forms of his fathers' in the clouds over-hanging Loch-na-Garr, and sings how the soul of one of his ancestral heroes 'rides on the wind.' It can scarcely have escaped the careful editor that the whole thought of Shelley's sixteen verses was 'lifted' out of Byron's eight verses.

CHAPTER IX.

MR. DENIS FLORENCE MACCARTHY *v.* THOMAS JEFFERSON HOGG.

Shelley's Matriculation at Oxford—Hogg's Matriculation at Oxford—
Hogg's First Arrival at Oxford—Lord Grenville's Election—Mr. Denis
Florence MacCarthy's Blunders—Hogg's 'New Monthly' Papers on
Shelley at Oxford—Mrs. Shelley's Reason for not Writing her Hus-
band's 'Life'—Peacock's Reason for not Writing it—Leigh Hunt's
Reason for not Writing it—Hogg undertakes the Task—Hogg's Two
Volumes—Their Merits and Faults—Hogg dismissed by Field Place
—His Mistakes and Misrepresentations—Some of his Misrepresenta-
tions adopted by Field Place.

IN a previous chapter it was stated that Shelley matriculated at Oxford,
and entered University College on 10th April, 1810,—a date given for
the first time to Shelleyan students. Hogg had then been a member of
the University and the same College for more than two months, having
matriculated on 2nd February, 1810,—another date never before given
to Shelleyan students. To those who, unaware how much readier the
Shelleyan enthusiasts are to abuse writers who differ from them than
to gather facts needful for the perfect statement of the poet's story, it
may well appear strange that, after the publication of so many books and
articles about Shelley, it should have been left for me to ascertain
from the archives of University College, Oxford, these two important
dates, by whose light the greater part of Mr. Denis Florence MacCarthy's
vehement manifesto against Hogg's account of his academic career is seen
to be one big tangle of blunderings.

Seeing the need for the discovery of these dates, I wrote a letter
that within forty-eight hours received this answer :

'TRINITY COLLEGE, OXFORD,
'12*th February,* 1884.

' DEAR MR. JEAFFRESON,

'The College Register of University College, Oxford, gives the
date of the matriculation of

'PERCY BYSSHE SHELLEY, 10th April, 1810.
'THOMAS JEFFERSON HOGG, 2nd February, 1810.

' I have this direct from the Master. This testimony, I suppose, will be
sufficient; so I return your stamps. I applied to the College first, and not
to the Registrar of the University.

'Ever yours truly,
'H. B. DIXON.'

In assuming that, because they were both first-year's men on making one another's acquaintance in the dining-hall of their College, Hogg and Shelley matriculated and went into residence on or about the same day, and that, as they met one another for the first time in October, 1810, at the same dinner-table, they both entered Oxford in the Michaelmas term of that year, Mr. Denis Florence MacCarthy followed half-a-score Shelleyan specialists in assuming as matters of course, what no old Oxford man would have thought of assuming, even as mere *primâ facie* probabilities. Shelley's academic senior by more than two months, Hogg was his superior in respect to 'residence' by a much longer time. After matriculating on 10th April, 1810, and passing a few days in the University, during which time he visited the Bodleian Library, Shelley returned to Field Place, kept 'grace-terms' in the country, and went 'into residence' in the following October. Hogg, on the contrary, went into residence on the day of his matriculation, and from that day till the next Long Vacation remained at Oxford, with the exception of the brief break of the Easter holidays, which he spent with friends who lived in counties more accessible to the undergraduate, than his own home in the northern shire. In Shelley's time, no less than in the present writer's time at Oxford, it was usual for freshmen, coming to the University from homes or schools at no great distance from Alma Mater, to 'go down' after matriculating, and keep 'grace-terms' in the country, before coming into residence. On the other hand, it was usual in pre-railway times for the academic freshman, who could not return to his people without a long and expensive journey, to matriculate and go 'into residence' at the same time.

For the information of those, who have been induced to regard Mr. MacCarthy's book of blunders as an authoritative performance, it may be well to add that the duly matriculated undergraduate, keeping 'grace-terms' in the country, was just as much a member of the University, as the freshman staying at his College. Both alike had entered the University, and become members of it. In respect to Hogg's time at Oxford, it is also well to remark that, though he did not matriculate till 2nd February, 1810, he came to Oxford from the north country in the previous autumn. Everyone, who has read his delightful 'two volumes,' remembers Hogg's account of his first arrival at Oxford, one 'fine autumnal afternoon.' He may have come to Oxford to read with a tutor before matriculation. Or on taking his first view of the University, he may only have been passing through the seat of learning, on his way to friends in some not remote county. Anyhow, it is certain that the youngster from the north country visited Oxford, and took something more than a mere tourist's interest in the place, at a time when the University was already, or was soon to be, agitated by the fierce conflict of parties, that resulted in the election of Lord Grenville to be Chancellor, in the place of the late Duke of Portland,—a fact to be remembered in connection with certain of the charges made against the biographer by Mr. Denis Florence MacCarthy.

The Duke of Portland died on 30th October, 1809 ; his successor in the Chancellorship (Lord Grenville) was elected after an unusually vehement contest on 14th December, 1809, by only thirteen votes over the number of votes given for Lord Eldon. If he was not at Oxford during the election, or during the canvass, Hogg was there shortly before the conflict of closely-matched parties, and was a member of the University when the new Chancellor had been chosen only seven weeks and one day. Let us now see the way in which Mr. Denis Florence MacCarthy presses charges of inaccuracy against Hogg, in respect to what the latter says about this election. After accusing Hogg of serious and suspicious misstatements on other matters, the author of *Shelley's Early Life* writes thus :—

'But even on questions which apparently he could have no motive in misrepresenting, he is just as inexact as Captain Medwin. The following is an instance of this . . . . . "During the whole period of our residence there," —that is, at Oxford, says Mr. Hogg, in one of those unguarded moments when he enables us to test his statements by reference to a fixed date,—"the University was cruelly disfigured by bitter feuds arising out of the *late* election of its Chancellor; in an especial manner was our most venerable college deformed by them, and by angry and senseless disappointment, Lord Grenville had just been chosen." . . . . A few words will show how utterly irreconcilable these statements are with the date of Shelley's entrance at University College. . . . . The candidateship of Lord Grenville, therefore, extended from the 30th of October to 14th of December, 1800. But in 1800, as we have seen, Shelley was at Eton and Field Place, *and did not go to Oxford until the end of October*, 1810—that is, exactly a year after the candidateship of Lord Grenville commenced, and ten months after he had been elected. Even the installation of Lord Grenville as Chancellor preceded *the entrance of Shelley into the University by four months.* That event took place on June 30, 1810. . . . . As Shelley *did not enter the University of Oxford until the end of October*, 1810, ... that nobleman (*i.e.* Lord Grenville) 'had not "just been chosen" as Mr. Hogg writes; *he had been elected ten months before.*'

Surely as he was speaking of the whole period, covering his own residence as well as Shelley's residence (*our* residence is the biographer's expression), Hogg was not without justification in speaking of an event, that had preceded his own entrance into residence by only seven weeks and one day, as a recent occurrence. Whilst censuring Hogg for errors of fact, Mr. Denis Florence MacCarthy persists in saying that Shelley did not go to Oxford, did not enter the University till the end of October, 1810, though he might easily have ascertained that the young poet went to Oxford, entered the University, put his name on the roll of University College, and as a member of the University visited the Bodleian in the preceding April, six months earlier than the time at which *Shelley's Early Life* represents him to have joined the University. Mr. MacCarthy greatly overstates the case in declaring Hogg as inaccurate as Medwin. Mr. MacCarthy himself (though curiously inaccurate), is nothing like so inaccurate as

Medwin. And Hogg (though he often trips and sometimes blunders seriously) is upon the whole nothing like so inaccurate as Mr. Mac-Carthy. There is no need to weary readers with a complete list of Mr. MacCarthy's exhibitions of inexactness. It is enough to have shown that if Hogg is at times faulty, his censor is by no means faultless.

It is not surprising that Hogg's memoirs of his old college friend are wanting in accuracy. Some nine years after the poet's death, some twenty years after his expulsion from University College, in consequence of the growing admiration of his writings, the increasing interest in his story, and the general disposition of the literary coteries to regard his failings charitably, pressure was put on Hogg to recall remote circumstances, and tell the world what he could remember of his friend at Oxford in the time of their closest intimacy. The result was that the busy lawyer in 1832 contributed the Papers on *Shelley at Oxford* to the *New Monthly Magazine*, at that time edited by Mr. Edward Lytton Bulwer, afterwards Lord Lytton. It was in the nature of things that the Papers, written after so long an interval of time, not from notes made at the time of each recorded incident, but from recollection, assisted by a few letters, should be much less than precisely accurate in all their numerous details. To impart spirit to these reminiscences, to endow them with the charm of the poet's personality, the writer every now and then called imagination to the aid of his memory. For instance, to enable readers to realize the disorderly appearance of the poet's college-room, and the confusion of its multifarious contents, the author of the Papers, without exceeding the license of a descriptive illustrator, threw into the schedule of effects certain articles of furniture, scientific apparatus, and personal apparel, which he would no doubt have declined to declare in an affidavit to have been items of the medley. It is obvious that such a picture was in some degree an imaginative sketch, in respect to its details. Yet Hogg's detractor has dealt with it as though it were an auctioneer's catalogue of lots. In judging the picture, the question to be asked is, whether the piece of descriptive writing gives the general appearance of the room, as Hogg remembered it more than twenty years afterwards. The very style of the writing is a frank announce-ment that the words must be trusted only for their general effect.

In like manner the conversations, which Mr. MacCarthy derides as ' invented conversations,' were of course given as nothing more than exhibitions of certain matters, and the kind of matters on which he remembered himself to have talked with the poet, and of the way in which they talked together to the best of his recollection after a lapse of more than twenty years. To the lawyer, familiar with questions of evidence, it never occurred that ' the conversations ' would be read in any other way. To the humourist (and that Hogg was a racy humourist is admitted even by his enemies) the bare imagination that any supremely matter-of-fact mortal would read ' the conversations,' as one peruses a short-hand reporter's notes of a legal cross-examination, would have been provocative of vehement laughter. The questions for

the critic to ask about these conversations are, Do they faithfully exhibit
the kind of subjects on which the two friends chatted?—the ways in
which the talk flowed?—the sentiments and manner of the young
poet? Are they, in fact, faithful exhibitions of what Hogg remembered,
or believed himself to remember, after a lapse of more than twenty years,
of the talk he and Shelley had with one another when they were undergraduates? No impartial and fairly intelligent reader of the Papers
will hesitate to answer these questions in the affirmative.

However defective, the Papers on *Shelley at Oxford* were greatly
beneficial to the reputation of the poet, whose writings had found few
readers outside the literary coteries during his life, whose name was still
associated in the minds of the majority of educated Englishmen with
atheism, conjugal faithlessness, and dangerous politics, rather than with
the highest poetry. Written lightly and circulated widely, the sketches,
dealing only with the Oxonian Shelley, created an impression that the
undergraduate had been treated harshly by the authorities of his
college, and left readers in a mood to discover that he had been too
severely punished for the indiscretions of later stages of his career.
Henceforth, instead of being confined to the coteries, the desire for larger
knowledge of the poet's personal story found a voice in general society.

It was felt that the Papers should be followed up and superseded by
a complete biography. By turns, and repeatedly, several of the persons,
who had known him most intimately, were urged to produce a worthy
record of so remarkable a poet. Mrs. Shelley, Peacock, Leigh Hunt,
and Hogg, were all entreated to write the sufficient memoir. William
Godwin's daughter would have written the poet's *Life* had not old
Sir Timothy Shelley informed her that, if she ventured to publish
anything in the way of biography about his family, she must go
her way without the income he provided for her own and her child's
maintenance. Peacock declined to write the *Life* because he had a
strong opinion that it would be impossible to tell the story honestly,
without setting forth matters that, for the poet's sake, had better be
unrecorded. Leigh Hunt (eventually the author of a flimsy and unsatisfactory memoir of the poet whose pocket had yielded him so many
guineas) was silent from the fear of provoking dangerous resentments.

'The book,' he remarked, in reference to Middleton's *Shelley and his
Writings*, in a letter dated to Edmund Ollier, 2nd February, 1858, 'is a
proof of what I have always said when applied to to write the *Life* myself,
viz., that it would be impossible to give a complete account of Shelley and
his connexions till the latter were all dead and gone; even if it was possible
then for any person to be so thoroughly well informed or impartial as to do
it, because facts would have to be so coloured as to misrepresent both living
and dead, some one way and some another; or the living would be forced
either to enter into the most unseemly and worse than useless wars with
one another, or to maintain silences the most difficult and distressing to keep
out of delicacy, and the most self-condemning in appearance with some, and
in reality with others.'

Whilst William Godwin's daughter was silent from pecuniary prudence, Leigh Hunt silent from fear of the consequence, and Peacock silent because he thought the book (which, if written, should be written honestly) had better not be written at all, Hogg was reluctant to produce the memoir, which the success of the Papers had caused most people to think should come from his pen. No one can charge him with intruding himself prematurely, or without invitation, into the chair, out of which he was thrust so discourteously by the very persons who had begged him to take it. The man of imperturbable temper and adamantine patience (as he is styled by Peacock) was not pricked into unauthorized action by the amateur biographers, who, sometimes without acknowledgment, and always without permission, pillaged his Papers. Medwin's *Life* appeared in 1847; and smiling at the *littérateur's* blunders, the man of imperturbable temper held his pen. He remained the man of adamantine patience, though rumours came to him that Mr. Middleton was at work on a *Life* of the poet, whom he had never known at all; that Trelawny was threatening to produce a book of gossip about the poet, whom he had known for only six months; and that the works of these gentlemen would be followed at no great distance by a work from the pen of the ' metropolitan versifier ' (Leigh Hunt), of whom he in due course remarked in the preface to his two volumes : ' If it were a question of assets, of faculties, of effects, the taking of an account of plunder,—an inventory of sums received, and of moneys to be received, refunded, and disgorged,—a mere calculation of the wind that had been raised, this indication of the person best qualified to be the biographer of a prince amongst poets would be judicious.'

It was not till Field Place felt the necessity of correcting the numerous misstatements about the man of genius by a complete and authoritative biography, that the largely employed lawyer declared his willingness to execute the difficult task, which had been deferred too long. Midway between sixty and seventy years of age, when he thus accepted the invitation of Sir Percy Florence and Lady Shelley, the man of many affairs, and an exacting avocation, did not set to work on the *Life* till nearly a quarter of a century had passed since the publication of the *New Monthly* Papers; till the poet had been dead nearly thirty-five years; till full forty-five years had passed since the poet, in the company of his future biographer, set their faces for London, on leaving University College, Oxford.

Though it took the outer world by surprise, the immediate result of the publication of Hogg's two volumes was less surprising to the literary coteries, and no matter of surprise whatever to the few members of those coteries, who, knowing that Hogg was a robust enemy of shams, knew that no biographer would satisfy Field Place, which should fail to accord with the straight-nosed pictures, and with the notion that Shelley was a being of stainless purity and angelic holiness.

If, in writing the *Life*, Hogg's first duty was to be thoughtful for the sensibilities of Field Place, his book must indeed be declared a bad one. Instead of giving readers the Shelley indicated by the frontispiece of the first volume, or the Shelley who, under auspicious circumstances might have been the Saviour of the World, or a Shelley who might have sobered down into a pheasant-shooting squire and Chairman of Quarter-Sessions, the biographer makes us acquainted with the wayward, freakish, impulsive, scarcely sane, and ever restless Shelley of the poet's early manhood,—the Shelley, whose great wit was divided from madness by a strangely thin partition ; the Shelley, whose earnestness was too often associated with perversity, whose winning candour was curiously allied with secretiveness, whose impulsive benevolence was perplexingly linked with indifference to the feelings and rights of particular individuals ; the Shelley, whose several amiable and generous traits were attended by qualities that were neither beneficent nor agreeable. Showing that this whimsical Shelley was a frequent utterer of untruths that were altogether or partly referable to delusions, Hogg also shows by evidence of the most conclusive kind that this perplexing Shelley could also utter untruths, knowing them to be untruths—was capable of telling fibs to escape a trivial inconvenience, —was capable of writing false and wheedling letters to get money, and of admitting with a singular, if not absolutely unique, shamelessness, that he had told a lie, or meant to tell a lie for a very slight reason.

No wonder that the biographer who dealt thus frankly with his friend's infirmities is distasteful to the enthusiasts of Mr. Buxton Forman's school. No wonder that his book was perused for the first time by Sir Percy Florence and Lady Shelley ' with the most painful feelings of dismay.' Their dissatisfaction with the biographer would have been more painful had all four volumes of the *Life* been published on the day, that saw the publication of the earlier half of the book. Fortunately for Sir Florence and Lady Shelley the biographer at the end of the second of the two published volumes was only coming to the part of the poet's story which they were especially desirous he should handle with extreme delicacy. There is much about William Godwin in the two volumes, and a little about his daughter. But the second volume closes at the moment when Shelley is only at the threshold of his passion for his familiar friend's sixteen-years-old child,—closes before he has told the ' marvellous tale' of his father's cruelty, and barbarous purpose of shutting him up in a madhouse, to the generous-hearted girl, in order to induce the naughty child to fly with him to the Continent in the company of her sister-by-affinity. It was obvious to Sir Percy Florence and Lady Shelley that they had chosen the wrong historian to write about Mary Godwin, the judicious treatment of whose scarcely edifying story was so needful for the honour of the Castle Goring Shelleys. It had been hoped by Field Place that Mr. Hogg would varnish ugly facts with specious phrases. Disappointed in this hope, it was obvious to Field Place that the indiscreet biographer must be sent about his business. Hogg having failed to write the *Life* into harmony with the pretty picture facing the title-page, as Arthur Pendennis wrote the verses to suit the picture of the country church, it was manifest to the authorities of Field Place that they must discharge their man of letters, and bide their time till they should find a fitter instrument and happier season for their purpose. This was done. Hogg was dismissed, and in these later years of grace Field Place has found in Mr. Anthony Froude a man of letters, capable of writing about the poet's flight with his intimate friend's sixteen-years-old daughter, as nothing worse than 'the sin of acting on emotional theories of liberty ;' capable of smiling at their concubinage as a pleasant passage of romance, because they were so young and enthusiastic.

Though a grievous injury was done to English literature when Hogg was treated in this manner, it must not be imagined that his book is devoid of serious faults. Containing numerous trivial inaccuracies, it contains also some grave blunders. The confusion of its materials may be compared to the state of disorder in which the author found his friend's room at the commencement of their acquaintance. The biographer was unwise to reproduce in the book his early Papers on *Shelley at Oxford* without first revising them carefully. Though he would have done ill to keep himself as much as possible out of view, and was right in regarding passages of his own story as part of his friend's story,—a part of it, moreover, that could not be omitted without serious injury to the biographical narrative,—he says far too much of himself. In some places, the biographer's egotism is grotesquely garrulous. It is no sufficient excuse for such egregious self-consciousness and self-intrusiveness, that the egotist is a droll, piquant, racy, exquisitely humorous egotist. None the less true, however, is it that,—their eccentricities and extravagancies notwithstanding,—the two volumes give us a substantially truthful view of Shelley in his youth and earlier manhood, and, in so doing, bring us face to face with the Real Shelley. No intelligent and impartial peruser of the two volumes ever closed them without feeling that Hogg's portraiture of Shelley is a performance, from whose lines no biographer of the poet can depart widely, without going widely astray.

There is no need to say more of the confusion, in which Hogg offered the excellent materials of his book to the world. But so much has been said about his dishonest treatment of letters, that some notice should be taken of his various ways of dealing with evidential documents.

It must be admitted that his printed transcripts of epistles are often inaccurate ; a considerable proportion of the inaccuracies being slips, for which the printer is not to be held accountable.

The letters are, in some cases, mis-dated, through the biographer's carelessness in taking a postal-date, or the date of an addressee's endorsement, as the date of the letter itself. Occasionally, also, he errs by giving, as an ascertained and exact date, what appears, on examination, to be nothing else than his own calculation of an approximate date.

Regardless of the paragraphical arrangement of a letter, when he is desirous of saving space, he does not hesitate to bring several written paragraphs into a single printed one,—an unobjectionable practice, when it does not affect the force of the written words, in the case of letters that are not exhibited in type as examples of epistolary style.

It is his practice to condense a letter, by picking out its most important passages, and putting them together (without points indicative of omitted words), as though they followed one another on the written paper, precisely as they appear on the printed page:—a most objectionable practice.

After condensing a letter in this manner, he sometimes exhibits the abridgment in a way to make readers think it an entire letter:—also a most objectionable practice.

In the case of one most important and interesting letter (of whose contents more will be said in a subsequent chapter), he changes names for purposes of concealment and mystification; but a fair consideration of his reasons for thus tampering with an important evidential writing, acquits him of dishonourable conduct in the curious and suspicious business.

Attention must also be called to the grounds for the gravest charge, that has been preferred against Hogg's editorial treatment of evidential writings. He has been declared guilty of altering such evidences by inserting in his printed transcripts entire sentences that do not appear in the manuscripts; and it cannot be denied that there are *primâ-facie* grounds for the serious accusation. On careful examination, some of the printed transcripts of the *Life* are found to contain passages (some of them long passages of several sentences) that do not appear in the originals of the transcribed documents. As these passages appear without any typographical indication that they are no part of the original writings, and have every *primâ-facie* show of being part of the transcripts in which they are inserted, they may be fairly described as 'interpolations.' It is not, therefore, surprising that Hogg has been charged with one of the gravest forms of editorial dishonesty. The reader's attention has already been called to one of these editorial notes,—a note printed, indeed, within brackets, but followed by no indicatory initials. In subsequent chapters, examples will be given of similar notes, printed without either brackets or initials. For the present, it is enough to say they may be found in several of Hogg's printed copies of documents. How can they be accounted for in a way, to clear the biographer of reasonable suspicion of misrepresenting the contents of evidential writings?

Instead of making his editorial comments on his transcribed documents in paginal foot-notes, it was Hogg's most objectionable and dangerous practice to insert them in the body of the transcripts. Of course, in doing so, it was his rule to put his initials after each editorial note, and to place each 'initialed' note between brackets. Thus exhibited between brackets, with the biographer's initials put immediately before the second bracket, an editorial note is recognized at a glance by the most careless reader, as no part of the transcribed document, but a mere editorial elucidation of the preceding passage. Printed as Hogg intended them to be, no one of these editorial notes could have been mistaken, even momentarily, for a part and parcel of the writing, in whose body it was inserted. But, unfortunately, for the biographer's reputation, these notes were not always printed as he intended them to be printed. In some cases the first bracket, in some cases both brackets, are omitted, though the initials are inserted. There are also cases where a scrap of editorial explanation is found without either brackets or initials. As Hogg was no regular author, but a slap-dash rough-and-ready legal draughtsman (plying his pen, in his proper vocation, with perfect confidence in the ability of solicitors and law-stationers to correct the literal slips of his compositions), he wrote copy for the press just as he slapt and dashed copy off for his ordinary clients. A careless writer, he was also a careless corrector of proofs. Hence it came to pass that editorial notes, which he meant to bracket and initial (notes, which, of course, should have been made at the foot, instead of in the body of his pages), came under the public eye without the brackets and initials, that should, and would, have distinguished them at a glance from the printed matter they were intended to elucidate. That this is the explanation of the interpolations in Hogg's transcripts, appears from—(1), the biographer's practice of peppering his transcripts with initialed and bracketed scraps of editorial comment; (2), the grammatical construction that distinguishes the interpolations from the text in which they are set; (3), the absolute inefficacy of the inserted passages for any end a dishonest interpolator could have in view; and (4), the conclusive fact, that, whilst it is a mere perplexing disturbance to the narrative, so long as it is taken for part of the transcript, each of the interpolations becomes an intelligible and more or less serviceable comment on the context, as soon as the reader puts it into brackets, and deals with it as an editorial note. In respect to these interpolations, and also in respect to all the other errors which the biographer's enemies are pleased to regard as deliberate misstatements, Hogg must be acquitted wholly of dishonest purpose. Had he been duly mindful for brackets and initials, the interpolations, of which so much has been said to his discredit, would never have exposed him to a suspicion, much less to a direct imputation, of editorial knavery..

It does not follow, however, that the *Life* is disfigured by no statements to be fairly rated as deliberate misrepresentations. Resenting the calumnies, that have been poured on Hogg since his death; resenting more especially the malice of those, who would fain extort evidence to the biographer's infamy from what is mere evidence of one of Shelley's wildest and most unwholesome delusions; I wish I were in a position to declare the volumes altogether pure of falsehood. It would have been better for Hogg's character in his life's closing years, and far better for his posthumous fame, had he in his mature age written with

candour and justice of the incidents that resulted in his academic disgrace, and of the individuals who only did their clear duty in bidding
him and Shelley leave Oxford.   But whilst lacking the courage to be
truthful about matters even more discreditable to himself than to his
friend, he wanted the highmindedness that would have enabled him to
speak fairly of the Master and Fellows, whom he remembered to his last
hour with a rancorous animosity that was singular in the man of usually
even and placable disposition.   The story of his academic disgrace was
one of the very few subjects, on which the man of imperturbable temper
and adamantine patience could not keep his temper.   Whilst throwing
off the papers for the *New Monthly*, Hogg surrendered himself the
more completely to his animosity against the Oxford dons, because he
could persuade himself that, in giving vent to his personal resentment,
he was only vindicating the honour of his friend.   The consequence
was an account of Shelley's academic misadventure, so veined with misrepresentation and loaded with untruth, as to defeat the purpose for
which it was written.   It is needless to say that the Shelleyan enthusiasts
have never protested against the egregious perversity and falseness of
this portion of the biography.   Attacking the book for its inaccuracy,
in respect to those of its passages that are substantially honest, they
have adopted as good history those of its pages that are distinctly
untruthful.   That Field Place saw nothing to censure in the faultiest
part of the biographer's performance appears from the way, in which
Lady Shelley reproduced some of its most glaring misrepresentations
in her *Shelley's Memorials*.

CHAPTER X.

Hogg's Toryism—Shelley's Liberalism—In Hogg's Rooms—Shelley's Looks and Voice—Patron and Idolater—The Ways of Passing Time—Hogg's Reminiscences—Nocturnal Readings and Conversations—Country about Oxford—Pistol Practice—Playing with Paper Boats—Windmill and Plashy Meadow—The Horror of it—Posthumous Fragments of Margaret Nicholson—University Tattle and Laughter—Eccentric Inseparables—Pond under Shotover Hill—Pacing 'The High'—Dons' Civility to Shelley—His Incivility to Dons—Uninteresting Stones and Dull People—'Partly True and Partly False'—The Fiery Hun!—'My Dear Boy'—Shelley offers his Sister to Hogg in Marriage—Hogg entertains the Proposal—End of Term.

THOUGH I have spoken warmly of Hogg's general honesty, and resent the calumnies that have been rained down upon him in the grave, I must admit that Hogg's friendship was so injurious that it might almost be called disastrous to the Oxonian Shelley. Though the youth who had distinguished himself by unruliness at Eton, whose views of life had come to him chiefly from morbid romances, whose natural perversity disposed him to revolt against control of every kind, was far more likely to abuse the liberty and privileges of the academic course than to employ them to his advantage, the conditions are conceivable under which he would have passed through the University with honour —or at least without discredit. It depended chiefly on the friendships he should form immediately upon coming into residence at his college, whether, taking a new moral and intellectual 'departure' he would disappoint the evil promise of his Eton days, or whether he would persist in the perversities in which he had been encouraged by Dr. Lind. For his welfare in the University, it was needful that the young man, so sympathetic and fervid, but absolutely wanting in common sense and mental sobriety, should have for his especial friend a man devoid of moral levity, and should live in a set of young men who, together with tastes congenial to his own, possessed the steadiness of intellect and temper, calculated to restrain and correct the erratic forces of his peculiar nature ;—young men who, by their example, rather than by their words, would dispose him to regard his University with pride, his College with affection, his tutors with loyalty. It was a great misfortune for Shelley that, on coming into residence, he found no such companions, and took for his chief associate,—indeed, his only familiar associate, —a young man, whose intellectual vigour and robustness were curiously allied with an intellectual levity and a cynical sprightliness, that rendered him a most baneful companion for a stripling of Shelley's equally fervid and wayward disposition.

A stronger contrast of character is seldom witnessed than the contrast to be noticed in the two undergraduates, who, through meeting casually, and talking together freely at the same dinner table 'in hall,' formed at once a close friendship, that (with the exception of the brief period of estrangement, which renders the story of their intercourse more singular and interesting), endured till death divided them for ever. Whilst Shelley was a Liberal, whose liberalism even at the commencement of this friendship was revolutionary in its aims and enthusiasm, Hogg was a caricature of Eldonian Toryism, who held Dissenters in disdain, snapt his fingers at Catholic Emancipation, and smiled contemptuously at every reference to Irish grievances. In political sentiment the Hogg, who wrote the *New Monthly* Papers on ' Shelley at Oxford' differed from the Oxonian Hogg, only as the Toryism of a middle-aged man differs from the Toryism of a boy. The election that ' had just taken place,' when he entered University College was a choice he disapproved ; though animosity against the Lord Chancellor, who deprived Shelley of his children, and animosity against those of the Chancellor's supporters who expelled Shelley and Shelley's friend from Oxford, caused him in later time to write of Eldon, as though the Chief of the Law were greatly inferior in culture and mental dignity to his victor in the academic conflict. Doubtless, on coming to Oxford immediately after the election of Lord Grenville, the young gentleman declared his disapproval of the triumph of the blue-and-buff faction :—not passionately, for passion seldom stirred his breast ; but with much droll ridicule of a business so eminently ridiculous, for even from his boyhood Mr. Hogg (a born humourist and cynic) turned everything, even his own religious convictions, to jest.

Whilst the Oxonian Shelley, already a half-fledged republican, talked tenderly of the poor and the populace, Hogg ever a provincial aristocrat (and by no means devoid of provincial vulgarity), regarded the populace with disgust, and maintained that all the poor wanted was to be kept in their proper places and to their proper work. Ever impatient, Shelley was fervid as fire itself, whilst Hogg, from youth to old age, was remarkable for imperturbable temper and adamantine patience, on every question that had no reference to his academic misadventure. Coming from the North of England to Oxford in the autumn of 1809, some weeks before he donned cap and gown in February, 1810, Hogg entered the University with the purpose of taking honours, and had acquired the reputation of 'a reading man' before the long vacation of 1810.

Coming to Oxford for residence in the autumn of 1810, when Hogg had acquired status and character amongst the younger members of his academic house, the sensitive, simple, never worldly-wise Shelley entered University College with a strong appetite for general knowledge, and an intention to peruse many books on many subjects for his own amusement, but with no ambition for academic honours, no intention of competing for them, no purpose of becoming, in the academic and limited sense of the term, 'a reading man.' Hogg had not been three months in University College, before the tutors saw he meant to put his name in a 'first class.' Shelley, on the other hand, had not been three weeks in College before the tutors saw he meant to go out with the 'pass men,' and were doubtful whether he would take a degree.

As it must be held in some measure accountable for the influence he acquired over Shelley, readers must assign considerable weight to the fact that Hogg was qualified by several matters—his seniority on the College books, priority in residence, greater knowledge of the University, higher status in the lecture-rooms,—to play the part of academic superior to his new acquaintance. Superlatively trivial to men of *the* world, the matters that gave Hogg this precedence and superiority over Shelley in University College, are no light affairs in the small world of the University, the still smaller world of a single College. The sensitive Shelley would not have presumed to invite Hogg to his rooms after their first meeting 'in hall.' It was for Hogg to pay the compliment to the freshman in his first term of residence; and no old University man will doubt that Shelley felt he received a considerable attention, when so notable a personage amongst the first-year's men as Mr. Hogg said to him, 'Come and have wine at my rooms.'

As Hogg and Shelley sat over their wine in consequence of this invitation, the host took an opportunity to examine the aspect of his new acquaintance more minutely, and to observe that his girlish pink-and-white complexion was much freckled. 'His complexion,' says Hogg, 'was delicate, and almost feminine, of the purest red and white; yet he was tanned and freckled by exposure to the sun, having passed the autumn, as he said, in shooting;' a piece of description that is referred to by 'the Shelleyan enthusiasts' as an example of Hogg's imaginativeness. No one (if we may credit Shelleyan enthusiasts) but a suspiciously imaginative historian would have ventured to say he could remember, after twenty years, the sun-spots of an old college friend's complexion. I venture to say that the disfigurement is a good example of the kind of things, likely to live in the memory of certain observers.

In respect to a part of what he says of the freckles in Shelley's skin, Hogg is corroborated in a remarkable manner by Medwin, who (his inaccuracy notwithstanding) was generally right in the main facts, and not always wrong in the details of his statements. 'He,' Medwin says of Shelley's shooting in the winter of 1809 and the autumn of 1810, 'had during September often carried a gun in his father's preserves; Sir Timothy being a keen sportsman, and Shelley himself an excellent shot, for I well remember on one day in the winter of 1809, when we were out together, his killing, at three successive shots, three snipes, to my great astonishment and envy, at the tail of the pond in front of Field Place.' The three successive and successful shots are good examples of the small incidents likely to live in a sportsman's memory. What old sportsman, with snow upon his head, cannot remember quite as vividly just as small matters, that occurred long since on the moors or during a run across country?

Another of the small matters of Hogg's *Life*, that unquestionably lived in his memory. He remembered how, in the early morning at the close of Shelley's first visit to his rooms, after 'lighting' the poet downstairs with the stump of a candle, he 'soon heard him running through the quiet quadrangle in the still night,'—adding in the words of truth's own music, 'That sound became afterwards so familiar to my ear, that I still seem to hear Shelley's hasty steps.'

The evidence is clear that whilst Shelley, the freshman (ever a feminine creature on one side of his nature), regarded Hogg

as an exemplary scholar, great thinker, and worthy leader,—
the self-sufficient, hard-headed, cynical, humorous youngster
from the North of England regarded Shelley as a delightful
plaything, a brilliant absurdity, a piquant joke. When the
' reading man,' who rose from his bed every morning as the
clock struck seven, had spent the first six hours of the day in
strenuous study and attendance at lectures, he went to his
' young friend ' for diversion, never before one o'clock, oftener
when the clock had struck two p.m. It amused the north-
countryman, as he lay back in the easiest chair of his young
friend's well-furnished and disorderly room, to watch his young
friend work fiercely at the handle of his electrical machine,
till the crackling and snapping sparks flew forth viciously ; to
see the youngster's long locks bristle and dishevel into wildness,
surpassing their usual disorder ; to observe the animation of
his countenance, the singular brightness of his prominent blue
eyes, and to hear him talk volubly for half-hours together, in
the thin shrill voice that often screamed as harshly as the
voice of a highly excited parrot, about the blessings that would
flow from chemistry to the ill-fed, ill-clad, ill-treated toilers
of the human race.

The excruciating voice, that was so 'intolerably shrill, harsh, '
and discordant ' to the north-countryman's sensitive ear at the
opening of his acquaintance with this eccentric and delightfully
unconventional undergraduate, became less disagreeable, even
in its sharpest notes, to the critical auditor as it grew more
familiar. Moreover, the voice was not always at torture-pitch.
It was only when he was under excitement that the youngster
afflicted his hearers by ' speaking ' (to use Peacock's description
of the poet's vocal peculiarity) ' in sharp fourths, the most un-
pleasing sequence of sound that can fall on the human ear.'
When he spoke calmly, the voice was not otherwise than
agreeable; when he read poetry that delighted him, the voice
became musical, ' was good ' (says Peacock) ' both in tune and
in tone ; was low and soft, but clear, distinct, and expressive.'
Hogg had not known his young friend many days without
discovering that the voice could be no less melodious and charming than harsh and screeching. In these vocal characteristics,
as in so many other matters, Shelley resembled Byron, who
used to shriek and scream in his frequent paroxysms of hysterical
rage, and yet had a voice sweeter even than his verse, when he

gossiped contentedly with women, and prattled lovingly with little children.

It is not wonderful that the self-sufficient, critical, humorous Hogg's interest in his young friend was composed equally of amusement and admiration, cynical curiosity and amiable contempt; a disposition to love him, and an even stronger disposition to laugh at him. There was so much to admire and love in the eccentric boy, who overflowed with pity for the miseries of mankind, and prattled with almost childish communicativeness about his cousin Harriett's beauty and his sister Elizabeth's perfections; so much that was inexpressibly ludicrous in the youthful chemist and scientific enthusiast who, believing in the 'Elixir Vitæ,' was at the same time an astronomer and astrologer—in the sceptical philosopher who, equally credulous and incredulous, spoke no less reverentially of dreams than irreverentially of the Scriptural miracles, could embrace any fable provided it were not one of 'the delusions' of Christianity, and had no doubt he ought to believe in ghosts, whilst deeming it questionable whether he ought to believe in God. Under Hogg's tuition this last question was erased from the list of Shelley's moot points. Having repudiated Christ at Eton, the freshman had not entered on his second term of residence at Oxford without finding himself under 'the necessity' of repudiating God; and, though he would probably have come to this conclusion by himself somewhat later in his career, it is certain he came to it the sooner for Hogg's assistance and encouragement.

It is uncertain what Hogg's real sentiments on matters pertaining to religion were at the close of 1810 and 1811. In later time he was one of those Tories who reflected with pride on the support their party had given Bolingbroke, and on the protection it had afforded Hume:—one of those Tories, of gentle birth and culture, who deemed it their peculiar privilege to think and say amongst themselves whatever they pleased on ecclesiastical polemics, provided they did nothing to weaken the popular belief in the doctrines of the Church of England, as by law established —doctrines that were so eminently conducive to social order, by disposing persons of the less fortunate classes to do their duty submissively in that state of life to which God had been pleased to call them. Whilst commiserating Shelley for being, by education and familiar conditions, one of those 'buff-and-blue folks' who naturally could not speak their own minds freely lest their words should be misconstrued into treason and infidelity, and could not, therefore, carry the poet safe through the difficulties arising out of his ill-advised publications, Mr. Hogg, the mature biographer, observed :—

'As to my own family, and my immediate connexions, we were all persons whose first toast after dinner was invariably " Church and State!" warm partisans of William Pitt, of the highest Church, and of the high Tory party; consequently we were anything but intolerant, we were above suspicion and ordinances. . . . My relatives felt that they had margin enough, plenty of sea-room, that whatever might be said or done, their good principles could not be doubted, but would always carry them through. . . . If the *Age of Reason* had been republished by myself or one of my earliest friends, the world would have supposed that it was put forth merely to show the utter futility and impotence and vanity of the author's arguments.'

The self-sufficient young gentleman, who quickened Shelley's steps to his final academic disaster, was the veritable father of the man who wrote thus lightly of what Tories (provided they were highly-educated gentlemen) might do within the lines of Free Thought. From strong, but not conclusive evidence, I think that in his Oxford days he might have summarized his creed by saying: 'There's nothing new, and there is nothing true ; and it don't much sinnify, provided we don't let vulgar people find it out.' Whatever his belief on sacred questions, he never allowed so immaterial a consideration to affect his course in discussion. Speaking first on one side of a question, and then on the other side, and then for a third time just to show he had been equally and utterly wrong in his arguments on both sides, Hogg always played the part Shelley wished him to play. What Shelley said, Hogg contradicted—never angrily (for his temper was imperturbable), never impatiently (for his patience was adamantine), never discourteously (for he was courteous by nature, and on principle), often lightly and with fine raillery (for he was a born humourist), always considerately (for the reading man delighted in his play-fellow). It was thus the two young men wrangled together amiably, keeping the ball of doubt flying to and fro between them till the one or the other sent it flying out of bounds. A game often congenial to clever young-sters, it was a game especially congenial to these two under-graduates; all the more so, because Shelley was altogether in earnest, Hogg altogether at play.

If the reading-man had reason to congratulate himself on finding so good a playmate for his hours of relaxation, the freshman may well have been flattered by the attention of a fellow-student, so considerably his senior in academic status and worldly wisdom. With all his imperfections, Hogg had no vice or fault to repel his young friend. Shelley, who would have held aloof from an undergraduate with a propensity to any kind of dissoluteness, found in Hogg a man no less temperate in eating and drinking than himself, no less incapable of uttering or relishing an obscene jest, no less averse to gambling with dice and cards, no less disdainful of the ordinary dissipations of academic idlers. On the other hand, Hogg's natural endowments and intellectual attainments were especially calculated to commend him to Shelley's confidence, and render him the object of Shelley's admiration. Shelley had enough of classical taste and culture to respect the reading-man for being so greatly his superior in Latin and Greek, and to be delighted at the moderate praise accorded by so considerable a scholar to his performances in Latin prose and Latin verse. But classical studies were not the only studies to interest Hogg. The reading-man delighted in English literature, amused himself occasionally by writing English verse, and had some thought of writing a book of poetry or romantic fiction, when he should have taken his 'first class.' Instead of being indifferent to his young friend's literary ambition, Hogg participated in it. The youngster who had already published a novel (what a novel it was!), and the young man who was thinking of writing a novel, were, in their simple, boyish way of regarding the matter, kindred spirits and men of letters. Their association at college would prove the first stage of a life-long friendship!

The relation in which Steerforth and Copperfield stand to one another in the earlier stages of their friendship is comparable with the relation in which Hogg and Shelley stood to one another at University College. Hogg patronized Shelley very much as Steerforth patronizes Copperfield; and just as Copperfield idolizes Steerforth, Shelley idolized Hogg. At the present time one may well smile at these relations between the humorous north-countryman, who never became anything more than a successful chamber-barrister, and the poet, whose name will never perish from the story of his race. But it is no unusual thing for time and the development of mental forces to reverse the relations of ancient comrades; placing the former idolater on the idol's pedestal, and converting the receiver of homage into the worshiper. Whilst the Hogg of University College gave promise of being a very remarkable personage, Shelley had given no promise of becoming a supremely great poet—on the contrary, had raised expectations that he would be a very contemptible poetaster. In 1810–11 Shelley was the one of these two friends to render worship, Hogg the one to receive it.

In the earlier weeks of their friendship, Hogg and Shelley used to exchange visits; but soon Shelley's room was the usual meeting-place of the two friends—the choice of the room being made partly (Hogg says wholly) because Shelley, still delighting in his scientific toys, liked 'to start from his seat at any moment' and play with his air-pump and electrical machine; and partly (we may surmise) because the hard reader wished to guard his severely studious hours from the intrusion of his choicest and most particular friend. But though they never met before luncheon, save when they passed one another at morning chapel, or on their ways to and from different lectures, Shelley and Hogg lived together as completely as they would have done, had they been 'chums' sharing a single set of rooms, like the 'chums' of older academic time.

Meeting at one or two p.m., they seldom separated before one or two a.m. In foul weather they read, talked, wrote letters in each other's company, without going out of college. They read together Locke's *Essay concerning Human Understanding*, Hume's *Essays*, several of Plato's Dialogues (by means of Dacier's translations), several of the works of Scotch metaphysicians, not worthy of being mentioned in the same sentence with Hume, treatises of Logic, and divers English poets and Latin poets. But Plato, Locke, and Hume were the authors who held their attention most often, stirred their minds most deeply, provoking them at every turn to pass from study to talk, and argue out the questions raised by printed text. Of Locke's and Hume's writings they made careful notes, that in some cases were precise abstracts of the author's several arguments on a question of supreme importance. That Hume whetted Shelley's appetite for sceptical literature may be inferred from the note, in which (on November 11th, 1810, *Sunday*) he begged Stockdale to look out for a translation into Greek, Latin, or any of the European languages, of a certain ' Hebrew essay, demonstrating that the Christian religion is false, that was mentioned in one of the numbers of the *Christian Observer*, last spring, by a clergyman, as an unanswerable, yet sophistical argument.'

When the weather was fair, or not so foul as absolutely to prohibit exercise in the open air, the two friends went for walks in the country,—sometimes for very long walks, that kept them for four, or even six hours, in the open air. Excellent pedestrians, they delighted in walking; and Shelley was never happier than when he and his peculiar comrade started out for the country in the early afternoon for an unusally long walk, with the intention of 'cutting hall' (the hour for the college-dinner in those days was 4 p.m.), and returning in the evening, for the equally welcome and needful supper, ordered to be ready for them on their return to the poet's first-floor rooms,* in the principal quadrangle of their college. In these long walks it was that the two inseparable undergraduates walked repeatedly over and about Shotover Hill; threaded meandering ways through Bagley Wood; traversed the farmstead in which the furious dog seized with his teeth, and almost tore off, the tail of the poet's brand-new blue coat; and leaped through the gap of an aged fence into the trim garden,—leafless on that mid-winter day, had it not been for the evergreen shrubs; flowerless, had it not been for the brumal flowers here and there faintly visible; but still trim, daintily kept, and eloquent of peaceful-ness, seclusion, and human care,—the garden where the poet gathered the first of those seeds of pathos and delicate senti-ment, that slowly germinating in his fancy, bore fruit long years afterwards in *The Sensitive Plant*.

It was in Hogg's memory, when he wrote the *New Monthly* sketches, how, after retreating from this tranquil spot as suddenly as he had entered it, Shelley spoke of the sacredness of the spot, that of course owed its attractiveness to the minis-trations of feminine goodness and beauty; and how, after making it the haunt of a single enchantress, he changed the picture so far as to give her a sister, fair and sensitive as herself, for the sharer of her gentle toil and pure enjoyment of the garden in brighter seasons.

* Hogg describes Shelley's rooms as 'being in the corner next the hall of the principal quadrangle of the University College.' 'They are,' he continues, ' on the first floor, and on the right of the entrance, but by reason of the turn in the stairs, when you reach them, they will be upon your left hand.'—Hogg's *Life*, v. 1, p. 67.

In another of these walks, the inseparable undergraduates came, in a desolate part of the country, on a little girl, so young and small that she might almost be called a nursling, who had been placed there in her weariness to await the return of her mother and some other women. Having waited till she imagined herself deserted, the cold, hungry, miserable child was weeping and wailing piteously, when Shelley accosted her (ugly little brat though she was), won something of her confidence, and induced her to accompany him to the nearest dwelling, where he restored her to comparative contentment with a bowl of warm bread and milk.

'It was,' says Hogg, ' a strange spectacle to watch the young poet, whilst . . . . holding the wooden bowl in one hand, and the wooden spoon in the other, and kneeling on his left knee, that he might more certainly attain to her mouth, he urged and encouraged the torpid and timid child to eat. The hot milk was agreeable to the girl, and its effects were salutary ; but she was obviously uneasy at the detention. Her uneasiness increased, and ultimately prevailed ; we returned with her to the place where we had found her, Shelley bearing the bowl of milk in his hand, even to the spot where the child was already being sought for by her mother and friends.'

To discredit this story, and press it into evidence that Hogg was an egregious liar, your true Shelleyan enthusiast does not hesitate in crying triumphantly, ' Is it possible for any man, after a lapse of two-and-twenty years, to remember whether his friend on a particular occasion knelt on his right knee or his left knee ?' Yet I conceive no judicial reader will deny that the story bears the brand of substantial truthfulness; that the incident was just the incident to live in the spectator's memory ; that the story accords with what has come to us from other sources of information respecting Shelley's womanly concern for children,—the feminine tenderness with which he nursed little Allegra in her infancy, and his own babes in their times of sickness.

Other pleasant examples are given by Hogg of the fine human interest Shelley took in the humble, and sometimes unlovely, children they encountered in their pedestrian excursions round about Oxford,—such children as the gipsy girl whom he visited in her parental tent, and her brother, the little gipsy boy, into whose hands he rolled the big orange, which he had brought out with him from Oxford, for his own refreshment during a long walk. It may serve the purpose of Hogg's detractors to decry these stories as manifest fabrications; but to me they are evidential of Hogg's substantial truthfulness, because whilst they commemorate just such characteristic trifles as are apt to survive far more important matters in our re-collections of the dead who were dear to us long ago, they are the mere trifles which no fraudulent tale-wright would think of inventing. Only to the narrator, who remembered them feelingly, would such trifles appear worthy of record.

The walks in the country round about Oxford took the longer time, because of two of Shelley's favourite diversions —his delight in pistol-practice, and the pleasure he found in folding and twisting pieces of paper into little boats, and putting them afloat on the surface of pond or streamlet.

His fondness for the former amusement affords another of his numerous resemblances to Byron. Like the Byron of Southwell and Cambridge, the Shelley of Field Place and Oxford, seized every convenient occasion for blazing away with powder and ball, and perfecting himself in the use of 'the hair-trigger,'—a practice that would have been more remarkable in each of the poets, had it not been usual in the days of duelling for youngsters to regard pistol-practice as an important part of the education of every gentleman, who in his way through life might at any moment be invited to exchange shots at ten paces. To the biographer of the two poets, their fondness for this military pastime is the more interesting, because they lived to fire away at the same mark day after day during their residence at Pisa. That the sport in which he delighted in the last year of his life was one of Shelley's favourite amusements at Oxford, we know from Hogg, who tells how the youthful poet of 'mild aspect and pacific habits,' used to equip himself for a country walk, with a pair of duelling pistols and a good supply of powder and ball. On coming to a solitary spot during a rural ramble, it was his use to fix a card, or some other suitable object, upon a tree or embankment, and fire away at it till his ammunition was exhausted. On one occasion he induced Hogg to have a shot at a slab of wood, about as big as a hearth-rug. Taking the pistol, Hogg discharged it at an unusally long range for pistol-practice, and sent his bullet into the very centre of the wooden target. Shelley was amazed and delighted at the goodness of his friend's firing, and running to the board gazed intently at the place of the bullet's lodgment. After satisfying himself that the ball was in the very middle of the board, he more than once measured the distance from the target to the spot where the trigger was pulled by the man, who had never before fired a pistol loaded with ball. 'I never knew any one so prone to admire as he was, in whom the principle of veneration was so strong,' Hogg remarks, in reference to the poet's expressions of surprise and delight at the excellence of his comrade's address with the weapon.

One may well smile at this tribute to the reverential disposition of the Oxonian, who despised the tutors of his college for their dullness, spoke contemptuously of his grandfather, held his father up to ridicule, wrote disdainfully of his mother's mental narrowness, and had fought the whole tribe of his Eton masters, from Dr. Keate to Mr. Bethell. But the tribute was not altogether undeserved. All through life Shelley valued men for their worth, and honoured superior men ungrudgingly for their superiority, provided they were not placed in authority over him, or had not provoked him to antagonism. Had Hogg been his tutor, Shelley would soon have discovered flaws in his friend's character, and unsoundness in his attainments,— would have found him overbearing, presumptuous, hypocritical, tyrannical.

Finding the pistol-practice lessen his enjoyment of their country walks, Hogg, with some difficulty, induced Shelley to relinquish the diversion; but the north-countryman was unsuccessful in his attempts to wean the poet from the other pastime, in which he delighted so keenly. On coming to a large pond in their rambles, Shelley, indifferent to the coldness of wind, even though it were a 'cutting north-easter,' drew up, took paper from his pocket, twisted it into a boat, and floated it out upon the glassy surface. If the frail bark succumbed quickly to the forces of wind and water, another bark of the same description was speedily fitted and launched for the perilous voyage. When the paper-boat was wafted safely to the opposite shore, no child could have been more delighted than the Oxonian student at so trivial a cause of satisfaction. Sometimes the player at this curious game floated several paper-boats out upon the water as nearly as possible at the same moment, and then watched the fortunes of his fleet with the liveliest interest. After leaving Oxford, Shelley often amused himself in the same manner, continuing to play thus childishly at the water's brink, till he had made away with all his provision of waste-paper to the last scrap. Even then he could not desist from the fascinating pastime; but would prolong his enjoyment with the sacrifice of letters written by his dearest friends, and fly-leaves torn from volumes that he had in his pockets. It was told of him for the first time by an imaginative humorist, and has been often repeated for true history by dullards, incapable of recognizing and appreciating a humorous invention, that on one occasion after consuming in this way all his store of comparatively valueless pieces of paper, he manufactured a toy-ship out of a bank-post bill for fifty pounds, which he committed to the water of the Round Pond in Kensington Gardens, when the miniature lake was more than usually agitated by a breeze from the north-east. 'The story, of course,' says Hogg, 'is mythic fable, but it aptly portrays the dominion of a singular and most unaccountable passion over the mind of an enthusiast.'

The pond at the foot of Shotover Hill, lying on the left of the pedestrian about to make the ascent, was one of the waters near which Hogg (of the adamantine patience) was often constrained to wait, whilst Shelley folded and twisted scraps of paper into boats, with fingers empurpled by the cold. By that same water the poet used to linger till dusk, 'repeating verses aloud, or earnestly discussing themes that had no connexion with surrounding objects.' Ever and again on these occasions the curious boy, who developed into so marvellous a man, would throw a stone as far away from himself as possible into the pond, and then exult in the splash and disturbance of the usually tranquil waters. Hogg could also remember how his friend, with the blue eyes and disorderly hair, used to split the slaty stones into thin and flat pieces, with which he would gravely make ducks-and-drakes on the water's surface.

That Shelley delighted in the scenery of the neighbourhood of Oxford we know from Hogg's assurances. That the scenes, which delighted him in 1810-11, lived in his memory we know from the poem that was in the main an outgrowth of his recollections of the quiet garden, to which reference has just been made; and from the way in which he used in later years to dream of one particular bit of Oxfordshire landscape.

'I have,' (Shelley wrote in the *Speculations on Metaphysics*, just five years after this Michaelmas Term), 'beheld scenes, with the intimate and unaccountable connexion of which with the obscure parts of my own nature, I have been irresistibly impressed. I have beheld a scene which has produced no unusual effect on my thoughts. After the lapse of many years, I have dreamed of this scene. It has hung on my memory, it has haunted my thoughts, at intervals, with the pertinacity of an object connected with human affections. I have visited this scene again. Neither the dream could be dissociated from the landscape, nor the landscape from the dream, nor feelings, such as neither singly could have awakened, from both. But the most remarkable event of this nature, which ever occurred to me, happened five years ago at Oxford. I was walking with a friend, in the neighbourhood of that city, engaged in earnest and interesting conversation. We suddenly turned the corner of a lane, and the view, which its high banks and hedges had concealed, presented itself. The view consisted of a windmill, standing in one among many plashy meadows, inclosed with stone walls ; the irregular and broken ground, between the wall and the road on which we stood ; a long low hill behind the windmill, and a grey covering of uniform cloud spread over the evening sky. It was that season when the last leaf had just fallen from the scant and stunted ash. The scene surely was a common scene ; the season and the hour little calculated to kindle lawless thought ; it was a tame uninteresting assemblage of objects, such as would drive the imagination for refuge in serious and sober talk, to the evening fireside, and the dessert of winter fruits and wine. The effect which it produced in me was not such as could have been expected. I suddenly remembered to have seen that exact scene in some dream of long ——

' Here I was obliged to leave off, overcome by thrilling horror.'

To this extraordinary revelation of one of the innermost chambers of a human soul by the soul's own self, Mrs. Shelley long after her husband's death appended this note :—

' I remember well his coming to me from writing it, pale and agitated, to seek refuge in conversation from the fearful emotions it excited. No man, as these fragments prove, had such keen sensations as Shelley. His nervous temperament was wound up by the delicacy of his health to an intense degree of sensibility, and while his active mind pondered for ever upon, and drew conclusions from, his sensations, his reveries increased their vivacity, till they mingled with, and were one with thought, and both became absorbing and tumultuous, even to physical pain.'

Why this horror, that caused Shelley to drop the pen, at this recollection of a common-place bit of landscape, justly styled ' a tame and uninteresting assemblage of objects,' beheld by him for the first time just five years ago ;—no, not this horror *at* the recollection of so tame a scene, but this horror *at* recollecting how often the uninteresting scene had recurred to him in his dreams? Those who would know the Real Shelley, whose long locks, peculiar dress, and eccentric aspect, were matters of tattle and laughter in the common-rooms of the colleges in 1810-11, should ponder this self-revelation of Shelley's own soul, and should also take heed of his widow's note upon it. Let readers recall what they have been told of the way in which Byron's memory, sensibility, and imagination acted and inter-acted upon one another; the memory stirring the sensibility, the sensibility quickening the imagination, the imagination stimulating the memory again and again, till the recollections of old impressions far surpassed the original impressions in vividness and intensity; and let them then observe how Shelley was similarly constituted, with a memory singularly retentive of particular impressions, a sensibility (apt to be roused to morbid activity by these recollected impressions), and an imagination no less quick at the instance of sensibility to intensify the pictures of memory. It was thus that the tame scene, so clearly and deeply printed in his mind as to be repeatedly offered by memory to his re-awakening consciousness, acquired a vividness that was in itself terrifying. But the terror begotten of this vividness was not the terror that made the poet drop his pen. Whilst his sensibility was being stirred to morbid and distressing activity by recollection and fancy, he was suddenly surprised by remembering how repeatedly the same tame scene had come back to him in dreams,—*i.e.* at the moment of the re-awakening of consciousness,—and in his agitation, heightened by perplexity at so singular a fact, the surprise affected him with horror, even as any surprise (one that is the merest trifle to a cool and self-possessed mind)—a surprise arising from the rustling of a leaf, the echo of a footfall, the shadow of a spray by moonlight,—is apt to plunge the agitated and unbalanced mind into the Horror of Perplexity.

Happy in themselves, Hogg and Shelley did not care to be happy with other undergraduates, either of their own college or of the other colleges. A few old Etonians, belonging to other colleges, occasionally visited University College, to see the whilom Atheist of their former school; but though Shelley was civil to them, and on the eve of his abrupt withdrawal from the University paid Halliday a farewell call, he showed no disposition to be intimate with them. Three or four other undergraduates, to whom the supremely self-sufficient Mr. Hogg refers loftily as harmless and inoffensive persons, also found themselves now and then in the young poet's rooms; but no cordial pressure was put upon them to come oftener. Mr. Hogg and the freshman were sufficient unto themselves.

Necessarily known, under these circumstances, within their own college as 'the Inseparables,' the two close friends were also known throughout the University as 'the Inseparables.' How could it be otherwise, when they were seen by walking men and riding men, day after day (weather permitting) walking along the roads and over the meadows round about Oxford? Whilst both were almost daily seen together, it was seldom that either of them was ever seen 'out of college' without the other. Men who thus 'keep themselves to themselves' are never popular with the multitude from whom they hold aloof. There was much curiosity about the two singular young men, after the publication of the *Posthumous Fragments of Margaret Nicholson* (published on, or just before, 17th November, 1810), of which they were generally understood to be joint-authors;— but the curiosity was not flattering nor even friendly. It was averred that they aimed at eccentricity in costume and deportment; that they thought too well of themselves, and said by their looks, 'We are superior to everybody;' that Shelley's turn-down collars (worn, of course, so that he might be taken for another Lord Byron, and capable of writing a better satire than the *English Bards*), and his blue coat with glittering (Birmingham steel) buttons, were unutterably ludicrous; that his shock of wildly flowing hair was a disgrace to the University; that known as Mad Shelley, before he was sent away from Eton in disgrace, he seemed bent on justifying the nickname.

If the gossip about the young poetaster and novelist had the note of malice, it had, also, the ring of sincerity, and was not altogether wanting in justice. Though the morning on which he awoke to find himself famous was still in the future, Byron had made himself a celebrity before he started for the East; and had not the success of the *English Bards and Scotch Reviewers* (published in 1809) brought his peculiar collars into vogue with young gentlemen of poetical aspirations, Shelley would never have thought of wearing them to everybody's amusement at the University. Possibly, his blue coat with glittering buttons was not more defiant of the academic orders

touching costume than other coats worn by modish Oxonians of
his period ; but the freshman who donned it must have meant
to be observed and talked about.   Even Hogg admits that his
young friend's appearance was peculiar even to eccentricity, and
that his long and bushy hair was remarkable, when all other
undergraduates wore their hair short, and that, in consequence
of the conspicuous superfluity of his tresses, the ' little round
hat upon his little round head ' had a 'troubled and peculiar' air.

Eccentric in his costume, Mr. Bysshe Shelley, of University
College, was even more eccentric in his demeanour in the public
ways.   The poor scholar who fights his way to higher knowledge, whilst toiling for his daily bread as a clerk or craftsman,
must needs read as he runs to and fro between his place of
nightly rest and his place of daily labour, must con the printed
page whilst eating his meals, and seize moments for study
without care for his spectators.   But though Hogg commends
the Oxonian Shelley for seldom appearing by himself in the
High Street without an open volume under his eyes, most
people will attribute the needless show of studious zeal to a
whimsical affectation rather than to sincere delight in learning,
and an insatiable appetite for knowledge.   Why could not
Mr. Shelley read his books in those pleasant rooms where he
spent so much time daily in writing letters for mere amusement, in correcting the proof-sheets of a comically bad novel,
in playing with his air-pump and solar microscope, and in
holding desultory conversations with an agreeable companion ?

To appreciate this comical parade of scholarly enthusiasm,
readers must remember how much time the undergraduate
consumed in playing with paper boats and ' making ducks-and-
drakes' at the pond under Shotover Hill.   Why did the freshman, so prodigal of precious hours, thus affect the part of a
student set on turning every minute of his time to the best
account?   What was his motive in figuring under the public
gaze in a character so widely different from his real character ?
In answering these questions, readers should forget, as far as
possible, the freshman's subsequent greatness, and thinking of
him as the Eton scatter-brain, judge him precisely as they would
judge any youngster, who should behave in the same absurd
fashion in this present year of grace.

The freshman, who read the Latin and Greek classics as he
paced 'the High,' had other ways of calling attention to himself

in the public places of Oxford. On their return from a stroll, in cap and gown, Shelley and Hogg were holding high discourse on certain Platonic questions, when they encountered on Magdalen Bridge, a woman with a child in her arms,—an infant that might have been taken clean out of her arms, had the eccentric freshman encountered no resistance from the lawful owner of the baby.

'Will your baby tell us anything about pre-existence, Madam?' the excited disputant asked in a piercing voice, as he suddenly caught hold of the long-robed infant.

The woman was still in the act of recovering the self-possession, of which so singular an assault had deprived her for a few moments; when Shelley repeated the question in the same penetrating tone and with unabated earnestness.

'He cannot speak, Sir,' the woman replied with respectful seriousness.

'Worse and worse!' cried the eccentric undergraduate, shaking his long locks in a manner that must have heightened the woman's perplexity and alarm. 'But surely, Madam, the babe can speak if it will, for he is only a few weeks old. He may fancy, perhaps, that he cannot, but it is only a silly whim; he cannot have forgotten entirely the use of speech in so short a time; the thing is absolutely impossible.'

'It is not for me,' replied the woman, eyeing the two youthful gownsmen, with mingled deference and consternation, 'to dispute with you, Gentlemen, but I can safely declare that I never heard him speak, nor any child, indeed, of his age.'

Having thus troubled and frightened the worthy woman, for no purpose, except that he might execute an awkward and feeble pleasantry, the gownsman, who liked to be talked about, pressed the baby's cheeks with his fingers, and turned away saying to his companion, 'How provokingly close are those new-born babes! But it is no less certain, notwithstanding their cunning attempts to conceal the truth, that all knowledge is reminiscence: the doctrine is far more ancient than the times of Plato, and as old as the venerable allegory, that the Muses are the daughters of Memory; not one of the Nine was ever said to be the child of Invention.'

Whilst the freshman amused himself at Oxford in ways glanced at in the foregoing pages, how did he get on with the tutors of his college, and the other academic authorities? That he had no cause to complain of their treatment of him during the earlier weeks of his brief time at Oxford, he admitted in clear and noteworthy terms, to the Etonian who inquired of him in Hogg's hearing, 'Do you mean to be an Atheist here, too, Shelley?'

To this inquiry, whether he meant to worry, harass, and defy the tutors of his college as he had worried, harassed, and defied the persons put in authority over him at Eton, the University College freshman answered decidedly, 'No! certainly not. There is no motive for it; there would be no use in it; they are very civil to us here; they never interfere with us; it is not like Eton.'

For the precise words of this reply, represented by Hogg as having been made by Shelley, the biographer was doubtless indebted in some degree to his imagination. But even the 'Shelleyan enthusiasts' will admit that the tenor of the reply was something Hogg might have remembered. Bearing in mind also that Hogg disliked the University College 'dons,' and held them in bitter remembrance as the authors of his own academic disgrace, the same enthusiasts will admit that he was not likely to have invented such a piece of testimony to the general inoffensiveness of 'the dons' he detested. Even by them, therefore, it will be admitted that at this early point of his brief 'residence' in college, Shelley admitted that the 'dons' of University College treated him, as gentlemen in their position should treat a gentleman in his position; that they did not 'interfere' with him, that he had no grievance against them, or any grounds for worrying them. They were not like the Eton masters. They were gentlemen. This admission is the more noteworthy because Hogg (wildly wrong-headed and considerably less than historically truthful in matters touching his own and the poet's expulsion from University College) in his bitterness against those same 'dons,' was at much pains to declare them no gentlemen.

If the 'dons' were civil to Shelley, it must be admitted that he was less than civil to them. One would like to be able to say otherwise; but the evidence is conclusive that the undergraduate was uncivil to the 'dons' of his college, and to 'dons' not of his college, both in his bearing towards them, and his speech of them.

On the very first evening of their acquaintance, Shelley

withdrew from Hogg's rooms at 6.45 p.m., immediately 'after wine,' in order to attend a lecture on mineralogy,—leaving his entertainer with a promise to return to tea. An hour later he reappeared, chilly and disappointed. The evening was raw and cold, and the lecture had 'bored' him. He would never listen to another lecture by the dull lecturer.

Coming close up to Hogg, and speaking in a shrill whisper, the young gentleman said with an arch look,—

'I went away, indeed, before the lecture was finished. I stole away for it was so stupid, and I was so cold, that my teeth chattered. The Professor saw me, and appeared to be displeased. I thought I could have got out without being observed; but I struck my knee against a bench, and made a noise, and he looked at me. I am determined that he shall never see me again.'

'What did the man talk about?' Hogg asked.

'About stones! about stones!' answered the freshman (just then affecting to be an enthusiastic student of natural science). 'About stones!—stones, stones, stones!—nothing but stones!—and so drily. It was wonderfully tiresome — and stones are not interesting in themselves!'

Discreditable to the youngster's intelligence and scientific knowledge, the story is highly discreditable to his breeding. Instead of being 'uninteresting things in themselves,' stones are things of extreme interest. If the lecture was dull, he was bound by academic etiquette and common social courtesy, to remain to the end of it. As the lecture was poorly attended, he was especially bound by politeness to hear it out to the last word. Leaving the lecture as he did, blundering out of the room with noise so as to attract the lecturer's attention, he was guilty of an extravagance of incivility and rudeness to one of the Professors * of his University. The freshman, who in the first week or ten days of his 'residence in college,' could behave in this way to the lecturer, who had bored him, was a freshman who on the slightest provocation would be 'an Atheist' at Oxford, in the same sense in which he had been an Atheist at Eton.

* The first Reader in Mineralogy of the University of Oxford, with a Grant from the Crown, was William Buckland, B.D., subsequently the famous Dean of Westminster. From the Oxford University Calendar, it appears that a Crown Grant was assigned to this famous Professor for lecturing on Mineralogy in 1813. Probably the same lecturer gave lectures in the same department of science before receiving the grant, and was the gentleman whose 'dullness' was so afflicting to Mr. Bysshe Shelley.

A few days after this incident, the freshman (the *brilliant* author of *Zastrozzi* and *St. Irvyne*) discovered that the tutors of University College were '*very dull people.*' One of these very dull people, in the performance of his official duty, sent for the freshman to speak with him about the subjects of study to which he should give his mind, and the lectures he should attend. The interview between the dull person and the brilliant Mr. Bysshe Shelley (author of *Zastrozzi* and certain *Original Poetry* that was not original) left the younger gentleman with a mean opinion of his intellectual adviser, and probably left the elder gentleman with a no less unfavourable opinion of his pupil. What took place at this interview shall be told here in the words of the pupil, whose *ex parte* account of the matter (given to his friend, Mr. Hogg) is by no means creditable to the narrator.—

'They are very dull people here!' the freshman remarked one evening soon after he came ' into college.' ' A little man sent for me this morning, and told me, in an almost inaudible whisper, that I must read. "You must read," he said many times in his small voice. I answered that I had no objection. He persisted: so, to satisfy him, for he did not appear to believe me, I told him I had some books in my pocket, and I began to take them out. He stared at me, and said that was not exactly what he meant. "You must read *Prometheus Vinctus*, and *Demosthenes de Corona*, and *Euclid!*" "Must I read *Euclid?*" I asked sorrowfully. "Yes, certainly ; and when you have read the Greek works, I have mentioned, you must begin *Aristotle's Ethics*, and then you may go on to his other treatises. It is of the utmost importance to be well acquainted with Aristotle." This he repeated so often that I was quite tired, and at last I said, "Must I care about Aristotle? What if I do not mind Aristotle?" I then left him, for he seemed to be in great perplexity.'

The reader may be left to fill in and expand this brief sketch of an interview between one of the tutors of University College and the freshman, who acknowledged that the same tutors were ' very civil' to the undergraduates of the college. However, filled in and expanded, it must remain the account of an interview, in which the tutor, behaving with proper considerateness, and in no degree going outside the lines of his official duty, was treated with freedom, bordering on gross impertinence, by the pupil. Can anyone peruse the brief account without coming to the conclusion that Shelley gave and meant to give Hogg the impression, that he had treated the tutor saucily, *smoked* him elegantly (if I may use a word of obsolete slang), or, as school-boys would say, 'checked him' to his face. Of course Shelley's words come to us through Hogg, who is stigmatized as a treacherous and false friend by the 'Shelleyan enthusiasts.' But even they will admit that Hogg (with a personal interest in making the world imagine that the authorities of University College treated him and Shelley with unprovoked harshness) was not likely to misrepresent Shelley in this particular matter to his disadvantage.

Having discovered that the tutors of University College were 'dull people,'—a sentiment in which his familiar friend concurred,—Mr. Bysshe Shelley reminded Hogg on a subsequent occasion how very dull they were. Hogg was looking over one of his friend's Latin exercises, a translation into Latin of a portion of a paper in the *Spectator*, when he drew Shelley's attention to 'many portions of heroic verses, and even several entire verses,' observing that they were 'defects in a prose composition.' Smiling archly, the freshman replied in his peculiar piercing whisper, 'Do you think they will observe them? I inserted them intentionally to try their ears! I once showed up a theme at Eton to old Keate, in which there were a great many verses; but he observed them, scanned them, and asked why I had introduced them? I answered, that I did not know they were there; this was partly true and partly false; but he believed me, and immediately applied to me the line, in which Ovid says of himself:

" Et quod tentabam dicere, versus erat." '

It was thus that the modest and loyal Shelley (as he is styled by 'the enthusiasts') dealt with the tutors who were very civil to him,—putting blemishes into his Latin exercises, in the hope that, by overlooking them, the dull people would afford him another occasion for ridiculing their dullness. Surely the freshman, who dealt with and talked of his tutors in this style, was ripe and yearning to rebel against them, even as he had rebelled against his masters at Eton. 'I answered,' he says of his reply to Dr. Keate, 'that I did not know they were there; *this was partly true and partly false,*'—words to remind the reader of the semi-delusions (as Peacock called them) of the poet's later time. 'This was partly true and partly false!' What an admission respecting the Etonian Shelley, who (to use

Lady Shelley's words), was 'more outspoken and truthful than other boys!'

Though they saw at once he had no intention of throwing himself heartily into the studies of the place, and had reason to smile at certain of his more grotesque eccentricities, the tutors of University College discovered no more serious cause for complaining of the freshman's behaviour during Michaelmas term. On the contrary, as they of course were not ignorant of the character he had borne, and the trouble he had given at Eton, and even of the circumstances that occasioned his premature withdrawal from the school, the tutors of the Oxford College may well have congratulated themselves on the general orderliness of his behaviour, and have imagined if they left him to his own course, and interfered with him as little as possible, the perverse and contumacious Atheist of Eton would go through an ordinary academic career without discredit. It is not to their shame that they neither detected nor suspected his latent genius, which, besides being latent, was so absolutely dormant, that it may be said to have had no existence up to a time, considerably later than his expulsion from Oxford. All they could say of him in the earlier of his two residence-terms was that he behaved fairly well.

Thus much they could say of him. Living almost entirely with a single friend (even as Byron in his earliest time at Cambridge lived in shy seclusion almost entirely with a young chorister and a single friend of gentle degree), he kept morning chapels with fair regularity, attended a sufficient number of the college lectures, 'pricked *æger*' (when he was quite well) no oftener than usage permitted, gave no noisy wine-parties, had no noisy acquaintances, never 'knocked' into college after the appointed hours for 'knocking in,' showed no propensity to any kind of dissipation. It was true that he appeared 'in hall' less often than so quiet a young gentleman might be expected to appear at the freshmen's dinner-table; but attendance 'at hall' was not insisted on. True, also, that he was understood to have written an extremely silly novel and a very absurd book of poems; but it was well and needful young men should amuse themselves, and better that they should amuse themselves with pen and ink than with dice and cards.

Throughout the term, Shelley was more occupied with his literary diversions than with the serious studies recommended by his tutor. Whilst correcting the proofs of the *Posthumous Fragments of Margaret Nicholson* (published *on* or a little before 17th November, 1810, by J. Munday, of the firm of Munday and Slatter, Printers and Booksellers, *Herald* Office, High Street, Oxford), he was in correspondence with Mr. John Joseph Stockdale, of Pall Mall, about *The Wandering Jew*, and writing verses that were shown to Hogg, and probably sent without delay to his sister Elizabeth and Miss Harriett Grove, to each of whom he wrote frequently. Before there was laughter in the colleges over the *Posthumous Fragments* (a performance that, doubtless, found more readers than admirers in the University), he had returned the amended manuscript of *St. Irvyne* to the Pall Mall publisher ; and before he had done with the proofs of that singular tale, or, at the latest, before the story was offered to the circulating libraries, he was at work upon another novel (which never saw the light, and probably was never finished),—the work of which he wrote to Mr. Stockdale on 18th December, 1810 :—

'I have in preparation a novel ; it is principally constructed to convey metaphysical and political opinions by way of conversation, it shall be sent to you as soon as completed, but it shall receive more correction than I trouble myself to give to wild Romance and Poetry.'

In the same term (probably during the second month of it) he found time to make, with Hogg's assistance, 'the very careful analysis' (mentioned in Hogg's *Life*) of Hume's *Essays*, to which he was chiefly indebted for the theological views of *The Necessity of Atheism*, and for the other arguments, with which he troubled the minds of the several indiscreet persons, whom he lured with delusive letters into confidential controversy on matters pertaining to religion.

From this survey of his literary diversions and other ways of spending his time during this academic term, it is obvious that the freshman had not many hours for strenuous study. Few, indeed, were the minutes left to him out of the twenty-four hours for any purpose, when he had spent *five* hours in bed, an hour in attending chapel and breakfasting, two or three hours in attending lectures, an hour in playing with his scientific toys, an hour or two in writing letters to some of his numerous correspondents, two hours in correcting proofs and producing fresh copy for the printers, four hours in walking (with 'breaks' for pistol practice, playing with paper boats, and 'making ducks-and-drakes' on the water), an hour at dinner and supper, from two to four hours in his usual evening-nap, and four hours in conversation with his peculiar friend. Some reading, together with much talk, was doubtless done by the friends during these last-mentioned four hours; but though it may be refreshing and otherwise serviceable, the reading, which two sociable and naturally loquacious fellow-students get through in each other's company, is never strenuous and 'hard reading,'—must ever be more or less light and desultory. The best apology to be made for the freshman's practice of conning the printed page in the High Street, is that his various diversions left him so little time for reading in his own rooms.

Whilst amusing himself with his young friend, whose eccentricities afforded him so much amusement, the lightly humorous and severely practical Hogg (ever with an eye to the 'first-class' and the 'fellowship,' that should serve him as stepping-stones to higher social success, if not to social great-ness) held to his hard-reading and was a prudent economist of the time, which the freshman spent in busy idleness. Rising from his bed at seven, and passing the earlier hours of the day on the work for which he had come to Oxford, the reading-man never entered Shelley's rooms before one p.m., and some-times kept away from them till a later hour of the afternoon. In the evening he resumed his studies, and pursued them with-out interruption, whilst Shelley took his evening-slumber, lying sometimes on a sofa, but oftener on the hearth-rug before the large fire, that, ever bright and fierce, never burnt too fiercely for his comfort. Suddenly overcome by drowsiness the slight and nervous stripling surrendered himself to torpor almost in an instant, and dropping on the sofa or rug, lay in deep lethargy for two or three (on some evenings for four) hours, stretched like a cat before the glowing fire. If he dropt off in this fashion at six o'clock, he slept for four hours; if he fell into slumber at eight o'clock he slept for only two hours. What-ever the time when it began, the nap of profound slumber——never a short one—ended at ten o'clock, or within a few minutes. That the heat of the glowing stove affected the sleeper agreeably, was obvious from the way in which he rolled away from any object that screened him from the fire, and

placed his little head so that it felt more sensibly the ardour of
the burning coals. Occasionally he talked in his sleep, more often
his rest was not less silent than long. Whilst the youngster
slept, the reading-man worked steadily at his books and papers.

Recovering consciousness as suddenly as he lost it, Shelley
was no sooner awake than he was restored to perfect mental
alertness. Rising to his feet with startling alacrity, he was
ready for talk as soon as he had rubbed his eyes and passed his
long fingers through his long hair. At the same instant, the north-
countryman looked up from his books and turned away from
his papers. On different evenings, the talk ran on poetry and
science, logic and history, morals and religion, man's relation to
the universe, the soul's immortality, the errors of the creeds,
and the reasons why a reasonable man should not believe in
anything. Sometimes the talk resulted in reference to books,
and the reference to books for particular passages led sometimes
to larger reading of them.   If it was not begun and perfected,
the ' very careful analysis ' of Hume's *Essays* was often referred
to, reconsidered and amended at these nocturnal conferences.

At other times, when the youthful philosophers were weary
of high and exhausting themes, the talk turned on their domestic interests, their kindred and prospects, their respective
homes and counties, the humours of Durham and Yorkshire, and
the manners of Sussex. When the gossip played about these
homely topics, the freshman was even more entertaining to his
delightful and incomparable friend, than when they discoursed on
loftier matters. Lying back in his chair, and laughing in his sleeve
as he tried to discriminate between the fact and fiction of
his companion's marvellous communications, Mr. Hogg, of
University College, learnt many things that were not altogether
true of Field Place, its inmates, and its traditions. From the
commencement of their friendship, it was obvious to the young
gentleman from the neighbourhood of Stockton-on-Tees, that
his friend's statements were to be taken with allowance for the
vigour of a fertile fancy, and the speaker's propensity for
drawing the colloquial long-bow. When the scientific enthusiast described with needless emphasis and much extravagant
gesticulation how nearly he had killed himself at Eton, by
inadvertently swallowing some mineral poison, the interested but
scarcely sympathetic listener suspected that a lively imagination
was in some degree accountable for the thrilling tale. The

stories about the 'Old Snake' were received in the same sceptical spirit by the auditor, who regarded the staggering legends as signally wanting in 'the commonplace truth of ordinary matters of fact,' though doubtless rich in 'the far higher truth of poetical verity and mythological necessity.' The Michaelmas Term was still young, when the same sceptical auditor listened with more interest than credulity to Shelley's account of the way in which he was saved from the madhouse, to which he would have been consigned by his inhuman father, had it not been for Dr. Lind's timely and intrepid action. Before the Term had grown old, Mr. Hogg had heard much, of which he believed little, to the discredit of the worthy, though curiously pompous gentleman, who retained the confidence of the New Shoreham electors, without possessing his eldest son's good opinion.

To say that Shelley told his whole heart and mind to his fellow-collegian during this season of their closest and most cordial intimacy, would be saying too much of a young man, whose candour was less real than apparent:—of the rash and seemingly reckless speaker who, resembling Byron in the freedom with which he talked of his private affairs to slight acquaintances and the whole world, resembled him also in having reserves from those to whom he was most communicative, even at the moments when he seemed most incapable of secresy or any other kind of self-restraint. Hogg, however, may well have imagined that nothing was withheld from him by the freshman, who, talking to him copiously of half-a-hundred matters he had better have kept to himself, submitted his letters from Field Place to so recent an acquaintance, letters from his father, and letters (containing specimens of her poetry) from his sister. Expressing great admiration of the young lady's verse and prose, Mr. Hogg was vastly tickled by the peculiarities of Mr. Timothy Shelley's epistles, which he turned to ridicule with much piquant sprightliness, and to the lively gratification of their writer's son.

Because these epistles began in kindly fashion with 'My Dear Boy,' the writer was suspected of wishing to imitate the style of Chesterfield's Letters, and also of thinking he resembled the courtly Earl in elegance, accomplishments, and worldly wisdom. It was easy, and no less pleasant than easy to the two undergraduates, to make fun of the epistles, so curiously deficient

in coherence and perspicacity.   Always *franked* by the member
for New Shoreham, the letters sometimes 'scolded the dear boy
nobly, royally, gloriously.'   One of these franked, furious and
fiery missives having moved Hogg to speak of it derisively, and
with a sprightly reference to a familiar line of Campbell's
' Hohenlinden,' Shelley henceforth took to speaking of his father
as ' the fiery Hun.'   The son had other nicknames for the
father, whom he so often offended,—sometimes unintentionally,
and sometimes with deliberate and malicious purpose to rouse
and exasperate the irritability, that afforded the two youthful
Oxonians so much diversion ;—the irritability which the son (of
whose poetical light and sweetness so much has been written
by fantastic adulators) was bound by filial duty to consider
tenderly and soothe to the utmost of his ability ; was bound by
honour and care for his own dignity to screen and palliate.
Writing and talking of him as ' the Fiery Hun,' Shelley could
also speak of his father contemptuously as ' Killjoy ' and ' the
Old Boy,' in the letters that passed between him and Hogg
after their dismissal from University College.

Whilst Hogg was exquisitely droll about the defects of
Mr. Timothy Shelley's letters, he of course heard all about his
friend's passion for his cousin, Harriett Grove, which, though it
never touched the boy's deepest and strongest affections, was
still a sufficiently fervid sentiment to justify him in thinking
it a grand and eternal devotion.   It is not surprising that
Shelley opened his heart on this interesting topic to his constant
companion.   On the contrary, it would be strange had he done
otherwise.   It is rare for a boy to pass through his first love-
fever without confiding to a sympathetic hearer of his own sex,
how he fares under the violent delights and still more violent
anxieties of his heart's unrest.   In speaking to his dear and
incomparable Hogg of Miss Harriett Grove's beauty and accomplishments, her irresistible voice and richly radiant tresses,
her composure that too nearly resembled coldness, and the
circumspection that might not be imputed to her for unkindness,
young Bysshe Shelley only did as most youngsters would have
done under similar circumstances,—as most youngsters under
similar circumstances will do, to the end of Time and Love.

But though he did nothing unusual or otherwise remarkable
in talking of his love and his Harriett's loveliness to his one
familiar male friend, Mr. Percy Bysshe Shelley did what few

young Englishmen of gentle lineage and culture would have done,—what no young gentleman could do, without lacking in some degree the delicate fastidiousness and proud reserve befitting a youth of breeding and quality,—when, out of fraternal concern for the young lady's welfare, and in the fervour of his generous affection for so incomparable a friend, he invited Mr. Thomas Jefferson Hogg to visit Field Place on the first convenient opportunity, for the express purpose of seeing the eldest daughter of the house, falling in love with her, and marrying her. It is not often that a young lady (*ætat.* sixteen, living under the protection of her father and mother) is thus offered in marriage by her elder brother (*ætat.* eighteen) to a young gentleman whom she has never seen. It does not seem to have occurred to Mr. Bysshe Shelley that his father and mother were entitled to a voice on the disposal of their daughter in marriage, that before entering on negotiations on so delicate a subject, with a gentleman of whose person and family they were alike ignorant, he should consult the Fiery Hun on the business, and learn from the Fiery Hun's wife, whether the arrangement would be agreeable to her feelings.

From what is known of Mr. Thomas Jefferson Hogg's character and lively humour in his later time, one may imagine that in the lightness and levity of his earlier time he was vastly tickled by his young friend's flattering proposal for this alliance of their respective houses ; that he saw the probable advantage of wedding the daughter of so wealthy a baronet, as Mr. Timothy Shelley would become on the death of his aged father; and that he was strongly predisposed to admire his young friend's sister, who was said to resemble her brother in the colour of her eyes and hair, no less than in the pink-and-white freshness of her complexion, and to surpass him greatly in facial comeliness, by virtue of the delicate symmetry of a countenance, whose most prominent feature was faultless in size and shape. Anyhow, the undergraduate from the northern county, who, on account of its remoteness, had no intention of returning to his father's roof at Christmas or Easter, consented readily to a project that, even if nothing more came of it, would enable him to pass the shorter vacations in congenial society at no inconvenient distance from the University.

It was doubtless a matter for regret and apologetic explanation with Mr. Bysshe Shelley, that, owing to the Fiery Hun's

peculiarities, he could not safely carry his friend with him to
Sussex at the close of the Michaelmas term, but was under the
necessity of preceding him to Field Place and foregoing the
delights of his society, until he should be authorized by the
capricious, and too often austere Killjoy, to invite him thither
for the gaieties of Christmas and the New-Year. The evidences
are not conclusive on the point; but they afford particulars from
which it may be fairly assumed that, for several days after
Shelley's withdrawal from the University for the Christmas
holidays, Hogg (whether lingering at Oxford, or staying at the
London Hotel, where he received several letters from Shelley in
the closing days of December, 1810, and the opening days of
January, 1811) looked to each successive post for an invitation
to Field Place, and to the presence of the young lady, with
whom he was predisposed to fall in love, and had promised to
fall in love, if he found it in his power to do so.

CHAPTER XI.

THE CHRISTMAS VACATION OF 1810-11.

Presentation copies of *St. Irvyne*—Shelley resorts to Deception—Shelley in Disgrace at Field Place—Harriett Grove's Dismissal of her Suitor—The Squire's Anger—Mrs. Shelley's Alarm for her Girls—Shelley's Troubles—His Rage against Intolerance—His Wild Letters to Hogg—'Married to a Clod'—Stockdale's Design—His Intercourse with Shelley's Father—More Negotiations with the Pall-Mall Publisher—Shelley a Deist—Controversial Correspondence—Shelley's Attempt to enlighten his Father—His Passage from Deism to Atheism—The Squire relents to his Son—Hogg invited to Field Place—Stockdale's Disappointment—Hogg invited to Field Place—Stockdale's Character—His Scandalous *Budget*.

LEAVING Oxford at the end of Michaelmas term, 1810, and journeying to Sussex by way of London, Mr. Bysshe Shelley was at Field Place on the 18th of December, on which day he wrote to Mr. John Joseph Stockdale, of Pall Mall, expressing approval of the publisher's advertisement of *St. Irvyne*, and begging him to send a copy of the absurd story to each of the three following persons :—Miss Marshall, of Horsham, Sussex ; Thomas Medwin, Esq., of the same place; and Thomas Jefferson Hogg, Esq., at the Reverend Mr. Dayrell's, Lynnington (a misspelling of Lillingstone) Dayrell, Buckinghamshire. At the same time the author requested that six copies should be sent to himself, and observed, at the close of his brief note, 'I will enclose the printer's account for your inspection in another letter;' words of some moment to the reader who would get a view of the circumstances that soon resulted in the young author's rupture with his publisher. Under ordinary circumstances, the printer's bill for printing a book published at the author's risk would be paid by the publisher, and would not come under the author's notice save as an item of his publisher's account. Paying the printer with a bill, or with ready-money, on which discount would be allowed, the publisher would charge the author with the full sum of the printer's account, making on the transaction a considerable profit (to the amount of the discount), if he pays the printer in ' cash ' and is promptly repaid by the author. Mr. Stockdale, of course, would not have been slow to arrange for getting this advantage, had he not by the middle of December discovered grounds for mistrusting the author's ability to pay the charges for which he was responsible; or had he not somehow come to the opinion that the author (a minor) should be pressed for immediate payment of the costs of producing a book, whose sale would necessarily be trifling. That Mr. Gosnell, of Little Queen Street, London (the printer to whom Mr. Stockdale had himself sent 'the copy' of *St. Irvyne*, after the MS. had been 'fitted for the press'), was thus asked to press the author for immediate payment for the printing, is alike significant of the publisher's distrust of the author's solvency, and of the publisher's unfavourable opinion of the book.

If he was not in trouble and disgrace at Field Place from the first moment of his return to his boyhood's home, Mr. Percy Bysshe Shelley did not pass many days of the Christmas vacation in Sussex, before his father spoke to him sharply, and his mother regarded him with sorrowful disapproval. A letter he wrote to Hogg on 20th December, 1810—a letter to be found in Hogg's *Life*—shows that, at so early a time of the holidays, he found himself in a position of divers annoyances, several humiliations, and much embarrassment. Acting in the name of their daughter, and also with the authority pertaining to them as her natural guardians, Mr. and Mrs. Grove, of Fern House, Wiltshire, had written to Field Place, expressing reasonable surprise and displeasure at their nephew's conduct in abusing the privileges of familiar intercourse so far and so outrageously as to write his cousin Harriett Grove (*ætat.* 17 to 18) letters, whose main purpose was to draw her into religious controversy, and lure her from Christianity,—the faith in which she had been educated; the faith of her parents and kindred. To Mr. and Mrs. Grove, it necessarily seemed that in thus acting towards their daughter, Bysshe had acted dishonourably, and shown himself unworthy of the love he required from her; unworthy even of the friendly intercourse with her, to which he had been entitled as her near kinsman. Under these circumstances, Shelley was informed that his correspondence with Miss Harriett Grove must be stayed at least for the present, and that his hope of marrying her must be dismissed for ever.

Holding old and wholesome views on certain questions of honour, though he certainly was no person to be compared with the Saviour of the World, Mr. Timothy Shelley concurred in the sentiments of Fern House on this affair, and told his son so in terms none too daintily worded. ‘The Fiery Hun’ blushed to think he had a son capable of sapping the faith and principles of a young lady, to whose familiar confidence he had been admitted under conditions of which no gentleman, old or young, was unmindful. To poor Mrs. Shelley, the case was even worse. Regarding the point of honour with her husband’s eyes, she thought also of the monstrous wickedness of her first-born child, who, throwing from him the truths of the Christian religion, had covered them with ridicule. In alarm, she thought of her girls. If Bysshe could act thus wickedly to his cousin Harriett, what was there to withhold him from acting in like manner to his sister Elizabeth? He and she were so closely attached to one another, that it was their practice to read and walk and write poetry together. During the whole of his single term of residence at Oxford, there had been letters passing between them. Had he already inspired the dear girl with sceptical sentiment? Instead of submitting to her father and mother, as Harriett Grove had done, the evil counsel he was giving her, had Elizabeth taken his impious words to heart? Was she pondering them secretly, and brooding over them, in doubt whether she should reject them as false, or hold to them as true? Or had she embraced them no less impetuously and strongly than furtively? Was she already a disbeliever?—an infidel? Then the terrified mother thought of her younger girls,—Mary, and Hellen, and Margaret. If he could tamper with the religious tenets of so young a girl as Elizabeth, still only sixteen years old, what was there in the tenderness of their infantile years to render Bysshe more heedful for the spiritual health and tranquillity of Elizabeth’s younger sisters?

It needs no lively imagination to conceive the terror that agitated this anxious mother, to realize the apprehensions that, fretting her spirits incessantly, gave her sleepless nights and sorrowful days. Instead of being touched and subdued by the words and looks, that made him cognizant of her maternal solicitude, the young gentleman (who might have been the Saviour of the World) wrote lightly to his fellow-collegian on January 11, 1811, about his mother’s alarm. She imagined him on the

high road to perdition. She fancied him set on making infidels
of his little sisters. Could anything be more laughable? It
was, however, no laughable matter to the poor lady; and it
should not have been a matter for laughter with her son.
Why was his mother a simpleton for allowing such fears to
trouble her, when the young gentleman was craftily and
insidiously sapping his eldest sister's belief in Christianity,
apportioning the new doctrine of Free Thought with nice
consideration for her girlish timidity, and for the weakness
of her intellect,—giving it in doses large enough to awaken and
stimulate curiosity, without stirring her to amazement and horror?

As he was working in this condescending and considerate
manner on Elizabeth's darkness and weakness on the 26th
of December, 1810, why was his mother a mere goose for fearing
he might be no less condescending, and considerate, and slily
beneficent to Elizabeth's younger sisters?

Moreover the time was near at hand when, in his fanatical
intolerance of all opinion from which he differed, the youthful
philosopher regarded Elizabeth's younger sisters as quite old
enough to digest the crumbs of truth, that fell from his lips.
With all her disposition to minimize and palliate the feelings
of her poet, Lady Shelley admits that such a youngster as the
Oxonian Shelley would be a perplexing member of any household with a brood of children to be thought for. Indeed, she
even goes the length of saying that, before accusing Mr.
Timothy Shelley of treating his heir with inadequate tenderness,
people should ask themselves how they would like to have in
their houses a Spinozist or a Calvinist, so set on making converts, as to seek them in the butler's pantry or the children's
schoolroom. Lady Shelley is even more particular, in moving
every Christian mother to think, how she would like to entertain for her guest a Spinozist, desirous of making her 'youngest
daughter' concur in his opinions.

Readers should bear in mind how clearly the author of
Shelley Memorials: From Authentic Sources, intimates that, instead
of being the absurd and laughable fancy her son declared it,
poor Mrs. Timothy Shelley's fear for the spiritual safety of her
younger girls was nothing less than a reasonable anticipation
of what actually took place in their schoolroom, in respect to
the youngest of them, before the poet turned his back on Field
Place for ever.

Just about the same time at which his attention was called
to his son's sceptical opinions, and his zeal for making converts
to them, by Mr. and Mrs. Grove, of Fern House, Mr. Timothy
Shelley received some information, touching the same matters
of painful interest from Mr. John Joseph Stockdale, of Pall
Mall. As the man of business, who lived to be one of the
blackest sheep of 'the trade,' was at no point of his career a
person of extraordinary worth, the readers of the present
chapter are not required to attribute the publisher's action in
this particular business to any sincere concern for the younger
gentleman's welfare, or for his father's happiness. Before he
became uneasy about the printer's bill, for whose payment he
was of course responsible, should the undergraduate of University College fail to pay it, Mr. Stockdale had been warned by
several circumstances to exercise greater caution in his dealings
with the young gentleman, whose *Original Poetry* had proved
so inconveniently wanting in originality. *Zastrozzi*, of which
he doubtless took a view after learning the name of its publisher, can scarcely have raised the author of the Victor-and-
Cazire book in Mr. Stockdale's estimation. The quality of *St.
Irvyne*, and the pains he had himself taken to fit it for the
press, cannot have disposed the man of business to think highly
of the author's ability. What he had heard about *The Wandering Jew* cannot have disposed the publisher to think less
contemptuously of the young gentleman's literary parts and
ambition. The note touching the Hebrew Essay to the discredit
of the Christian religion, was only one of several matters, to
indicate to the publisher that his youthful client's reading
would possibly result in perilous writing. One can imagine
how the publisher of novels and inferior poetry received the
suggestion that he should publish the novel on *Metaphysical and
Political Opinions*. On the approach of the Christmas holidays
(1810–11), it was clear to Mr. Stockdale he had better press for
a pecuniary settlement with Mr. Percy Bysshe Shelley; and in
case the young gentleman was not likely to pay his debt, to
take measures for getting the money out of the young gentleman's father. Hence, the publisher's earlier interviews with
the Member for New Shoreham, who was instructed that his
son had fallen into evil hands at Oxford, and was a supporter
of sceptical philosophy. How little the publisher got by
his pains, and how he avenged himself on the Member of

Parliament, whom he failed to bleed, are matters for subsequent
pages.

When he wrote to Hogg on the 20th of December, 1810,
Shelley had endured and was still enduring several sharp
annoyances. Angry words had escaped ' the Fiery Hun,' who
scolded his son for writing ridiculous books when he should be
reading learned ones at Oxford; scolded him for running into debt
with a publisher and printer, whom he had no means of paying;
scolded him for adopting the damnable opinions of Hume, Paine,
and the other infidels ; scolded him royally for his most ungentlemanlike behaviour, in trying to lure his cousin Harriett
from the sound Christian principles in which she had been
educated by her most virtuous and exemplary parents. It was
the way of fathers to scold their sons thus royally at the beginning of the present century ; and it being part of the paternal
style of George the Third's time, no sound-hearted and loyal-
hearted son ever resented so wholesome, though somewhat
turbulent, an exercise of paternal authority. Now-a-days,
fathers bring, or try to bring, their disorderly sons to meet
contrition, with less noise and more dignity, but with speech
quite as galling at the time, and more likely to rankle in the
memory. To argue that Mr. Timothy Shelley was brutal and
wanting in natural affection, because he scolded his naughty
boy in this manner, is wild nonsense. However roundly he was
spoken to, Mr. Bysshe Shelley received nothing more than he
deserved. For awhile the father threatened to take his son
from Oxford at once, but the threat was not carried out. It
would have been better for Shelley had his father held to the
threat. Mr. Bysshe Shelley's grand averment that the menace
was withdrawn, because he 'would not consent to it,' is a delicious
piece of puerile ' bounce.'

Shelley had reason for discontent. Forbidden to write to
his cousin Harriett, he imagined, for a few days, he had loved
her vehemently. Dismissed by her on account of his opinions,
he deemed himself the victim of religious intolerance. By turns
he thought of committing suicide, and wreaking his vengeance
on the religion, which he held accountable for his greatest
trouble. Swearing on what he was pleased to call the altar of
perjured love, he vowed he would put an end to religious intolerance, by slaying secretly, stabbing secretly, the creed and
the sentiment which generated religious intolerance. Dismissing

the thought of killing himself, he confirmed himself in his
purpose to kill superstition; and whilst maturing his plans for
the achievement of this resolve, he determined to pursue his
literary enterprises.   But as 'the Fiery Hun' disapproved
of his dealings with publishers, he determined to conceal his
literary designs from his parents.   On this point he wrote with
instructive frankness to Hogg. 'There is now,' he wrote to his
friend, 'need of all my art: I must resort to deception.'   The
deception he practised was to work on a new novel, with a view
to early publication, whilst telling his father and mother he
had no intention of publishing anything again. 'Inconveniences
would now result from my owning the novel,' he wrote to
Hogg, 'which I have in preparation for the press. I give out,
therefore, that I will publish no more.' It pleased him to know
that every one believed his false statement, with the exception
of the few, who, being in his confidence, knew that it was a
falsehood.   One of the persons thus taken into his confidence
was his sister Elizabeth (*ætat.* 16), whom he thus educated in
deceit, by telling her how he was deceiving their parents. This
was the course taken by the singularly outspoken and truth-
loving Shelley in his own home,—towards his father and
mother on the one hand, and towards his sister on the other.
At the same time, whilst deceiving his father and mother, he
was debating how he could impose his new book on a publisher
by misrepresenting the tendency and purpose of the work. He
was afraid that, though a thick-skulled man, Stockdale would
detect the falsehood of the statement he was ready to make
about the book.

What further evidence can readers of ordinary intelligence
and temper require that, instead of being more outspoken and
truth-loving than other people, the poet suffered from a deficiency of that repugnance to untruth which is the prime
characteristic of English gentlemen; that he was capable of
telling untruths, and did tell them, for small ends that would
not draw Englishmen of average veracity a single hair's-breadth
out of truth's clear and straight path? Of course the facts,
which cannot fail to bring impartial readers to this painful
conclusion, are regarded in another way, by those 'Shelleyan
enthusiasts' who idolize the author of *Laon and Cythna* as a
being worthy of being likened to the Saviour of the World.
The facts that to impartial minds are evidential of the poet's

untruthfulness, the most extravagant of the Shelleyan zealots regard as so much evidence that their idol possessed an inordinately powerful imagination. What stronger evidence can there be of the overpowering vigour and sway of his fancy, than that so lofty and faultless a being could imagine himself capable of deceiving his publisher, of telling falsehoods to his father and mother, of educating his younger sister in untruth; and could, moreover, deliberately write himself down guilty of these flagrant offences, of which so faultless a being must have been innocent as the new-born babe?

Scarcely less noteworthy than his avowal of the deceit he is practising on his father and mother, are the terms in which Shelley refers to the abrupt termination of his correspondence with Miss Harriett Grove, and declares his purpose of avenging himself on Intolerance for the annoyance that has come to him from the lady's disapproval of his religious scepticism.

As Miss Harriett Grove had never promised to be his wife, but had on the contrary persisted in assuring her cousin Elizabeth that she might not anticipate a successful issue to her brother's suit, this talk about 'perjured love' was very much out of place. Still it did no harm; and as the young gentleman felt it needful to swear on something, and was precluded by the exigencies of the case from swearing 'on the book,' he, perhaps, exercised a wise discretion when he elected to 'swear on the altar of perjured love.' To swear what? That, because he was very much annoyed at being sent about his business by Miss Harriett Grove, and at being otherwise reprimanded for troubling her mind with sceptical sentiments, he would make war upon Intolerance, would fight Intolerance to the bitter end, would be the death of Intolerance, would 'stab the wretch in secret.' This was the oath sworn on the altar of perjured love! Having suffered, more in self-love than in any other of his affections, from a young lady's disapproval of his religious opinions, and from her parents' no less cordial repugnance to those opinions, Mr. Bysshe Shelley regarded himself as a victim of religious intolerance. Yet further,— seeing that Christians, intolerant of opinions antagonistic to their religious tenets, would not be intolerant Christians were it not for their Christianity, he determined to render them tolerant by slaying the religion which he regarded as the source of their intolerance. 'Indeed, I think it,' he wrote, 'to the benefit of society to destroy the opinions which annihilate the dearest of its ties,'—*i.e.* the ties uniting such lovers as Mr. Bysshe Shelley and Miss Harriett Grove were, before religion separated them. As the war against Christianity had begun long before the poet's severance from his cousin, which was, indeed, one of the consequences of the war, it would, of course, be absurd to attribute the poet's hatred of the religion to the anger begotten of his dismissal by Miss Grove. But in accounting for the vehemence with which Shelley pushed the war, and the spirit in which he extended the field of his operations, and from being the enemy of a single faith became the foe of all religions, readers must make allowance for the sense of personal injury which animated him to swear he would slay Religious Intolerance.

In the letters which Shelley poured upon Hogg, from the 20th of December, till the end of the academic vacation, one comes upon much more about Harriett Grove, and his correspondence with her. To skim these flighty and rhapsodical letters is to miss the information that may be extracted from them. But to study them carefully is to take the present writer's view of Shelley's regard for his cousin, from the summer of 1810.

It is clear the cousins never plighted troth to one another. On 23rd December, 1810, Shelley wishes to know, whether he did wrong in luring his cousin to correspond with him, in order that they 'might see if by coincidence of intellect,' it would be well for them 'to enter into a closer, an eternal union;' the desire for information being clothed in words, amounting to an admission there had been no regular engagement. In the same letter, speaking of Miss Grove's coldness, Shelley speaks also of the failure of his sister's efforts to make the self-possessed beauty regard him with feelings warmer than those of cousinly kindness. That the young gentleman's strongest affections were not concerned in the affair appears from the fact that, within eight days of swearing on the altar of perjured love, he could write with comparative calmness of his inability to fall in love at present with any other young lady.

In language that may be suspected of having contributed something to Lord Dundreary's colloquial style, he wrote to Hogg, on 28th December, 1810, 'at present a thousand barriers oppose any more intimate connexion, any union with another, which, although unnatural and fettering to a virtuous mind, are nevertheless unconquerable.' After writing thus calmly, however, he relapsed into moods, of alternate dejection and fury. He 'slept with a loaded pistol and some poison last night' (*i.e.* 2nd January, 1811), 'but did not die.' Again he vowed vengeance on the religious intolerance that had robbed him of his Harriett. On the 11th January, 1811, he wrote fiercely to Hogg, 'She is gone! She is lost to me for ever! She is married! Married to a clod of earth; she will become as insensible as himself; all these fine capabilities will moulder!'

It may not be inferred from the words 'She is married,' that the gentlewoman had already become a wife, or that Shelley meant to do more than announce her engagement to Mr. William Helyar, of Coker Court, Co. Somerset, whose wife she became in November, 1811, two months after the future poet's Scotch marriage to Harriett Westbrook. Bearing in mind the old distinction between marriage and its celebration, and remembering, at the same time, the ancient doctrine of the Church, that a mere matrimonial contract was wedlock—though not yet celebrated and sanctified into *holy* wedlock—readers must take the words as a mere declaration that Miss Grove had plighted her troth to her future husband. The old ecclesiastical law, which made matrimonial pre-contract a sufficient ground for nullification of marriage, was based on the doctrine that an interchange of nuptial promises was, in itself, marriage. In his 'anti-matrimonialism'—a sentiment growing more and more powerful in the author of *Zastrozzi* and *St. Irvyne*—Shelley, disdainful of the ecclesiastical celebration, looked upon the interchange of promises ('the engagement' of ordinary parlance) as the real marriage; and in doing so he was (strange to say) in accord with the canonists, and with the old matrimonial law that, surviving in North its extinction in South Britain, was, even to yesterday, generally known as 'the Scotch marriage-law.'

The clod of earth had a good many acres of land in Wiltshire, Somerset, and Devonshire, and instead of being the senseless and soulless wretch it pleased Mr. Bysshe Shelley to imagine him, was a gentleman of good repute in the three shires, for each of which he was a magistrate. Heir to an ample estate, he married Miss Harriett Grove in November

1811, and living with her till death divided them, was never moved to transfer his affections to another lady. Would life have gone thus pleasantly with the gentlewoman, who became the mother of children fair and gracious as herself, had she yielded to the suit of her scatter-brain cousin?

Whilst he was fuming over his sentimental misadventure, and writing extravagant nonsense about the 'altar of perjured love,' not so much because he felt his cousin's unkindness acutely, as from a notion that the poetical proprieties required him to use the language of indignation and wretchedness, Mr. Bysshe Shelley made frequent mention of his sister Elizabeth in the letters he sent in steady stream to the young gentleman, who had been entreated to fall in love with her.

It sadly disarranged the brother's plans for his sister's welfare, that he could not invite his peculiar friend forthwith to Field Place. The reason why he could not do so was that his father, already instructed by Stockdale to attribute his son's scepticism to the influence of his Oxford friend, had declared his opinion of Mr. Hogg in terms, which satisfied Bysshe he had better not ask for permission to summon the incomparable Hogg to Sussex. But though he could not bring them together for the present, the match-making brother did his best to inspire his sister and his college-friend with a sentimental regard for one another, that could not fail to result in mutual love, so soon as they should come together. Speaking to his sister of his friend in terms of vehement admiration, he read her the letters that came to him in steady stream from his idolized and incomparable Hogg. That Hogg (whose sense of humour was allied with a liberal measure of romantic sensibility) delighted in the notion of becoming his friend's brother-in-law, and during the holidays even went so far as to bind himself to fall in love with Miss Shelley, appears from the letter in which Shelley overflowed with gratitude for so great a concession to his wishes. 'How,' wrote Shelley to his friend, 'can I find words to express my thanks for such generous conduct with regard to my sister, with talents and attainments such as you possess, to promise what I ought not, perhaps, to have required, what nothing but a dear sister's intellectual improvement could have induced me to demand?' At Oxford it had been enough for Shelley to declare a hope that Hogg would become his brother-in-law. From Field Place, during the Christmas holidays, the enthusiastic stripling begged Hogg to promise he would satisfy the hope.

Whilst he thus arranged a match between Hogg and his sister, Shelley knew that his friend was a Freethinker on questions relating to religion. From what had recently taken place in respect to his sceptical correspondence with Miss Harriett Grove, he knew that his father and mother concurred with his uncle and aunt Grove in regarding religious scepticism with repugnance and horror; knew that his father and mother would regard their eldest daughter's marriage to a Freethinker as a terrible and supreme calamity. Yet he was coolly and secretly scheming for such a marriage of their sixteen-years-old daughter, and was cautiously 'illuminating' her out of the Christian religion, and otherwise training her to become the fit wife of a man, whom he had good reason to know her parents would never consent to accept for their son-in-law. The young gentleman does all this in absolute indifference to the rights and feelings of his own father and mother—with absolute carelessness for the serious trouble he is preparing for his father, the agonizing sorrow he is preparing for his mother. Am I wrong in saying that the young man (*ætat.* 18), who acted in this manner to his father and mother and his younger sister, was guilty of domestic treason?

What was the literary enterprise on which Shelley was at work during the earlier weeks of this Christmas recess (1810-11)?—the work that was offered to Mr. Stockdale during the recess?—the work about whose publication Mr. Hogg, whilst staying at a London hotel, had several interviews with the Pall-Mall publisher, who, sixteen years later, professed to have been most unfavourably impressed by the Oxonian's appearance, speech, and manner, at those interviews? The general opinion of the 'Shelleyan enthusiasts' is that the work thus submitted to the bookseller was *The Necessity of Atheism*, the pamphlet that resulted in Shelley's expulsion from his college? Mr. Garnett has no doubt that the work was 'either the unlucky pamphlet which occasioned Shelley's expulsion from Oxford, or something of a very similar description.' Mr. Denis Florence MacCarthy goes a step further, and speaks of it roundly as the manuscript of *The Necessity of Atheism*. That the manuscript, which afforded Stockdale another opportunity for warning Mr. Timothy Shelley to remove his son from Mr.

Hogg's pernicious influences, was a sceptical performance is unquestionable. But there are grounds for a strong opinion that it was neither *The Necessity of Atheism*, nor any tract written on the same lines as that notorious pamphlet. The evidence is conclusive that up to the time, and beyond the time, when Stockdale was invited to publish the pamphlet, Shelley believed in the existence of a supreme Deity. He had for a considerable period ceased to be a Christian. But he still believed in God. To hold, therefore, that the manuscript declined by Stockdale was *The Necessity of Atheism*, or 'something of a *very similar description*,' is to hold that whilst believing in God Shelley wrote a book to prove there was no God; that whilst believing in the existence of the Deity he set himself deliberately to work, to force other people into pure atheism. I cannot believe with Mr. Garnett, and Mr. Denis Florence MacCarthy, that Shelley was capable of such amazing impiety. Nothing is stranger in Shelley's story than that the hardest things said of him should, in so many cases, be uttered by his extravagant idolaters. My conception of the Oxonian Shelley is that he was an impetuous, unruly, combative young scatterbrain; disloyal and deceitful to his parents; certainly capable of falsehood in comparatively small matters to other people; but I cannot believe he could have been so false to his own soul, so prodigiously false to his own convictions on the most awful of all solemn subjects, as to write and seek a publisher for a serious argument against the belief in God, whilst he himself believed in the Deity.

Let us see from evidences, known to Mr. Garnett, when he wrote his *Shelley in Pall Mall*, what were some of Shelley's views respecting God, in the Christmas holidays of 1810-11. On 26th December, 1810, he writes to Hogg from Field Place :—

'Thanks, *truly* thanks, for opening your heart to me, for telling me your feelings to me. Dare I do the same to you? I dare not to myself, how can I to another, perfect as he may be. I dare not even to God, whose mercy is great.'

On 3rd January, 1811, the future poet writes to the same correspondent :

'The word "God," a vague word, has been, and will continue to be, the source of numberless errors, until it is erased from the nomenclature of philosophy. Does it not imply "the soul of the universe, the intelligent and necessarily beneficent, actuating principle." This it is

impossible not to believe in.　I may not be able to adduce proofs ; but,
I think, that the leaf of a tree, the meanest insect on which we trample,
are, in themselves, arguments more conclusive than [any] which can be
advanced [. . . .] that some vast intellect animates infinity.　If we
disbelieve this, the strongest argument in support of the existence of a
future state instantly becomes annihilated.'

Nine days later (12th January, 1811), the future poet writes
from Field Place :—

'I here take God (*and a God exists*) to witness, that I wish torments, which beggar the futile description of a fancied hell, would fall
upon me ; provided I could attain thereby that happiness for what I
love, which, I fear, can never be !　.　.　.　I wish, ardently wish, to
be profoundly convinced of the existence of a Deity, that so superior a
spirit might derive some degree of happiness from my feeble exertions ;
for love is heaven, and heaven is love　.　.　.　.　I think I can prove
the existence of a Deity—a First Cause.'

After declaring thus emphatically his belief in the existence
of a Deity, Shelley goes on to argue in defence of his conviction.

Thus Shelley is found declaring his belief in the existence
of God so late as 12th January, 1811, when the work declined
by Stockdale (the work said by Mr. Garnett to have been either
The Necessity of Atheism, 'or something of a very similar description '), must have already been in the publisher's hands.
The post did not travel seventy years since so quickly as it
travels in these railway times; the work, whatever it was, could
not have been written in a day; brief though it is, *The Necessity
of Atheism* could not have been designed and put on paper in
a single morning ; yet, on 14th January, 1811, Shelley could
write indignantly to Hogg :—

' S[tockdale] has behaved infamously to me ; he has abused the
confidence I reposed in him in sending him my work; and he has made
very free with your character, of which he knows nothing, with my
father.'

Moreover, on the 12th January, 1811, Hogg (who saw Stockdale
about the work during his stay in Lincoln's Inn Fields) had
left London some six or eight days.　It is, therefore, certain
that Shelley was believing in the existence of God at a time
when Mr. Garnett represents him as set on teaching men
that atheism was a necessity.

When did Shelley discard the reasons which had hitherto
constrained him to believe in the existence of God?　Clearly at

some time subsequent to 12th January, 1811. Who caused him to discard them ?—Mr. Thomas Jefferson Hogg. To readers of Shelley's afore-mentioned letter of 12th January, 1811, it is obvious, from the arguments with which he essays to demonstrate the reasonableness of his belief in a Deity, that, though still clinging to his belief in God, he was already troubled by, and battling with, his doubts on the subject. His mind had been so troubled for several days. On 6th January, 1811, he had written from Field Place to Hogg, 'I will consider your argument against the non-existence of a Deity.' In reply to Hogg's arguments for *The Necessity of Atheism*, Shelley does his feeble best (on 6th January, 1811) to demonstrate their unreasonableness. If Shelley's arguments were sufficient for their purpose, Hogg had argued with less than his usual ability. Shelley's arguments are puerile, and he clearly felt their insufficiency, when he followed them up with these words: 'But I will write again; my head is dizzy to-day, on account of not taking rest, and a slight attack of typhus.' Hence it appears that from 6th to 12th January, Hogg was arguing against the existence of God, and Shelley was more earnestly than strenuously arguing for the belief in Deity. If he was dizzy on 6th January, after replying to Hogg, he was yet more so on 12th January, 1811, after striving to prove the existence of God.

The poor lad's head was dizzy, but not from want of sleep, or from typhus fever : Mr. Thomas Jefferson Hogg had dizzied it with his ingenious arguments against the existence of Deity. One can conceive how the clever, hard-headed, humorous young gentleman from the neighbourhood of Stockton-upon-Tees, smiled over his friend's letters, and exulted at the signs of his plaything's perplexity. It mattered not a rush to Mr. Hogg, of University College, Oxford, on which side of a question he argued. Having done his best to dizzy his young friend out of his belief in God, and convince him of the necessity of atheism, Mr. Hogg tacked about, and five or six days later amused himself by constructing some equally ingenious arguments to convince his young friend of the necessity of Christianity. On the 12th of January, 1811, after fighting desperately for the preservation of his belief in God, the poor boy with the dizzy brain writes to his tormentor : 'But now, to your argument of the necessity of Christianity, I am not sure that your argument does not tend to prove its unreality.'   All through this perilous game Hogg was at play, whilst Shelley was in earnest,—far too much in earnest to be capable of publishing a tract against God's existence, whilst he believed in it. What was sport to Hogg was death to Shelley,—at least, to his happiness in this world.

Towards the close of the Christmas vacation, Mr. Timothy Shelley seems to have worked off his anger with his son, and taken him into affectionate consideration—though, of course, neither into high favour nor perfect confidence. Having thrown off his wrath in scolding with tongue and pen, the Member of Parliament for New Shoreham relented to his scatterbrain boy, so far as to talk with him sympathetically on the very questions that had caused their disagreement. This change of feeling may have resulted in some degree from the advice of judicious counsellors. The Duke of Norfolk, whose opinion was weighty with Mr. Timothy Shelley in his private concerns, no less than in his political affairs, may have been one of these judicious counsellors; for his Grace had already displayed a kindly interest in the future poet, and in later time was at great pains to mediate between the father and son, and recover them from open war to an appearance of mutual friendliness. The Horsham miser, whose word of definite command was law to the son he hated, may also have used his influence in favour of the grandson, for whom he cherished in his cold and selfish breast a secret and curiously malicious tenderness. An atheist himself, who, on the approach of death, spoke with equal confidence and contentment of his own utter annihilation, the aged baronet was in no degree shocked by the youngster's religious opinions. On the contrary, he contemplated them with self-complacence as the fruits of his own teaching and example, and as indications that the lad would develop into a creditable chief of the Castle Goring Shelleys. Approving his grandson's heterodoxy, and liking him none the less for being a thorn in his father's side, Sir Bysshe may be assumed to have given the Squire of Field Place a significant hint that the boy was not to be rated and denounced out of his grandsire's favour. In accounting, however, for the alteration of Mr. Timothy Shelley's demeanour to his heir, it is only fair and reasonable to suppose that the change was in some degree due to the paternal affectionateness and good sense of this gentleman, who could not shut his eyes to the fact that he was his son's father. Anyhow, it is inconsistent with much which has been written of the father's invariable harshness to the youthful poet, that towards the middle of January, 1811, he could invite his son to a friendly conference on the evidences of Christianity.

Ever in the humour for controversy, it is needless to say that Mr. Bysshe Shelley (whose great grievance against the 'dons' of University College was that they expelled him *without* arguing with him) accepted this invitation without requiring his father to repeat it. For a few minutes the youngster's brain and heart kindled with a desire to enlighten his father out of his Christian darkness, and the hope that by winning so strange a convert he should make himself master of the religious position at Field Place. For a few minutes the discussion was more than satisfactory and encouraging to the beardless apostle of Free Thought. Admitting it was absurd to believe in witches and ghosts, Mr. Timothy Shelley allowed that the mediæval miracles were the mere offspring of vulgar fancy and vulgar credulity. But on being pressed to take the same view of the Scriptural miracles, the worthy gentleman faced about, and held stoutly to his delusions, making it only too manifest that he could not be argued and illuminated out of them.

By the considerations which determined him to ascertain his son's religious opinions, the Squire of Field Place was also brought to see that, instead of denouncing his son's familiar friend without knowing him, even as he had denounced his religious views without apprehending precisely what they were, it would be better for him to look Mr. Hogg clearly in the face, make his acquaintance, talk to him in friendly wise, and judge for himself how far the young gentleman from the neighbourhood of Stockton-upon-Tees had been fairly described, and how far misrepresented, by the Pall-Mall bookseller. Mr. Timothy Shelley was far too robust and intelligent a gentleman to put implicit reliance in Mr. Stockdale's judgment, and to have perfect confidence in the honesty of the publisher, who, after giving a 'minor' pecuniary credit for conveniences scarcely to be rated as 'necessaries' for an Oxford undergraduate, was now looking to the minor's father for payment of 'the little account.' Quite shrewd enough to see Mr. Stockdale's motive and game, Mr. Timothy Shelley, whilst listening to him with abundant civility, and thanking him with all the customary courtesies for his valuable information, saw the necessity of checking the publisher's statements with intelligence, gained from other, and possibly less equivocal, sources. Acting like a sensible man of affairs and the world, the Member of Parliament made inquiries about Mr. Stockdale, and also inquiries touching Mr. Thomas Jefferson Hogg, and Mr. Hogg's people in Durham Co. and Yorkshire; the result of the inquiries being that he thought none too well of the bookseller, and a good deal better of Mr. Hogg. Hence it was that, whilst adopting a conciliatory tone to his son on the religious questions, Mr. Timothy Shelley ceased to speak harshly, and began to speak civilly to his son, of Mr. Thomas Jefferson Hogg, whom he now knew by good report, as well as by ill report, though only by report.

At the same time, it became obvious to the Squire of Field Place that he had better have the friendly regard of the young gentleman, who certainly had considerable influence over his son. Hence it was that the Squire, little imagining the conspiracy for marrying his eldest daughter to the young gentleman he had never seen, told Shelley to invite his college-friend to Field Place for the next Easter vacation :—a concession that, attended with other indications of the Squire's change of feeling for Hogg, caused Shelley to think his father must have received a favourable account of the Durham Co. and Yorkshire Hoggs, from some of his friends in the House of Commons.

The visit was never paid by Hogg; but to the date of the catastrophe, which, driving them from Oxford, was quickly followed by incidents that rendered Hogg no person to be welcome at Field Place, the friends looked forward to the Easter recess as a time that would be fruitful of opportunities for the accomplishment of their designs on the eldest daughter of the house.

The knavish publisher of 41 Pall Mall, had small reason to congratulate himself on the success of his machinations for separating Bysshe Shelley from his friend; for rendering Hogg the object of Mr. Timothy Shelley's strongest aversion; and for inducing the Squire of Field Place to pay the costs and charges of the publication of *St. Irvyne.* Instead of separating the two undergraduates, the schemer had the pleasure of knowing they were even closer friends at the beginning of February than they had been in the earlier weeks of December. Instead of rendering Hogg especially distasteful to Mr. Timothy Shelley, the schemer had only stimulated the Member for New Shoreham to make inquiries, which disposed him to think favourably of his son's friend. Instead of making Mr. Timothy Shelley mistake him for a worthy man, who was entitled to handsome reward for important service, the schemer got never a shilling for his pains. For breach of confidence and slanderous tattle, Hogg whipt the dirty fellow with a scorching letter. For the same offence the paltry creature was punished in the same manner by Shelley. Having heard the tale-bearer out to the end of his cunning talk, Mr. Timothy Shelley saw no reason why he should pay a sixpence of the bill which he had declared no affair of his, on the first hint that he would act gracefully and generously by settling the claim. Having exhausted his store of pleasant words for such a creature, Mr. Timothy Shelley turned from the man with a sufficiently frank avowal of contempt.

Mr. John Joseph Stockdale was no person to smart acutely from disdainful words. He was, of course, uneasy to think he had provoked the enmity of the two young men, who a short while hence might be able to injure him in his business; but, had it not been for this consideration, he would read their angry letters with more amusement than annoyance. Mr. Timothy Shelley's scorn would have passed over his thick skin without causing him aught more than transient uneasiness, had it been accompanied with a cheque for the required sum. But it galled Mr. John Joseph Stockdale to miss the trick for which he had played so meanly,—galled him all the more because he was conscious of having played his poor cards badly. It must be confessed that the cards were no less weak than dirty. A cleverer rogue than Mr. Stockdale would have failed to win with them. Had he, in 1811, been the rich man he became in later times, Mr. Timothy Shelley might well have declined to pay the publisher's demand, and thereby encourage other literary speculators to produce his son's works in the expectation of being paid by his father. But till Sir Bysshe passed from the world, the Squire of Field Place, far from being wealthy for his station, was in no position to spend a hundred guineas lightly. Under these circumstances, the gentleman with several children and a pecuniary prospect that might even yet be darkened by the caprice of his eccentric father, was more than barely justified in saying that his son's publisher must look to his client, not to his client's father, for remuneration. It was

not in Mr. Stockdale to take this obvious and reasonable view
of a simple question.   The money Mr. Timothy Shelley refused
to give him was regarded by Mr. Stockdale as money basely
and fraudulently withheld.   To the publisher's imagination the
sum he failed to extort became a sum of which he had been
robbed; the injury done him being the more outrageous and
exasperating because he had rendered the doer of the wrong
an important service.

In 1827, when the poet had been dead between four and
five years, the publisher took his revenge on the perpetrator
of so monstrous an injustice.   By that time the embittered
knave had dropt from the ways of decent trade, and was
falling to the deeper disrepute in which he soon passed from
view.   A fabricator of scandalous literature as well as a publisher of it, he had already produced the *Memoirs of Harriet
Wilson*, when he started the *Budget*, that bears his name,
as a vehicle for airing a vanity, which had in some degree
deranged a mind long fretted by imaginary grievances, and
as an instrument for venting his spite on those who had
provoked his displeasure, no less than as means of drawing
relief to his indigence from the lovers of personal gossip.
In this sordid serial, the broken and utterly discredited libeller produced a mendacious narrative of his transactions
with Shelley and Shelley's father.   As he could get nothing
in 1827 by abusing Shelley, it is not surprising that he spoke
well of him at the instigation of self-interest, vanity, and spite.
The man knew enough of the literary coteries to know the tide
of social feeling had so far turned in Shelley's favour that,
whilst disparagement of the poet would not fail to offend, praise
of him would not fail to conciliate the readers, most capable of
commending the *Budget* to public favour.   For the same reason
vanity prompted the fellow to represent himself as the original
discoverer and earliest fosterer of the poet's genius.   In prais-
ing the poet he was also actuated by spite against the poet's
father, whose treatment of his son would appear harsh and
hateful, in proportion to the strength of the reader's conviction
that the poet deserved different usage.   On the other hand,
though chiefly actuated by malice, the libeller was also animated
by vanity and self-interest in what he wrote to Sir Timothy
Shelley's discredit; for whilst it afforded him a pleasant sense of
his own importance to speak authoritatively of a baronet's mis-

demeanour, the slanderer knew the growing appetite for words
to the poet's credit was attended with an even keener appetite
for evidence to his father's discredit. Hence, whether he spoke
of the poet or the poet's father, he spoke at the instance of
self-interest, vanity, and malice.

Such was the man, such were the motives of the man, in
whose malignant and nauseous gossip about the poet and his
father, Mr. Garnett discovers 'traces of sincere affection' for
the author of *Laon and Cythna.* Not content with gushing
over Stockdale's 'sincere affection for the young author whose
acquaintance was certainly anything but advantageous to him in
a pecuniary point of view,' Mr. Garnett deals with the words of
this professional slanderer as good evidence, that in their bitter
differences the poet was guiltless of serious offence, and that the
poet's father was greatly to blame.

'Stockdale,' says Mr. Garnett, of this creditable witness to character
and want of character, 'had frequent opportunities of observing the
uneasy terms on which the two stood towards each other, and unhesi-
tatingly throws the entire blame upon the father, whom he represents as
narrow-minded and wrong-headed, behaving with extreme niggardliness
in money matters, and at the same time continually fretting Shelley by
harsh and unnecessary interference with his most indifferent actions.'

What a use to make of the words of a slanderer-by-trade, a
libeller surcharged with rancorous enmity against the poet's
father! To insult Shelley by making his character depend in
any degree on the words of such a rascal as Stockdale, it is
necessary that a man of letters should be a 'Shelleyan
enthusiast.'

It is not a fact that 'Stockdale had frequent opportunities
of observing the uneasy terms on which the two stood to each
other.' With the exception of the two or three occasions when
the father and son came together to the Pall-Mall shop, Stockdale never saw them together. Doubtless there was uneasiness
between them on those occasions, for they met on matters of disagreement, and in the presence of the man who, for his own
advantage, was doing his best to render the father more than
usually distrustful of, and anxious about, his son. The whole
period of Stockdale's acquaintance with Mr. Timothy Shelley
was covered by the few weeks, during which time they
exchanged letters and had two or three conferences touching
the poet's affairs,—the few weeks during which the unscrupu-

lous tradesman was vainly endeavouring to wheedle the Member of Parliament into paying the minor's bill for the publication of *St. Irvyne.* What opportunities can so brief and slight an intercourse have offered the publisher for using influence to dispose Mr. Shelley to be a better father? To believe the fellow's impudent statements, one must believe that during those few weeks he assumed an almost parental authority over the gentleman on whose pocket he had designs. In 1827 sixteen years had elapsed since this slight intercourse of less than two months. How strange that after so many years, Stockdale should have had so clear a memory of the incidents of this slight intercourse,—so distinct a recollection of the peculiarities of the gentleman with whom he spoke on three or four occasions, and exchanged perhaps as many letters! How strange that ' the Shelleyan enthusiasts '—so suspicious and distrustful of the accuracy of Hogg's recollections of his most familiar friend whom he knew thoroughly—should accept so readily the publisher's recollections of the gentleman, of whom he knew scarcely anything!

The same reflections are applicable to Stockdale's vivid recollections of the Oxonian Shelley, and to Mr. Garnett's reliance on the accuracy of those recollections. Though they exchanged letters in January, 1811, and had some disagreeable correspondence in later months of the same year, it does not appear that Shelley ever set eyes on the Pall-Mall publisher after December, 1810. The whole period of their personal intercourse cannot have exceeded four months :—months spent chiefly by Shelley at Oxford or in Sussex, whilst the publisher was attending to his affairs in London ? To assume that during these four months they had a dozen meetings is to assume too much. It is more probable that they talked with one another on seven or eight several occasions. What opportunities could such an acquaintanceship afford the publisher for knowing his young client in such a way, that sixteen years later he could recall him clearly ? Is it reasonable to suppose that the publisher during these interviews (and from several letters in no degree calculated to fill their receiver's breast with tender emotion) conceived a strong affection—or any affection whatever—for the boy out of whom, or rather out of whose father, he meant to ' make a bill ? '

One might as reasonably imagine a money-lender overflowing with love for any young gentleman ' in his teens,' to whom he lends 50*l.* on the usual terms. Are London publishers so very different from other men of business, that they do business with youthful poets and novelists from impulses of affection, altogether pure of self-interest? I know something of London publishers: few men have better reason to think and speak well of them; to my last hour of consciousness I shall never recall a particular London publisher, without remembering him as one of the trustiest and dearest of the many friends who have contributed to my happiness; but still my impression is, and my experience has been, that a publisher's regard for a young author has a tendency to rise and fall with the sale of the young author's works. *St. Irvyne* having fallen dead from the press, even as Mr. Stockdale expected it to do, I have no doubt that Mr. Stockdale merely regarded his young author as a simpleton, whom he would not trust on any future occasion (during his minority) to pay the printer's bill. To do Stockdale justice (and even to such a worm I would not be less than just) it should be remarked that he is no such preposterous 'humbug' as Mr. Garnett's words imply. Though he whines hypocritically about 'his too conscientious friendship' for Mr. Bysshe Shelley, of University College, Oxford, the professional libeller does not profess to have loved the youth, with whom he was doing 'risky business.' In 1827, the disposition to think tenderly of Shelley had not gone so far as to produce a crop of 'Shelleyan enthusiasts' capable of believing that the publisher loved the author of *St. Irvyne.* Had Stockdale claimed credit for loving the dear boy, who came to his shop about the *Original Poetry* that was not original, the original readers of the *Budget* would have derided him, and denounced his *Budget.* Though he says civil things of Shelley, to heighten the effect of the uncivil things said of Shelley's father, Stockdale forbears to descant on his affection for the future poet. It is enough for him to say, 'Even from these boyish trifles' (*i.e. St. Irvyne,* and the *Victor-and-Cazire Book*), 'assisted by my personal intercourse with the author, I at once formed an opinion that he was not an everyday author.' In saying this (as he meant the ambiguous words to be construed in the way most complimentary to the poet) the budgeteer told a lie,—but a lie not too outrageous to be believed. Further (to insult Sir Timothy Shelley, who in the scribbler's opinion had refused to discharge 'every honest claim upon him'), the libeller spoke highly of the poet's 'honour and rectitude,' declaring him a man to 'vegetate, rather than live, to effect the discharge of every honest claim upon him.' But to speak of a man in this style is not to show signs of loving him. I know an author who certainly is no 'everyday author,' and would (I am sure) be at great pains to pay his creditors twenty shillings in the pound; but far from loving him, I would any day rather go without my dinner than eat it in his company.

Truth to tell, the 'traces of a sincere affection for the young author,' which Mr. Garnett has discovered in Stockdale's words about Shelley, are so far from being distinctly apparent, that I have vainly sought for them in the pages, where they are so manifest to the author of *Shelley in Pall Mall*. I think Mr. Garnett goes a little too far in saying—

'Percy Shelley captivated all hearts: the roughest were subdued by his sweetness, the most reserved won by his affectionate candour. . . . . In spite of his disappointment, Stockdale really appears to have been captivated by Shelley, and to have been not more forcibly impressed by the energy of his intellect than by the loveliness of his character.'

Gentlemen given to gushing often say more than they mean. I cannot conceive Mr. Garnett means all he says in his perplexing article. I have vainly worked through Stockdale's *Budget* in search for the proofs, that Stockdale was forcibly impressed by the intellectual energy and moral loveliness of the author of *St. Irvyne*. But the 'Shelleyan enthusiasts' are so apt to weaken their case by exaggeration; they are so excessive in their statements. The notion that Stockdale the Libeller was a man to be captivated by moral beauty is comical.

CHAPTER XII.

MR. MACCARTHY'S DISCOVERIES TOUCHING THE OXONIAN SHELLEY.

A Poetical Essay on the Existing State of Things—Evidence that the
Poem was Published—Reasons for Thinking it may never have been
Published—Reasons for Thinking that, if the Poem was Published, it
was promptly Suppressed—Did Shelley contribute Prose and Poetry
to the *Oxford Herald?*—Spurious Letter to the Editor of the *Statesman*
—Shelley's First Letter to Leigh Hunt—His way of Introducing himself to Strangers—Did he at the Same Moment Think Well and Ill of
his Father?—Miss Janetta Phillips's Poems—E. & W. Phillips, the
Worthing Printers.

BEFORE returning from Field Place to Oxford at the close of the
Christmas Vacation (1810–11), readers who, in addition to a perfect
view of Shelley's life at the University, wish to have a knowledge of all
that has been written about that part of his career, will do well to
consider certain matters with which Mr. Denis Florence MacCarthy
may be said to have cumbered the highway of the poet's academic
story. Considerations of prudence for himself, and of care for the
interests of his readers, forbid the present writer to pass over these
matters in silence, as though he were not cognizant of their existence.
At the same time, he is disinclined to notice them in a chapter, where
they would interrupt the narrative of the undergraduate's second term
of residence at University College. He therefore decides to deal with
them in a separate chapter, that may be lightly 'skimmed' or altogether
skipt by the busy peruser of these volumes, whose curiosity respecting
the poet's life is unattended by a keen appetite for details of Shelleyan
controversy.

I. With magniloquence, that may seem comical to persons deficient
in Mr. Forman's ability to venerate every scrap of paper blotted by the
poet's pen, Mr. MacCarthy declares himself to 'have discovered the
surrounding light that indicates the presence of a star,' without being
so fortunate as to have 'detected its nucleus.' This is only Mr.
MacCarthy's figurative and beautiful way of saying that, without
coming upon a copy of the work, he has come upon evidence that
Shelley, towards the close of his second term of residence at Oxford,
published *A Poetical Essay on the Existing State of Things*, for the
benefit of Mr. Peter Finerty, then undergoing imprisonment in Lincoln
Gaol for libel on Lord Castlereagh,—that this poem was a very beautiful

poem,—and that it differed from all the poet's earlier and all his later writings, in having a quick and large sale.

Readers, who take Mr. MacCarthy's view and estimate of the evidence, have no doubt that the sale of this remarkable poem, after paying the costs of its production, yielded nearly one hundred pounds to the fund that was raised for Mr. Finerty's sustenance and comfort in captivity. To persons who remember the wretched quality of the Oxonian Shelley's prose and verse, it can scarcely be obvious why a lost poem by his still feeble pen should be likened to a star, and why the shadowy evidence that he wrote the poem should be comparable with the surrounding light of the heavenly body. Let that pass, however; and let it be conceded that evidence of so successful a poem, by the youthful and hitherto unfortunate aspirant to literary fame, would be a matter of some interest, even to persons in no degree touched with Shelleyan madness. What is the evidence that Shelley produced this successful poem, no copy of which has ever come under the notice of living man? The evidence consists of,—

(*a*) This advertisement in the 9th March, 1811, number of the *Oxford Herald* :—

'Literature. Just published, Price Two Shillings, *A Poetical Essay On The Existing State of Things*.

"And Famine At Her Bidding Wasted Wide
The Wretched Land. Till In The Public Way,
Promiscuous Where The Dead And Dying Lay,
Dogs Fed On Human Bones In The Open Light Of Day."

By A Gentleman Of The University Of Oxford. For assisting to Maintain In Prison Mr. Peter Finerty, Imprisoned For A Libel. London : Sold By B. Crosby and Co., And All Other Booksellers. 1811.'

(*b*) Four advertisements of the same poem in London newspapers; two of them being in the *Morning Chronicle* for 15th and 21st March, 1811, whilst the other two may be found in the *Times* for 10th and 11th April, 1811.

(*c*) These words by an anonymous writer in the *Dublin Weekly Messenger* of 7th March, 1812 :—

'We have but one more word to add. Mr. Shelley, commiserating the sufferings of our distinguished countryman, Mr. Finerty, whose exertions in the cause of political freedom he much admired, wrote a very beautiful poem, the profits of the sale of which, we understand, from undoubted authority, Mr. Shelley remitted to Mr. Finerty. We have heard they amounted to nearly an hundred pounds. This fact speaks a volume in favour of our new friend.'

(*d*) The fact that Shelley sent from Dublin a copy of the paper containing these words, and particularly called Godwin's attention to the article in which they appeared.

(c) The fact that during his imprisonment Mr. Finerty had the sympathy of the *Dublin Weekly Messenger*.

These are all the facts Mr. MacCarthy produces in evidence that Shelley wrote a poem no living man ever saw, no single person of any time is known to have seen. Of course the gentleman, who is so severe on Hogg's inaccuracies, blunders and contradicts himself in marshalling so slender an array of facts. For instance, after stating (p. 100) precisely and correctly that the earliest of the five advertisements of the poem appeared in the *Oxford Herald* of 9th March, 1811, he avers a few pages later (p. 105) that this same earliest advertisement appeared in the paper of 2nd March, 1811.

How does this curiously inaccurate gentleman reason from his facts? To Mr. MacCarthy it appears indisputable that the poem must have been written and published, as the five advertisements declare it ' Just Published.' But it is no uncommon thing now, it was no rare thing eighty years since, for publishers to announce books as ' just published,' before their actual day of publication. Books have been printed and so announced, and yet at the last moment have been withheld from publication. Moreover, it would be no new thing for a literary adventurer to advertise that a work by his pen would shortly appear, without having any intention or power to fulfil the promise of the announcement. The books of the British Museum Library would be more numerous by several thousands, had authors invariably acted up to their advertisements.

Underscoring the words ' undoubted authority,' Mr. MacCarthy intimates that Shelley himself must have been the ' undoubted authority.' The assumption is reasonable, but it is only an assumption. Could he be proved to have been the sure authority, it would still be noticeable that, though he declared the poem had been published for Mr. Finerty's benefit, some other person may have been the journalist's authority for saying the profits amounted to nearly 100*l.* For, whilst declaring ' from *undoubted authority*,' that Shelley sent the profits to Mr. Finerty, the article-writer is curiously silent as to the quality of his authority for writing, ' *We have heard* they amounted to nearly an hundred pounds.' In fact, his language implies that, whilst having the best authority for the first, he had not the best authority for the second, statement.

Again, arguing from Shelley's veracity, Mr. MacCarthy insists that by sending the article to Godwin without disclaiming any of the grounds on which he is commended in it, Shelley endorsed the whole statement, and pledged his honour to its truth.

' This statement, too, it should be remembered, is authenticated by Shelley himself, for he sends the paper containing it to Godwin, and pointedly refers to the article in which it is given.'

Was Shelley so precisely accurate in all his statements, that we should be bound to believe the words, if he could be shown to have written them himself? To readers who have given due consideration to a certain letter referred to in the last chapter, it must be comical to hear the author of *Shelley's Early Life* arguing that the words of the *Dublin Weekly Messenger* must be true, because in sending the paper to Godwin, the poet did not warn him of their inaccuracy. Readers will have stronger reason for smiling at Mr. MacCarthy's simplicity, when they know more about the earlier of Shelley's letters to Godwin,—letters overflowing with the most staggering misrepresentations.

Yet further, it is argued by Mr. MacCarthy that, having the friendliest relations with the *Dublin Weekly Messenger*, Mr. Finerty was doubtless a regular and attentive reader of the paper, must therefore have seen the words relating to the profits of the poem, and would of course have contradicted them had they been untrue. As Mr. Finerty did not contradict the words, his silence must be regarded as tantamount to direct testimony from his pen, that the poem was published for his benefit, and yielded a sum of nearly one hundred pounds to the fund raised for his benefit.

'Nothing,' says Mr. MacCarthy, 'published in the *Weekly Messenger* could possibly have escaped his notice. It is incredible that he would not have contradicted this statement of the presentation to him of the profits of a poem if it were not true.'

Against this series of assumptions and the argument founded upon them, several considerations may be urged. (1) Because the *Dublin Weekly Messenger* favoured his cause, it does not follow that a copy of the paper was sent to Mr. Finerty every week during his imprisonment in Lincoln Gaol. (2) There is no evidence that the paper was usually sent to him every week (in times when the rates of postage were heavy), or even that it was sent on any single occasion to him during that term. (3) As he was treated with extraordinary severity during his imprisonment, it is by no means so certain as the author of *Shelley's Early Life* imagines, that the prisoner was allowed to see newspapers containing expressions of sympathy with and admiration of him. (4) On the contrary, though he may have seen the copies of the *Dublin Weekly Messenger* that contained no reference to his case, it is highly improbable that during his imprisonment he was allowed to see the copies of the journal which spoke of him eulogistically. (5) It is conceivable that, if he saw the words of the Dublin newspaper during his imprisonment, he knew them to be inaccurate, and yet refrained from contradicting them. He may have read the words in prison without knowing whether they were true or false, as the business of collecting the money for his benefit was in the hands of a committee. He may have known that Shelley published a poem for his advantage, and known also that the publication yielded no profits : in which case he would not have been so ungracious as to contradict the statement of the amount of the profits, and thereby call attention to the literary miscarriage of a well-wisher who, besides subscribing a guinea to the Finerty Fund, had also recommended the fund to public favour in the unsuccessful work. If he saw the words of the Dublin newspaper, and knew them to be untrue, the inaccuracy was no reason why he should call attention to a misstatement that could do him no harm, was on the contrary calculated to stimulate the feeling in his favour, and could not be corrected without risk of giving annoyance to the young gentleman who anyhow had subscribed a guinea to the Finerty Fund.

Whilst the evidence of the publication of a poem is far from conclusive, the evidence is very strong that, if a poem was published, its sale must have fallen far short of the number indicated by the *not* authoritative words (the statement made on mere hearsay talk) of the anonymous writer of the *Dublin Weekly Messenger*. *If* the poem was published at all, it appears from the advertisements to have been offered for sale at the price of two shillings a copy. If a poem was published, it was probably not a poem of many thousands, or even many hundreds, of lines. Let us suppose that a poem was published, and the costs of printing, producing, publishing, and advertising the work were 50*l.*—a moderate sum at which to put the expenses, if the poem contained from five hundred to a thousand lines. Allowances to the trade being taken into account, there must have been a sale of at least two thousand copies at the rate of two shillings a copy, for the sale to bring in 50*l.* for expenses of publication, and 100*l.* for the Finerty Fund. The sum accruing to that fund from the sale is put by the anonymous writer of the *Dublin Weekly Messenger* at something less than 100*l.* On the other hand, account must be taken of copies sent to reviewers and copies *given* by the author to his friends;—copies that, without being paid for, passed into circulation. These copies may be computed as equal to the number by which the actual sale of the work fell short of 2000 copies,—*i.e.* the sale that would have yielded a clear 100*l.* (over the 50*l.* for costs) to the Finerty Fund. What is the evidence that so large a number of copies of the poem cannot have been put in circulation?

' "It is," says Mr. MacCarthy, in the preface to *Shelley's Early Life*, "needless to say that this interesting volume is not to be found in any of our public libraries. To the courteous librarians of the Bodleian at Oxford, and of University College" (*sic*) " at Cambridge, I have specially to return my thanks for the search they had kindly made for it. A printed circular sent by myself to almost every second-hand bookseller in the three kingdoms was equally unsuccessful. To advertisements in the public journals, and special inquiries instituted by Mr. Quaritch, Piccadilly; Mr. Stibbs, Museum Street; Messrs. Longmans, Paternoster Row, and others, no reply has been received." '

Mr. Denis Florence MacCarthy seizes every occasion for inaccuracy, and now and then makes an occasion, in the absence of a decent opportunity, for blundering. What does Mr. MacCarthy mean ' by University College at Cambridge?' Oxford has a college styled University College; there is a college so called in London; but

Cambridge has no University College. By the charitable writer of the present page, it is assumed that by 'University College *at* Cambridge,' Mr. MacCarthy (who is so merciless and malignant to Hogg for his occasional inaccuracies) means The Cambridge University Library. Let it be so assumed by the reader.

It follows, that some years since Mr. Denis Florence MacCarthy sought by printed circular for a copy of this Shelleyan poem (which possibly was never published) in the shop of nearly every second-hand bookseller in Great Britain and Ireland; that he caused the Librarians of the Bodleian Library, and the Cambridge University Library, to search for a copy of the poem in their libraries; that he induced Mr. Quaritch of Piccadilly, Mr. Stibbs of Museum Street, and the Messrs. Longmans of Paternoster Row, ' and others,' to make search by advertisements and special inquiries, for a copy of the poem,—without coming upon a copy after all the trouble.

Yet more :—Hogg never heard of this poem; Peacock never heard of it, so far as the evidences go ; no one of the poet's friends or relations appears ever to have heard of it ; no review of the poem has come to light ; and (more remarkable yet !) no one of the many published lists of subscriptions to the Finerty Fund, to be found in the *Morning Chronicle*, and other papers of the period (examined by Mr. MacCarthy), makes mention of any single contribution amounting to 100*l.*,—of *any* contributions whatever as the result of the sale of the poem.

What a labour of searching for a copy of the poem, and for evidence about the poem, that may never have been written! Surely the searching would have resulted in the discovery of a copy, had 2000 copies passed into circulation, or in the discovery of some stronger evidence of the poem's publication, had the sale of the work yielded any considerable sum of money to the Fund, which amounted in the course of twelve months to something more than 1000*l.*

The evidence is not even conclusive that Shelley had a serious intention to produce a poem for Mr. Finerty's advantage. He may have put forth the advertisements to whip up the public interest in the movement for the unfortunate journalist's benefit. Evidence so weak can only be used conjecturally. I am disposed to regard the advertisements as *bonâ-fide* advertisements, and to think they referred to some poem published by Shelley for the alleged object. The author may also have published the poem with an eye to his own advantage; may have hoped to use the excitement of a political stir as a means of floating into circulation a poem, which, in case it succeeded, the 'Gentleman of the University of Oxford' could claim in his own name. He had been for some time thinking of publishing a satirical poem. 'I am,' he wrote to Hogg from Field Place, on 20th December, 1810, ' composing a *satirical* poem. I shall print it at Oxford, unless I find, on visiting him, that R. is ripe for printing whatever will sell. In case of that, he is my man.' There is evidence (though of a doubtful quality) that he wrote the first sketches for a poem, which eventually took shape in

Queen Mab, in the summer of 1810. Much of that poem would answer to the title of *A Poetical Essay on the Existing State of Things*.

Shelley put so many fictions into his earlier letters to Godwin, that the reader, who is not a 'Shelleyan enthusiast,' hesitates to trust any statement of those highly imaginative epistles, that is not supported by another witness. But he may have been writing truth at Keswick on 16th January, 1812, when he wrote of himself as the author of the *Essay on Love*, a little poem. This 'little poem,' if it was ever written, may have been the same poem as the *Political Essay on the Existing State of Things*, if the latter was ever written. Were it announced to-morrow on good authority that a copy had been recovered of the poem by Shelley, for a copy of which Mr. MacCarthy made so vain a search, I should expect to learn that the poem, published for Mr. Finerty's benefit, proved to be poetry that was subsequently worked into *Queen Mab*. If the *Poetical Essay* (of March and April, 1811) contained some of the more violent and outrageous passages of *Queen Mab*, the same considerations that caused the poet's Oxford bookseller to destroy all the copies of *The Necessity of Atheism*, that were in his hands, would determine him to destroy at the same time all the copies of the *Poetical Essay* lying in his premises.

II. What evidence does MacCarthy produce that Shelley was a contributor of poetry and of prose articles of literary subjects to the *Oxford Herald*, whilst he was an Oxford undergraduate?

(1) Mr. MacCarthy's sole reason for attributing the *Ode to the Death of Summer* to Shelley's pen, is that it possesses the 'peculiar Shelleyan flavour by which we can so easily recognise his later poems,' the qualities of feeling and expression, which justify the author of *Shelley's Early Life* for saying,—

'As Pope said of Chapman's translation of the *Iliad*, that it was " something like what one would imagine Homer himself would have writ before he arrived at years of discretion ; " so this little poem may be offered as something like what Shelley would have sung before he attained the full faculty of lyrical expression.'

But whilst there is no positive testimony that the Oxonian Shelley could give his verses the peculiar flavour for which Mr. MacCarthy commends the 'Ode,' which appears in the *Oxford Herald* of 22nd September, 1810, the poems of *St. Irvyne*, published three months later, may well dispose critical readers to question, whether the author of the novel was capable of producing verses, having any resemblance to the poetry of his later time. It may, of course, be urged that the verses, put into the ridiculous romance, were the nerveless efforts of a considerably earlier period ; but it is difficult to believe that, could he have produced the *Ode to the Death of Summer* in September, 1810, the Oxonian Shelley could a few weeks later have offered the public such feeble effusions as the *St. Irvyne* verses.

(2) Whilst Shelley's title to be regarded as the author of *The Ode*

rests on the 'Shelleyan flavour' of the poem, which in that respect differs from all the poetry known to have proceeded from his pen before the end of 1810, his claim to be regarded as one of the producers of the 'prose essays on some of the older English poets' (which appeared in the *Oxford Herald* during his residence at the University) rests on the fact that one of these essays is signed, 'P. S.' 'One of the papers, signed "P. S."' says Mr. MacCarthy, 'appeared during the period of Shelley's residence. and may possibly have been written by him.' It is quite as probable that some Peter Smith, or other person with P. S. for his initials, wrote the verses.

(3) Consisting altogether of the two initial letters, the evidence which disposes Mr. MacCarthy to rate the poet with the literary essayists of the Oxford newspaper, cannot be declared convincingly cogent and conclusive. It is, however, far less weak and shadowy than the evidence that the undergraduate of University College, Oxford, produced the English translations from the Greek *Anthologia*, which appeared in the *Oxford Herald* of 5th January, and 12th January, 1811, with the signature 'S' attached to each set of verses. After identifying Shelley with the translator by this solitary letter, Mr. MacCarthy next argues that, having been thus detected in translating verses of the Greek *Anthologia*, Shelley may be fairly suspected of being, and indeed assumed to be, the translator of the epigram by Vincent Bourne, that appeared in English dress in the *Oxford Herald* of 23rd February, 1811 (signed 'Versificator'); and also the translator (signing himself 'Versificator') who produced the English versions of two epigrams from the Greek *Anthologia*, that appeared in the *Oxford Herald* of 9th March, 1811. To those, who hesitate in declaring Shelley the producer of the two January translations, because his sur-name began with the letter 'S,' it may well appear considerably less than manifest that Shelley should be regarded as the producer of Versificator's translations, because he had a taste for making verses. After arguing that 'S' was Shelley, because the Shelleys resembled the Smiths in one interesting particular, and that 'Versificator' must have been Shelley, because Shelley had as good a right as any one else to style himself so, this perplexing Mr. MacCarthy (who is of so much account with the Shelleyan experts) tells us in a note, that some one, during Shelley's time at Oxford, sent a translation from Vincent Bourne to the *Oxford Herald*, signed 'S. S.—Edmonton.' On such trifles and trifling, weeks and months were wasted by the Shelleyan expert, who, with all his boastful show of laborious research, never troubled himself to find out, when Shelley and Hogg became members of their University.

III. For reasons, with which there is no need to trouble the reader of the present chapter, Mr. Denis Florence MacCarthy holds a strong opinion that the spurious letter, alleged to have been written by Shelley from University College on 22nd February, 1811, to 'The Editor of the *Statesman*,' may have been a genuine performance, although it appeared for the first time to the public in the notorious *Letters of Percy*

Bysshe Shelley (1852), that passed through Mr. Robert Browning's editorial hands only to provoke the scrutiny, that was followed quickly by their suppression. Maintaining that the letter may have been genuine, Mr. MacCarthy is only a few degrees less confident that the epistle *was* the genuine performance of the undergraduate who, ten days later, wrote Leigh Hunt the epistle that seems to have been studied by the manufacturer of the forgery.

Opening with a long paragraph, whose style affords conclusive evidence that it was not composed by the Oxonian Shelley, the epistle of the earlier date closes with the following sentences taken verbatim from the letter of later date :—

'The ultimate intention of my aim is to induce a meeting of such enlightened, unprejudiced members of the community, whose independent principles expose them to evils which might thus become alleviated; and to form a methodical society, which should be organized so as to resist the coalition of the enemies of liberty, which at present renders any expression of opinion on matters of policy dangerous to individuals. . . . . Although perfectly unacquainted with you privately, I address you as a common friend to liberty, thinking that, in cases of this urgency and importance, etiquette ought not to stand in the way of usefulness.'

Whilst these two sentences accord in style with the rest of the letter to which they properly belong (the genuine letter addressed to Leigh Hunt on 2nd March, 1811), they are preceded in the spurious epistle of later manufacture and earlier date (22nd February, 1811) with writing of this incongruent style :—

'Sir,—The present age has been distinguished from every former period of English history by the number of those writers who have suffered the penalties of the law for the freedom and spirit with which they descanted on the morals of the age, and chastised the vices or ridiculed the follies of individuals of every rank of life, and among every description of society. In former periods of British civilization, as during the flourishing ages of Greece and Rome, the oratorical censor, and the satirical poet, were regarded as exercising only that just pre-eminence to which superior genius and an intimate knowledge of life and human nature were conceived to entitle them. The *MacFlecknoe* of Dryden, the *Dunciad* and the satirical imitations of Pope, remained secure from molestation by the Attorney-General; the literary castigators of a Bolingbroke and a Wharton enjoyed the triumph of truth and justice unawed by *ex-officios;* and Addison could describe a coward and a liar without being called to account for his inuendos by the interference of the judicial servants of the king. But times are altered, and a man may now be sent to prison for a couple of years, and ruined perhaps for life, because he calls a spade a spade, and tells a public individual the very truths that are obvious to the most partial of his friends.'

So fine a judge of 'Shelleyan flavour' as Mr. Denis Florence MacCarthy ought surely to have observed how greatly this piece of writing differs in style and quality from the prose of Shelley's novels,

his Oxonian letters to Stockdale and Hogg, his Irish addresses, and all
his prose writings of the same period. Instead of discovering the
difference, however, our nice *connoisseur* of 'Shelleyan flavour,' and the
historic probabilities, exclaims in a rapturous note to the last sentence of
the quotation :—

'This passage proves almost conclusively that the person addressed as
"Editor of the *Statesman*" must have been Mr. Finnerty. The public
individual of whom he published those obvious truths that were pronounced
a libel by Lord Ellenborough was Lord Castlereagh. The former editor
of the *Statesman*, Mr. Lovell, was suffering imprisonment for a different
offence.'

There is no evidence that Mr. Finerty was, or ever had been, the
editor of the *Statesman*. There are no grounds for thinking he ever
had been the editor of that paper. Mr. Denis Florence MacCarthy
admits he has no reason to think Mr. Finerty ever was editor of the
Statesman. Yet he insists that this spurious letter (genuine epistle as
he thinks), dated 22nd February, 1811, to the Editor of the *Statesman*,
must have been addressed to a man (who was *not* that paper's editor),
because it contains a reference to the imprisonment of some person in
terms quite as applicable to an imprisoned journalist who *had never been*,
as to an imprisoned journalist *who had been or was* editor of that paper.

Nothing in the letter to the Editor of the *Statesman* implies that
the imprisoned journalist had been in any way connected with the
paper, or that the writer of the letter believed the imprisoned journalist
to have been connected with the paper. Yet Mr. MacCarthy is at great
pains to show how the Oxonian Shelley may have come to imagine that
the cruelly entreated Mr. Finerty was editor of the paper, with which
he in fact is not known to have had any professional connexion. The
libel on Lord Castlereagh, for which Mr. Finerty was sent to prison,
having been published in the *Statesman* as well as the *Morning
Chronicle*, it was natural for Shelley (argues Mr. MacCarthy) to
assume that Mr. Finerty was editor of the *Statesman*. Shelley was
by no means such a fool as the 'Shelleyan enthusiasts' would have us
think him. The youngster reasoned wildly sometimes, but he was not
likely to think a journalist must be the editor of one paper because
he had been sent to prison for libelling a Minister in another
paper. Knowing well enough that Mr. Finerty (in whose concerns he
took a lively interest) had been committed for eighteen months to
Lincoln Gaol on 7th February, 1811, Shelley was not likely · to
imagine a fortnight later he was the Acting Editor of the London
Statesman. Knowing right well Mr. Finerty had been sentenced to
eighteen months, Shelley was not likely so soon after the sentence to
imagine the journalist had been sent to prison for *two years*. To read
Mr. MacCarthy's perplexing pages is to see that the gentleman was not
more successful in confounding his readers than in confounding himself.
Yet because he threw a new kind of mud on Shelley's earliest biographer,

this superlatively inaccurate and stupefying writer has been cried up as a great Shelleyan authority.

After setting forth the words of the spurious epistle, Mr. MacCarthy remarks in his usual style of laborious inaccuracy :—

'This letter, whatever its claim to authenticity may be, is dated February 22nd, 1811. Six days later—*that is,* on the 2nd of March in the same year —Shelley addressed, for the first time, another newspaper editor then personally unknown to him, but who became a few years later one of his most valued and intimate friends—Leigh Hunt.'

February 22nd, 1811. Six days later—that is, on the 2nd of March in the same year!—What particularity and what curious persistence in blundering! The gentleman, who is so severe on Hogg for an occasional slip, is more than usually fortunate when he is only twenty-five per cent wrong in a calculation of days. Mr. MacCarthy, however, is right in holding there is no reason to doubt the genuineness of the youthful Shelley's first letter to the Editor of the *Examiner*. Written in the Oxonian Shelley's best, but far from strenuous, style, the epistle (of 2nd March, 1811) to Leigh Hunt—the epistle Leigh Hunt never answered—could not have proceeded from any hand but Shelley's hand. Strangely ingenious things have been done in the way of Shelleyan forgeries, but no fabricator of spurious letters and other materials for fictitious biography would have thought of manufacturing the delicious bit of puerile bounce that makes the letter end in this droll fashion :—

'My father is in parliament, and on attaining twenty-one I shall, in all probability, fill his vacant seat. On account of the responsibility to which my residence in this University subjects me, I, of course, dare not publicly avow all I think; but the time will come when I hope that my every endeavour, insufficient as they may be, will be directed to the advancement of liberty.   'Your most obedient servant,
'P. B. SHELLEY.'

From his Eton days to a time considerably subsequent to his expulsion from Oxford, it was Shelley's practice to open correspondence with strangers by telling them how greatly he differed in his worldly circumstances and prospects from ordinary young men. In this strain of boyish boastfulness, he is known to have approached so many people, that it is reasonable to suppose it to have been his usual device for putting himself in the favourable regard of persons, whose acquaintance he sought. To the Messrs. Longman, of Paternoster Row, he wrote from Eton: 'My object in writing it was not pecuniary, as I am independent, being the heir of a gentleman of large fortune in the county of Sussex.' To Stockdale he introduced himself by word of mouth in much the same fashion. In the earliest days of their acquaintance, Hogg heard not a little from Sir Bysshe Shelley's grandson, of matters redounding to the dignity of the Castle Goring Shelleys; the romantic traditions of his house; the arguments with which the Duke of Norfolk urged him to look to politics as his proper field of action. 'My father is in parliament,' he writes on 2nd March, 1811, to the editor of the *Examiner*, whom he has never seen, 'and on attaining twenty-one I shall, in all probability, fill his vacant seat.' Ten months later (10th January, 1812), he is writing to William Godwin, whilst seeking the philosopher's friendship by letter before seeing him,

'I am the son of a man of fortune in Sussex . . . . . . It will be necessary, in order to elucidate this part of my history, to inform you, that I am heir by entail to an estate of 6000*l.* per annum. My principles have induced me to regard the law of primogeniture as an evil of primary magnitude.'

In the musical egotisms of his poetry, the ear catches the same note of boastful arrogance and self-complacence. Whilst preaching the gospel of love, and proclaiming his determination to sacrifice himself for the good of others on the first convenient opportunity, Shelley knew how to remind his hearers that he would sacrifice a great deal more than the common sort of philanthropists; and there were moments when, not content with virtue's peculiar and sweetest reward,—an approving conscience, he was more eager to provoke, than avoid, the plaudits of the multitude.

The reader of the epistle to Leigh Hunt may well smile at the youngster's announcement that, in the course of two years, he would probably occupy a seat in the House of Commons, through his father's timely retirement from political life. It is not the wont of even the most affectionate father to be so considerate for his heir-apparent; and though he was a much kindlier and more generous parent than the 'Shelleyan enthusiasts' like to admit, Mr. Timothy Shelley, of Field Place, was by no means a likely man to retreat into private life, in order that his eldest son might become Member of Parliament for New Shoreham in his twenty-second year. Delighting in the status of a member of elective assembly, the self-complacent and rather pompous gentleman plumed himself on standing well with his 'party' and 'Mr. Speaker,' and being so highly respected by 'the house' and 'the country' that he gave peculiar weight and moral influence to the committees to which he was appointed. By no means so destitute of imagination as numerous detractors have declared him, Mr. Timothy Shelley resembled his son in an aptitude for conceiving whatever tended for the moment to put him on good terms with himself. To hear Mr. Timothy Shelley repeat over his second bottle the compliments whispered into his ear by Mr. Speaker, was to infer that, if his words were reported accurately, Mr. Speaker was an habitual and extravagant flatterer, or had some unaccountable partiality for the Member for New Shoreham. To believe all the Member for New Shoreham said of himself, was to believe, that no committee was appointed in the Lower House until he and Ministers had spoken together respecting its constitution, that few nice questions of foreign policy were decided until Ministers had asked him what might, and what might not, be done. The kindly gentleman, who declared he had furnished Archdeacon Paley (or 'Palley,' as the Member for New Shoreham pronounced the name) with all the main arguments for the 'Evidences,' could persuade himself that his smile or frown determined the course of Ministers and Administrations. Whilst the Oxonian Shelley liked to imagine himself in parliament, his father delighted in imagining himself the very soul of parliament. So imaginative a father was not likely to vacate his seat for the advantage of so imaginative a son.

The mere absence of reasonable grounds for the statement would not, however, justify a confident opinion that Shelley was guilty of deliberate untruth when he wrote on 2nd March, 1811, that, on coming of age, he would probably succeed to his father's vacant place in the House of Commons. Enough has been said in previous pages of this work to show that, together with a capacity for saying what he knew to be untrue, the Oxonian Shelley, no less than the Shelley of later time, possessed a fancy so curiously vigorous and fertile of inventions, that it may be held in some degree accountable for some of his numerous misstatements. In their desire to shield him from the obloquy of wilful and habitual untruthfulness, some of the poet's friends have, no doubt, exaggerated this consequence of his imaginative energy. In maintaining that his friend cordially detested falsehood, and in respect of his frequent inaccuracies of statement, was the mere 'creature, the unsuspecting and unresisting victim, of his irresistible imagination,' Hogg not only went beyond his evidences, but traversed and contradicted them in a manner to provoke suspicion of his own honesty. Even where he admits that the inaccuracies were referable, in a large measure, to untruthfulness, Peacock betrays a similar disposition to make the utmost of the singular imaginativeness, which he held no less accountable for the poet's frequent deviations from veracity.

By those who would rate none too highly the testimony of these two notable witnesses to the poet's character, allowance must of course be made for the partiality of friendship. On the other hand, it must be remembered that, whilst affording them opportunities for studying his character closely, their intimacy with so singular and interesting a companion, offered them the strongest inducements to judge him fairly and know him thoroughly. If it must be conceded that Hogg and Peacock would never have thought of referring their friend's imperfect veracity to his excessive imaginativeness, had he been nothing more to them than a slight acquaintance, it must also be conceded that the circumstances of their close and affectionate intercourse with the poet, qualified them to give the true explanation of his most perplexing utterances and most pitiable infirmity. Having regard to the general trustworthiness of the witnesses, and also to the several obvious considerations which may well dispose the reader to receive their evidence with suspicion and incredulity, I cannot question that, however much they overstated their respective opinions out of tenderness for the poet's fame, both Hogg and Peacock had reasonable grounds for believing that a quick and undisciplined fancy was far more, or scarcely less, accountable than moral obliquity for their friend's untruthful assertions. For the moment, therefore (*but only for the moment*), let it be assumed that, whilst penning the lines to Leigh Hunt, the undergraduate of University College really believed he was likely to take his father's seat in parliament in the course of the next two or three years.

The assumption puts the reader face to face with another difficulty. The Oxonian Shelley, who made this remarkable announcement to Leigh Hunt, was the same Oxonian Shelley, who used to declare himself indebted to Dr. Lind's timely intervention for preservation from the madhouse, to which his father meant to consign him. Whilst there is evidence of some sort that one of Shelley's hallucinations haunted him from boyhood to the last month of his existence, there is no evidence of any kind that his most transitory hallucinations perished within a few days of the hour, when he first came under their power. It took him more than a year to get the better of his morbid fancy that Hogg was set on seducing his first wife. It took him several weeks to survive his equally ludicrous and distressing fancy, that he was stricken with leprosy. There is no ground for suspecting he was visited by hallucinations so fleeting that they might be styled 'illusions of the hour.' If, at the time of writing to Leigh Hunt, he really believed he would enter parliament in his twenty-second year, the hallucination must be regarded as holding his mind for a considerable period, concurrently with the hallucination touching his father's determination to confine him for life as a lunatic. If there are grounds for thinking he really hoped to enter parliament so soon through his father's affectionate consideration, the grounds are still stronger for thinking he really apprehended incarceration in a madhouse, through his father's cruelty. To believe his father capable of retiring from parliament for the advantage of a son who had occasioned much trouble and reasonable displeasure, it was necessary for Shelley to think his father a rare example of parental devotion and beneficence. To believe his father capable of locking him up in a madhouse, at the instigation of resentment and notions of domestic policy, it was necessary for Shelley to think his father a monstrous example of parental malice and cruelty.

If he thought his father capable of such self-sacrifice for his boy's happiness, Shelley must have thought his father an admirably good parent. If he thought his father capable of such barbarity to his own offspring, Shelley must have deemed his father a superlatively cruel and wicked parent. To have believed his father capable of the parental self-sacrifice and the parental cruelty, Shelley must in the same moment of time have regarded his father as one of the very best and one of the very worst parents. It is not in the power of human sanity or human madness to think thus differently of the same person at the same moment. If Shelley really believed his father was watching for an opportunity to shut him up in a madhouse, he was fibbing when he wrote to Leigh Hunt, that his father would probably soon retire from parliament in his favour. If Shelley believed what he wrote to Leigh Hunt, he was fibbing when he talked to Hogg and others of his cruel father's malignant purpose to shut him up in a lunatic asylum. Strange creature though he was, it is difficult to believe even of Shelley that, whilst seeing his father's goodness, he could be so malignantly wicked to do his utmost to persuade his friends of his father's inordinate badness. Perhaps it is even more difficult to imagine, strange being though he was, that whilst thinking his father an execrably bad parent, Shelley would be so perverse as to invent the story, which went to prove his father an extraordinarily good one.

To escape from this tangle of difficulties, from this dilemma of *four* horns, readers are at liberty to assume that the Oxonian Shelley believed no tittle of either of the marvellous stories. Dismissing the assumption that the youngster wrote to Leigh Hunt in good faith and simple honesty, they may take it as proved that, in bragging about the seat he would have in parliament as soon as he should have taken his degree, the undergraduate was fibbing, in order that the newspaper editor should form something more than an adequate notion of his correspondent's importance. They may also take it as proved, that the undergraduate was no more sincere in talking about his wicked father's design to lock him up in a madhouse, than in writing that his father would probably retire from parliament in his favour. The time, doubtless, came when Shelley believed his worst fictions to his father's discredit, even as tellers of untruths usually come in course of time to believe the fabrications which they persist in repeating steadily and earnestly :—even as ' the nobleman, who recently languished in captivity at Portland,' has doubtless succeeded in persuading himself that he is the veritable Sir Roger Tichborne.

But before fancies, born of fierce and violent resentments, acquired the complexion and force of hideous truths to his disordered judgment, it is conceivable—ay, it cannot be doubted—that Shelley passed through states of mental and moral disturbance, which were fruitful of impressions and misconceptions, so curiously composed of fact and fancy, of truth and chimera, that he might be well described as a victim of semi-delusions. Between the period when he was altogether sane and the period when he suffered from steady hallucination, at least on one subject, and transient hallucinations on other subjects, there was a period during which he was neither absolutely free from delusions nor wholly possessed by any delusion respecting his father's character and conduct.

IV. Yet another ' discovery ' respecting the Oxonian Shelley, for which the ' Shelleyan enthusiasts' overflowed with gratitude to Mr. Denis Florence MacCarthy. To believe all that is told to his honour in *Shelley's Early Life* is to believe that Shelley made himself responsible for the costs and charges of publishing the little volume of verse, which gave Miss Janetta Phillips her modest place in literary annals. That

Miss Janetta was writing poetry whilst Shelley kept terms at Oxford, that she rose to a high place in his poetical regard in the spring of 1811, and that whilst waging war with bigotry and superstition in academic circles, he was at much pains to get subscribers for her book of poems, are matters of historic certainty. In the April of that year, when Miss Elizabeth Shelley was fast falling from her brother's favour, he wrote to Hogg, ' Elizabeth is, indeed, an unworthy companion of the Muses. I do not rest much on her poetry now. Miss Phillips betrayed twice the genius; greater amiability, if to affect the feelings is a proof of the excess of the latter.' The long list of subscribers to *Poems by Janetta Phillips*. Oxford: Printed by Collingwood and Co., 1811, affords conclusive evidence that, whilst regarding her poetical ability with approval, Shelley bestirred himself in Oxford, London, and Sussex, to further Miss Janetta's literary venture. Subscribing himself for six copies of the work, he induced his sister Elizabeth to put her name down for a copy of the metrical effusions, which ' betrayed twice the genius' of her compositions. Miss Hellen Shelley at the Clapham Boarding School, and her friend Miss Harriett Westbrook, also produced half-crowns from their little purses for the benefit of Miss Janetta Phillips. Other members of Shelley's circle ordered the book at his instance. Mr. Medwin, of Horsham, ordered a copy; Mr. Charles Grove took a copy; Mrs. Grove, of Lincoln's Inn Fields, put her name down for three copies. It was, doubtless, at Shelley's solicitation that his Oxford bookseller consented to subscribe for Miss Janetta's little volume. It is probable that the young lady had other friends besides Shelley in the University, where she found no less than eighty subscribers for her *Poems*. Still, it may be safely assumed, she was considerably indebted to Shelley's influence in the colleges for the sympathy and money of so many gownsmen. That Shelley admired Miss Janetta's poetry, and pushed the fortunes of her book to the utmost of his ability, is certain.

But what proof is there that he generously took upon himself the charges of publication, and thereby incurred a debt that drained his pocket a few months later? What are the facts that to this extent ' exhibit Shelley in the amiable light of being an active encourager of a youthful muse?' Here is Mr. Denis Florence MacCarthy's evidence to the fact. In one of the undated letters, which he wrote in the summer (say July) of 1811, from Radnorshire to Hogg at York, Shelley says—' I have at this moment no money, as Philipps' and the other debt have drained me.' What evidence to the point! In the spring of the year Miss Janetta Phillips published a little book, which was so largely subscribed for that, besides paying the charges of production, it must have put a good many guineas into the author's pocket. Three or four months later Shelley writes from Wales that ' Philipps' and the other debt have drained' him so completely that he is without money. It follows, according to Mr. MacCarthy, that at the time of writing the letter Shelley was suffering from his generosity to Miss Janetta Phillips.

The 'Shelleyan enthusiasts,' who mistook Mr. MacCarthy for a prophet because he wrote abusively of Hogg, may be assured that neither of the debts referred to in the epistle had anything to do with Miss Janetta Phillips's book. Printed whilst the young lady's poetry was passing through the press at Oxford, Shelley's tract on *The Necessity of Atheism* —the publication that resulted in his expulsion from University College, Oxford—was printed by E. and W. *Phillips,* of Worthing. I have not thought it worth my while to inquire about Miss Janetta's parentage and history ; but I should not be surprised to learn she was the daughter of one of these Worthing printers, and that Shelley's efforts for the success of her book proceeded in some degree from friendliness for the printers, who were just then rendering him secret and confidential service. One thing is certain about Miss Janetta. Though it occasioned him considerable trouble at the moment, the publication of her poems caused him no subsequent discomfort. The debts, referred to in the letter, were the debt to Stockdale for the production of *St. Irvyne,* and the debt to the Messrs. E. and W. Phillips, of Worthing, for printing *The Necessity of Atheism.* Mr. MacCarthy's precious discovery is 'a mare's-nest' for the cynical reader to chuckle over.

CHAPTER XIII.

SHELLEY'S SECOND RESIDENCE-TERM AT OXFORD.

Harriett Westbrook—Her Character and Beauty—How Shelley came to care for her—Her Subscription for Janetta Phillips's Poems—Shelley's first Visit to Harriett's Home—His Intention to compete for 'the Newdigate'—Thornton Hunt's scandalous Suggestion—Obligations of the Oxford Undergraduate—Mary Wollstonecraft on the Guinea Forfeit —Shelley's False Declaration—His numerous Untruths—*The Necessity of Atheism*—Was it a Squib?—Lady Shelley's Inaccuracies—Mr. Garnett's Misdescription of the Tract—His Misrepresentation of Hogg—The *Little Syllabus* printed at Worthing—More Untruths by Shelley—The Tract offered for Sale in Oxford—Shelley called before 'the Dons' —His Expulsion from University College—Hogg's Impudence and Craft—His Misrepresentations—Shelley and Hogg leave Oxford.

THOUGH he had not yet seen the child who, in the following September, became his first wife, Shelley was enough interested in her on 11th January, 1811, to write to his publisher, Stockdale :—'I would thank you to send a copy of *St. Irvyne* to Miss Harriet Westbrook, 10, Chapel Street, Grosvenor Square;' an order he would scarcely have given, had not circumstances already caused him to think of her with peculiar friendliness. At their boarding-school on the north side of Clapham Common, near the 'Old Town,' Miss Mary Shelley (*ætat.* 13) and Miss Hellen Shelley (*ætat.* 11) had several schoolmates, of whose looks and doings they would naturally prattle to their elder brother during the Christmas holidays, as they sat about the Christmas fire. How was it that, of all the girls about whom his sisters may be assumed to have spoken in his hearing, Harriett Westbrook was the one he selected for a compliment that must have greatly pleased her? Mary and Hellen were the only persons (with the exception of their elder sister— possibly one of Harriett's school friends in earlier time) who can be conceived to have gossiped with him about the loveliest of Mrs. Fenning's pupils, in a way to inspire him with interest in her. The fair inference from the reasonable assumptions is that of all the school-girls, of whom his sisters spoke, Harriett

Westbrook seemed the fairest and most fascinating to him and them.

Let it be assumed that, of all their friends at the Clapham boarding-school, Harriett was the only girl of whom the sisters spoke to their brother. In that case, the question arises, why the sisters, so uncommunicative about the others, were eloquent about the girl who soon became their brother's wife?—eloquent about her in a way to make him desirous of knowing her? The question must be answered in a way more or less favourable to the notion that Harriett stood well in the opinion of the sisters.

There is another reason for thinking Harriett Westbrook was at this point of her career peculiarly acceptable to the young ladies of Field Place. Older than Miss Mary Shelley by two years at least, more than three years older than Miss Hellen Shelley, Harriett Westbrook, besides being one of the older girls of Mrs. Fenning's seminary, was the acknowledged 'beauty' of the school; and beauty in a senior school-girl always disposes the juniors of the school to regard her favourably, when it is not associated with any irritating moral defect. Harriett's temper was by no means faultless, but as she was the only serious sufferer from her propensity to imagine herself an ill-used damsel, it did not lessen the natural influence of her personal attractiveness.

Fretful towards herself, she was never peevish or wilfully unkind to others. Her prevailing mood was tranquil melancholy; and there were times when she played the rebel with a serene sullenness that made worthy Mrs. Fenning wonder what would be the end of so perplexing a young lady. When she was more than usually miserable about nothing at Clapham, this young lady (who eventually committed suicide) used to think she might as well destroy herself, would even tell the governesses she rather thought she should destroy herself. But the announcements of suicidal purpose were made in so placid and passionless a manner, that they caused little or no alarm. Even in her naughtiest humours she was gentle in speech and bearing to her classmates, and not devoid of frigid decorum to those who were in authority over her. In her brighter seasons she was childishly charming,—so winning and cooingly docile, that Mrs. Fenning and the subordinate teachers quickly relented to her smiles, and forgiving her in five minutes for all the trouble she had given throughout twice as many weeks, fell to kissing and petting her, as though she were the veriest darling. How could this darling, so irresistible to the governesses she harassed, be otherwise than popular with the girls whose tempers she never tried?

One of those beauties, who are seen oftener on the walls than the floors of drawing-rooms, less a thing of real life than a picture, this girl of curious and memorable loveliness lived in the recollections of her Clapham schoolmates, when forty years and more had passed over her grave. Rather below the average stature of womankind, shapely as a sculptured Venus, graceful in her movements, she would have possessed all the finer elements of womanly loveliness, had she not lacked the air and style of mental force and moral dignity. In 1856 Miss Hellen Shelley recalled Harriett* Westbrook, whom she saw for the last time in 1811, as 'a very handsome girl, with a complexion quite unknown in these days—brilliant pink and white,—with hair quite like a poet's dream, and Bysshe's peculiar admiration.' It lived also in Miss Hellen's recollection that Mrs. Fenning, and her assistant-governesses, used to talk about Harriett's beauty, and even spoke of her as qualified to 'enact Venus' at a *fête champêtre*. In colour her eyes resembled Shelley's prominent blue eyes, and the profusion of hair, that was his 'peculiar admiration,' was light brown.

When she committed to paper (in her fifty-seventh year, or thereabouts) whatever she could remember of the beautiful girl, whom she never beheld after they became sisters-in-law, it lived in Miss Hellen Shelley's recollection that her brother was said to have married her because her name was Harriett. It is in the way of lovers to delight in the names of those they idolize, even when their devotion is rewarded with coldness. To the last, Byron's ear discovered music in 'Mary,' the name of the wee Scotch lassie whom he loved in his tenth year. One can readily imagine that the charm of her name was the first influence to

---

* Biographers differ in spelling Harriett in the case of Miss Westbrook, and also in the case of Miss Grove. Hogg says Harriett Westbrook signed herself 'Harriet,' though Shelley instructed Mr. Medwin the elder to give the name a second *t*. Like Mr. Rossetti, I comply with Shelley's wish. Miss Grove's Christian name is spelt with a second *t* in the Grove genealogy of Burke's *Landed Gentry*, a record corrected by the representative of the family.

make Shelley an attentive listener to his sisters' gossip about 'the beauty' of their college friend. It is conceivable that their talk about this lovely Harriett of the Clapham boarding-school was accountable for the frame of mind in which Miss Harriett Grove's discarded suitor wrote from Field Place to Hogg on 28th December, 1810 : '*At present*, a thousand barriers oppose any more intimate connexion, any union with another ;' words that would scarcely have fallen from his pen within a fortnight of his final rejection by the Wiltshire 'belle,' had he not already recovered from the first and keenest misery of the misadventure, so far as to be capable of looking forward to a future time when his 'union with another' Harriett would be possible.

Is it not conceivable, also, that in their sympathy with his distress for the loss of Harriett Grove, and in their affectionate desire to restore him to his usual cheerfulness, the sisters at Field Place conspired to remind him that their cousin Harriett was not the only beautiful Harriett in the universe, and to lure him into consoling himself for Harriett Grove's disdain with Harriett Westbrook's devotion? No doubt Miss Hellen Shelley and Miss Mary Shelley were full young for match-makers. But girls sometimes take to match-making, no less than to flirtation, before their teens. Little Hellen (*ætat.* 11) may not have been taken fully, or even at all, into the confidence of her elder sisters on the romantic project. They may have encouraged her to prattle about Harriett Westbrook without letting her suspect their purpose.

The evidence of this conspiracy on the part of three, or two, of Shelley's sisters for marrying him to Miss Harriett West-brook, is fragmentary and flimsy ; but few readers will question that divers facts point to the existence of an influence at Field Place that not only disposed, but determined, the poet to seek the young lady's acquaintance. But for his sisters he would, probably, have never heard of Harriett Westbrook. Their speech about her must be held accountable for his desire to know her. On 11th January, 1811, he requested Stockdale to send her a copy of *St. Irvyne*. What but his sisters' talk about her can have disposed Shelley to pay so considerable a compliment to the young lady, of whom he would probably never have heard, had it not been for them ?

Just about the time when he paid her this remarkable atten-tion, Miss Harriett Westbrook subscribed for a copy of the poems, on the point of being published, by Miss Janetta Phillips, a young lady in whom he was warmly interested; a young lady of whom she doubtless heard through him or his sisters, and whose name would probably have never come to her ear had it not been for him or them. It is suggested by Mr. Denis Florence MacCarthy that Harriett Westbrook gave her name to the roll of Miss Janetta Phillips's subscribers at the instance of Miss Hellen Shelley, and that the copy of *St. Irvyne* sent to Miss Harriett Westbrook was Shelley's acknowledgment of her expression of concern in the enterprise of his literary *protégée*. Probably the affair should be taken the other way about. It is more likely that Miss Harriett's subscription to Miss Janetta's poems was consequent on Shelley's gift of the copy of the novel. There is no evidence that subscribers for Miss Janetta's poems were being sought so early as the Christmas holidays (1810–11), and there is good evidence that the list of those subscribers was not completed and made out for publication till after Lady-day, 1811. I am, therefore, more disposed to think Miss Harriett Westbrook subscribed for the poems at Shelley's instance, and in acknowledgment of his civility in sending her the copy of *St. Irvyne*, than to regard the gift of the novel as the author's acknowledgment of her complaisance in subscribing for the poems. But if Mr. Denis Florence MacCarthy is right on this point, Miss Harriett Westbrook's act in subscribing for the poems *may be* regarded as an act, done less for the gratification of one of Shelley's sisters than for the gratification of Shelley himself, and *must be* regarded as an act done, more or less, for the gratification of the young man of whom she can have heard only through his sisters. Hence the young lady's subscription for the poems becomes another indication of the existence of an influence at Field Place, disposing the poet to entertain feelings of friendliness for 'the beauty' of the Clapham boarding-school. Why, it has already been asked, was Miss Harriett Westbrook the only one of his sisters' school-fellows to whom he sent a copy of his novel? Why, it must be also asked, was she the only one of their school-fellows to subscribe for the poems, for whose success he was so desirous? The questions can only be answered in a way, pointing to the existence at Field Place of an influence, to which the act of subscription was directly, or indirectly, referable.

Whilst readily admitting that the facts of the case sustain

and justify a strong opinion that Miss Hellen Shelley (*ætat.* 11), and Miss Mary Shelley (*ætat.* 13), talked about their school-fellow Harriett, so as to make their brother curious about and interested in her, readers may fairly object (in respect to Miss Elizabeth Shelley) that it is unusual for a young gentlewoman of the mature age of sixteen years to use her influence, or be in a position to exercise any influence, over her brother (*ætat.* 18) to make him fall in love with a young lady he has not seen. It may also be further objected that, as she is not known to have been personally acquainted with Miss Harriett Westbrook, it is especially difficult to imagine that Miss Elizabeth Shelley made any efforts to compass her brother's marriage with her younger sisters' school-fellow. There is force in both of these objections. It must, however, be remembered that, as she had been a pupil at the Clapham Common school, Miss Elizabeth Shelley (now in her seventeenth year) may have been at school with Miss Harriett Westbrook, still only in her sixteenth year. She may (in the absence of evidence to the contrary) be fairly assumed to have known Miss Harriett Westbrook by personal observation as well as by report—to have remembered, as a delightful little girl, the same Harriett who was an unutterably beautiful ' great girl ' in the eyes of Mary and Hellen.

It is of more importance for readers to remember how unusual were the relations in which Elizabeth stood to her elder brother. It is on the record (so as to put the facts beyond dispute) that, throughout his suit to and correspondence with his cousin Harriett, Shelley made a confidante of his sister respecting his passion for that lovely girl; that he especially commissioned his eldest sister to plead for him to the object of his passion ; and that in his disappointment at the failure of his suit to his cousin, he threw himself on his sister for sympathy, consolation, and counsel. It is no less clear on the record that, during those Christmas holidays of 1810–11, Miss Elizabeth Shelley, whilst sympathizing with his sorrow, was for some days in fear that in the agitations of his grief he would destroy himself. It matters not that Shelley never seriously thought of committing suicide ; it is enough that his sister believed him to be meditating and capable of self-destruction. ' My eldest sister,' Miss Hellen Shelley wrote in 1855, or thereabouts, ' has frequently told me how narrowly she used to watch him, and accompany him in his walks with his dog and gun.' Moreover, whilst Shelley was in his trouble seeking consolation and counsel from his eldest sister, he was influencing her to fall in love with a young man she had never seen, and to that end was speaking to her of his friend Hogg in terms which made her fully aware of his purpose. Under these circumstances it would not be surprising, could it be shown that sister (whom for *her* happiness he was training and luring to love a man she had never seen) conceived a purpose of turning the tables upon him, and making him (for *his* happiness) fall in love with a girl on whom he had not set eyes. Under these circumstances, what more natural than for her to do him a service corresponding to the service he was set openly on doing her?

Anyhow, it is certain, that having conceived an interest in Miss Harriett Westbrook, when he can have known nothing of her except from his sisters, Shelley did not return to Oxford at the close of the Christmas vacation, without having seen the young lady, and made arrangements for corresponding with her.

In his article on *Shelley in Pall Mall*, Mr. Garnett is good enough to promise that, when it shall suit his convenience to do so, he will lay before the world 'an interesting but unpublished document,' in evidence that the poet first saw Harriett Westbrook in January 1811. It is very kind of Mr. Garnett to make this promise; but as it has been known for more than a quarter of a century to all the world (with the exception of Shelleyan specialists) that Shelley made Miss Harriett Westbrook's acquaintance in that month, Mr. Garnett may as well keep his 'interesting but unpublished document' to himself, if it cannot afford any further information about the poet. In an extremely entertaining letter, to which reference has been made in a previous chapter of this work (a letter to be found in Hogg's much-abused *Life of Percy Bysshe Shelley*), Mr. Charles Henry Grove, the poet's cousin, says:—

'During the Christmas vacation of that year, and in January 1811, I spent part of it at Field Place, and when we returned to London, his sister Mary sent a letter of introduction with a present to her schoolfellow, Miss Westbrook, which Bysshe and I were to take to her. I recollect we did so, calling at Mr. Westbrook's house.'

It has been often represented that Shelley was indebted to 'little Hellen' for his first introduction to the girl who became, a few months later, his first wife. It has been no less often represented that Shelley made his first wife's acquaintance only a few weeks before their marriage; that he made her acquaintance *at* Mrs. Fenning's house ; and that he was inveigled into the marriage without being allowed the usual opportunities for studying the girl's character. Readers, therefore, will do well to observe that he saw her for the first time under her father's roof; that he made her acquaintance there because he went there for the purpose of making it; that, on the occasion of this first visit to Mr. Westbrook's house, he went there with a letter of introduction to the young lady from his sister Mary; that he, on the same occasion, brought the young lady a present from his sister Mary ; that he made this call upon the young lady in the company of one of the gentlemen of his family ; that this visit must be assumed to have been paid with the cognizance of Miss Elizabeth Shelley (his eldest sister) ; that, from the date of this visit, he and the young lady were in the habit of exchanging letters ; that he did not marry her till he had corresponded with and otherwise known her intimately for eight full months ; that he did not marry her till he had lured her from Christianity into atheism ; that, instead of marrying her (a sixteen-years-old child) with her father's consent, he stole her from her father's keeping, even as (less than three years later) he lured another sixteen-years-old girl from the roof of her father, who was his intimate friend.

All these statements are matters of fact, and yet Mr. Garnett says the time will come, when ' it will for the first time be clearly understood how slight was the acquaintance of Shelley and Harriet, previous to their marriage ; what advantage was taken of his *chivalry of sentiment*, and her compliant disposition, and the inexperience of both.'

Returning to Oxford for the Lent term, after making Miss Harriett Westbrook's acquaintance, Shelley returned to the same kind of life, in which he found various excitements and congenial diversions in the eight weeks preceding the Christmas holidays. There was no diminution in his familiarity with and affection for Hogg. Again, the young men took long walks in the neighbourhood of Oxford, and committed boyish extravagances of costume and demeanour that made the gownsmen titter over their wine in the common rooms. They still hoped to be brothers-in-law, and looked forward to the Easter Vacation as a time for winning Miss Elizabeth Shelley's acquiescence in their project for the union of their respective families. They wrote letters, and got through a good deal of desultory reading, in company with one another. They resumed their old practice of talking with much volubility and vehemence on subjects of which they knew little, from ten p.m. till two hours past midnight. Whilst Hogg persisted in reading for honours, Shelley turned over a good many books for amusement. Instead of writing to Miss Harriett Grove, he wrote letters to Miss Harriett Westbrook. At the same time he was making efforts to lengthen the list of subscribers for Miss Janetta Phillips's poems.

Having in the Christmas holidays scolded off his reasonable displeasure with his heir, and taken him once again into his favour, Mr. Timothy Shelley wrote the youngster letters of good advice, begging him to read hard and distinguish himself at the University; letters which the son and his friend turned to excellent fun. Whilst the Squire of Field Place thus evinced a disposition to live on better terms with his boy, there were signs of a corresponding disposition on Shelley's part, to live on better terms with his father. Anyhow, it was partly to please the Member of Parliament for New Shoreham, that the undergraduate promised to compete for the next Prize Poem,—a promise that vastly delighted the elder Mr. Shelley, who honoured letters without being qualified to excel in them, and desired very much to speak of his son as an Oxford Prizeman. The subject for ' the Newdigate,' was *Parthenon*, and as soon as Shelley had consented to his father's desire, so far as to say he would go in for the Prize (eventually awarded to Mr. R. Burdon, of Oriel College), the jubilant Squire of Field Place went off to his particular friend, the Reverend Edward Dallaway, Vicar of Leatherhead, and historian of Sussex, and begged the sound scholar and famous antiquary, to put his erudition at the service of the poetical undergraduate. The result of this kindly busy-bodyism on the part of an honest gentleman, who certainly sometimes did his best to be a good father to a worse than indifferent son, was that Mr. Percy Bysshe Shelley, of University College, received a long letter from Mr. Dallaway, together with charts, sketches, and documents, which might have been useful to the young poet, had he remained long enough at the University to complete the poem (which he began), and send it in to the judges.

In one respect, the present writer may have described Shelley's academic life too favourably. Too much may have been said of the purity of the poet's personal tastes, and of his aversion to pleasures that are fascinating only to the sensual. If he has erred in this particular, the writer has not failed through ignorance of matters, making for another and less agreeable view of the undergraduate's ways of amusing himself at Oxford, but through a determination to say nothing on insufficient evidence to the discredit of a remarkable man, whose life affords too many occasions for necessary censure.

When anything is needlessly blurted to Shelley's shame, the injurious statement is usually made by one of his idolaters, acting the proverbial part of a 'candid friend.' It is so in the case of what has been urged against the prevailing testimony to the purity and refinement of the Oxonian Shelley's personal habits and tastes.

'Accident,' says Mr. Thornton Hunt—one of Hogg's vituperators, and one of Shelley's idolaters—'has made me aware of facts which give me to understand that in passing through the usual curriculum of a college life in all its paths, Shelley did not go scatheless; but that, in tampering with venal pleasures, his health was seriously and not transiently injured. The effect was far greater on his mind than on his body.'

It is needless to specify the pleasures to which Mr. Thornton Hunt points. The pleasures which may be bought, and often attract young men in their hours of idleness, and sometimes result in consequences permanently injurious to their health, are not so numerous as to make the reader doubtful as to the nature of the pleasures thus boldly indicated. But Mr. Thornton Hunt's statement has features which will dispose readers to question the sufficiency of his information. As Shelley never passed 'through the usual curriculum of a college life,' he can scarcely have passed through it 'in all its paths' (whatever that may mean):—but let that pass. It is enough that Mr. Thornton Hunt is unambiguous as to the class of the pleasures. It is not, however, so clear how those pleasures, which can only injure the mind through the body, should in Shelley's case have been so much less baneful to the body than the mind. As Mr. Thornton Hunt seems to have gained his facts from a loose talker or writer, it is only fair and charitable to the poet to suppose that his 'frank friend' got his facts from an altogether unreliable reporter. It may, of course, be that in a transient fit of rakishness Shelley was so unfortunate as to-encounter mischance, which habitual rakes may be so lucky as to escape. But the abundant evidences to the point satisfy me that 'rakishness' was foreign to Shelley's general way of living at the University,—that, in respect to common kinds of dissipation, his habits accorded with the manners of Victorian much more closely than with the manners of Georgian Oxford.

To pass from a matter about which Mr. Thornton Hunt might as well have been silent, to an affair of several incidents, which, though notorious, must be recorded precisely and fully, because they have never been narrated correctly ;—the incidents that closed with Shelley's expulsion from University College, Oxford.

Whilst rejecting, with his usual good sense, Hogg's apologetic and untruthful account of Shelley's motives and purpose in writing and publishing (for he did both) *The Necessity of Atheism*, Mr. William Rossetti remarks :—

'In this case, as in others, the honestest and boldest course is also the safest: and we shall do well to understand once for all that Percy Shelley had as good a right to form and expound his opinions on theology as the Archbishop of Canterbury had to his. Certainly Shelley differed from the Archbishop, and from several other students of, and speculators on the subject, past and present ; but, as there was no obligation on him to agree with all, or any of them, so there is nothing to be explained away or toned down when we find that in fact he dissented.'

Had Mr. Rossetti been educated at Oxford or Cambridge in his boyhood, he would not have put these words in print. Like the Archbishop of Canterbury, or any other man, Shelley had, of course, a natural right to hold and declare what he believed to be the truth on questions of religion. In civilized communities, however, natural rights are in some cases necessarily put under limitations, or altogether taken from individuals,—are partially or wholly relinquished by individuals,—for the welfare and good order of the societies of which they are members. Archbishop Manners Sutton had, no doubt, like every other man, a natural right to his own opinions on matters pertaining to religion, and to proclaim those opinions. But this right was limited in his case not only by obligations put upon him as a citizen, but also by official obligations put upon him as Primate of the Anglican Church. So long as he remained in his sacerdotal office he was bound in conscience to hold no opinions at variance with the doctrines of the Church of England, and bound even more stringently in conscience, and by social law, to refrain from publishing opinions calculated to discredit those doctrines. Had he relinquished his sacred office and orders, he would have recovered that much of his natural right to think and say anything he believed to be true, which was not denied to him by mere obligations of citizenship. On returning as far as possible to the position and quality of a layman, he would have recovered the right of a layman to limited freedom of speech on matters of religion,—*i.e.* so much of the natural right to free thought and utterance as in his time was allowed by the law of the land to every person of his nation. But, so long as he remained Archbishop, his natural right to be heterodox, and to teach heterodoxy, was wholly dormant.

In like manner, as a member of the University of Oxford (a society he had joined of his own free will; a society from which he did not wish to be withdrawn when, in December, 1810, his father threatened to withdraw him from it), Mr. Percy Bysshe Shelley was bound to act as though he were a sincere son of the National Church, and to do nothing that was likely to put his orthodoxy in suspicion. Far from being under 'no obligation to agree with all or any' of the doctrines of the Church of England (as Mr. Rossetti avers), he was under clear, strong, and stringent obligations to agree with every one of those doctrines. It may have always been, and recent legislation has declared that it *was* (if not in Shelley's time, at least in later time) unjust and impolitic in the law of the land to confine the Universities within limits, and hold them under restrictions, that rendered them at most nothing more than superb seminaries for the larger part of the nation, instead of seats of learning for the whole nation. In the present work, however, there is no need to ask whether those limits and restrictions were ever needful, or whether they were salutary after ceasing to be needful, or whether they should have been removed sooner than the recent year (1871) that saw the abolition of the University Religious Tests. It is enough for Shelley's biographers to know that, when the poet matriculated at Oxford, no one was allowed to enter the University without solemnly declaring himself a member of the National Church, and subscribing the Thirty-nine Articles in demonstration of the truth of his declaration. Conformity to the doctrines and uses of the Church was the condition of admittance to the University.

It was also the condition under which every matriculated student continued to enjoy the privileges and partake of the benefits of the University. Every member of the University, besides being a member of the Church, was required to be a communicant of the Church,—taking the Sacrament at appointed times in the chapel of his college.

In respect to this last particular, it was usual for the academic 'dons' to have regard for the religious scruples of undergraduates, whose consciousness of evil living made them feel they would be guilty of presumption in coming to the Lord's Table. On going to the Dean of his college, or his tutor, and making confession of his unfitness to communicate, the undergraduate of light manners and tender conscience received permission to be absent from the approaching celebration, on the understanding that he made a suitable contribution to the alms, gathered on the occasion for charitable uses. In most colleges it was understood that the undergraduate who thus avoided the communion should give a guinea to the offertory; a requirement to which the applicant for the dispensation could not object on conscientious grounds. Hence the usage which in course of time gave occasion for the statement that the dispensation was *bought* for a guinea, and the still more perverse statement that undergraduates took the Sacrament at the Universities *in order* to escape the exaction of twenty-one shillings. In her remarks on the defective discipline and morality of our national seminaries, in the *Vindication of the Rights of Woman*, Mary Wollstonecraft says, 'What good can be expected from the youth who receives the Sacrament of the Lord's Supper to avoid forfeiting a guinea, which he probably afterwards spends in some sensual manner?' The offering, which Mary Wollstonecraft regarded as a guinea forfeit, was in its origin nothing else than the voluntary donation of the conscientious student who said to his tutor, 'Though I am not worthy to be a partaker of the Holy Communion, I may be permitted to give to the poor.'

Of Shelley, indeed, it is not unfair to say that he was quite capable of taking the Sacrament in order to have a guinea the more for his pleasure. It is certain that, whilst openly deriding Christianity, and denying the existence of God, he could take the Sacrament, from a lighter motive than a desire to husband his pocket-money. The levity with which he could take the Sacrament, and afterwards allude to the act as a pretty piece of drollery, is (to use no stronger language) startlingly offensive. Whilst lodging in Poland Street, Oxford Street, immediately after his expulsion from University College, Oxford, he wrote to Hogg (24th April, 1811) of Harriett Westbrook and her elder sister:—

'My little friend, Harriet W., is gone to her prison-house. She is quite well in health; at least, so she says, though she looks very much otherwise. I saw her yesterday. I went with her sister to Miss H.'s [? F.'s] and walked about Clapham Common with them for two hours. The youngest is a most amiable girl; the eldest is really conceited, but very condescending. *I took the Sacrament with her on Sunday !!!*'

With the same levity, he took the Sacrament, seven or eight weeks later, in Sussex, after returning to Field Place. Writing to Hogg from Horsham on 16th June, 1811, he says, 'I am going to take the sacrament. In spite of my melancholy reflections, the idea rather amuses and soothes me!!!' This from the youthful zealot and martyr for Free Thought, who, according to some of his idolaters, was driven from Oxford because his singular earnestness and sincerity would not permit him to acquiesce hypocritically in a faith he disbelieved, or in usages he deemed superstitious!

Whilst the University was held within these religious limits, it was one of the prime duties of the academic authorities to take due care for the maintenance of the religious uniformity required by the law of the land. For the wisdom or impolicy of the law they were no more accountable than any judge is accountable for the justice or impolicy of the law he is appointed to administer. It was not for them to make reply or reason why, but to see that the law for uniformity of religious sentiment was duly respected by the gownsmen of every academic grade. Had the Master and Fellows of any college winked at any irregularities tending to defeat the law within their house, they would have been guilty of a heinous breach of trust. It is needful to insist on this obvious fact, because, through the influence of books and articles, written for the most part by gentlemen who were not educated at either Oxford or Cambridge, the notion has arisen that the Master and Fellows of Shelley's college might with propriety have forborne to call him to account for publishing a work at Oxford to demonstrate the necessity of atheism; that they are chargeable with mischievous indiscretion, and a flagrant excess of duty, in taking notice of the tract he wrote and offered for sale at Oxford. Mr.

Garnett is of opinion that by merely leaving Shelley alone 'the Oxford authorities . . . might have preserved an illustrious modern ornament of their University.' To think with Mr. Garnett on this point is to forget that to preserve to the University a young gentleman who might one day write excellent poetry was not the first duty of those authorities. It is to forget that they were bound to have due care for the religious order and discipline demanded by the law of the land.

It is easier to discover laxity and indifference than the vexatious indiscretions of an excessive zeal in the measures employed by those authorities for the maintenance and preservation of religious uniformity. Acting too much rather than too little like men of the world, too little rather than too much like cloistered enthusiasts, they allowed their undergraduates as far as possible to go their own way, reading whatever they pleased, saying whatever they liked amongst themselves. When he remarked approvingly of the authorities of his college, 'They are very civil to us here : they never interfere with us,' Shelley described precisely the method of academic government, that, according to Mr. Garnett, would have preserved Shelley to the University. In respect to affairs of religion no less than other matters, the undergraduates were treated civilly ; put as gentlemen upon their honour, taken as gentlemen at their word, allowed the largest possible liberty, interfered with as little as possible. At matriculation the undergraduate was subjected to no searching examination, for the discovery of the weak points of his orthodoxy. It was enough that he made the usual declaration and subscription with the simple honesty and good faith to be looked for in young Englishmen. After matriculation he was allowed an almost perilous freedom. He did not live, like the students of some religious seminaries, under constant surveillance and espionage. He had no fear that, during his absence from his rooms, strange eyes would inspect his private books and search his private papers. He was not harassed with divinity lectures, attended with questions nicely devised for entrapping him into revelations of theological unsoundness. Heterodoxy was not sniffed, scented, hunted down and punished in him and his companions, as heresy was detected and denounced in the colleges of the sixteenth century by spies and eavesdroppers. It was enough for the 'dons' of his particular college and the other authorities of the University,

that he attended chapel with sufficient frequency, and took the
Sacrament in accordance with the rules of 'the house.' Just as
he was credited with sincerity at matriculation, when he
subscribed the Articles, it was assumed that he attended chapel
as a sincere member of the Church of England. If he asked
for exemption from attendance at the next celebration of the
Lord's Supper, the request was not regarded as an indication of
heterodoxy. Throughout his terms, in the absence of clear and
unlooked-for evidence to the contrary, it was inferred from his
fair observance of religious forms, that he was an honest Church-
man. To what further point could *laisser-faire* indulgence be
carried with safety? In this manner Shelley was treated in
respect to matters of religion by the rulers of his college, who
are said to have worried him with vexatious interference and
insulting requirements. The boy of eighteen years was dealt
with in this fashion. Yet we are told that all would have gone
well with him at Oxford, had the Master and Fellows of the
University only left him alone.

Because religious uniformity was maintained with the least
possible interference with the liberty of individuals, it would be
a mistake to imagine it was not maintained effectually. Of late
the fashion has arisen to speak of the religious forms, that were
used for the preservation of this uniformity, as vain and idle
forms. A moment's consideration will satisfy the fair and
judicial reader that this fashion is an unjust one. Surely the
forms were not vain and idle, that excluded from the Universities the young men of our non-conforming families; that
yearly drove to other and inferior seminaries some three or four
hundred young men of our fairly prosperous families, who, but
for those forms, would have sought their higher education at
Oxford and Cambridge. To assume that those forms were less
influential within the Universities than in families having no
connection with the Established Church, is to assume that
English Dissenters surpassed English Churchmen greatly in
truthfulness.

Doubtless the Oxonians of Georgian England comprised a
small percentage of undergraduates who were extreme free-
thinkers, and a more considerable percentage of young men,
who, after subscribing the Articles in levity, and with an imperfect knowledge of their contents, passed their academic
terms in frivolity and dissoluteness. But it cannot be doubted

that the religious requirements and observances of the University
operated as an efficacious discipline on the majority of the
students. The same requirements and observances were also
influential on every undergraduate, whatever his secret sentiments and his manner of living, in reminding him that the
University was a school for members of the Church of England
and for no other persons, that as a member of the University he
was bound to live in apparent conformity to the National Church,
and that he would forfeit his right to remain in the University
by repudiating the doctrines of the Church. In Shelley's
academic time, every undergraduate knew that by publishing a
work to discredit the fundamental doctrines of Christianity he
would render himself liable to banishment from the University,
and that the authorities of his college would be constrained by
their official obligations to take prompt action for his punishment, and in case he persisted in his flagrant heterodoxy to
expel him. It is certain that Shelley's view of his academic
obligations and responsibilities differed widely from Mr.
Rossetti's erroneous view of them. That he published *The
Necessity of Atheism* anonymously, that he made a secret of his
authorship of the work, that he declined to answer 'yea' or
'nay' to the inquiry whether he wrote the tract, are sufficient
testimony that he was alive to the nature and consequences of
the offence of which he had been guilty. Evidence under
Shelley's own hand has already been produced that, instead
of imagining himself at liberty to hold and expound any
opinions he pleased, he was well aware that, as a member of the
University, he was precluded from publishing certain opinions.
On 2nd March, 1811, at the very moment of publishing *The
Necessity of Atheism*, he wrote from University College, to Leigh
Hunt: '*On account of the responsibility to which my residence in
this University subjects me, I, of course, dare not publicly avow all
that I think.*' The writer of these words was better informed
than most of his biographers respecting the obligations of an
Oxford undergraduate.

Had he been so remarkably out-spoken and truth-loving,
as Lady Shelley declares him to have been, Shelley would not
have entered Oxford with a falsehood on his lips, by a solemn
declaration that he believed what he disbelieved. Though he
believed in the existence of God till the later part of the Christmas vacation (1810-11), he had ceased to believe in the divinity

of Christ before he went to Oxford. At the time of his matriculation he was not a Christian; yet he went before the authorities of University College and of the University, and declared himself a believer in Christianity, and an honest member of the Church of England. How are we to account for the conduct of this singularly out-spoken and truth-loving Shelley in stating thus deliberately and solemnly what he knew was untrue?

It may be said that other young men in 1810 told the same untruths for their convenience and advantage. Doubtless, a few other young men were guilty of the same untruths. But no one has ventured to extol them for singular candour, veracity, and moral courage. How came the singularly out-spoken and truth-loving Shelley to utter the solemn falsehoods? Had he been so out-spoken and truth-loving, surely he would have said, 'I will not go to Oxford, because I can only enter the University by means of enormous untruths.' In the year of his matriculation every English county had young men, every considerable English town had young men, who would gladly have gone to Oxford and Cambridge for the advantages of University education, could they have done so without falsehood;—young men who entered on the battle of life with inferior culture and at serious disadvantages, because to get admittance to the Universities it would be necessary for them to be untruthful. No one has ever thought of commending these young men for any peculiar elevation of character, because they refrained from telling a lie and entering on a course of hypocrisy, that would in some considerable respects have been beneficial to them. They deserved no such commendation; for their conduct merely proved they were not wanting in the ordinary truthfulness and honesty, which parliament assumed ordinary Englishmen to possess, as a matter of course, when it was determined to exclude Non-conformists from the Universities. How came the singularly out-spoken and truth-loving Shelley to be so much less than ordinarily truthful in this business?

It cannot be pleaded in his excuse, as it can be pleaded in behalf of the many youngsters who subscribed the Articles with commonplace carelessness, that he had not given much consideration to the Articles and Christian evidences; that he took it for granted they were all right; that, though he may have been wrong to trust in so serious a business to vague and general impressions, he did not know the Articles comprised tenets from

which he differed. It cannot be urged in palliation of his falseness that by declining to go to one of the Universities he would
have thrown away his only or his best chance of rising to a
position of dignity and comfort. Nor can it be suggested that,
knowing his father wished him to go to the University, and to
distinguish himself there, so dutiful and loving a son did not like
to disappoint his sire's paternal ambition. Shelley went to Oxford
merely to please himself; and, in order to have the pleasure of
living at Oxford with congenial companions, he entered the
University under cover of falsehood, declaring he was a Christian
when he knew he was not a Christian. He entered Oxford
under cover of this falsehood, well knowing that to a man of his
opinions the usual residence at Oxford would be a course of
hypocrisy. Other young men (though, unless I err, *not many
young men*) have done likewise. But it would be absurd to
commend them for being especially out-spoken and truth-
loving.

During the Michaelmas term of 1810, Shelley amused himself by luring persons, whom he knew only by name and reputation, into corresponding with him on religious questions, just
as in former time he had drawn strangers into controversy on
questions of natural science. Addressing these people under a
false name and address, he caused them to imagine they were
replying to the letters of a person, troubled with doubts and
honestly desirous of information and guidance for the solution
of the difficulties. To account for the secresy and misrepresentations, with which Shelley approached the individuals he thus
lured into religious controversy, it is recorded in Hogg's *Life*
that, whilst at Eton, the youthful disputant about gases was
threatened by an angry chemist with exposure to Dr. Keate,
who would not fail to whip him into a healthier state of mind.
On being thus reminded how unfavourable the discipline of his
school was to equally frank and free inquiry, the schoolboy
adopted a course that, without affecting the freedom of his
inquiries, would guard him from some of the consequences of
perilous frankness. An anonymous letter-writer at Eton to save
his skin, Shelley was an anonymous letter-writer at Oxford to
save his credit for religious conformity with the 'dons.' Instead
of using only one *nom-de-plume* in these affairs of deceitful correspondence, Shelley employed several *aliases* for his more effectual
concealment; and whilst using different names he misdescribed

himself in various ways to the persons with whom he held intercourse through the post.

Whilst some of his correspondents were given to understand that he was a sceptical layman, others were led to imagine him a sceptic in holy orders. The prelates and other learned divines who answered his letters answered them under misconceptions, arising chiefly or altogether from his misstatements. At least on one occasion he signed with a woman's name, that of course accorded with the tenor, tone, and handwriting of the epistle to which it was appended. The bishop, whom the poet thus lured in controversy (*vide* Medwin's *Life*, I. p. 119), was under the impression that his correspondent was a gentlewoman. Referring to the day he passed with his cousin at Oxford in Lent term, 1811, Medwin remarks :—

' He showed and read to me many letters he had received in controversies he had originated with learned divines ; among the rest with a bishop, under the assumed name of a woman. . . . . It is to be lamented,' Medwin adds, ' that all his letters written at this time should have perished, as they would throw light on the speculations of his active and inquiring mind.'

Whether they would materially enlarge our knowledge of the poet's intellectual and moral constitution is questionable ; but it cannot be doubted the recovery of the vanished epistles would afford some curious examples of the untruthfulness of which the singularly outspoken and truth-loving Shelley was capable. Instead of expressing, or hinting disapproval of his cousin's duplicity, Mr. Medwin only regrets so few illustrations of so droll a practice should have been preserved. To Mr. Medwin the whole business of these Shelleyan fabrications appears equally innocent and diverting ; and in this respect he resembles the Shelleyan enthusiasts of later time, who regard the same evidence of the truth-loving Shelley's staggering untruthfulness, merely as so much testimony that he was an exceedingly clever and amusing young gentleman, and that the learned divines whom he tricked with untruths must have been stupid fellows and sad simpletons.

To persons of sufficient culture and sensibility, as well as of sufficient sobriety, to delight in Shelley's poetry, without at the same time thinking he might have been the Saviour of the World, it is not obvious why Shelley should be held guiltless of untruth when he wrote to a Bishop of the Church of

England that he was a lady, and as a lady threw himself upon the same Bishop's charitable consideration. Of course Shelley had a powerful imagination. That is a fact which the Shelleyan enthusiasts take care we should not forget. But it is inconceivable (*surely* it is inconceivable even to the Shelleyan enthusiasts) that, whilst writing to the Right Reverend Father in God, the undergraduate of University College, Oxford, believed that he really was a young lady, and that as a young lady he might claim a large measure of the Bishop's charitable aid and sympathy. To sober and fairly intelligent persons it appears, that, whether it is composed to win confidence which shall be fruitful of a few half-crowns, or to win such confidence as shall dispose its receiver to expend time and labour for the sender's advantage, a letter of false pretences is an act of imposture, of which rogues are likely, and no quite honest gentleman is at all likely, to be guilty. For myself,—in the course of every year I receive several letters from strangers asking me to give them money; and as many letters from strangers of education and apparent honesty asking me to give them time and labour and judgment, for their assistance in their literary enterprises. I answer some of the former letters after inquiry, and I answer all the latter letters without suspicious inquiry, from a mere wholesome habit of believing what people say. But should it come to my knowledge that a writer of any of those latter letters had lured me by false representations into troubling myself about his affairs, I should naturally think the letter-writer an impostor, and think myself the victim of imposture.

The letters that passed between Hogg and Shelley during the Christmas vacation (1810-11) afford evidence that throughout the holidays the future poet found diversion in incidents arising out of his deceitful and delusive correspondence with persons, to whom he was not known personally. Respecting one of his correspondents — the 'W.' whom Mr. MacCarthy mistook for William Godwin—Shelley wrote on 20th December, 1810 :—
'I wrote to him when in London, by way of a gentle alterative. He promised to write to me when he had time, seemed surprised at what I said, yet directed to me as the Reverend : his amazement must be extreme.'

No one knew better than this interesting young gentleman, what good cause W. had for amazement with his reverend correspondent. After the Christmas vacation, Shelley returned to University College with a strong disposition to enlarge his correspondence with strangers, and to extend the field of his operations for disturbing people in their religious opinions. Having left Oxford in December, believing in the existence of God, he returned to Oxford in January with the conviction that there was no God. In Michaelmas term (1810) he had regarded Christianity as a rather narrowing and otherwise baneful delusion, from which people should be weaned. In Lent term (1811) he regarded all religions as unutterably hateful, as alike injurious to human nature and destructive to human happiness. Anger at the religious steadfastness and intolerance, which determined Miss Harriett Grove to dismiss him from her acquaintance, had determined him to kill every religion, so that no religion should be left for people to be intolerant about. Having left Oxford, in December, with an opinion that all religions were equally ridiculous, he returned to Oxford, in January, with the opinion that all religions were equally detestable,—with the resolve to *slay* religious intolerance, to *stab her secretly*, by secretly stabbing and slaying the religious faith that, besides being the generator, was the vital force, of religious intolerance. To slay intolerance, the arch-enemy and arch-destroyer of the sweetest human affections and the most sacred social ties, he would slay creed,— stabbing her secretly, whilst wearing the disguise of a Christian. In December (1810) it satisfied him to deride Christianity; at the end of January (1811) he was determined to kill the belief in God. Any reader who thinks I have overstated the purpose of this undergraduate (whose feeble pen had produced nothing stronger than *St. Irvyne*), will cease to think so, after perusing attentively and judicially the letters which he wrote to Hogg, during the Christmas holidays.

In the execution of this determination to slay the belief in God (by stabbing it secretly), this singularly outspoken and truthful Shelley, whilst still pretending to be a Christian by remaining at Oxford and attending the religious services of his college chapel, wrote (with Hogg's help) *anonymously*, and circulated *secretly* with anonymous or false letters, the following tract (which readers of this work should peruse deliberately) on

THE NECESSITY OF ATHEISM.

'A close examination of the validity of the proofs adduced to support any proposition, has ever been allowed to be the only sure way of attaining truth, upon the advantages of which it is unnecessary to descant; our knowledge of the existence of a Deity is a subject of such importance, that it cannot be too minutely investigated; in consequence of this conviction, we proceed briefly and impartially to examine the proofs which have been adduced. It is necessary first to consider the nature of Belief.

'When a proposition is offered to the mind, it perceives the agreement or disagreement of the ideas of which it is composed. A perception of their agreement is termed belief, many obstacles frequently prevent this perception from being immediate, these the mind attempts to remove in order that the perception may be distinct. The mind is active in the investigation, in order to perfect the state of perception which is passive; the investigation being confused with the perception has induced many falsely to imagine that the mind is active in belief, that belief is an act of volition, in consequence of which it may be regulated by the mind; pursuing, continuing this mistake they have attached a degree of criminality to disbelief of which in its nature it is incapable; it is equally so of merit.

'The strength of belief like that of every other passion is in proportion to the degrees of excitement.

'The degrees of excitement are three.

'The senses are the sources of all knowledge to the mind, consequently their evidence claims the strongest assent.

'The decision of the mind founded upon our own experience derived from these sources, claims the next degree.

'The experience of others, which addresses itself to the former one, occupies the lowest degree.—

'Consequently no testimony can be admitted which is contrary to reason, reason is founded on the evidence of our senses.

'Every proof may be referred to one of these three divisions; we are naturally led to consider what arguments we receive from each of them to convince us of the existence of a Deity.

'1st. The evidence of the senses.—If the Deity should appear to us, if he should convince our senses of his existence, this revelation would necessarily command belief:—Those to whom the Deity has thus appeared, have the strongest possible conviction of his existence.

'Reason claims the 2nd place, it is urged that man knows that whatever is, must either have had a beginning or existed from all eternity, he also knows that whatever is not eternal must have had a cause.—Where this is applied to the existence of the universe, it is necessary to prove that it was created; until that is clearly demonstrated, we may reasonably suppose that it has endured from all eternity.—In a case where two propositions are diametrically opposite, the mind believes that which is less incomprehensible, it is easier to suppose that the universe has existed from all eternity, than to conceive a being capable of creating it; if the mind sinks beneath the weight of the one, is it an alleviation to increase the intolerability of the burden?—The other argument which

is founded upon a man's knowledge of his own existence stands thus:—
A man knows not only he now is, but that there was a time when he
did not exist, consequently there must have been a cause.—But what
does this prove? we can only infer from effects causes exactly adequate
to those effects:—But there certainly is a generative power which is
effected by particular instruments ; we cannot prove that it is inherent
in these instruments, nor is the contrary hypothesis capable of demonstration; we admit that the generative power is incomprehensible, but to
suppose that the same effect is produced by an eternal, omniscient,
Almighty Being, leaves the cause in the same obscurity, but renders it
more incomprehensible.

'The 3rd and last degree of assent is claimed by Testimony—it is
required that it should not be contrary to reason.—The testimony that
the Deity convinces the senses of men of his existence can only be
admitted by us, if our mind considers it less probable that these men
should have been deceived, than that the Deity should have appeared to
them—our reason can never admit the testimony of men, who not only
declare that they were eye-witnesses of miracles but that the Deity was
irrational, for he commanded that he should be believed, he proposed the
highest rewards for faith, eternal punishments for disbelief—we can only
command voluntary actions, belief is not an act of volition, the mind is
even passive, from this it is evident that we have not sufficient testimony,
or rather that testimony is insufficient to prove the being of a God, we
have before shewn that it cannot be deduced from reason,—they who
have been convinced by the evidence of the senses, they only can believe it.

'From this it is evident that having no proofs from any of the three
sources of conviction : the mind *cannot* believe the existence of a God,
it is also evident that as belief is a passion of the mind, no degree of
criminality can be attached to disbelief, they only are reprehensible who
willingly neglect to remove the false medium thro' which their mind
views the subject.

'It is almost unnecessary to observe, that the general knowledge of
the deficiency of such proof, cannot be prejudicial to society : Truth has
always been found to promote the best interests of mankind.—Every
reflecting mind must allow that there is no proof of the existence of a
Deity.   Q.E.D.'

On a separate leaf between the title-page and the first page
of the text of the tract the author put this

'Advertisement :—As a love of truth is the only motive which
actuates the Author of this little tract, he earnestly entreats that those
of his readers who may discover any deficiency in his reasoning, or may
be in possession of proofs which his mind could never obtain, would
offer them, together with their objections, to the Public, as briefly as
methodically, as plainly as he has taken the liberty of doing.   Thro'
deficiency of proof,—An Atheist.'

In the middle of the title-page appears this title, 'Quod clarâ et perspicuâ demonstratione careat pro vero habere mens omnino nequit humana.'—*Bacon de Augment. Scient.*; whilst at the foot of the same page appears this announcement :—'Worthing.—Printed By E. & W. Phillips. Sold in London and Oxford.' It having been so often asserted that this tract was neither published nor printed with a view to ordinary publication, readers should take note of the words, 'Sold in London and Oxford.' The promise of these words was fulfilled, at least so far as Oxford was concerned. Duly advertised in the *Oxford Herald* of 9th February, 1811, on the eve of its publication, the tract was offered for sale at Oxford in the usual way. Even by Mr. Buxton Forman it is admitted that the tract 'was "on sale" in Oxford for twenty minutes.' Mr. Forman does not say who counted the minutes. Possibly the expression was merely meant by Mr. Forman to signify that the work was on sale for part only of a single day. That it was no longer on sale within their jurisdiction was, of course, due to the authorities of the University, whose prompt action for the suppression of the work may be presumed to have been the direct or indirect cause of the destruction of the copies of the pamphlet, lying in the hands of the author's Oxford bookseller.

However they may differ about the literary style and logical force of this tract, all fair readers must allow that it exhibits no signs of levity, no indication of having been thrown off in jest as a satire on the class of performances to which it really belongs. From the first line to the last, it accords with the Atheist's declaration (in the advertisement) that he is actuated by a love of truth, and is earnestly desirous that its arguments may receive serious consideration. Yet it has been described as a mere harmless piece of fun.

The Shelleyan apologists call attention to the brevity of the monograph, as though it were a fact in Shelley's favour. It is suggested that serious books are long books of many pages with many words on a page; and that so short an essay (even if it was wrong of Shelley to produce it) should be regarded as a trivial performance, and its publication as nothing worse than a trivial indiscretion; the implication being that the Master and Fellows of University College were guilty of monstrous injustice and cruelty in expelling the author of so small a work. In thus prating about the insignificant size of the work, these apologists resemble the peccant maid-servant, who pleaded that, if she had given birth to an infant without having gone through any form of lawful marriage, it should be remembered, in palliation of the misdemeanour, that her baby was an unusually little one. Writing from those 'authentic sources,' which have afforded her much strange misinformation, Lady Shelley assures us that the little pamphlet was a 'publication consisting of only two pages;' whereas if she will only return to her original sources and count the duly numbered pages, the author of *Shelley Memorials* will discover that the text of the small treatise occupies *seven pages*, besides the title-page and the page exhibiting the 'advertisement,' which is no immaterial part of the composition. How came Lady Shelley to count the pages so carelessly? Lady Shelley is curiously wrong on other points about this little pamphlet. 'In point of fact,' we are told by the lady who suffered so acutely from Hogg's inaccuracies, 'the pamphlet did not contain any positive assertion.' Why, the tract is made of positive assertions; it would not be easy for Lady Shelley to find another tract of the same length, containing a greater number of positive assertions. The tract concludes with a sentence of these words :—' Every reflecting mind must allow that there is no proof of the existence of a Deity ;' words followed by what the lady calls 'a Q. E. D.' What more does this assertion require to render it 'positive?' Speaking from her original sources, Lady Shelley tells us that Shelley wrote the little pamphlet 'hastily,' and 'with his habitual disregard of consequences.' How a pamphlet, made up out of the 'very careful analysis' of Hume's *Essays*, which Shelley and his friend had prepared in the previous term, can be said to have been written hastily, is not apparent.

Hogg's narrative, and the extant letter that passed between him and Shelley in the Christmas holidays, abound with evidence that the latter came gradually to his opinions touching the non-existence of Deity, and that the pamphlet was the result of much deliberation. It is no less certain that instead of publishing the tract with 'habitual disregard of consequences,' Shelley gave much thought to the consequences of a discovery that he wrote it. Publishing it anonymously, he was at much pains to keep the authorship a secret. Yet further we are assured by Lady Shelley :—

'The publication . . . . seemed rather to imply, on the part of the writer, a desire to obtain better reasoning on the side of commonly received opinion, than any wish to overthrow with sudden violence the grounds of men's belief.'

The reader who knows the circumstances under, and the end for, which the pamphlet was produced, and has perused the *ipsissima verba* of the tract, may be left to form his own opinion of this example of the way in which the authorities of Field Place would write the poet's history.

I would not be wanting in courtesy to Mr. Garnett of the British Museum, of whom I would say nothing worse than that he is wildly and inexplicably inaccurate in what he has written about *The Necessity of Atheism*. There is a curious discrepancy between Lady Shelley's account and Mr. Garnett's description of the famous tract. Whilst Lady Shelley regards the pamphlet as a serious attempt to strengthen the evidences of the existence of the Deity, by eliciting ' better reasoning on the side of the commonly received ' view, Mr. Garnett declares that the essay was a mere piece of caustic playfulness. ' After Hogg's account of it,' says Mr. Garnett, in his article on *Shelley in Pall Mall*, ' it is sufficiently clear that this alarming performance was nothing else than a squib, prompted by the decided success of the burlesque verses the friends had published in the name of " My Aunt Margaret Nicholson." ' A squib, in the sense suggested by Mr. Garnett, is a flash of humour, a lampoon, a slight satire, a little censorious writing. A learned gentleman, Mr. Garnett knows well enough what ' squib ' means, when it is applied to a little book. Yet he tells the readers of *Macmillan's Magazine* that Shelley's serious argument against the belief in God was a mere product of caustic fun and humorous sprightliness. What a charge to make against Shelley! Mr. Garnett is one of Shelley's friends, admirers, idolaters ; and he declares that Shelley made a jest of the most solemn and awful of all momentous questions ; was so droll a fellow that he styled himself an Atheist, and argued against the existence of the Deity in pure sportiveness. This is how Shelley is dealt with by one of his peculiar friends !

What does Mr. Garnett mean by giving Hogg as his authority for saying that *The Necessity of Atheism* was a squib, when Hogg is at pains to say the tract was no such thing ? Hogg writes lightly and seriously by turns of the tract, as he does of other matters of the poet's story. He speaks of the pamphlet as 'a small pill that worked powerfully.' To minimize the importance of the work, for which he was even more accountable than Shelley ; to make the least of the serious offence, touching his own character no less hurtfully than Shelley's reputation, Hogg calls it a 'little pamphlet, 'a. general issue,' 'a compendious allegation in order to put the whole case in proof,' 'a formal mode of saying, you affirm so-and-so, then prove it,' 'a little syllabus,' 'an innocent and insignificant thesis propounded for the delectation of lovers of logomachy,' a tract that 'was never offered for sale.' In this style Hogg speaks lightly of the work, that was the central incident of the painful business, about which he felt too acutely and personally to his last hour, to be able to speak of it truthfully. The whole affair was one of the few subjects on which the otherwise substantially honest biographer was untruthful. Consequently, had he called the tract a squib, in some sentence at discord with his other statements about the pamphlet, Mr. Garnett would not have been justified in fathering his own discovery on an authority, so unworthy of perfect credit on this particular subject. But Hogg nowhere calls the tract a squib. On the contrary, he guards against any such misconstruction and misinterpretation of his lighter remarks, and is at pains to say that, so far as Shelley was concerned, the pamphlet was an altogether serious performance.

'In describing briefly the nature of Shelley's epistolary contentions,' Hogg says, 'the recollection of his youth, his zeal, his activity, and particularly of many individual peculiarities, may have tempted me to speak sometimes with a certain levity, notwithstanding the solemn importance of the topics respecting which they were frequently maintained. The impression that they were conducted on his part, or considered by him, with frivolity, or any unseemly lightness, would, however, be most erroneous; his whole frame of mind was grave, earnest, and anxious, and his deportment was reverential, with an edification reaching beyond the age—an age wanting in reverence.'

Be it remembered that, in the later weeks of Shelley's second term of residence, the printed tract was a main feature and chief instrument of the 'epistolary contentions' to which the biographer refers? How then came Mr. Garnett to give Hogg as his authority for saying this 'grave, earnest, and anxious Shelley' diverted himself at Oxford with writing a squib on the most awful of all sacred subjects? How are we to account for so staggering a misrepresentation of the evidence of Hogg's book? In his article on *Shelley in Pall Mall*, Mr. Garnett speaks no less strongly than precisely of the evidential force of certain Shelleyan documents, not under the view of the public. What value should we assign to evidence, respecting documents we cannot examine, from a gentleman who can misrepresent in so extraordinary a manner the evidence of a printed book open to the whole world's scrutiny?

When *The Necessity of Atheism* had been printed by Messrs. E. and W. Phillips, of Worthing, it was Shelley's practice to send a copy of the performance to any notable divine or other personage whom he wished to draw into a controversial correspondence, together with a brief note (under a false signature and address), saying—

' That he had met with that little tract, which appeared, unhappily, to be quite unanswerable. Unless,' Hogg continues, ' the fish was too sluggish to take the bait, an answer of refutation was forwarded to an appointed address in London, and then in a vigorous reply he would fall upon the unwary disputant, and break his bones. The strenuous attack sometimes provoked a rejoinder more carefully prepared, and an animated and protracted debate ensued; the party cited, having put in his answer, was fairly in court, and he might get out of it as he could.'

It was thus that ' the innocent and insignificant thesis propounded for the delectation of lovers of logomachy' (Hogg's description of the tract) was floated into circulation, by force of lie upon lie. Instead of being ' propounded for the delectation of lovers of logomachy,' it is stated by Hogg himself that the tract was composed and put in type because Shelley, finding strangers slow to notice a written challenge to argument, conceived they would be attracted by a printed syllabus. True, so far as it goes, this statement gives only part of the truth. Seeing that a printed scheme for disputation would be more attractive, Shelley saw also that he could not spare the time to produce a manuscript syllabus (written by his own hand) for each of the many persons whose bones he was set on breaking.

The day on which the undergraduate of University College received his first lot of printed copies from the Worthing printers is unknown; but it cannot have preceded by many days the appearance in the *Oxford Herald* (9th February, 1811,) of this advertisement:—' Speedily will be published, to be had of

the Booksellers of London and Oxford, *The Necessity of Atheism.*
"Quod clarâ et perspicuâ demonstratione careat pro vero habere,
mens omnino nequit humana."—*Bacon de Augment. Scient.*'
Probably the appearance of this advertisement in the Oxford
newspaper followed closely upon the arrival at Shelley's rooms
in University College of the first lot of printed copies from
Worthing. Anyhow, the authorities of the University were
advertised, so early as the 9th of February, that a work, to
demonstrate the necessity of atheism, would be speedily offered
for sale within their jurisdiction. Inserted in a newspaper,
read by many members of the University, this advertisement
came quickly under the eyes of the Vice-Chancellor and Proctors
of the University, the Heads of Houses, and all other persons
especially concerned in the maintenance of academic discipline
at the seat of learning. There was gossip in the common-
rooms. Sitting over their port, Doctors of Divinity and Masters
of Arts exchanged sentiments respecting the audacious announcement. The proctors took counsel with their pro-proctors,
and the acutest and most discreet of 'the bull-dogs' was ordered
to keep a sharp look-out for the first copy of the atrocious
publication that should be offered for sale in any bookseller's
window. Of course it was the opinion of the authorities that
Mr. Munday, the proprietor of the *Oxford Herald*, knew the
atheist's real name; at least could say what induced him to
put such a staggering advertisement in his paper. It cannot
be questioned that Mr. Munday's shop, the office of the *Oxford
Herald*, was watched day and night by persons who were instructed to take note of all individuals visiting the printer's
premises. Doubtless, also, the people at the Post Office were
affected by the measures, taken by the academic authorities for
the discovery of the person or persons, who should venture to
sell atheistical literature in the City of the Church. The Vice-
Chancellor and Proctors have good and sufficient means of
observing what is done at Oxford in this present year of
grace, and had even better means of observation seventy years
since.

Whilst the academic authorities were taking measures for
the discovery of any persons who should trouble the University
with an atheistical publication, Shelley was sending out copies
of the tract, and replying to the letters of his numerous correspondents. Each of the copies so sent forth by the author was

commended to the careful consideration of its recipient by several falsehoods,—the untruths of the printed advertisement, and the untruths of the letter accompanying the work. It was untrue that the author's 'only motive' in putting the tract in circulation was 'a love of truth;' he was actuated by resentment against the religious earnestness which had caused Miss Harriett Grove to dismiss him from her acquaintance, and by a desire to slay what he called bigotry and intolerance. It was untrue that he hoped earnestly the recipient of the pamphlet would show him defects in his arguments; all he desired being a reply that would afford him an opportunity for breaking the replicant's bones! It was untrue that he had come accidentally on the little tract, which he had written himself. It was not true that the apparent conclusiveness of the arguments caused him unhappiness. The name appended to his letter was a false name; the address from which he pretended to write was a falsehood. When he pretended to be a woman he was guilty of another falsehood. The most offensive of all the falsehoods was the profession that he was suffering from his religious doubts, and sincere in asking the stranger to aid him in dispersing them.

It has been repeatedly urged, in palliation of the falsehoods Shelley employed in provoking and prosecuting 'his epistolary contentions,' that the scholars of former time, who brought about the revival of letters or were the offspring of the revival, contended with one another by epistles as well as by word of mouth, and that their letters, instead of being signed with their rightful Christian names and surnames, were usually signed with fanciful names of their own manufacture. The apology, were it true to the facts of the ancient fashion, would not justify Shelley's deceits; but it is a misrepresentation of the innocent usage of the old disputants. The mediæval scholar, who wrangled and wrote under an assumed name, held steadily to his adopted name, so that he was known by it and by no other name in the Universities and scholarly guilds. When Gerard's illegitimate son had once styled himself Desiderius Erasmus, in accordance with the innocent though fantastic and pedantic fashion of his contemporaries, he was styled so to his dying hour. The man who thus takes a name and sticks to it, whether he be a soldier or lawyer, a politician or dramatic actor, is guilty of no falsehood. Erasmus did not change his name every day of the week from a deceitful motive; he did not use a score of *aliases* at the same time; it was not his habit to write to charitable people saying that he was a woman, and whilst feigning to be some one else to pretend he was living in one place whilst he was living in another place. In his epistolary diversions the singularly outspoken and truth-loving Shelley was guilty of all these various forms of misrepresentation. He used a score of different names, misrepresented his sex, told fibs about his address, said he was unhappy at what caused him delight, declared himself to have come accidentally on the book written by his own hand, declared to strangers that he was actuated solely by love of truth at the moment when he was boasting to Hogg that he was animated by hatred of religion. It cannot be denied that he was habitually guilty of all these different forms of deceit. It is admitted he was guilty of them, even by those who extol him for his singular frankness and sincerity.

The end to Shelley's Oxford career came suddenly. From the day of his return to College after the Christmas vacation, things had gone pleasantly with the undergraduate. When Medwin, on passing through Oxford, spent a day with his cousin, he found him agreeably diverted with the incidents of his controversial correspondence with learned divines, including the Bishop who thought him a woman. He was exchanging letters with charming little Harriett Westbrook. His efforts for the benefit of Miss Janetta Phillips had been successful. He was on friendly, if not affectionate, terms with his father, and was at work on the poem for the Newdigate Prize. In spite of all Mr. Denis Florence MacCarthy says to the contrary, he delighted as much as heretofore in the society of Hogg. The term was drawing to an end, and in a week or two the young men hoped to be at Field Place, in the society of the young lady, whose assent to their wishes would make them brothers-in-law. Nothing had occurred to forewarn him of the storm so soon to break in fury upon him, when, one fine, bright, cheery morning, Mr. Percy Bysshe Shelley received a summons to appear before the Master and some of the Fellows of his College in their common-room. It does not appear that, together with the summons, Shelley received an intimation of the business that made the Master and 'dons' wish to see him. It is more than probable that the messenger who brought the summons left the undergraduate to conjecture, why he was required to meet the magnates of the College in their common-room soon after the usual hour for breakfast. He can scarcely be supposed, however, to have gone to the common-room without an apprehension that *The Necessity of Atheism* had something to do with the summons. His suspense was of no long duration. The Master and two or three Fellows were awaiting his arrival when he entered the room, and, on his appearance, the Master produced a copy of *the Little Syllabus.*

How the pamphlet came to the Master's hands is unknown to the present writer. There is reason to think the work had not been on sale in Oxford for many days, though its speedy publication had been advertised in the *Oxford Herald* on the 9th of the previous month. There is reason for thinking that 25th March, 1811, the day of Shelley's expulsion, was also the day on which the tract was first offered for sale in Oxford. After the author's disgrace, no tradesman of the city would have ventured to offer the work to customers in the ordinary way of business. As the University police were doubtless on the look-out for the publication, it is not to be supposed that the tract had been long on sale before it came to the Master's hands. I should not be surprised to learn that the first copy displayed in Mr. Munday's shop-window was snapped up by an officer of the University within a few minutes of its appearance there, and that the policeman's act was speedily followed by the delivery of a notice, that determined Mr. Munday to lose no time in destroying all the copies of the work remaining in his possession. In fact, I should not be surprised to learn that Mr. Buxton Forman had good authority for the precise number of minutes which he represents (figuratively or literally) as covering the time during which the tract was on sale at Oxford. To imagine all this is, of course, also to conceive that the authorities of University College had already completed their inquiries respecting the work, had discovered the author, and at the break of the 25th day of March, were only waiting for an act of formal publication, to take promptly a course of action on which they had previously decided.

Anyhow, they were ready for decisive action on the young author's appearance before them. They certainly acted on that occasion with vigour and apparent promptitude; but it does not follow that they acted without due inquiry and deliberation.

Anyhow, they fastened the deed on the doer. They knew that Shelley was one of the authors, if not the sole author, of the tract. If, as Shelley and Hogg averred, the sentence for Shelley's expulsion was signed and sealed before he entered the common-room, the fact merely shows that the authorities came there only to act on the result of previous inquiry. The fact does not indicate precipitation or prejudgment of the case,—*i.e.* judgment before sufficient inquiry and clear discovery. It is not wonderful the Master and Fellows knew all about the matter; for at Oxford the academic authorities had great facilities for inquiry into such a business. Through inquiries and observations at the Post Office, the University police could easily discover to whom Shelley was writing letters,— to what address in London he was sending letters. It was easy work in the course of a few weeks to gather information from persons who had received copies of *the* pamphlet, together with letters in the author's handwriting. It was also easy for the Master and 'dons' of University College to gather additional information respecting Shelley's previous history. There *is* now, and *was*, seventy years since, close and confidential inter- course between the authorities of the Universities and the authorities of the public schools. A boy does not leave Eton with a very bad character and enter Oxford with a good one. From the date of his matriculation the 'dons' of University College knew what kind of boy Shelley was at Eton. As soon as he began to trouble them at Oxford, they knew what to expect from him, and how they must deal with him.

How did the outspoken and truth-loving Shelley act when the Master, taking the tract from his pocket, inquired whether he wrote it? Did he, in a manner becoming a martyr for the truth's sake, reply, ' Yes, sir, I wrote the pamphlet, and it declares faithfully my sincere convictions'? Did he in a manner suitable to a gentleman (interrogated by his collegiate superiors on a matter about which they had a clear right to question him, and about which they were bound to question him) answer frankly, ' Yes, sir, and I am prepared to take the consequences of my act'? Not a bit of it. The frank, out- spoken, fearless Shelley shuffled and quibbled like an attorney's copying-clerk. He asked the Master's purpose in putting the question. He told the Master to produce his evidence. He blustered about the injustice and illegality of the Master's proceedings. Then, losing his temper, he became abusive. He accused the Master (who was only doing his duty) of tyranny, injustice, and vulgar violence. He asked for the production of evidence, demanded a formal trial, and yet refused to plead 'Not Guilty.' All that is known respecting what passed between the Master and Fellows on the one hand, and the contumacious undergraduate on the other hand, within the four walls of the common-room, comes to us from Shelley himself, by way of Hogg's pen. One would fain have a more reliable witness. But in default of better testimony, we must be content with the report of Shelley's evidence against himself.

It had been arranged between the two friends that Hogg should come to Shelley's rooms at an unusually early hour on the Lady-day of 1811. In accordance with this appointment, Hogg (little imagining what was even then going on in the common-room) entered his friend's apartment, whilst the latter was with 'the dons,' or on his way back from his interview with them. In a minute Shelley rushed into the room, terribly agitated.

'I am expelled,' he cried in a shrill voice, 'I am expelled! I was sent for suddenly a few minutes ago; I went to the common-room, where I found our Master and two or three of the Fellows. The Master produced a copy of the *little syllabus*, and asked me if I were the author of it. He spoke in a rude, abrupt, and insolent tone. I begged to be informed for what purpose he put the question. No answer was given; but the Master loudly and angrily repeated, " Are you the author of this book ? " " If I can judge from your manner," I said, " you are resolved to punish me if I should acknowledge that it is my work. If you can prove that it is, produce your evidence ; it is neither just nor lawful to interrogate me in such a case and for such a purpose. Such proceedings would become a court of inquisitors, but not free men in a free country." " Do you choose to deny that this is your composition ? " the Master reiterated in the same rude and angry voice. Shelley (Hogg continues) complained much of his violent and ungentlemanlike deportment, saying, " I have experienced tyranny and injustice before, and I well know what vulgar violence is; but I never met with such unworthy treatment." I told him calmly, but firmly, that I was determined not to answer any questions respecting the publication on the table. He immediately repeated his demand; I persisted in my refusal; and he said furiously, " Then you are expelled ; and I desire you will quit the college early to-morrow morning at the latest." One of the Fellows took up two papers, and handed one of them to me ; here it is.' He produced a regular sentence of expulsion, drawn up in due form, under the seal of the college.

Here we have Shelley's account of the affair; or, to speak precisely, Hogg's report of Shelley's account of the affair. There appears no reason to question the substantial accuracy of the narrative. Allowance for prejudice and partiality must, of course, be made by the reader, especially in respect to those words that relate to the demeanour of the Master and Fellows. One can believe the authorities were gracious neither in their looks nor their voices. There was no reason why they should affect complaisance. If they were rude and harsh in style, Shelley admits that he was insolent and abusive. It is noteworthy that as soon as the collegiate powers, to whose ' civility ' he had borne witness on a previous occasion, presumed to exercise authority over him, the undergraduate (of whose sweet gentleness we have heard so much) flew at them in a manner that was neither gentle nor sweet. In a moment he became the same contumacious youngster who had given his Etonian masters so much trouble. There is no reason to suppose that Hogg misreported Shelley, or that Shelley was inaccurate in the words, ' One of the fellows took up two papers and handed one of them to me.' The other paper was doubtless a similar writ of expulsion that had been prepared for delivery to Hogg. It follows, therefore, that before Shelley entered the common-room, the authorities had determined to dismiss both of the undergraduates from the college, and that Hogg learnt he was under sentence of banishment from Shelley's lips.

Like a true Durham-and-Yorkshireman, Hogg seized the bull by the horns. Seeing he would be expelled, was in fact already under sentence of expulsion, he saw it would be to his advantage to make it appear that he had been expelled for loyalty to his friend. It would discredit him with his kindred near Stockton-on-Tees to be expelled for conspiring with Shelley to teach atheism ; on the other hand it would be rather to his credit with them, and all other robust hearers of the affair, to be expelled for sticking pluckily to a comrade in trouble. Seeing the politic course he took it boldly. Instead of going to his own rooms, where he would either find a written summons or a messenger inviting him to the conclave of 'dons' in the common-room, this smart young man seized a pen, and forthwith wrote the Master and Fellows an impudent letter, enjoining them to reconsider their action towards Shelley, recall their sentence of expulsion, retrace their steps, and behave better in the future. Never was an undergraduate, already under sentence of expulsion, guilty of more extravagant insolence to the authorities of his college. That Hogg was guilty of this act of cunning effrontery to the Master and Fellows, about whose insolence and vulgarity he is so indignant, we know from his own boastful confession.

'I wrote,' he says, 'a short note to the Master and Fellows, in which, as far as I can remember a very hasty composition after a long interval, I briefly expressed my sorrow at the treatment my friend had experienced, and my hope that they would reconsider their sentence, since, by the same course of proceedings, myself, or any other person, might be subjected to the same penalty, and to the imputation of equal guilt. The note was despatched; the conclave was still sitting; and in an instant the porter came to summon me to attend, bearing in his countenance a promise of the reception which I was about to find. The angry and troubled air of men, assembled to commit injustice according to established forms, was then new to me; but a native instinct told me, as soon as I entered the room, that it was an affair of party; that whatever could conciliate the favour of the patrons was to be done without scruple; and whatever could tend to impede preferment was to be brushed away without remorse. The glowing Master produced my poor note. I acknowledged it; and he forthwith put into my hands, not less abruptly, the little syllabus. "Did you write this?" he asked, as fiercely as if I alone stood between him and the rich see of Durham. I attempted, submissively, to point out to him the extreme unfairness of the question; the injustice of punishing Shelley for refusing to answer it. . . . . When I was silent, the Master told me to retire, and to consider whether I was resolved to persist in my refusal. . . . . I had scarcely passed the door, however, when I was recalled. The Master again showed me the book, and hastily demanded whether I admitted or denied that I was the author of it. I answered that I was fully sensible of the many and great inconveniences of being dismissed with disgrace from the University, and I specified some of them, and expressed a humble hope that they would not impose such a mark of discredit upon me without any cause. I lamented that it was impossible either to admit or deny the publication, —no man of spirit could submit to do so;—and that a sense of duty compelled me respectfully to refuse to answer the question which had been proposed. "Then you are expelled," said the Master angrily, in a loud, great voice. A formal sentence, duly signed and sealed, was instantly put into my hand; in what interval the instrument had been drawn up I cannot imagine. The alleged offence was a contumacious refusal to disavow the imputed publication. My eye glanced over it, and observing the word *contumaciously*, I said, calmly, that I did not think that term was justified by my behaviour.'

This is the substance of Hogg's prolix account of his own
expulsion; an account at conflict in one important particular
with Shelley's narrative of his expulsion, and affording several
grounds for declaring it untruthful. Two writs—one of them
certainly a writ of expulsion, and the other presumably a writ
of expulsion—having been drawn up before Shelley entered the
common-room, and Hogg having been told that whilst the one
writ was given to Shelley the other was reserved by the 'dons,'
the north-countryman had good ground for thinking the writ so
reserved was the writ eventually given to him. If his account of
the affair was truthful, in respect to the brevity of the conference
and quickness of the proceedings, a third writ could not have
been made out and sealed during so short and stormy a conference. There is no reason (apart from certain words of
Hogg's narrative that seems to have been written disingenuously) for thinking a third writ was substituted for the reserved
writ. Hogg cannot be supposed to have thought a third writ
was so substituted. He must have assumed at the time that the
writ, put into his hand, was the reserved writ of which Shelley
had told him. In suggesting that the writ put into his hand
was drawn up during the warm colloquy (*in what interval* of it
he could not *imagine*), Hogg must be thought to have written
disingenuously, the object of the disingenuous writing being to
cover a misdescription of the instrument itself. The writ having
been penned before Shelley entered the common-room, it cannot
have alleged that the sentence of expulsion was consequent on
a 'contumacious refusal to disavow the imported publication.'
Possibly the offence was not specified in the document. But
if it was mentioned the instrument must have declared the
sentence consequent on the atheistical writing. Hogg's motive
for misdescribing the document is obvious. Smarting under the
imputation of atheism, the Church-and-State Tory freethinker
to the last represented himself to society as a sufferer from
loyalty to his friend, and he misdescribed the writ so as to
make it harmonize with the creditable view of his case.

The evidences are conflicting in some particulars and deficient in others, but the case may be stated thus :—Hogg and
Shelley were the joint authors of the atheistical pamphlet, the
former being on the whole the more culpable. This tract was
put in circulation, and announced for sale, in Oxford. Having
obtained proof that the tract was the production of the two

undergraduates, the authorities of University College determined to expel the joint-authors as soon as the work should be offered for sale within the academic bounds. Acting on this resolve they sent in the forenoon of Lady-day for the culprits, summoning Shelley first as the one who had employed the printer, and been the busier in putting the tract in circulation. To put himself in a position to say that he had not been expelled for writing the atheistical tract, but merely for declining on grounds of principle to say whether he was concerned in the publication, Shelley refused to answer 'ay' or 'nay' to the Master's questions. For this contumacy alone the authorities would have been justified in dismissing him from the college. But using the writ drawn up before the refusal to answer questions, they expelled him as the joint author and promulgator of an atheistical work. Hogg was dealt with in like manner, and for the same reason, although he tried at the time to put his inevitable punishment on another ground, and subsequently took credit to himself for standing chivalrously by his friend, when he might (as he averred) have escaped punishment by a less generous course. That he knew he was under sentence of expulsion before he wrote the insolent letter to the 'dons' is sufficient proof that he was actuated by no chivalrous motive in writing the epistle. To urge that the 'dons' prejudged the case and acted with indecent precipitation, because they drew up the instrument of expulsion before sending for the offenders is absurd, because they knew the delinquents could not clear themselves. Events justified the action of the 'dons.' The culprits offered no defence, could not offer any, did not venture to say that they were innocent of the charge. The 'dons' had traced the offence to its actual doers before dismissing them from the college. No one who apprehends the legal constitution of the University, the obligations of the authorities, and the obligations of the undergraduates, can question that the writers of the tract were properly dismissed from University College, as persons who were no longer members of the Church of England, or deny that the Master and Fellows were under the circumstances bound to tell the pamphleteers to go about their business.

In his letter, dated 16th February, 1857, from Torquay (a letter already referred to more than once in these pages), Shelley's cousin, Charles Henry Grove, says, indeed, of *The*

Necessity of Atheism and its consequences, 'The pamphlet had
not the author's name, but it was suspected in the University
who was the author; and the young friends were dismissed
from Oxford, for contumaciously refusing to deny themselves
to be the authors of the work;' words of evidence that Shelley's
attempt to misrepresent the cause of his dismissal from the
University was not unsuccessful within the lines of his domestic
circle; or at least of evidence that his near relatives liked to
attribute his expulsion to contumacy rather than to atheism.

The account, given by Shelley of his expulsion to Peacock,
differed notably in certain particulars from the substantially
accurate account he gave on the morning of its occurrence
to his fellow-collegian. To Thomas Love Peacock, the poet
averred that 'his expulsion was a matter of great form and
solemnity,' and that 'there was a sort of public assembly,
before which he pleaded his own cause in a long oration, in
the course of which he called on the illustrious spirits who
had shed glory on those walls, to look down on their degenerate
successors.' Yet further, in confirmation of this extravagant
story, Shelley showed Peacock an Oxford newspaper, or what
appeared to be an Oxford newspaper, containing a full report
of these theatrical proceedings, together with his own oration
at great length.

'His oration,' Peacock adds (*vide Fraser's Magazine*, of June,
1858) 'may have been, as some of Cicero's published orations were, a
speech in the potential mood; one which might, could, should, or
would, have been spoken; but how in that case it got into the Oxford
newspaper passes conjecture.'

To the young gentleman, who made the Bishop imagine
him a lady, and had confidential relations with John Munday
(the Oxford bookseller and printer of the *Oxford Herald*), it is
no injustice to suggest that, instead of being a veritable copy of
the *Herald*, the paper exhibited to Hogg may have been a 'bogus'
copy of the journal, made up in accordance with Mr. Percy
Bysshe Shelley's instructions, for his private use. No reader,
acquainted with Oxford and the ways in which things are done
in the University (and in 'the city' whose people stand, or
used to stand, in wholesome awe of the academic authorities),
can need assurance that the business of the expulsion was a
strictly private affair; that no proceedings in the case afforded
diversion to a public assembly; that Mr. Percy Bysshe Shelley

delivered no grand oration on the degeneracy of collegiate establishments; and that it is highly improbable any Oxford printer ventured to offer the readers of any *bonâ fide* Oxford journal any 'such speech in the potential mood.'

On the morning following their expulsion (the morning of 26th March, 1811), Percy Bysshe Shelley and Thomas Jefferson Hogg, formerly of University College, Oxford, made the journey to London on the outside of a stage-coach. Thus Shelley passed in disgrace from his University at the close of his second residence-term; an event that may be regarded as the termination of the first period of his literary career. What a disastrous period it was! How fruitful of misadventure, ridicule, catastrophe, and shame! No literary aspirant, destined for imperishable fame, ever made a more inauspicious beginning. In his first voyages on literary waters, Byron encountered stormy weather and rough usage. His first book of poetry resembled Shelley's maiden volume, in being suppressed for fear of consequences. Ere his first razor had lost its edge, he was assailed by the *Edinburgh Review*. But having weathered the gale, that almost wrecked *The Hours of Idleness*, he enjoyed merry seas and favourable breezes. A notability before starting for Greece, he returned from the 'pilgrimage,' to spring to the highest pinnacle of fame. On leaving Oxford, Shelley had produced the *Victor-and-Cazire* book (suppressed for want of originality); two of the feeblest and absurdest novels ever written in the English tongue; the *Posthumous Fragments of Margaret Nicholson*, that, despite all Hogg says to the contrary, made him the laughing-stock of Oxford; the advertisements of the *Poetical Essay* that never saw the light; and (with Hogg's help) the *little* syllabus that brought him to *great* grief,—to about the greatest disgrace a young man can undergo at manhood's threshold, without falling in the grip of the criminal law.

CHAPTER XIV.

THE SPRING AND SUMMER OF 1811.

Arrival in Town—The Poland-Street Exiles—The Squire's Correspondence with Hogg's Father—His gentle Treatment of Shelley—Dinner at Miller's Hotel—Hogg's Testimony to the Squire's Worth—Shelley's Nicknames for his Father—Shelley rejects his Father's Terms—Shelley offers Terms to his Father—The Squire's Indignation—He Relents—He makes Shelley a Liberal Allowance—Lady Shelley's Misrepresentations—The Exiles about Town—The Separation of 'The Inseparables'—Shelley's Intimacy with the Westbrooks—John Westbrook's Calling and Character—Taking the Sacrament—Harriett Westbrook's Conversion to Atheism—Her Disgrace at School—Shelley's Measures for illuminating his Sister Hellen—Tourists in Wales—The Change in Elizabeth Shelley—Arrangements for a Clandestine Meeting—Mrs. Shelley's Treatment of her Son—Captain Pilford's Kindness to his Nephew—Harriett Westbrook's Appeal to Shelley—Her Decision and Indecision—From Wales to London—Hogg's Influence—The Elopement to Scotland—Hogg starts for Edinburgh.

Leaving Oxford on 26th March, 1811 (Tuesday), the expelled Oxonians reached London at the close of the day, and after dining at the coffee-house near Piccadilly (where they put up for the night) took tea in Lincoln's Inn Fields with Shelley's cousins, described by Hogg as ' taciturn people, the maxim of whose family appeared to be, that a man should hold his tongue and save his money.' Though the Groves never wasted words, it is conceivable that their extreme taciturnity on the present occasion was in some degree due to Hogg's embarrassing presence. In the hearing of the stranger, whom they most likely held accountable for the catastrophe that had befallen their kinsman, they could scarcely talk, even in their usual guarded manner, of the news the visitors brought with them from the seat of learning. ' Bysshe,' says Hogg, ' attempted to talk, but the cousins held their peace, and so conversation remained cousin-bound.' The position so fruitful of embarrassment cannot have induced the two comrades in misfortune to prolong the visit to a late hour; and it may be presumed that before midnight they were at Piccadilly, in the beds for which the long day on the roof of the stage-coach had disposed them. The next morning they sallied forth to look for lodgings, and before dusk they were settled in the Poland Street lodgings, where they lived together till about 18th April, 1811. Hogg says they 'lived together nearly a month,' before he went off to North Wales, whence he journeyed to York, to make the acquaintance of the provincial conveyancer who had undertaken to introduce him to the mysteries of the law. But as they did not take possession of the lodgings till 27th March, 1811, and Shelley's first letter addressed to his absent friend is dated 18th April, 1811, their joint-tenancy of the Poland Street rooms barely exceeded three weeks.

Mr. Timothy Shelley was not in town when his scapegrace heir alighted from the coach in Piccadilly; but the news of 'the late occurrence at University College' was not long in travelling to the Squire of Field Place, who, putting pen to paper just about the time when the naughty boys were settling into their temporary quarters in Poland Street, wrote from Sussex a characteristic note, recalling the invitation Mr. Thomas Jefferson Hogg had received to visit Field Place in the Easter holidays. Nine days later (5th April, 1811) the honest and kindly gentleman was in town, and writing from the House of Commons a no less characteristic and even more comical letter (*ride* Hogg's *Life*) to Hogg's father. Thinking it needful in the highest degree that the Oxonian 'Inseparables' should be separated, Mr. Timothy Shelley invited Mr. Hogg, senr., to co-operate with him for that end. 'These youngsters,' the Member for New Shoreham wrote from the House of Commons, 'must be parted, and the fathers must exert themselves.' On the same day the Member for New Shoreham (who without seeing his son had corresponded with him since Lady-day) wrote his 'dear boy' a kindly, reasonable, and affectionate letter, to be found in Hogg's book. Alluding briefly to his son's serious disgrace, the father expressed sympathy with the offender under the shame and trouble he had brought upon himself by 'criminal opinions and improper acts,'—no harsh words, surely, for the description of the youngster's misconduct. In this letter (worded the more cogently because Shelley had already shown his resolve to oppose his father's wishes) the Squire of Field Place set forth the terms on which he would forgive his errant child: (1) Shelley was directed 'to go immediately to Field Place and abstain from all communication with Mr. Hogg for some considerable time. (2) The Squire wrote to his son, 'Place yourself under the care and society of such gentleman as I shall appoint, and attend to his instructions.' The gentleman, who has been charged with driving his boy from his boyhood's home for publishing *The Necessity of Atheism*, only required that the lad (*ætat.* 18) should go straight home, forego the pleasure of Hogg's society for a time, and pursue his studies under the direction of a private tutor. Were these terms hard and unreasonable? After setting them forth, the Squire no doubt wrote a few big words about his boy's unjustifiable and wicked and diabolical opinions, in the fashion of fathers of the period. But these were the father's terms:—Go home, where you will see me next Thursday; keep clear for awhile of your partner in mischief, and be a good boy with the tutor who will be found to take charge of you.

On the morrow (6th April, 1811) the honest and troubled gentleman wrote again (*vide* Hogg's *Life*) to Mr. Hogg the Elder, urging that their boys should be parted, instead of being allowed 'to go into professions together,' as they wished. It was the Squire's intention to use Paley's arguments for the correction of his dear boy's erroneous views; to make his young man read Paley's *Natural Theology*; to go through the *Natural Theology* with him. 'I shall,' wrote the sorrowful father of Field Place to the other sorrowful father near Stockton-on-Tees, 'read it with him. A father so employed must impress his mind more sensibly than a stranger.' This is droll and comical from one point of view, no doubt. But it is also pathetic, and very much to Squire Timothy's credit.

Hitherto Mr. Timothy Shelley had not seen his son since 'the late occurrence at University College;' but on the day following the date of his second letter to Mr. Hogg, senior—*i.e.* on 7th April, 1811, the first Sunday of the month—the young men dined with the Member for New Shoreham, by invitation, at his hotel (Miller's) on the Surrey side of the river, hard by Westminster Bridge. Leaving Poland Street at an early hour, the two youngsters prepared themselves for the repast, to which they had been bidden, with a long walk, during which Shelley read aloud several passages, to the excessive ridicule of the Jews and their religion, from some critical work on the Old Testament.

On coming to Miller's Hotel, with faces brightened by exercise in the spring breezes, and complexions reddened by laughter at their author's satirical jocosities, they were welcomed with kindness by Mr. Timothy Shelley, and with cordiality by Mr. Graham, the Squire's 'factotum.' The reception was courteous, but the genial warmth and courtesy of Mr. Shelley's manner did not render Mr. Hogg blind to its comical extravagances. 'He presently,' Hogg remarks of the Squire's demeanour, 'began to talk in an odd, unconnected manner; scolding, crying, swearing, and then weeping again; no doubt, he went on strangely;'—even as honest gentlemen of an old school were apt to do under impulses of strong and conflicting feelings. Glad to see his boy who had offended him, angry with himself for letting this pleasure appear, and feeling it incumbent on his parental dignity to affect an air of sternness, Mr. Timothy Shelley was stirred far too deeply to play the part he wished to play, and 'broke down' in an absurd and rather ludicrous fashion, scolding a little, swearing a great deal, and blubbering hysterically in his want of self-control. Most young men would have been touched by these exhibitions of feeling, but to Hogg and his friend nothing was more obvious than that the 'old boy' was going on strangely.

'What do you think of my father?' Shelley inquired in a whisper of Hogg, whilst the senior was contending with too powerful emotion.

'He is not your father,' Hogg replied slily in reference to the Pater Omnipotens, of whom they had been reading in the satirical treatise on their way to the hotel. 'It is the God of the Jews: the Jehovah you have been reading about!'—an answer that tickled Shelley's never fine sense of humour so acutely, that he slipt from the edge of his chair, and 'laughing aloud with a wild, demoniacal burst of laughter,' measured his length on the floor, to the surprise and alarm of his father, and Mr. Graham, who hastened to raise him from the ground. If Mr. Shelley the Elder 'went on strangely,' Mr. Shelley the Younger cannot be said to have behaved in an orderly and commonplace manner.

Dinner being announced, just as Mr. Timothy Shelley and his factotum had raised the younger Mr. Shelley to his feet, the party went to the meal, which passed off agreeably. After dinner (in the absence of Percy Bysshe), Hogg had some friendly conversation with the Member for New Shoreham, about his perplexing son.

'You are a very different person, Sir,' said the Squire, 'from what I expected to find; you are a nice, moderate, reasonable, pleasant gentleman. Tell me what you think I ought to do with my poor boy. He is rather wild; is he not?'

'Yes, rather.'

'Then, what am I to do?'

'If he had married his cousin, he would perhaps have been less so; he would have been steadier.'

'It is very probable that he would.'

'He wants somebody to take care of him—a good wife. What if he were married?'

'But how can I do that? It is impossible. If I were to tell Bysshe to marry a girl, he would refuse directly. I am sure he would. I know him so well.'

'I have no doubt he would refuse, if you were to order him to marry; and I should not blame him. But if you were to bring him in contact with some young lady, who, you believed, would make him a suitable wife, without saying anything about marriage, perhaps he would take a fancy to her; and if he did not like her, you could try another.'

It has been remarked by Mr. Rossetti that this conversation accords in some of its particulars with Thornton Hunt's unsatisfactory evidence, that Shelley indulged at Oxford in dissipation, hurtful to his health. Hogg's admission that Shelley had been ' rather wild,' followed immediately by advice that he should be happily married to a young lady qualified to ' take care of him,' would bear this construction; but it may admit of a different interpretation. Young men may be rather wild without being rakish; and rakishness is not the only kind of wildness for which early marriage is often prescribed as a remedy.

Shelley's reappearance (after executing the errand on which his father had sent him) having put an end to the talk about various young ladies, any one of whom might be appointed to wean him from wildness, tea was served; and after tea there was some conversation on matters pertaining to religion, of which Hogg gives the following example:—

'There is certainly a God,' ejaculated the Squire of Field Place abruptly; 'there can be no doubt of the evidence of a Deity; none whatever.'

No one showing any disposition to question the assertion, the Squire, turning sharply upon Hogg, inquired, 'You have no doubt on the subject, sir; have you?'

'None whatever.'

'If you have, I can prove it to you in a moment.'

'I have no doubt.'

'But perhaps you would like to hear my argument?'

'Very much.'

'I will read it to you, then,' exclaimed the Squire, taking out a sheet or two of letter-paper, on which he had jotted down some familiar arguments taken from Paley's *Natural Theology*.

'I have heard this argument before,' remarked Shelley in an under-tone to Hogg.

A minute or two later, whilst the Squire was still delivering from notes *his* demonstration of the existence of a Deity, Shelley repeated to Hogg, 'I have heard this argument before.'

'They are Paley's arguments,' said Hogg.

'Yes; you are right, sir,' assented the Squire, as he folded his paper and restored it to his pocket;—adding with delicious frankness and self-complacence, 'They are Palley's arguments; I copied them out of Palley's book this morning myself; but Palley had them originally from me; almost everything in Palley's book he had from me.'

For a pleasant quarter-of-an-hour readers should refer to Hogg's diffuse and piquant account of the meeting and talk at Miller's Hotel, but enough has been taken from the humorous narrative to show how little reason Lady Shelley had for reprehending the severity, which distinguished the Squire's treatment of Shelley, immediately after his expulsion from Oxford.

On Hogg, the born humourist, it is needless to say that Shelley's father made a most agreeable impression,—none the less agreeable because his hearty air, grotesque speech, extravagant emotionality, and egregious self-complacence, afforded so much food and many occasions for merriment. To the young man from the north country it was manifested his friend's father was by 'no means a bad fellow!' In later time Hogg used to think with cynical sadness and humorous regret how differently life might have gone with Shelley had he only borne himself to his sire as leal and loving sons are wont to bear themselves to their fathers. Thus thinking, it was small comfort to the biographer to reflect how impossible it was for a man of

Shelley's brilliant genius and poetic sensibility to pursue the path of homely filial duty. Small blame to Hogg that he refrained from reflecting severely on the failings of the son who, instead of gossiping sociably with his sire over the daily bottle or two of old port, was quick to show contempt for his understanding, and 'to take umbrage at the poor man's noise and nonsense.' Loyalty to the former friend forbade the historian to utter all he knew and felt on this subject. It was enough for him to intimate lightly that Shelley was no less to blame than his father for their bitter severance. 'It is,' says Hogg, 'only fair to the poor old governor to add that he was the kind master of old and attached servants, and that his surviving children speak of him at this hour with affection.'

It is, however, a matter of reproach to Hogg, that, taking this view of the elder Mr. Shelley in 1811, he never appears to have urged his friend to behave with filial loyalty and dutifulness to a substantially good father; that, on the contrary, he encouraged the son to make a jest of his sire, to exhibit him to the ridicule of his acquaintance, to write of him in terms of vulgar flippancy as 'the old boy,' 'the old fellow,' 'the old buck,' 'old Killjoy,' 'the enemy,' and 'a practitioner of the most consummate hypocrisy,' —all which expressions are used to the Squire's discredit in his son's familiar letters to his especial friend, Mr. Thomas Jefferson Hogg.

Seven days had not passed since the dinner at Miller's Hotel, before the conflict of the father and son resulted in distinct issues. To the paternal order that he should 'go immediately to Field Place,' Shelley replied that for the present it was his intention to stay in Poland Street. To the requirement that he should 'abstain from all communication with Mr. Hogg for a considerable time,' Shelley (*ætat.* 18) responded that he could not for a moment think of foregoing the pleasure of his friend's society. To the requirement that he should submit to the government of the tutor to be selected for him, Shelley replied he would do no such thing. Rejecting his father's requirements, and assuming that he was the person to offer the terms of reconciliation, Mr. Percy Bysshe Shelley demanded (1) unrestrained freedom of correspondence with Hogg, and (2) freedom to choose his own profession, as soon as Hogg should enter one of the Four Inns of Court, or apply to any other calling. On these terms, he would consent to visit

Field Place and receive his father into favour. On receiving his son's ultimatum, the Squire of Field Place wrote (14th April, 1811) in great excitement to Mr. C. (a gentleman who acted for Mr. Hogg the Elder) a letter of lively animadversion on the presumption of the two disrespectful, undutiful, 'opinionated youngsters.' To his son's ultimatum, the Squire of Field Place replied by stopping his pocket-money, and bidding him keep away from his boyhood's home. There being evidence of all this, surely there is good evidence that the future poet was not banished from his home, and denied the society of his mother and sisters, at the instigation of religious intolerance, *because* he published *The Necessity of Atheism.*

How, then, did Mr. Timothy Shelley deal with his son on his expulsion from Oxford, when the eighteen-years-old boy was lodging in Poland Street? Did he denounce and discard him? On the contrary, he invited him and his friend in trouble to dinner. Did this hard-hearted, unnatural father at once forbid the boy to come into his presence, and order him to keep away from the home of his infantile years? On the contrary, he bade him go quickly to his mother and sisters, and resolve to be a better boy under the private tutor, who would soon be found to take charge of him, than he had been under his masters at Eton and his tutors at Oxford. Did he speak of the boy as hopelessly bad and unreasonable? By no means. Taking a cheery view of the case, he thought the boy could be brought out of his spiritual disease and mental disorder by a course of 'Palley.' And believing that the course of 'Palley' would operate more quickly and efficaciously if the reasonings of the divine were enforced by the luminous comments of an equally sagacious and affectionate father, the honest gentleman got down his copy of Paley's *Natural Theology* and worked away at it so that he might be ready to be his boy's preceptor. The absurdity of his proceedings and purpose must be admitted. No doubt, he went on strangely at Miller's Hotel. His notion that with Paley's help he could recover his son from infidelity, and bring him back safe and sound to orthodoxy, is exquisitely droll. But one looks in vain to discover unnatural harshness and cruelty in his measures for his son's benefit. Urging that this troubled father should not be utterly condemned for his action to his son, and speaking of 'some excuse' that may be fairly made for his conduct, Lady Shelley (writing from those

'authentic sources' which afford her so little information) says:
—'Still, it is to be regretted that a milder course was not
pursued towards one who was peculiarly open to the teachings of
love.' If Mr. Shelley did and said a few unreasonable things,
when his conciliatory action was answered with unqualified
rebellion, it cannot be denied that the line of action he proposed to take to his boy at the end of March and the beginning
of April was reasonable, moderate, generous, and affectionate.
What could be milder than his requirements, that the eighteen-
years-old boy should go home to his mother and sisters, read
with a tutor, and desist from intercourse with Hogg 'for some
considerable time,'—*not for ever*; not for many years; but for
some considerable time,—say, till he should come of age and be
master of his own actions?

Was this third requirement preposterous? Mr. Shelley
had grounds for thinking Hogg a hurtful companion for his
boy. Whatever his grounds for it, the opinion was just.
Hogg's influence *had been very harmful* to Shelley. But for
Hogg, it is possible that Shelley would never have been an
atheist. It is certain that if he had gone to atheism without
Hogg's help he would have gone to atheism at slower pace. It
is certain that Hogg was the influence which moved him to the
deed that had caused his expulsion from University College. The
two youngsters had got into trouble and dark disgrace together.
What was there harsh in the demand that the disastrous association, which had been fruitful of so much evil in less than
six months, should be broken for 'some considerable time?'
Paternal authority is an empty name, if a father in Mr. Timothy
Shelley's position may not say to an eighteen-years-old son in
the future poet's position, 'Now, my boy, I will do my best for
you; but, at least for some time, you must forbear from
intercourse with that young scapegrace who was your associate
in the ugly business which occasioned your expulsion from
Oxford.'

When Lady Shelley speaks of Shelley as 'one who was
peculiarly open to the teachings of love,' she is not writing
true biography, but biographical romance. From the moment,
when he comes clearly before us, to the moment when he sunk
beneath the angry waves, Shelley never paid any heed to the
teachings of the love, if they admonished him to do what he
could not do, without sacrifice of his own strongest feelings.

Like Byron he had no care for the feelings of the man or woman with whom he came into conflict. In his contention with his father it never seems to have occurred to him that his father had feelings to be considered, rights to be respected. As he wished to associate with the friend whom he was still set on marrying to his sister Elizabeth (without consulting her parents on the subject), he thought it monstrous that he should be required to cease from associating with him for a considerable time. He would not assent to so intolerable a demand. Hogg was everything to him,—his father nothing to him but a dolt, a fool, an ass, a tyrant. It was preposterous that his father should presume to offer him terms. It was for him to offer terms to his father. Mr. Percy Bysshe Shelley's terms were that his father should make him a sufficient allowance; that he, Mr. Percy Bysshe Shelley, should live where he pleased and do what he pleased; and above all, that he should be free to maintain the closest intercourse with his dear friend, Mr. Thomas Jefferson Hogg. This was modest from a young gentleman (*ætat.* 18), immediately after his expulsion from his Oxford College!

The ever-choleric Mr. Timothy Shelley was furious for several days, for some few weeks, at these proposals from the young gentleman whom he had hoped, with 'Palley's' help, to bring round to religious orthodoxy; and in his wrath, he said and did foolish things after the wont of extremely angry fathers. He vowed he would 'stop the supplies,' and so far as his own pocket was concerned, he did stop them for some few weeks; during which time the naughty boy lived comfortably enough on money lent him by Hogg (who was in funds), money sent to him by his sisters, and money given to him by his uncle, Captain Pilfold. On 18th April, 1811, when his father was in the purple stage of his fury, Shelley received a present of money from his mother, which, however, he returned from some scruple of delicacy or dignity. 'Mr. Pilfold,' he wrote on that day from Poland Street to Hogg, 'has written a very civil letter; my mother intercepted that—sent to my father, and wrote to me to come, inclosing the money. I, of course, returned it.' The 'stopping of the supplies' from the paternal purse made them flow in all the more plentifully — from irregular sources. The exile from his home was therefore in easy circumstances so far as money was concerned. The pictures of the future poet languishing in penury, and menaced with starvation, whilst his wealthy father fared sumptuously, may be tossed aside with other biographic fictions.

Whilst he received no money from his father, the exile of 15 Poland Street was also under order to keep away from Field Place and its inmates,—an order that may perhaps be referred rather to the Squire's wrath, no less than to a sincere belief that the youngster's presence there would do his sisters any serious injury; though, doubtless, Mr. Shelley the Elder attributed the prohibition to the more creditable motive. It is also conceivable how the Squire explained the apparent inconsistency of his conduct in forbidding the boy to do at the end of April, what he had wished him to do a fortnight earlier. At the beginning of the month, when he hoped to find his son comparatively docile and tractable after his humiliating misadventure at Oxford, the Member for New Shoreham doubtless imagined the scapegrace (out of respect to a paternal injunction to that effect) would refrain from talking with his sister Elizabeth on religious questions. His son's defiance of parental authority, in respect to his intercourse with Hogg, may have caused his father to assume he would be no less unwilling to respect parental orders touching his intercourse with his eldest sister,—an assumption that would put Mr. Timothy Shelley in the way to argue that he was only actuated by care for his daughter, in forbidding her brother to approach her. If the Squire of Field Place put the matter thus to his own conscience, he only contrived to deceive himself as resentful gentlemen are wont to deceive themselves. Anyhow, he was determined for a few weeks to keep the brother and sister apart.

The order to keep away from Field Place and from his sister, of course, made Shelley desirous of visiting them. In no hurry to return home, whilst his father wished him to go there quickly, Shelley had no sooner been commanded to refrain from entering Field Place than he resolved to go there.

On hearing that, if he tried to visit his sister at Field Place, she would be removed from home, the young gentleman declared he would follow her, whithersoever she should be taken. Jubilant over an assurance that 'the estate was entailed on him,' —totally out of the power of 'the enemy' (*i.e.* his father) he declared his intention of entering the enemy's dominions (*i.e.* Field Place) as soon as he wished to do so. He would walk into **Field Place**, whether his father liked or disliked it. And on this point he was as good as his word : for returning to the place something sooner than the Squire wished to see him there, he chuckled over the inefficacy of his father's arrangements for putting restrictions on his intercourse with his eldest sister.

The quarrel of the father and son was at its fiercest heat when, on 24th April, 1811, they met one another in the passage of John Grove's house, in Lincoln's Inn Fields ; a scene occurring which (if Shelley reported it truthfully to Hogg) was creditable to neither of them, but far more discreditable to the good feeling of the son than to the good sense of the sire. If the father did ill in returning an inquiry for his health with a look as black as a thundercloud, the son did worse by answering the look with a bow, whose extreme lowness rendered the formal show of obeisance a mere act of insult.

That even in his wrath the Squire of Field Place was not wholly unreasonable is shown by the shortness of the time that had elapsed since he 'stopt the supplies,' when he consented to make his son an allowance of 200*l.* a-year. Only five days after the exchange of offensive greetings in John Grove's passage, the future poet was in high hope that his father would forthwith allow him 200*l.* a-year.

Sixteen days later (15th May, 1811), the arrangement was made on conditions that left Shelley free to live and go wherever he liked, so long as he kept away from York, whither Hogg had gone for twelve months, to read law and acquire the rudiments of legal draughting in a conveyancer's chambers. The scapegrace of Field Place had reason to exult at the liberal terms, for which he was indebted no less to his father's placability than to the Duke of Norfolk's influence over the Member for New Shoreham. So soon did the cruel and parsimonious father renew the current of 'supplies,' after stopping it in a season of fierce anger. No more than seven weeks and two days had passed since his expulsion from Oxford, when the future poet was enjoying a sufficient income, granted on no ignominious conditions.

The smallness of this allowance having been often adduced in evidence of Mr. Timothy Shelley's niggardliness to his eldest son, readers should recall what they have already been told respecting the pecuniary circumstances of the Squire of Field

Place up to the date of his father's death, till which event he was by no means wealthy for his social position. Dependent on his father, who, loving money more passionately as his fingers grew more feeble, was incessantly bickering with his heir-apparent about the excesses of his expenditure, Mr. Timothy Shelley (with several children on his hands) could not make his son a larger allowance. Two hundred a-year was a far better bachelor's income seventy years since than it is now-a-days. Thirty years later it was still regarded as more than a sufficient allowance for a briefless barrister. Shelley was still only eighteen years old when it was allotted to him. Moreover at the time of the arrangement, it was not contemplated that it would be his only means of subsistence; for it was made in anticipation that he would be a frequent visitor at his father's house. Had he from early boyhood lived harmoniously with his father, and been a loving and dutiful son, Shelley in his nineteenth year could not reasonably have looked for a larger income from his father during his grandfather's life. Getting so handsome an allowance from his father so soon after his expulsion from Oxford, he was treated in money-matters with liberality by the father, who is generally conceived to have treated him with vindictive stinginess.

These are the facts of the matter about which Lady Shelley writes in these words :—

'Exasperated by his son's refusal to conform to the orthodox belief, he' (*i.e.* Timothy Shelley) 'forbade him to appear at Field Place. On the sensitive feelings of the young controversialist and poet, this sentence of exclusion from his boyhood's home inflicted a bitter pang; yet he was determined to bear it, for the sake of what he believed to be right and true.'

As Lady Shelley's published book about her husband's father is still regarded as a work of authority, readers should examine this curious conglomerate of misrepresentations. (1) Instead of being exasperated by his son's avowal of atheism, Mr. Timothy Shelley, though naturally shocked and grieved by the incident, treated the eighteen-years-old youngster with affectionate consideration and tenderness, in respect to that serious offence. (2) Instead of excluding him from Field Place for that reason, he told him to go home quickly, when the boy's Atheism was his only reason for displeasure. (3) Mr. Timothy Shelley's vehement anger with the youngster was due to his contumacious refusal to comply with the reasonable requirement touching his intercourse with Hogg. (4) Lady Shelley speaks of 'the young controversialist,' as though the profession of atheism were one of the Liberal professions, and as though Mr. Timothy Shelley should have been grateful to the boy for embracing so honourable a vocation. (5) Instead of inflicting a bitter pang on his sensitively affectionate feelings, the sentence of exclusion from his boyhood's home merely caused Shelley a little irritation and a vast amount of amusement. (6) Instead of 'determining to *bear it*, for the sake of what he believed to be right and true,' Shelley resolved to treat the sentence of exclusion with contempt; to go to Field Place whenever it should please him to go there, 'to enter his father's dominions, preserving a quaker-like carelessness of opposition . . . . and turning a deaf ear to any declamatory objections,'—and he was as good as his word. The sentence of exclusion had been delivered barely a month, when (15th May, 1811) Shelley was back at Field Place ; from which date till the middle of July, 1811, when he went to stay with his cousins at Radnorshire, he remained in Sussex staying alternately with his uncle Pilfold at Cuckfield, and with his mother and sisters in the home of his boyhood, from which he is said to have been so barbarously excluded. The sentence ceased to be operative as soon as the exile cared to disregard it. Keeping out of his father's way, so long as the 'old buck' was in his hottest 'rage' (to use the gentle Shelley's nice way of talking of his father and his father's displeasure), the exile of Poland Street went down to Field Place as soon as he thought life in the country would be pleasanter than life in London. The sentence of exclusion was from the first a mere *brutum fulmen*. It is absurd to speak of this exclusion as a real exclusion. At the worst it was nothing more than such an exclusion from his boyhood's home, as most undergraduates undergo, when they are 'rusticated' for one or two terms.

It is needful to return to Poland Street, and the time when the exiles lodged there. Reading divers books, besides *The English Bards and Scotch Reviewers*, writing letters, and blotting no little paper in the composition of essays that never found publishers, the expelled students lived as far as they could in the manner of Oxonians. The cousins Grove dropt in upon them in the afternoons, and were less taciturn than they had been in Lincoln's Inn Fields on the evening of March 26th. Sometimes by themselves, sometimes with a Grove to conduct them by ' the shortest cuts,' the exiles perambulated the town, and amused themselves after the manner of young gentlemen from the country, thrown upon the London pavements seventy years since. One day they dined in the chambers of a smart Templar (given to talk about duchesses and countesses) on ' steaks and other Temple messes.' Another day they roamed about Kensington Gardens to the delight of Shelley, who was charmed with the sylvan aspect of the timbered lawns. On a third day they walked out to Mrs. Fenning's boarding-school for young ladies on Clapham Common, where Shelley saw his little sister Hellen, scampering about with her light locks streaming over her shoulders. One of their favourite places for lounging was St. James's Park, where Bysshe, after watching the soldiers at drill, inveighed against standing armies, as hostile to the liberties of the people. At least on one occasion Shelley was seen at the British Forum near Covent Garden, where he harangued the assembled Radicals on the vices of all governments :—the sentiments of the orator being so acceptable to his auditors that, when he ceased to scream at them in his shrillest notes, they rushed upon him to discover who he was and whence he came,—inquiries to which the apostle of liberty (with a large stock of *aliases* at command) replied with a false name and address.

Because the *Poetical Essay on the Existing State of Things* was advertised in the *Times* of the 10th April, and 11th April, 1811, and because Hogg says never a word about that perplexing publication (that in all probability was never published), Mr. Denis Florence MacCarthy maintains that the poem was on sale during that month in London, and that (without letting Hogg know aught of the matter), Shelley made daily runs from Poland Street to Messrs. B. Crosby and Co.'s shop, to inquire how much the sale of the poem was doing for Mr. Finerty's advantage. It may be taken for certain that if Shelley made daily calls on the booksellers, Hogg knew why his friend called on them. It may also be assumed that, instead of appearing in the *Times* because the poem was then on sale, the advertisements appeared in the morning journals because their insertion had been ordered (with the usual prepayment) from Oxford some three weeks earlier, when there was, perhaps, an intention to publish the poem, that probably never was published. But if he never crossed the bookseller's threshold, Shelley was seen more than once at Mr. Abernethy's anatomical lectures, and oftener in the dissecting-room of St. Bartholomew's Hospital, where Charles Henry Grove (nearly two years Shelley's junior) was at that time a medical student.

Hogg would have us believe that to his people in Durham Co. and Yorkshire, Mr. Timothy Shelley (known to them by his not uniformly perspicuous epistles) appeared a 'bore of the first magnitude, and a serious impediment to carrying into effect any ordinary arrangement.' Facts, however, make it certain that Mr. Hogg, the Elder of Norton, agreed with this bore of the first magnitude in thinking their boys must be parted, and kept from one another, at least for a considerable period. The letter, in which Mr. Shelley spoke his mind to his afflicted fellow-sufferer, through the afflicted fellow-sufferer's London agent, was dated 14th of April, 1811. Four days later (18th April, 1811), Mr. Thomas Jefferson Hogg was on the roof of a stage-coach, journeying from London towards North Wales, where he was allowed to visit a few friends, before going into pupilage under the conveyancer at York. The dates are eloquent. The joint rebellion against parental authority, which put Shelley in conflict with the Squire of Field Place, was fruitful of a paternal command to Mr. Thomas Jefferson Hogg, that he should pack his traps and move out of London without delay. Mr. Thomas Jefferson Hogg did as he was bid, and for nearly twenty weeks the young men were separated. Thus rudely severed by domestic tyranny, they cheered one another through the post.

On Hogg's withdrawal from London, Shelley had more time and a stronger disposition for the society of the Westbrooks, of Chapel Street, Grosvenor Square. Something has already been said of charming Harriett Westbrook, of the influences that caused Shelley to be curious of her, of the circumstances under which he made the young lady's acquaintance, and of the correspondence he held with her through the post during his second term of residence at Oxford. But the time has come for further particulars about the family, of which the poet became a member by marriage. The family consisted of Mr. John Westbrook (who must have been in the main a respectable person, as so little has been discovered to his discredit by the many persons who, at divers times, have hunted for evidence against him), his wife Mrs. Westbrook ('a nonentity,' as Mr. Rossetti styles her, so far as the Shelleyan drama is concerned), his daughter Harriett

—the pretty child with whom Shelley fell in love, and her elder sister Elizabeth,* who has the reputation of making up the match, and the misery between her sister and the poet. The private residence of these people was in Chapel Street, Grosvenor Square,—not far from Mr. Westbrook's place of business in Mount Street.

Who was John Westbrook?—What was John Westbrook?—What was his place of business? Mr. Westbrook was a successful taverner, and as he was sometimes styled 'Jew Westbrook,' though he was Christian, it may be assumed that he was a taverner who (after the wont of successful tavern-keepers in London's western quarters, in the earlier decades of the present century) lent money to those of his modish and more trustworthy customers, who cared to borrow it of him 'on the usual terms.' The development of modern club-life has affected in various ways the character and quality of the taverns in the western quarters of London, and nearly extinguished the sociable, and, in some degree, confidential relations that sometimes existed between the keepers and frequenters of those places of entertainment. Before clubs were numerous, modish gentlemen about town lived very much at their favourite taverns (or coffee-houses as they were usually styled), eating and drinking and seeing company at them, using them in fact very much as a gentleman about town now-a-days uses his club. Using his coffee-house in this fashion, it was natural for the gentleman about town, after losing heavily at cards, or emptying his pockets at the hazard-table, to look to his tavern-keeper for relief from urgent financial embarrassment. On the other hand, the business of a money-lender fitted in excellently well with the business of coffeehouse-keeper. Living sociably with his regular customers, who gossiped *of* one another as well as *with* one another, the tavern-keeper gathered from their gossip no little information that saved him from losses in the money-lending department of his business. Mr. Westbrook was a coffeehouse-keeper whose daughters had heard him spoken of as 'Jew Westbrook.' As he

* There has been uncertainty about this lady's name. Styled 'Emily' in at least one of Shelley's letters, she is usually styled Eliza in Shelleyan biography. But her real Christian name was Elizabeth. In her affidavit of 10th January, 1817, preserved at the Record Office, the name is so spelt. It has already been remarked in this work that, though usage has made the two several and different names, 'Eliza,' 'Elizabeth,' Isabel, and Isabella, are various forms of the same name, Iza.

was a Christian by profession and bore a surname which countenances the assumption, it may be assumed that he was sometimes spoken of as 'Jew Westbrook,' not because he was of Israel, nor because he had an Israelitish look, but because he was known to lend money: 'Jew' being a familiar designation in the days of our grandfathers for every man of business who lent small sums of money, for short periods, on personal security.

Mr. Westbrook's two-fold vocation may not have been in the highest social favour, but it was followed by many respectable men, and there is evidence that Mr. Westbrook was one of its most creditable followers. Living with the fear of God and good society before his eyes, he shaped his ways discreetly. Whilst his tavern was well spoken of for its wines and dinners, no evil stories were told of the transactions of the little parlour in which he counted out his money. With the views and tastes of a self-respecting and slightly ambitious tradesman, he was not wholly without the manners and feelings of a gentleman. Mrs. Westbrook (the nonentity) may have been a cook in early life; if so, she was a good cook, for Mr. Westbrook was not at all likely to have married a bad one. If he was a butler before keeping a tavern, we may be sure he was an honest butler. Without having grown inordinately rich by lawful business, he had acquired the measure of wealth that is styled a 'comfortable independence' or 'moderate fortune.' It is to his credit that on rising to easy affluence he withdrew his wife and daughters from the coffee-house, which was necessarily at times a rather noisy place, and planted them in a private house, where they lived as far as possible after the manner of gentle people. It is to his credit that he was at pains and charges to rear his daughters as far as possible to be ladies. Miss Elizabeth Westbrook and Miss Harriett Westbrook were every whit as well educated as Shelley's sisters, that is to say, in all matters of book-learning and school-culture.

Mr. Percy Bysshe Shelley, late of University College, Oxford, had not been a week in Poland Street without calling at the house, where he made the acquaintance of the young lady, with whom he had been corresponding for more than a couple of months. In walking out to Clapham Common he was moved by a desire to see his sisters' schoolfellow no less than by a desire to see his sisters. If she was not a weekly boarder at the Clapham School, Harriett used to visit her father's house in Chapel Street, Grosvenor Square, during the scholastic terms, and on these trips to town used to bring the poet money from his sisters. He saw her also during the Easter holidays.

Having seen something of the Westbrooks, whilst Hogg was staying in Poland street, Shelley saw more of them when Hogg had left London. Hogg had scarcely started for North Wales, when Miss Elizabeth Westbrook called upon the future poet at his lodgings, bringing her sister with her. On the evening of the 18th of April, 1811, the day of Hogg's departure, Shelley wrote to his friend, 'Miss Westbrook has this moment called on me with her sister. It certainly was very kind of her.' Three days later (Sunday, 21st April, 1811), Shelley 'took the Sacrament' with the lady who had paid him so acceptable an attention. Another three days later (24th April, 1811), Shelley wrote to the same correspondent of the elder Miss Westbrook's kindness, charity, and goodness. In a subsequent letter, re-calling words he had uttered to her discredit, he commended her for cleverness. Thinking so well of the lady, with whom he had so lately taken the Sacrament, it was natural for Shelley to think he ought to illuminate her, as well as her sister, out of the Christian religion. Resolute to kill religious intolerance by killing creed, and to slay creed by converting people to his own views, he thought he should deal heavy and crushing blows to prevalent superstition by withdrawing John Westbrook's daughters from the faith in which they had been educated. 'The fiend, the wretch,' he wrote of Christianity to Hogg on 28th April, 1811, 'shall fall! Harriett will do for one of the crushers, and the eldest, Elizabeth, with some training, will do too.'

From the date of Hogg's departure from London (18th April) to the middle of May, when he went into Sussex, Shelley saw much of both sisters. Seeing Harriett in Chapel Street, he saw her also at the Clapham school, which he described as the young lady's 'prison-house.' Accompanying Elizabeth in an excursion to the 'prison-house,' he on one occasion spent two hours, walking about Clapham Common with the two sisters. On another occasion, he hastened in the evening (at the elder sister's invitation) to Chapel Street, where he found Harriett ill and suffering from headache. After talking for some time with the elder sister, on love and other interesting subjects, he found himself closeted with Harriett, in the absence of Elizabeth, who left the boy and girl together: her complaisance going so far that Shelley sate in private conference with the beauty of the Clapham boarding-school till past midnight. Shelley, of course, availed himself of so good an opportunity for enlarging the child's views of love and religion. By this time, Harriett had learnt a good deal on these matters from her future husband, and had proved so apt a pupil as to be in disgrace at Clapham for uttering sentiments of his teaching. The girls of the school were holding aloof from Harriett, on account of her awfully wicked opinions: some of them even going so far as to call her 'an abandoned wretch.' Shelley was under the impression that his little sister Hellen was the only one of the girls brave enough to hold friendly intercourse with Harriett, under the odium she had provoked. In his delight at his little sister's courage, he determined to seize the earliest opportunity of illuminating her out of the Christian faith. 'There are,' he wrote to Hogg, 'hopes of this dear little girl: she would be a divine little scion of infidelity. I think my lesson to her must have taken effect.' Thus he was already taking measures to convert his little sister (still in her thirteenth year) to atheism. At Keswick (1811–12) Shelley told Southey (*vide Correspondence of Robert Southey with Caroline Bowles*, 1881) that he endeavoured to make proselytes to atheism in Mrs. Fenning's school; that he succeeded in making a proselyte of Harriett; and that he married her, because she was expelled from the school for accepting his doctrine, and doing her best to induce her schoolfellows to accept it. 'One of the girls,' Southey wrote to Shelley in August, 1820, 'was expelled for the zeal with which she entered into your views, and you made her the most honourable amends in your power by marrying her. . . . . . I had this from your own lips.' The words thus spoken by Shelley to Southey must be read with suspicion, like all Shelley's other statements about himself and his own affairs. There is the more need for caution in this case, as Shelley certainly suffered from delusions at Keswick, and made Southey other statements clearly referable to hallucination. But his statements at Keswick, respecting his measures for making proselytes at Clapham in the previous spring, are notably confirmed in some particulars by what he wrote at the time to Hogg, of his measures for illuminating Harriett Westbrook and his little sister Hellen.

Writing from Field Place to Hogg on 16th June, 1811, Shelley says, 'I shall see you in July. I am invited to Wales, but I shall go to York; what shall we do? How I long again for your conversation!' the invitation being to Cwm Elan, the place of his cousin, Thomas Grove, five miles distant from Rhayader, Radnorshire, whither he went for three or four weeks, towards the middle of July; one at least of his motives for the trip to Wales being that he might stay with the Westbrooks at Aberystwith. Writing from Field Place on 21st June, 1811, to Hogg, at York, Shelley says, 'I shall leave Field Place in a fortnight. Old Westbrook has invited me to accompany him and his daughters to a house they have at Aberystwith, in Wales. I shall stay about a week with him in town; then I shall come to see you and get lodgings.' Hence, at the date of this epistle, the writer's purpose was to leave Field Place somewhere about 5th July, and, after staying a week under Mr. Westbrook's roof, in Chapel Street, Grosvenor Square, to go *via* York to Wales, for the visits to Cwm Elan and Aberystwith. Changing his plans (for reasons to be mentioned in a later page), he deferred the visit to York, and went by a less circuitous route to Rhayader in Radnorshire, whence he wrote to Hogg somewhere about the middle of July, 'Miss Westbrook, Harriett, has advised me to read Mrs. Opie's *Mother and Daughter*. She has sent it hither, and has desired my opinion with earnestness.' A few days later he wrote to Hogg, without dating his letter, 'I shall see the Miss Westbrooks again soon; they were very well in Condowell, when I heard last; they then proceed to Aberystwith, where I shall meet them.' Yet some other few days later (also in an undated epistle), he writes to Hogg, 'Your jokes on Harriett Westbrook amuse me; it is a common error for people to fancy others in their own situation, but if I know anything about love, I am *not* in love. I have heard from the Westbrooks, both of whom I highly esteem.' This disclaimer by Shelley of love for Harriett Westbrook, when he had for months been in love with her, may well remind readers of the way in which Byron disclaimed (in his private journal) all love for Miss Milbanke, when he had for months been loving her. 'I am *not* in love,' Shelley wrote from Wales within six weeks of eloping with

Harriett Westbrook. 'What an odd situation and friendship is ours! without one spark of love on either side!' Byron wrote in his journal of the lady, to whom he had already made one offer and was still yearning to make his wife.

Including the time spent in journeying to and fro between London and Cwm Elan, Shelley spent some three weeks and three or four days on the Welsh trip, which he made in the hope of staying with the Westbrooks at Aberystwith. Leaving him in Radnorshire readers should return to the spring of the year, in order to take a view of the future poet's relations with his sister, his mother and his Uncle Pilfold, from the date of his expulsion from Oxford to the midsummer of 1811.

Mr. Timothy Shelley's withdrawal of the invitation he had given Hogg to visit Field Place, and his subsequent conflict with his son, did not cause the young men to relinquish their hope of becoming brothers-in-law. On the contrary, the new obstacles to the achievement of their purpose only quickened their desire for the realization of the romantic project. Whilst Shelley yearned to call Hogg his brother, the vein of romance, that mingled with the north-countryman's lively humour and cynicism, caused him to be enamoured of the young lady, who was known to him only through her poetical compositions, her letters to her brother, and his report of her personal, mental, and moral endowments. But the brother, who loved her passionately so long as she worshipped him without presuming to oppose him in anything, had not been many days in conflict with his father, before he was disappointed in his sister, discovered faults in her poetry, suspected he had thought too highly of her intellect and courage, saw reason to bewail her mental narrowness, and to fear she was not worthy to be the wife of his incomparable friend. What caused this change of feeling and opinion?

On seeing the goal to which her brother's influence and cautious teaching would carry her, Elizabeth started back in horror. Trustful in his superior wisdom so long as he only required her to think the legends of Christianity were in some particulars fabulous, she fell away from her confidence in the brother who had proclaimed himself an atheist. Instructed that Hogg's influence had brought her brother to this extreme point of infidelity, she was of opinion that her father was right in determining to separate Bysshe from so hurtful a friend.

Thinking that in this determination her father was only showing proper care for his son's welfare, she thought Bysshe's opposition to his father's will undutiful and wicked. She was not brave enough to deny the existence of God; she had the courage to tell her brother he was not behaving like a good son. In the religious conflict, she was on the side of the Almighty. In the domestic conflict, she went with her father. No wonder Bysshe was disappointed by her servility and meanness of spirit. Hogg had barely left London when he was informed by Shelley of his sister's deflection from the path of religious freedom and philosophy,—that she was lost to them. Hogg's reply to this melancholy announcement was to the effect that, though lost for the moment, she was *not* lost for ever,—a sentiment which, on 26th April, 1811, moved the exile of Poland Street, to reply, 'She is *not* lost for ever? How I hope that may be true! but I fear I can never ascertain; I can never influence an amelioration, as she does not any longer permit a *philosopher* to correspond with her. She talks of duty to her *Father*. And this is your amiable religion.'

Instead of writing to him in her old vein of enthusiastic and worshipful admiration, Elizabeth had the presumption to remind him of his and her duty to their parents; sending him the letters that moved him to charge her with 'talking cant and twaddle.' Had he not cause to think with sorrow and bitterness of the ' young female,' who, after asserting for a brief while her ' claim to an unfettered use of reason,' had returned to the sway of the bigots. How could he be sanguine of again reclaiming her from the darkness of mediæval superstition to the clear sunshine of philosophy, when to do so he must conquer her countless hateful prejudices, teach her to despise the world's opinion; nerve her to repudiate the doctrines of 'the tremendous Gregory,' and purge her mind of the absurd notion that she ought to respect her father's wishes. Fretted by her letters, he was depressed by her subsequent silence. On returning to Field Place in the middle of May, 1811, it was a relief to him to learn that, instead of resulting from unconcern for his misery, this silence was due to an attack of scarlet fever. At times, during her convalescence from this illness, he could hope faintly that even yet she would show herself worthy of his former confidence, and not unworthy to be the wife of his incomparable Hogg. But these passages of flickering hope closed in a renewal of his conviction, that she was far too weak a creature for the high place and service to which he had too hastily appointed her. There were moments when, instead of thinking her changed for the worse, he attributed her apparent deterioration to his own recently acquired power of perceiving mental and moral infirmities to which he had been formerly blinded by fraternal partiality. Possibly the sister, whom he used to adore and extol to Hogg, had been a creature of his imagination. Obviously it was his duty to put this view of the case before Hogg, so that so excellent a man should not be under misconceptions, arising from a friend's imaginativeness and delusive speech, link himself for life with an uncongenial and miserably insufficient spouse. To Shelley it was no small trouble that his pen was powerless to make Hogg believe, either that Elizabeth was greatly altered, or that she had been greatly misrepresented to him. Whilst the humorous Hogg laughed secretly at the change of Shelley's regard for his sister, the romantic Hogg declined to think either that she had changed for the worse, or that she had been offered in delusive colours to his fancy. To the humorous and romantic law student, it was clear that the change in Elizabeth was wholly referable to her brother's changefulness, and to the lightness and activity of his imagination. Whilst Hogg refused to be enlightened, Shelley despaired of showing him by written words, so much less potent than speech, how ' a change, a great and important change, had taken place in' the girl who had been offered to him in marriage. Oh, that he could speak with his dear Hogg face to face! 'Unwilling as I am,' Shelley wrote from Horsham, on 16th June, 1811, 'conviction stares me in the face. *Oh, that you were here !'*

This wish may have caused Hogg to entertain the notion of making a clandestine visit to Field Place, to inspect the home of the young lady he hoped to marry, and to get a furtive view of her personal attractions, which were still known to him only by her brother's report. Or the wish may have been followed by a definite proposal from Bysshe that his friend should come to him. Anyhow, the friends now entertained a project for seeing one another in Sussex.

The Squire having recalled his invitation to Hogg, and Shelley (in consideration of his 200*l.* a-year allowance being under bond to hold no personal communication with his former college-friend), Hogg could not visit Field Place openly. It was therefore arranged that he should enter the house secretly, and by night, and that during his clandestine sojourn in the mansion, he should share Shelley's study and bedroom,—two rooms never entered by Elizabeth (under the new rules for limiting her intercourse with her brother), and never entered by any one but Shelley himself, and the servant who attended to them. Taking his sleep by day, it was arranged that Hogg should take his exercise by night, when he would be able to pass through a window into the garden without fear of being observed. Through the same window, commanding a view of the lawn, he would be able to get a view of Elizabeth, when she walked in the garden. This project for a secret meeting of the separated 'Inseparables' at Field Place was dropt, probably on account of the risks the conspirators would run in carrying it into effect. But though it was not pursued to a point, at which the intruder could have been ejected ignominiously from the Sussex mansion, the boyish scheme came to the Squire's knowledge,—possibly from the lips of a treacherous servant, in whom the future poet had confided; but more probably from a letter Shelley had written and forgotten to post to his especial friend. The project for a clandestine meeting at Field Place having fallen to the ground, Shelley (albeit, bound by honour, and the terms of his 200*l.* a-year allowance to have no personal intercourse with Hogg) bethought himself he would go to Wales *viâ* York, and pass a few days with his peculiar friend at the archiepiscopal city. Could he do so without risk of forfeiting his allowance, he would go there openly *on* the way to Wales. Should ' old Killjoy' be too sharp for him he would outwit the 'old buck' by running from Wales to York under the assumed name of Peyton, in order that his movements should be less likely to come to the knowledge of the tyrant, who eventually threatened to stop the allowance, should his son carry out his purpose of paying Hogg a visit.

Too prudent to take openly a step that might result in a withdrawal of the allowance, and at the same time too wary to ask for a direct liberation from his promise to keep away from Hogg, the wily and diplomatic Shelley bethought himself of alluding to his purpose of visiting York in a letter, which his father might neglect to answer, or might answer without referring to the particular project. In either of those cases silence could be construed as consent; and to any subsequent expressions of displeasure at his breach of a chief article of their agreement, the son could reply by pleading that he had not gone to York without giving his father timely notice of his wish, or without grounds for supposing he had his father's tacit permission to go there. In thus 'trying it on' with 'the old buck,' at a peculiarly inauspicious moment, Shelley encountered a rebuff for which he was not unprepared. Instead of overlooking the announcement, or treating it with indifference, the Squire of Field Place answered promptly, 'Go to York if you like; but *not* with my money.' Finding his father thus resolute in holding him to the terms of their compact, Shelley deferred his trip to the north, and went straight to Radnorshire. At the same time he determined that before many weeks had passed he would go to York under a false name, and breaking his promise do secretly what he dared not do openly. 'Do not think, however, but that I shall come to see you long before you come to reside in London; but open warfare will never do, and Mr. Peyton, which will be my *nom-de-guerre*, will easily swallow up Mr. Shelley.' In a later letter from Radnorshire, Shelley says of his motives for deceiving his father in this business :—'When I come, I will not come under my own name. It were to irritate my father needlessly; this is entirely a *philautian* argument, but without the stream, of which he is the fountain-head, I could not get on. We must live; that is, we must eat, drink, and sleep, and money is the necessary procurer of these things!' This from the young gentleman whose averseness to underhand ways is extolled so cordially by Lady Shelley!

Whilst the future poet was thus at open war and hollow truce with his father, the evidence is conclusive that he was treated (from the date of his expulsion from Oxford to the date of his first marriage) with sympathetic and conciliatory tenderness by his mother, who has been charged by successive historians with coldness and severity towards her perplexing and troublesome son. In the letter (of 28th April, 1811), which declares his disgust at the intolerance of his sister, who 'talks cant and twaddle,' Shelley speaks of his mother as a woman 'who is mild and tolerant,' though 'narrow-minded.' On the 15th of May, when the exile has come to terms with his father, and returned to the home from which he had been so inhumanly excluded, Shelley writes to Hogg, 'My mother is quite rational.' She says, 'I think prayer and thanksgiving are of no use. If a man is a good man, philosopher, or

Christian, he will do very well in whatever future state awaits us. This I call liberality.' It was not in the nature of the callow philosopher and atheist, who wrote so bitterly of his sister's 'cant and twaddle,' to bear this evidence to his mother's liberality, had she vexed him with sorrowful censure or irritated him with bootless opposition. Between the naturally indignant father and the unnaturally rebellious son, this anxious and sorely troubled wife and mother seems to have played a difficult part with exemplary dutifulness and affectionateness to the husband she honoured and the boy she loved. It is conceivable, that once and again the Squire of Field Place may have had grounds for charging her with defective loyalty during the cruel contention, but the unruly boy certainly had no right to complain of the imperfect devotion of the mother who, in her desire to hold his affection and confidence, assured him she was tenderly interested in his friend at York.

Yet biographers have insisted that Shelley suffered in heart and fortune from the intolerance and frigid hardness of his mother; the intolerant mother who spoke to him on their differences of religious opinion with so much leniency and forbearance and large-hearted sympathy that he was constrained to extol her liberality: the unsympathetic mother who won so large a measure of his confidence, that he submitted some of Hogg's letters to her perusal, and (probably because he had cautiously sounded her on the subject) was assured she would not use her influence to prevent the marriage of his sister to his friend.

To complete the view of the future poet's relations with the principal members of his familiar circle, one must glance at the way in which he was treated by his Uncle Pilfold, and the characteristic way in which he repaid the cheery sailor for his good services. Instead of eyeing him askance, regarding him coldly, holding aloof from him, denouncing him as an incorrigible young reprobate, this kindly uncle grasped his nephew by the hand, as though it were a greater honour to be expelled from Oxford than to win 'the Newdigate.' Welcoming the boy to his house, the old sailor opened at the same moment his heart and his purse to the youngster in disgrace. When Mr. Timothy Shelley's wrath at his boy's rebellion had in ten days or a fortnight scolded off its fiercest heat, Uncle Pilfold became a mediator between the father and son, inducing the former to

let the boy have intercourse with his sister, and at the same
time making the latter see that he must concede something to
his father who, though he had gone a deuced deal too far in stopping the supplies, was not without grounds for displeasure. 'I
am now with my uncle,' the future poet wrote from Cuckfield to
Hogg, on Sunday, 19th May, 1811; 'he is a very hearty fellow,
and has behaved very nobly to me, in return for which I
illuminated him. A physician, named Dr. J——, dined with
us last night, who is a red-hot saint; the Captain attacked him,
warm from *The Necessity*, and the Doctor went away very much
shocked.' Grateful for his uncle's kindness, Mr. Percy Bysshe
Shelley rewarded him with characteristic munificence,—by
illuminating him out of Christianity.

What reason had Shelley to complain of the way in which
he was treated by his kindred in the season of his heavy disgrace? Expelled from Oxford for the gravest offence of which
an undergraduate could be guilty, he was enjoined by his father
to go home before being placed under a sufficient tutor. Having
refused to obey his father's orders, he was angrily told to keep
away from the home he had declined to visit, when ordered to
do so. Consenting for a few weeks to this barbarous exclusion from
his boyhood's home,—an exclusion which he knew he could terminate at any moment by simply walking into the house, and which
he did terminate by that simple process,—the exile passed a few
weeks very agreeably in London. During this so-called exclusion
and banishment he was in affectionate communication with his
mother, his sisters, his Uncle Pilfold, and his cousins Grove.
On returning to his 'boyhood's home,' within a month or five
weeks of the sentence of exclusion, he was received with a
measure of affectionate indulgence and consideration by his
mother, that may well have surprised him. He was also treated
affectionately by his sister Elizabeth, though she kept away
from his study, and instead of assenting to his sceptical opinions,
met them with much exasperating 'cant and twaddle,' and made
him despair of illuminating her into a fit mate for his incomparable Hogg. At the same time he was treated with substantial kindness by his father (who, in return for a liberal
allowance, only required him to desist for awhile from personal
intercourse with Hogg), and with a flattering show of sympathetic concern by his father's patron,—the Duke of Norfolk.
Unless Shelley's cousin, Charles Henry Grove, is in error as to

the year, his Grace of Norfolk and the Squire of Field Place talked (in the spring of 1811) over a plan for bringing the youngster into Parliament, on the earliest opportunity, as Member for Horsham. It was thus that the future poet was persecuted by his kindred, and thus that he endured persecution at their hands in the months ensuing immediately on his expulsion. There must be an end of the wild nonsense about the poet's sufferings for truth and conscience at this stage of his career. Perhaps no youngster was ever treated more tenderly by his nearest kindred, so soon after earning signal disgrace by extravagant misbehaviour.

Relinquishing his design to go to York before going to Radnorshire, when he saw the breach of promise and act of disobedience would be fruitful of pecuniary inconvenience, Shelley went (as we have seen) direct to Cwm Elan, Rhayader, in the middle of July, 1811, with the intention of staying there till the Westbrooks should have arrived at Aberystwith, when it was his purpose to run over to them, and enjoy the society of the young lady, with whom he was not at all in love. Had the Westbrooks' movements accorded with Mr. Bysshe Shelley's anticipations and wishes, there is reason to think he would have eloped with the sixteen-years-old school girl from Aberystwith, instead of eloping with her from London. Possibly on leaving town he had not fully made up his mind to do so. Possibly he took coach for Radnorshire, with no more definite programme of proceedings than that in the course of three weeks he should be with the Westbrooks at Aberystwith ; after which event he would, somehow or other, be happy with Harriett for ever. It is, however, sufficiently manifest from the records, that he accepted his cousin's invitation to Cwm Elan, because it afforded him a pretext for going to Wales, which would cover the real purpose of the journey from his father, and because the neighbourhood of Rhayader would be a convenient resting-place, whence he could slip away to Aberystwith, some thirty miles distant. Moreover, it is clear in the superlative degree that Shelley and Harriett had both set their hearts on meeting one another at Aberystwith ; and that it was an occasion of the sharpest disappointment to both of them, when, after proceeding towards Aberystwith, as far as the place, called Condowell in one of Shelley's letters, Mr. Westbrook suddenly faced about, and returned to London, with the intention of sending his younger daughter again to boarding-school, when she imagined herself to have 'left school for good.'

What caused this sudden relinquishment of Mr. Westbrook's plans for his summer holidays is matter for conjecture. But from matters of indisputable record, it may be safely inferred that the worthy taverner returned to town because he thought it better Mr. Bysshe Shelley and his younger daughter should not come together at Aberystwith; and that he was bent on sending her again to school, because he thought a regular and professional schoolmistress better qualified than Miss Elizabeth Westbrook to take good care of the giddy girl. Possibly Mr. Westbrook had peeped into one of the several letters which Shelley sent the sisters from Rhayader, and learnt from it enough to convince him he had better return abruptly with his daughters to London. Anyhow he decided to do so, alike to Shelley's annoyance and Miss Harriett's chagrin.

Like Byron, Shelley never brooked aught that thwarted his will, or in any way threatened to withhold from him a pleasure, on which he had set his heart. On being told she must go back to London and to school, instead of onwards to Aberystwith, Miss Harriett Westbrook wrote to Shelley for advice. On receiving Harriett's shocking intelligence, Shelley overflowed with indignation at the monstrous cruelty of the father, who could think of sending his sixteen-years-old daughter to school for another half-year. Should she, Harriett asked in her letter, submit to her father's tyranny or resist it? Shelley, of course, answered, 'Resist it.' At the same time he wrote to Mr. Westbrook a letter which, though it was intended to mollify the stern and inhuman parent, only confirmed him in his hideous and revolting purpose. Powerless to subdue by tears and tragic threats the father, who only fumed and sneered at Percy's mollifying epistle, Harriett wrote to Shelley that she threw herself on his protection, and would fly with him anywhere. Shelley was delighted. For weeks and months he had been nursing the hope that his darling Harriett would rise so far superior to the dwarfing prejudices, which disposed ordinary women to prefer wedlock to Free Love, as to commit herself to his custody without regard to the laws of Priests and the requirements of tyrannic custom. For weeks and months he had been educating her to see in Love a sufficient sanction of the union requisite for fulfilment of its desire. And here was

the fruit of his instruction. Snapping the ties of parental
tyranny and filial thraldom, Harriett had thrown herself on him
for protection, and would fly with him anywhere,—to be happy
with him for ever. Had he not reason, in the first and liveliest
exultations of his triumph, to write to Hogg, 'Gratitude and
admiration, all demand, that I should love her for *ever?*' How
could he be sufficiently grateful to the girl who had thus surrendered herself to his honour, in her absolute confidence in his
goodness? How could he sufficiently admire the girl, whose
magnanimity had enabled her to say to him, 'Do your will with
me; take me on your own terms, so long as you are good
enough to make me yours?' If Shelley went to Wales, without
a project for elopement with Harriett Westbrook, he certainly
returned from Radnorshire to London, with the intention of
taking her from her father at the earliest opportunity.

With the judicial fairness and critical moderation, that are
not the only qualities to distinguish him from the poet's other
worshipful biographers, Mr. Rossetti hesitates in inferring
from Shelley's words ('she . . . . . threw herself upon my protection') that, whilst writing to Shelley at Cwm Elan, Harriett
Westbrook was ready to be his mistress. Reminding his
readers that, instead of being the girl's own words, the phrase
is at the utmost nothing more than Shelley's 'summing up' of
her expressions,—Shelley's way of packing into half-a-dozen
words the most momentous of her passionate communications,—
Mr. Rossetti also bids his readers qualify their censure of her
indelicacy with considerations, arising from the reflection that
'the school-girl of sixteen, hardly more than a child,' had been
'lately philosophised out of the ordinary standard of propriety'
by Shelley himself.

The biographer who writes with so much conscientious circumspection cannot be charged with straining words to Harriett's
disadvantage. Still I am disposed to think he goes something
too far. More doubtful even than Mr. Rossetti, I hesitate to
accept or reject his inference from the words which, instead
of being the school-girl's own words, are nothing more than
Shelley's summary of them. The inexact Shelley's mere summary of the written words is no evidence to be accepted with
unqualified confidence in its accuracy. Moreover, could it be
shown that the summary was a fair representation of the
purport of her written words, it would still be conceivable

that in her haste and excitement the angry girl put them on paper without seeing their full force and realizing to what they committed her. Yet, further, it may be urged in palliation of the child's want of maidenly decorum that, if she was ready for flight without marriage at the moment of penning the letter, she changed her mind on coming out of her anger against her father, and subsiding to a temper that permitted her to reflect with comparative calmness on all that had passed between herself and her lover. Instead of finding her ready to fly with him on any terms, when he saw her in London after his return from Wales, Shelley found her in a state of indecision. 'My unfortunate friend, Harriett,' he wrote from London to Hogg at York, on 15th August, 1811, 'is yet undecided, not with respect to me, but herself.'

But though I am far from confident that Harriett ever threw herself on Shelley's protection in the sense imagined by Mr. Rossetti, or even gave Shelley sufficient grounds for saying she had done so, I am in no degree disposed to suspect Shelley of wilfully misrepresenting the nature of her confidence in, and appeal to, him. On the contrary, I have no doubt that Shelley meant to make his friend at York understand the girl was ready to become his mistress, and that he felt himself justified by the words of her letter in crediting her with this readiness. I have no doubt that the future poet wrote to Hogg in perfect good faith, and for the mere purpose of letting his correspondent see the exact state of the case. The evidences leave no room for doubt that, after spending weeks and months in training and educating his sister's schoolmate to take a philosophic view of marriage, he accepted with equal sincerity and delight the expressions of her tempestuous letter as a declaration that she was willing to be his mistress, or (in the language of the Free Lovers) to become his wife without the intervention of the priest and the sanction of legal matrimony. Under this impression he wrote to Hogg from Rhayader with jubilant boyishness,—' We shall have 200*l.* a-year; when we find it run short, we must live, I suppose, upon love! . . . . We shall see you at York. . . . . I can get lodgings at York, I suppose.' Under the same exhilarating impression he journeyed from Wales to London, thinking how he and Harriett would be journeying northwards a week or ten days later, how happy they would be for ever in lodgings at York, and how furious his tyrannical father would be on hearing he had carried Harriett away from her tyrannical father and taken her to the city he was forbidden to enter,—to the dear, delightful, incomparable Hogg, with whom he was forbidden to have personal intercourse. But on arriving in town he found Harriett in no humour for immediate elopement. She was undecided, not in respect to her choice of a lover, but in respect to the time *at* which, and the terms on which, she should commit herself to his custody.

It is, therefore, by no means so manifest to me as it is to Mr. Rossetti, that had he cared to take advantage of her simplicity and romantic trustfulness, Shelley could easily have seduced his sister's schoolfellow, or, rather (I beg pardon of the Free Lovers), could have made her his wife without marrying her.

'If the calculating habit is still strong upon us,' says Mr. Rossetti, 'we may compute what percentage of faultlessly Christian young heirs of opulent baronets would have acted like the atheist Shelley, and married a retired hotel-keeper's daughter offering herself as a mistress. To deny that the act was foolish would be absurd under any circumstances, and doubly so when we reflect upon the ultimate issue of it to Shelley and Harriett themselves ; let us then distinctly recognize that it was foolish, and no less distinctly that it was noble.'

With all his desire to deal fairly with Harriett Westbrook's reputation, Mr. Rossetti is less than fair to her in arguing that up to the moment of her Scotch wedding she was ready to become Shelley's mistress, because she threw herself on his protection (by letter) three weeks earlier. Ladies have a proverbial right to change their minds ; and if we must concede that Harriett had a mind to be Shelley's mistress when he was at Rhayader, it cannot be questioned she had changed her mind on that particular matter before he came to her again in London. Living in Chapel Street, Grosvenor Square, under the eye of an elder sister, who, possessing her confidence, knew how to keep her well in hand, Harriett was not so completely at Shelley's mercy as Mr. Rossetti would have us think. It is inconceivable that Shelley would have been allowed to possess himself of the school-girl on terms which wanted the elder sister's approval ; and it is not to be imagined that Miss Elizabeth Westbrook, favouring Shelley's suit, partly from romantic affectionateness, and partly from social ambition, would have consented to an arrangement for making her sister the mere kept mistress of a gentlemanly scapegrace, who might one day become a baronet. The elder Miss Westbrook was no person to allow herself to be treated as a nonentity, or aught less than a very considerable personage, in an affair touching her dignity and self-respect so delicately and deeply. Under these circumstances it is in the highest degree improbable that Miss Westbrook, who facilitated the elopement which promised to make her younger sister eventually a lady of title and estate, would have permitted herself to be made the sister of such a person as Harriett would have become, on passing to Shelley's keeping without marriage.

There are other reasons for questioning whether Shelley should be credited with nobility of conduct, in forbearing to do what he would not have been permitted to do. Had he in May or June made Harriett his mistress *without* marrying her, he would only have acted in accordance with his notions of morality. He did no more at the end of August or the beginning of September when he made her his wife *by* marriage. If he should be credited with distinctly noble conduct merely for taking what he thought the right course in September, he would have been no less distinctly noble three months earlier for merely taking what he thought the right and moral course in May and June. Had the future poet, however, made the girl his mistress in either of those last-named months, Mr. Rossetti would scarcely have ventured to credit him with distinct nobility of action in doing so, merely because he conceived himself under a moral obligation to do so. It should be observed that Shelley's sentiments respecting marriage were during this period of his career greatly modified by Hogg's arguments against them; and that, in commending the future poet's conduct in making Harriett Westbrook a wife instead of a mistress, Mr. Rossetti applauds him for conduct largely, if not altogether referable to Hogg's influence, and may, therefore, be said to give Shelley the praise that should rather be given to his friend.

The evidence of Hogg's beneficial, though only transient, influence on his friend in this respect is conclusive. The shrewd and humorous north-countryman, who nursed the hope of marrying his friend's sister Elizabeth, was, at this stage of his story, a robust and resolute defender of matrimony and the laws for its protection; and in the many letters that passed between him and Shelley in the spring and summer of 1811, he seized every opportunity for combating and correcting what he deemed his friend's perverse and erroneous views on the usages and ethics of marriage. It is to Hogg's credit (at least in the opinion of those who regard marriage with reverential jealousy) that on seeing his friend more and more strongly set on some kind of domestic association with Harriett Westbrook, he made the most strenuous efforts to induce him to marry the girl in a legal way, instead of uniting himself to her in a way that would, at least in law and social sentiment, render her only his mistress. Besides being strenuous, these efforts were successful. Having regard to the miserable consequences of the match, some readers may, perhaps, regret that Hogg was so busy and successful. Perhaps it would have been better for both parties to the disastrous union, had Hogg left ill alone. Had the north-countryman been less energetic, it is conceivable that Mr. Westbrook's pretty daughter would have escaped the misery of being Shelley's wife, without falling to the shame of being his mistress. But Hogg's action was none the less meritorious, because it may have been hurtful to the friend he wished to serve.

Shelley's stay in Radnorshire did not end before he admitted the force of his friend's demonstrations of the convenience and beneficence of lawful marriage. In the very letter that declared his puerile delight in Harriett's appeal to him for protection from her inhuman father, he says, 'We shall see you at York. I will hear your arguments for matrimonialism, by which I am now almost convinced.' Some ten days later (15th August, 1811), when he had passed through London, made a flying visit to Horsham and Cuckfield, and returned to town for stolen interviews with Harriett, he wrote to his incomparable Hogg at York, stating most precisely that he had relinquished his purpose of making Harriett his mistress, and had determined to make her his wife, in pure submission to Hogg's counsel, and to the force of the arguments with which that counsel was enforced. 'I am become,' Shelley wrote, 'a perfect convert to matrimony, not from temporising, but from *your* arguments. . . . . The one argument, which you have urged so often with so much energy; the sacrifice made by the woman. so disproportioned to any which the man can give,—

this alone may exculpate me, were it a fault, from an inquiring submission to your superior intellect.' Shelley's words respecting himself and his own affairs must of course be always used with caution and lively suspicion. But the words written by him *to* Hogg himself on 15th August, 1811, are good evidence that, on finding Shelley set on taking Harriett Westbrook to himself, either as a mistress or as his wife, and strongly disposed to take her in the former capacity, Hogg used all his power to make him see that he was bound to marry her.

It does not speak much for Shelley's innate chivalry and generous tenderness for womankind, of which so much extravagant stuff has been written by his idolaters, that he could not discover for himself the most obvious considerations why no man of honour should place a woman of sensibility and refinement in the ignominious position of a kept mistress; that he could not without Hogg's assistance see, how much the woman sacrifices of her social dignity and legal rights, who humours masculine insolence and selfishness, by sinking to a position, which, giving her all the trials and responsibilities, withholds from her all the higher privileges of a wife. On the other hand, it is something to the credit of the youngster, who could not discover these facts for himself, that he could see them when they were pointed out to him, and was withheld by the timely expostulations of sober common-sense from the sin of acting on his 'hasty decision.'

In the letter, from which the last extract is taken, Shelley says, 'I am now returned to London; direct to me as usual at Graham's. My father is here; wondering, possibly, at my London business. He will be more surprised soon, possibly.' At the same moment, on the same sheet of paper, he chuckles over the surprise his speedy elopement with Harriett Westbrook will occasion his father, and pretends to think it unlikely he shall soon be called upon to make a choice between Marriage and Free Love. It was like Shelley, to contradict himself in this fashion almost in the same breath.

The particulars of Shelley's movements between the 15th of August and the end of the month are unknown, with the exception of a few details, which, in the absence of positive testimony, the imagination would furnish as matters of course. For the expenses of the elopement, Shelley obtained 25*l.* from Tom Medwin's father (the Horsham attorney), who lent him

the money without knowing or suspecting the purpose for which
it was needed; a slender sum, that seems to have been reduced
considerably before the future poet paid the fares for two
inside places in the mail from London to Edinburgh. There
were secret interviews between the lovers; interviews of
which Mr. Westbrook probably knew nothing, and Miss Eliza
Westbrook was doubtless cognizant, even when she was not
present at them. Charles Henry Grove (younger than Shelley
by something less than two years) was in his cousin's confidence during these days of pleasant excitement and romantic
conspiracy, and accompanied the future poet on some of his
visits to Harriett. There were understandings and misunder-
standings, decisions and changes of purpose, arrangements and
re-arrangements. Then came the hour of early morning when
Harriett Westbrook, in all the brightness of her still childish
beauty—the lovely girl who, a few years later, escaped from
unendurable shame and wretchedness by self-murder—stept
from her father's house, and entered the hackney-coach, that
conveyed her, together with the two cousins (Shelley and
Charles Henry Grove), to the 'Green Dragon,' in Gracechurch
Street, where they remained all day, till the northern mail
was packed and ready to start. Another minute, and the two
childish adventurers were at the outset of their long journey
for Edinburgh, *vid* York, whilst the guard's horn sounded
cheerily, and Charley Grove (left standing on the pavement)
waved a last farewell to the departing vehicle.

It is a question whether the elopement was made at the
end of August or in the beginning of September. I have
little hesitation in saying Harriett left her father's house in
September; none in saying she was married to Shelley in
Edinburgh in the first week of that month. The girl may
have crossed her father's threshold on the morning of Saturday
31st August, but it is more probable she did so on Sunday
the 1st, or Monday the 2nd of September. On passing through
York at midnight, after spending an entire night and the
following day (allowance made for the usual stoppages) in the
coach, Shelley, with care for the replenishment of his almost
empty purse, wrote a hasty and careless note to Hogg, begging
for the loan of 10*l.*, and saying that he and Harriett would
'have 75*l.* on Sunday.'

'On Sunday,' of course, meant 'next Sunday.' After

answering the brief note, as soon as it was brought to him on the following morning by a messenger from the Inn, Hogg packed his portmanteau, and in the afternoon of the same day 'in the first week of September,' was on the road to Edinburgh, where he arrived some two or three days before the Sunday, when Shelley hoped to get the 75*l*. Dating from Field Place on Sunday, 8th September, 1811, immediately on hearing his son and Hogg were together in the Scotch capital, Mr. Timothy Shelley wrote from Field Place on 8th September, 1811, to Mr. John Hogg, of Norton: announcing that Shelley had ' withdrawn himself from ' the writer's ' protection, and set off for Scotland with a young female.'

Hogg is certain that he answered Shelley's note immediately on getting it, that he started for Edinburgh in the afternoon of the same day, and that he made the journey to Edinburgh in the first week of September. Mr. Timothy Shelley's letter makes it certain the young men were together in Edinburgh in that week. Had the ' on Sunday ' of Shelley's note pointed to Sunday, 1st September; had he written for the 10*l*. for his expenses *till* that Sunday, Hogg's run to the Scotch capital would have been made in the last week of August.

CHAPTER XV.

MOTIVE AND INFLUENCES.

The fatal Marriage — Was Shelley trapt into it ? — Mr. Garnett's Assurances
— The Fiction about Claire — Lady Shelley's Use of Hogg's Evidences —
The Prenuptial Intercourse — Was it slight ? — Shelley's Opportunities for
knowing all about Harriett — His Use and Abuse of those Opportunities
— Mr. Westbrook's Action towards Shelley — His endeavour to preserve
Harriett from Shelley — Eliza Westbrook's part in making up the Match
— The Tool's Reward — The Etonian Free Lover — The Social Condition
of the Westbrooks and Godwins — Harriett Westbrook's Beauty — Her
Education — Her Knowledge of French — Her quick Progress in Latin —
What Wonder that Shelley fell in love with her ?

THUS it was that Shelley carried off Mr. Westbrook's sixteen-
years-old child, and made her his wife, instead of acting on
'the hasty decision,' from which Hogg dissuaded him. Did
he take this momentous step inconsiderately? On a slight
acquaintance with the young lady? Under circumstances that
denied him fair opportunities for observing the temper and
studying the character of the girl whose singular beauty had
fascinated him? Was he lured, drawn, inveigled, into the
marriage by influences, stronger than those that are usually
employed by a girl's nearest relatives for compassing what
they think a good match for her? The enthusiasts, who draw
their inspiration on Shelleyan questions from Field Place, do
not hesitate to answer all these questions in the affirmative.

Mr. Garnett (*vide* his *Shelley in Pall Mall*) assures us that
whenever certain documents, hitherto withheld from the world,
shall be made public, *i.e.* when Field Place shall issue its
authoritative biography for the ending of all controversies on
Shelleyan matters, ' it will for the first time be clearly understood how slight was the acquaintance of Shelley with Harriet,
previous to their marriage ; what advantage was taken of his
chivalry of sentiment, and her compliant disposition, and the
inexperience of both ; and how little entitled or disposed she
felt herself to complain of his behaviour.' It is certain that
before submitting to what she could not prevent, Harriett

complained with passionate vehemence of her husband's behaviour to her. Let that matter, however, pass for the present. What are the grounds for saying that unfair advantage was taken of Shelley's inexperience, and that Shelley, by reason of the slightness of his acquaintance with her, when he stole her from her father, knew much less of Harriett than young men usually know of girls they are on the point of marrying?

Strange things may of course be looked for from the people, who have recently required the world to believe that, instead of taking Claire from London to Byron at Geneva, Shelley and Mary Godwin were taken (like two little children) *by* Claire to Switzerland,—and so taken there *by* her, although they (as the Field Place story goes) disliked her exceedingly, even to the point of disgustful aversion. But even the authorities of Field Place will scarcely declare the documents published in Hogg's *Life* to be spurious documents. They will scarcely declare that Hogg (the writer with a peculiar style from which he could not liberate himself for an instant) forged the multitude of letters, published in his book as letters written to him by Shelley,—the epistles, some of which Lady Shelley herself used for evidential purposes in writing her *Shelley Memorials*,—the epistles which are so Shelleyan in thought and diction, feeling and language, form and style, that no other human being but Shelley could have written them. Field Place has dared to do strange things, but its daring will stop short of this extravagance. To produce documents, drawn by Shelley's hand or at his dictation, in contradiction of these letters, would not be to discredit the letters, but only to produce fresh illustration of one of Shelley's most perplexing infirmities,—fresh evidence that he often made statements contrary to the truth.

From documentary evidences of unimpeachable genuineness and irresistible cogency, it is certain that Shelley made Harriett Westbrook's acquaintance in January, 1811, eight lunar months before his elopement with her; that he corresponded with her between the day on which he made her acquaintance and the date of his expulsion from Oxford; that in the spring of 1811 he saw her repeatedly at her home and elsewhere,—receiving her at least on one occasion at his lodgings in Poland Street, attending her from her father's house to her school on Clapham Common, walking about with her on Clapham Common, and sitting up with her (at least on one occasion) till past mid-

night, at Chapel Street, Grosvenor Square, in the absence of a
third person ; that he corresponded with her from March to
September; that the wooing, which began at Oxford by letter,
if not on the occasion of their first meeting, was strenuously
prosecuted by Shelley to the day of the elopement ; that he had
opportunities for seeing and influencing her, which enabled him
to illuminate her out of Christianity and (to use Mr. Rossetti's
expression) to ' philosophise her out of the ordinary standard of
propriety'; that he had opportunities, and used them, for making
her think lightly of the matrimonial rite; that he had opportunities, and used them, for encouraging her in rebellion against
her own father; that instead of being kept in the dark as to the
chief, and indeed the only important defect of her temper—a
constitutional proneness to discontent—he was peculiarly interested in her manifestations of this significant quality, and sym-
pathized cordially with her groundless grievances and imaginary
sorrows. Though he was uncertain as to the day on which Shelley
determined to win Harriett Westbrook's affections, Hogg had no
doubt his friend had begun to woo the girl before he left Oxford.
' Shelley's epistles show the progress of his courtship,' he says,
' and that his marriage was not quite so hasty an affair as it is
commonly represented to have been. The wooing continued for
half-a-year at least, and this is a long time in the life,—in the
life of love, of such young persons.' The interval, between
Shelley's withdrawal from Oxford and his marriage at Edinburgh, wanted at least three weeks of an entire half-year. Yet,
Field Place requires us to believe slightness was a principal
characteristic of the prenuptial intercourse of these young
people !

How about the charge of inveiglement ? No one has ever
suggested that Mr. Westbrook was an accomplice in measures
for luring the heir of the heir to a wealthy Sussex baronetcy into
wedlock with his younger daughter. On the contrary there were
reasons why he should regard any such project with disfavour. If
he was not a gentleman, Mr. Westbrook was a man of the world,
who came in contact with gentlemen, and knew something of
the ways of the higher world and fashionable society, from the
gossip of the gentlemen who used his public-house. The west-
end taverner, who had risen to comfortable circumstances by
attention to his affairs, was not the man to be keenly desirous of
having for his son-in-law the scatterbrain youngster who only

the other day was expelled from Oxford.   He had seen too many
youngsters of quality drop to grief and ruin, not to know that a
young gentleman of Shelley's parentage and expectations and
story might prove a very poor match for a prosperous tradesman's daughter.   He knew the value of his money too well, not
to be aware that his pretty daughter, to whom he could make
a good allowance during his life and perhaps leave ten thousand
pounds at his death, might do much better for herself than
marry the harum-scarum son of the Member for New Shoreham.   Mr. Westbrook did not need to be told that, so married,
his pretty daughter and her children might drain his pocket to
his last hour.   Like a prudent man, he did nothing to hurry
his daughter into the unfortunate marriage.

When Shelley came to Chapel Street with his sister's present
and letter of introduction in his hand, he was received with
courtesy at the taverner's private house.   Mr. Westbrook received the youngster with civility in the ensuing spring : a
civility that would have seemed less 'strange' to Shelley (vide
Letter to Hogg, of 28th April, 1811), had he not been conscious
how little he deserved it.   Though he writes disdainfully of the
tradesman, whom he calls alternately a coffeehouse-keeper and
ex-coffeehouse-keeper, and charges him with pitiful stinginess
to his daughter, whose disobedience raised her so considerably in
the scale of social dignity, Hogg forbears to accuse Mr. Westbrook of imposing his younger daughter on the youth of quality,
who made her so poor a husband.   According to Hogg, Miss
Elizabeth Westbrook made up the match, her father being
guilty of nothing worse than prudent and hypocritical anger at
the event on which he secretly congratulated himself.   Perhaps
Mr. Westbrook, after the elopement, made the most of Harriett's
unfilial disobedience, and feigned more displeasure than he felt
at her misbehaviour, in order to have and preserve a good pretext for tightening the string of his purse.   But no one can
suspect him of busying himself to bring about the match.   Com-
pelling Harriett to return to her prison on Clapham Common
after the Easter holidays, he did nothing to facilitate their intercourse, before Shelley, in the middle of May, went from town to
Sussex.   At the beginning of August, on finding how matters
had been going on with the lovers, without his consent or
suspicion, Mr. Westbrook determined to send Harriett again to
school, returned with his wife and daughters to Chapel Street,

and on Shelley's reappearance in the neighbourhood of Grosvenor Square, shut his door against him.

Miss Elizabeth Westbrook no doubt had a hand in making up the match. But what of that? To make matches is the privilege and convenient diversion of mature woman-kind, and a successful taverner's daughter is not to be denied the rights and privileges of her sex, because her father is a licensed victualler. In doing what she did to oblige Shelley in the matter, she was moved partly by affection for her sister, and partly by a desire to become, sooner or later, the sister-in-law of a wealthy baronet, the sister of a lady of quality. Actuated by ambition and sisterly affection, Miss Elizabeth Westbrook obeyed precisely the same motives that determine any gentlewoman of high condition to make the heir of a peerage, or any other highly eligible *parti*, duly sensible of her eldest daughter's manifold graces and virtues. Standing to Harriett in the relation of a mother rather than a sister, Miss Elizabeth Westbrook merely did for her younger sister's advantage and her own gratification, what a mother bent on marrying her daughter advantageously is permitted to do for the achievement of her purpose. Shelley besought Miss Westbrook for opportunities of seeing Harriett, as he was disposed to love her, and Miss Westbrook gave him what he wanted.

If this is to lure and inveigle a young man into wedlock, the elder Miss Westbrook was guilty of that offence. But I cannot think her action should be described by such offensive words. She did not seek Shelley; it was he who in a very remarkable way sought her and her people out. He was not the mild and compliant youth to be led into wedlock against his will, because a rather mature maiden told him it would be good for him. Miss Elizabeth Westbrook of all women was the least qualified to exercise such control over him. She was not beautiful, and at the outset of their acquaintance she was by no means acceptable to Shelley. He thought her affected, and suspected her of unamiability. He felt for her a dislike that almost amounted to repulsion, and would soon have quickened into aversion, had she irritated him by opposing his scheme. Till he had made her clearly understand he did not visit Chapel Street to talk of love with her, but to talk of it with her sister, and she had consented to his design, Shelley saw nothing to approve and much to disapprove in the elder Miss Westbrook. On changing his mind about her, he found the lady amiable merely because she acquiesced in his scheme. When a person consents to be the tool of another, the tool usually has a reward. Sometimes in addition to the reward agreed upon by both parties, the tool has in view an end unimagined by the person using the tool. Sometimes also it happens that, turning the tables, the tool becomes the tyrant of its former employer. It was so in the present instance. After Shelley's marriage, Miss Elizabeth Westbrook insisted on the reward of former services, and for a while exacted heavier payment for them than Shelley was willing to pay. Amiable in his eyes, whilst she was only his tool, Miss Westbrook soon grew hateful to him when she had become his tyrant.

Why should we assume, why was it ever assumed, that Shelley was inveigled and drawn into the association, which was so completely an affair of his own desire and contrivance? The notion that he *was made* to do the thing which he did of his own accord, and in spite of numerous obstacles, probably originated from regard for the disparity of the Westbrooks and Shelleys in respect to social station. The disparity, no doubt, was considerable. Though he was not of aristocratic ancestry as biographers have so stubbornly declared, the young man who, besides being the son of a Member of Parliament, stood in the direct line of succession to a good estate and a hereditary dignity, married greatly beneath him when he took a licensed victualler's daughter for his wife; and in the majority of the cases, where a young man marries a girl so greatly his inferior in social quality, the marriage is found on inquiry to have been brought about by the artifice and influence of a third person. Shelley's marriage, however, was one of those unequal marriages that are distinctly referable to other causes. Having in his boyhood a sentimental repugnance to lawful matrimony, that had steadily grown in power from the time when he wrote *Zastrozzi*, the Oxonian Shelley had no sooner been discarded by Harriett Grove, than he desired a conjugal partner, whom he could attach to himself by a tie less enduring than the bond of marriage,—a girl, in fact, with whom he could live in Free Love. He could not hope to find such a partner in his own social grade. The prejudices against Free Love were stronger in Shelley's time, even as they are at the present time, in the higher than in the lower grades of English society. In descending from his own social grade, to the grade of the prosperous London *bourgeoisie*, he descended no lower than the highest social grade, in which he could conceive it possible for him to find a girl of beauty, culture, refinement, and delicacy, whom he would be allowed to 'philosophise out of the ordinary standard of propriety,' till she should 'throw herself upon him for protection.' To win Harriett Westbrook, he descended (at least in the eyes of fashionable society) no lower, than he descended to win Mary Godwin. Of course, in being a very considerable man of letters, Godwin (in the opinion of the present writer) was greatly Mr. Westbrook's superior; but this superiority was in Shelley's time more obvious to persons of education moving in the middle way of life, than to people of fashion and patrician quality. Moreover, Godwin's superiority to Mr. Westbrook in this particular was attended with circumstances that would render 'society' more than usually indifferent to it. By birth and familiar associations, William Godwin and Mr. Westbrook were of the same social degree. They were also of the same social degree in respect to the avocations, by which the one had acquired sufficient affluence, and the other maintained his family in Skinner Street. Whilst the prosperous man of business lived with the port and bearing of a gentleman in Chapel Street, Grosvenor Square, the man of letters was a struggling and needy bookseller in the city. In eloping with Mary Godwin in 1814, the poet associated himself with a family no less distinctly beneath people of quality than the family from which he took his first wife. Yet it has never been suggested that he was lured and inveigled into his alliance with the Skinner Street family.

The notion that Shelley was 'caught' and 'trapt,' inveigled and drawn against his will into his first marriage, becomes still more ludicrous, when regard is had to the personal charms of Harriett Westbrook,—charms that, had she been of far lowlier origin, would account for the young man's action in making her his wife. Shapely in figure and graceful in her movements, she possessed a face of singular loveliness, and the air of high breeding that is so often wanting in damsels of high birth. It is no exaggeration to say that she was a rare and faultless example of the girlish beauty, which was most delightful and charming to Shelley. Her features were delicate and regular; her light-brown hair was of a colour peculiarly acceptable to her admirer; no girl ever had a more transparent complexion, or alluring lips; and in her sunnier moods, her countenance brightened with looks curiously expressive of intellectual alertness and childish *naïveté*. At the same time in a laugh, equally spontaneous and joyous, and a voice so musical, that people delighted in hearing her read unentertaining books for the hour together, she possessed two natural endowments that have been known to inspire passion, when they have been associated with features plain even to ugliness. The air and style of this lovely girl were such, that fifteen months after their wedding, Shelley wrote of her and them, 'The ease and simplicity of her habits, the unassuming plainness of her address, the uncalculated connexion of her thought and speech, have ever formed, in my eyes, her greatest charms.' Speaking of the pleasure he experienced in hearing her read aloud, Hogg says, 'If it was agreeable to listen to her, it was not less agreeable to look at her; she was always pretty, always bright, always blooming; without a spot, without a wrinkle, not a hair out of its place.' Peacock admired the taste and simplicity with which she arranged her light-brown tresses, and the simple elegance of her costume. Be it also remarked that for a girl of her period (more than seventy years since) Harriett was well educated,—writing excellent letters of gracefully fluent penmanship: so familiar with French, that during her six weeks' stay at Edinburgh, she found a congenial occupation in translating one of Madame Cottin's novels into English; fond of reading sound literature by herself, no less than to attentive auditors; and possessing so much taste and aptitude for study that Shelley delighted in teaching her Latin, and brought her so quickly forward in it, that before the end of 1812, she was reading the Horatian Odes with interest, if not without difficulty.

Such was the Harriett Westbrook of 1811 and 1812. And yet Field Place cannot account for Shelley's weakness in wedding so lovely and winsome a creature, without assuming that he was 'caught' and inveigled into the match by a designing third person,—the artful and scheming Elizabeth Westbrook.

CHAPTER XVI.

EDINBURGH, YORK, AND KESWICK.

The Scotch Marriage—The Trio at Edinburgh—' Wha's the Deil?'—Posting from Edinburgh to York—Dingy Lodgings and Dingy Milliners—Shelley's run South—Did Harriett accompany him?—The Squire stops the Supplies—The Earl's Description of Harriett Westbrook—The Squire's Anger at the *Mésalliance*—The Course Shelley could not take—Eliza Westbrook in Possession—The Ouse at full Flood—One too many—Designs on Greystoke Castle—Shelley's Appeal to the Duke of Norfolk—The Codicil to Sir Bysshe's Will—The Flight to Richmond—Miss Westbrook strikes her Enemy—The Trio at Keswick—Shelley's affectionate Letters from Keswick to Hogg at York—John Westbrook's Daughters at Greystoke Castle—Ducal Benignity and Policy—The Calverts of Greta Bank—Shelley's Means during his first Marriage—How to live on Three-Hundred-a-year—How not to live on Four-Hundred-a-year.

DURING the latest stages of their long journey in the London and Edinburgh mail, Shelley and Harriett had for their travelling companion a young Scotch advocate, who, on being taken into their confidence, told them the right and speediest steps to marriage in accordance with the usage of the land. Hence, on embracing his friend in the handsome front-parlour of a high and roomy house in George Street, and taking his first view of Harriett, ' bright, blooming, radiant with youth, health and beauty,' Hogg was in the presence of husband and wife.

For particulars of the way in which the young people spent the next three weeks in the Scotch capital, readers must go to Hogg's much-abused book. For the purpose of the present chapter, it is enough to indicate how life went there with the trio, who in the dead season of a never too lively city, laughed over trivial matters with youth's light-heartedness, and found in themselves all the society they needed. Hogg's only disappointment was that Harriett's disinclination for exercise denied him opportunities for the long walks he had hoped to take in the surrounding country. Otherwise he was abundantly happy in regarding the happiness of the incomparable Shelley, and in studying the charms, the character, and endowments of the girl his friend had taken for better or worse. Rising for an early breakfast, passing the morning in studious or literary labour (Shelley was busy on his translation of a treatise by Buffon; Harriett on her translation of Madame Cottin's *Claire d'Albe*), and dining in the middle of the day, they spent the afternoon in exploring the high-ways and by-ways, the grand places and the nooks and corners, of the picturesque town. Having taken tea freely and talked philosophy with equal freedom, the young men surrendered themselves to the music of their official reader (Harriett of the clear and mellifluous voice), till the deepening shades of evening reminded them it was time to admire the stars, and gaze at the famous comet that gave our grandfathers the wine, whose flavour lingers on tradition's tongue.

For their higher happiness indebted to the heavens and themselves, these young people were indebted to Scotch sabbatarianism for some of their heartiest peals of laughter. With unintentional profanity the future poet was laughing in his own peculiarly shrill and vehement fashion in Prince's Street, on the day that is still the saddest of the seven in North Britain, when he was admonished for his scandalous levity by the austere wayfarer, who remarked, 'You must not laugh openly in that fashion, young man: if you do, you'll most certainly be convened;'—a warning that may have been fruitful of the curiosity, which determined Shelley on a subsequent Sabbath to go to kirk, for the purpose of hearing the servants and children catechized on matters touching religion.

The drollery of Hogg's account of this visit to the kirk is due to the narrator's lively humour, rather than to any unusual absurdity in the proceedings for instructing an assemblage of servants and children in the rudiments of theology. From dullness and shyness, the pupils were slow in catching their catechist's meaning, and still slower in answering the questions that were shouted to them by a teacher, whose Scotch accent was the more effective on his auditors from the south, because at moments of displeasure, his vocal pitch indicated that he was not devoid of Scotch irritability. In asking his class 'Who is the devil ?' this catechist cannot be said to have travelled beyond the lines of ordinary official routine; but his vocal peculiarities and the sharpness of his manner gave the simple question a startling piquancy and grotesqueness, that, sending Shelley into shrieks of laughter, drove him to the open streets where, though inopportune, and highly scandalous, such laughter would be less outrageous than in a place of religious instruction.

Six weeks having slipt away quickly, after the wont of time that passing agreeably passes without exciting incidents, the morning came, on which the trio entered a postchaise and began the return-journey to York. Hogg would have preferred the mail or the slowest stage-coach to the private chaise,—a mode of travelling scarcely appropriate to the financial position of the three travellers; the law-student, who had nothing more than a liberal allowance for a student from his father, and the happy pair, who had married on the 200*l.* a-year, which they had reason to apprehend would be withheld from them by the indignant Squire of Field Place. But Harriett had suffered too much on her northward journey to be desirous of resuming her seat in the mail, whilst as a matron of only sixteen summers she wished to travel in a way more befitting a gentlewoman of quality. So Shelley, who hated restraint of any kind, and Hogg, ever averse to costly ostentation, consented to the young lady's desire for a chaise, in which they could converse freely, and she could read one of Holcroft's novels to them. Whatever the book had been, Hogg would have enjoyed hearing it read by so charming a reader. But the tale was tedious to Shelley, who, after sighing in a significant way, vainly entreated Harriett to skip some of the less entertaining parts of the narrative. The conflict on so trifling a matter may be noticed as an indication that, even thus early in their married life, the poet and his bride had trivial differences, in which she had her own way, and he was constrained to let her have it. Not that Harriett insisted on reading aloud the whole of the time from Edinburgh to York. There were moments when, if not glad to give her throat a rest, she was pleased to enlarge her knowledge of rural matters by listening to the talk of her travelling companions. How much it needed enlargement at this point of her career, appears from the earnestness with which the little Cockney (as Shelley styled her) besought her husband to teach her how to discriminate between turnips and barley.

Hogg's comfortable lodgings in York having been let 'over his head' during his absence in Scotland, the trio had no sooner alighted from the last of their successive post-chaises, than they went forth in the rainy twilight to look for other rooms. Hogg suggested, was indeed urgent, that they should pass the night at an inn, and defer the search for lodgings till the morrow. But Shelley flatly refused to acquiesce in the proposal; —a refusal that may well have perplexed Hogg at the moment, as the cause of the future poet's impatience to get into rooms in a private house did not appear till the following morning. Shelley declaring thus stoutly for an immediate entrance on lodgings—any lodgings rather than rooms in a tavern for a single night,—and Harriett of course concurring with her husband, Hogg was in a minority, and could not decline to join them in the search for a temporary home, which, in the course of the damp and chilly October evening, made them the joint-tenants of certain rooms in 'the dingy dwelling of certain dingy old milliners' (the Misses Dancer of Coney Street), who, in the course of a week or ten days, were as glad to be quit of their lodgers, as the lodgers were glad to be quit of the austere and reasonably suspicious needlewomen.

On the morrow Hogg, who had overrun his leave of absence by a few days, went early to the chambers of the conveyancer with whom he was reading; but he did not return thus early to the scene of legal labour and study, without having heard of Shelley's intention to start for London by the next night-mail. The future poet's announcement of this intention to run southward, whilst leaving his bride at York under his friend's care in the rooms they had occupied for a single night, of course showed Hogg why Harriett's youthful and erratic husband had been so urgent for an immediate choice of lodgings,—so averse to tarrying in a tavern for a few hours. On the journey from Edinburgh to York, Shelley had been secretly nursing his project for running off to London and Sussex,—to see his father's attorney (Mr. Whitton), to take counsel with his Uncle Pilfold, and to come to a financial understanding, either by personal interview or through the attorney's intervention, with the Squire of Field Place. The charges of six weeks' residence at Edinburgh, followed by the charges of the southward journey, had reduced his money in hand to so insignificant a sum, that, on approaching York, he could not think of taking Harriett with him on the meditated trip to Middlesex and Sussex. It was manifest to him that she must remain at York, whilst he went on the expedition for 'raising supplies.' At the same time it was obvious, even to the harum-scarum Shelley, that he could not with propriety leave his girlish bride in a York tavern, where she would not fail to become the one subject of gossip, with the landlady and her chamber-maids, the gentle folk of the coffee-room, the bagmen of the commercial-room, the tipplers and loiterers at the public bar. Left to the accidents of life in a tavern, the lovely school-girl—staying by herself in a provincial hotel, without husband or lady's maid, without any companion of her own sex—would be liable to various kinds of insult and annoyance, from which she would be secure in a quiet lodging-house. Hence Shelley's determination to lose not an hour in settling his bride in lodgings after their arrival at York, as he was set on leaving her for a while, in little more than four-and-twenty hours.

Hogg had several reasons for opposing his friend's resolve to go south so abruptly. Seeing what mischief might be made by gossips at York, and by gossips in London and Sussex, of the young husband's voluntary withdrawal from his childish wife, at a moment when she stood in peculiar need of his presence,— when nothing short of overpowering necessity should make him leave her side for an entire day,—and when the very circumstances of their union required them to be more than ordinarily thoughtful for appearances and the world's opinion, Hogg saw the impropriety and insufficiency of the arrangements for her comfort during Shelley's absence. Whilst he was too much a man of the world to think himself the fittest guardian for the lovely girl, on the point of being thrown so completely and unceremoniously on his hands, or to imagine the ladies of York would think him so, Hogg had grounds for a strong opinion, that his friend would gain nothing more by interviews with Mr. Whitton and Mr. Whitton's client than he could gain from them by letters sent through the post,—that he would, in fact, be wasting on a profitless journey the few guineas still remaining to him of borrowed money,—the last lingering guineas, which in a few weeks he might need for bare necessities. Under these circumstances, it is not strange that the more worldly-wise of the two youngsters advised his comrade to postpone the journey for a few days. Even so short a time would have given Hogg opportunities for introducing the Shelleys to ladies of the northern city; for inducing some of those ladies to take an interest in Harriett who, wedded woman though she was, needed a chaperon as much as any recently emancipated school-girl; and for withdrawing from a domiciliary relation to the young lady that, during Shelley's absence, was likely to give rise to equally egregious and undesirable misconceptions in the northern capital. In pleading for delay, Hogg could not, of course state frankly his reasons for the prayer. The questions at issue were too delicate for candour. All the north-countryman could do was to recommend postponement. Of course, the counsel was in vain.

Holding to his purpose, Shelley went for the south, leaving his bride and the incomparable Hogg fellow-lodgers in the same dingy dwelling, and sharers of the same dingy parlour. Surely the circumstances of the case may be held to justify, or at least to excuse, suspicion on the part of the two ancient and austere milliners, careful for their own characters and the reputation of their house in a provincial city, abounding, like all other provincial towns, with people more curious about their neighbours' doings than heedful of their own affairs. Here is the case from a milliner's point of view.—Late one evening, Mr. Hogg (a sprightly young bachelor of the city) enters the house, in the company of Mr. Shelley (a very young gentleman, looking no older than his wife) and Harriett Shelley (looking less than her sixteen summers) ; the entrance of the trio being covered with assertions that the sprightly Mr. Hogg's juvenile friends are husband and wife. Twenty-four hours later, the young gentleman with the aspect of a schoolboy goes off by the London mail, leaving the sixteen-years-old girl in the house, under the charge of the sprightly Mr. Hogg, whose way of saying strange things makes it doubtful to maiden ladies of mature age and lowly station, whether they should smile or frown. Who is the young lady ? Who the young gentleman who has gone off to London ? Are they really husband and wife ? If so, why has the young gentleman gone off without her ? Why has he left her under the care of the sprightly Mr. Hogg, of all people in the world ? Can it be that the Scotch marriage, instead of making her the very young gentleman's wife, made her the sprightly Mr. Hogg's wife ? The austere and suspicious milliners may well have asked themselves these and half-a-hundred other questions.

Whilst Shelley was away, Harriett spent lonely days at York. The weather was rainy, but there were hours when the sky cleared or its clouds forbore to spend themselves on the roofs and open spaces of the city. It speaks for the girl's uneasiness in a position from which she should have been preserved, and also for her sense of womanly fitness and delicacy, that during her boyish husband's absence she kept herself within the doors of the dingy lodging-house,—forbearing to visit the Minster and other sights of the city, and declining the many invitations Hogg gave her to take exercise in the open air under his escort. In Edinburgh she took daily walks, usually with her husband and Hogg, sometimes with no other companion than her husband's friend ; but at York, during her husband's absence, she remained at home. ' When it was fair,' says Hogg of her *triste* and uneventful days at York, ' she did not go out, having unfortunately transplanted her London notions of propriety to York : she considered it incorrect to walk in the streets of that quiet city by herself.'   As Shelley was certainly absent from York on one Sunday (20th October, 1811),—a day on which Mr. Hogg's work at chambers did not preclude him from walking about the town — it may be fairly assumed that Harriett's notions of propriety forbade her to walk in the streets with him no less than by herself. Certainly in her circumspection the sixteen-years-young gentlewoman gave the grim and vigilant milliners no grounds for speaking of her with disapproval, apart from the fact that she continued to share the same parlour with Mr. Hogg. In this matter, how could the poor child do otherwise ?   How could she help herself ?

Having so much of her own company by day, whilst her fellow-lodger was ' at chambers,' Harriett may well have enjoyed Hogg's company in the evening, when they talked together of her husband, and his projects for the regeneration of human kind, her papa and his affairs, her Clapham boarding-school and its discipline, her mamma and sister,—the mamma who looked so ladylike in black satin, and the sister Eliza (in the fulness of her Christian name, Elizabeth) who had so elegant a figure and so noble a crop of black hair. When these and other domestic topics did not hold their attention, Harriett's fellow-lodger used to sit with unqualified contentment for hours together, whilst she read aloud to him Holcroft's *Anna St. Ives,* Dr. Robertson's historical works, and other staid and instructive books. It may be inferred from expressions in Hogg's book that, though she often read aloud to him at Edinburgh, Harriett read aloud to him at York, during Shelley's absence from the city, more copiously than during any other time of their acquaintance. Noteworthy, also, is it, that (by Hogg's admission), Harriett's audible readings became much less frequent and lengthy when Miss Westbrook appeared upon the scene, just four-and-twenty hours before Shelley returned to the city, and that they ceased almost entirely before the Shelleys went away abruptly to Keswick. Possibly, Hogg was wrong in attributing this change of Harriett's conduct altogether to Miss Westbrook's influence. Possibly, also, he was mistaken in attributing the copiousness of Harriett's audible readings, during her husband's absence, altogether to her delight in reading aloud. Harriett read no less clearly than musically. 'Hers,' says Hogg, 'was the most distinct utterance I ever heard.' It is conceivable that, instead of reading thus distinctly either for her own pleasure or for Mr. Hogg's pleasure, Harriett at York read thus audibly for the protection of her own character, and the edification of hearers listening in the passage outside the parlour door.

It cannot be doubted that the poor child, left as she should not have been left, in a position of vexatious and humiliating embarrassment, knew that she, Hogg and her husband were each and all objects of suspicion to the austere and dingy milliners. So placed, she was, of course, painfully jealous for her reputation, and resolute that she would shape her course, so as to be able to extort evidence to her goodness from the very women who suspected her of evil. Never leaving the house, she put it beyond the power of the austere milliners to accuse her of going about the town in pursuit of pleasure. Never receiving any visitor but her fellow-lodger, she confined the milliners' suspicions within narrow limits. Whilst she and her fellow-lodger were together, it was her practice to be incessantly conversing with him or reading to him in a voice, clearly audible outside their room,—so that the milliners should have the evidence of their own ears, that she and her fellow-lodger were no fit objects of suspicion. I have no direct and con-clusive evidence that Harriett talked and read aloud for this end. But that she talked and read aloud mainly for this end, is a fair inference from what Hogg says of her talking, reading, and other behaviour during her husband's absence. Reading Hogg's evidence in this way, I have no doubt it was to Harriett's relief, if not at her suggestion, that Miss Westbrook, immediately after her arrival at York, forbade the readings as exercises too exhausting for her sister's nervous system.

In passing through London, Shelley made attempts to see Miss Westbrook and Mr. Whitton, and, probably, saw both of them. If he did not see the attorney, he communicated with him by letter, saying that he should quickly return from Sussex to London. If he saw Miss Westbrook, one may be sure she told him plainly he had done ill in leaving his bride at York under Hogg's care, at a moment when he was especially bound to be thoughtful for her comfort and character. It cannot be doubted that, on coming to Cuckfield, he found his Uncle Pilfold of Miss Westbrook's opinion on this matter. If the old sailor did not say so in words, we may be sure the expression of his countenance told his nephew, that he should not have come to Sussex without his wife; that in leaving her at York he had given people another reason for talking lightly of her and to his disadvantage; that he would do well to withhold from the Field Place and Horsham people a matter they would not fail to report with unfavourable comments, should it come to their knowledge. Under these circumstances it was natural for the young gentleman to take measures to make the Field Place and Horsham people imagine that Harriett had accompanied him to Sussex. The evidence in his own hand-writing, which has caused some writers to imagine she accompanied him to Sussex, is only evidence of the pains taken by Shelley to conceal the indiscretion of which he had been guilty. Dating from his uncle's house at Cuckfield, on Monday 21st October, 1811, the future poet wrote Mr. Medwin (the Horsham attorney) a letter which has been produced in testimony that, instead of being at York (as Hogg truthfully represented), Harriett was on that day with her scatterbrain husband under Captain Pilfold's roof.

Instructing the lawyer that Mrs. Shelley spelt her Christian name with a second t, Shelley further instructed him to prepare a deed of marriage settlement (assigning 700*l.* a-year for Mrs. Shelley's provision during her life, in case of her husband's death). Further, Mr. Medwin was directed to address to his youthful client 'at Mr. Westbrook's, 23 Chapel Street, Grosvenor Square.' After giving these directions, and announcing his purpose of remarrying Harriett (by English form) in the course of three weeks or a month, before which renewal of his nuptials he intended to execute the settlement, Shelley added: 'We most probably go to London to-morrow. We shall probably see Whitton, when I shall neither forget your good advice, nor cease to be grateful for it.'

The instructions by the nineteen-years-old boy for a deed of settlement on his wife, to be executed by him in a few weeks, are amusing. What induced him to say she spelt her Christian name with two t's, when she spelt it in the ordinary manner with only one, is unknown. The main object of the epistle was the purpose of the two delusive sentences beginning with 'we,'—sentences intended to create an impression, or to confirm Mr. Medwin in the impression, that Harriett had accompanied the writer from York. Even in the absence of evidence to the point, the young gentleman (who ten months earlier 'resorted to deception' in order to escape a trivial annoyance) might be presumed to have written other letters to make the Horsham and Field Place gossips imagine his wife was with him in Sussex and London, when she was at York. Taken by itself the evidence that, instead of leaving her at York, Shelley took Harriett with him to London and Sussex is considerable. Indeed, standing by itself, it would justify the historian in representing that the boyish husband carried her southward in his company. But the counter evidence that he left her in York is so much stronger, that I do not hesitate in adopting Hogg's narrative, and in regarding the contradictory evidence as fallacious testimony, arising from Shelley's wish to conceal, and his measures for concealing, the impropriety of which he had been guilty.

Shelley had better have remained at York in submission to Hogg's counsel, instead of spending the greater part of his few remaining guineas on the costly journey, from which he got nothing but disappointment. Refusing to see him, the Squire of Field Place declined for the present to hold any communication with him except through Mr. Whitton. At the same time the Squire declined to give his unruly son any more money, till he should promise to amend his ways and submit himself to his father's authority with fit expressions of penitence. Acting doubtless at his client's instance, Mr. Whitton begged he might not be troubled with a call from his client's son, who could say all that was needful under the circumstances on a sheet of paper. The attitude of the Squire and the attitude of the attorney are clearly defined in two notes dated by the latter to Mr. Percy Bysshe Shelley on the same day (23rd October, 1811); the one note being addressed to the poet at Cuckfield, the other being directed to him at the Turk's Coffee-House, Strand.

The young gentleman, who in August chuckled over anticipations of his father's surprise and fury at his runaway match with an innkeeper's daughter, had not made his account for his father's steady persistence in displeasure. The young gentleman who had just travelled southward by mail from York, to talk matters over and settle them with the 'old boy' (Shelley's expression), found the 'old buck' (also Shelley's expression) in no haste to talk matters over, found him resolute to leave matters as they were till he could rearrange them in his own way. Kept at a distance in this way by ' old Killjoy ' (also one of the son's nicknames for his sire), Mr. Percy Bysshe Shelley was treated with similar insolence by old 'Killjoy's' attorney, who enjoined him to say what he wished to say in writing. It was Mr. Percy Bysshe Shelley's turn to feel surprise and indignation. Baffled and resentful the young gentleman returned to York with a heavy heart and a light purse.

At length there was war to the bitter-end between the long-suffering father who had endured so much, and the son, who had now exhausted his sire's patience. At length he was excluded from Field Place, *not* for his religious opinions, *but* for his successive extravagances of deceit, disloyalty, and disobedience to an affectionate father, and for the *escapade* by which he sought to introduce a tavern-keeper's daughter to his mother's drawing-room as the young lady, who in the course of time would be Lady Shelley of Field Place.

Successive writers have insisted that the poet would never have been drawn into this disastrous marriage had it not been for the excessive chivalry of his nature, that placed him at the mercy of the designing, artful, unscrupulous Eliza Westbrook. A chivalrous boy usually has some care for the feelings and dignity of the women of his own blood and hearth. If Shelley really surpassed other boys in chivalry, even as he surpassed them (according to Lady Shelley) in truthfulness and candour, he would surely have been more thoughtful for his mother's feelings and his sister's dignity, than for Miss Westbrook's wishes. It does not appear to have occurred even for a single moment to this chivalrous youth that, in choosing a wife, he should not be absolutely

without concern for his mother's sensibility, his sister's honour
and social interest. From first to last he seems to have assumed
that his own feelings were the only sensibilities for which he
was required to think. By those who (with the present writer)
think Shelley ran away with Harriett Westbrook because he was
thoroughly in love with her, it may, of course, be urged in his
excuse that love is proverbially selfish, and that in choosing
their wives young men are always more bent on pleasing themselves than on pleasing their mothers and sisters. But such
considerations cannot be urged in the youngster's behalf by
those, who maintain (with Mr. Garnett) that, instead of marrying the young lady, because he desired her passionately, Shelley
fell with passionless weakness into the *mésalliance* through Miss
Eliza Westbrook's artful treatment of his sense of chivalry.
Moreover, even by those who believe him to have been honestly
in love, it must be conceded that he was less thoughtful for his
mother and sisters, than a generous and chivalric young man
must necessarily be when he is choosing a wife.

Had he thought for a moment how the *mésalliance* would
affect his mother, he must have seen it would occasion her
sorrow and acute mortification. Had he given a thought for the
interests of his sisters, he must have seen the match would be
greatly injurious to them. Had he taken thought for the
honour of the family, which his father and grandfather had
raised to the dignity of a territorial house, he must have seen
that the gentlewomen of many of the neighbouring families
would be slow to recognize and visit John Westbrook's daughter.
If he thought with indifference of these sure consequences of the
mésalliance, the chivalrous Shelley was strangely wanting in
chivalric care for the women of his nearest kindred. If he did
not think of them at all, his selfishness exceeded the selfishness
permitted to lovers.

When ' society ' is invited to consider and pass judgment on
a new *mésalliance*, it is in the nature of things for the unpleasant
and reprehensible features of the affair to be magnified and
multiplied by social sentiment. On hearing that young Shelley
of Field Place had surpassed all his previous offences by running
off to Scotland with an innkeeper's daughter, to his father's unutterable wrath and his mother's grief and dismay, the Sussex
families imagined something far more shocking than the actual
incident. Knowing nothing of Harriett's beauty and refinement,

of her father's respectability, and the care expended on her education, the people of the county houses thought of what was least agreeable in inns and innkeepers, and of all that was most disagreeable in the smart girls usually employed in the inns along the posting roads of the country; and having thus surrounded themselves with more or less repulsive recollections of simpering damsels, the Sussex families leapt to the conclusion that the boy, who was expelled from Oxford last spring, had thrown himself into the arms of some pert barmaid or saucy chamber-woman. In the correspondence (preserved at the Record Office) touching the box of Shelley's pamphlets, that was opened by the Surveyor of Customs at Holyhead in March, 1812, a letter is preserved, which affords curious evidence respecting the view taken of Shelley and his marriage by the great families of the poet's county. Dating from Stanmer, near Brighton, on 8th April, 1812 (just seven months after the elopement) the Earl of Chichester—the chief of Sussex Pelhams and Postmaster-General (in conjunction with . . . .)—wrote to Mr. Francis Freeling, Secretary of the Post Office :—

'DEAR FREELING,—I return the pamphlet and declaration. The writer of the first is son of Mr. Shelley, Member for the Rape of Bramber, and is by all accounts a most extraordinary man. I hear that he has married a servant, or some person of very low birth.'

It was thus that the chief of a great Sussex family wrote, and the Sussex quality spoke, of the lovely girl, whose marriage had raised her to the honour of being so quaintly and disdainfully misdescribed. For a few weeks known by report to the county families as an innkeeper's daughter, she was vaguely remembered by them a few months later as 'a servant, or some person of very low birth.' A year later the Castle Goring Shelleys were known in county houses, lying outside the immediate neighbourhood of Horsham, as people who made low marriages. Such was the kind of discredit that came to Shelley's kindred from the alliance he had formed in absolute carelessness for their feelings and interests.

A man of the world (albeit an eccentric one), the Squire of Field Place was aware of the disrepute that would come to him and his house from his son's latest escapade. He was also precisely the man to feel acutely the disrepute, which he had reason to fear would be hurtful to his girls. The son of the man who had founded a new family, the heir of the old man who had gathered together enough wealth for the sufficient endowment of half-a-dozen baronets, the *protégé* of the Duke of Norfolk, who had for several years regarded him with growing complaisance, and a Member of Parliament, who had contrived to persuade himself he was no ordinary Borough-Member, the honest, kindly, hearty Squire of Field Place, had hoped that his boy would, under his Grace's favour, pass directly from his nonage to public life; that his girls (the eldest of them already a beauty, the three younger ones bearing on their childish faces the promise of uncommon womanly loveliness,) would marry into the best families of the county, with whose history his name had been so long associated, though none of his father's lineal ancestors had ever held place amongst its aristocracy. Doubtless, the simple, sport-loving, and mildly ambitious Englishman had cherished the hope that his son, or one of his son's sons, would wear a coronet. And now all these pleasant and not inordinate hopes were dissipated by his perverse boy's marriage with the girl, with whom the county families would decline to associate,—the girl who would be called the Field Place 'barmaid,'—the girl who, so soon after her discreditable marriage, lived in the minds of the Sussex grandees as a servant or other low person.

The Squire's mortification might be deemed his fitting punishment, had he in pride of purse borne himself insolently to former friends; had he, on rising to friendship with 'the great,' fawned and cringed to their grandeur; had he, in his desire for the elevation of his offspring and the aggrandisement of Castle Goring, attempted to force his son into a distasteful union, requiring him to marry for more money or higher rank. But the honest gentleman had committed none of these faults. Addressing the great without sycophancy, he lived in good-fellowship with all men. Instead of trying to force his son's affections, he would have been content to see him marry Harriett Grove,—a girl of no fortune, and of a family something nearer doubtless, but only something nearer, the aristocracy than the small squireens and gentle yeomanry from whom he was himself descended. All he had asked of the boy, who with good conduct would succeed to a noble fortune, was to marry a gentle-woman, fit to be his mother's daughter and the sister of his sisters. And what had the boy done? He had run off with a barmaid!—for, of course, to the Squire, in his fury, John Westbrook's lovely child was nothing better than a barmaid.

In the autumn of 1811 the Squire of Field Place could not comfort himself with reflecting that, if he was a much worried father, he was worried by a marvellously clever boy whom it was an honour to have begotten; for at that time Shelley had done nothing to indicate he would win a place amongst men of genius, or even figure amongst men of considerable parts. His Eton career had been worse than disappointing; his Oxford career had been eminently disgraceful; his novels were ludicrous performances; *The Necessity of Atheism* was not an achievement on which his father could be expected to think with complaisance. At the worst he had, from his fifteenth year, been a bad boy; at the best he was a mere scatterbrain. Having pardoned the boy repeatedly for serious misdemeanours; having again and again relented towards him and, saying 'let bygones be bygones,' given him a fresh start, is it wonderful that Mr. Timothy Shelley determined to make no more bootless concessions, to accept no more imperfect recognitions of his authority, to have done with half-measures, and to insist on his son's unqualified submission as the prelude to a renewal of their intercourse? The father has been charged with enormous severity to his son, because he required him to behave like other sons, and held steadily to his determination to keep his son at a distance, until the youngster had promised to show ordinary consideration for the feelings of his parents. When Percy said, 'Out of regard to my feelings give me a good allowance, and let me bring my wife to Field Place,' what was there so monstrous in the Squire's answer, 'Out of regard to my feelings, your mother's feelings, your sisters' welfare, forbear from giving expression to sentiments that offend me, shock her, and bring social disrepute to your family?' What should the father have done? Hogg was of opinion that the Squire should have given his son a handsome allowance, and left him at liberty to say and do what he liked. Bearing in mind that Shelley was still only nineteen years of age, most readers of this page,—certainly most fathers with unruly sons still in their nonage,—will see reasons for differing from Mr. Hogg on this matter.

If Miss Eliza Westbrook was desirous of a good pretext for hastening to York and taking the young couple under her protection and government, she found her desire in the singular circumstances under which her sister (a mere child) had been left at York. Packing her trunks, Miss Westbrook took the road along which her sister had travelled seven or eight weeks earlier. She was in possession of her darling, and at war with Hogg in the dingy lodging-house, whilst Shelley was still on his way back to the northern city, with a light purse and a heavy heart. On returning to the dingy house, the boyish husband found both sisters in the dingy parlour.

Having been told by Harriett that her sister was 'beautiful, exquisitely beautiful,' with an elegant figure, dark bright eyes, and a profusion of black hair, Hogg was surprised by the indications of age in her countenance which, instead of being lovely, was chiefly remarkable for marks of small-pox, and the not translucent pallor common in faces disfigured by that malady. To Hogg (a prejudiced and strongly biased witness against the woman he loathed) it appeared that, though dark, Eliza Westbrook's eyes were dull and meaningless ; that, though black and glossy, her hair was coarse ; that her figure was meagre, prim, and graceless ; that her personal charms existed only in her younger sister's imagination.

History has still to discover the year of Miss Westbrook's birth ; but it may be safely assumed she was not so old as Mr. Hogg imagined,—that she was over five-and-twenty, and under thirty years of age. It may also be assumed that her appearance was less repulsive to other people than to Mr. Hogg. If Harriett's fancy erred in one direction, Mr. Hogg's animosity erred in another. If Harriett's partiality caused her to think too well of her sister's appearance, Hogg's resentment inspired him to speak too unfavourably of Miss Westbrook's looks.

Miss Westbrook and Hogg were enemies even before they set eyes on one another. The lady had travelled to York to encounter the enemy of her sister's reputation. On hearing she would soon appear in the dingy lodging-house, Hogg knew that on her arrival he would be face to face with a foe. At the moment of their first meeting, Shelley's incomparable friend and Shelley's sister-in-law exchanged glances of aversion. When he bowed before her, at their introduction to one another in the dingy parlour, the 'barmaid by origin' (to use Hogg's words) scarcely deigned to notice him.

'I thought Bysshe was to have brought you with him,'

observed Hogg to the lady, who, in her haste to shelter her darling, had not waited to travel with her brother-in-law.

'Oh dear, no!' Miss Westbrook replied, with cold and disdainful significance.

'Shall I make tea?' Hogg inquired, glancing at the tea-things on the table; and as he was not forbidden to do so, he brewed the tea, and brought Miss Westbrook a cup of the beverage, which she regarded contemptuously when it was placed before her. This was embarrassing to the gentleman who was joint-tenant of the dingy parlour.

If it was not farce, what followed this meeting of the enemies was very broad comedy. Miss Westbrook, thinking Hogg in the way, was of opinion he ought to get out of the way as quickly as possible. Thinking Miss Westbrook had come where she was not wanted, Hogg was of opinion she ought to be ordered back to London. On reappearing in the dingy lodging-house just twenty-four hours after Miss Westbrook's arrival, Shelley found himself between an incomparable friend who said, 'You must get rid of Miss Westbrook,' and an incomparable sister-in-law who said, 'You must get quit of Mr. Hogg.' As Harriett was on her sister's side, the future poet could not act on Hogg's advice. There was another reason why the youthful husband could not deal thus summarily with his sister-in-law.

Thinking that Miss Westbrook should be sent back immediately to London, and seeing that Shelley was scarcely the person to tell her and constrain her to go home, Hogg was of opinion that his friend ought to put strong pressure on his bride, to tell her sister she must retire from the scene where she was unwelcome,—that he should say firmly to Harriett, 'Choose between me and your sister: I leave York if she doesn't. If you wish me to remain by your side, you must tell your sister to go and leave us alone.' Five-and-forty years later, when he reviewed this critical passage of the poet's career, and all the miserable consequences of Miss Westbrook's transient power of him, Hogg felt as firmly as ever that Harriett's husband might have preserved his conjugal contentment for a much longer period, by saying stoutly to her 'either Eliza goes or I go,' and showing he would forthwith act on the menace, if the intruder did not at once retire. The happiness, coming to him from his marriage, might not have been great and enduring

under any circumstances; but by shaking Eliza from him at
York, he would have rid himself of the creature, whose scheming spirit and false tongue made it so miserably brief and insufficient. This was Hogg's one-sided and possibly erroneous
view of the case. Holding it honestly, he may well have
deplored the weakness that incapacitated 'the divine Shelley'
for casting from him so promptly the influence which extinguished for ever his confidence and delight in his young wife,
after having placed him for a while at war with the friend, who
induced him to make the lovely child his wife, when he was
thinking of making her his mere mistress.

Thinking Eliza should be dismissed in this fashion, Hogg
doubtless told Shelley so. As Shelley, whilst differing from
Byron in being able to keep a secret, resembled him also in a
habit of blabbing to others what he should have kept to
himself, it may be assumed that, if he did not impart it
directly to Miss Westbrook, he communicated Hogg's counsel
to his wife, without requiring her to act upon it. Further, as
Harriett's confidence in her sister was perfect at this point of
their curious story, it cannot be questioned, that whatever
Shelley told his wife of Hogg's view of the position, was
speedily communicated by her to Miss Westbrook.

It is not probable that under any circumstances Shelley
would just then have concurred in Hogg's opinion, and decided
to act upon it. But even if he approved the advice on general
grounds, circumstances forbade him to adopt it. Returning to
York with an almost empty purse, and no hope that it would
be speedily replenished by his father, Shelley could not afford to
quarrel with his sister-in-law, who had a little money in her
pocket, and was influential with her father, to whom he was
already looking for pecuniary relief. Though he could lend
Shelley 10l. from time to time, Hogg (as he tells us) was
unable to provide him with enough money for his own and his
wife's maintenance. At that moment, the law-student's store of
money in hand had been reduced to a trifle by the charges of
his recent trip to Scotland. Captain Pilford had already done
his utmost for his nephew's pecuniary relief. Having incurred
the Squire's vehement displeasure by lending Shelley the 25l.,
which enabled him to fly with Harriett to Edinburgh, Mr.
Medwin (the Horsham attorney) was in no mood to incense his
powerful neighbour and relative to fiercer wrath, and to provoke

further censure from the Squire's patron, the Duke of Norfolk, by lending the young gentleman any more money. Under these circumstances, Mr. Percy Bysshe Shelley could not afford to quarrel with Miss Westbrook, the only person to whom he could just then look for the relief of his immediate necessities, —'the influence' through which he was hoping to get a regular allowance from his father-in-law.

Seeing that Shelley would not put the needful pressure on his wife, the brilliant thought occurred to Hogg that, doing what his friend dared not do, he would indicate the 'necessary course' to Harriett, and urge her with equal delicacy and firmness to take it. Miss Westbrook spent much time in brushing the black hair, which Harriett regarded admiringly, and Mr. Hogg spoke and wrote about with profane flippancy. One day, whilst the elder sister was brushing her hair, Hogg persuaded Mrs. Shelley to walk with him to the old Roman bridge, and have a look at the Ouse, which had just then overflowed its banks, and was in divers ways behaving with picturesque and sensational extravagance.

'Is it not an interesting, a surprising sight?' remarked Harriett, whilst viewing 'the floods' from the middle of the bridge.

'Yes,' returned Hogg, 'it is very wonderful. But, dear Harriett, how nicely that dearest Eliza would spin down the river! How sweetly she would turn round and round, like that log of wood! And, gracious heaven, what would Miss Warne say?'—Miss Warne being a maiden lady (daughter of a London taverner) who held so high a place in Miss Westbrook's affection and esteem, that the latter, in her ordinary talk on things in general, was in the habit of referring admiringly to the lady's discretion and faultless taste.

At this piquant suggestion, that it would be well to pitch Eliza into the river, and give Miss Warne a fine opportunity for saying something remarkable, Harriett (says Hogg) 'turned her pretty face away, and laughed—as a slave laughs, who is beginning to grow weary of an intolerable yoke.' It speaks much for Hogg's rashness, that he ventured to speak in this fashion of Miss Westbrook to her younger and admiring sister; —for his self-sufficiency, that he imagined a few words from him would put the girl in revolt against her only sister;—for the excessive familiarity of his bearing to her, that he addressed her as 'dear Harriett,' as he spoke thus lightly of the 'dearest

Eliza,' and her super-excellent Miss Warne;—for his vanity and ignorance of human nature, that he imagined Harriett would respect his confidence so far as to keep his saucy words from her sister. Of course the sixteen-years-old girl did not deem herself under an obligation of honour to withhold from her only sister the flippant utterances of so recent an acquaintance. Honour and loyalty required her to tell Eliza that Hogg wished to separate them,—was set on compassing their estrangement. On learning that Hogg meant Shelley and Harriett to discard her, Miss Westbrook resolved that they should discard him. Whatever may be thought of the means she used for the achievement of her end, it cannot be denied, that she could plead extreme provocation in excuse of what was reprehensible in her extreme measures;—and that it was natural for her to determine her sister and brother-in-law should banish the man who wanted them to dismiss her. It was a fight between an angry and unscrupulous young woman and an overbearing young man. The fight was sharp and short: for the moment, the victory was with the woman.

In fighting Mr. Hogg,—in taking for his humiliation and discomfiture a course, which she probably never thought of taking till he struck her, and possibly would never have thought of taking, had he treated her in a courteous and conciliatory manner,—it is conceivable that Miss Westbrook persuaded herself she was actuated by pure concern for her sister's happiness, and righteous disapproval of masculine wickedness, and in no degree whatever by personal spite and resentment. The lady was in just the position to imagine she did altogether for her sister's good what she did chiefly for the gratification of her own vindictiveness. Travelling northward to guard her darling from Hogg's indiscretion, she made the journey in a mood to suspect him of something worse than indiscretion. By no means wanting in self-esteem, or disposed to underrate her charms, the lady naturally inferred from Hogg's desire to extrude so fascinating a person as herself from so small a circle, that her presence was distasteful to him, because it promised to defeat his insidious designs on Harriett's honour and happiness. The young man, who would deprive Harriett of her sister's society and protection, desired to get the dear child into his power,—to have her at his mercy. For what end did he desire to have the dear child in his power, at his mercy? The answer to this question determined Miss Westbrook to preserve the dear child from a villain.

Tractable and docile in the hands of the elder sister, whom she admired and loved enthusiastically, the dear child in perfect simplicity and purity of thought provided Miss Westbrook with evidence that Shelley's incomparable friend was a young man of incomparable wickedness. Here are the damnatory admissions and confessions of the younger sister. Mr. Hogg had been extremely attentive to her in Edinburgh, and also (during her husband's absence) at York. At Edinburgh he had taken her for walks, unattended by Shelley. He certainly admired her beauty, for he had said so outright on several occasions. He had paid her extravagant compliments,—indeed compliments so extravagant, that they caused her embarrassment. He was very kind and attentive to her; but she had often wished he would not commend her so immoderately to her face. She had refused to take walks with him in York during Shelley's absence, but it cost her no little effort to hold to her decision on this point, so urgent was he in begging her to walk abroad. When he was not at Chambers, or on the way to and fro between them and the dingy lodging-house, Hogg had spent all his time at the house. Taking tea with her every evening, he had passed the whole of each evening in the dingy parlour with her, till she retired to rest for the night. It had been very awkward for her, to live in the same house and share the same parlour with him, during her husband's absence :—all the more awkward, because he persisted in paying her such extravagant compliments. The milliners had been disobliging and suspicious in their bearing to her. Possibly they would have been less so, had Hogg left her under their protection altogether, or been less attentive to her in her husband's absence. Such were Harriett's admissions and confessions to her sister,—admissions and confessions made afterwards to her husband. Miss Westbrook knew how to manipulate and dress up these simple admissions into evidence to Shelley, that his friend's gallantry to Harriett had been excessive, that his admiration of her was embarrassing to Harriett, that he might have been more thoughtful for the delicate sensibilities of the simple and innocent child, that they had been too much together for her contentment and reputation, that the dear child had been worried and harassed by her admirer, that her husband should put a distance between them. Care for the dear child's nerves and feelings required that she should be removed from York as soon as possible.

Committing herself to no statement of fact, in which her sister would not concur, Miss Westbrook was careful to say nothing that would make Shelley suspicious of his wife's goodness, or render him wrathful with Hogg. It was enough for the present to suggest that Harriett's mere beauty had inspired Hogg with a sentiment of strong admiration, trembling on the verge of passion;—that, without doing or saying aught to justify Shelley in quarreling with him outright, Hogg had permitted Harriett to see the state of feeling which he should have been most careful to conceal from her; that Harriett was secretly troubled by her sense of Hogg's regard for her;—a regard for which of course she was in no degree to be blamed, and he was to be pitied rather than condemned. Of course Miss Westbrook (a clever woman) knew how the seeds of distrust and jealousy would grow in the breast to which she was committing them; knew that by charging Hogg at first with nothing worse than weakness, she would be able to persuade Harriett's boyish and fanciful husband a few weeks or months later, that his incomparable friend was a false friend.

Whilst he was being thus educated to regard his friend with distrust and pity, Shelley was living with his wife and her sister in Mr. Stickland's (? Strickland's) lodging-house, Blake Street, York;—lodgings to which they migrated from the dingy dwelling of the austere milliners, within a day or two of Shelley's return from London. Though certain expressions of Hogg's second volume would countenance a contrary opinion, it is not probable that he was permitted to accompany them to this new abode. In the absence of definite evidence to the point, it may be assumed from divers circumstances that, whilst the newly constituted trio rested in Mr. Stickland's house, the fourth member of the party had quarters elsewhere. If it was so, however, Hogg was a daily visitor on uneasy terms at the Blake Street lodging-house; talking as freely as heretofore with his friend and Harriett, but painfully conscious that they spoke less unreservedly with him, and that forces were in operation to sever him from them. There seems to have been no distinct rupture between Hogg and his friend, before the latter went off abruptly for Keswick.

It having been decided by the trio, that they must get away from York and Hogg, they spoke openly to him of their intention to migrate to Keswick. He was pressed to go thither with them,—pressed the more cordially because the trio knew his legal studies and other obligations constrained him to remain at York. But whilst telling him of their intention to go to Keswick, and begging him to accompany them, they forbore to tell him their real reason for selecting Keswick as their next resting place. To the last, Hogg was under the impression that they were drawn to Keswick by the picturesqueness and the poetical associations of the district, dwelt in and beloved by Wordsworth and Southey, Coleridge and De Quincey; and under the quite erroneous notion that they were pining for the beauties of Derwentwater and the Lodore Falls, he urged 'them to postpone their journey to the lovely region till a season more favourable for the enjoyment of its scenery. ' If you dislike York,' he urged, 'and the neighbourhood of York, so much do not remain there—quit it at once; but go to the south, to a part of the world with which you are acquainted, and where you are known; to a milder and more genial climate, and where you will be nearer your supplies? Why expose youselves to the bleak north at this unkindly season ? Why go out of the way of everybody and of everything ? Why go out of the reach of money, and bury yourselves alive amongst rude and uncivilised barbarians?' The counsel (adds Hogg bitterly and compassionately) was offered in vain.

To Miss Westbrook the advice was only another reason why she and her young charges should go farther north. On leaving Mr. Hogg at York, for them to do the very thing he urged them not to do would be a fit humiliation to the overbearing gentleman. It would show him how lightly they regarded his opinion, and make him feel that he was the discarded one. That he might take this view of their action was another reason with Miss Westbrook, why he should be kept in ignorance of its chief object. When he told them, with mingled pomposity and vehemence, that in going to Keswick they would be going 'out of the way of everybody and everything,—out of the reach of money,' and into the society of 'rude and uncivilised barbarians,' the trio smiled in their sleeves at one another. And well might they do so, as they were set on the journey because they hoped it would bring them to the house of somebody of no common account, to society in the like of which their monitor had never moved, and to the money which they so urgently needed. Think-

ing the while of Greystoke, and the Duke of Norfolk, and the exalted people they hoped to meet at 'the Castle,' the sisters could
scarcely keep their smiles in their sleeves, as Mr. Hogg prated
of 'rude and uncivilised barbarians.' Had he known that the
march on Keswick was a march on Greystoke Castle; that the
march on the northern potentate had for its end the conciliation
of the southern powers; that instead of going to Keswick for the
pleasure of drinking tea with Southey, the trio were going
thither to fix themselves on the great Duke, who would in ten
days or a fortnight be at his northern seat, Hogg would either
have refrained from opposing the project, or would have opposed
it on other grounds.   It shows how completely he had fallen out
of favour with the trio, how completely Eliza and Harriett had
extruded him from Shelley's confidence, that Hogg had no notion
why his companions were set on going to the lakes at a time
when the hardiest tourists were leaving them.

From Blake Street, York, without conferring with his
incomparable Hogg on the matter, Shelley on 28th October,
1811, wrote (*vide Notes and Queries*, second series, Vol. vi., p. 405)
to his father's patron, the Duke of Norfolk, entreating his Grace
to use his influence again, even as he used it in the last spring,
to mediate between the writer and his too indignant father, and
induce the same too indignant father to allow his son a sufficient
income.   A letter to be looked up by readers, who have the
Notes and Queries volumes on their shelves, this remarkable
epistle from the future poet to his father's patron comprises
these extremely noteworthy words :—

'. . . . . . . As I experienced from you such an undeserved instance
of friendly interposition in the spring, as I am well aware how much my
father is influenced by the mediation of a third person, and as I know
none to whom I could apply with greater hopes of success than to yourself, I take the liberty of soliciting the interference of your Grace with
my father in my behalf. You have probably heard of my marriage. I
am sorry to say that it has exasperated my father to a great degree,
surely greater than is consistent with justice, for he has not only withheld the means of subsistence which his former conduct and my habits
of life taught me to expect as reasonable and proper, but has even
refused to render me any the slightest assistance. He referred me on
application to a Mr. Whitton, whose answer to my letter vaguely complained of the disrespectfulness of mine to my father. These letters
were calculated to make his considerations of my proceedings less
severe. My situation is consequently most unpleasant; under these

circumstances I request your Grace to convince my father of the severity of his conduct, to persuade him that my offence is not of the hideous nature he considers it, to induce him to allow me a sufficient income to live with tolerable comfort. I am also particularly anxious to defend Mr. Medwin from any accusations of aiding and assisting me, which my father may bring against him. I am convinced that a statement of plain truth on this head will remove any prejudice against Mr. M. from the mind of your Grace. That he did lend me 25*l.* when I left Field Place is most true. But it is equally true he was ignorant of my intentions; that he was ignorant of the purposes to which I was about to apply the money . . . .'

Every sentence of this extract from an important letter should be carefully weighed by the reader who would apprehend precisely the relations of Mr. Timothy Shelley and the poet, and observe the pains taken by the Duke of Norfolk in mediating between the father and son. The letter shows to whose influence Shelley attributed, and no doubt justly attributed, the quickness with which his father relented to him in the spring. In this respect the Squire suffers in some degree from the testimony of the epistle, which denies him the credit that would otherwise seem due to his clemency and financial liberality to the son, who had so recently exasperated him by rebellious extravagances. It does not follow that left to himself the Squire would not in a somewhat longer time have subsided from his wrath, and treated his boy with the same generosity. It must, however, be conceded that the Duke's counsel was accountable for the quickness with which the Squire dismissed his anger, and offered the terms which Shelley accepted with exultation, calling the terms 'very good ones,' when he wrote of them exultingly to Hogg in the middle of May. On the other hand, by all who would take an impartial view of the father's treatment of his son, it must be admitted that the Squire's readiness in deferring to his patron on so delicate a question was creditable to his moderation, was at least incompatible with the violent and stubborn wrong-headedness with which he has been unfairly charged. Indicative of a disposition to do what was right by his boy, this readiness indicates a conscientious desire to be preserved by judicious counsel from the vehemence of his own temper, and withheld from errors to which he might be betrayed by the fervour of his feelings. The evidence is conclusive that Shelley was not more quick than his father to have recourse to the Duke's mediation; a fact which must be at least allowed to indicate a desire on the father's part, that his behaviour to his son should be such as a fair and high-minded arbitrator would approve. The evidence is no less conclusive that Mr. Timothy Shelley's treatment of his son had the Duke's approval; and that his sense of the Duke's approval caused him to look to his patron as a friend, who would defend his paternal character from social reprehension.

It is noteworthy that, whilst thanking the Duke for his good services of the previous spring, Shelley speaks of the pecuniary arrangement resulting from his Grace's intervention as a 'reasonable and proper' arrangement. Even more noteworthy is it that, instead of attributing his father's anger and withdrawal of the allowance to disapproval of his religious and philosophical views, he attributes them altogether to indignation at his marriage, and displeasure at his letters. It is not suggested by phrase or word that the rupture was due in any degree to differences of opinion on matters of creed. The letter's only complaint against Mr. Timothy Shelley is that his indignation is 'greater than is consistent with justice' (words of admission that the writer had given his father cause for serious, though less extravagant, displeasure) : the letter's only prayer is that the Duke will address himself to the pecuniary consequence of this displeasure. The Duke is not asked to modify the Squire's religious intolerance, but to moderate his anger at the *mésalliance*, and induce him to allow his son 'a sufficient income to live with tolerable comfort.' There is no suggestion that he was shut out of his 'boyhood's home' on account of his heterodoxy. On the contrary, the writer speaks of himself as leaving that home of his own accord to make the match, on which he had not spoken to his father. Writing to the Duke, who knew the truth of the case, Shelley could not venture to be otherwise than precisely truthful on these points. In the letter, therefore, we have Shelley's sincere view of his relations with his father, and see how he spoke of them to well-informed persons. By-and-by it will be seen how he wrote of those relations to William Godwin, who did not know the truth of them.

Just two days before Shelley dated his letter (of 28th October, 1811) from York to the Duke of Norfolk, old Sir Bysshe Shelley executed a noteworthy codicil to the will, by which he had directed that all persons entitled to lands, &c. (designated A in my abstract of the will), whose consent

and co-operation should be needful for the purpose of the testament, should join in settling the same lands A precisely as the
lands, &c. (designated C) were ordered by the same will to be
put in strict settlement. It was observed in the aforementioned
abstract, that the testator's grandson (Percy Bysshe) was
tenant in tail in remainder expectant on the deaths of his father
and grandfather, of two lots of real estate, designated A and B.
By the will he was required to resettle, in accordance with the
testator's purpose, the lands, &c., A; no requirement being made for
the resettlement of lands, &c., B. By the codicil, which old Sir
Bysshe executed on 26th October, 1811, it was directed that any
person, being tenant for life at the same time of A, B, and C,
and every person or persons being tenant in tail of A and B,
and at the same time tenant for life of C, should settle A *and* B
as C, within a year of so becoming entitled and capable of joining in the resettlement. It was further provided by this noteworthy codicil that, if any such entitled person or persons
should refuse or neglect to settle A and B as C, then the estates
of such person or persons and their respective issue under the
will in estates C, should be forfeited, and the remainder
expectant on such estates should be accelerated. Yet, further,
it was directed by this remarkable codicil that if, by reason of
alienation or charge any person, at the date of the codicil
interested in remainder to any estate in A and B should not be
able to settle A and B *as* C, there should then be the same
forfeiture of the estate and estates of such person and his issue
under the will, as if he had refused or neglected to settle A and
B *as* C. As this last provision was aimed directly at the future
poet, though he is not mentioned by name in the clause, and as
readers of this work should be under no uncertainty respecting
the provision, by which the poet may be said to have disinherited
himself and his issue from participation in his grandfather's
very large property, it is well to put on the present page the
ipsissima verba of the provision, which runs thus :—

'Provided always and I do hereby declare,' says old Sir Bysshe
in this momentous codicil, 'my will and mind to be that, if any person
or persons who is or are now entitled in remainder under or by virtue
of the said Indenture of Appointment of the twentieth day of April,
one thousand seven hundred and ninety-one, and the said Indenture
of Release of the thirtieth day of April, one thousand seven hundred
and eighty-two respectively, to any estate or estates of and in the
hereditaments therein respectively comprised hath or have or shall alien

or charge the same whereby he or they may be prevented from making
or causing to be made the resettlement hereinbefore by me directed to
be made of the said settled estates, then and in such case, from and
after the expiration of the time before limited or mentioned for making
such resettlement, the uses or use estates or estate by my said will
directed to be limited to or for the benefit of the person or persons who
hath or have so aliened or charged or shall so alien or charge as aforesaid and his or their issue shall, notwithstanding he or they may
be personally willing to make such resettlement as aforesaid, cease
determine and become absolutely void, and that the manors and other
hereditaments by my said will devised and directed to be settled in
trust as aforesaid shall in such case immediately thereupon go over in
the same manner as I have hereinbefore directed the same to go over
in case such person or persons had refused or neglected to make such
resettlement as aforesaid, and I do hereby expressly declare that my
intentions in respect to the resettlement of the said settled estates shall
be carried into effect by proper clauses and provisoes to be for that
purpose inserted in the settlement in and by said will directed to be
made as aforesaid.'

It is obvious that differences on questions of religion or
politics were in no degree accountable for the codicil, by
which the future poet was required to resettle the real estates,
that would devolve on him absolutely after the lives of his
father and grandfather.   Himself an atheist and materialist, it
mattered nothing to old Sir Bysshe, whether his grandson believed
in fifty gods or one God, or chose to deny the existence of a
supreme Deity.   Himself a man of the people, the son of a
Yankee apothecary by the miller Plum's widow, old Sir Bysshe
was not so strongly prejudiced in favour of aristocratic persons
and institutions, as to be greatly incensed by his grandson's
folly in wedding a publican's pretty daughter.   It was a
matter of comparative indifference to the aged cynic, whether
the boy held to the Whigs, went over to the Tories, or, declaring
against both political parties, joined the red Republicans.   The
one thing he required of his eldest son's eldest son, was that
on coming of age, the youngster should join in a resettlement
of the settled estates, that would make them part and parcel
of the big entailed property of the Castle Goring Shelleys.
Let him be compliant on that point, and the youngster had his
grandsire's permission to be as wilful as he pleased on all
other matters.   On the other hand, should he prove rebellious
and undutiful in respect to this one requirement, neither he
nor his issue should profit by the grand estate that would be

created for the perpetual dignity of the house, founded by his grandfather. For all the veteran cared, the youngster might think, say, write, do whatever he pleased, provided he forbore to cross the purpose of his elders on the one matter of business. Should he refuse to exchange his larger estate in the settled lands for a contingent life interest in them, he must be content with that estate (which, though a comparatively small affair, was sufficient to maintain a baronet's dignity), and forego all interest for himself and issue in the lordly revenue, to which he would otherwise succeed in the course of nature.

Having formed this scheme for the honour of his descendants, at a time when he never imagined the little Brentford schoolboy might decline to further it, Sir Bysshe was not the man to relinquish any part of his grand ambition out of deference to the whim and wildness of an unruly stripling. From the boy's action in wedding a girl of Harriett Westbrook's condition, without the consent or knowledge of his parents, it was obvious to the veteran, that his grandson's regard for the feelings and wishes of his nearest kindred were not likely to be largely operative in determining him to concur in the proposed re-settlement of family estate. From the circumstances of the *mésalliance*, the veteran had also reason for thinking it probable that the youngster would raise money on his future resources even in his minority; and, unless pressure was put upon him at the earliest moment to resettle the estates A and B, would be under the control of money-lenders, soon after the attainment of his majority. Hence the old man's resolve that the strongest possible appeal should be made at the earliest moment to the young man's self-interest to put it out of his power to squander the estates, in which he was interested as tenant in tail in remainder expectant. The stringent codicil was old Sir Bysshe's answer to his grandson's mad-cap elopement; and in taking this action on the boy's latest escapade, the founder of the poet's mushroom 'house' had no consideration whatever for the young man's religious or political opinions.

It is uncertain on what day the trio left York. Mr. Denis Florence MacCarthy is certain they departed on Friday, 29th October, the day next after the date of the epistle to the Duke of Norfolk, and perhaps the inaccurate writer does not err on this point. Anyhow it is unquestionable that they had left York several days, when the Duke's reply (dated 7th

November, 1811) came to Hogg's hands, and was forthwith (on the 9th or 10th of the month) forwarded to Shelley, at Keswick. Moreover, enough is known of the droll circumstances of the departure, which may indeed be called a flight, and of the manner in which His Grace the Duke of Norfolk answered Shelley's judiciously worded letter.

Charles, the eleventh Duke of Norfolk, a keen politician, and methodical man of affairs, kept a diary; and on 7th November, 1811 (when he was in his sixty-sixth year) he made this entry in the personal record, 'Wrote to T. Shelly that I would come to Field Place on the 10th, to confer with him on the unhappy difference with his son, from whom I have a letter before me.—To Mr. B. Shelley in answer that I should be glad to interfere, but fear with little hope of success; fearing that his father, and not he alone, will see his late conduct in a different point of view from what he sees it.—That I propose going into the North next week, and will come to York to see him, provided he will inform me when I may find him there.'

Written to Shelley himself, a letter of this sentiment and tone shows, even more forcibly than the Earl of Chichester's gossiping note, written to his official subordinate, what view the great Sussex families took of the young gentleman's latest *escapade*. To the Duke no less than the Earl, the marriage with the innkeeper's daughter appeared a discreditable business; and though in writing to Shelley, he of course made no mention of her low origin, the Duke told him frankly the marriage was an affair about which his father had reason to be indignant. In saying the Squire would not be singular in declining to take Shelley's view of the matter, the Duke declared, as plainly as courtesy allowed him, that he could not take that view. Shelley's view, as exhibited in the letter, was a mere opinion that his father's anger exceeded just and reasonable displeasure; and from this opinion the Duke dissented. Having in the meanwhile dined with the angry father at Horsham, the Duke, thirteen days later (23rd November), wrote Shelley another letter, inviting him, his wife and sister-in-law, to Greystoke Castle, some twelve miles from Keswick. Of this invitation, Shelley wrote on 26th November to Mr. Medwin, the Horsham attorney, 'We dine with the Duke of N. at Graystock this week,' words implying that this first invitation was only for dinner. On the same day (26th November), the Duke appears from another entry of his journal to have sent the trio a second invitation, which enabled Shelley to write on Saturday (30th November) to the Horsham lawyer, 'We visit the Duke of N. at Graystock to morrow. We return to Keswick on Wednesday,' words indicating an extension of the invitation, and a stronger disposition on the Duke's part to befriend the young people.

What was there comical in the departure from York? Having gone to chambers one morning under the impression that the trio would leave York on the morrow, Hogg was not a little surprised at his dinner-hour to discover that, whilst he was at work over legal papers, his friends had gone away in a post-chaise for Richmond. 'When I returned to dinner, such was the precipitation of the young votaries of the Muses, that the birds were flown,' says Hogg, in language which, at the first glance, seems to imply that he lived in the same house as the trio, till the moment of their departure. But though the evidence is less than conclusive, I have grounds for thinking that, after retiring from the dingy abode of the dingy milliners, Shelley and the sisters rested in a tenement which Hogg did not enter except as their visitor. If I am right on this point, it would seem that on returning to the lodgings, where he was a daily visitor, he went there by invitation to a farewell dinner, instead of returning to his proper place at the common board. Anyhow it is certain that, on going to the Blake Street lodging-house, he learnt that the friends with whom he meant to dine had taken their departure. The birds had flown, to Hogg's surprise and perplexity. Had they at the last moment changed their plans? or had they gone away in accordance with pre-arrangements, that had been withheld from him? The blood may well have brightened Hogg's cheek, as he asked himself these questions. His annoyance was not diminished by the short note left for him by the fugitives, who merely informed him they were off to Keswick, and would pass the next night at Richmond, whither he had better follow them speedily, if he would attend them to the lakes.

As the trio knew he could not leave York, it was impossible for Hogg to regard their invitation as sincere or flattering. Moreover, he could not be indifferent to the signal affront they had offered him in running away without a word of farewell. That the incident was Miss Westbrook's work he had no doubt;

that Mrs. Shelley was an accomplice in her sister's scheme for
his humiliation he may well have suspected. Nor could he
acquit Shelley of being a partner to the insult. It is thus that
human schemes miscarry, and human hopes perish into disap-
pointments. For months Shelley had looked forward to the
pleasure of settling in York, and living there 'for ever,' with
his incomparable Hogg and his dearest Harriett. What was
the end of this scheme for perpetual felicity? After so brief a
stay in the ancient city, Shelley was posting to Richmond with
his wife and sister-in-law, in order to get away from the friend
whom he had been so quickly taught to think a dangerous
companion for his childish wife.

In the absence of conclusive testimony, the known circumstances of the flight admit of several different explanations,
provoke many curious conjectures. One may imagine that
Shelley, Harriett, and Miss Westbrook, were confederates on
equal terms, and in perfect mutual confidence, for Hogg's
humiliation. Or one may conceive Shelley was not admitted
to the confidence of the ladies, until they had arranged all the
particulars of the departure. Readers are at liberty to imagine
no deception was practised by the trio, or any person of the
trio, on Hogg, when he was informed the departure would be
made twenty-four hours later. It is conceivable the suddennes
of the departure was no less real to the fugitives than apparent
to Hogg. Possibly no one of the three was aware two hours
before the departure that they would sleep the next night at
Richmond. Shelley may have been looking for days to the
particular hour at which his chaise eventually rattled out of
Blake Street, as the particular hour at which he would start
from York. His taste for making mysteries about nothing would
countenance an opinion that he misled Hogg as to the pre-
appointed day. It makes little for the contrary opinion that,
writing ten days or so later from Keswick, he declared himself
to have had no part in concerting the departure from York,
or the later departure from Richmond. On the other hand,
it is conceivable he was carried off at a moment's notice and
in high excitement from York by his clever and irresistible
sister-in-law. There are divers other points of this business,
in respect to which the ingenious reader may be left in the
free exercise of his imagination, and at perfect liberty to think
what he pleases.

VOL. I.   B B

My own hypothetical view of the business is, that Shelley was kept almost to the last moment in ignorance of the time appointed for the departure; that on this matter he was in the confidence neither of his sister-in-law nor of his wife during the last days of his sojourn at York; that, in respect to this affair, Harriett submitted to the judgment and will of her elder sister, who was for the moment the controlling member of the trio; and that in thus concealing part of her intentions from Harriett's boyish husband, Miss Westbrook was actuated partly by malice against Hogg, and partly by prudent regard for the difficulties she might reasonably anticipate in tearing the incomparable Hogg and the incomparable Shelley asunder, when the moment for severance should arrive. Playing her game no less cautiously than boldly, Miss Westbrook (whilst at York) could not venture to do more for the severance of the friends, than to hint to Shelley that Harriett had been placed in a false and embarrassing position towards Hogg, that one consequence of this false position was Hogg's inordinate and inconvenient admiration of Harriett, that, without doing anything distinctly culpable (Harriett's goodness precluding any such contingency), Hogg had been too demonstrative of a far too affectionate interest in his friend's wife. The sum of the maiden lady's case against her 'enemy' at York was, that he had been wanting in discretion and delicacy and chivalric self-control. At York she could not go much beyond this in her statements to Hogg's discredit, without inspiring her pupil with suspicions of his wife's delicacy and discretion; and to urge only thus much in support of her counsel for prompt withdrawal from Hogg's society, was to forbear from stirring Shelley to resentments, that would at once put it out of his friend's power to keep him at York in opposition to her wish and purpose. Hence, Miss Westbrook had reason to apprehend Shelley might even at the last hour decline to quit York, unless she eventually effected her object in his friend's absence, and with an abruptness for which neither of the young men was prepared. It is therefore conceivable that four-and-twenty hours before he intended to leave the city, Shelley was surprised by his sister-in-law with an announcement that Harriett's nerves required them to clear out of York instantly. To the execution of such a *coup-de-main*, the aggrieved and angry lady would also be strongly moved by a desire to inflict sharp annoyance on her adversary. This hypothesis accords with Shelley's emphatic assertion that the flight from York was no affair of his arrangement.

That Shelley did not leave York in any mood of vehement animosity against Hogg, or with any disposition to accuse him of serious misconduct towards Harriett, is shown by the affectionate warmth with which he wrote from Keswick to his incomparable friend. 'You were surprised,' he wrote immediately after his arrival at Keswick, 'at our sudden departure; I have no time, however, *now* either to account for it or enter into an investigation which we agreed upon.—With real, true interest, I constantly think of you, believe me, my friend, so sincerely am I attached to you.'

A few days later Shelley wrote to his friend at York:—'We all greatly regret that "your own interests, your own real interests," should compel you to remain at York. But pray, write often; your last letter I have read, as I would read your soul. . . . . Yours most affectionately, most unalterably, ... In another of his undated letters from Keswick to his friend at York, Shelley writes in this vein of affectionateness:—'If I thought we were to be long parted, I should be wretchedly miserable,—half mad! . . . . Cannot you follow us?—why not? But I will dare to be good,—dare to be virtuous; and I will soon seize once more what I have for a while relinquished, never, never again to resign it.' In another letter, Shelley says to his friend at York: —'I did not concert my departure from Richmond, nor that from York. Why did I leave you? I have never doubted you,—you, the brother of my soul, the object of my vivid interest; the theme of my impassioned panegyric.' In another letter he writes to his friend:—' I do not know that absence will certainly cure love; but this I know, that it fearfully augments the intensity of friendship.' These passages from letters which, though undated, were obviously written in the time between the future poet's first arrival at Keswick and his visit to Greystoke,— letters affording evidence that, during the earlier weeks of the residence at Keswick, Hogg was writing to Harriett with her husband's cognizance and approval, epistles which she submitted to his approval.

Possibly the trio would have tarried a few days longer at York, had they not felt it would favour their designs on Greystoke Castle that they should be at Keswick, when the Duke's reply to Shelley's appeal (of October 28th) should come to their hands. Knowing the Duke would be journeying to Cumberland in the course of the next month (November, 1811), the trio had reason for hoping his Grace would propose to see them on his way through York. On receiving this expression of the ducal pleasure, it would be well for them to be already at Keswick, so that the meeting should take place in the neighbourhood of Greystoke, if not *at* the Castle itself. Anyhow, they were at Keswick when the Duke's offer (7th November, 1811) to see Shelley at York came to the hands of the conspirators, whose reply (dated from Keswick) may be said to have forced the Squire's patron to invite them to his Cumberland place—barely twelve miles from that town. That the Duke, on the 23rd of November, invited the trio to meet him at the Castle appears from his diary; but this first invitation seems to have been regarded by the adventurers as nothing more than an invitation to dinner. 'We dine,' Shelley wrote to Mr. Medwin, of Horsham, on 26th November, 1811, 'with the Duke of N. at Graystock this week.' A few hours later he received the letter from Greystoke, which enabled him on the last day of the month to write to the same correspondent:—'We visit the Duke of N. at Graystock to-morrow. We return to Keswick on Wednesday.'

Coming to them at a time when they had reason to be thankful for small mercies, the Duke's second invitation may be supposed to have cheered the trio, whose spirits had been already raised from the deepest dejection by another reassuring incident. Influenced possibly by prompt intelligence that his daughters had been invited to the Duchess of Norfolk's dinner-table, Mr. Westbrook had sent his son-in-law a few pounds. The gift may have been accompanied (as Shelley, in his letter of November 30th to the Horsham attorney, avers it to have been) with an intimation that it was not to be regarded as the first of a series of similar benefactions; but, however guarded and qualified it may have been with cautious words, the re-mittance was an occasion for thankfulness to the trio, who had for several days needed money for their immediate necessities. Enabling them to pay their few debts in Keswick, the gift enabled them to go to Greystoke, albeit (to use the future poet's words) the visit was paid almost with their very last guinea.

Going to the Castle on Sunday, 1st December, 1811, for

three nights, the trio stayed there for eight or nine days;—an extension of the visit which, whilst certainly indicative of the Duke's growing disposition to befriend the young couple, may also be thought to indicate that he and the Duchess were favourably impressed by John Westbrook's daughters. Seeing in her rare beauty a palliation of the youngster's reckless act, the host and hostess must have been surprised by the charm of Harriett's simplicity, the music of her voice, the refinement of her tone. At a glance it was obvious to them she was no saucy barmaid. Before the Sunday dinner was over, they saw she was one of those girls of lowly origin, who under auspicious influences may win the confidence and love of the high-born. Though she lacked her sister's manifold charms, it was no less manifest to the Duke and Duchess that, instead of being such a young woman as the mere knowledge of her father's calling had predisposed them to find her, Miss Westbrook was a person of education and cleverness who might figure creditably in the drawing-rooms of the subordinate Sussex gentry. And in their judgment of Shelley's womankind, the Duke and Duchess had the concurrence of the several other gentle people who were staying in the Castle, —of Lady Musgrave, of Edenhall and Hartley Castle, Co. Cumberland; James Brougham, brother of Henry, the future Lord Chancellor; and Mr. Calvert, of Greta Bank, near Keswick, a Cumberland squire, who, differing widely from Mr. Timothy Shelley in mental and moral characteristics, seems to have stood towards the Duke of Norfolk in Cumberland somewhat in the same relation in which the Sussex Squire stood to his Grace in the southern county.

Why did the Duke of Norfolk show so much concern and take so much trouble in the domestic affairs of Field Place? This question should be answered precisely, as the extravagant notions of the poet's ancestral quality are mainly referable to misconceptions respecting the nature of the intercourse of the ducal Howards and the Castle Goring Shelleys. Having taken Sir Bysshe and the Squire of Field Place under his protection, and in a certain sense into his familiar friendship, the Duke was doubtless moved to trouble himself about the Squire's dealings with the future poet, by a genuine desire for Mr. Timothy Shelley's welfare. Nor can it be questioned that the powerful noble was influenced at the same time by affectionate interest in the youth, whose cordial looks and bearing, ever conciliatory to strangers and slight acquaintances, were none the less pleasing to the Duke, because the boy's manner towards his father's patron was gracefully expressive of ingenuous reverence for the age, experience, and rank of so august a personage. But it would be a mistake to suppose his Grace's treatment of the Shelleys was chiefly due to these amiable and altogether disinterested motives. A keen politician, who was charged by his enemies with sacrificing his religious convictions to his political interests, the Duke cared for men in proportion as he saw they might be serviceable to his ambition. Having raised the Shelleys to a higher grade of local quality, because they could be useful to him, the Duke continued to cherish them for the same end. The mushroom house, which he had dignified with the bloody hand, was dear to the Duke as an instrument for advancing his own greatness, and promoting the grandeur of the Howards. To such a patron the estate, which at any moment might devolve on the Member for New Shoreham, represented money and influence that would be employed by the second baronet at elections for the advantage of the Norfolk connexion. The estate that might come to-morrow to the Squire of Field Place was so much social power that, two or three years later, might, by a gun-accident, a fall in the hunting-field, a violent and fatal illness, pass from Sir Bysshe's son to the unruly boy, who under the new circumstances might be no less serviceable to the Howards than his father promised to be. In Squire Timothy the Duke had a loyal adherent and thorough Whig partisan; in the Squire's boy, who had come to grief at Oxford and made a runaway match with an inn-keeper's daughter, the Duke saw a youngster who, after running through the fever of red-republicanism, and surviving his freakish infidelity, would take sober views of politics and religion, and settle down into as good a Whig as his father, and on nearing middle-age be more desirous of ranking with the peers than with the poets of his country. Hence the pains taken by his Grace last spring to mediate between the father and son, to induce the former to give his boy a sufficient allow-ance, and to talk the latter into a disposition to live quietly and with due regard for his ultimate interests, until he should be of an age to enter Parliament and sit there like a sensible fellow for a pocket-borough. Hence also the Duke's readiness to act again as mediator between the angry sire and contumacious son. The same view must be taken of the Duke's condescension,—and, an even more remarkable fact, the Duchess's condescension,—in asking John Westbrook's daughters to Greystoke Castle.

As he lived at Greta Bank, less than a mile from the town of Keswick, and was at home when the trio became his near neighbours, it is not surprising that Mr. Calvert had made Shelley's acquaintance before meeting him at the Duke of Norfolk's table. An observant and energetic man, ever vigilant of the life, and keenly interested in the improvements, of his neighbourhood, the Squireen of Greta Bank was certain, under any circumstances, to hear of the arrival of so singular a party of tourists within a fortnight of their coming to the town, at so inclement a season. It is, however, probable that the Duke of Norfolk's useful neighbour at Keswick was the sooner cognizant of the strangers and their proceedings, because he had been asked by his Grace to be on the look-out for them. Circumstances indeed warrant something more than a suspicion that Harriett and her sister were not invited to Greystoke till the Duke had learnt from Mrs. Calvert that John Westbrook's daughters had the looks and manners of gentlewomen. Anyhow Shelley and Harriett had encountered Mr. Calvert on the hills about Keswick before meeting him at the Castle; and on talking with him at Greystoke it was soon apparent to the future poet that much of his private affairs had come to the knowledge of his new acquaintance. The 'elderly man,' whose looks impressed Shelley so agreeably, may be presumed to have gained his surprising knowledge of the youngster's concerns from the Duke of Norfolk. Other circumstances indicate that, before the Shelleys came to Greystoke, the Duke and his useful neighbour had conferred together on what had better be done for the suitable entertainment of the adventurers from Southern England.

The results of the march on Keswick justified the enterprise from which Hogg had vainly tried to dissuade the trio. Whilst Harriett's rare beauty and simple girlishness palliated to her august host and hostess the *escapade* that had stirred the Squire of Field Place to natural indignation, Shelley's speech was no less conciliatory than the tone of his letter to his father's patron. If she did little to enhance the effect of her sister's loveliness and her brother-in-law's discreet behaviour, Miss Westbrook was by no means the combative and offensive person she had shown herself to Mr. Thomas Jefferson Hogg at York. The young woman, who ruled her brother-in-law for many months, was clever enough to appear a fairly sensible and meritorious person for a few days to the Duchess of Norfolk and Lady Musgrave. Having consented to receive the trio under his roof, the Duke could not have declined to befriend them any further, even if they had offended him. But the prolongation of the visit to the ninth day is conclusive evidence that the visitors won the favour of their entertainers. Another and even stronger indication of ducal benignity appears in the arrangement that was made (certainly with the Duke's approval, and probably at his instance) for providing the trio with a comfortable home during their sojourn at Keswick, where they seemed likely to linger to a time considerably later than the day, on which they eventually started from Cumberland for Ireland.

Before the visit at Greystoke came to an end, it was settled that the trio should move from their (second) uncomfortable lodgings in Keswick to rooms under Mr. Calvert's roof at Greta Bank, to which the Duke's useful neighbour agreed to welcome them in the twofold character of guests and lodgers ;—as guests receiving Mrs. Calvert's hospitable courtesies, and at the same time as lodgers rendering their entertainer a payment, that would enable them to live in his house for a considerable period (for several months, even for two or three years) without incurring an oppressive sense of pecuniary obligation.. That a gentleman of Mr. Calvert's social position consented to receive the trio on these terms is of itself a clear indication, that the domiciliary arrangement was expected to last for more than a few weeks. It is also conceivable that the Duke approved the pecuniary arrangement as a compact, that would render it easier for him to induce Mr. Timothy Shelley to renew the yearly allowance to his son. On hearing that his son and daughter-in-law had been received on such terms by one of his patron's friends, the Squire of Field Place would of course feel it incumbent on his honour to put his son in a position to fulfil his pecuniary obligations to the Duke's friend. This view of the pecuniary arrangement, and of the effect it could not fail to have on Mr. Timothy Shelley, accords with the ungracious terms in which the renewal of the allowance was soon afterwards announced to Shelley by his father's man of business. Writing on 28th January, 1812, to William Godwin, Shelley says of his father's action in this matter, 'A little time since he sent to me a letter, through his attorney, renewing an allowance of two hundred pounds per annum, but with this remark " that his sole reason for so doing was to prevent my cheating strangers." ' The strangers thus pointed to in the lawyer's letters were doubtless the strangers (Mr. and Mrs. Calvert) who had taken the trio into their house.

The date of this letter, whose needless offensiveness (offensiveness, by the way, that may have been exaggerated by Shelley) was perhaps referable to the attorney's ill-breeding rather than the Squire's harshness, is unknown ; but it may be assumed that the allowance was renewed soon after the arrangement with the Squire of Greta Bank came to Mr. Timothy Shelley's knowledge, *i.e.* within two months of its withdrawal. The Squire of Field Place having thus again given his son an income (revocable at will) of 200*l.* per annum, Mr. Westbrook (no doubt mollified and flattered by the Duchess of Norfolk's civility to his daughters) appears to have determined to act with equal liberality to his daughter Harriett and to raise her husband's annual revenue to 400*l.* It has been questioned by successive biographers whether John Westbrook acted thus liberally. Even by Mr. Rossetti (an authority, from whom I never venture to differ without carefully reviewing the facts) it is doubted whether the poet had so good an income during his first marriage. But I see no grounds for thinking his yearly income in that term of his career was less than 400*l.*

Shelley had no obvious motive to overstate his means to William Godwin and Miss Hitchener in 1812. On the contrary, there were considerations that would dispose him to understate his income to those correspondents. Yet he assured both of them in that year that he had a yearly allowance of 400*l.* Writing on 14th January, 1812, on information given him by Shelley, Southey says Mrs. Shelley's father allowed her and her husband 200*l.* a-year. A fortnight later (28th January, 1812) Shelley in the letter to Godwin, speaks of his father's renewal ('a little time since') of 'an allowance of two hundred pounds per annum.' On the 14th of the next month Shelley wrote to Miss Hitchener that he had '400*l.* per annum.' Five months later (5th July, 1812) he wrote from Lynmouth, North Devon, to William Godwin, ' I am, as you know, a minor, and as such depend upon a limited income (400*l.* per annum) allowed me by my relatives.'   During the three first months of his married life (*i.e.* the months preceding the renewal of his father's 200*l.* a-year and his father-in-law's first concession of a similar allowance) Shelley received considerably more than 100*l.* from different sources (*i.e.* 25*l.* from Mr. Medwin, spent on the charges of the elopement; 10*l.* from Hogg; 75*l.* sent to him at Edinburgh; the money [say 25*l.*] provided by Miss Westbrook for expenses at York and the journey to Keswick; and the 'small sum' [say another 25*l.*] sent to him at Keswick towards the end of November by Mr. Westbrook,—sums amounting to 160*l.*)   There is no reason to suppose that Mr. Timothy Shelley withheld the allowance of 200*l.* a-year after its renewal, or that Mr. Westbrook failed to give the other 200*l.* a-year, till the poet's rupture with his first wife in the spring of 1814.   Surely then there are good grounds for saying Shelley had at least four hundred a-year from the date of his first marriage to the time of his quarrel with Harriett :—an income (equivalent to 600*l.* or 700*l.* a-year at the present time) that certainly acquits Mr. Timothy Shelley of the charges of scandalous and hurtful niggardliness to his perplexing and contumacious son.

Further evidence to the same conclusion is afforded by Shelley's way of living throughout the period, when he is generally supposed to have suffered severely from insufficient means.   So long as he tarried under Mr. Calvert's roof he lived well within his average monthly income; but with the exception of this brief period of about three months, Shelley's way of living from the September of 1811 to the midsummer of 1814 was a way in which he could not have persisted on less than 400*l.*, even if no regard is had to the costly extravagances with which he indulged his wife in the later and inharmonious months of their conjugal association.   To subsist on 200*l* or 300*l.* a-year, it would have been necessary for Shelley and Harriett to live in one place and in the same small house, practising the petty domestic economies by which a little money may be made to go a long way.   But instead of living in this manner, they chose a life of restless vagrancy—a way of living that of all modes of existence is the one most impoverishing to gentle folk of limited means.   Economical in clothing and parsimonious in diet, they were prodigal in travelling expenses.   Wandering hither and thither, from London to Edinburgh, from Edinburgh to York, from York to Keswick, from Keswick to the Isle of Man, from the Isle of Man to Dublin, from Dublin to Wales, from Wales back to Ireland, now lingering at Killarney, and now worshiping Nature in North Wales, they were incessant tourists at a time when touring (in respect to charges of locomotion) was far costlier than in these later years of grace. As tourists in Scotland, Ireland, Wales and England, and in a later stage of their joint-career as strangers in London, they spent yearly on hotel-keepers and lodginghouse-keepers twice the sum that would have maintained a cottage with two servants and a pony carriage in a Sussex village. At the same time it must be remembered that, though he seldom spent a shilling for pleasures on which young men of his degree are apt to spend many pounds, Shelley was by no means a man without 'personal expenses.' Giving much to beggars and other victims of distress, he was an habitual buyer of books, and in the execution of his literary enterprises, spent much on printers. Though he rarely bought wine, he often bought a costlier drink—laudanum, for his own drinking. How could he live in this way on 400*l.* a-year? Of course his expenses exceeded 400*l.* a-year. Of course in his wanderings he resembled the eighteenth-century poet, who dragged at each remove a lengthening chain of debt. But how could he have met the immediate, urgent, unavoidable and not-to-be-deferred charges of such incessant touring on less than four hundred a-year?

CHAPTER XVII.

GRETA BANK.

Shelley wishes for a Sussex Cottage—His Friends at Keswick—Southey at Home—Poet and Schoolmaster—Southey's Way of handling Shelley—Shelley caught Napping—Mrs. Southey's Tea-cakes—Eggs and Bacon on Hounslow Heath—At Home with the Calverts—Shelley's remarkable Communications to Southey—His Story of Harriett's Expulsion from School—The Story to Hogg's Infamy—Mr. MacCarthy on the *Posthumous Fragments*—Miss Westbrook's transient Contentment—Shelley's *For Ever* and *Never*—His Interest in Ireland—Burning Questions—Southey and Shelley at War—The *Address to the Irish People*—Letters to Skinner Street—Godwin tickled by them—Shelleyan Conceptions and Misconceptions—Shelley forgets all about Dr. Lind—Preparations for the Irish Campaign—Letter of Introduction to Curran—Project for a happy Meeting in Wales—Miss Eliza Hitchener—Bright Angel and Brown Demon—Shelley's Delight in her—His Abhorrence of her.

FROM Shelley's letter of 26th November, 1811, to Mr. Medwin, of Horsham, it appears that the trio came to Keswick with the purpose of journeying southward, and settling in some picturesque nook of Sussex, when they should have succeeded or failed in the main object of their expedition to the Lake country. The Horsham attorney was instructed to look out for a cottage, adapted to their means and requirements, near St. Leonard's forest or in any other part of the county, where they would be at a distance from soldiers and workshops, and have rural quietude with good scenery.

It would have been well, perhaps, for Shelley and his chances of domestic contentment, had they held to this plan, and settling down in a peaceful Sussex village, avoided the life of comfortless vagrancy, in which he spent the rest of his life. It would have been better still, perhaps, both for him and Harriett, had they been content to lead tranquil and studious days at Greta Bank for two or three years in the society of the Southeys at Keswick, of De Quincey and Wordsworth at Grasmere, of Coleridge and John Wilson. But it was not in his nature, nor, perhaps, was it possible to a young woman of her peculiar temper, to be happy for many months together, in any place that wanted the charm of novelty. Anyhow, instead of biding his time at Greta Bank till De Quincey and Wordsworth, Coleridge and Wilson, had come about them, Shelley surrendered the advantages of the home, that had been provided for him by ducal favour, and left Cumberland at the beginning of February without making any acquaintances at Keswick with the exception of the Calverts from whom he parted regretfully, and the Southeys from whom he parted in no kindly temper.

Either through the carelessness of the original writer (who may have made the common mistake of pre-dating the epistle by an entire month), or through the carelessness of the copyist of the document, a wrong date (10th October, 1811) is given in Mr. Denis Florence MacCarthy's *Shelley's Early Life*, to the extract from an unpublished letter, in which the poetical aspirant says of the author of *Thalaba*, 'Southey hates the Irish; he speaks against Catholic Emancipation. In all these things we differ. Our differences were the subject of a long conversation.' As Shelley had not seen Southey on 10th October, 1811, as he made Southey's acquaintance at Keswick, which he entered for the first time on some day of the following month (November, 1811), he cannot have talked in the earlier days of October, 1811, with the celebrated man of letters on questions touching Catholic Emancipation and the discontents of the Irish Catholics. The long conversation and differences about those topics may have been affairs of November, but it is more probable that the famous poet and the unknown literary aspirant had no angry altercations about Ireland's wrongs and Robert Emmett's story before the last month of 1811.

It is, however, certain that they differed on these subjects, and that their differences of opinion were fruitful of overbearing speech on Southey's part,—and of much vehement and bitter speech from Shelley.

Shelley came to Keswick with a disposition to have the friendliest relations with the man of letters who two years since had been his favourite English poet, and whom he regarded as a great man till personal intercourse extinguished the favourable opinion. And whilst Shelley went to 'the lakes' in a mood to render homage to Southey's greatness, Southey was by no means disinclined to receive the homage in those portions of his laborious time, in which he condescended to have speech with inferior mortals. But, notwithstanding Shelley's readiness to admire and Southey's readiness to be admired, no one familiar with their peculiar infirmities of intellect and temper would have predicted that the two men would prove congenial companions. In return for his worship and deference, the vehement and romantic Shelley looked for encouragement and sympathy from the famous scholar and poet. Hoping for a cordial welcome to the great man's heart and library, Shelley was reprimanded with a look of mingled surprise and displeasure for his presumption in taking books from the great man's shelves. The welcome accorded to him by the man of fame was attended with limitations and conditions. The house was open to him, but only at times when the master could see him. The library was open to him for the perusal·of such books as their owner put into his hands, or rather for such passages of them as were submitted to his consideration. Eager for approval and acutely sensitive of disrespect, the youngster was quick to perceive that Southey listened to his words with supercilious curiosity and amusement, and in replying to them felt himself talking to an intellectual inferior,—to a mere whimsical scatterbrain singularly devoid of mental discretion; to a youth whose exuberant speech ran on matters of which he knew very little. Taking this view of his young friend, Southey (whose dictatorial air and eloquence had, in his thirty-eighth year, assumed all the overbearing insolence that distinguished him in later time) gave his young friend much equally wholesome and unacceptable admonition, that would have been less ineffectual for good and far less effectual for harm, had it been given in a less offensive manner.

Whilst he never failed to take something more than his proper share of the conversation, in whatever company he found himself at this period of his life, the argumentative Shelley liked to imagine he controlled the minds of the listeners, who were more often silenced than swayed by his excessive loquacity. With comical and characteristic self-complacence he wrote of Mr. Calvert and the Duke of Norfolk's other guests, soon after the visit to Greystoke Castle, 'We met several people at the Duke's. One in particular struck me. He was an elderly man, who seemed to know all my concerns, and the expression of his face, whenever I held the argument, *which I do everywhere*, was such as I shall not readily forget.' The young gentleman who, 'holding the argument everywhere,' pursued his customary course even in the presence of ducal quality, met in Southey's house with an entertainer, no less fond of holding the argument; with a host not at all disposed to be overtalked by a boy, barely half his own age. In Southey, the poet usually went hand-in-hand with the pedagogue; but in his dealings with Shelley, the poet disappeared in the pedagogue, the scholar merged in the schoolmaster,—sometimes in the angry schoolmaster. Instead of withdrawing into silence, Southey met the youngster's vehement assertions with scornful counterstatements, traversed his arguments with caustic speech that turned them to ridicule, or raising his voice poured upon him torrents of invective, that only stung and lashed the beardless disputant to wilder extravagances of speech.

Some of Southey's donnish ways to the irrepressible lad were superlatively exasperating. One of the schoolmaster's tricks was to stop the course of controversy by taking down a book, opening it, and reading a passage in a tone, which implied that the quotation closed the discussion for all minds, accessible to reason. At other times, when Shelley had talked himself purple, this exasperating Southey was content to remark in a tone of galling pity and tenderness, 'No doubt, no doubt; I thought and spoke in just the same way when I was your age.' Few forms of dissent are more irritating to a callow disputant than a suggestion that he thinks what he thinks and says what he says, merely because he is very young and inexperienced. Whilst Southey was writing with sublime compassionateness of the young 'man at Keswick, who acted upon him as his own ghost would,' Shelley wrote from Greta Bank to a correspondent, whose personal acquaintance he had still to make :—'Southey, the poet, whose principles were pure and elevated once, is now the paid champion of every abuse and absurdity. I have had much conversation with him. He says, " You will think as I do when you are as old." I do not feel the least disposition to be Mr. S.'s proselyte.' Recalling how he had dealt and differed with Shelley in Keswick, Southey (vide *The Correspondence of Robert Southey with Caroline Bowles*, 1881) wrote to the author of *Laon and Cythna* in June, 1820 :— 'Eight years ago you were somewhat displeased when I declined disputing with you on points which are beyond the reach of the human intellect,—telling you that the great difference between

us was, that you were then nineteen and I was eight-and-thirty.'
Southey's letter about his own ghost was dated 14th January,
1812; Shelley's letter to Godwin, about 'the poet, whose principles
were pure and elevated once,' was dated just two days later, 16th
January, 1812. Whilst Shelley was nothing more respectable to
Southey than a young simpleton of parts, who might survive his
folly and become a sensible man, Southey was nothing less contemptible in Shelley's eyes than a literary hireling, who defended
every abuse and absurdity he was ordered to defend.

Few were the words spoken in later time to Southey's
advantage, many the words spoken to his ridicule, by the
younger poet, with whom he had wrangled so hotly on the
marge of Derwentwater. One of Shelley's stories, to his enemy's
discredit, was the droll account of the way he was led by Southey
into his little upstairs study, locked into the narrow chamber, and
then 'read' into unconsciousness by his merciless captor; the
thing thus read to the captive's stupefaction being one of the
captor's poems in manuscript. Charmed with the beauties of
his own creation, the author read on slowly and distinctly, till
the listener would fain have escaped from the scene of his
punishment; read on till the listener nodded from drowsiness,
instead of approval; read on till the whilom unwilling listener
had ceased to listen; read on till the same whilom listener slipt
from his seat to the floor; and still read on till, on looking up
from his manuscript for something more flattering than silent
admiration, he looked in vain for him who should have given it.
The Southey of this comical anecdote may well have been surprised at the listener's unaccountable disappearance. How had
he escaped?—Not by the door, for it was locked; nor by the
window, for it was barred; nor by the chimney, for it was too
narrow. The poet's wonder at the listener's disappearance was
exchanged for wonder at his insensibility and indifference to
what was loveliest in poetic art, when, on looking under the
table, he discovered the whilom listener, lying at full length on
the carpet, and wrapt in profoundest slumber. It is suggested
by the humorous Hogg that, if Shelley had kept his chair and
consciousness, during the reading of the long poem, he would
never have been placed by the naturally indignant bard on the
roll of the Satanic School.

Mr. Denis Florence MacCarthy, by the way, discovers cause
for virtuous indignation at Hogg's monstrous untruthfulness, in

representing that the poem, which acted thus soporifically on Shelley, was *The Curse of Kehama*. The poem of *The Curse* had been published long before Shelley set foot in Southey's house. Even whilst he was at Oxford, Shelley had taken from a printed copy of *The Curse* four lines to serve as a motto for the title-page of his own sublime and undiscoverable poem (that possibly was never written), *On the Existing State of Things*. It is infinitely absurd to suppose Southey read in manuscript one of his *old* poems to Shelley at Keswick. In saying Southey was guilty of this offence, Hogg said what was untrue. It follows that Hogg was a reckless writer, false biographer, and bad man. The fun of the matter is that Hogg does not say the poem *was The Curse of Kehama*. On the contrary, he is at pains to say he is uncertain whether it was *The Curse*, or some other of the poet's metrical performances. 'The poem, if I mistake not, was *The Curse of Kehama*,' are the words of the biographer, who is so rashly assailed for inaccuracy, though in his mere repetition of Shelley's piquant anecdote, he is so careful to say the poem of the story may *not* have been the *Curse*. It is thus that, in his passion for defaming Hogg, Mr. Denis Florence MacCarthy pelts him with any stone, or stick, or bit of dirt that comes to hand.

The incident of the story, if it was a real one, cannot be supposed to have taken place when Mrs. Southey regaled the stranger from southern England with the tea-cakes, which he devoured so ravenously, after abusing them with the vehemence of unqualified prejudice. Had he at that time offered her husband the affront of going to sleep at the poetical-reading, the lady would scarcely have pressed Shelley so cordially to partake of the tea and hot buttered tea-cakes, blushing with currants, or sprinkled with caraway seed, with which she and her poet were regaling themselves, at the close of washing-day.

'Why! good God, Southey!' the younger poet is reported to have exclaimed, with a look of disgust at the unromantic fare, 'I am ashamed of you! It is awful, horrible, to see such a man as you are, greedily devouring this nasty stuff.'

'Nasty stuff, indeed!' cried Mrs. Southey. 'How dare you call my tea-cakes nasty stuff?'

To assuage the lady's wrath, Shelley scanned the cakes, sniffed their savour, took up a piece of one of them, and ate it. Scent and palate convincing Shelley that it was an occasion for prompt recantation of a sentiment formed from the mere appearance of things, he went to work at the remaining tea-cakes, devouring them even more greedily than Southey. Another plate of the hot and buttered cakes being brought to the board, Shelley took something more than his full share of them, and was hoping for the appearance of yet a third plate, when he learnt that more could not be had, the whole batch having been eaten to the last fragment and crumb. Hogg had the story of Mrs. Southey's tea-cakes from Harriett (West-brook) Shelley, who added, naïvely, ' We were to have hot tea-cakes every evening " for ever." I was to make them myself, and Mrs. Southey was to teach me.'

The story has considerable biographical value, as an example of Shelley's alternate abstemiousness and self-indulgence in food. Resembling Byron in habitual abstinence and indifference to the quality of the fare that sustained him, Shelley also resembled Byron in occasional acts of feasting that might almost be called excesses of greediness. Hogg gives a piquant account of a meal Shelley made off eggs and bacon, in the parlour of a humble inn on Hounslow Heath, at a time subsequent to his union with William Godwin's daughter, when, as a vegetarian, he had for a considerable period regarded pork with abhorrence. Entering the modest tavern, at a moment when Hogg was about to assail a goodly dish of the gross and abominable meat, the hungry poet eyed the bacon with disgust, looked at it with curiosity, sniffed its alluring savour, regarded it longingly, just as he had in former time regarded Mrs. Southey's tea-cakes. 'So this is bacon,' he observed daintily, taking a morsel of the meat on the end of a fork, and putting it into his mouth. Having tasted fat, he fell from the purity of abstinence to the uncleanness of carnal enjoyment. Having consumed a liberal portion of his friend's dish, he ordered another dish on his own account, and devoured it voraciously. Sharpened with what it fed upon, his appetite caused him to cry aloud, 'Bring more bacon;' an order that was speedily followed by the appearance of a third dish. After despatching this third dish, the poet demanded a fourth, when to his lively annoyance he learnt there was no more bacon in the house. It was debated whether the landlady should not be sent to Staines for more bacon; but Hogg prevailed on his friend to put a bridle on fleshly appetite, and set forth for his cottage at Bishopgate and Mary's well-furnished tea-table. On coming to that tea-table, Shelley astonished his wife by exclaiming eagerly, 'We have been eating bacon together on Hounslow Heath, and do you know it was very nice? Cannot we have bacon here, Mary?' On hearing he could not have bacon till the morrow, but must for the present be content with tea and bread and butter, the poet replied plaintively, 'I would rather have some more bacon.' When a worthy book shall be written on the Feasts of the Poets, it will not fail to tell how Byron, after long spells of fasting, used to devour huge messes of broken potato and stale fish, drenched with vinegar. Nor will it omit to record how Shelley ate poor Mrs. Southey out of buttered tea-cakes, and gorged himself with fried bacon at a pot-house on Hounslow Heath.

Whilst they dispose me to think the famous feast on tea-cakes cannot have preceded the hour when Shelley fell asleep under Southey's poem, circumstances also incline me to think the acrimonious disputations on Irish affairs must have followed the first day of Shelley's entertainment at Greta Bank. Anyhow, it is certain that the Shelleys and Southeys were on friendly terms, when the former took up their abode in Mr. Calvert's house. The garden at Greta Bank was the 'pretty garden' of the piquant story known to every reader of De Quincey's curiously inaccurate paper about Shelley. It was to a question, put to her by one of the Southey party, then calling upon her in her new quarters, that Mrs. Shelley replied, with winning childishness, 'Oh, no, the garden is not ours; but then, you know, the people let us run about in it, whenever Percy and I are tired of sitting in the house;' an utterance that, coming from the girlish wife, may well have amused the married ladies to whom it was made.

Nor is it conceivable that Southey and Shelley had exchanged hot and disdainful words on questions of Irish politics, when the younger poet, overflowing with pitiful speech on subjects about which he should not have uttered a syllable to so slight an acquaintance, told Southey the story of Harriett's conversion to Atheism, and the still more revolting tale of Hogg's attempt to seduce her. By the first of these excesses of communicativeness, Southey was informed how Shelley had busied himself in making proselytes in Mrs. Fenning's boarding-school; how Harriett Westbrook was expelled the school for accepting his doctrine and aiding him in his purpose; and how he had married her, in order to render her the *amende honorable* for the disgrace and trouble he had brought upon her. The second of the amazing stories was, that on their journey from Edinburgh to York Hogg had attempted to debauch his friend's bride, so soon after her marriage. Telling these things to his wife's discredit and Hogg's infamy, Shelley spoke frankly of his disapproval of marriage. About the same time, either from Shelley's own lips, or from the lips of some other informant, it came to Southey's knowledge that, since coming to Keswick, Shelley had told his wife expressly, that he regarded the marriage-rite as a ceremony of no binding force, and that he should leave her on ceasing to love her. Having no doubt the statements thus made to Harriett *at* Keswick were a mere repetition of statements made to her by Shelley *before* their marriage, Southey had reasons in 1820 for declining to believe that, after deciding to wed one another by lawful form, either she or Shelley had entered the compact on the Free Love understanding that they should be at liberty to separate on ceasing to like one another. One could wish Southey had stated more precisely how much of his knowledge of Shelley's nuptial and pre-nuptial relations to Harriett came to him from Shelley's own lips, and how much from other informants. It is, however, certain that Southey received from Shelley's own tongue, his information, or misinformation, touching the circumstances of Harriett's alleged expulsion from school, touching Shelley's alleged motive for marrying her, and touching the attempt said to have been made by Hogg on her honour. Whether the allegation to Hogg's infamy should be deemed good evidence against the law-student is a question to be considered in a subsequent chapter. For the present, it is enough to observe that Shelley spoke to Southey at Keswick on divers delicate personal matters, about which even he would scarcely have opened mind and heart to so recent an acquaintance had they already squabbled fiercely on Irish affairs.

Because Shelley introduced a virtuous Irishman into the later part of *St. Irvyne*, and published in the *Posthumous Fragments of Margaret Nicholson* some metrical trash about a banshee's moan, and a white courser, bestridden by a shadow sprite, Mr. Denis Florence MacCarthy would have us believe, that Shelley did not leave Oxford without seriously interesting

himself in the history and legends of Ireland, and entertaining
a purpose to redress the wrongs of her miserable people. Here
are Mr. Denis Florence MacCarthy's own words :—

'One of them' (*i.e.* the poems of the *Posthumous Fragments*)
'*The Spectral Horseman*, is interesting as showing that at this early
period, Shelley had begun to take that interest in the history and legends
of Ireland, which led to such extraordinary results two years later. We
have here "The Banshee's moan on the storm;" "A white courser," like
that of O'Donoghue, "bears the shadowy sprite;" "The whirlwinds howl
in the caves of Innisfallen,"—

> "Then does the dragon, who, chained in the caverns
> To eternity, curses the champion of Erin,
> Moan and yell loud at the lone hour of midnight."

Fragments, page 25.

'Extravagant as all these passages are, they show Shelley's sympathies for Ireland had already been awakened, and that his practical
efforts for her benefit at a later period were not the result of any sudden
or passing caprice.'

What evidence that a youngster—living in the times of
Moore, and Maturin, and Sydney Morgan; in times when the
popularity of the 'Irish Melodies' had called into existence a
score imitators of their author; in times when romantic Irish
ballads and patriotic Irish ballads lay on every drawing-room
table; in times when to humour the prevailing taste for fiction
about Ireland, and to profit by the demand for Irish tales at
circulating libraries, Lady Morgan christened one of her stories
The Wild Irish Girl, though no such girl played a part in the
narrative,—was a serious student of Irish history and legends,
and had entered on a course of inquiry and thought, that naturally resulted in a resolve to visit Ireland, for the purpose of
striking the manacles from the bruised and bleeding limbs of
Fair Erin! Thus is it that Shelley's story has been told by his
fanciful idolaters.

The instruction given (November 26th, 1811) to Mr. Medwin,
the Horsham lawyer, to find a Sussex cottage for the poet's
habitation, is a sufficient proof that Shelley at that time designed
to settle ere long in his native county. When a man speaks to
his lawyer on such a matter, he may be assumed to mean what
he says. Shelley's written words to the man of business were:
'We do not intend to take up our abode here for a perpetuity,
but should wish to have a house in Sussex. Let it be in some

picturesque, retired place—St. Leonard's Forest, for instance. Let it not be nearer to London than Horsham, nor near any *populous* manufacturing town. We do not covet either a propinquity to *barracks*.' The young man who wrote with this amplitude and precision must have meant what he said. He could not afford to hire a house and let it stand empty. With no purpose of staying a long time at Keswick, he wished for a house in Sussex to retire to, in the company of his wife and sister-in-law, when he should withdraw from the lakes. This was his plan when he entered Keswick; and when he had been there some weeks.

What made him relinquish this scheme for a home? Probably he relinquished it at the advice and with the approval of his wife and her sister, and also in accordance with his own judgment, immediately after the visit to Greystoke Castle, and Mr. Calvert's offer to take them into his house. When they had been received at the Castle—not for a mere formal dinner, not for a brief three nights' stay, but for a visit of several (eight or nine) days—the prospect of living for a considerable time at Keswick must have been acceptable to both the sisters; to the gentle and lovable Harriett, who had several reasons for thinking such a residence would be for her husband's advantage,— and to the scheming and ambitious Eliza, who, in some degree sincerely desirous for Harriett's and Percy's welfare, was chiefly ambitious of taking rank with gentlewomen. Exulting in her reception at Greystoke Castle,—a reception that qualified her to speak of the Duchess of Norfolk as her friend, and gave her the castle-mark of gentility in the eyes of the 'highest quality' of and near Keswick—Miss Westbrook, we may be sure, was in no hurry to withdraw from the neighbourhood, that was the scene of her sweetest social triumph; from the town that necessarily rated her one of the Greystoke circle. It was manifest to the prudent and ambitious Miss Westbrook, that nothing could be more favourable to her own hopes, and aims, and interest, than such a residence at Keswick as would plant her amongst the local 'quality,' and result in future invitations to the Castle,— nothing more certain to please her money-grubbing and upward-looking father; nothing more likely to conciliate Percy's wrathful father; no course more likely to end in her own admission to Field Place during the life of Percy's mother.

At the same time it was no less manifest to Miss Westbrook

that a better place of residence than Keswick could not be found for her youthful and erratic brother-in-law during the next two or three years. Living in Sussex he would be a perpetual irritant to his irritable father. Living in Cumberland he would be out of his father's way, and under the fewest temptations to exasperate him to fiercer anger. Not only would he be out of his father's way in Cumberland, but living there, in a certain sense, under the Duke of Norfolk's patronage, he would be passing his time under conditions most likely to confirm the Duke in his friendly disposition towards him, and therefore most likely to result in the reconciliation of the father and son. At Keswick her brother-in-law would have literary society, form literary friendships, and have access to the libraries of his literary friends. On hearing her brother-in-law enjoyed the Duke of Norfolk's favour, and meant to remain for a considerable time at Greta Bank, Miss Westbrook was hopeful that Mr. De Quincey would soon call upon him. On their return to the lakes, Mr. Samuel Taylor Coleridge and Mr. John Wilson would make his acquaintance. Mr. Wordsworth might hold aloof from the new-comers for a time, but in some way or other he would extend the hand of good-fellowship to them, soon after Coleridge's reappearance in his favourite haunts. Living with such friends, Percy would read many books, and write a wonderful poem, that, raising him yet higher in the omnipotent Duke's good opinion, would restore him to his father's favour, and open the doors of Field Place to his wife and her sister. These were Miss Westbrook's views of the position and prospect. No one can say they were unreasonable views. Had they been so, Harriett would have accepted them out of her usual submissiveness to so incomparable a sister. But there was no need for Miss Westbrook to force her views of these matters on her sister, who, without guidance or instruction of any kind, had come to the same conclusions. Harriett and Eliza had seldom been of different opinions on anything up to this point of their story. At least for once, the concurrence of their sentiments was in no degree due to the elder sister's authority.

Whilst Harriett and Miss Westbrook both liked the notion of living at Keswick for a considerable period, Shelley also favoured it. One consequence of Shelley's enthusiasm and nervous vehemence was that, whilst he was the most changeable of mortals in some matters, he seldom did a thing once without at the same time intending to do it 'for ever.' A restless vagrant from his manhood's threshold to his death, he seldom entered a picturesque place without declaring he would live in it 'for ever.' He was perpetually doing things 'for ever,' and undoing them a few days or weeks later. He never made a friendship with man or woman without vowing the league should be perpetual. He went to York with the intention of living there 'for ever.' He declared he would love Hogg 'for ever.' He vowed he would live 'for ever' in friendship with Miss Hitchener, of Hurstpierpoint, and no long time afterwards vowed just as passionately and sincerely to hate her 'for ever.' It mattered not to him in periods of passionate excitement, that in his opinion love and all other sentimental preferences were mere consequences of perception and wholly independent of volition. It mattered not that 'Love was free,' and that in his judgment 'To promise for ever to love the same woman was not less absurd than to promise to believe the same creed,' because such a vow excluded its maker from inquiries he might be constrained to make, and from new judgments he might be compelled to form, and was therefore by the nature of things powerless to bind its utterer when the mental perceptions required him to disregard it. All the same, he never desired human affection without praying for it, in order that he might enjoy it ' for ever,'—never wished vehemently for anything without hoping, in his emotional intensity, to get happiness from it 'for ever.' He promised to love Harriett Westbrook 'for ever,' whilst believing himself to be so constituted that at no distant time he might be powerless to love her at all. In the same spirit, with the same fervour, and the same perception of love's fickleness and instability, he carried off Mary Godwin with avowals that he would love her 'for ever.' When Claire, in the 'Six weeks' tour,' exclaimed with delight at each new scene of loveliness, ' Let us live here,' the lively and humorous girl was laughing in her sleeve at Shelley's practice of declaring he would 'live for ever' in any place, that pleased him greatly at first sight. Allowance must be made for Shelley's vehement emotionality and extravagance of diction by readers who would not be misled by his use of ' ever ' and 'never' in matters of his own personal story.

In the absence of positive evidence to the point, I have little doubt that Shelley entered the rooms assigned to him in Mr. Calvert's house with a declaration that he would inhabit them 'for ever,' and that the sisters who had him in their keeping entered the same rooms with a strong opinion that he would do well to inhabit them for a considerable time. He would scarcely have remained in them for seven weeks had he not taken possession of them with the intention of occupying them for as many years. How was it then that he withdrew so soon from so eligible an abode? Certainly the cause was neither a sudden dislike of Keswick, nor a diminution of his affectionate regard for Mr. and Mrs. Calvert. There exists testimony in his own handwriting that he left Keswick with regret, and the Calverts with a hope to see more of them. 'I hope,' he wrote to a friend from Whitehaven on 3rd February, 1812, as he was on the point of sailing for Ireland, ' some day to show you Mrs. Calvert; I shall not forget her, but will preserve her memory as another flower to compose a garland which I intend to present to you.' How came he then to tear himself away at the beginning of February, 1812, from a place he liked, · and from friends in whom he delighted? How was it that, on tearing himself from this place and these friends, he went off to Ireland,—an expedition he certainly cannot have thought of making when, on 26th November, 1811, he wrote to Mr. Medwin, of Horsham, about a house in Sussex? How are we to account for the change of purpose that sent him on a mission to Ireland for the Repeal of the Union and the Emancipation of the Catholics? Successive writers have either declared their inability to answer this question, or have answered it in the wrong way.

Confessing his inability to answer the question, Hogg conjectures that some Irish frequenter of the Mount Street coffeehouse, or some Hibernian Hampden, encountered by Shelley on the hills of Cumberland, may have inspired Shelley with an ambition to settle all the Irish questions, and put a period to all the Irish grievances, by making the voyage to Dublin, and speaking words of wisdom to its inhabitants. Mr. Denis Florence MacCarthy is certain that this new project for the pacification of Ireland was the natural result of Shelley's Oxonian study of Irish history and legends; that the poet went to Ireland of his own mere motion, after coming slowly and dispassionately to a strong and reasonable opinion that he would do Ireland good service, by visiting her capital, and in the course of a few weeks converting her children to moderation, temperance, industry, orderliness, and universal political amenity. The present writer is no less certain that Shelley's Oxonian concern for Irish literature had nothing to do with his marvellous scheme for settling Irish difficulties; that his premature departure from Keswick was mainly due to his dislike of Southey; and that his Irish mission was the outcome of sentiments arising from his acrimonious disputations with the same poet on questions of Irish politics.

It is not surprising that the man of letters and his young friend exchanged their views on questions that engaged the attention of all persons interested in the politics of the United Kingdom. It would have been strange had the *Quarterly* Reviewer and the literary aspirant—the mature Tory, who spoke disdainfully of his former republicanism as mere boyish effervescence, and the youthful enthusiast of the revolutionary school—differed amicably on matters, so calculated to stir the ·temper of either disputant. Whilst they were alike fervid and intolerant, each had a manner peculiarly irritating to the other, as soon as their pulses quickened under verbal contention. Overbearing and contemptuous, even to those who agreed with him, Southey soon grew insufferably dogmatic and disdainful to the boy who had the presumption to contradict him. Never remarkable for a reverential and conciliatory demeanour to those of his elders who ventured to teach him what he did not wish to be taught, Shelley soon ceased to show his opponent the respect due from him to a man, so greatly his superior by age, experience, and achievement. Southey's attempts to snub his young friend into submissiveness, and lecture him into sensible views, only stirred and stung Shelley to declare in shriller notes his repugnance to the views that were forced upon him in so dictatorial a manner. On finding that in Southey's study and presence he was expected to hold silence and take instruction, the young gentleman (*ætat.* 19), who deemed himself qualified 'to hold the argument everywhere,' became furious. Of course, everything Southey said in this insolent style, against the Irish, only made Shelley think, or confirmed him in thinking, the reverse. The more insultingly he was told that all Ireland needed was firm government and the steady maintenance of existing laws, the more clear was it to Shelley that Ireland's chief need was the gentle rule of new and humane laws. Southey's assertions that

easoning was wasted on the Irish, for whose government the
bayonet was the best instrument, only made Shelley more
positive that the Irish were a gentle, generous, and reasonable
people, who could be reasoned into virtuous behaviour, and be
cured by sympathetic and persuasive speech of their faults and
failings,—faults and failings chiefly, if not altogether, due to
the tyranny under which they had groaned so long.

To show that he was altogether right, and the exasperating
Southey altogether wrong, about Ireland and the Irish, Shelley
set to work with his pen on the production of *An Address to the
Irish People*, that, written at Keswick in the last month of 1811
and the first month of 1812, was printed and published at
Dublin in February, 1812. As the words of this curious and
delightfully boyish composition fell to the paper, it struck the
author that it would be well for him to visit Ireland, and enforce
with his persuasive tongue the wholesome admonitions of his
pen,—and very pleasant for him, and Harriett, and Eliza, to
observe in the streets of Dublin the first signs of that conversion
of the Irish people to thrift, industry, temperance, and tolerance, which could not fail to be the immediate consequence of
the publication of so excellent an essay. This notion of going
to Ireland, for the purpose of contributing to, and witnessing
the success of, his pamphlet, was the more agreeable to Shelley
because he was eager to get away from the odious Southey, and
because, in going to Ireland (of all places of the earth's surface)
to get out of the renegade's way, he would exhibit, in a
singularly telling and emphatic manner, his contempt for all
that had been urged to the discredit of the dear Irish people
by the malignant apostate from pantisocratic and other republican principles. Under these circumstances, is it wonderful
that the later slips of the *Address* were written in the midst
of arrangements for the author's expedition to the land, that
could be so speedily recovered from rancour and wretchedness
to contentment and prosperity?

Whilst writing the *Address to the Irish People* at Greta
Bank, Shelley found other employment for his pen, in producing
verses to Robert Emmett's glorification, with other additions
to the collection of poems which he designed to publish in
Dublin; and in throwing off letters to Miss Eliza Hitchener, of
Hurstpierpoint, near Brighton, and to a certain famous author
and struggling bookseller, who must have experienced emotions

of amusement and self-complacence on perusing the first of the
letters, in which the author of the *Necessity of Atheism*
approached William Godwin with expressions of profoundest
reverence, several months before he was permitted to gaze on
the altogether human lineaments of the divine philosopher.

In the first of these letters (a letter dated from Keswick on 3rd
January, 1812, though it is one of the many blunders of Mr. Kegan
Paul's book about Godwin to insist that it was written from
Keswick ten months before Shelley set foot in the place) Shelley
assures the addressee of the epistle that 'the name of Godwin
has been used to excite in him feelings of reverence and admiration;' that he has been 'accustomed to consider' the
sublime Godwin as 'a luminary too dazzling for the darkness
which surrounds him;' and that after long regarding the sublime
Godwin regretfully as one of 'the honourable dead,' as a
personage 'the glory of whose being had passed from this
earth of ours,' he has learned with 'inconceivable emotions' that
so great a benefactor of his species still has an earthly existence
and an earthly habitation in Skinner Street, in the City of
London. 'It is not so,' ejaculates the writer of the adulatory
epistle; 'you still live, and, I firmly believe, are still planning
the welfare of human kind.' It was in this strain of extravagant and obsequious reverence that Shelley approached, in
January, 1812, the man whose house he entered some months
later, whose hospitality he accepted freely as it was proffered,
and whose sixteen-years-old daughter he lured into Free Love
two and a half years later. It is also well for the reader to
know and remember, that at the time of writing this characteristic epistle, the singularly truth-loving Shelley had not recently
discovered with inconceivable emotion that Godwin was still
living and following his trade in Skinner Street. The evidences
are clear that the sentimental words about the writer's regret
for the death of the too dazzling luminary were untrue words.

The dazzling luminary, who would perhaps have left the
letter unanswered, had not its adulation tickled his self-complacence agreeably, replied in terms that caused the young
enthusiast to produce an autobiographic fragment for his
correspondent's enlightenment. Writing from Keswick on
10th January, 1812, to the philosopher of Skinner Street,
Shelley (after the customary announcement of his filial relation
to 'a man of fortune in Sussex') remarks that his habits of

hinking never coincided with his father's habits of thinking;
hat it was his misfortune in childhood to be 'required to love,
>ecause it was his duty to love' his father, a system of coercion
vhich, of course, rendered it impossible for him to love his
ather; and that he published his two novels (*St. Irvyne* and
Zastrozzi) before he was seventeen years of age,—a statement
iot a little wide of historic truth. Instead of publishing these
>ooks when he was at Eton, and only sixteen years of age, he
vas seventeen years and ten months old when he published the
arlier story, and eighteen years and four months old when he
>ublished the later tale, both romances having appeared whilst
ie was a member of University College, Oxford. These in-
ccuracies are followed in the letter by a more remarkable
xample of the writer's inaccuracy in statements touching his
>ersonal affairs. Representing that he read Godwin's *Political
Justice*, and adopted its views, whilst he was at Eton, he adds,
No sooner had I formed the principles which I now profess
han I was anxious to disseminate their benefits. This was
lone without the slightest caution. I was twice expelled, but
ecalled by the interference of my father.' All this is repre-
ented to have taken place at Eton before he 'went to Oxford;'
et it is certain that he never published anything controversial
>n the questions raised in the *Political Justice* whilst he was at
Eton, and no less certain that he was not twice expelled from
he school for doing so. Though he left Eton prematurely,
ind with a bad name, his dismissal from the school differed so
videly from expulsion, that he would not have been justified in
peaking of himself as having been expelled once.

In the same letter (of 10th January, 1812, to Godwin)
Shelley says of the circumstances of his expulsion from Oxford,

'I printed a pamphlet, avowing my opinions and its occasion.
. . . . . Mr. ——, at Oxford, among others, had the pamphlet; he
howed it to the Master and the Fellows of University College, and I was
ent for. I was informed that in case I denied the publication, no more
vould be said. I refused and was expelled.'

It is scarcely needful for me to remind the readers of
his work, that the collegiate authorities never told him he
:ould escape punishment by disclaiming the publication;
iever urged him to deny the publication; never expelled him
or refusing to deny it. The whole statement is untrue in

every particular. What made him pen these untruths, with or without cognizance of their absolute untruthfulness? Even taking the most charitable view of his friend's most perplexing infirmity, Hogg maintains that Shelley had no intention of misstating the case when he misstated it so egregiously.

'This is incorrect,' says Hogg; 'no such offer was made, no such information was given; but musing on the affair, as he was wont, he dreamed that the proposal had been declined by him, and thus he had the gratification of believing that he was more of a martyr than he really was.'

Yet further Shelley writes in the same delusive style in the same epistle :—

'It will be necessary, in order to elucidate this part of my history, to inform you that I am heir by entail to an estate of £6000 per annum. . . . . . . My father has ever regarded me as a blot, a defilement of his honour. He wished to induce me by poverty to accept of some commission in a distant regiment, and in the interim of my absence to prosecute the pamphlet, that a process of outlawry might make the estate on his death devolve to my younger brother. These are the leading points of the history of the man before you. . . . . . . I am married to a woman whose views are similar to my own. To you, as the regulator and former of my mind, I must ever look with real respect and veneration.'

Readers should notice and remember each of the several untruthful statements of this extract. (1) It was untrue that the Squire of Field Place had 'ever regarded' his son 'as a blot and defilement of his honour.' (2) It was untrue that the Squire had endeavoured to force his son to accept a commission in a distant regiment in order that, during his absence on military service, he might deprive him by legal process of his birthright to the advantage of his younger brother. (3) It was untrue that the Squire had put pressure on his son to enter the army, though it has been suggested by one of the poet's several friendly biographers that, soon after his expulsion from Oxford, it may perhaps have been suggested to the unruly boy that he should adopt the military profession, like his cousin Tom Medwin, who went from the University into a cavalry regiment. (4) The father who had dealt so leniently and tenderly with his son on first hearing of his academic disgrace, never for an instant entertained a thought of compassing the

prosecution of the author and printer of the scandalous tract.
Of the malicious purpose and scheme, attributed to the kindly
though irascible Squire of Field Place by the boy to whom he
had been a considerate and good father, Hogg says justly :—

'It is only in a dream that the prosecution, outlawry, and devo-
lution of the estate could find place. The narration of such proceedings
would have been too strong and strange for a German romance ; it
would have been too large a requisition upon the reader's credulity to
ask him to credit them in the father of *Zastrozzi*. . . . .'

One may well smile at such egregious ignorance of law
and affairs in the self-confident youth, who was preparing to
visit Ireland in order to Emancipate the Catholics, Repeal the
Union, and instruct the whole Irish people in political science.
It is, however, no matter for smiling that this young scatterbrain, whom his adulators compare with the Saviour of the
World, penned these egregious inventions to his father's discredit in a letter to a person, with whom he had no domestic
connexion,—to a stranger, of whom he knew nothing, save
that he was a writer of entertaining and clever books.

Readers must settle for themselves whether the untruthful
statements were sheer and wilful untruths, or the fruits of misconception scarcely compatible with mental sanity, or products
of a state of mind that would justify the critic in adopting
Peacock's term, and speaking of them as results of 'semi-
delusion.' On these points there may be room for differences
of opinion ; but it must be obvious to all judicious readers that
in putting the erroneous statements on paper, the generous and
chivalric Shelley was actuated by a desire to exhibit his father
as an unnatural and treacherous parent to the man of letters, to
whom the epistle was addressed. Had the Squire of Field
Place been the bad father Shelley declared him, it was not for
Shelley to say so in a letter to a stranger. Even to his nearest
and dearest friend—even to so familiar a comrade as Hogg, in
the time of their most affectionate intimacy—Shelley would
have been silent on so painful and shameful a subject, had he
been the loyal and chivalrous being his idolaters would have us
think him.

Readers may also reflect on the different strain in which
Shelley, only a few weeks earlier, wrote of his father to the
Duke of Norfolk. Godwin, the stranger, is informed by Shelley

that his father regards him as a blot and defilement; that his father had striven to force him out of the country into distant military service; that his father had designed to institute legal proceedings against him for writing *The Necessity of Atheism*; that his father had desired to despoil him of his birthright, and place his younger brother next in succession to the family estate. These statements are made to the stranger, who is not likely to know the real causes of his correspondent's estrangement from his father. But in Shelley's letter to the Duke of Norfolk, who knows all about the domestic question and the Squire's treatment of his son, it is not suggested by Shelley that 'the pamphlet' had anything to do with his father's anger. On the contrary, his father's extreme displeasure with him is attributed to the real cause—his marriage, and the circumstances of the *més-alliance*. Why this difference? To those who answer that, whereas Shelley was in his right mind when writing to the Duke of Norfolk, and labouring under delusions when writing to William Godwin, it must appear curiously significant and suggestive of another conclusion—that he wrote truthfully of his affairs to the correspondent who (to his knowledge) knew the truth of them, and altogether untruthfully about his affairs to the person whom he had reason to think ignorant of them.

Godwin's answer to the letter containing these inaccurate statements is not extant; but it is on the evidences that the philosopher's reply indicated surprise at, and disapproval of, the terms in which his youthful correspondent had spoken of his father. Finding he had exhibited himself in an unfavourable light to the author of *Political Justice*, Shelley hastened to retrieve the false step, and recover his correspondent's good opinion by writing (14th January, 1812), in his third letter from Keswick to Skinner Street:—

'You mistake me if you think that I am angry with my father. I have ever been desirous of a reconciliation with him, but the price which he demands for it is a renunciation of my opinions, or, at least a subjection to conditions which should bind me to act in opposition to their very spirit. It is probable that my father has acted for my welfare . . . . .'

Neither misconception nor semi-delusion can be pleaded for Shelley's statement that he was not angry with his father. It was not true that he had 'ever been desirous of a reconciliation

with his father.' The two statements were untruths, told by
Shelley in order to set himself right with his correspondent.
For the same purpose he now admits that his father (charged
in the previous letter with an execrable design for depriving
him of his birthright) may have acted for his welfare.   Other
words of the extract should have the reader's thoughtful consideration.   One of the charges against the Squire of Field
Place being that, after banishing his son from his boyhood's
home at the instigation of religious intolerance, he required his
son's renunciation of his sincere opinions as the condition for their
reconcilement, it is well for readers of the poet's story to take
especial notice of his admission that, instead of being required to
renounce his opinions, he was only required to 'submit to conditions which should bind him to act in opposition to their very
spirit,' words of qualification which, coming from Shelley, are
sufficient evidence to the moderation and reasonableness of the
conditions.   There is a wide difference between a demand for
the renunciation of opinions and a demand for abstinence from
noisy and aggressive assertion of them ; and the father who
requires a youngster in his nonage to hold his pen and tongue
on certain subjects of difficult and perilous controversy is guilty
of no despotic excess of paternal authority.   The forbearance
which Mr. Timothy Shelley had required of his son was in
truth nothing more than the forbearance which William
Godwin was already urging the youngster to exercise for
his own advantage.   'I will not again,' Shelley writes to his
newly selected Mentor, 'crudely obtrude my peculiar opinions
or my doubts on the world ;' a promise which he, of course, had
no intention of keeping ; a promise he was, even at the moment
of making it, on the point of breaking in the imbecile *Address
to the Irish People.*   Had he made the same promise to his father
and kept it, there would have been peace between them,—at
least on mere matters of opinion.

Writing to William Godwin, on 16th January, 1812, a letter
that affords some curious examples of the obsequious adulation
with which he approached the man of letters, whose friendship
he was desirous of winning, Shelley remarked :—

'I have known no tutor or adviser (*not excepting my father*) from
whose lessons and suggestions I have not recoiled with disgust. The
knowledge which I have, whatever it may be (putting out of the
question the age of grammar and the horn-book), has been acquired by

my unassisted efforts. I have before given you a slight sketch of my earlier habits and feelings—my present are, in my opinion, infinitely superior—they are elevated and disinterested; such as they are, you have principally produced them.'

'I have known no tutor or adviser (*not excepting my father*) from whose lessons and suggestions I have not recoiled with disgust.' This language is no less comprehensive than precise. Including all his schoolmasters and other official teachers, it includes all his advisers and social monitors—includes even his own father. How about Dr. Lind?—the wise, the humane, the gentle and large-minded Dr. Lind? the physician who trained him in science and philosophy, and carried him through brain-fever at Field Place? the benign hermit of *Laon and Cythna*, the persuasive teacher of *Prince Athanase?* Readers cannot need to be reminded of all Shelley told Hogg and his second wife about the wise physician's influence on his mental and moral development; of the poetic egotisms of *Laon and Cythna* and *Prince Athanase*, that glorified the doctor for having been the beneficent illuminator of his pupil's young mind; the poetic egotisms which Mrs. Shelley accepted, and the present Lady Shelley regards, as severely accurate autobiographic evidence. Taking them *au pied de la lettre* Lady Shelley argues from these scraps of egotistic verse as though they were historic *data* of unimpeachable authority. Lady Shelley is confident that Dr. Lind ('the erudite scholar and amiable old man,' as she styles him) was one of Shelley's Eton tutors, —a tutor in whom he delighted at school, and remembered in after-life with love and veneration. Yet Shelley assures us that up to January, 1812, he never had tutor or adviser of any kind from whose lessons and suggestions he had not recoiled with disgust. Did Shelley really recoil with disgust from the hard-swearing doctor who taught him to curse his father?—from the enlightened physician who guided his 'scientific studies?' Or had he clean forgotten the doctor and all his virtuous ways when he was writing from Keswick to William Godwin? To those who answer this last question in the affirmative, it must seem strange that Dr. Lind, with all his virtue and wisdom, was so completely forgotten by the young gentleman, whom he had influenced so strongly and agreeably so few years since. If Dr. Lind was so great a power in the poet's education as trustful readers of his poetry imagine, it is passing strange that Shelley never remembered him when he was recalling his teachers and their services in the first month of 1812. By those who attribute the frequent inaccuracies of his personal statements to a fertile fancy, an innocent and unconscious inventiveness, it must be considered that Shelley's unruly and too vigorous imagination was suspiciously associated with an unreliable (though often strongly retentive) memory,—that whilst curiously apt to imagine things had taken place which had never occurred, he was also at times strangely forgetful of matters that he might well have been thought certain to remember.

On learning from this same Keswick letter of 16th January, 1812, that Shelley had made up his mind to go shortly to Dublin, with his wife and sister-in-law, for the purpose of furthering, to the utmost of their joint powers, the cause of Catholic Emancipation, Godwin (who seems to have been vastly delighted with the letters from Keswick, whilst seeing much to disapprove in them) sent his youthful and enthusiastic correspondent a letter of introduction to Curran, the Irish Master of the Rolls. In the letter which acknowledged the note of introduction as 'a great and essential service,' Shelley (28th January, 1812) referred apologetically to the lawfulness of his union with Harriett Westbrook, as a concession he made to despotic usage from 'considerations of the unequally weighty burden of disgrace and hatred, which a resistance to this system' (*i.e.* of lawful wedlock) 'would entail upon his companion' in connubial felicity. Yet further in defence of his politic 'submission to the ceremonies of the Church,' and in reference to the uneven consequences of the other and in some respects better course, he remarked, 'a man in such a case, is a man of gallantry and spirit—a woman loses all claim to respect and politeness. She has lost modesty, which is the female criterion of virtue, and those, whose virtues extend no further than modesty, regard her with hatred and contempt.'

Unaware how completely Godwin had abandoned certain of his earlier views respecting wedlock (*i.e.* (1) that in the existing state of English society the existence of mutual love was a sufficient sanction of the conjugal association of a man and woman; (2) that where such love existed it was better for spouses to live together in the liberty of Free Love than in the bondage of lawful marriage; and (3) that the institution of lawful matrimony was a demoralizing interference with the liberty of individuals), Shelley regarded his marriage as a domestic incident, from which he would suffer in the philosopher's esteem, unless he were duly informed of the considerations which had determined Harriett's husband to accommodate his conjugal arrangements to the prejudices of society. But though he wrote thus apologetically of his marriage, in order to place himself higher in the philosopher's favour, Shelley wrote honestly. From his Eton days he had been a favourer of Free Love. But for Hogg, he would have taken Harriett to his embrace without marrying her. He did not relinquish his purpose of uniting himself to her in the loose and easy fashion, until Hogg had made him see the enormity of the disadvantages that would ensue to him and her from the arrangement. The principal reasons he gave in January, 1812, for having married her were the same reasons he gave in the previous August for determining to marry her.

Another thing to be noticed in this statement to Godwin is its evidence how precisely he saw, and how fully he realized, the shameful character of the position held by a woman living conjugally with a man not her lawful husband,—the position in which he, ere long, placed his intimate friend's sixteen-years-old daughter. Whilst the male partner of such an association merely acquired a reputation for gallantry and spirit, the female lost all title to social respect. Whilst he became the gallant keeper of a mistress, she became nothing less contemptible than a kept mistress. The youngster of birth and breeding, who saw this in the January of 1812, saw it no less clearly in the summer of 1814, when he determined to become the gallant keeper of a mistress, and, in violation of one of the most sacred laws of hospitality, prevailed on his intimate friend's sixteen-years-old daughter to accept the position of a mistress.

Shelley did not leave Keswick without a plan for making away with time agreeably in the ensuing summer, when he should have emancipated the Irish Catholics, repealed the Act of Union, and withdrawn from the land he had endowed with perpetual felicity. On 16th January, 1812, he wrote to Godwin: 'In the summer we shall be in the north of Wales. Dare I hope that you will come to see us? Perhaps this would be an unfeasible neglect of your avocations. I shall hope it until you forbid me.' Twelve days later (28th January, 1812), whilst referring lightly to this project for a meeting in Wales, Shelley ventured to express his hope that in the ensuing summer he and Harriett would entertain Mr. and Mrs. Godwin, and their children, in the same romantic spot, where it was their purpose to receive another 'most dear friend.' This 'most dear friend' was Miss Eliza Hitchener of Hurstpierpoint in Sussex, whose acquaintance Shelley had formed whilst staying under his Uncle Pilford's roof at Cuckfield.

Philosopher, Deist, and Republican, Miss Eliza Hitchener kept a school for little girls at Hurstpierpoint, and seems to have enjoyed, in her particular parish of Sussex, a larger measure of social respect than was accorded to her father, the keeper of a public-house in the same neighbourhood, who had been in some way or other concerned in the contraband trade of the Sussex coast, before he changed his name from Yorke to Tichener and joined the noble army of licensed victuallers. Thus much was discovered about Miss Hitchener and her father from the letter, written by Joint-Postmaster-General, the Earl of Chichester, to the Secretary of the General Post Office on 5th April, 1812 :—' Miss Hichener,' the Earl wrote, ' of Hurstpierpoint, keeps a school there, and is well spoken of ; her Father keeps a Publick House in the neighbourhood ; he was originally a smugler, and changed his name from Yorke to Tichener, before he took the Publick House.' The statesman, who spelt smuggler with a single ' g,' and described Mrs. Shelley as ' a servant, or some person of very low birth,' cannot be said to merit unqualified confidence for the accuracy of his spelling and personal intelligence ; but he may have been right in representing that the whilom ' smugler' and his daughter assumed different surnames. As an instructress of children, Miss Hitchener may have had a professional motive for getting away from her papa's assumed surname, even as he had a sound prudential motive for getting away from a proper name, disagreeably familiar to the ' smuglers ' of the Sussex coast.

Anyhow, the lady figures as Miss Eliza Hitchener in Shelleyan annals. Opinions differ respecting Miss Hitchener's character and conduct. Shelley had not known her long before he thought much ill of her. But there are sufficient grounds for a confident opinion that she was neither the angelic creature he imagined her, whilst cherishing her with platonic affection, nor the superlatively evil being he imagined her when he came to denounce her, in shrillest notes of abhorrence, for being a brown demon and an hermaphrodite.

CHAPTER XVIII.

SHELLEY'S QUARREL WITH HOGG.

Shelley's Suspicion of Hogg — His Conviction of Hogg's Guilt — Did Hogg make the Attempt — The Manipulated Letter — Hogg's Object in publishing it — His Purpose in altering it — The Great Discovery — Evidence of Hogg's Guilt — Sources of the Evidence — Shelley's Correspondence with Miss Hitchener — His Letters from Keswick to Hogg — Their vehement Affectionateness — Eliza Westbrook in Office — Shelley under Training — Sisters in Council — Shelley's Conferences with Harriett — Proofs of Hogg's Innocence — *Primâ Facie* Improbability — Why Hogg was not charged at York — His Arraignment at Keswick — Condemned in his Absence — The Reconciliation — Divine Forgiveness — Hogg's Restoration to Intimacy with Harriett — Shelley's subsequent Intimacy with Hogg — Hogg's Intimacy with Mary Godwin — Shelley's Acknowledgment of Delusion — He begs Pardon of Hogg — Hogg's Denials of the Charge — Hypothetical Letters — Concluding Estimate of Harriett's Evidence — If Hogg should be proved Guilty — Consequences to Shelley's Reputation.

WHILST telling William Godwin of his benevolent purpose towards Ireland, Shelley was silent on the subject to the incomparable Hogg. How was this? Hogg had fallen out of Shelley's favour. Incomparable till circumstances caused Miss Eliza Westbrook to regard him with enmity, Hogg became incomparably evil in Shelley's eyes before the trio bade the Calverts farewell with tearful emotion, and set their faces for Whitehaven. What evil had the alternately ductile and unmanageable Shelley been educated into thinking of his no longer incomparable friend?

There is no need to answer the question, readers having been already informed that Shelley did not leave Keswick, without coming to the conviction that Hogg had attempted to seduce Harriett, either on the journey from Edinburgh to York, or in the last-named city. Shelley did not charge Hogg with seducing Harriett, but only with *attempting* to seduce. Had he charged Hogg with the larger offence, he would have preferred against his familiar friend the accusation that, even when it is supported by considerable *primâ facie* evidence, is so often found on enquiry to have proceeded from unreasonable marital jealousy. In charging him with the mere attempt, Shelley charged his friend with an offence which, though no less flagitious, is by no means so easily proved as the more comprehensive crime. There are crimes, whose preliminary circumstances are necessarily too manifest and unequivocal to admit of any doubt of the culprit's purpose. But seduction is one of the secret and insidious offences, that are seldom preceded by circumstances affording evidence of clear and unmistakable attempt to perpetrate them. No doubt cases arise from time to time, where a seducer's measures for the accomplishment of his purpose may be fairly described as a manifest attempt to commit the crime. But these cases are rare. In most cases, where a man is charged with attempting to seduce, the accusation rests altogether on circumstances that, admitting of another construction, are compatible with the innocence of the accused person.

To Field Place, animated by bitter memories of the biographer's 'two volumes;' to the Shelleyan enthusiasts, quick to think evil of the personal historian, who, refusing to write the poet's life into harmony with the straight-nosed pictures, gave them a faulty instead of a faultless Shelley; and to the Free Lovers, who, disliking Hogg for his ridicule of their substitute for lawful marriage, see, in his alleged attempt on Harriett's virtue, a way of accounting creditably for the instability of the poet's devotion to his first wife,—Shelley's conviction is a sufficient proof of Hogg's guilt. Years since, it was enough for Hogg's enemies to hint vaguely that his intimacy with Harriett was in no slight degree accountable for the briefness of Shelley's affection for her. Of late, they have spoken of Hogg's iniquity with greater freedom and boldness. No long while since, an *Edinburgh* Reviewer declared roundly that Hogg essayed to seduce Harriett within a few weeks of her wedding. At the present time it is the fashion of the Shelleyan specialists to speak of Hogg's egregious and revolting turpitude, as a matter admitting of no doubt. To readers, however, who, whilst delighting in Shelley's verse, are neither Shelleyan zealots, nor Free Lovers, nor Field Place partisans, it may appear well to make some enquiries respecting the nature and quality of the evidence that Hogg was so monstrous an example of perfidy and uncleanness. If Hogg (who, from certain points of view, was a typical English gentleman) can be proved innocent of the

flagrant iniquity, with which he has been charged, it is desirable
for the credit of his nation and race, that his innocence should
be established.   Even by his most vehement admirers it is
admitted that, during his brief stay at Keswick, Shelley suffered
from hallucination on another matter :—that he imagined he
suffered from a violent assault, when no violence had been done
him.   According to one of his letters (26th January, 1812)
Shelley, only a day or so earlier, was assailed by a robber, from
whose felonious hands he escaped by falling fortunately *into*
Mr. Calvert's house.   No robbery had been attempted on the
poet's person: no robber had assaulted him.   He was the victim
of hallucination, in thinking himself attacked by a robber under
the very eaves of his dwelling-place, and in imagining he
escaped his assailant, by dropping within the bounds of his own
temporary home.   The whole affair was the mere whimsey of
his own freakish imagination.   If the fancy originated in
nervous derangement caused by opium, it was none the less
a delusion.   This affair happened closely upon the time when
Shelley came to think so ill of Hogg.   Even by the most
cautious readers it will be admitted that the young man,
who experienced an imaginary attack on his person, was a
likely young man to experience a no less imaginary attack on
his honour.   The evidence is superabundant that Shelley suffered
at times from grotesque delusions.   This is admitted by his
more discreet apologists, who use the mental infirmity to account
for circumstances that, but for the infirmity, would prove him
superlatively untruthful.   To show, therefore, that Shelley was
deluded in thinking Hogg an incomparable villain, is only to
exhibit him as suffering from mental disorder, to which he was
certainly liable.   Moreover, it is my purpose to show that my
view of the circumstances, resulting in the transient severance
of the two friends, is not more favourable to Hogg's reputation,
than needful for Shelley's honour.

What is the evidence that Hogg made *the attempt* ?   At this
distance from 1811, the evidence must be sought for in MSS. or
printed pages, exhibiting,—(1), words written by Shelley, or
credibly reported to have been spoken by him ; (2), words
written by Hogg, or credibly reported to have been spoken by
him ; (3), words written by Harriett, or credibly reported to
have been spoken by her; (4), words written by persons, who (like
Southey at Keswick, or Miss Hitchener at Hurstpierpoint)

derived their information directly or indirectly from Shelley, Hogg, or Harriett, or from more than one of them, or credibly reported to have been spoken by persons, so informed directly or indirectly by Shelley, Hogg, or Harriett ; (5), words proceeding from persons who, without being known, may be reasonably assumed to have derived their information from Hogg, Shelley, or Harriett. Of statements made by unreliable diarists, letter-writers, and other literary tattlers, who merely recorded gossip that came to them from uncertain sources, no account should be taken. There exists no small mass of matters (written or printed), to be placed in one or another of these five classes of evidential statements. It is in the nature of things that the information gained from such sources should be more or less unsatisfactory. No one of the givers of information can be cross-examined respecting his or her testimony ; much need though there is for such cross-examination, in order to render the evidence fairly reliable. For the production of a credit-worthy account of the most puzzling business of Shelley's perplexing story, all one can do is to pick out from a mass of matters the apparently credit-worthy statements, and deal cautiously, whilst dealing inferentially, with them.

Were evidence weighty in proportion to the number of the sources, from which it is gathered, the evidence of Hogg's guilt would not be light. But the testimony of a single scrap of paper may countervail and even annihilate the testimony of a hundred different documents. One fact in this affair of manifold uncertainties is, however, indisputable:—that for several months from some date of his residence at Keswick, Shelley believed Hogg to have made an attempt on Harriett's honour. Shelley spoke and wrote too freely of Hogg's iniquity for there to be any room for doubt whether he really thought so ill of his friend. And it cannot be questioned, that, had Shelley been constituted like most other young Englishmen of his social degree,—had he been as discreet in judgment, as accurate in statement, as unlikely to be carried away from common-sense by the forces of a lawless imagination, as exempt from proneness to delusion, as most young English gentlemen,—his bare utterance of his deliberate conviction, that Hogg had essayed to compass Harriett's dishonour, would be strong *primâ facie* evidence that the conviction was no less reasonable than dismal. But Shelley was not constituted like other young men. Instead of being evenly balanced, his mind was often swayed by delusive fancies. He was habitually inaccurate in his statements. At the very time of thinking so ill of his friend, he suffered from hallucination on another subject. Instead of being an accurate observer of facts, he could believe himself assailed by a robber, when no one attacked him. The young man who thought Hogg capable of trying to seduce his wife, was the young man who thought his father was set on locking him up in a lunatic asylum. To see how far Shelley's conviction about Hogg was reasonable or unreasonable, it is needful to know the facts that determined his judgment in the matter. My view of those facts will soon be given. But before it is submitted to readers of this chapter, it is well for them to be reminded that the original mere facts, pointing to Hogg's infamy, can, in the first instance, have been known to no one but Hogg, Harriett, and Shelley. It is inconceivable that Hogg attempted to seduce Harriett under the very eyes of her sister. Whatever he *did* to provoke the hideous charge must have been done at some time prior to Miss Eliza Westbrook's arrival at York ; and her knowledge of the criminatory facts must have been derived from one or more of the three. As Hogg cannot be imagined to have given her any evidence against himself, she must have gained her knowledge of the criminatory facts from Shelley or her sister, or from both. Shelley's knowledge of *facts*, which he came to regard as evidential of his friend's guilt, may have resulted altogether from his own personal observation ; but he may be presumed to have gathered the knowledge from his wife's words, no less than from personal observation. Hogg certainly was not likely to tell his friend, or any other person, anything that could fairly be construed into evidence that he was a villain. As the criminatory *facts* (*i.e.* of Hogg's conduct) cannot have been known in the first instance to anyone but Shelley, Hogg, and Harriett, all our knowledge of those facts (in whatever forms and through whatever channels it has reached us) must have proceeded originally from Hogg, Shelley, or Harriett. It is not to be supposed that Hogg either confessed having made the attempt, or admitted to anyone that he had done aught incompatible with his innocence of so serious an offence. It follows, therefore, that our knowledge of facts, in any degree evidential of Hogg's guilt, is referable, in some way or other, to the *ex-parte* statements of the husband or wife, or both of them.

That Shelley went from York to Cumberland without thinking that Hogg had made an attempt on Harriett's virtue, appears,—(1), from the passionate affectionateness with which he wrote to Hogg from Keswick; (2), from the fact that, for some time, Hogg was permitted to write letters to Harriett at Keswick; (3), from the fact that Harriett was permitted and encouraged by her husband to answer the letters she received at Keswick from Hogg. It is inconceivable that Shelley would have allowed his young bride to correspond with the man who, to his belief, had only a few weeks since tried to seduce her; that he would himself have continued to write letters, over-flowing with protestations of friendship and love, to the man whom he regarded as having essayed to compass her ruin and her husband's dishonour. Is it suggested that Shelley's peculiar notions, touching the intercourse of the sexes, qualified him to live in amity with a man so lately desirous of seducing his wife? There is conclusive evidence that he was not a man to consent thus tamely to his own dishonour. On coming to the conviction that Hogg had been guilty of *the attempt*, Shelley broke with him promptly, and ceasing to correspond with him denounced him for a villain. It was thus Shelley acted towards Hogg, after he had been fully educated into thinking Hogg had not only admired Harriett with embarrassing and dangerous fervour, but had actually tried to seduce her. Here, surely, is sufficient proof that, had he thought so ill of Hogg on leaving York, he could not have written affectionately to him from Keswick, and at the same time have encouraged Harriett to correspond with him.

Whilst requiring Hogg to keep away from Harriett, till his admiration of her should have survived an enthusiasm too passionate for her ease and his safety, Shelley wrote to him from Keswick, 'Think not I am otherwise than your friend:—a friend to you now more fervent, more devoted than ever, for misery endears to us those whom we love. You are, you shall be, my bosom friend:'—words to be found in the heart of the long and remarkable epistle, which Hogg published in the second volume of the unfinished *Life* (*vide* pp. 490–497), describing it as a 'Fragment of a Novel,' and saying of it lightly—'This epistle from Albert to Werter is forcibly written, with great power and energy; but it wants the warmth, the tenderness, of Goethe and Rousseau.' The more effectually to disguise the real nature of the composition from his ordinary readers, the biographer substituted 'Charlotte' for 'Harriett' in his printed copy of the epistle.

What was the object of this mystification? Why did Hogg thus misdescribe the letter, and substitute Charlotte for Harriett? These questions are answered in two very different ways,—by the wildest of the Shelleyan idolaters, who believe that the biographer (unquestionably guilty of declining to write Shelley's story into harmony with the delusive portraits) must have been an unutterably wicked person; and by those of the poet's discreet admirers, who, whilst recognizing in Hogg's *Life* many inaccuracies and a considerable element of untruthfulness, believe the book to have been written on the whole with a sincere design of giving the world a fair view of the poet's life and nature.

By the wildest of the Shelleyan idolaters it is maintained that Hogg had scarcely set eyes on his friend's girlish bride, when he tried to lure her from the ways of wifely goodness; that entertaining this infamous design on the young lady, who but for him would not have been married at all, Hogg set about seducing her either at Edinburgh, or on the road from Edinburgh to York, or in the dingy dwelling of the dingy milliners; that Shelley withdrew her precipitately from York, in order to remove her from the baneful influence of his false friend; and that, after vainly combating Hogg's wicked passion with affectionate expostulations, Shelley broke with the man who had proved himself so unworthy of his regard, and ceasing to answer his letters, held no intercourse with him for a considerable period. To those, who take this view of Hogg's character and of the incidents that unquestionably resulted in a temporary estrangement of the two friends, it appears obvious that the misdescription and misleading alterations of the letter proceeded from Hogg's desire to conceal the shameful circumstances that caused it to be written.

On the other hand, to those who can admire Shelley's poetry without shutting their eyes to his various infirmities, and who on more than sufficient grounds hold a strong opinion that Hogg never entertained evil designs on his friend's wife, and that Shelley was under an equally absurd and monstrous hallucination in thinking his familiar comrade capable of such wickedness, it is no less obvious that the mystification Hogg practised in his way of dealing with the epistle, instead of resulting from care for his own honour, proceeded altogether from delicate concern for the poet's reputation.

In the absence of positive evidence to the point, I do not hesitate to assume, as a matter of course, that whilst writing his friend's history Hogg was aware of the gravest and most revolting suspicions entertained of him by Shelley. It may be just conceivable, but it is in the highest degree improbable, that Hogg survived Shelley without discovering the worst of the several evil things the poet thought, said, and wrote of him, towards the close of 1811 and in the earlier months of 1812. But even if it could be proved that, whilst discharging the functions of his friend's biographer, Hogg was in this most improbable ignorance, it would be none the less certain that he was aware Shelley had deemed him an unsuitable companion for Harriett; had, in consequence of the monstrous notion, ceased for several months to correspond with him; and had moreover been deplorably communicative to certain of his acquaintance respecting his reasons, for breaking in so singular a manner with so particular a friend. Aware that he had for a time been the victim of Shelley's marital jealousy, and that the disturbance of their friendship was known in the esoteric Shelleyan coteries to have resulted from this jealousy, the biographer reasonably determined (for his honour's sake no less than for the sake of his friend's honour) to exhibit to those coteries a document, so largely and precisely eloquent of the feelings and considerations that occasioned the breach. At the same time it was no less natural for the personal historian to shrink from calling universal attention to a matter, so little calculated to win respect and sympathy for the poet in whose honour the history was being written.

Wishing to deal frankly with the coteries, and less than frankly with the multitude, Hogg bethought himself how he could enlighten the coteries on a matter about which they had a claim to information, without offering Shelley to the whole world's amusement in the equally ludicrous and ignoble character of an unreasonably jealous husband. Hence the biographer's determination to misdescribe and manipulate the document, so that, whilst accepted in the coteries for what it was (viz. the poet's confidential letter on matters of the nicest indelicacy), it should be read by the multitude, as what it was not,—a mere scrap of romantic fiction.

Several years have now passed since the Shelleyan enthusiasts, with much clucking over their own critical sagacity, discovered that the 'fragment of a novel' was a manipulated letter, and that Mr. Hogg was an inordinately deceitful person in dressing the letter so delusively. From every point of view the affair is one of the broadest comedy. The discoverers of the real letter under the false label were comically jubilant over their cleverness in discovering what was put under their noses,—jubilant like children, crying with delight at finding what was hidden from them only that they might have the pleasure of finding it. It was droll to see how, in their eagerness to expose the biographer's dishonesty, these discoverers revealed to the irreverent multitude what the biographer hoped the enthusiasts of the coteries would keep to themselves, out of tenderness for the poet's reputation. It was very droll to observe how Hogg was denounced for tampering fraudulently with the document, which he published thus cautiously for the enlightenment of the initiated Shelleyans,—could have safely withheld, as it was his own property; and would not have published even in so guarded a way, had he not desired to afford sufficient information, on a matter respecting which he had not the hardihood to be fully communicative.

It being certain that sooner or later the world will be authoritatively assured of the sufficiency of Shelley's reasons for thinking Hogg designed and tried to seduce the girlish bride; and that the allegations to this effect will be made with the two-fold object of destroying the biographer's credit and raising suspicions of Harriett's discretion and modesty, even from the very commencement of her association with the poet, it is right that readers should be forewarned and fore-armed against such preposterous assertions, by a further exhibition of the influences that caused Shelley to think so ill of his heretofore closest friend, and by an adequate exposition of the superabundant reasons for declaring Hogg wholly and absolutely innocent of the wickedness, which has long been charged against him.

Enough has been said in a previous chapter of the incidents and influences, that caused Shelley to regard his wife's intimacy with his friend as an association which, already fruitful of

embarrassment to the former, threatened to become no less fruitful of moral injury to the latter. There is no need to remind
readers of the train of circumstances closing with the flight
from York to Keswick, or of the abundant documentary evidence
that Shelley arrived at Keswick with undiminished confidence
in his friend's loyalty and honour, though with a lower respect
for his discretion, considerateness, and moral robustness. Had
he on entering Keswick imagined that Hogg had deliberately
contemplated to lure Harriett from the ways of wifely dutifulness, and even taken steps to compass her seduction, Shelley
could not have written to him from Keswick with the passionate
affectionateness, that animates each and all of the several extant
letters he sent his friend at York during the earlier weeks of
the residence at Keswick.

The *Fragment of a Novel*, which I regard as the last of
the extant series of undated epistles from Keswick, affords
abundant evidence that, almost up to the moment of the cessa-
tion of his correspondence with Hogg, Shelley accused his
friend of nothing worse than indiscretion, weakness, insincerity,
imbecility :—*i.e. indiscretion*, in allowing so much of passionate
fervour to qualify his admiration of Harriett ; *weakness*, in pro-
longing the intimacy that was causing him perilous excitement ;
insincerity, in trying to disguise from himself the nature of the
feelings into which he had been betrayed ; and *imbecility*, surpassing mere weakness, in declining to combat the feelings
whose indulgence tended to wickedness. The force of some of
the writer's expressions, no doubt, exceeds the force of anything
in his earlier expostulations with Harriett's too frank and impulsive admirer ; the greater energy of the language showing
that Shelley was fast nearing the time, when he passed suddenly
from the state of mind in which he accused Hogg of nothing
worse than indiscretion, weakness, insincerity, and imbecility,
to the state of mind in which he charged him with villany.

But even in this far more cogent and strenuous epistle one
comes upon expressions that expressly acquit Hogg of the
wickedness of wishing to seduce a simple girl, who had been
his friend's wife for only a few weeks. In answer to language,
by which Hogg appears to have repelled an ungenerous suspicion, Shelley says in the letter, 'I admit the distinction which
you make between mistake and crime. I acquit you heartily
of the latter.' Whilst penning them, the writer of these words

could not have imagined Hogg guilty of a design on Harriett's virtue. In reply to other words, by which Hogg seems to have attempted to disperse certain of his correspondent's absurd fancies, Shelley says, 'I hope I have shown you that I do not regard you as a smooth-tongued traitor; could I choose such for a friend? could I still love him with affection unabated, perhaps increased?' Curious and abnormal creature though he was, Shelley could not have written thus, whilst believing his correspondent guilty of the darkest treason.

After speaking of a letter Harriett has received from Hogg, Shelley says, 'Harriett will write to you to-morrow.' Could Shelley have in this manner sanctioned his wife's correspondence with a man whom he believed guilty of trying to seduce her? Shelley's idolaters answer this question in the affirmative. They are welcome to their opinion; but they must not ask me to insult him by holding it.

Within a few days of writing thus strenuously to Hogg, that he loved him as deeply and passionately as ever, and that his wife would write to him on the morrow, Shelley assured Miss Hitchener of Hurstpierpoint, that this same Hogg had attempted to seduce Mrs. Shelley. Taking possession of Shelley's mind, at Keswick, towards the close of 1811, this morbid fancy held it for several months. The poet's correspondence with the Hurstpierpoint schoolmistress affords conclusive testimony that, instead of being a quickly transient delusion, arising from an overdose of opium, and perishing with the nervous disturbance caused by the drug, this ghastly hallucination occupied the future poet's brain, at least, from the middle of his sojourn at Keswick till the close of the ensuing spring.

It is in the nature of things for Platonic friendships to be mistaken by ordinary observers for less amiable and orderly attachments. When a young gentleman is seen sauntering about sylvan glades and rural lanes with a pretty milliner on his arm, or is known to be corresponding through the post with a publican's daughter, the world is slow to think the intimacy of the young people, wholly independent of the motives and considerations that are usually more or less operative, when a young man of gentle rank lavishes attention on a young woman of plebeian quality. On the contrary, judging from appearances, with no excessive care for exceptional idiosyncrasies, the world is apt to refer the unequal association to certain of the most familiar affections. Though the avowal may move some readers to smile at my simplicity, I have little doubt Shelley's liking for Miss Eliza Hitchener was from first to last a purely Platonic preference. It would, however, have been strange, had the people in and about Cuckfield and Hurstpierpoint taken this charitable view of an intimacy, that, causing no little gossip in and around those parishes, moved local tattlers to declare Miss Hitchener no better than she ought to be. Readers may not suppose that this view of Miss Hitchener's character and relations with the poet was confined to the haunters of her father's tavern. Having for some time regarded her nephew's civility to the schoolmistress with suspicion, Mrs. Pilfold held a strong opinion in the spring of 1812, that the continuance of the intimacy, now he had married Harriett Westbrook, would be simply scandalous. Whether the lady wrote to her nephew on the subject does not appear. Anyhow, he learnt through some channel enough of his aunt's unfavourable opinion of the curious friendship, to hold her chiefly accountable for certain Cuckfield gossip that, moving him to indignation in April, 1812, caused him, on the 29th of that month, to write from Nantgwilt to his friend at Hurstpierpoint, 'I unfaithful to my Harriett! You a female Hogg! Common sense would laugh such an idea to scorn, if indignation would wait till it could be looked upon!'—words of evidence that at least to the end of April in 1812, the writer was held firmly by the fancy that caused him to break with Hogg towards the close of the previous year.

Eliza Westbrook was chiefly accountable for Shelley's passage from the state of mind, in which he regarded Hogg as nothing worse than Harriett's inconveniently emotional but loyal admirer, to the state of mind, in which he regarded him as a treacherous libertine, set on seducing her. Even as she had been at York the influence to carry Shelley from a condition of unqualified confidence in his friend's discretion and moral robustness into a condition of feverish apprehension for the consequences of his tempestuous sentimentality, Eliza Westbrook became at Keswick the baneful tutor, who educated him into thinking Hogg an egregious villain.

From the moment of her arrival at Keswick, to the moment when she could congratulate herself on having effected her purpose, the woman whom Hogg had hoped and tried to separate from her sister and brother-in-law, found her chief occupation in bringing Shelley to the conviction that Hogg was a black-hearted knave. In justice to the woman who accomplished this evil work, it should be remembered that she had received no ordinary provocation. She may have imagined she was rendering good service to her childish and inexperienced sister. Though she was a person of some culture and more than average cleverness, it is not to be supposed that John Westbrook's elder daughter had, together with the superficial refinement, acquired the delicate sensibility of a gentlewoman. Whilst there is nothing to countenance an opinion that Miss Westbrook was remarkable for mental purity and elevation, there is abundant evidence that in feeling and temper she resembled the average womankind of the London *bourgeoisie*. Born in a tavern, reared from infancy to girlhood's later term in a bar-parlour, and shaping her course in accordance with Miss Warne's canons of feminine propriety, she held on numerous questions the views and notions, generally favoured, by people of the decent but unrefined class, in which she had found her earliest teachers. It was natural for her to think no young man could approach her beautiful sister without regarding her passionately, and seizing the earliest occasion for the gratification of his desire. Taking this view of Hogg and his peculiar intimacy with Harriett, it is conceivable that Miss Westbrook was at times less mindful of her strictly personal reasons for disliking the young gentleman, than of the dangers from which she desired to save her sister. It is not surprising that she resolved to put an end to an intimacy so likely to tarnish Harriett's reputation, and even make her a faithless wife.

Nor is it surprising that Miss Westbrook accomplished at Keswick the purpose she formed at York,—the purpose she could scarcely have accomplished at York, or anywhere else, so long as Shelley was in daily personal intercourse with his incomparable friend. At York, with his radiant smiles and racy humour, his cordial looks and sympathetic hints, Hogg was more than a match for the enemy who, so long as he was on the spot to answer precise charges of wickedness, could only hint that her dear Harriett was embarrassed by his extravagant gallantry. But at Keswick Shelley was altogether at the mercy of the quick-witted spinster, who, recalling to his memory countless trivial incidents, knew well how to give them a suspicious colour, and manipulate them into evidence that, instead of being **Harriett's** chivalric admirer, **Hogg** had been her wicked pursuer.

Resembling Byron in being easily governed by any woman with whom he was thrown, so long as he was pleased with her, Shelley went to Keswick in the best of humours with his wife's sister. Grateful to her for favouring his pursuit of Harriett, and cheering him in sisterly fashion at a moment of many troubles, he magnified her considerable cleverness into marvellous sagacity, and discovered angelic sweetness in her transient complaisance. At Keswick, and for several weeks after leaving Keswick, the youngster, who had found a tyrant in his kindly father and rebelled against his mother's mild control, surrendered himself to the government of his wife's sister with comical submissiveness. When a freakish and petulant man consents to petticoat rule, he usually reserves his freedom of action in regard to a few matters of minor importance. But for awhile no spirit of petty mannishness put a limit to Miss Westbrook's authority over her brother-in-law. Pleased to be managed by her in great things, such as his attitude towards Hogg, he was no less pleased to be governed by so wonderful a woman in the smallest things. So long as he delighted in his marvellous sister-in-law, Shelley was content to go about with empty pockets, and take his sixpences from the diplomatic Eliza as he wanted them. 'Eliza,' he wrote meekly from Dublin to Miss Hitchener, 'keeps our common stock of money for safety in some nook or corner of her dress, but we are not dependent on her, although she gives it out as we want it.'

Of course the lady, who gave money to her two children as they wanted it, was aware that, to control them for any considerable period, she must be mindful of their humours and govern them with gentleness; that to retain her power over them she must drive with a light rein and seldom crack the whip. Having opened Shelley's eyes to Hogg's iniquity, she was clever enough to see and say what he saw and said on questions of poetry and social science. To reward her brother-in-law for banishing the perfidious Hogg from his breast, she promised to receive Miss Hitchener to her heart in the ensuing summer, when the Sussex schoolmistress should come to them in North Wales. In his altercations with Southey she was, of course, altogether on her brother-in-law's side. If she doubted whether *The Address* would do all the author hoped of it, for the good of the Irish people, she kept the doubt to herself. It may also be assumed confidently that, on entering Dublin with Harriett's husband, she had never expressed in his hearing any misgiving of his ability to emancipate the Catholics and cancel the Act of Union. Miss Westbrook did not govern her erratic brother-in-law for any long period; but her control over him would have been less enduring by several months, had she not known that to rule a freakish and wayward man on matters of moment a woman must agree with him on matters about which she is indifferent.

How far in her measures for Hogg's humiliation Miss Westbrook was aided by Shelley's bride; how far the assistance Harriett gave her sister to this end was given with a clear knowledge of the object for which the latter was working; and how far Mrs. Shelley was in her sister's confidence, are questions for differences of opinion. It cannot, however, be questioned that, either with malice aforethought, or in the heedlessness of girlish simplicity, Harriett contributed to the matters of testimony which brought the future poet to the amazing conclusion that Hogg, at some time or times before the flight from York, had wished and essayed to seduce her. It is conceivable that from first to last in this unsavoury business the sisters were in perfect mutual confidence; but I cannot believe that so young a girl as Mrs. Shelley deliberately conspired with her sister at York to trump up so monstrous a charge against her husband's closest friend. I can, however, imagine that in her amazement at the view taken by Shelley of some of her admissions respecting Hogg's demeanour to her, she may have lacked the courage to protest against the misconstruction put on innocent occurrences, and may have been betrayed by such weakness at Keswick into acquiescing in a hideous story which she knew to be untrue. I can imagine that *after* her arrival at Keswick she was schooled and terrorized by her elder sister into conspiring with her to impose the vile romance on her husband. After practising alternately on Harriett's imagination and Shelley's imagination, Miss Westbrook may, by sheer force of will, have constrained Harriett to think that, to preserve her husband's confidence, it was necessary for her to affect to think what he thought of Hogg,—that by speaking in Hogg's defence she

would cause Shelley to suspect her of having connived at his
wicked design.   Miss Westbrook may even have talked Harriett
at Keswick into thinking Hogg had tried to make her a faithless wife.   It must be remembered how young and inexperienced Harriett was,—and how greatly under her sister's
influence.

But I think it more probable that Harriett was never admitted fully into her sister's confidence,—was never permitted
either by Miss Westbrook or Shelley to know all the evil they
thought of Hogg.   Perplexed by the conditions of her recent
association with Hogg, it was natural in the young wife at York
to wish to escape for awhile from an intimacy that, during her
husband's absence, had exposed her to the suspicion of the
prying milliners.   On Miss Westbrook's arrival at the lodging-
house, it was natural for the girlish bride to speak to her sister
of the uneasiness and the mingled feelings of irritation and
shame she had experienced.   On Shelley's reappearance it was
no less natural for her to speak to him on the same subjects.
She may have felt that her position would have been less trying
if Mr. Hogg had been something less attentive to her ; that he
would have shown greater delicacy in either withdrawing from
the lodgings, or spending his evenings elsewhere so long as
Shelley was away.   Feeling this, she may have said so to Shelley
as well as to her sister.   It cannot be questioned that she joined
her sister in urging Shelley to withdraw hurriedly from York ;
but in doing so Harriett may not have been actuated, like her
sister, by a desire to offer Mr. Hogg a great affront.   She may
have been told by Miss Westbrook that Hogg was aware what
would take place during his absence.   Anyhow it is certain that
Harriett left York without thinking Hogg guilty of harbouring
infamous designs on her honour, and also without conceiving
her sister and Shelley suspected him of such wickedness.   Had
she thought either the one or the other, it is inconceivable
that she would have written friendly letters to him from
Cumberland.

At Keswick, during the earlier weeks of November, Shelley
and Harriett had several conversations about Hogg and his
behaviour to her ; conversations in which they reviewed all the
circumstances of his sojourn with them at Edinburgh and at
York ; conversations in which Shelley questioned and cross-
questioned her respecting the incidents of her life in the dingy

lodging-house, whilst he was absent from the cathedral town; conversations in which they examined critically the letters Hogg had sent her from York since her arrival at Keswick. Whilst there is good reason to believe Harriett spoke freely with her husband in these Cumberland conferences, there is no reason to think she spoke otherwise than honestly. But it is in the nature of such conferences (where the memory of one speaker feeds the curiosity of another) to magnify words and deeds of no moment into matters of the highest moment, and to play strange tricks with the colour and quality of remembered circumstances. Unconscious inventiveness is ever at hand to help the memory. If Harriett's recollections were severely historic, and wholly free from the delusive effects of mental excitement, she was a strangely cold and unsympathetic young woman. Instead of being offered to a listener of sober intellect and judicial temper, her recollections were offered to a young man of quick fancy, impetuous spirit, vehement emotionality. Given to such a mind, the recollections were necessarily fruitful of false impressions.

In these conversations Harriett unquestionably played into the hands of Miss Westbrook, and greatly furthered her elder sister's machinations for Hogg's chastisement; but I have a strong (though possibly erroneous) opinion that this aid was rendered by Mrs. Shelley in ignorance of all her sister's purpose. She certainly had no strong liking for Hogg. She disliked him to the extent of wishing to be relieved of an embarrassing intimacy with him, and may even have desired her husband to regard him coldly. In proportion as she is young and foolish, a bride is apt to regard her husband's closest male friend with jealousy and antagonism. Harriett was a mere girl, and no wiser than most girls of her age. Of her own mere motion she would have been sure to think Hogg was overvalued by her husband. Living so much under Eliza's influence she necessarily wished him to stand lower in her husband's favour. But I cannot think she did or said anything for the purpose of causing Shelley to imagine Hogg had made an attempt on her virtue.

Whilst these conversations (having for their avowed object the discovery of the degree in which Hogg's admiration of Mrs. Shelley had exceeded the limits of conventional propriety and virtuous behaviour) gave an unhealthy direction to the thoughts of the girlish bride, they worked the nervous and emotional Shelley into states of excitement favourable to Miss Westbrook's designs. Each of his conversations with Harriett may be presumed to have been followed by confidential talk with Eliza, in which Shelley gave her the particulars of Harriett's latest admissions, and she (in Harriett's absence) taught Shelley what views to take of those admissions, what inferences he should draw from them. The preciseness with which Shelley wrote to Miss Hitchener about Hogg's iniquity justifies a strong suspicion that Miss Westbrook's operations on her brother-in-law's jealousy and credulity closed with some definite statement to Hogg's infamy. It is difficult to imagine that even Shelley could have been brought to the final conviction by mere hints and inferential suggestions. On the other hand, it is difficult to conceive any statement, likely to have been made by Miss Westbrook for her brother-in-law's conviction of Hogg's guilt, that would not have rudely shaken his confidence in the virtue of his wife, who had herself written to Hogg from Keswick in friendly terms. It is enough that the moment came when Shelley wrote of Hogg to the Hurstpierpoint schoolmistress, 'He attempted to seduce my wife.'

Chivalry being the last quality I should think of attributing to Shelley, it is not for me to show how his action in writing thus grossly on so delicate a subject is compatible with the chivalric delicacy and generosity for which he is so extravagantly applauded by his idolaters. It is for them to explain how so chivalric a creature wrote thus coarsely to the Sussex schoolmistress, whom he had known for only a few months. Chivalry influences a man's demeanour to men as well as to women,—to his enemies and friends of the sterner sex as well as to the women whom he reverences, and the women whom he holds in disesteem. It is also a self-respecting quality, disposing a man to be thoughtful for his own honour. People's notions differ, of course, about chivalry, as well as everything else; but most readers will concur with the present writer in thinking that, on discovering in his familiar friend such guilt and baseness as Shelley imagined himself to have discovered in Hogg, a chivalric man would punish the traitor in accordance with prevailing laws of honour, or decide to leave him to the punishment of his own conscience, and then be silent for ever of him and his infamy. Living in the days of duelling, it was open to

Shelley, if not incumbent on him, to do his best to slay the man, whom he believed to have meditated and essayed his wife's seduction. It was open to him to refrain from this vindictive course on conscientious grounds; but it was *not* open to him, as a man of honour and chivalry, to tattle and gossip of such an affair to any sempstress of his acquaintance. Whether he fought Hogg, or left him to go his own way to perdition, he should, out of tragic regard for their former friendship, and sublime pity for the once-loved friend, have committed the ghastly business to *altum silentium*. Had he been a chivalrous man, he could not have written about a matter, implicating his wife's honour and delicacy in so hideous a way, to a young woman of Miss Hitchener's social degree.

Writing to Miss Hitchener letters on this subject, about which he should have told her nothing, Shelley, of course, wrote to other persons, on the same unsavoury business. As the monstrous story came to Southey's ears from Shelley's own lips, whilst 'the trio' were at Keswick, it is not unfair to assume that Harriett's husband was no less communicative on the revolting topic, by word of mouth, to divers persons, who, knowing little of him, had no personal knowledge whatever of Hogg. There is rumour in the air that other letters by Shelley, in addition to those he is known to have sent Miss Hitchener, will be produced, sooner or later, in evidence of Hogg's criminality. But instead of being evidence that Hogg felt and acted vilely, such letters will only be so much additional evidence that Shelley thought unjustly and ignobly of his old college-friend, who at no point of his career was any more guilty of trying to seduce his friend's wife, than the Squire of Field Place was guilty of wishing to lock his son up in a madhouse. At the most, such letters, even though numbering several hundreds, can only afford additional evidence respecting the strength of Shelley's unreasonable conviction, and the number of the persons to whom he wrote about the unreasonable conviction.

Why is it so certain that in thinking thus ill of Hogg, Shelley was only labouring under an hallucination,—the wildest and most grotesque, though not the most obstinate, of the several hallucinations that possessed him at different times of his career?

(1.) Though the *primâ facie* improbable often happens in this strange world, the charge against Hogg is discredited by its egregious improbability. No one has ever questioned the force and sincerity of Hogg's affection for Shelley up to the time of the poet's first marriage. Nothing has ever been proved against Hogg to countenance even a suspicion that he had in early life any strong propensity for vicious ways,—unless freedom in philosophic speculation is to be designated a vice. A young gentleman by birth and culture, he had the tastes and habits of a gentleman. His moral influence over Shelley had been in some particulars distinctly beneficial. It was due to him that, instead of making Harriett a mere mistress, Shelley made her his wife. There was a vein of poetry, a strong vein of romance, in Hogg's comparatively cold nature. In 1811, he and Shelley were both at a time of life when well-born and well-bred youngsters are influenced most strongly by generous sentiments. They had been close friends at College; and it is no exaggeration to say, that the mutual affection of two such college friends surpasses the love of brothers. Their romantic love of one another having continued without abatement until the September of 1811, Shelley married a charming girl,—marrying her lawfully (instead of taking her without a marriage-rite), only because Hogg argued him into doing so. Hastening to Edinburgh to rejoice in his friend's happiness, Hogg there sees his friend's wife for the first time, almost, if not actually, on the morrow of her marriage. He is charged with pursuing her wickedly from so early a date of their acquaintance; that he (*ætat.* 19) tried to seduce her before he had known her more than eight weeks. Is it probable that he did any such thing?

(2.) Only eight weeks elapsed between Hogg's first introduction to Harriett, at Edinburgh, and her departure from York. It is curious that the persons who insist most strongly on the truth of the accusation are the persons who insist most strongly that, instead of passing all this short time in Hogg's society, Harriett spent some ten days of it in journeying with her husband fro and to, between York and Sussex. The story, which Southey heard, was that the attempt on Mrs. Shelley's virtue was made during the journey from Scotland. But let no deduction be made from the eight weeks. Is it conceivable that in so short a time Hogg did that of which he is accused?

(3.) Certainly nothing took place either at Edinburgh or York under Shelley's observation, to induce him at either of those places to believe his friend so wicked. This is proved by the fact that he wrote to Hogg from Keswick a series of vehemently affectionate letters,—letters he could not have written whilst believing Hogg guilty of the most revolting offence a man can commit against his friend. It is certain that before she left York nothing had occurred to make Harriett imagine herself so injured and outraged as the accusation represents her to have been. For otherwise, it is inconceivable she would at Keswick have corresponded with him through the post. No less certain is it that nothing occurred at York under her observation, which Miss Westbrook could venture to report to Shelley, as certain evidence of the crime charged against Hogg a few weeks later; for had any such thing occurred, she would not have failed to report it to Shelley at once, and forthwith put his guilt beyond question.

(4.) It follows that Shelley's conviction of Hogg's guilt cannot have resulted immediately from observations, made either by him or by Harriett, before they left York. At best it was due to his recollections of matters which at Keswick he imagined to have taken place several weeks since at Edinburgh or York, or between the two places; to similar recollections by Harriett; to Miss Westbrook's statements, and to Shelley's inferences from those recollections and statements. Hogg during his absence was, in fact, arraigned and tried at Keswick for flagrant treason against his friend, and his friend's wife, in a court where Shelley sat as judge and acted at the same time as witness; where Miss Westbrook acted in the threefold capacity of accuser, judicial-assessor, and witness; and where Harriett was a witness,—perhaps, only a subordinate witness. Shelley's evidence for the prosecution consisted of his recollections of matters that, at the time of their occurrence, cannot have made him think Hogg seriously at fault. Mrs. Shelley's evidence consisted of her recollections of matters, that did not prevent her from corresponding with Hogg after her arrival at Keswick. Miss Westbrook's statements consisted in equal parts of recollection and invention, and of inference from her own recollections and inventions, and from the recollections of the other two witnesses. No defence was offered for the absent Hogg. What was the evidential value of Shelley's recollection,—the reminiscences of the man who could not at any time of his life be trusted to give an accurate account of any business in which he was strongly interested? What was the evidential value of Mrs. Shelley's recollections,—the recollections of the sixteen-years-old girl,

who wrote friendly letters from Keswick to the man, soon to be
declared guilty of having attempted to seduce her before she
left York? What evidential value may be assigned to Miss
Westbrook's statements? How about the judicial faculty of
the judge? What witnesses! What evidence! What a tribunal!

(5.) But the strongest evidence that Shelley's conviction of
his friend's guilt was mere hallucination remains to be stated.
In a few months, certainly less than twelve months, he had got
the better of the morbid fancy that caused him to break for a
while with Hogg, and, having come out of the delusion and
returned to his right mind, he at once declared in the most impressive manner that he had thought and spoken of Hogg with
injustice. And having so declared in the most impressive
manner his own error and his friend's innocence, Shelley
held steadily to this declaration to his last hour. How was the
declaration made? By deeds as well as by words.

(6.) Migrating from York to London, when he had passed
twelve months in the chambers of his first legal instructor,
Hogg became a Middle Temple law-student in the late spring,
or early summer, of 1812. Eating his dinners in the hall of
his Inn, and spending his days in the chambers of the Special
Pleader with whom he was reading, the hard-working student
usually passed his evenings in rooms he occupied in a lodging-
house, at some distance from the Inns of Court. Having
recently returned from the country, at the close of the Long
Vacation of 1812, Hogg was sitting in his quiet lodgings late
one evening at the beginning of November, with a book under
his eyes and a tea-pot near at hand, when he heard a violent
knocking at the street-door. Another minute and some one
ran furiously upstairs. Another instant, and Percy Bysshe
Shelley rushed into the student's room. Certainly for more than
nine months, possibly for eleven months, Hogg had received no
letter from his friend, had heard nothing of his movements.
For so long a period—a long period in the life of the young—
there had been a total severance of the two friends. How
much Hogg knew then of Shelley's reasons for ceasing to write
to him does not appear. But he knew Shelley was deeply offended
with him, and knew the displeasure was connected with his atten-
tions to Harriett. Though, from concern for his friend's honour,
he could not tell the ludicrous and painful story outright in pages
designed to commemorate the poet's finer and nobler qualities,

Hogg indicates thus much in the *Life* with sufficient clearness to all readers capable of reading 'between the lines' of a printed record.   For more than nine months, possibly for eleven months, the friends had lived asunder; and now they were together again, by the act of the one who had caused the severance.   Having got the better of his hallucination, and come to London in his right mind, Shelley had hunted for Hogg at Lincoln's Inn; hunted for him at the Temple; discovered the chambers where he was a student; declined to wait till the morning for the much-desired interview with his old college chum; constrained 'the clerk at chambers' to give him Hogg's address; and gone off impetuously in quest of the incomparable Hogg at his lodgings, though it was already near the hour when quiet lodging-houses were usually closed for the night.   Thus it was that Shelley returned to the friend whom he had charged with trying to seduce his wife.   Surely, this return to friendly relations with the man whom he had imagined capable of such iniquity should be regarded as a declaration of Hogg's innocence, as an avowal by Shelley that he had misjudged his friend, and in consequence of monstrous misconception had calumniated him.

(7.) Shelley's merciless, slanderous idolaters say otherwise. These 'friends' (may heaven preserve all future poets from such friends!) insist that, when he thus threw himself into his friend's arms, Shelley still believed Hogg had tried to seduce his wife; still believed him capable of trying to seduce her, and was only showing his superhuman generosity and his divine faculty of forgiving, when he thus *forgave* the man who, twelve months since, had tried to perpetrate so foul and revolting a crime.   Not by the men who are mindful of his human infirmities, but by the men who declare his virtuous nature had no alloy of evil, is it asserted that Shelley rushed into Hogg's arms with these words on his lips: 'It is true you strove to corrupt my bride twelve months since; but I forgive you that little error; so let by-gones be by-gones, and once again let us be "friends for ever!"'   Superhuman generosity! divine faculty of forgiveness!   If this is divine forgiveness, I can only say that, so far as I am concerned, divine beings are welcome to their monopoly of so vicious a virtue.   It is a matter for congratulation that human nature is seldom capable of such generosity.   I am alive to Shelley's failings, but I decline to join with his idolaters in crediting him with so peculiar a generosity—a generosity only to be possessed by the meanest of mankind.

(8.) Having thus returned at a late hour of the evening to Hogg's heart, Shelley insisted the next day on taking him to an hotel near St. James' Palace, in order that he should there be re-introduced to Harriett, and once again brought into close and affectionate intimacy with her. Can I be wrong in saying that, in thus re-introducing Hogg to his wife, Shelley declared his previous conviction of his friend's guilty purpose to have been pure misconception?—that Shelley could not have been so careless of his wife's honour, her virtue, his own honour, as to have thus restored Hogg in the November of 1812 to his previous intimacy with Mrs. Shelley, whilst still believing he tried to seduce her in the October of 1811? The Shelleyan zealots declare me altogether wrong. They maintain that in the November of 1812 Shelley still believed Hogg made an attempt on Harriett's virtue in October, 1811, still believed him capable of so dark a crime. They admit it was strange and remarkable that, under these circumstances, Shelley should have again invited Hogg to live, and made him live, in close intimacy with Harriett—still in her eighteenth year. But they insist that a sufficient explanation of conduct so strange and remarkable is afforded by Shelley's superhuman generosity and divine faculty of forgiving.

(9.) Having thus returned to friendship with Hogg, Shelley lived in friendship with him to the last;—so living in friendship with him (the Shelleyan zealots insist) whilst he all the while believed him to have tried to seduce Harriett within eight weeks of her marriage.

(10.) After breaking with Harriett, and joining hands in Free Love with Mary Godwin, Shelley took an early occasion for inviting Hogg to live as intimately with Mary, as he had in former time lived with Harriett. Is it conceivable that Shelley would have invited to this intimacy with his second spouse the man whom he still believed guilty of trying to corrupt his first spouse?

(11.) By his will (dated 18th February, 1817, when he, Hogg, and Mary Godwin were living in affectionate intimacy: and proved more than twenty-two years after his death, *i.e.* on 1st November, 1844), Shelley left Hogg a legacy of 2000*l.*—a substantial proof of the affectionate regard in which Shelley to his last hour held his old college friend. It is unusual for a testator to bequeath 2000*l.* to a man whom he believes to have tried to seduce his wife.

(12.) Declaring by acts, and by steady persistence in the friendship never again to be broken or shaken, that he had misjudged Hogg and quarrelled with him through misconception, Shelley by his pen put it upon record that he had wronged his early friend in thinking him vile and treacherous. Of all the egotisms of *Laon and Cythna*, few are of greater biographic value than the stanzas in which the author, speaking of himself in the character of Laon, records how in his youth he was so far misled by envious and deceitful tongues as to bewail the falsehood of his heart's dearest friend, and in due course discovered that, instead of having been really found false, his comrade had only seemed so. In the second canto of the poem it is written:—

> ' Yes, oft beside the ruined labyrinth
>   Which skirts the hoary caves of the green deep,
>   Did Laon and his friend on one grey plinth,
>   Round whose worn base the wild waves hiss and leap,
>   Resting at eve, a lofty converse keep :
>   And that his friend was false, may now be said
>   Calmly—that he like other men could weep
>   Tears which are lies, and could betray and spread
> Snares for that guileless heart which for his own had bled.'

It is not till he has been torn from Cythna, confined on the column's dizzy height, freed from bondage, cured of madness, and despatched to lead the revolutionary patriots of the Golden City, that Laon encounters again the friend from whom he parted in grief and misconception, and discovers how wrong he was to think evil of him. Recounting in the poem's fifth canto the incidents of his first night and morning in the patriots' camp, Laon says:—

> ' And now the Power of Good held victory,
>   So, thro' the labyrinth of many a tent,
>   Among the silent millions who did lie
>   In innocent sleep, exultingly I went ;
>   The moon had left Heaven desert now, but lent
>   From eastern morn the first faint lustre showed
>   An armèd youth—over his spear he bent
>   His downward face.—"A friend!" I cried aloud ;
> And quickly common hopes made freemen understood.

> I sate beside him while the morning beam
> Crept slowly over Heaven, and talked with him
> Of those immortal hopes, a glorious theme!
> Which led us forth, until the stars grew dim:
> And all the while, methought, his voice did swim,
> As if it drownèd in remembrance were
> Of thoughts which make the moist eyes overbrim:
> At last, when daylight 'gan to fill the air,
> He looked on me, and cried in wonder—" Thou art here!"
>
> Then, suddenly, I knew it was the youth
> In whom its earliest hopes my spirit found;
> But envious tongues had stained his spotless truth,
> And thoughtless pride his love in silence bound,
> And shame and sorrow mine in toils had wound,
> *Whilst he was innocent, and I deluded;*
> The truth now came upon me, on the ground
> Tears of repenting joy, which fast intruded,
> Fell fast, and o'er its peace our mingled spirits brooded.'

Thus it was that, in the poem written during the six brightest months of 1817 (*i.e.* of the summer following the execution of his will), Shelley gave a penitential account of his quarrel *with*, and transient severance *from*, his heart's best friend, taking all the error and shame of the miserable affair to himself; acknowledging he did his friend black injustice in thinking him false, confessing his weak submissiveness to the false and envious tongues that misled him; declaring himself altogether *deluded*, and Hogg altogether innocent of the offences charged against him — altogether blameless in the whole wretched business, unless it was that he had been silent from a proud sense of injury, when by free and candid speech he might have utterly discredited the 'envious tongues,' and dispelled the misconceptions and delusions resulting from their slanderous activity. In the way of poetry, what fuller acquittal, what larger acknowledgment of the wrong done him, could Hogg require than the single line: 'Whilst *he* was innocent and I deluded?'

(13.) Some readers may think the acknowledgment would have been more effective in simple prose,—may think the avowal suffers in force from the artificiality of its terms,—may think it a pity Shelley did not say in less artful language what he put so gracefully in verse. One may be sure the impetuous Shelley poured the same confession in half a hundred forms of vehement speech into Hogg's private ear. Moreover, he did not pass from the world without putting the same pathetic confession and prayer in less than forty words of strenuous prose. When Hogg, some thirty-five long years after the poet's death, came for the first time on the MS. of *An Essay on Friendship*—the essay mentioned in a previous chapter of this work—he found these dedicatory words on the paper: 'I once had a friend, whom an inextricable multitude of circumstances has forced me to treat with apparent neglect. To him I dedicate this essay. If he finds my own words condemn me, will he not forgive?' In Shelley's hand-writing, these words may well have affected Hogg acutely and profoundly! Penned for his eye, they penetrated his heart! No writer (that I am aware of) has ventured to deny boldly and honestly that this dedicatory note was meant for Hogg, or even to question seriously whether it was not intended for some one else; but petty scribblers by the score have sneered at Hogg's egotism and impudence in taking to himself the dedicatory note, that certainly was meant for no one else.

What more can readers require in the way of evidence that, in respect to the morbid notion which caused his transient quarrel with Hogg, Shelley was the victim of monstrous hallucination? Those who require more evidence on this point, are persons to whom The Real Shelley will never be known.

In arguing this case, I have striven to argue evenly on both sides, as though I were retained by both plaintiff and defendant to discover the truth. I have kept cautiously within my evidences. Possibly, evidences touching the matter have not come under my notice. But I do not think I have missed any writing likely to affect my arguments or conclusions materially. All reliable information respecting the affair must come to us in some way or other from Shelley, Harriett, or Hogg. Any additional statement from Shelley to Hogg's disadvantage would be the mere statement of a sufferer from delusion. Possibly, papers exist, in which Harriett, whilst stating precisely that Hogg attempted to seduce her, gives minute particulars of the alleged attempt. Let us assume that, in her correspondence with Miss Hitchener, and other persons, she was thus communicative, and that Field Place is in a position to produce a bundle of letters, in each of which she accuses Hogg of trying to seduce her, and describes minutely the means by which he tried to achieve his purpose. Such letters, however numerous and precise, would be the mere statements, in chief, of a witness, whom it is impossible to cross-examine,—a witness whose veracity is not unimpeachable; a witness who has been freely charged by Shelleyan apologists with untruth, in respect to several of her numerous statements to her husband's discredit; a witness, moreover, who, to use Mr. William Rossetti's words, was, in her seventeenth year, philosophized by Shelley himself out of the ordinary standard of feminine propriety. It is no uncommon thing for a young woman to imagine an attempt has been made on her honour, when no such attempt has been made. Women have been known to imagine themselves the victims of seduction when no one has seduced them. A case occurred no long while since in one of our law courts, where evidence of a woman's criminal intercourse with her alleged seducer was afforded by notes, made in her own hand-writing, in her private diary, and yet it was proved conclusively that her own written confessions of guilt were romantic and purely imaginative records of incidents that had never really taken place. Some women have a curious aptitude for suspecting men of wishing to seduce them; and it would not be unfair to suggest that the sixteen-years-old school-girl, to whose thoughts Shelley had given an unwholesome direction, was capable of entertaining such a suspicion groundlessly. Moreover, the discovery of such letters should neither occasion surprise, nor dispose the judicial reader to regard them as conclusively evidential of Hogg's guilt; because, if she wrote about the matter at all in her letters, the girl who, from terror or motives of policy, or from imaginative influences, certainly acquiesced in the charge against Hogg, even if she did not deliberately conspire with her sister to trump it up, would naturally write in accordance with the accusation, to which she was a party.

How about Hogg,—the third of the sources of information? He denied the charge. His way of dealing with the Keswick letters was a denial of the charge,—as clear, precise, and strenuous a denial as he could give to the accusation, respecting which he could not, for Shelley's honour's sake, speak precisely to the whole world. He denied the charge again by the way in which he took to himself the dedicatory note to the *Essay on Friendship*. He could not have denied the charge more precisely to the coteries, and every individual cognizant of the vile slander, without exhibiting the poet to the whole world's derision.

What if evidence should even yet be produced that Hogg actually made the attempt? For argument's sake, let us conceive what is in the highest degree improbable, and suppose that letters, written by Hogg himself to Shelley and Harriett, are, even now, put before the world by Field Place, to the conclusive demonstration of the writer's guilt,—letters placing it beyond question that he really made the attempt. What then? The result would comprise the absolute destruction of Shelley's right to be rated with men of honour, or even with men of common decency. Such letters would prove that, within a few days of an attempt on his wife's virtue, and in sure cognizance of the attempt and the maker of it, Shelley wrote in terms of passionate affectionateness to the culprit. They would prove that, knowing Hogg had, only a few weeks since, tried to debauch his bride, Shelley wrote to him, ' You are my bosom friend.' They would prove that in less than fourteen months from the attempt, Shelley survived his faint annoyance at the affair so completely as to be capable of throwing himself into Hogg's arms, saying to him, ' Let us think no more of that unlucky business,' and forthwith inviting him to renew his intimacy with the girl, whom he had tried to seduce. What is the only construction to be put on the conduct of the husband, who brings again into familiar intercourse with his wife the very man whom he knows to have recently tried to seduce her ? It cannot be urged that Shelley acted thus on sufficient proof that Hogg was an altered man ; for there had been no intercourse between them, by letter or otherwise, since Shelley left Keswick. Yet more,—such evidence of Hogg's guilt would prove that, in introducing him to Mary Godwin, Shelley brought into close intimacy with his second spouse, the man whom he knew to have tried to seduce his first wife within a few weeks of her wedding. Such evidence would, of course, cover Hogg with dark disgrace. But it would, at the same time, cover Shelley with blackest infamy. The Shelleyan enthusiasts would have been less eager to prove Hogg guilty of *the attempt*, had not animosity against Hogg blinded them to what would ensue to Shelley's reputation, should they succeed in proving the charge.

END OF VOL. I.

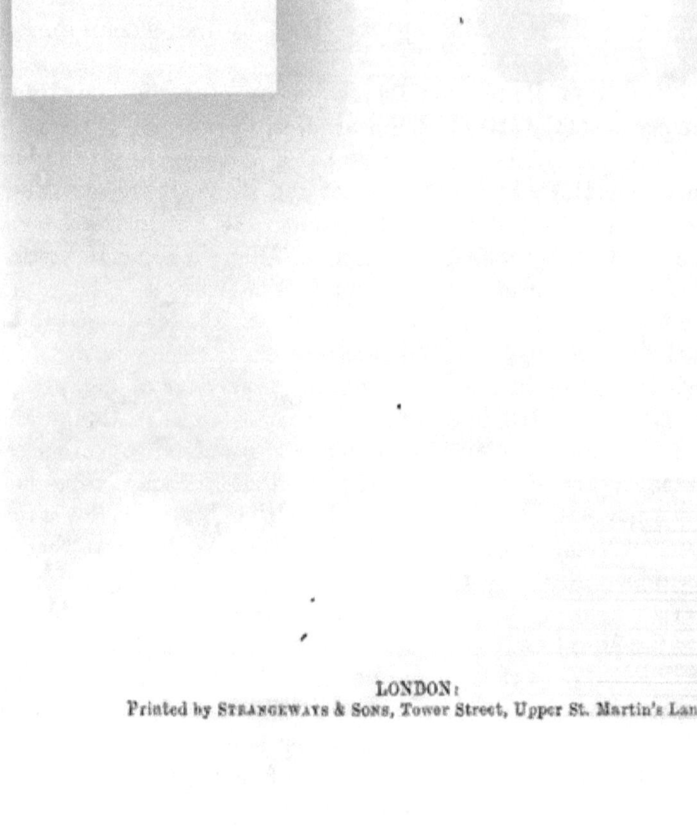

LONDON:
Printed by STRANGEWAYS & SONS, Tower Street, Upper St. Martin's Lane.